PENGUIN CLASSICS

THE TALE OF TALES

GIAMBATTISTA BASILE (1575–1632) was born near Naples, Italy, and during his life was an accomplished poet, courtier, and feudal administrator. Today he is remembered not for his "official" literary output but for *The Tale of Tales*, the first integral collection of fairy tales published in Europe. Gathered by Basile probably during his travels through the Mediterranean region, the tales were written in the nonstandard Neapolitan dialect and published by Basile's sister two years after his death. They include the first literary versions of Sleeping Beauty, Cinderella, Hansel and Gretel, Rapunzel, and many other classic tale types. Notwithstanding the subtitle "Entertainment for Little Ones," they were written not for children but for entertainment and conversation in the sophisticated courts and academies that Basile frequented, and their often flawed heroes and heroines make their way through dark fairy-tale landscapes that mirror the troubled world in which he himself lived.

NANCY L. CANEPA is an associate professor of French and Italian at Dartmouth College. She is the author of *From Court to Forest: Giambattista Basile's* Lo cunto de li cunti *and the Birth of the Literary Fairy Tale* and the editor of *Out of the Woods: The Origins of the Literary Fairy Tale in Italy and France.*

JACK ZIPES is a preeminent fairy-tale scholar who has written, translated, or edited dozens of books, including *The Original Folk and Fairy Tales of the Brothers Grimm.* He is a professor emeritus of German and comparative literature at the University of Minnesota.

CARMELO LETTERE is an Italian artist. Originally from Lecce, Italy, he now lives in New Hampshire.

GIAMBATTISTA BASILE

The Tale of Tales

OR ENTERTAINMENT FOR LITTLE ONES

Translated with an Introduction and Notes by
NANCY L. CANEPA

Foreword by
JACK ZIPES

Illustrations by
CARMELO LETTERE

PENGUIN BOOKS

PENGUIN BOOKS

An imprint of Penguin Random House LLC
375 Hudson Street
New York, New York 10014
penguin.com

First published in the United States of America by Wayne State University Press 2007
Published in Penguin Books 2016

THE LIBRARY OF CONGRESS HAS CATALOGED
THE WAYNE STATE UNIVERSITY PRESS EDITION AS FOLLOWS:
Basile, Giambattista, ca. 1575–1632.
[Pentamerone. English]
Giambattista Basile's The tale of tales, or, Entertainment for little ones /
translated by Nancy L. Canepa ; illustrated by Carmelo Lettere ; foreword by Jack Zipes.
p. cm.
Includes bibliographical references and index.
ISBN 978-0-14-312914-1
I. Canepa, Nancy L., 1957– II. Title. III. Title: Tale of tales.
IV. Title: Entertainment for little ones.
PQ4607.B5P413 2007
398.20945—dc22
2006032926

Printed in the United States of America
5   7   9   10   8   6   4

Set in Sabon LT Std

Alle mie monacielle,
Camilla e Gaia

Contents

Illustrations

Foreword

The Rise of the Unknown Giambattista Basile

It is not an exaggeration to claim that, along with E. T. A. Hoffmann, Giambattista Basile is the most talented and innovative of all the fairy-tale writers in Europe up through the present day. Nobody wrote and invented tales with such gusto, style, and profound social criticism as did Basile. Only Hoffmann was able to match his brilliant irony and adroit use of fairy-tale motifs, often turning them upside down and inside out. But it was Basile who paved the way for Hoffmann and many other writers of literary fairy tales. However, Basile has remained fairly unknown because he wrote in Neapolitan dialect, and many of the jokes, references, and barbs in his tales are difficult to decipher, even by those who know the dialect well and have a comprehensive knowledge of folklore and fairy tales.

Historically, Basile's *Lo cunto de li cunti* became gradually known in other European countries through translations and word of mouth. Aside from some of the important French fairy-tale writers of the 1690s such as Mme d'Aulnoy, Mme Murat, Mlle Lhéritier, and Charles Perrault, the omniscient Brothers Grimm were the first important folklorists and writers to praise and comment on Basile in 1811. Jacob Grimm even translated one of Basile's tales into German in 1814 and thought of translating all the tales in *Lo cunto de li cunti*, but he eventually settled on writing the introduction to Felix Liebrecht's translation in 1846. In England, there was an adulterated translation of selected tales for young readers, *The Pentamerone, or, The Story of Stories: Fun for the Little Ones* (1848), by John Edward Taylor with illustrations by George Cruikshank. The first complete translation of *Lo cunto de li cunti*, by this time better known as *The Pentamerone*, was by Richard Burton in 1893. Typically, Burton took great poetic license, and though his translation has its charm, it is chock-full of errors, embellishments, and distortions. The book did not attract many readers, and Basile remained virtually unknown in England and America until the twentieth century.

By 1925, the great Italian critic and philosopher Benedetto Croce translated Basile into Italian, and in 1932 the British scholar Norman

Mosley Penzer translated Croce's version of *The Pentamerone* in two volumes with voluminous notes. Although this translation is excellent, there are many errors because Penzer worked from the Italian translation, not from the Neapolitan editions of *The Pentamerone*. He was also hampered by the fact that very little scholarly work had been done on Basile's original use of folklore, Baroque literature, poetry, and courtly customs. Once again, despite Penzer's major contribution, Basile remained a ghostly figure even among folklorists and literary experts, perhaps in part due to fascism and the outbreak of World War II in 1939 that hindered cultural exchange in Europe and America during that time.

It was not until the 1970s, 1980s, and later that scholars in Europe and America began taking a new interest in Basile, and numerous essays and books appeared that reflected a deeper appreciation and knowledge of Basile's extraordinary accomplishments. In Italy, Mario Petrini, Michele Rak, and Ruggero Guarini published new translations and/or editions of *Il Pentamerone* in 1976, 1986, and 1994. In France, Myriam Tanant and Françoise Decroisette produced their translations in 1986 and 1995. In Germany, the renowned folklorist Rudolf Schenda supervised a collective translation completed by leading German scholars and folklorists in 2000. In memory of Schenda's unfortunate death that same year, Michelangelo Picone and Alfred Messerli published a significant collection of essays on Basile with the title *Giovan Battista Basile e l'invenzione della fiaba* (2004); the essays were based on talks delivered at a special 2002 conference in Zurich honoring Schenda. Among the leading Basile scholars who contributed an essay to this volume was Nancy Canepa, who had already published the most complete critical study of Basile, *From Court to Forest: Giambattista Basile's "Lo cunto de li cunti" and the Birth of the Literary Fairy Tale,* in 1999. This comprehensive work has been responsible for finally drawing the attention to Basile in the English-speaking world that he deserves.

Now, thanks again to Canepa, we have the first full, accurate, and annotated English translation of Basile's *Lo cunto de li cunti* based on the original Neapolitan texts. This work is a prodigious accomplishment. Not only has Canepa masterfully captured the tone and style of Basile's complex and pungent tales, but she has also provided important footnotes to understand the recondite meanings and references in Basile's tales. In fact, her translation is steeped in knowledge of Italian history, literature, and customs. Basile lived and wrote during a period of great upheaval, and he traveled north as a soldier and then returned to Naples, where he worked as an administrator at various courts in the region and also wrote poetry. His wide experience imbued his tales with an unusual folk tone and high literary rhetoric. He was obviously at home on the streets and at courts, and one can sense his zest for life and his understanding of the intrigues of his times and his awareness of the survival strategies that people of all classes employed to taste a bit of happiness. Basile's tales do not always end happily. Like Brueghel, he was too wise and wry to paint pictures of sweet idyllic country and court scenes. His plots reverse expectations; his language is an unusual stylized Baroque version of the Neapolitan dialect, at times mellifluous, at times coarse and provocative; his critical commentary on his era was so ahead of his time that it still has a bearing on contemporary society. Unlike the tales of the Brothers Grimm, Basile's stories are more down-to-earth and more honest depictions of how people desperately sought the help of the fates and fortune to endure the trials and tribulations of life and to reap some benefits. His tales are not easy to translate into our vernacular and into the metaphors of our day and age. But Nancy Canepa has managed to do this, and Basile can now speak to us as he has never spoken before.

JACK ZIPES

Illustrator's Note

In the varied course of its four hundred years, Basile's *The Tales of Tales* has enjoyed unusual popularity as well as noteworthy marginality, above all with regard to the creation of national values. This condition of neglect has allowed for a better preservation of its qualities up to our own time, just as nature does with its own treasures, where the effort required to attain access to these treasures prepares one to possess them.

This particular collection of fairy tales cannot be recommended as light reading. The difficulty of access to a plebeian language, the learned virtue of design, and the classical sense of allegory all demand a patient approach. The forms of Basile's text are a refined study in expression, not mere appearance. Those who fail to recognize this higher goal and wish for something more facile, moralized, or manipulated would do better to stay away.

Basile's text lacks any anxiety about being easily popularized. Forms of laughter, for instance, are at the limits of the possible: from aristocratic humor to the roughest of comic constructions; from the luminous detachment of irony to the folly of a sneer; from triumphant royal laughter to the trivial convulsions of a practical joke to the devastating sound of a staged fart. In Basile's text an uncontainable, unseemly, and impure world unfolds in elegant and anticlassical fashion; today, after centuries of disputes and oblivion, there is general agreement that *The Tale of Tales* is a Neapolitan classic—not of the Neapolitan dialect, but of the Neapolitan language.

THE VERNACULAR OF THE MODERNS

Basile parodied both Petrarch and Boccaccio, and thus drew critically on both models. His point of departure was the variety of processes that had led to Tuscan becoming the "learned" language of Dante. He intended to demonstrate that the "illustrious vernacular" was suitable not only for Dante's Aristotelian "tragic" mode but also for the comic; Basile's program was, in fact, to make Neapolitan it-self an "illustrious vernacular," using the comic-jocose tradition to create the new model of the literary fairy tale.

Basile was not the only one in the Naples of his time with this sort of program. But it should be remembered that outside Naples the names that have come to be associated with him are figures of abso-lute historical significance: Teofilo Folengo, François Rabelais, Fran-cisco Quevedo, Miguel de Cevantes, William Shakespeare.

The Tuscan literati, as well as all of the various schools that pre-ceded them and of which they were the culmination, disputed the preeminency of academic Latin as the sole learned language and ar-gued for the eloquence of the vernacular. They were also disputing an archaic system—one that rested on the heritage of the imperial uni-versality of Rome, for which the Roman Church had continued to answer as feudal relationships with other empires were forged and against which the new bourgeoisie of the Italy of the communes was reacting. The confrontation was now extended to the question of the legitimacy of the common idiom.

For Dante and Petrarch and the Italy of their time the vernacular was an active and well-defined cultural and political project— expressed, for example, in Dante's *Convivio* and *De vulgari eloquen-tia*. The Neapolitan literati of the 1600s followed in their footsteps (although their objectives were not identical, their "Italy" was still stably divided), and they, too, revisited the ideal of the polis, even if in an appropriately more unconventional fashion. Or, in other words, the Neapolitans shared an ideal with the earlier authors, an ideal that considered language to be intimately linked to the work of construct-ing the polis, as well as an inner fatherland.

If spoken language opens a space that is the domain of ethics, let-ters articulate this space. And the site where spoken language en-counters linguistic signification, where voice and sign come together, was just as relevant in the establishment of civic morality as it was in the edification of personal thought. In the case of Basile and the Ne-apolitan language, the experience of refining a language contributed in intimate and latent form to the creation of the ideal of a redemp-tive ethos that, in effect, would never realize itself historically in the formation of a paradigmatic language and literature (as occurred with the Tuscans), but instead became historically inscribed— perhaps in more modern fashion—as an exploration of the poetic value of "different" languages. The Neapolitan of *The Tale of Tales* articulates itself as the language both of the marvelous and of experi-ence, the language of oral folktales and of childhood, and thus be-comes, in its own way, an ethical experiment as well as a peculiar cultural quest, even if the magnitude of the phenomenon and its effects on civic custom are not as easy to understand as in the case of Dante and Petrarch.

With Basile takes place, perhaps, the leap that is necessary in order for voice to flow toward an unconditional exercise of thought. As such, the successful example that *The Tale of Tales* provides must be understood in its historical context and should stand as an authoritative model of how spoken language may realize, in the sign, sound integrated with thought.

THE IMAGE, THE LETTER, AND THE SIGN

The letter is the stylized image that voice and sign transmit. The act of sublimating an archetype and formalizing an art through the combination of letters is fascinating and remote, and already presented itself in complete form in the West with the Greeks. Greek civilization realized, at its apogee, a stylistic synthesis of unpredented historical value. Moreover, it took the idea of nature as mysterical center, common to the Egyptians and all the ancient world, and translated it into a more historical and less cosmic mimesis. If on the one hand writing lost its formal and sacral ties to the symbol, toward which it previously tended, on the other hand it affirmed itself as the secular instrument that we still consider it today. Cognitive and speculative paths were disciplined; knowledge became articulated and developed. Nature was no longer only celebrated but observed and investigated in an esthetic and scientific sense. Allegory, with its different levels of reading, is a testing ground for religious and protoscientific authority. With the Greeks it expanded its contexts and interpretative adaptations to comprehend various solutions: the lyric, the epic, and above all the tragic, the prince of genres for the Greeks, born to make intelligible the mysterious and hybrid dialogue between gods and men that distinguished myth.

The fundamental particularity of literature, its tendency to fix the characters of experience, is also its most notable vocation. This experience, whether it is personal or shared, by definition annuls itself at the same time that it is perceived. The same experience that nourished rhetorical and literary codes in specific historical periods finds, in other contexts, other expressions, redefining its formal values and requiring different sorts of synthesis: new literature, new ideals, new paradigms.

The *cuntu* (tale) was traditionally an oral genre (and still is today in places where it is possible to adapt its memory) of southern Italy, a

form of ritualized narration that had its own discreet, concealed pro-
tocol. By convention, it is situated between the fairy tale and the Boccaccian novella. This fact is registered in the formal choices present
in *The Tale of Tales,* some of which may be uncomfortable for us
today. It also explains the text's explicit parody—an allusion to the
popular sources and common roots of Basile's opus and Boccaccio's
Decameron.

Even when narration is more stylized, as in the case of a fairy tale,
people continue to talk about themselves: memories, voices, words.
In the words of Jack Zipes,

> Once there was a time when folk tales were part of communal property
> and told with original and fantastic insights by gifted storytellers. . . .
> Not only did the tales serve to unite the people of a community and
> help bridge a gap in their understanding of social problems in a lan-
> guage and narrative more familiar to the listeners' experiences, but
> their aura illuminated the possible fulfillment of utopian longings and
> wishes which did not preclude social integration. . . . In fact, folk tales
> were autonomous reflectors of actual and possible normative behavior
> which could strengthen social bonds or create more viable ones. Their
> aura depended on the degree to which they could express the needs of
> the group of people who cultivated them and transformed them through
> imaginative play and composition in "socially symbolic acts," to bor-
> row a term from Fredric Jameson. In many respects the aura of the folk
> tale was linked to a community of interests which has long since disin-
> tegrated in the Western world.[1]

Although the *cuntu* can also be addressed to children, it intends to
entertain everyone. It is, ultimately, an act of affabulatory convention
and social magnetism. In *The Tale of Tales* the tale-telling is always
enthusiastic, vital, and pleased with itself, and the storytellers engage
in cheerful rhetorical competition. But Basile did not "collect" his
tales only to fix the memory of orality. *The Tale of Tales* is a literary
locus where the tales and novellas of both oral and written tradition
re-encounter the mythological fable, with its metamorphoses, but
even more its science of allegory—the chemistry of sentiments that
constitutes it is fantastic.

Moving toward a conception of literature based on place and perhaps identity, Basile's enterprise aspired to attain the social and ex-
pressive depths of dialect. Today, not only in Italy but everywhere,

---

1. Jack Zipes, *Breaking the Magic Spell: Radical Theories of Folk and Fairy Tales*
(Lexington: University of Kentucky Press, rev. ed. 2002) 6.

we know that to write "differently" does not lead to a disintegration of the common language but, on the contrary, opens up a path, through writing, to territories where the "official" language cannot arrive because of its ingrained rigidity or arrogance. In places where, as in schools, the hegemonic culture feigns magnanimity while knowing in advance that the institution must ultimately serve the cruel laws of its historically established authority, to write differently makes it possible to diffuse literacy in the social and mental territories cut off from history and that have no recognized authority of their own. And yet, in the longer, but still human, duration, every contribution enriches, with or without suffering, the common language, just as in nature every tributary, whatever its course, ends up in the principal river.

UNITARY IDEALS AND DIALECT

With the push toward Unification and national ideals in the 1800s (and later with the advent of the Nationalists and the Gentile reforms) came the aspiration to unite culture and territory by means of a rigid cultural and institutional centralization; and even when persistent civic disorder or a cautious moral restlessness made assimilation impossible, the sense of a national interest was imposed. And so dialects were deprived of their dignity as languages, and the people who spoke them of their words. From then on the sounds of the dialects were progressively delegitimized in Italy, until from traditional sources of literary enrichment they had become sites of inarticulate laments. An artificial distance between the learned tradition and natural and social experience was thus formalized, in an institutional and in a moral sense, starting from the schools.

In the meantime, the question of a common language had become less of a purely scholarly topic of discussion when, in peasant and bourgeois society, mass knowledge and the access to it became the declared locus of social struggle. When literacy, too, became a means of social amelioration and redemption, it was historically clear that the control of knowledge could no longer base itself on an exclusive and unlimited right.

The greatest quality of the popular imaginary—miraculously made literature in *The Tale of Tales*—is an inner authority that expresses itself in the power to bring together. It is a presence that unites and strengthens, beyond both subjective values and the boundaries of folklore and against every disintegrative dynamic, a sense of relation and of human reciprocity. In particular, the spirit that animates this text disposes those who read it toward a sort of critical vigilance of the unwritten values of spontaneous cohesion. More precisely, it encourages a wariness toward whatever leads to a consideration of the individual as unreliable or extraneous, toward whatever pushes in the direction of believing that a new culture inhabited by living people is a danger to the larger group, toward conditions in which civic decay leads to a state of criminality or in which rejection is expressed in the form of a prejudicial and senseless negation of all that is excellent, out of an abstract and private sense of social order.

A SCHOOL WITHOUT *THE TALE OF TALES*

In 1960 I attended first grade on the outskirts of Paris, in Ivry sur Seine. I started second grade, but wasn't able to finish it, because we returned to Italy, to our town outside of Lecce. My younger brother Roberto and I spoke only French, and we played by ourselves until the school year began.

It is commonly thought that children learn and forget quickly. But I had to repeat first grade. Among the myths and pomp of a sandstone country palace, where my school was solemnly located, words changed sound once again.

One day I drew a rooster and caused, among my classmates and the teacher, a reconciling and redemptive enthusiasm. I had found a way to prove myself and to communicate with them, and at the same time to attenuate my difficulties with the linguistic transition. But a misunderstanding was also born, and it remained latent and unrepeatable until only recently. That rooster, which I now evoke with affection, was not the rustic animal that everyone thought it was, but the symbol of France, and, together with the merlons of the Bastille, at the time one of my favorite subjects.

Between 1963 and 1965 I attended second and third grades in a new school building on the outskirts of town. So as to better remember those years I did some research on the class registers, where I discovered new memories and interesting information on the educational system.

MISS ANGIOLINA'S PROSE AND THE UNIFIED STATE AS NEUROSIS

Miss Angiolina P., born in T., was an esteemed mother and teacher. After the bell rang she calmly walked back to her honest but modest house not far from the school. She had a good opinion of me. Back then, the grades at the end of the year weren't only expressed with numbers that went from 1 to 10, but at the end of the list of grades for each subject the evaluation was summed up with a series of adjectives. Mine for second grade were the following: "studious, neat," and for third grade: "good student, intelligent, disciplined." Already in second grade there were no negative traces of my re-adaptation; no signs of delay or anything else. I was a boy like everyone else! A dream come true. With a variety of adjectives that went from "slow" or "not very intelligent," for the worst of us, to "intelligent" and "studious," almost all of us, in fact, were admitted to third grade.

The notes from those registers are the most authentic profile possible of the teaching practices in that school of my early years, as well as of the climate of that Italy, now small and distant. On November 25, 1963, our second-grade year, the class register declares, in a note indirectly addressed to the principal,

> In October and November each part of the scheduled program was completed with good results on the part of the class. There are some members of the class who study, but many who are not able to follow, and a few whom I despair of saving, like M., because he is truly of scarce intelligence; R., because of his many absences; T., because he is incorrigibly lazy; and I., because he is in need of particular care, constant study, and much will, all of which are entirely lacking in him. P., F., P., and A. are street boys who do not study, and I have never, in spite of promises of gifts and other things, had the pleasure of hearing them recite a memorized poem. It appears that once they leave school they lose all memory of it, and in class they are disruptive, especially the last two.

In January, "after a medical visit," a boy is transferred to a special education class; another two change schools. A note about a boy who's never in school states that the parents (peasants) "although repeatedly called, have never presented themselves at school." In March, when this boy has been absent twenty-five days in three months, it is specified that "his recovery is therefore quite impossible." In the same note, again addressed indirectly but with all probability to the principal, "special" praise goes to the son of a doctor "who has been able to fill many gaps." The absent boy has sixty-one absences by the end of the year. He was even absent the day of the final exams.

In the third grade, six children stay back. Of those who pass, only eight or nine enjoy the full esteem of the teacher, and the remaining ones manage to scrape by. The adjectives used to describe their performance suggest fatigue and severe care on the part of the teacher.

On October 31, 1964, it is noted, "Two of those who have repeated are lazy, actually extremely lazy, as are two other much older boys, whom I passed only in order to encourage them." On March 20,1965, the teacher writes,

> We are at the end of the second quarter and there is not much left of the curriculum to cover. Many students, spurred on by me and by their families, have armed themselves with the best of will and have improved; six students, on the other hand, are incorrigible, and there's nothing that can dissuade them from their lack of interest for school: they are often absent, they come to school without their smocks (I've even given smocks to some of them), and they are disruptive in class and make it very difficult to maintain discipline.

In May 1965, at the end of the year, she adds, "The six students who have made poor progress are in the same conditions as before; they have accumulated numerous absences, principally due to negligence on the part of their families."

Based on the "Insufficency Report" compiled by Miss Angiolina for each of the children who stayed back, it would appear that Italian schools rejected those children on the basis of the quality of their family life. But perhaps this is an example, typical of those years, of a provincial school and a provincial petite bourgeoisie, which tells also of the historically difficult relationship between Italy as a national state and its more Mediterranean provinces.

The truth is that the petite bourgeoisie avoided with disdain its private heritage of an impoverished past, localized in the recent memory of World War II. The early 1960s were the years in which the presence or absence of a television set at home became the cause and effect of a radical difference in attitudes and social behavior. There was a push toward mass consumption and standardization; growth boomed as the Italy of those years struggled in its feverish adaptation to modernity, which on the whole it greeted and interpreted as historical emancipation and social redemption. At the same time, the individual became a fragment of the mass, and his or her needs were anticipated in order to render consumption uniform and to treat differences as the fruit of historical backwardness or ideological dissent.

Television arrived in Italy in 1954. In 1965 broadcasts were limited to the afternoon hours on just one channel, which telecast many popular programs. The *Zecchino d'Oro,* even then watched by many, was a singing competition for children. A classroom version of this program was mentioned among the activites in the 1965 class register, right after the songs in honor of the Madonna in May. These were also the years in which, in somewhat contradictory fashion, equality among children was promoted in the public school system created by Giovanni Gentile. Ballpoint pens took the place of fountain pens and inkwells. Boys and girls were rigidly separated—a mandatory black smock (white for girls) with a white collar and light blue bow (pink for girls) and a book bag made up the uniform. The bow could be a little frivolous, or elegant, or else signal negligence and thus announce the drama of dereliction; the way it was folded could influence the fate of the child wearing it.

"INSUFFICIENCY REPORTS," THE IDIOTS OF *THE TALE OF TALES,* AND THE REINCARNATION OF A SAINT

Pierino shaved his eyebrows because they bothered him. Barefoot, he ran after diffident animals in the steppes at the outer limits of our town, which lacked all buildings but were full of obstacles. The teacher reported that he was "easily irritable," "quite lazy," "not very intelligent," and "not bad at drawing." And further: "Immature in his reasoning and ability to reflect, lacking in ideas." If this isn't prime material for one of Basile's ogres. . . . Pierino's family was healthy but "not at all educated." Instinctive parents!

The first tale of *The Tale of Tales* is the well-known "Tale of the Ogre" (1.1), and Pierino would have been an Antuono of more than pleasing temperament for the illiterate ogre who is the pedagogical genius of the tale. And there were other children, like Antonio, who fell under a spell as they listened to the teacher with their mouths hanging open, until a trickle of saliva dropped from their lips and caused them to wake up and participate, laughing themselves, in the general class hilarity. A clearer idea of what I mean can be found (putting aside all closer resemblances) in the credulous fixity of Vermeer's girls: *Girl with a Flute, Girl with a Red Hat.*

Saint Giuseppe of Copertino, the most saintly idiot in the world, was born in our parts, in Copertino in the province of Lecce, and was a contemporary of Basile. He is the saint of enchantment, of mystical raptures, flights, and other "certified" natural phenomena— the same ones traditionally evoked by the fairy tale and other accounts of spiritual peculiarity. When he was a boy he was called "open-mouth," just like Antonio, and the difficulties in performing his ministry in the church of the time are documented in the acts of the Inquisition. Even if he was "of scarce intelligence," Antonio was promoted, perhaps secretly helped, by Saint Giuseppe himself, who

as the universal protector of students might have appeared before
Miss Angiolina. And how not to think of Peruonto (tale 1.3), flying
though the air astride his bundle of kindling?

Saint Giuseppe of Copertino didn't help Bruno, unfortunately.
Skin and bones, a slacker, full of sudden comic outbursts that were
like nervous tics, Bruno was considered "apathetic" in class and fell
"gravely" ill for nearly two months. He was "good-natured, sincere,"
and according to the teacher "of average intelligence." But to no
avail, since none of this "is applied to bettering his scholastic results."
The teacher might have asked him to chant a nursery rhyme in dialect
like "Spingula malingula," familiar and at the same time obscure in
its reference to a historical fact of epochal and local relevance, as it is
customarily done, with little pinches on the bony finger joints of a
child sitting on one's knees ("Spingula malingula / stocca stuccante /
Fierru felante / cozza nuta / stampagnata / iessi fore / ca si cacciata / si
cacciata / te l'Albania / iessi fore te casa mia"), instead of expecting a
sonnet stammered in an embarassing Italian, toward which Bruno
stoically confirmed his indifference. Perhaps just this small thing, in
its humbleness, could have constituted a gesture of foundational importance, like all acts of love.

Giovanni Battista was also of average intelligence, but he was "extremely negligent" and had "no sense of duty." Among the salient aspects of his immaturity was an "inability to observe, to apply himself,
and to use his will." What can have happened to him in Germany,
where he went with his family? Did he find a pot of gold coins there
to bring home to his mother, thinking they were beans, just like Vardiello (tale 1.4), even if he didn't have the help of an imp?

The families of Annunzio and Cesare are cited with varying degrees of revulsion. The two boys lived with their large families in
modest houses in the same medieval neighborhood. In the square
near the church there was an iron fountain decorated with a fasces
where people got their drinking water. In far-off 1963 the only public
water source for the populous community of the village was the fountain, and with its crowded theater of everyday, plebeian reality it was
not distant from the comic spirit of the more noble fountain of oil of
the frame tale's king of Hairy Valley. Cesare was "good-natured,
docile," and "delicate; pale." He had "some will," but too little, and
he was "not very intelligent." Yet "his scholastic results could be sufficient if he studied," even though he was unable to "comprehend"
and "memorize" and was "lacking in ideas." In another note the
teacher indicated that he was "in need of physical, emotional, and
moral assistance," and his family "poor, uninterested in the boy's appearance, cleanliness, and scholastic progress." For Annunzio the

tone was cold and bureacratic. The impression was that he had never been considered a presence, a boy in flesh and blood, but only a formality. These last cases bring to mind Pacione of "The Five Sons" (tale 5.7), who has five good-for-nothing sons whom he can no longer support, and decides to get them off his back by sending them out into the world to learn something. "But take care," says the affectionate parent, "not to agree to serve for more than a year, and when the time is over I will be at home waiting for you to show me your skills."

It was more than a suspicion that many children had difficulties understanding their teachers and following, without huge efforts, the curriculum. This was due both to the use of Italian, presented as a virtuous ideal as well as an integral antagonist of the culture of dialects, and to inappropriate cultural models, often offered without any sort of context. The pressure and the pedagogically inopportune imposition of guilt on the children and their families were evident. Too many paid the price of exclusion only because they chose a natural faithfulness to the values of their families and to the codes of their culture of origin, reacting with passive resistance or indolence. The school was extraneous, other, and as it excluded the child it deprived the adult and the community of civic prerogatives and a sense of their own history. In doing so it inhibited, as we would say today, self-esteem, instead promoting conflict and division in the children, which in turn prepared them for the very real separation from their community that would inevitably occur in the future.

Whoever reads Basile's tales can't fail to see the direct ties they have with southern Italian folklore. And we should remember with pride the debt that the European imaginary owes to both our culture and Basile. But we should remember above all that *The Tale of Tales* is more, and to this it owes its present and perennial greatness.

Benedetto Croce's 1925 Italian translation of the Neapolitan tales was a late attempt to recover the collection's legitimacy, denied to it in the 1800s in one of the first post-Unification histories of literature, written by Francesco de Sanctis. This might have created the authority necessary to renew efforts to popularize the collection and to help it to become, in the 1960s (and not only in the extended area where the language in which it is written is spoken), a scholastic point of reference, alongside exclusive post-Unification models like Alessandro Manzoni and Edmondo de Amicis. An assimilation of the lessons of *The Tale of Tales,* those that are closest and most familiar to us, would extend education to include an open, more critical form of knowledge. The school should be the first insitution in which the state gives proof of its magnanimity and its strength.

The Tale of Tales is a model for the promotion of literacy in dialect. Initiatives leading to its pedagogical use are welcome; let us hope that every dialect in Italy one day has its own version, with or without eclogues and even without the interference of Basile himself. I hope that at least in high schools students demand, just as they do with the Italian and Latin classics, the Neapolitan version in which *The Tale of Tales* was written. Why? Because Basile's unique merit lay in his ability to carve out, preserve, and restore, in universal form and with extreme lightness, a way of being Italian, and at the same time in his ability to give the gift of exhilarating pages to readers of every time and place.

PERENNIAL IMAGES: ILLUSTRATION AND THE LANGUAGE OF FAIRY TALES

Language and speech are a double reality. Pure and mute experience finds an untranslatable epiphany of being in the symbol. The word itself, in the fairy tale, can become allegory and thus correspond to the eloquence of the symbol. At the beginning word and myth were, perhaps, two forms of the same mystical necessity. Language that unfolds in allusions in order to express the universe describes the fixity of an image. Sound is united with word in a sudden illumination.

But it is clear that the fairy tale contemplated the internal processes and laws of nature. Mythological archetypes still inhabit the degraded myths of the *cunti,* even when they are reduced to the affairs of the small private worlds, historically more probable, of the novella, and when the authority of fairy-tale symbolism is personified in figures of everyday experience. Basile has no doubts; he takes the action of history, the declared cause of the wearing down of symbols, as a sign of the evolution of the genre. It matters little if it is history that becomes fairy tale or fairy tale that becomes history: the rewriting exalts the value of the open container.

This allegorical symbolism is a dissipated and tenacious virtue—a secret that travels with us, we who are oblivious and happily unaware of it—a presence as obstinate and fearful as a dragon in a cave or, worse, as being at the end of a chain held by some perverse god. It is an enemy to consciousness, often dominating and periodically killing it. But there is no death that is more universal and less absolute than this, since it is suffered at the culmination of an Edenic fullness, and the memory of this wholeness is dispersed but not lost in experience. Consciousness and history are the plane trod on by existence, but where we go to sleep at night and with whom, or where intimacy reposes in the contracted time of non-being, is a liminal mystery: the common and monstrous locus of the "solidarity of consciousness" of the civic being, and one of the nodes of modernity. The relationship between the imaginary constructions of fairy tales and dreams is a truly extraordinary and still open opportunity for excavation and research on the essence of things.

Lévi-Strauss sees in myth "a verbal entity which, within the sphere of language, occupies a position akin to that of the crystal in the world of physical matter. In relation to language [*langue*], on the one hand, and speech [*parole*], on the other, its position indeed resembles that of the crystal: an intermediary object between a statistical aggregate of molecules and the molecular structure itself." He identifies myth with "the mode of discourse in which the formula *traduttore, traditore* has practically no meaning."[2]

Infancy and myth are interpenetrated, in terms of their meaning and of their value as objects temporarily translated but at the same time coincident. With respect to langauge both are pertinent to nature and to history, but with opposite dynamics. Infancy, as Giorgio Agamben states in his essay "Infancy and History," is "precisely the reverse engine, transforming pure pre-Babel language into human discourse, nature into history"; myth partipates in a mute eloquence, translating human discourse, momentarily, into the pure language of nature.[3]

The fairy tale cannot do without the mysterical-initiatory qualities of myth, which, for its very nature, takes upon itself secrecy and silence. Agamben:

> The ancient world interprets this mysterical infancy as a knowledge that cannot be spoken of, as a silence to be kept. [. . .] the un-speakable of infancy [becomes] a secret doctrine weighed down by an oath of esoteric silence. This is why it is the fable, something which can only be narrated, and not the mystery, which must not be spoken of, which contains the truth of infancy as man's source of origin. For in the fairy tale man is freed from the mystery's obligation of silence by transforming it into enchantment: it is not participation in a cult of knowledge which renders him speechless, but bewitchment. The silence of the mystery is undergone as a rupture, plunging man back into the pure, mute language of nature; but as a spell, silence must eventually be shattered and conquered. This is why, in the fairy tale, man is struck dumb, and ani-

---

2. Cited in Giorgio Agamben, *Infancy and History: The Destruction of Experience,* trans. Liz Heron (New York: Verso, 1993) 60.
3. Agamben 60.

mals emerge from the pure language of nature in order to speak. Through the temporary confusion of the two spheres, it is the world of the *open mouth* (from the Indo-European root **bha* (from which the word fable is derived), which the fairy tale validates, against the world of the *closed mouth,* of the root **mu.* [. . .] Indeed, it can be said that the fairy tale is the place where, through the inversion of the categories: closed mouth/open mouth, pure language/infancy, man and nature exchange roles before each finds their own place in history.[4]

That is why Antuono is confused when he meets the ogre (tale 1.1), and asks him, fortuitously: "How far is it from here to the place where I have to go?" And Basile's ogre, out of a sense of investiture that finds no justification in his grotesque appearance, does not shirk his responsibility but, on the contrary, adopts Antuono into his fold.

CARMELO LETTERE

---

4. Agamben 61.

Acknowledgments

This translation has been an idea since I began to study Basile's work in the 1980s. By the time my critical study of *The Tale of Tales* appeared in 1999 (*From Court to Forest: Giambattista Basile's Lo cunto de li cunti and the Birth of the Literary Fairy Tale*), interest in Basile was on the rise, and dedicating myself full time to translating *Lo cunto* became an imperative. As happens with most projects of this sort, it has been a longer journey than expected. But it has also been an exciting and tremendously satisfying one. In many ways, my reading of Basile has culminated during the last five or six years, for there is no activity like translation to compel one to consider more deeply the linguistic and cultural strata present in every single word of a text.

I am most grateful for the various forms of assistance that have helped bring the translation to its happy conclusion. These included a National Endowment for the Humanities Summer Fellowship (1999) and a Dartmouth College Senior Faculty Fellowship (2003), both of which awarded me precious time to devote to the translation in its early and later stages, and the Ramon and Marguerite Guthrie Fund of the French and Italian Department at Dartmouth, which liberally subsidized some of the costs associated with preparing the manuscript for publication. I also benefited enormously from participation in a 2002 conference dedicated to Basile at the University of Zurich and organized by Michelangelo Picone and Alfred Messerli; the many conversations about Basile with scholars from a wide range of disciplines were enriching and inspiring.

As always, Wayne State University Press has been marvelously amenable to work with, and I thank the various people there who have patiently supported me from beginning to end, in particular the past and present directors, Arthur Evans and Jane Hoehner, editors Kathy Wildfong and Annie Martin, and Don Haase, editor of the WSUP fairy-tale series. Thanks also to Jack Zipes for a friendship and steady faith in my work that go back to the early Basile days, as well as for his wise counsel and the stupendous example he sets for all fairy-tale scholars.

Carmelo, Gaia, and Camilla have co-inhabited this project day in and day out: Carmelo as generous interlocutor on critical, linguistic, and artistic matters; Gaia as acute but fresh reader and cultivator of both the fairy tale and the joys of language; and Camilla, born mid-project, as bearer in her own spirit of the frank truths enveloped in the fairy tale and its characters. Without the passion and force of our own daily narratives the impetus to bring Basile's tales to a wider audience would not have been.

NANCY L. CANEPA

Introduction

Just how do we explain the appearance of the extraordinary creation that is *Lo cunto de li cunti, overo Lo trattenemiento de 'peccerille (The Tale of Tales, or Entertainment for Little Ones)*? Written in the early years of the seventeenth century and published in 1634–36 after the death of its author, Giambattista Basile (1575–1632), it is the first integral collection of authored, literary fairy tales in western Europe. This unique status extends in many other directions as well. *The Tale of Tales* is a masterpiece of Italian literature written not in standard Italian but in the dialect of Naples; thoroughly engaged with the aesthetics of the Italian Baroque, it nevertheless situates itself playfully at its linguistic margins. The marvelous dimensions depicted in its fairy tales stand in marked contrast to the realistic representation that was the heritage of Boccaccio and the novella tradition, still dominant at Basile's time. And Basile's tales are inhabited by supernatural creatures and propelled by forms of magic entirely dissociated from any religious system, at a time when the strict orthodoxy of the Counter-Reformation influenced public and private expression. *The Tale of Tales* is a work that simultaneously evokes the humus of seventeenth-century Naples—its landmarks, customs and daily rituals, family and professional life—and conjures forth a fantastic world whose absolute originality still holds strong attraction today. Finally, this collection, written four hundred years ago in an obscure language, offers us intriguing hints of the links between certain forms of folkloric and early modern narrative and the experimentalism, in both structure and content, that marks more recent narrative traditions, from modernism on.

Basile was a man of multiple literary personas. On the one hand he lived the typical life of a courtier in a turbulent period of Italian history, migrating from city to city and producing many works for many patrons. On the other, he authored a collection of fifty tales that today is recognized as a landmark in the history of the literary

Jacobus Pecini · fecit Venetiis 1641

An engraving of Basile

fairy tale—preceding Charles Perrault's much shorter *Histoires ou contes de temps passé* (*Stories, or Tales of Past Times*) by more than half a century and Wilhelm and Jacob Grimm's *Kinder- und Hausmärchen* (*Children's and Household Tales*) by almost two centuries. The stories of *The Tale of Tales* are like no other fairy tales: imbued just as much with the formulas of elite literary culture as with those of folkloric traditions and orality; closer to Rabelais and Shakespeare (Basile has been called a Mediterranean Shakespeare) than to most other fabulists; bawdy and irreverent but also tender and whimsical; acute in psychological characterization and at the same time encyclopedic in description; full, ultimately, of irregularities and loose ends that somewhat magically manage to merge into a splendid portrait of creatures engaged in the grave and laborious, gratifying and joyful business of learning to live in their world—and to tell about it. And reading Basile's text is an experience like no other, a roller-coaster ride in which the reader glides along smoothly for only brief stretches of what is, overall, a decidedly vertiginous experience.

Basile's work has been familiar since the nineteenth century to a small group of specialists of folklore and early modern Italian literature, but it was only in the 1980s that it attracted more sustained scholarly attention in the English-speaking scholarly world. As *The Tale of Tales* has begun to be awarded the attention it deserves, readers unfamiliar with Neapolitan or Italian still, however, have no access to a complete, modern, authoritative translation. The most recent English translation of *The Tale of Tales* dates from 1932; it has its charm but is sorely antiquated as well as lacking in the explosive verve of the original (besides having been out of print for decades). The present effort is, thus, long overdue and will, I hope, spread the riches of this remarkable collection.

BASILE'S LIFE

Giambattista Basile was born to Cornelia Daniele and her husband (of whom we know only the surname) in or around 1575, outside Naples in the village of Posillipo. With its population of 200,000, Naples was at this time one of the largest and most animated cities of Europe and a major cultural center of the Italian Baroque. Basile was one of many—perhaps seven—brothers and sisters; the family was most likely of the Neapolitan middle class that had been expanding in size throughout the course of the sixteenth century.[1] Giambattista spent his professional life at courts in Italy and abroad, as did most of his siblings, three of whom were singers and one a composer.

Very little is known about Basile's early years (up to about 1608), and in the absence of documentary evidence scholars have depended on autobiographical references in his works themselves. Around 1600, if not before, Basile probably left Naples to seek his fortune elsewhere, as he had been unsuccessful in finding a noble patron in his native city. He expressed his bitterness at this departure in *Le avventurose disavventure* (The adventurous misadventures [1611]) in a scene set in Naples where the autobiographical character Nifeo explains to another character,

> You will hear, then, that I first opened my eyes to daylight on this very shore. It should cause no marvel that I am not recognized as a countryman here, for I have roamed afar for so long that my dress and manners appear different from those here. [. . .] When I had journeyed half of my life's way, a new spirit inflamed in me the desire for higher study, and although I knew I was a swamp bird, I strived to equal the most noble swans. But when I thought most surely that my fatherland was going to confirm me in winning laurels, I then saw that those who should have loved me most ignored me. (Ah, the harsh conditions of our age, in which the most noble virtues of children are abhorred by their own mothers!) And so I arranged to flee the ungrateful shores and search for my fortune elsewhere.[2]

After a number of intermediate stops (we know neither where nor when) Basile ended up in Venice, where he enrolled as a soldier of fortune and was soon after sent to Candia, a Venetian outpost and strategic point of defense against the Turks. There he served and entered the graces of the Venetian nobleman Andrea Cornaro, who invited him to become a member of his Accademia degli Stravaganti. This was Basile's debut in literary society, and it offered him experiences that would subsequently prove precious, such as "the association with a 'frontier' civilized society that was composite and plurilin-

---

Unless otherwise noted, all references throughout this volume to Croce are to his 1925 edition of *Il Pentamerone*, and all references to Rak are to his 1986 bilingual edition of *Lo cunto de li cunti*.

1. The biographical information included in this section is based principally on the studies by Benedetto Croce (1891), Vittorio Imbriani, Michele Rak (1986), and Salvatore Nigro (1979).

2. Cit. Fulco 1985, 402.

gual . . . and the source of much material . . . that would later be used in *The Tale of Tales*."[3]

By 1608 Basile was back in Naples, where he finally managed to get a foot in literary circles, probably due to the fact that his sister Adriana, a singer, was on her way to becoming a celebrated diva. With her fame came connections and influence, and she was energetic in seeing that her brother's talents were better appreciated. In Naples Basile continued to exercise the profession of courtier, writing songs, devices, anagrams, and occasional verse for the celebration of significant events in the life of his patrons; organizing festivities and spectacles; and undertaking administrative and secretarial tasks.

The first known works by Basile are three letters in Neapolitan, dated 1604 (he wrote several others between 1604 and 1612), which, together with the dedication "A lo re de li viente" (To the king of the winds), were published as the preface to his friend Giulio Cesare Cortese's Neapolitan mock epic, *La vaiasseide* (The epic of the servant girls), in 1612. Here Basile also used for the first time the anagrammatic pseudonym with which he later signed all of his Neapolitan works: Gian Alessio Abbattutis ("abbattuto" means dejected or depressed). Basile's first work in Italian, the poem *Il pianto della vergine* (The tears of the virgin), was published in 1608. In this same year he composed a number of courtly and encomiastic works, and 1609 saw the first edition of *Madriali et ode* (Madrigals and odes), a volume of limited literary interest that nevertheless constituted another milestone in his literary career.[4]

In 1611 Basile published a marine pastoral set in Posillipo, *Le avventurose disavventure*. This genre, a variation on the ever-popular pastoral in which shepherds become fishermen, nymphs, mermaids, and so forth, shared many motifs—kidnapping, misplaced love, disguise, capricious fortune, final recognitions, and marriages—with the fairy tale. The choice of marine pastoral was also an attempt to rewrite a conventional genre in a distinctly Neapolitan key, an enterprise that not only allowed for a "native" space of literary creativity but also aggressively promoted local historical identity and popular cultural heritages, all of which would, later, receive their most exhaustive and spectacular expression in *The Tale of Tales*.[5]

In 1611 Basile became a founding member of the Neapolitan Acca-

---

3. Rak 1048.
4. See Rak, 1046–53, for a complete list of all Basile's published works, including single poems and other short compositions (*villanelle, canzonette,* etc.).
5. Rak, *La maschera* 65.

demia degli Oziosi, one of the most important academies of its day
and a crossroads of Italian and Spanish culture. Basile's personal device was a snail at the foot of a mountain, and his academic name "Il
Pigro," the same he had used at the Stravaganti in Candia. In 1612
were published the *Egloghe amorose e lugubri* (Amorous and lugu-
brious eclogues), the musical drama *Venere addolorata* (Venus afflicted), as well as numerous occasional pieces. Later in this same
year Basile traveled to Mantua to join his sister Adriana, who had
been part of the Gonzaga court for several years and had acquired a
feudal estate. In 1613 Basile, too, received the favors of the new duke
Ferdinando, who named him one of his court gentlemen. He also
continued to publish; the *Opere poetiche* (Poetic works) of 1613 contained re-editions of most of Basile's works of 1608–12.

By the end of 1613 Basile was back in Naples, and in subsequent
years served as feudal administrator for various landed nobles of the
kingdom of Naples. In 1615 he was in Montemarano (province of
Avellino); in 1617 in Zuncoli, under the Marquis of Trevico, Cecco di
Loffredo; in 1618 with the prince of Avellino, Marino Caracciolo;
and in 1619 he was named governor of Avellino. Although these were
"prize" jobs for someone like Basile, this life of continuous changes
of residence and allegiance must have been tiring; much of the anti-
court sentiment that permeates *The Tale of Tales* and the other dialect works was probably based on experiences accumulated during
these years.

Indeed, Basile declared his profound disillusionment with court
life in the facetious dedication ("A lo re de li viente") to Cortese's *La
vaiasseside*, one of the most important works of the nascent dialect
tradition.

> It would be a good idea never to publish anything, but if this mistake re-
> ally has to be made, my view is that the dedication should be to the wind.
> He must, indeed, be the greatest man in the world, for I hear him men-
> tioned by everyone, who all say they work for him. Just look at those who
> serve in the courts: you serve now, you serve later, you serve today, you
> serve tomorrow, . . . and then, suddenly, it's night for you, you're told to
> turn yourself around and get out! You can truly say that you've served the
> wind, and God only knows how many of those fellows there are who, in-
> stead of awarding you satisfaction, at the last minute send you away with
> an accusation of theft. The lover paces the floor, coughs, sneezes, runs,
> perspires, pines away, swells up with emotion, and when he expects at
> least a wink of the eye from his coy sweetheart, he finds that he has la-
> bored in vain, for the wind! [. . .] And so the poor poet—sonnets over

here, verses of every other sort over there, madrigals for this one and *bar-zellette* for that one—as soon as he collects his wits finds himself with an empty head, a shrunken stomach, and ragged elbows, one foot sunk in misery, . . . and always naked as a louse. Everything he does goes to the wind, just as my own affairs have.[6]

At this time Basile also embarked on philological editions of a selection of classic texts of the sixteenth-century Petrarchan and mannerist lyric traditions (Pietro Bembo, Giovanni della Casa, Galeazzo di Tarsia). The intensive cataloguing evidenced in these philological works was paralleled by, and perhaps preparatory to, the cataloguing of popular material that provided the foundation for Basile's two major dialect works, *Lo cunto de li cunti* and *Le muse napoletane* (The Neapolitan muses), on which Basile had probably started working as early as 1615 and which he may have been reading to friends and colleagues in the Neapolitan academies.

The third part of Basile's *Madriali et ode* came out in 1617; in 1619 he published *Aretusa,* a pastoral idyll; and in 1620, he wrote the musical drama *Il guerriero amante* (The warrior lover) specifically for performance by his sister Adriana, by this time a coveted national star. It was through her intercession with the viceroy Antonio Alvarez de Toledo that Basile, after serving for a few years (1621–22) as royal governor of Lagolibero (in the Basilicata region), acquired the far more prestigious position as governor of Anversa in 1626. In 1624 Basile published *Immagini delle più belle dame napoletane ritratte da' loro propri nomi in tanti anagrammi* (Images of the most beautiful Neapolitan ladies, portrayed by their own names in anagram), appearing on the frontispiece of this work, for the first time, as "Count of Torone," a designation that signaled his entrance into the "titled" bourgeoisie. He published fifty more *Odes* in 1627; and among Basile's final works was one of the first musical dramas to be performed in Naples, *Monte di Parnaso* (Mount Parnassus [1630]), set to music by Giacinto Lombardo. In this period Basile also wrote a version of Heliodorus's *Aethiopica,* titled *Del Teagene,* which was published posthumously in 1637.

Basile's last job was at the court of the duke of Acerenza, Galeazzo Pinelli, who named Basile governor of Giugliano (in the province of Naples) in 1631. But it was a short-lived position. After the eruption

---

6. *Lo cunto de li cunti,* ed. Petrini 575–76. Another acid depiction of court life can be found in the eclogue "The Crucible" as well as in a number of the tales themselves (e.g., tale 3.7, "Corvetto").

of Mount Vesuvius in 1631, a flu epidemic, so severe in its effects that it was compared by many to the plague, hit Naples and the surrounding areas, and Basile was one of its victims. He died on February 23, 1632, and was buried, after an elaborate funeral, in Giugliano's Santa Sofia church.

One of the only bits of documentation of Basile's life by his contemporaries is a "capsule" from the collection of biographies *Glorie degli Incogniti,* published by the homonymous Venetian Accademia degli Incogniti in 1637.

After he had applied himself, in the flower of his youth, to chivalrous pursuits just as much as to the study of the choicest letters, he became the true epitome of an exquisitely refined gentleman. Along with the knowledge of the most noble disciplines, he also learned several languages. [. . .] The literary merits of Giovan Battista were rendered more worthy of respect by his eminently courteous manners, by the sincere affection that he showed toward his friends, and by his perpetual cheerfulness of spirit, for which he was deemed the life of conversations. And so he conquered not only the affection of the gentlemen and ladies that he frequented in private, but also the grace of the most exalted, who held him quite dear. And although fortune did not fail to test him by acquainting him with the hostility that she often declares to great minds, keeping him constantly distracted in troublesome occupations, he never lost heart. Up to his last breath he maintained a very peaceful tenor of life, since at the time that death took him from the living he was nourishing substantial hopes.[7]

After Basile's death, Adriana was instrumental in getting *Del Teagene* published, and she probably also arranged for the publication of *Le muse napoletane* (1635) and *Lo cunti de li cunti* (1634–36). We might wonder at Basile's lack of editorial self-promotion with regard to the dialect works, considering his otherwise meticulous management of his literary affairs. Perhaps he did not deem them appropriate to publish or, possibly, felt that there was less need for their diffusion on a wide scale. Basile's ideal audience, in fact, consisted of the communities revolving around the small courts where he served and the Neapolitan academies of which he was a member; the preferred mode of consuming a work like *The Tale of Tales* was, most likely, the oral setting of "courtly conversation."[8]

---

7. Cit. Imbriani 36–37.
8. Rak 1057.

PUBLISHING HISTORY

Basile's Italian works, so well received during his own life, ceased to be republished shortly after his death and by the end of the seventeenth century had fallen into oblivion. The popularity of *The Tale of Tales,* on the other hand, has through the centuries steadily increased. There is no trace nor any mention in early biographical material on Basile of an autograph or indeed any sort of manuscript, and thus little is known about the time or modality of the composition of *The Tale of Tales.* It was initially published as five separate volumes: the first and second days in 1634 by the Neapolitan press of Ottavio Beltrano; the third in 1634 by Lazzaro Scorriggio, also of Naples; the fourth in 1635 by Scorriggio; and the fifth in 1636 by Beltrano. The Neapolitan bookseller and champion of Neapolitan culture Salvatore Scarrano was the author of a dedication appearing in day 1 in which *Lo cunti de li cunti* was referred to with an alternate name of *Pentamerone,* although it is uncertain whether this was done on the initiative of the editor or by Basile himself. In this dedication Scarrano also makes much of the "great delight and happiness" bound to be caused by Basile's ornamentation of his "little tales" with "so much word-play and so many sayings and so many extravagant conceits." This is no easy task, he continues, quoting from a letter by the eminent humanist Pico della Mirandola, since "to write in an erudite manner of funny things and fairy tales requires a sharper intellect than to hold forth on very serious subjects or to discourse eloquently. It is, in fact, more difficult to mold a beautiful statue out of mud than out of bronze or gold."

Later editions of *The Tale of Tales* were based on this *editio princeps,* and in the seventeenth century there were many of them: in 1637 a partial edition of the first two days (published separately), the first edition of which had already sold out (Beltrano); and complete editions in 1645 (Camillo Cavallo of Naples), 1654 (Cavallo), 1674 (Antonio Bulifon of Naples, with the primary frontispiece title given, for the first time, as *Il Pentamerone*), 1679 (Bartolomeo Lupardi of Rome), and 1697 (Mechele Loise Mutio of Naples). Basile's opus thus appears to have encountered near immediate success; already by the 1637 edition the editor notes how the first volumes were "received by the world with great applause, because of the poetic brilliance and skill found therein and because of the new genre, which will make them, I believe, immortal."

Throughout the seventeenth century *The Tale of Tales* acquired some popularity outside Naples, perhaps due to the fact that the general public had a passing familiarity with Neapolitan, which was fre-

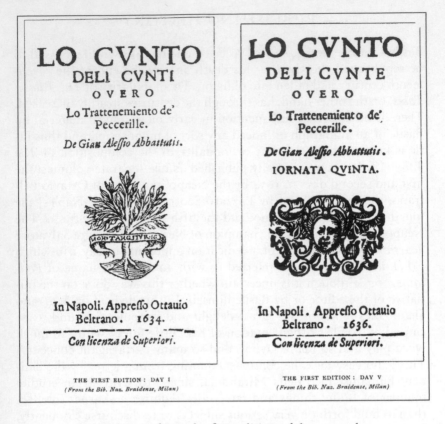

THE FIRST EDITION : DAY I
(From the Bib. Naz. Braidense, Milan)

THE FIRST EDITION : DAY V
(From the Bib. Naz. Braidense, Milan)

Frontispieces from the first edition of days 1 and 5.

quently used at the time in theater, especially the commedia dell'arte. The eighteenth century saw six more Neapolitan editions, two in Bolognese dialect, and six editions of an abridged Italian translation. In the next century there was another edition in Neapolitan, four more in Bolognese, and three in Italian; the first important editions in other European languages also began to appear. Felix Liebrecht's German translation was published in 1846, followed by recastings of the same translation in 1888 and 1909. Basile's work was first translated into English as the *Pentamerone* by John Edward Taylor in 1848 (with illustrations by George Cruikshank), and reedited in 1850, 1852, and 1902; in 1893 Sir Richard Burton published a new translation.

The twentieth century produced three more English editions: the first in 1911, which included only thirty of Taylor's translated tales;

the second in 1927 and 1928, a version of Burton's translation; and the third the complete, new translation (though from Benedetto Croce's Italian, not the original Neapolitan) by Norman Penzer in 1932. In 2001 Jack Zipes published a Norton anthology titled *The Great Fairy Tale Tradition: From Straparola and Basile to the Brothers Grimm*, in which he included Italian translations of twenty-three of Basile's tales.

In Italian, the eminently readable and excellently annotated (though not always faithful to the original) translation by the literary historian, critic, and philosopher Benedetto Croce dates from 1925. In the last several decades in particular Basile has begun to receive the scholarly attention he merits, which has resulted in a number of new editions. These include Mario Petrini's philological Neapolitan edition (1976), Michele Rak's bilingual edition (with his own Italian translation) in which he supplements Croce's apparatus with extensive notes and an introduction of his own (1986), and Ruggero Guarini's translation (1994). The Neapolitan composer and musicologist Roberto de Simone issued a provocative "rewriting" of *The Tale of Tales* in 2002, and there have been other recent initiatives aimed at familiarizing a younger readership with Basile's work, such as the publication, one day at a time (the first in 2004 and the second in 2005), of an abridged and simplified version by L'Isola dei Ragazzi.

As for elsewhere in Europe, where there has also been considerable recent appreciation of Basile, a French translation by Francoise Decroisette was published in 1995, and a team led by the folklore scholar Rudolf Schenda produced a new German translation in 2000.

BASILE AND NEAPOLITAN

Italian dialects, especially major ones like Neapolitan, were not at Basile's time nor indeed have ever been limited to the function of jargon or street lingo or, as in other nations, markers of class. Moreover, although a dialect is commonly understood to be "one of the subordinate forms or varieties of a language arising from local peculiarities of vocabulary, pronunciation, and idiom" (*Oxford English Dictionary*), most Italian dialects differ significantly from standard Italian in morphology and syntax as well, resulting at times in mutual incomprehensibility among dialect speakers from different regions. In Basile's time, as until relatively recently (the political unification of Italy into a nation-state took place in 1861, along with the institution of mandatory schooling and national conscription, both factors that encouraged the use of a "national" language), the majority of Italy's population spoke exclusively dialect, which was in effect their "mother tongue." Even "bilingual" Italians generally spoke dialect in many more contexts than they did Italian—in the family, with friends, and to do business in their native cities. Indeed, it was only with the advent of television nearly a century after unification that it could be truly said that Italian entered in full force into the households of Italians, and today a good deal of private and public affairs are still conducted in dialect in many places.

Before the mid-nineteenth century "Italian" was thus above all the language of literature and of a relatively small elite of intellectuals, nobles, and statesmen. Although it originally owed much linguistically to the Tuscan dialect of the "three crowns" of vernacular literary tradition—Dante Alighieri (1265–1321), Giovanni Boccaccio (1313–75), and Francesco Petrarca (1304–74), literary Italian has been throughout the centuries a work in progress. Indeed, the *questione della lingua,* or language question, remained a central fixture of cultural debate in Italy from Dante onward; one of its principal discussions revolved around whether one regional variety of the vernacular should form a common foundation for written and spoken Italian (and, if so, which), or whether, instead, a hybrid, composite vernacular containing elements from various sources should be adopted.

But by Basile's time there existed literary corpi not only in "Tuscan" Italian (which included among its Renaissance additions Machiavelli, Ariosto, Castiglione, and Tasso) and in Latin; there had already been literary experiments in a number of dialects as well. In the case of Neapolitan, some sort of tradition had been in place for several centuries, although it is generally agreed that "modern" dialect literature, or a literature that could rival the Tuscan tradition in artistic sophistication and complexity, was born at this time due to the efforts of Basile and his contemporaries Giulio Cesare Cortese and the pseudonymous Felippe de Scafato Sgruttendio. Among the dialect genres that enjoyed great popularity at Basile's time were the *villanelle,* lyric variations on pastoral themes; the *canzune massicce,* or "massive songs," longer poetic works similar to the epic; and the later *farse cavote* or *cavaiole,* theatrical farces deriving their name from the proverbially slow-witted inhabitants of Cava, in the province of Salerno. The thematic core of these works was, not surprisingly, description of life in Naples and the surrounding areas, and ranged from celebration of people and places to "micro-historical" chronicles of real or invented events, just as the register could range from the comic, traditionally the domain of nonstandard literary languages, to the pathetic. This literature evolved at the margins of insti-

tutionalized genres for the obvious reason that its local themes and
language made a wide diffusion difficult, but also for the less obvious
reason that in a period in which Spain was striving to consolidate its
colonialist regime in southern Italy, a literature whose depiction of
local realities was often veined with anti-Spanish and anticolonial
sentiment was regarded suspiciously by official culture. The dialect
writers of Basile's generation, in particular, showed themselves capable not only of creating a rapport with "high" tradition in the form of
parody but also of employing sophisticated formal resources—often
borrowed in part from the same elite tradition—to construct a thematics of difference in works that were themselves the foundations of
an alternative tradition.

THE NOVELLA HERITAGE

While it is undebatable that the complex interplay among traditions
and sources is one of the distinctive features of *The Tale of Tales,* the
generic line in which it most obviously situates itself is that of the novella, or short story. Following Boccaccio's groundbreaking model of
the *Decameron* in the mid-fourteenth century, the novella thrived in
Italy and in Europe throughout the following centuries. The first part
of the sixteenth century, especially, saw the publication of numerous
new collections as well as an explosion of the popularity of the genre
amid a reading public whose size and avidity for *novità*—just what
the novella purported to offer—were growing. The novella was in
many ways the ideal genre for satisfying the Renaissance curiosity
about the human being in his or her multifarious social and ethical
roles as protagonist of history. Due to a number of factors, among
which were the Counter-Reformation and changing economic conditions, by the late sixteenth century the "bourgeois realism" of Boccaccio's model was, however, on the wane, and the generally
optimistic vision of human peregrinations ending in equilibrium gave
way to a much more turbulent view of the relationship between man
and his surroundings, in which it was often disequilibrium and unreined instinct that triumphed. At the same time that the forms and
functions of the novella were being rearranged, the narrative content
of the tales themselves was also expanding to include materials
gleaned from the most diverse traditions. Italian authors augmented
the traditional Boccaccian repertoire of *beffe* and amorous intrigue
more and more with motifs borrowed from contemporary chronicles,
chivalric epics, and folklore.

The Tale of Tales marks a generic crossroads, appearing as the Italian novella was waning in both influence and production. It was one of the last great expressions of a tradition in which Italian authors were the most admired and imitated in Europe; it is undeniable both that Basile himself conceived of his collection in this manner and that "you cannot read the *Pentamerone* without thinking of the *Decameron*."[9] This is evident, for example, in the structure of the collection and in Basile's predilection for middle-class heroes; several of the tales even resemble novellas more than they do fairy tales (the tragic "Face," "The Buddy," an urban novella, and "Sapia," which bears similarity to tale 3.9 of the *Decameron*). But *The Tale of Tales* is also one of the first expressions of a nascent genre in which Basile's brilliant but nearly solitary example would have its greatest influence outside of Italy.

Why the choice of the fairy tale to fill the void left behind by bourgeois realism? One explanation sees the attraction to the enchanted realms of the fairy tale as an attempt to both evade and compensate for a dire social reality in which mobility was evermore restricted and active virtue seemed to count for less and less; a reality where magic became one of the only viable means to achieve social betterment and a privileged life. Others suggest, in like fashion, that by choosing to write fairy tales authors like Basile withdrew from engagement with the pressing social issues of their times. The attraction to a genre that depicts worlds driven by magic and imbued with the marvelous can certainly be read in autobiographical terms as the search for consolation from the harsh injustices encountered in the "real world": in the case of Basile, frustration with court life. Ultimately, though, I would agree with those who contend that Basile's work is profoundly and polemically engaged with the social reality in which it was produced.

> The fairy tale tells of the changes brought by modernity, the first effects of which make themselves visible in the realm of the family as a result of the cultural battles between urban groups and between the city and the country. The fairy tale tells the story of this historical drama through the metaphor of the journey and signals the possibility of violating the static grid of the social classes . . . the poor may become rich, peasants may become city-dwellers.[10]

Indeed, a substantial number of Basile's tales not only parodically disfigure representatives of social and political authority and the hierarchies of power in which they operate, but they also figure different

---

9. Getto 381.
10. Rak, *Napoli gentile* 299.

paradigms of social interaction where virtuous ingenuity becomes a winning quality.

It is not surprising that a seventeenth-century author such as Basile was drawn to a genre in which a reassuring happy ending is a standard feature. His was an age wrought by socioeconomic turmoil, an age in which vast cultural transformations could and did engender an anguished sense of the unstable, ever-shifting nature of things, and a pessimistic erosion of confidence in the human capacity to fathom reality and to act with the benefit of that knowledge. The fairy tale simultaneously embodies such anxieties and responds to them. No matter how much the fate of its typical protagonists seems controlled by inscrutable forces, they ultimately emerge triumphant in their quest to overcome even the most insurmountable of obstacles, often aided by the "magic" of powers newly discovered within themselves.

BASILE AND THE HISTORY OF THE LITERARY FAIRY TALE

Although Basile's authored tales are among the earliest in western Europe, the fairy tale as genre had existed, in both literary and oral forms, for thousands of years before Basile. The oldest example of an "Italian" literary fairy tale is the story of "Cupid and Psyche" embedded in Apuleius's second-century Latin novel *The Golden Ass*, which offers a prototype of the motif of the mysterious groom found in later classics such as "Beauty and the Beast." By Basile's time there were also, of course, well-established traditions outside of Europe that had already produced collections like the *Arabian Nights* and the *Panchatantra*.

The advent of vernacular culture, in particular from the thirteenth century on, marked the point at which the mediation between popular and literary traditions began to express itself in the form of inclusion of fairy-tale elements in the short narratives of the novella tradition. Early collections that contained motifs and compositional devices common to the fairy tale included the anonymous late thirteenth-century *Novellino,* Giovanni Boccaccio's *Decameron* (1349–50), and Ser Giovanni Fiorentino's *Pecorone* (second half of the fourteenth century). A number of the *cantari,* epic or romantic ballads that in their early form were recited in town squares by minstrels, also had a fairy-tale structure; the *cantari,* in turn, were one of the most important influences on Italian chivalric epics, which emerged in the fifteenth century and were populated by dragons, ogres and ogre-like wild men, miraculous animals, and fairies. But although from the late fifteenth century on there was an increasing interest in fables of the Aesopian mold (e.g., Girolamo Morlini's Latin *Novellae* [1520]), and general interest in popular culture and folkloric traditions permeated the Renaissance, until the second half of the sixteenth century the novella generally favored realistic subjects. Giovan Francesco Straparola was one of the first to include entire fairy tales in a novella collection. His *Le piacevoli notti* (*The Pleasant Nights* [1550–53]) is an eclectic mix of various forms of short narrative, and of the seventy-four tales approximately fifteen are fairy tales. Even if Straparola's tales are not as innovative as Basile's, he undoubtedly had a significant influence both on Basile, who reworked several of the tales, and later fabulists like Perrault and the Grimms.

The spread of print culture, the anthropological interest that the continuing geographical discoveries inspired, and the attraction to the marvelous that permeated late Renaissance and Baroque culture were contributing factors to the reevaluation of native folkloric traditions and the attempt to transport them onto the printed page. And Basile's work signals precisely this passage, from the oral folktale to the artful and sophisticated "authored" fairy tale. Despite its subtitle, "Entertainment for Little Ones," *The Tale of Tales* is not a work of children's literature, which did not yet exist as a genre, but was probably intended to be read aloud in the courtly conversations that were an elite pastime of the period and whose dynamics we can find described in the frame tales of many novella collections (Basile's included). But Basile did not merely transcribe the oral materials, which he most likely heard in and around Naples and on his travels through Italy and the Mediterranean. He transformed them into spectacularly original tales marked by an irresistible comic verve; pyrotechnical rhetorical play, especially in the form of extravagant metaphor; and meticulous attention to the rituals of everyday life and popular culture of the time. Their moral indeterminacy can be surprising in a form often so given to explicitly drawn lessons; their characters likewise do not always meet our expectations of fairy-tale characters; and a parodic intertextuality that has as its principal targets courtly culture and the canonical literary tradition contributes further to the distinctive flavor of the tales. *The Tale of Tales* contains the earliest literary versions, in the West, of many celebrated tale types— Cinderella, Sleeping Beauty, Rapunzel, All-Fur, Hansel and Gretel, among others—which on the whole outdo their better-known counterparts in sheer narrative exuberance.

In the years following its publication *The Tale of Tales* inspired much admiration but few further experiments with the genre; the only other Italian fairy-tale collection of the seventeenth century is Pompeo Sarnelli's *Posilicheata* (An outing to Posillipo [1684]), comprised of five tales told in Neapolitan by peasant women at the end of a country banquet described in the frame story. The enormous production and popularity of fairy tales in seventeenth- and eighteenth-century France saw no parallel phenomenon in Italy, and it was nearly a century and a half before the advent of another major Italian fairy-tale opus, Carlo Gozzi's *Fiabe teatrali* (*Fairy Tales for the Theater* [1760–70]), several of which were directly derived from Basile.

With the explosion of interest, in the nineteenth century, in the archaeology of popular traditions such as folk songs, oral poetry, legends, folktales, and fairy tales, Basile received new attention. Jacob and Wilhelm Grimm, pioneers in this field, wrote what has become one of the most famous collections of fairy tales in the world, *Children's and Household Tales;* one of their unfinished projects was an unabridged translation of *The Tale of Tales.* In Italy, too, there was an abundance of studies and compilations of tales, especially following the period of Italian unification (1861–70) and the concurrent attempts to "rediscover" the roots of national identity. These include Laura Gonzenbach's *Sicilianische Märchen* (*Sicilian Tales* [1870]), Vittorio Imbriani's *Novellaja fiorentine* (Florentine tales [1871]) and *Novellaja Milanese* (Milanese tales [1872]), the multivolume *Fiabe novelle e racconti popolari siciliani* (Fairy tales, novellas, and popular tales of Sicily [1875]) by Giuseppe Pitrè, and others. Although the hybrid character of Basile's tales—equally marked by the personality of their author and the impersonality of the "raw material," as one early scholar, Imbriani, commented—distinguishes them from the sort of tales collected by these folklorists, without exception they recognized Basile as a groundbreaking figure whose mark on the subsequent tradition, both oral and literary, was undebatable.

The first significant critical work on Basile of this period was Imbriani's lengthy essay titled "Il gran Basile: Studio biografico e bibliografico" (1875). But it was Benedetto Croce, whose lifelong passion for Neapolitan culture culminated in a number of essays on Basile, who had by far the largest role in bringing *The Tale of Tales* to the attention of the scholarly community, if not the general public. In 1891 he published an edition of the first two days, with an extensive apparatus; a version of the introduction to this edition, "Giambattista Basile e il *Cunto de li cunti*," was later included in the 1911 volume *Saggi sulla letteratura del Seicento*. In 1925 Croce's complete Italian translation was issued, with another landmark essay, "Giambattista Basile e l'elaborazione artistica delle fiabe popolari" (later appearing in *Storia dell'età barocca in Italia*). Croce, for whom the

Baroque was synonymous with artistic and moral aberration, defined Basile as an "unconscious ironizer" of the aesthetic codes of his period and considered *The Tale of Tales* the most supreme expression of the Italian Baroque for the very reason that in it the Baroque "dissolves" in a "merry dance."

As Croce was reevaluating Basile's work in its literary and cultural context, the fairy tale was sparking interest in the fields of narrative theory and psychology. Vladimir Propp's *Morphology of the Folktale* (1928) provided the groundwork for a rigorous structural analysis of the fairy tale that was later appropriated by scholars not only of folktales and fairy tales but of other narrative forms as well. Both Sigmund Freud and Carl Jung occupied themselves with the inner meaning of fairy tales and folk motifs, and each had disciples who dedicated full-length studies to the analysis of fairy tales.

By mid-century Basile had been canonized as a key source in Italo Calvino's masterly compilation, *Fiabe italiane* (*Italian Folktales*), published in 1956 and often considered the Italian equivalent of the Grimms' collection; and in the last several decades many of the prejudices expressed by earlier scholars have given way to a more nuanced consideration of Basile's work and the age in which he created it. In Bruno Porcelli's words,

> The art of *The Tale of Tales* is no longer considered to be in opposition, whether voluntarily or involuntarily, to the tastes of its age, but in full harmony with them. Today it is all too easy to maintain that the comic and grotesque elements of the work are not an ironization of this or that element (literature, or contemporary social reality, or the popular material of the fairy tale), but that they express the need, common to so many seventeenth-century authors, to explore, by means of the comic and the grotesque, a new world, to discover expressive forms different from the traditional ones.[11]

During the same period folklorists such as Max Lüthi and Lutz Röhrich were bridging more traditional folklore studies to the fields of literary criticism and cultural history, Lüthi by emphasizing the "literariness" of the fairy tale, and Röhrich by addressing the relationship between the folktale or fairy tale and the reality in which it was created. The most recent studies of Basile have capitalized on these sorts of methodological shifts, offering detailed analyses of the ways in which Basile "reconstructs" the oral, popular tradition of folktales to produce the new genre of the literary fairy tale; of the re-

---

11. Porcelli 197–98.

lationship between the seemingly fantastic universe represented in the tales and the sociohistorical reality in which they were written; and of how Basile's narrative strategies suggestively foreshadow certain postmodernist narrative techniques.

Although critical work on Basile in the English-speaking world still remains scarce (the only full-length study is my own), there are signs that this may change. In this century, Basile has already been the subject of a major international conference in Zürich (2002), a volume of essays, many articles, and a number of new translations into various European languages.

THE STRUCTURE OF THE COLLECTION

The Tale of Tales shares many structural features with the *Decameron* and other novellas as well as fairy-tale collections. The most apparent of these is its framed structure, in which the urgent circumstances of one tale—in this case, also a fairy tale—generate the telling of the rest of the tales, which in their turn lead to a resolution of the dilemma presented in the opening installment of the frame. (Basile's reelaboration of the framing device is, in reality, closer to the tradition of Eastern collections like the *Arabian Nights* than to the more typical novellistic framing technique of a simulation of reality with respect to the "fiction" of the tales within, such as we find in the *Decameron*.) In *The Tale of Tales* the frame centers around a number of common fairy-tale motifs—"the princess who would not laugh" and "the supplanted bride," among others—and unfolds in this way: after many unsuccessful attempts to make his daughter Zoza laugh, the king of Hairy Valley finally has a fountain of oil erected before his palace. An old woman stops to collect some oil, but her jar is broken by a rock hurled by a court page, who after her outraged reaction continues to taunt her. She responds by lifting up her skirts and exposing, to the courtly audience, her "woodsy scene," which sets Zoza laughing. At this ultimate offense the old woman lays a curse on Zoza: she must depart on a quest for her destined husband, prince Tadeo, and wake him from the deep sleep in which he lies by filling a pitcher with her tears. After many adventures Zoza finds Tadeo and sets to her job, but just as she is finishing she falls asleep and the pitcher is taken by a slave, Lucia, who at that moment happens to be passing by. Lucia marries Tadeo and becomes pregnant; determined to win back Tadeo, Zoza moves into a palace across from Tadeo's and uses three magic objects she has previously obtained from fairies to attract Lucia's—and Tadeo's—attention, finally casting a spell on

Lucia that makes her crave tales. One of the most telling anti-Boccaccian moments occurs at the end of the frame, when Tadeo summons the ten "most expert and quick-tongued" tale-tellers of the city, who come in the form of grotesque crones: "lame Zeza, twisted Cecca, goitered Meneca, big-nosed Tolla, hunchback Popa, drooling Antonella, snout-faced Ciulla, cross-eyed Paola, mangy Ciommetella, and shitty Iacova." They, he and Lucia, and the rest of his court then convene around a fountain outside his palace to hear tales. At the beginning of the fifth day, as Lucia is nearing her time to give birth, Zoza substitutes for an ill teller; after the ninth tale she tells her own story and reveals the slave's deceit. Lucia, still pregnant, is buried alive from the head down, Zoza takes her rightful place as wife to Tadeo, and *The Tale of Tales* ends.

The collection is thus divided into five days (and there is certainly a playful false modesty toward Boccaccio in this precise halving), each containing ten tales, one per teller. Each tale is introduced by a rubric that sums up the story and a preamble that includes a summary of the audience's reactions to the previous tale as well as reflections on the teachings of the tale to come (often leading to discussions of favorite Renaissance and Baroque topics such as fortune and virtue, wit, envy), and concludes with a moralizing proverb. Days 1–4 open with a description of the various pastimes of the group—banquets, songs, and dances—and conclude with the performance of extrinsic works, lengthy satiric dialogues that in spite of their decidedly unpastoral nature go by the name of "eclogues" and are recited by characters who are servants of Tadeo's court but not tellers themselves. Whereas in the tales proper the way in which characters are depicted and their adventures unfold only hint at Basile's views, the eclogues give full rein to Basile the moralist and commentator on social ills. The first, "The Crucible," has as its theme the contrast between appearance and reality, a favorite Baroque topos; the second, "The Dye," deals similarly with the ways in which the true motivations of individuals are masked and made to seem their opposite by society; "The Stove" treats the fleeting nature of all worldly institutions and pleasures, which ultimately result in tedium; and "The Hook" presents a theme of the greed and thirst for material wealth that lead to the search for personal profit by any means possible. The eclogues thus provide a counterpoint to the narratives by which they are surrounded: satires in the grotesque-pessimistic Baroque mode, they are a darker and more realistic note amid the optimistic fantasy of the tales.

Elements of an overall narrative organization, both within the confines of each day and from day to day, are present, although not to the degree of the rigorous thematic arrangement of a collection like the *Decameron*. References to the frame tale are found throughout *The Tale of Tales,* providing a constant reminder of the genetic link between the tales and what has spawned them as well as increasing the suspense around the ultimate destinies of Zoza and Lucia. A certain thematic progression is also evident, beginning with the tales of social rise that dominate day 1: seven of these tales feature an initially poor, simple-minded, or neglected protagonist who by means of a magic helper ends up in a socially superior position. In day 2 Basile takes the reader into more "fantastic" realms, where the emphasis, in the protagonists' journeys, is less on the final social legitimation of the traveler than on the adventures encountered in the course of the journeys themselves. The esoteric and, in general, magic are also more pervasive in these tales, as is discussion of the effects of envy and gratitude. Day 3 expands the theme of violation of conventional hierarchies to include tales of protagonists (mostly female, bourgeois, or both) who actively rebel against destinies that have been prearranged for them (usually marriage) by astutely manipulating their surroundings and fashioning their own fates, thus adopting strategies very different from the heroes of the first two days, who much more passively await their change of fortunes. The preambles move away from discussion of envy, gratitude, and fortune and instead figure their tales as parables of obedience and disobedience, in which the latter brings the most rewarding results. Day 4 is almost entirely devoted to stories of both magical and not so magical transformations, while at the same time continuing to showcase the active human intervention that characterizes the tales of the third day. Day 4 thus legitimates, by promoting them to the level of bona fide metamorphoses, the transgressions of natural and social boundaries that in day 3 have a more individual character. Finally, the tales of day 5 have much less of an apparent organization around central themes or motifs but instead constitute the culmination of the experiments with themes and rhetorical techniques introduced in the first four days. It is significant that the two tales that do share a similar motif focus on the creation of a spouse out of "raw" materials gleaned from the organic world or from the imagination (5.3 and 5.6)—an apt metaphor for Basile's fairy-tale project itself.

READING *THE TALE OF TALES*

Let us begin with a very basic question: what is the meaning of the second part of *The Tale of Tales*'s title, "Entertainment for Little

Ones"? To those familiar with fairy tales through later collections such as the Grimms' *Children's and Household Tales* (first ed. 1812), Perrault's *Stories or Tales of Past Times* (1697), or the anthologies of tales so widespread since the early twentieth century, reading *The Tale of Tales* can be a revelation. The tales were and are clearly not addressed to an audience of children, and adult readers may find themselves more intellectually and aesthetically engaged by this dense and willfully labyrinthine text than they had imagined they could be by a collection of fairy tales. Even if the title does refer to one of the possible functions of the fairy tale—to entertain children—and children were certainly included in oral storytelling activities at Basile's time and long before, they became the target audience only later, in the eighteenth and above all nineteenth centuries. Thus, the collection is decidedly *not* for little ones. The frequent mentions of "nursery stories" and the old wives who tell them refer instead, I believe, to the variety of languages and genres that merge in *The Tale of Tales*. When, for instance, at the end of the frame story prince Tadeo calls for tales "of the sort that old women usually entertain the little ones with," he speaks of the larger popular or folkloric culture; it was common practice during Basile's time to conflate children's culture with "low" culture, which was often seen as childlike or primitive. At the same time, masking the tales as children's pastime could have been an effective strategy for encouraging acceptance of this absolutely novel genre by the literary elite among whom the tales originally circulated.

Basile's audience would have been determined by its taste or lack of taste for such an idiosyncratic genre; it would also, of course, have been limited by its ability to actually read, or understand, a work written not in standard Italian but in a dialect. By using Neapolitan to re-create his narrative material, Basile thus not only simulated the oral tale-telling situation (in which the "mother tongue," not the acquired "Tuscan," would have been used) but also asserted his faithfulness to the native culture that nurtured those tales. And, as we have seen, Basile was not alone in this sort of self-conscious adoption of dialect as a literary language.

Basile's project is a fascinating early example of an "ex-centric" text (a term coined by Linda Hutcheon in her discussions of post-modernism), a work that highlights its own marginal or hybrid status and exploits it as a means for a critical engagement with dominant traditions and discourses. Even if the audience for such a work was probably closer in reality to the elite group of the frame tale (prince Tadeo and members of his court) than to the one Tadeo conjures up in his speech on tale-telling (solidly middle class, with its artisans, merchants, doctors, and lawyers), it was an audience of eclectic aesthetic tastes representative of the evolving literate public as a whole in a period that brought significant shifts not only in the system of genres, but also in the reception of cultural products.

That *The Tale of Tales* begs a sophisticated audience is quite apparent from the language in which it is written. Hyperbolic description, long-winded accolades, flamboyant metaphor, bloated word lists, endless strings of insults, and deformative citations of the most diverse authors and traditions can at times overshadow the bare storyline to the point of rendering it almost an afterthought. The *way* the tales are narrated is just as spectacular as *what* is narrated therein; episodes are memorable as much for how they are drawn as for the events they evoke. Who can forget the poignant farewell pronounced by Cienzo in "The Merchant" (1.7) as he leaves his beloved Naples, in which he recalls the prime landmarks of his city as well as its abundant culinary wonders? Or the account, somewhere between repulsive and hilarious, of a king's tryst with a haggard old woman in "The Old Woman Who Was Skinned" (1.10)? Or the pages of insults heaped on a sponging neighbor in "The Buddy" (2.10)? Basile's very Baroque pyrotechnics may please more or less, but it cannot be denied that they are part and parcel of the stories he tells (which make some recent attempts at abridgment seem so awkward).

Another technique for engaging polemically with convention is found in the intertextual references woven through the tales, which generally serve to bring the themes, characters, and language of the "illustrious" traditions of classical antiquity or the Renaissance down to the level of everyday—(albeit fairy-tale)—reality and frequently to laughable parody. For example, in "The Myrtle" (1.2) a prince attacks a group of envious courtesans who have tried to end his beloved fairy's life: "with the heart of Nero and the cruelty of Medea, [you] made an omelet of that pretty little head and minced up these lovely limbs like meat for sausage." Nero and Medea, emblems of ferocious cruelty, here give added force and solemnity to the prince's imprecations—at least until the courtesans' evil actions are likened to those of an overzealous cook. Or, in "The Goose" (5.1), a prince who stops in an alley to relieve himself and then uses what he thinks is a dead goose to wipe himself ends up with the beak of the very live goose stuck to his underside, "like a feathery Salmacis to a hairy Hermaphrodites." The reference is to the nymph Salmacis, who prayed to keep the unwilling Hermaphrodites in her arms forever, resulting in the fusion of the two into a hermaphrodite; the incongruous juxtaposition of the two contexts creates an irresistibly comic effect, in which a dramatic story of amorous aggression is demoted to an aggressive but mundane search for toilet paper.

Basile's manipulation of Renaissance classicism is even more ambitious; the overblown descriptions of princesses and hags, gentle beauties and ogresses that are a distinguishing feature of *The Tale of Tales* reveal a reworking of the literary portraits that were a centerpiece of the Renaissance love lyric. The sort of rhetorical acrobatics we find in *The Tale of Tales* was very much part of the Baroque aesthetic, and Basile misses no chance to exhibit his virtuoso skills in passages like the two below. The first depicts the heroine of 4.5, "The Dragon."

She was the most resplendent thing you could find on the whole earth: her hair was a set of handcuffs for the cops of Love, her forehead a tablet on which was written the price list for the shop of the Graces of amorous pleasures, her eyes two lighthouses that signaled the vessels of desire to turn their prow toward the port of joys, her mouth a honeycomb between two rose hedges;

The second describes the ugly and envious co-protagonist of 3.10, "The Three Fairies."

[She] was the quintessence of all cankers, the prime cut of all sea orcas, the cream of all cracked barrels. Her head was full of nits, her hair a ratty mess, her temples plucked, her forehead like a hammer, her eyes like a hernia, her nose a knotty bump, her teeth full of tartar, and her mouth like a grouper's; she had the beard of a goat, the throat of a magpie, tits like saddlebags, shoulders like cellar vaults, arms like a reel, hooked legs, and heels like cabbages. In short, she was from head to toe a lovely hag, a fine spot of plague, an unsightly bit of rot, and above all she was a midget, an ugly goose, and a snot nose.

What is striking, besides the sheer length of these descriptions, is the range of metaphorical fields that they comprehend—in the first, for example, those of law enforcement, commerce, navigation, and agriculture—and, specifically, the contamination of registers. It is this sort of playful admixture that highlights not only Basile's strategy of deformation with regard to tradition but also the important role that the exploration of untrod stylistic territory has in the project of forging a new literary genre.

Perhaps the most ubiquitous metaphorical play is found in the many descriptions of the sun's movements, interpolations common enough in the epic and the pastoral, but wielded to novel effect in *The Tale of Tales*. As has often been commented, barely a fairy-tale event goes by without the sun rising or setting on it. But far from serving exclusively as an oblique meditation on time—a favorite Baroque obsession—these periphrastic interpolations are employed as pretext for the encyclopedic survey of daily activities, trades and professions, and social customs and practices that together constitute a whole other collection of "micro-narratives" of the busy, polymorphous material world that was the kingdom of Naples of Basile's time. Thus we hear of what happened "before Dawn had hung the red Spanish coverlet from the window of the East, to shake out the fleas" (5.8), or when "the Sun, like an unsuccessful whore, began to change quarters" (2.6), or "as soon as the Sun opened its bank to pay out the deposit of light to the creditors of the day" (4.9), and so forth.

Metaphor is found when a word or groups of words are used not in their customary or literal sense but in a context where they assume another meaning, so that identity between two unlike terms is established (such as the relationship between "mouth" and "honeycomb" in the description above). It is a trope of transformation and transport (*translatio*); dissimilar objects—often vastly so with the *metafora ingegnosa* of the Baroque—are united in an attempt, more than to describe or imitate the "real" worlds of phenomena, to effect, in the words of Frank Warnke, an "imaginative modification" of the same,[12] and thus create "marvel" through the unusual couplings. The metamorphosis effected by metaphor (the honeycomb that becomes a mouth, or vice versa) also highlights the transformations endemic to the fairy tale itself, on the thematic plane: the endless possibilities for its characters and locales to become what they are not by crossing seemingly insurmountable geographical, class, and even species lines (peasants become royalty, humans bears, and so forth). And as we have seen, the narrative representation of metamorphosis is paralleled by a radical experimentation with metaphor that goes beyond the strictly textual to include the "transformation" of multiple languages and traditions into a uniquely woven end product.

The stylistic hybridity of *The Tale of Tales* also comprehends the appropriation of techniques common to oral narration, a logical choice considering the associations of both the genre (the fairy tale) and the language (Neapolitan) with oral culture. We have already considered how the frame scene in which the tale-tellers are selected both cites the oral archetype—a group of old wives telling fairy tales—and revises it by placing this activity in a very different context of orality, the court conversations or "entertainments" theorized by Baldassar Castiglione and others and intensely practiced at the courts and academies that Basile frequented.

It may be argued that some of the "rougher" aspects of Basile's style

---

12. Warnke, *Versions of Baroque* 19.

that are immediately apparent—the long, run-on sentences often connected by unsophisticated coordination of the "and" and "but" variety, extensive use of participial constructions, inconsistencies of tense
and agreement, replication of lexical elements, and the like—can be
attributed to a lack of final textual revision on the part of the author.
But the reader will find that many of the "characteristics of orally
based thought and expression" as described, for example, by Walter
Ong are fully at home in *The Tale of Tales*'s "additive rather than sub-
ordinative" syntax, its "aggregative rather than analytic" style that
makes use of "epithets and other formulary baggage," the predilection for "agonistically toned" exchanges, redundancy and *copia,* the
interplay between repetition and variation, the tendency to catalogue
and list, its episodic structure, and so forth.[13] For example, one of the
foundational conceits of Basile's literary project—exploring the treasures of Neapolitan culture—is frequently expressed in the form of
parenthetical lists: of medicines, contemporary fashions, birds, fish,
culinary specialties, games, songs, dances (these last especially evident
in the introductions to days 2, 3, and 4), and more. Among those, the
most encyclopedic catalogues of *The Tale of Tales* are of linguistic
items such as oaths, proverbs, and, above all, tirades of insults pos-
sessing a near physical force (another characteristic of oral culture,
according to Ong). This one, for example, is delivered at the climax of
tale 2.10 to a parasitic friend who refuses to take no for an answer.

> Now we've really filled the spindle! [. . .] You act like an occupying sol-
> dier who wants to scare us out of our possessions! A finger should have
> been enough, but you took the whole hand. [. . .] He who lacks discre-
> tion owns the whole world, but he who will not measure his actions is
> measured by others, and if you have nothing to measure with, we have
> reels and rolling pins! And finally, you know what they say: "A nice face
> deserves a nice pounding"! [. . .] You can go find a toothpick if you
> think this inn is open for your rotten gullet! [. . .] And if you're a dinner
> spy, a bread gobbler, a table cleaner, a kitchen sweeper, a pot licker, a
> bowl shiner, a glutton, a sewer pipe; if you're ravenous and have a wolf's
> appetite [. . .] then go to some other parish, go pull up the trawl net, go
> pick rags from the garbage dump, go look for nails in the street gullies,
> go collect wax from funeral candles, and go unplug latrine pipes so you
> can fill your gorge. May this house be like fire to you! [. . .]

Even the pervasive punning and wordplay whose urbane manipulation of Baroque conceit was one of the reasons Italo Calvino deemed

---

13. Ong, *Orality and Literacy* 31–57.

Basile "an odd Mediterranean Shakespeare" may constitute a simulation of the need, on the part of the oral storyteller, to use every means at his disposition—and the showier the better—to keep his audience's ears perked.

On the shore of thematics and characterization, the reader is presented with a morally ambivalent universe in which, for the very reason that their humanity is portrayed with some degree of complexity, protagonists and antagonists undercut our expectations of classic fairy-tale types such as the strong and ingenious hero, the passive and obedient heroine, the upright and just king, the evil ogre, and the like. In this Basile may actually be closer to the paradigms of oral storytelling of his time (when, we should remember, children were a negligible share of the audience), but if we contrast his moral vision to that of authors with whom the fairy tale is more readily associated today—the Brothers Grimm, above all—the differences are enormous. All of Basile's tales except one or two end well and in this sense affirm that the actions of the winning protagonists are the "right" ones for attaining marriage and riches. But *how* the heroes reach that end tends to be far more convoluted, ethically, than the itineraries of their brothers and sisters in the Grimms' tales. "The Cinderella Cat" (1.6), for instance, is the earliest European version of one of the most beloved tales of the canon, familiar to many in later versions in which the heroine is painted as a virtuous martyr: a girl "whose gentleness and goodness were without parallel" (Perrault); "good and pious" (Grimm). The protagonist of Basile's tale, on the other hand, is a conniving strategist; hardly helpless and even less virtuous, her final triumph results from a criminal intervention in the events of the story. She first attempts to better her lot by killing her stepmother, under the guidance of her teacher (and soon-to-be stepmother number two), and then, when her loyalty is not repaid, claws her way into an even more attractive milieu. Thus, regardless of the final moral, which states "those who oppose the stars are crazy"—only one of many that prove to be inaccurate fits for their tales—Basile's "Cinderella" tells the story of a worldly young woman's construction of her own destiny.

In general Basile's characters exhibit more down-to-earth behavior than many of their counterparts in later collections; they are flesh-and-blood creatures involved in fairy-tale adventures but also in the affairs of everyday life. They emote and are long-winded about it; they express affection and amorous passion, are cruel and vengeful, whine and complain, gossip, browbeat, and nag: in short, everything that we have always suspected is behind the black-or-white, good-or-bad exteriors of the more famous Cinderellas and Sleeping Beauties—

and perhaps, that we're secretly relieved to find. They also have sex, and revel in it, another aspect of Basile's collection that a modern public, brought up on a different fairy-tale diet, may not anticipate. And the sex scenes are among the most enchanting—and grotesque— of the book. In "The Myrtle" (1.2), for example, we hear of a prince's nighttime encounter with a mysterious creature.

[W]hen he felt that certain business drawing close and touched it, he realized what a smooth job it was; and where he imagined he would be squeezing hedgehog needles he found a little something that was more mellow and soft than Tunisian wool, more yielding and pliable than the tail of a marten, more delicate and tender than the feathers of a goldfinch. [. . .] [T]hinking that it might be a fairy (as in fact it was) he wrapped himself around it like an octopus, and as they played at "Mute sparrow," they also tried out "Stone in your lap" [two children's games, here used with sexual connotations].

At the other extreme, in "The Old Woman Who Was Skinned" (1.10) we find a king's similarly mysterious encounter with a paramour who turns out to be an ancient woman:

When Night arrived [. . .] the old woman smoothed back all the wrinkles on her body and gathered them behind her shoulders in a knot, which she tied tightly with a piece of twine. [. . .] The king was more than ready to light the fuse on his artillery, and as soon as he heard her come and lie down he smeared himself all over with musk and civet and sprayed himself from head to toe with cologne water, and then raced to bed like a Corsican hound. And it was lucky for the old woman that the king was wearing so much perfume, on account of which he wasn't able to smell the fumes coming from her mouth, the stink of her little tickly areas, and the stench of that ugly thing. But no sooner had he lay down than, feeling around, he became aware of that business on the back of her neck and discovered the dried tripe and deflated bladders that the wretched old woman kept in the back of her shop. Keeping his composure, he decided not to say anything right then, since he needed to have a clearer idea on the matter. And so, pretending not to notice, he cast anchor at Mandracchio when he had believed he would be on the coast of Posillipo, and sailed forth on a barge when he had thought he would be charting his course on a Florentine galley.

Although noble-spirited and courageous heroes are certainly not absent from *The Tale of Tales,* a significant number of winning protagonists are simpletons who possess few redeeming qualities. The hero of the very first tale (1.1), Antuono, is described as "such a bird-brain and muttonhead that he couldn't even throw a snowball." After his exasperated mother kicks him out of the house, Antuono moves in with an ogre, where he grows big and fat and receives from the ogre a number of magic gifts that make his fortune—without, however, undergoing any significant change for the better in the course of the story. Likewise, his fellow numskull Peruonto (1.3), who is considered "the most dismal creature, the greatest yokel, and the most solemn idiot that Nature ever created," is also banished by his mother, but in the course of his wanderings he makes a princess laugh with his absurd antics and eventually marries her.

On the contrary, there are a striking number of female protagonists who, with the sole aid of their intelligence (which thus substitutes for the magic that lesser heroes need), succeed in turning events to their advantage, often in spite of having to deal with hostile family members and male contenders whose social class and power far exceed theirs. We find one of these unexpectedly modern heroines in "Viola" (2.3), where a working girl makes fun of a king who greets her every day, and then manages to playfully skirt every trap he sets for her, bringing the prince to this conclusion: "I give up and you win, and now that I truly realize that you know more than I do, I want you without further ado for my wife!" The authority of Sapia (5.6) is even more evident: she is hired as a tutor for a doltish prince who, under her guidance and fueled by a slap she gives him when her patience is exhausted, becomes one of the most learned men of his kingdom. Even after he determines to avenge himself for the insult by marrying her so that he can maltreat her freely, she one-ups him and he is forced, at the end, to admit the superiority of her wisdom.

Kings and other representatives of power often have problems living up to the royal ideal of responsible management of subjects and reign, principally because they are either oblivious to their monarchic duties or driven to emotional excess by their thirst for power. The diminished authority and distracted nature of Basile's kings are underlined, structurally, by the fact that they are absent at the start of about half of the tales, appearing only subsequently and in minor roles as accessories to the hero's rise. The composite portrait that these kings form is of a dysfunctional system of power that, perhaps, figures the general sociopolitical crisis—of the Spanish monarchy and of the local nobility—that was playing itself out in the kingdom of Naples of Basile's time. Examples of deficient kings include the king of High Mountain (1.5), who fattens up a flea by feeding it daily with his own blood until it grows to monstrous proportions and he has it skinned; when he organizes a contest for guessing the origin of the skin an ogre wins, and the king forces his daughter to marry him. The king of Strong Fortress (1.10) obsesses about the mysterious neighbors that live under him until he finally convinces one of them to go to bed with him, only to discover, in the grotesque scene already considered, that she is a decrepit hag. Courtiers, a professional category with which Basile was intimately acquainted, fare no better, tending to be indecisive or envious and vengeful. In "Corvetto" (3.7), for instance, a virtuous courtier with magical powers bypasses the traps that the other, inferior courtiers lay out for him, and ultimately marries the daughter of his king.

Conventional antagonists are sometimes not so evil, either, as we can see from a survey of Basile's preferred villain, the ogre. The ogre in "Viola" (2.3) is a vassal of the king who lives in a garden adjacent to Viola's house, into which she is lowered by her envious sisters in the hope of eliminating her. The ogre, however, in an irresistibly comic scene in which he accounts for Viola's sudden appearance with the theory that one of his farts has impregnated a tree and thus generated the girl, tends to her with the loving attention of a father. In "Green Meadow" (2.2) we encounter an ogre couple that, in a reversal of the usual order of aggression, is "cannibalized" by the heroine of the tale, who needs their fat to cure an ailing prince. These ogres are presented as enlightened commentators on the doings of civilized society; during an affectionate after-dinner conversation the ogre complains to his wife that "everything is topsy-turvy and all awry," since "you hear of things that would make you jump out of your clothes: buffoons rewarded, scoundrels esteemed, lazybones honored, assassins protected, counterfeiters defended, and respectable men barely appreciated or esteemed."

Like the ogres, we, too, have the impression, when reading *The Tale of Tales,* that reigning hierarchies—literary, social, existential—have gone a bit topsy-turvy, and that this not only serves the purpose of reinforcing the alternative construct of a marvelous fairy-tale world, but also constitutes a vigorous engagement with the here and now. The degree to which real and fantastic, human and supernatural, nature and art, good and evil merge and are even mirrored one in the other, in an endless play of intersections, makes this a world of permeable boundaries and questionable closures, despite the token, rhetorical "happily-ever-after" with which most of the tales do end. The recognition that a clear-eyed affirmation of the most repellent, wondrous, confounding, *essential* aspects of human existence does not tally with a neat packaging of moral lessons is, perhaps, not always easy. But it does hold a remarkable affinity with our own (post)modern sensibility that so often expresses itself in paradox, contradiction, parodic transgression, a taste for the hybrid, and a distrust of ready-made categories. It is for this reason that the journeys of initiation narrated in *The Tale of Tales* bear, at the end, a certain familiarity to our own conflicted dialogue with the world around us.

THIS TRANSLATION

The recent critical attention that Basile has received is certainly as exciting as it is merited, but as Basile's star has risen there has been no corresponding attention to making his work itself more accessible. The lack of an up-to-date translation of *The Tale of Tales* is not only a serious impediment to further textual analysis on the part of scholars who lack familiarity with Neapolitan or Italian, but also deprives the more general public of tale enthusiasts—not to mention fabulists and storytellers—of a text of infinite resources and riches.

The only complete English translation of *The Tale of Tales* of the twentieth century was published in 1932 by the British folklorist Norman Penzer; it is twice removed from the Neapolitan original since Penzer translated from Benedetto Croce's 1925 Italian translation. Although quite readable and often elegant, the deficiencies in voice, vibrancy, and accuracy with respect to the original are significant in Penzer's version. Let us look at a representative passage. In "The Old Woman Who Was Skinned" (1.10), a king's attention is occupied by his mysterious downstairs neighbors, until, in the original,

> Era arredutto a termene che non poteva fare no pideto senza dare a lo naso de ste brutte gliannole, che d'ogne poco cosa 'mbrosoliavano a le pigliava lo totano: mo decenno ca no gesommino cascato da coppa l'aveva 'mbrognolato lo caruso, mo ca na lettera stracciata l'aveva 'ntontolato na spalla, mo ca no poco de porvere l'aveva ammatontato na coscia.

Penzer translates,

> The King was brought to this point: that he was not even able to sneeze without upsetting these old hags, for they grumbled and complained about everything. First they said that a sprig of jessamine had fallen from the window and bruised their heads, then that a torn letter had hurt their shoulders, and then that some powder had crushed their hips.

In the present translation the passage reads,

The king was reduced to such a state that he couldn't even fart without causing those old pains in the neck to wrinkle their noses, for they grumbled and threw themselves about like squid over the smallest thing. First they said that a jasmine flower fallen from above had given one of them a lump on her head, then that a torn-up letter had dislocated one of their shoulders, and then that a pinch of dust had bruised one of their thighs.

For my translation I have used as primary text the 1634–36 *editio princeps* that belongs to the Biblioteca Nazionale Braidense of Milan. The process of translation was painstaking due to the many degrees of difficulty of the text, but especially to the fact that the original is written in a seventeenth-century dialect often creatively manipulated by its author himself. My own familiarity with Neapolitan comes from some direct experience with related Italian dialects, but above all from long hours spent with Basile's Neapolitan texts, texts contemporary to *The Tale of Tales* (in both Neapolitan and Italian), Neapolitan dictionaries and grammars, and the existing Italian and English translations.

Once the essential semantic and syntactic hurdles had been confronted it was necessary to pose what is, perhaps, the translator's most important question: to what degree should the text be "familiarized"? Translating Basile's early modern version of a nonstandard language into standard American English is especially fraught with the risks of assimilating the status of Neapolitan to that of a dominant language. Specialists in Italian literature know that Basile's text has virtually no precedents, or epigones, for that matter, in Italian literature, and this exceptionality derives in part from its hybrid linguistic status. Should the translator attempt to reproduce Basile's every stylistic quirk, every note of his polyphonic opus, possibly to the detriment of fluidity, or, instead, to smooth the rough edges and coax the text into more orderly submission?

The temptation to "domesticate" in the direction of rendering a more polished, easy to read, and accommodating translation is one that most of Basile's early translators, and some of his later ones, succumbed to. Even Croce, certainly not naïve about the risks inherent in passing from one language to another—and a fellow Neapolitan to boot—tended to deal with difficult, or racy, passages by either simplification, elimination, or, above all, sanitation of the original. One example may suffice. At the beginning of "The Goose" (5.1), two penniless sisters spend their last resources to buy a goose, which as soon as they get it home awards them a big surprise. In the original we find,

Ma, scoppa dì e fa buono iuorno, la bona papara commenzaie a cacare
scute riccie, de manera che a cacata a cacata se ne 'nchiero no cascione.
E fu tale lo cacatorio che commenzaro ad auzare capo e se le vedde lu-
cere lo pilo. . . .

Croce's Italian translation reads,

Ma spunta l'alba e fa buon giorno: la buona oca cominciò a fare scudi
ricci, di modo che, a poco a poco, esse ne empirono un gran cassone; e
fu tale quell'evacuazione che cominciarono ad alzar la testa e si vide
loro rilucere il pelo.

All derivatives of the verb *cacare* (to shit) present in the original are
expunged in Croce, resulting in a reduced, flattened rendition, as we
see repeated in Penzer's translation (based on Croce).

But dawn comes and it turns out a fine day: the worthy goose began to
make golden ducats, so that, little by little, they filled a great chest with
them; and, such was that excrement, that they began to carry their
heads high with shining countenances.

Finally, my translation from the original:

And when morning breaks it's a nice day, for the good goose began to
shit hard cash until, shitload upon shitload, they had filled up a whole
chest. There was so much shit, in fact, that the two sisters began to raise
their heads and see their fur shine.

On a more specific level, considerable challenges present themselves
on every page of *The Tale of Tales* in the form of sophisticated punning and wordplay, citation of the most diverse registers and techni-
cal vocabularies, references to places, people, and usages of Basile's
time, and so forth.

I have opted for a productively foreignizing translation, in which I
attempt to preserve the distinctive tone, as well as the idiosyncrasies,
of Basile's literary language, a language that is "strange" even in
Italy, where all Italians except erudite Neapolitans read him in translation. Nonetheless, a good deal of the cultural references in *The Tale
of Tales* may be unfamiliar to the reader of today, and to embrace a
defamiliarizing strategy to the point of further obscuring these seems
irresponsible. Elucidation of what otherwise might appear to be esoteric references with little meaning has thus been a priority, but I have
preferred, as have most previous editors, to do this outside of the text

in the form of abundant notes, for the simple reason that the material peripheral to the bare plot of the tales forms an entire subtext unto itself that warrants an attentive, "parallel" reading. I have made ample use of the excellent (and exhaustive) notes by Benedetto Croce, Norman Penzer, Michele Rak, Roberto De Simone, and Ruggero Guarini and Alessandra Burani, adding my own when necessary.

In his criticism of "domesticating translation," Lawrence Venuti discusses a term coined by Gilles Deleuze and Félix Guattari: "minor literature." The authors of such literature "are foreigners in their own tongue," and produce

> stylistically innovative texts that make the most striking intervention into a linguistic conjecture by exposing the contradictory conditions of the standard dialect, the literary canon, the dominant culture, the major language. . . . Certain literary texts increase this radical heterogeneity by submitting the major language to constant variation, forcing it to become minor, delegitimizing, deterritorializing, alienating it.[14]

This is precisely Basile's operation as he fashions his Neapolitan not in a space radically separate from the "major" language (Italian) and its traditions, which would make of him a mannered naïf, but in constant dialogue with these. A deceptively fluent translation that purported to re-create a transparency and accessibility that were absent in the original text would thus be the most unfaithful to the spirit and letter of *The Tale of Tales*.

That said, I beg no excuse if what I have produced does not, at the end, leave the reader feeling rewarded by the treasures found in Basile's tales. For with all of its circumlocutions, digressions, extrapolations, and proliferations—all of its marvelous excess—*The Tale of Tales* can be a rocky ride, but never a tedious one.

NANCY L. CANEPA

---

14. Venuti, *The Scandals of Translation* 10.

The Tale of Tales

I

THE FIRST DAY

INTRODUCTION TO
THE TALE OF TALES

[Frame Tale]

A seasoned proverb of ancient coinage says that those who look for what they should not find what they would not, and it's clear that when the monkey tried putting on boots it got its foot stuck,[1] just like what happened to a ragged slave girl who although she had never worn shoes on her feet wanted to wear a crown on her head. But since the millstone grinds out the chaff and sooner or later everything is paid for, she who deceitfully took from others what was theirs ended up caught in the circle of heels,[2] and however steep her climb up was, her tumble down was even greater. It happened in the manner that follows.

It is said that there once was[3] a king, the king of Hairy Valley, who

---

This tale corresponds to Aarne/Thompson tale type 437, The Supplanted Bride. References to tale types follow the classification of Aarne and Thompson (*The Types of the Folktale*) and will henceforth be designated in the form "AT 437." For these indications I have relied heavily on Rudolf Schenda's German edition of *The Tale of Tales* (2000).

Croce notes, with regard to the frame tale, "The beginning is common to a great number of fairy tales [princesses or fairies who do not laugh are also found in tales 1.3, 1.10, 3.5, etc.]. For the adventure of the old woman, see, especially, Giuseppe Pitrè's *Fiabe e leggende poplari siciliane* 13 and 66, and Vittorio Imbriani's *Novellaja fiorentina* 24. [. . .] Also very common is the particular of the three objects given by the fairies to attract the attention of the lost lover" (*Lo cunto de li cunti,* 284).

1. "Travelers and naturalists narrate that hunters, when they see a monkey, put on and take off a pair of boots, which they then leave in sight of the monkey after having smeared them with bird-lime. The monkey, attempting to imitate them, remains ensnared in the unusual footwear. There is, perhaps, also an echo of the ancient fable, told, among others, by Firenzuola, of the monkey and the oak tree, and of Margutte's adventure with the Barbary ape (in Luigi Pulci's *Morgante* 19, 147–48)" (Croce 539).

2. "A game played by children in which they hold hands in a circle, and kick away one of the players who tries to enter the circle from outside it. The child who lets the outside player in must then go outside the circle" (Croce 3).

3. The majority of Basile's tales start with the formulaic "dice ch'era na vota" ("it is said that there once was"), evoking the temporal distancing of the fairy tale but also the oral tradition ("It is said") in which fairy-tale types had thrived for centuries before (and after) Basile. The corresponding Italian "c'era una vota" is usually translated into the English "once upon a time," though I have preferred a more literal translation.

had a daughter named Zoza, who, like a second Zoroaster or Hera-clitus,[4] had never been seen to laugh. Hence her miserable father, whose sole life breath was his only daughter, left nothing undone in his attempts to banish her melancholy. He tried to whet her appetite first with stilt walkers, then with hoop jumpers, acrobats, Master Ruggiero,[5] jugglers, strongmen, a dancing dog, Vracone the jumping monkey, the ass that drinks from a glass, bitchy Lucia,[6] and then with this and then with the other thing. But it was all a waste of time, for not even Master Grillo's remedy,[7] not even the sardonic herb,[8] not even a sword in her chest would have made the corners of her mouth turn up. Finally, not knowing what else to do, as a last resort her poor father ordered that a great fountain of oil[9] be erected before the palace gate, with the idea that as the passersby came and went like ants along the street they would be sprayed and, so as not to lubricate their clothes, would hop about like crickets, jump like goats, and run

---

4. "Zoroaster, or Zarathustra, was the prophet of the esoteric doctrine of the Maz-daic religion of pre-Islamic Iran (X–VI c. BC), according to which the child prophet laughs in his cradle, surrounded by light. [. . .] Heraclitus of Ephesus (c. 550–480 BC) was the Greek philosopher legendary for his enigmatic thought and his refusal to dif-fuse his writings" (Rak 26). In Roman times he was known as the "weeping philoso-pher." The reason for the reference to Zoroaster, who *does* laugh, is unclear.

5. "A popular singer and leader of musicians of the time, mentioned also by [Basile's contemporaries] Del Tufo, Cortese, and Sgruttendio. He gave his name to a sort of dance" (Croce 3).

6. "In the sixteenth and seventeenth centuries the Moorish 'dance of Lucia' was widely performed in Naples. It derived from the ecstatic dances of possession charac-terized by continuous spinning, like those that today are still performed by dervishes. Already 'desacralized' in the sixteenth century, it was transformed into a ritualistic Carnival performance. . . . The ambiguous character of Lucia was played by a man in blackface, dressed as an Oriental woman, whose song and movements referred to the sexual act, birth, death, and resurrection. The accompanying chorus insulted Lucia with the epithet of 'bitch.' . . . Later this dance was confused with the dance of Sfessania, which took its name from the city of Fez in Morocco" (De Simone 7). Jacques Callot, the French artist and contemporary of Basile, did a series of engrav-ings of the Sfessania in 1620. The list of "acts" intended to amuse Zoza is a compen-dium of the various forms of street theater in vogue at the time.

7. "The work *Opera nuova piacevole et da ridere de un villano nomato Grillo quale volse diventar medico* (Venice, 1521) was reprinted many times in this period. This Grillo, among other things, cured a king's daughter by some strange means, causing her to burst into laughter" (Croce 4).

8. *erva sardoneca* (Neap.): A plant of Sardinia believed to cause convulsive laughter in whomever ingested it (Rak 27).

9. "Fountains of oil and, much more often, of wine were one of the most common displays used in seventeenth-century festivities. The 'pleasure' derived on the one hand from the precious foodstuffs that were obtained, but on the other from the ob-servation, from afar, of the throngs of people and the incidents to which such an ap-paratus, like other similar displays, gave rise. Experiments with mechanical fountains were, in these decades, in a phase of expansion" (Rak 27–28).

like hares, slipping and bumping into each other, and that in this way something might happen to make his daughter laugh.

The fountain was thus constructed, and one day while Zoza was sitting at the window as sourly as a pickle an old woman chanced to pass by. She began to fill a jar she had brought with her, sopping up the oil with a sponge, and as she was busily going about her task a certain devil of a court page threw a stone at her with such precision that it hit the jar and broke it to pieces.

At that, the old woman, who had no hairs on her tongue and let no one ride on her back, turned to the page and began to say, "Ah, you worthless thing, you dope, shithead, bed pisser, leaping goat, diaper ass, hangman's noose, bastard mule! Just look, even fleas can cough now! Go on, may paralysis seize you, may your mother get bad news, may you not live to see the first of May![10] Go on, may you be thrust by a Catalan lance[11] or torn apart by ropes (so that no blood will be wasted), may you suffer a thousand ills and then some with winds in your sails! May your seed be lost! Scoundrel, beggar, son of a taxed woman,[12] rogue!"

After hearing this juicy outburst, the lad, who had little hair on his chin and even less discretion, repaid her in the same coin, saying, "Why don't you shut that sewer hole, you bogeyman's grandmother,[13] blood-sucking witch, baby drowner, rag shitter, fart gatherer?" When this news hit home the old woman became so angry that, losing her phlegmatic compass bearings and charging from the stable of patience, she raised her stage curtain and revealed a woodsy scene about which Silvio might have said, "Go and open eyes with your horn."[14] And at this spectacle Zoza started laughing so hard that she nearly lost her senses.

When she saw herself being made fun of, the old woman flew into such a rage that she turned to Zoza with a frightful face and said, "Begone, and may you never pluck a blossom of a husband unless you take the prince of Round Field." Upon hearing those words,

---

10. "A popular feast-day. In Naples every house became a tavern, with green branches over the door; races were run, greased poles were set up, and other merrymaking took place. The first of May was, in fact, celebrated everywhere, and Tuscan literature abounds with references to it" (Croce 539).

11. "The murderous efficacy of Catalan arms was proverbial" (Croce 5).

12. "Neapolitan prostitutes of the time paid a tax of two carlins per month" (Croce 5).

13. *parasacco* (Neap.): "The name of a devil or other evil spirit which nurses used to frighten children with, saying that he will open his sack, push them inside, and carry them off" (Croce 5).

14. Verses from scene 1, act 1 of Giovan Battista Guarini's *Pastor fido* (1590), a pastoral drama that was immensely popular at this time.

Zoza had the old woman called over, for she wanted to know at all costs whether the old woman had insulted her or laid a curse on her.

The old woman answered, "Now you should know that the prince I mentioned is a splendid creature named Tadeo, who on account of a fairy's curse gave the last brushstroke to the canvas of his life and was laid in a tomb outside the city walls. Inscribed on the stone is an epitaph proclaiming that any woman who within three days fills the pitcher that hangs there on a hook with her tears will bring him back to life and win him for her husband. And since it's impossible that two human eyes can piddle enough to fill a pitcher that holds half a bushel—unless they belonged to that Egeria[15] who, I've heard, became a fountain of tears in Rome—this is a curse that I have put on you, because you mocked me and made fun of me, and I beg the heavens that it hits you square on as a vendetta for the offense done to me." As she was saying this she fled down the stairs, fearing a beating.

At that same moment Zoza began to ruminate and chew over the old woman's words, and a little demon entered her lovely head. And after spinning many thoughts and milling countless doubts about the matter, she finally found herself pulled by the winch of that passion that blinds judgment and enchants discourse, and when she had taken a fistful of gold coins from her father's treasury, she slipped out of the palace and kept on walking until she came to the castle of a fairy.

She unloaded her heart's torments on the fairy and, out of compassion for such a beautiful young woman, who had been thrown off her horse by the two spurs of her tender age and her blinding love for things unknown, the fairy gave her a letter of presentation for a sister of hers, also a fairy. And after bestowing all sorts of compliments on her, the next morning—when Night had the birds emit the proclamation that whoever had seen a herd of wandering black shadows would be amply rewarded—she gave her a lovely walnut and said, "Take this, my dear girl, and hold it dear; but open it only in a moment of great need."

And with another letter she entrusted her to another sister. After a long journey Zoza arrived, was welcomed with the same affection, and the next morning received another letter for another sister, together with a chestnut and the same warning she had been given with the walnut. When she had walked a way, she arrived at the castle of the next fairy, who caressed her a thousand times over, and the next

15. "The nymph Egeria wept so much at king Numa's death that Diana transformed her into a fountain" (Croce 6). See Ovid's *Metamorphoses* 15.479–551.

morning when she was leaving presented her with a hazelnut and the same warning to open it only under the knife of need.

Once she had these objects, Zoza threw up her legs and traveled through so many countries and crossed so many woods and rivers that after seven years—just when the Sun, having been awakened by the roosters' trumpets, was putting on its saddle and preparing to make the usual deliveries[16]—she reached Round Field with barely a tail left on her. And there, before entering the city, she saw a marble tomb at the foot of a fountain that, imprisoned in porphyry, was crying crystal tears.

She took the pitcher that was hanging there, put it between her legs, and began to trade lines from the *Menaechmi*[17] with the fountain, hardly lifting her head from the edge of the pitcher, so that it took her less than two days to fill it to within two fingers of the rim— just two more fingers and it would have been full. But she was exhausted from all that crying, and without meaning to she was hoodwinked by sleep and forced to rest for a couple of hours under the tent of her eyelids.

In the meantime there arrived a certain cricket-legged slave girl[18] who often went to that fountain to fill her urn and who knew about the epitaph business, since talk of it was everywhere. When she saw Zoza crying so hard to make those two trickles of tears, she sat for a long time and spied on her, waiting until the pitcher was almost full so that she could wrench that fine booty from Zoza's hands and leave her with a fistful of flies.

As soon as she saw that Zoza was asleep, she took advantage of the opportunity and skillfully slipped the pitcher out from under her, placed her own eyes above it, and, in four snaps, filled it. The moment it was full to the brim the prince got out of his coffin of white stone as if he were awakening from a long sleep, took hold of that mass of black flesh, and carried her off to his palace where, amid festivities and royal fireworks, he made her his wife.

---

16. One of the first of hundreds of metaphorical descriptions of the Sun's rising or setting, a stylistic trademark of *The Tale of Tales* (see introduction).

17. This Roman comedy (sometimes also translated as *The Doubles*) by Plautus (c. 250–184 BC) had an enormous influence on Renaissance theater and at this time continued to be performed in many imitations and variations.

18. "One of the terms used to indicate the physical characteristics of the numerous members of the population of Naples who were of Middle Eastern [or North African] origin, for the most part purchased in slave markets or taken as booty in the course of sea raids or naval battles" (Rak 29). Later in the frame this slave speaks in the Neapolitan-Moorish patois that, besides being spoken in Naples and other ports of Italy where Moorish slaves lived, was also used in comic theater of the time. Such speech is also found in tales 6, 9, and 10 of day 5.

But when Zoza awoke and found the pitcher overturned, and with it her hopes, and saw the coffin open, her heart squeezed shut so tightly that she nearly unpacked the parcels of her soul at the customshouse of Death. Finally, realizing that there was no remedy for her ills and that all she had to complain about were her own eyes, which had insufficiently guarded the calf of her hopes,[19] she set off, one foot after another, until she arrived at the city. There she heard of the prince's festivities and of the fine sort of wife he had taken, and at once imagined what must have happened, exclaiming with a sigh that two black things had brought her to her downfall: sleep and a slave.

Even so, in her attempt to defy Death, against which every animal defends itself to the best of its abilities, she moved into a fine house across from the prince's palace, where although she could not see her heart's idol she could at least contemplate the walls of the temple that held the desired prize. And one day she was sighted by Tadeo, who like a bat was always flying round that black night of a slave but became an eagle when he fixed his eyes upon Zoza—that monster of nature's bounty, that "I'm out"[20] of the game of beauty.

When the slave realized what was going on she raised all hell and, as she was already pregnant, threatened her husband, saying, "If you no move from windowsill, me punch belly and little Georgie kill." Tadeo, who was concerned about his heir, trembled like a reed at the thought of causing his wife any displeasure and tore himself from the sight of Zoza like a soul from its body.

When Zoza saw that sip of broth taken away from her weak hopes, she knew not what course to follow in the moment of extreme need. But then she remembered the fairies' gifts, and opened the walnut. Out came a tiny little man, as big as a doll, the most delicious little plaything in the world, who got up on the windowsill and began to sing with so many trills, warbles, and embellishments that he sounded like Compar Biondo, he surpassed Pezzillo,[21] and he left Cieco di Potenza and the King of Birds far behind.

The slave happened to see and hear this, and became pregnant

---

19. "An allusion to the myth of Argus and the cow Io that was stolen from him by Mercury" (Croce 8).

20. "The expression is taken from certain card games, in which the player who has obtained the points needed to win throws his remaining cards on the table, saying: 'I'm out'" (Croce 8).

21. *compa' Iunno . . . Pezzillo* (Neap.): "Two popular singers of humble origins who were famous in Naples at the time. They are also mentioned in tale 6 of day 4, and in other places in the works of Basile, Cortese, and Sgruttendio [other seventeenth-century Neapolitan authors]. . . . The other two subsequently mentioned were probably similar figures" (Croce 540).

with such longing that she called Tadeo and said to him, "If me no have singing devil from sill, me punch belly and little Georgie kill." The prince, who had let himself be harnessed by the Moorish slave, immediately sent someone to ask Zoza if she was willing to sell it, to which she answered that she was not a merchant but that if he wanted it for a gift, he could take it as an homage. Tadeo, who yearned to keep his wife happy so that she could bring her pregnancy to term, accepted the offer.

Four days later Zoza opened the chestnut, and out came a hen with twelve golden chicks, which she put on the same windowsill. When the slave saw them she felt a craving all the way down to the little bones in her feet, and after she called over Tadeo and showed him what a lovely thing it was, she said, "If you no hen get from sill, me punch belly and little Georgie kill."

Tadeo, who let this bitch give him the runs and pull on his tail, again sent someone to Zoza to offer her whatever price she was asking for such a lovely hen. Her answer was the same as before: he would have to accept it as a gift, since any talk about buying it was a waste of time. The prince thus had no choice in the matter and out of need was forced to beat down all discretion, and as he snatched up the lovely morsel he marveled over the generosity of this woman, since women are by nature so greedy that all the gold bars in India are not enough to satisfy them.

After just as many days went by, Zoza opened the hazelnut, out of which came a doll that spun gold, an object amazing beyond all imagination. No sooner had it been placed on the windowsill than the slave caught a whiff, called Tadeo, and said to him, "If you no buy me dolly from sill, me punch belly and little Georgie kill."

Tadeo let himself be wound like wool and pulled by the nose by the arrogance of this wife who rode him like a horse, but since he did not have the courage to send for Zoza's doll he decided to go in person, recalling the mottos "No better messenger than yourself," "If you want something, go yourself; if you don't, send someone else," and "If you want to eat fish, you have to get your tail wet." He beseeched her endlessly to pardon his excesses, caused by the cravings of a pregnant woman; Zoza, who now that the cause of her misfortunes stood in front of her was in raptures, forced herself not to give in to his pleas, so that she might still her oars and enjoy at greater length the sight of her lord, who had been robbed from her by an ugly slave. Finally, she gave him the doll as she had done with the other objects, but before parting with it she begged the little piece of clay to instill in the slave's heart the desire to hear tales.

Tadeo, who discovered himself with the doll in hand without having shelled out a penny,[22] was astonished at such kindness and offered Zoza his state and his life in exchange for so many favors. He returned to the palace and gave the doll to his wife; as soon as she took it in her arms to play with it assumed the appearance of Cupid, in the form of Ascanius, in Dido's arms.[23] And it put fire in her chest; she was struck by such a burning desire to hear tales that, unable to resist and fearing that she might touch her mouth and give birth to a querulous son capable of infecting an entire ship of poor souls,[24] she called her husband and said, "If people no come and with tales my ears fill, me punch belly and little Georgie kill."

In order to do away with this March cure[25] Tadeo immediately issued a proclamation: all the women of the land were to come to his palace on such and such a day. And that day—at the rise of Diana's star, which awakened Dawn so that she might adorn the streets where the Sun was to promenade—they all gathered in the appointed place. But since Tadeo did not think it proper to detain such a mob to satisfy his wife's whim, and since, moreover, the sight of such a crowd suffocated him, he chose just ten women, the best of the city, the ones who appeared to be the most expert and quick-tongued. They were: lame Zeza, twisted Cecca, goitered Meneca, big-nosed Tolla, hunchback Popa, drooling Antonella, snout-faced Ciulla, cross-eyed Paola, mangy Ciommetella, and shitty Iacova.[26]

Once he had written down their names and sent the other women away, together with the slave they all arose from under the canopy and made their way with measured step to a garden of the same pal-

---

22. *uno de ciento vinte a carrino* (Neap.): one of the 120 *calli,* or *cavalli,* that made up a *carlino* or *carlin* (a coin); hence, a minuscule sum.

23. Basile makes reference to the episode from book 1 of Virgil's *Aeneid,* in which Dido is made to fall in love by Cupid, who appears in the form of Aeneas's son Ascanius.

24. "A reference to the popular belief that if pregnant women desire but cannot obtain something and by accident touch themselves on a part of their body, on the corresponding part of the child's body the mark ('the craving') of the desired thing will appear. Here the slave was afraid that if she touched her mouth, her child would be born with a disposition for querulous requests, which was in the mother's own nature" (Croce 11).

25. I.e., a bother. "Various popular beliefs about March and its misfortunes circulated at this time: for example, it was believed that in March the infirm, especially those suffering from syphilis, suffered more intensely" (Guarini and Burani 25).

26. These are all derivatives of noble names common in Naples (Lucrezia, Francesca, Domenica, Vittoria, Porzia, Antonia, Giulia, Paola, Girolama, Giacoma), which Basile ironically distorts, just as the women themselves are "deformed" versions of the conventional group of noble tale-tellers found in the frames of many novella collections (e.g., Boccaccio's *Decameron*), as is evidenced by both their social class and their physical irregularities.

ace, where the leafy branches were so entangled that the Sun was unable to separate them with its rod. After taking their seats under a
pavilion topped by a pergola of grapevines in the middle of which
flowed a large fountain, schoolmaster of courtiers whom it daily instructed in the art of murmuring, Tadeo began to speak in this manner: "There is nothing in the world more delicious, my illustrious
women, than to hear about the doings of others, nor without obvious
reason did that great philosopher[27] set the supreme happiness of man
in hearing pleasant tales; since when you lend an ear to tasty items,
cares evaporate, irksome thoughts are dispelled, and life is prolonged.
And it is because of this desire that you see artisans leave their workshops, merchants their commerce, lawyers their cases, and shopkeepers their businesses, and go open-mouthed to barbershops and gossip
circles to hear false news, invented broadsides, and airy gazettes.[28]
For this I must apologize on behalf of my wife, who has gotten the
melancholic urge to hear tales stuck in her head. And so if it be your
pleasure to shatter the jug of the princess's fancy and to hit the bull's-
eye of my cravings, you will content yourselves for these four or five
days before she empties her belly to each tell one tale a day, of the sort
that old women usually entertain the little ones with. We will always
meet in the same place, and after we gulp down our food the talk will
begin, and each day will end with a few eclogues, which will be recited by our own servants.[29] And thus our lives will be spent merrily,
and woe to those who die."

At these words the women all accepted Tadeo's orders with a nod
of their heads; in the meantime the tables were set and the food arrived, and they began to eat. After they finished slurping it up, the
prince signaled to lame Zeza to fire her weapon. She bowed down
low to the prince and his wife, and began to speak in this manner:

---

27. "Aristotle; but the reference is certainly jocose" (Croce 12).

28. "*Avvisi* were hand-written news-sheets, and also sometimes the dispatches of
diplomatic agents. *Gazzette* were printed newspapers, which at this time were just
beginning to appear" (Croce 12).

29. *sfrattapanelle* (Neap.): lit., "bread evicters." "Servants were given seven loaves
of bread at the beginning of the week, that were to last them seven days (bread was
baked on Saturday and distributed on Sunday); thus their alternate name of *settepanelle* [seven breads]" (Croce 12).

I

THE TALE OF THE OGRE

First Entertainment of the First Day

After Antuono of Marigliano is kicked out by his mother for being the ringleader of all oafs, he enters into the service of an ogre, from whom he receives a gift whenever he wants to go back and see his home. Antuono is tricked each time by an innkeeper, but finally the ogre gives him a club that punishes him for his ignorance, makes the innkeeper do penance for his ruses, and brings Antuono's family riches.

"Whoever said that Fortune is blind knows a lot more than master Lanza,[1] stick it to him! For she certainly strikes blindly, raising people you wouldn't deign to kick out of a bean field to great heights and beating to the ground people who are the flower of mankind, as you shall now hear.[2]

"It is said that in the town of Marigliano[3] there once was a respectable woman named Masella. Besides her unmarried daughters, six little farts as thin as poles, she had a son who was such a birdbrain and muttonhead that he couldn't even throw a snowball. And so she sat around like a sow with a bit in her mouth, and there wasn't a day that she didn't say to him, 'What are you doing in this house? Damn

---

AT 563: The Table, the Ass, and the Stick. Penzer notes that "this is one of the most widely spread tales in the whole collection," mentioning tale 36 from the Grimms' *Children's and Household Tales* ("The Magic Table, the Golden Donkey, and the Club in the Sack"), as well as many other Italian versions (1:24).

1. A well-known Venetian ballad singer and oral storyteller of the time (Croce 15).
2. The preambles include discussion of topics that range from the classic Renaissance themes of *fortuna* and *virtù*, to envy and ingratitude (also very much present in writings on the court of this period), to more concrete observations on the ills and virtues exemplified in the present or previous tale. Starting with the preamble to the next tale (1.2), these introductions are generally divided into three "narrative moments": a description of the reactions of Tadeo and his court to the preceding tale (often with comments on the performative skill of the teller), Tadeo's call for silence, and the next teller's "moral introduction" to her tale.
3. A town in the province of Caserta, about twenty kilometers from Naples (Croce 15). The towns from which the protagonists of the tales hail are, when mentioned by name, either real geographical locales, such as this one (and this is somewhat surprising in the often spatially abstract world of the fairy tale), or more fantastic places, such as "High Mountain" (1.5) or "Long Pergola" (1.9).

the bread you eat! Clear out, you big piece of you know what; make
yourself scarce, Maccabee; go fall in a hole, troublemaker; get out of
my sight, chestnut-guzzler! Someone must have switched you in the
cradle; in exchange for an adorable dollikins and a pretty little baby
I got a big lasagna-gobbling pig.' But even with all this, Masella
talked and he just whistled.

"Seeing that there was no hope that Antuono[4] (that was her son's
name) would get it into his head to do any good, one day that was
like any other she gave his head a good washing without soap, took a
rolling pin in her hand, and began to measure him for a jacket.[5] Antuono found himself fenced in, stockaded, and staked when he least
expected it, and as soon as he could get out of her hands he threw up
his heels and walked so far that around dusk—when the lamps began
to be lit in Cynthia's[6] shop—he reached the foothills of a mountain
so high that it butted horns with the clouds. Here, atop an enormous
poplar root at the foot of a grotto decorated in pumice stone, there
sat an ogre; and oh, dear mother, what an ugly one he was!

"He was a little old midget; a bunch of dried twigs; his head was
bigger than an Indian squash, his forehead all lumpy, his eyebrows
joined; his eyes popped out of his head, his nose was dented by two
horse's nostrils that looked like two sewer mains, his mouth was as
big as a grape press, with two tusks that hung all the way down to
the little bones of his feet; his chest was hairy, his arms like spinning
reels, his legs vaulted like a cellar, and his feet as flat as a duck's. In
short, he looked like a wicked spirit, an old demon, a filthy pauper,
and the spitting image of an evil shade, and he would have made Roland[7] tremble with fright, Skanderbeg[8] quake with terror, and the
most skilled wrestler grow pale.

"But Antuono, who wouldn't budge even at the crack of a sling-
shot, bowed his head and said to him, 'Good day, sir, what's up?
How are you? You want anything? How far is it from here to the
place where I have to go?' The ogre, when he heard this speech

---

4. The name "Antuono" was also used as a common noun, to refer to a simpleton
(Croce 16).
5. I.e., to give him a beating.
6. The goddess of the moon, Diana.
7. Roland was the protagonist of the French epic (c. 1100) *Chanson de Roland* and
of its countless imitations and spin-offs not only in the "high" epic tradition (e.g.,
Ariosto's *Orlando Furioso*) but also in popular poems and in theatrical renditions by
mountebanks and puppeteers.
8. Or Iskanderbeg, the commonly used name of Giorgio Castriota (1403–68). "This
Albanian national hero [who in the fifteenth century repulsed numerous Turkish in-
vasions in Albania] was very popular in Naples because of the help he gave to Ferdinand of Aragon [king of Naples] in defense of his throne" (Guarini and Burani 29).

straight out of the blue, began to laugh, and since he liked the beast's temperament, he said to him, 'Do you want to work for me?' And Antuono replied, 'How much do you want a month?' And the ogre came back with, 'Take care to serve me honorably; we'll get along fine and you'll see good times.' The deal was thus closed and Antuono stayed on to serve the ogre, where food was thrown in his face, and as far as working went he lived like a sheep at pasture. And in four days he grew as fat as a Turk, as big-bellied as an ox, as bold as a rooster, as red as a lobster, as green as garlic, as round as a chestnut, and so massive and burly that he could barely see past his nose.

"But before two years had gone by he became bored by all the plenty and felt a craving and a great longing to go take a peek at Pascarola,[9] and with all that thinking about his little home, he was almost reduced to his original state. The ogre, who could see straight through to his innards and recognized by smell that his ass was itching like someone poorly attended to, called him over and said to him, 'My dear Antuono, I know you're burning with desire to see your flesh and blood. Since I love you like the pupils of my eyes I will thus be happy if you go for a little visit and have this pleasure. So take this ass, which will save you the fatigue of the journey, but mind you, never say, "Giddy up, shit gold" to it, or you'll regret it, on the soul of my grandfather.'

"Antuono took the donkey and, without even saying, 'Good evening,' climbed onto its back and set out at a trot. But before he had gone a hundred yards he got off the jackass and started saying, 'Giddy up, shit gold,' and he had barely opened his mouth when the animal began to shit pearls, rubies, emeralds, sapphires, and diamonds, each as big as a walnut. With his mouth hanging wide, Antuono stared at those lovely bowel movements, at the superb diarrhea and rich dysentery of the little ass, and with great joy he filled up a saddlebag with the jewels. Then he got back on and set off at a good pace, until he arrived at an inn where, after dismounting, the first thing he said to the innkeeper was, 'Tie this ass at the trough and feed it well, but see that you don't say, "Giddy up, shit gold," or you'll regret it. And store these little things of mine in a safe place.'

"When he heard that extravagant request and saw the jewels,

---

9. Croce considers it a mistake that Basile has Antuono return to Pascarola (another nearby town) instead of Marigliano. Such inconsistencies, which we find throughout *The Tale of Tales,* may indeed be due to a lack of final editing but in some cases could also be intentional. Here, for example, the fact that Antuono wants to "return" to a different town may suggest, as subsequent events will prove, that he is not yet ready to return home.

which were worth hundreds,[10] the innkeeper—an expert at his trade,[11] a harbor fish,[12] well experienced with acid and the crucible[13]— became curious to see what the words meant. So after he fed Antuono well and gave him as much to drink as he could, he had him stuffed between a straw mattress and a thick blanket, and no sooner did he see that his eyes had grown heavy and that he was snoring at top speed than he ran to the stable and said to the ass, 'Giddy up, shit gold.' With the medicine of those words the ass performed the usual operation, tapping its bowels of streams of golden shit and bejeweled excrement. When the innkeeper saw the precious defecation, he decided to substitute the ass and trick that moron Antuono, since he figured it would be a simple task to blind, swindle, bamboozle, trick, cheat, hoodwink, and embroil him, passing off baskets for lanterns in the eyes of a fat pig, bumpkin, macaroni head, booby, big sheep, and sucker like the one that had fallen into his hands.

"And so, upon waking the next morning—when Aurora went to empty her old man's urinal, full of fine red sand, at the window of the Orient—Antuono rubbed his eyes with his hand, stretched for half an hour, and after a dialogue between sixty yawns and as many farts, he called the innkeeper and said, 'Come here, pal: frequent bills make for long friendships; let us stay friends and our wallets do battle; draw up my bill and be paid.' And so, after so much had been calculated for bread, so much for wine, this sum for soup, that one for meat, five for the stabling, ten for the bed, and fifteen to your health,[14] he shelled out the beans. Then he retrieved the false ass, together with a sack of pumice stones in place of the gemstones, and raced off in the direction of his village. And before he even set foot in the house

---

10. *valevano quattrociento* (Neap.): lit., "were worth four hundred." The expression possibly derives from a popular ditty (Guarini and Burani 31).

11. *de li quattro dell'arte* (Neap.): "In the hierarchy of the guilds of crafts and trades there were, at the top, the consuls and the 'four of the trades' " (Croce 18).

12. "Fish that lived in harbor waters were believed to have the gift of special craftiness" (Guarini and Burani 31).

13. "The 'coagulant' (*quaglio*) and the 'crucible' (*coppella*) were the acid and the vessel that goldsmiths used to assay gold and silver; *quaglio* is also rennet, yeast, or sperm, all substances associated with the idea of extreme sagacity and shrewdness of the dishonest and deceptive sort" (Guarini and Burani 31).

14. Del Tufo (in *Ritratto di Napoli nel 1588* 81) describes a Neapolitan innkeeper in the act of settling accounts with his patron: "At last he comes to settle the bill with an eager and joyful face, and says to each of them: 'Four and four makes eight, and thirteen makes twenty-one. Four for the bread and six for the wine makes ten; six more for the *escapece;* seven for the roast and three for the stew and six for fruit and cheese and roast provolone; and, without a thought to the innkeeper who earns not a rag and to the health of my patrons, two more, and may it do you well: that's right, if I haven't counted wrong, you owe me eight carlins' " (Croce 541).

he began to shout as if he had been stung by a nettle bush, 'Hurry, Mommy, hurry; we're rich! Get out the tablecloths, unfold the sheets, spread the blankets, for you're about to see some treasures.'

"With great joy, his mother opened a chest that held her marriageable daughters' trousseaus, and she pulled out sheets so fine that if you blew on them they floated on air, freshly laundered tablecloths, and blankets of stunning beauty, arranging them in a nice display on the floor. Antuono placed the donkey on top of them and began to intone 'giddy up, shit gold'; but with all the 'giddy up, shit gold's that you like, the donkey paid no more attention to those words than it would have to the sound of a lyre.[15] Nonetheless, after repeating the words three or four times, which was the same as throwing them to the wind, he took hold of a nice club and began to pester the poor beast, planing it down, touching it up, and padding it so well with blows that the poor animal lost control down below and took a fine yellow crap on the white cloths. When she saw the animal's bowels thus tapped, poor Masella, who had founded her hopes on enriching her poverty and now found herself with such a liberal foundation that her whole house reeked, grabbed a stick and, not giving him time to show her the pumice stones, patched Antuono up so well that he immediately beat it back to the ogre's.

"The ogre saw Antuono coming, more at a trot than a walk, and since he knew what had happened because he was enchanted, he gave him a juicy scolding for having let himself be fooled by an innkeeper, calling him a good-for-nothing, oh-dear-mother-drink-this-one-up, birdbrain, jackal, idiot, piece of junk, noodlehead, chestnut guzzler, simpleton, boor, and nitwit, who in exchange for an ass well lubricated with treasures had allowed himself to be given an animal lavish with makeshift mozzarellas. Antuono swallowed this pill and swore that never ever again would he allow himself to be conned and made fun of by a living man.

"But before another year had gone by he got the same headache and was dying to go see his people. The ogre, who had an ugly face and a kind heart, gave him not only permission to go but a lovely tablecloth as well, saying, 'Take this to your mother, but be careful not to act like a donkey as you did with the ass, and until you're at home say neither "open" nor "close, tablecloth," because if you get into any more trouble it'll be at your own expense. Now go with my best wishes, and come back soon.'

"So Antuono left, but not far from the grotto he put the tablecloth

---

15. "Asinus ad lyram": Latin proverb (Croce 19); used for an awkward or unintelligent person.

on the ground and quickly said 'open' and 'close, tablecloth.' And when it opened up, lo and behold! There was such beauty, such magnificence and elegance that it was an incredible thing. Seeing all that, Antuono immediately said, 'Close, tablecloth,' and after everything was closed up inside of it he hotfooted it in the direction of the same inn as the other time, where, upon entering, he said to the innkeeper, 'Here, put away this tablecloth and see that you don't say "open" and "close, tablecloth."' The innkeeper, a thrice-baked rogue, said, 'Just leave it to this fellow,' and after he stuffed Antuono and made sure he had grabbed the monkey by its tail,[16] he sent him off to bed, got the tablecloth, and said, 'Open, tablecloth.' And when it opened, the tablecloth brought forth so many precious things that it was stupendous to behold. Then the innkeeper found another tablecloth similar to the other, and after Antuono awoke he palmed it off on him. Antuono hoofed it out of there and arrived at his mother's house saying, 'Now we'll really give our poverty a kick in the face; now we'll really find a remedy for our rags, tatters, and patches!'

"That said, he spread the tablecloth on the ground and began to say, 'Open, tablecloth.' But he could have said it from today till tomorrow and he would have been wasting his time; it yielded neither a crumb nor a bit of straw. And so, seeing that his business was going against the nap, he said to his mother, 'Bless the new year, the innkeeper has stuck it to me again! But watch out; there are two of us! Better if he had never been hatched! Better if he had fallen under the wheel of a cart! May I lose the best piece of furniture in my house if when I stop by that inn to get my refund for the jewels and the stolen donkey I don't make dust of his dishes!' Hearing this new asininity, Antuono's mother began to spit fire and said to him, 'Knock it off, accursed son! Go break your back! Get out of my sight; I'm losing my guts, I can't stomach you anymore; my hernia is swelling and I get a goiter when you're underfoot! So cut it short, and may this house be like fire to you, for I'm going to shake you out of my clothes and pretend I never shat you!'

"Poor Antuono saw the lightning and didn't want to wait for the thunder and, as if he had stolen a load of fresh laundry, he lowered his head and threw up his heels and raced off toward the ogre's house. When the ogre saw him arrive at a listless pace and with a lackluster demeanor, he played him another piece[17] on the cymbals, saying, 'I

---

16. I.e., got him drunk (Guarini and Burani 34).

17. *recercata* (Neap.): type of instrumental composition, usually contrapuntal, with complexly interwoven melodic lines (similar to a motet for voices); it can be fugal or canonic or can more generally refer to a prelude.

don't know what keeps me from tearing out one of your orbs, you fart throat, gas mouth, filthy gullet, hen's ass, ta-ta-ta-ta, trumpeter of the Vicaria:[18] you make a public proclamation about every private matter, you vomit whatever's in your stomach, you can't even hold down a chickpea! If you had kept your mouth shut at the inn, none of this would have happened to you, but since you used your tongue like the sail of a windmill, you've ground to dust the happiness that this hand gave you!'

"Poor Antuono tucked his tail between his legs and sucked up the music. He stayed in the ogre's service without event for another three years, thinking about his home as much as he thought about becoming a count. And still, after all that time the fever returned, and once more he got the whim to take a spin back home. So he asked leave of the ogre, who was happy to rid himself of such a bother by letting him go, and gave him a lovely carved club, saying, 'Take this in remembrance of me, but be careful not to say "up, club" or "down, club," because I want nothing more to do with you.' Taking it, Antuono answered, 'Go on, I've cut my wisdom teeth; I know how many pair three oxen make! I'm not a little boy anymore, and whoever wants to cheat Antuono can kiss his own elbow first!' At this, the ogre answered, ' "The praise of masters lies in their works; words are female and deeds are male." Let's wait and see. You heard me better than a deaf man: "A man forewarned is a man half-saved." '

"As the ogre went on talking Antuono slipped off toward his house; before he was half a mile away he said, 'Up, club!' This was no mere word, though, but the art of enchantment. As if it had a little imp[19] in its core, the club began to polish poor Antuono's shoulders so that the blows seemed to shower down from the open sky, each stroke waiting for the next. Finding himself pounded and dressed like a piece of Moroccan leather, the wretched fellow immediately said,

---

18. "The public crier of the grand Court of the Vicaria of Naples, who issued proclamations to the sound of a trumpet" (Croce 21).

19. *scazzamauriello* (Neap.): the name, in Naples, of a domestic imp or sprite also called the *monaciello*. "According to popular imagination this little creature, dressed like a priest with a red skullcap, furtively frequented houses, and especially kitchens and hearths, where he performed minor mischief (moving objects or making them disappear, turning on and off the stove, turning on the faucet, and so on). Sometimes he snuck into women's beds, to the great despair of their husbands, who didn't even dare to make the sign of the cross. Astute and capricious, the *monaciello* was sometimes indulgent with women: he would warn them of some imminent disaster, suggest the way to avoid danger or cure an illness, give the numbers for the next lottery, indicate the spot where a treasure was buried, etc." (Guarini and Burani 36).

'Down, club!' and the club ceased writing counterpoint on the staves[20] of his back. And so, after he learned the lesson at his own expense, he said, 'May he who flees become lame; on my word, this time it won't get away from me! He who will have a bad evening has not gone to bed yet!' Thus saying he arrived at the usual inn, where he was received with the warmest welcome in the world, since it was clear what that pork rind would render. As soon as he arrived Antuono said to the innkeeper, 'Here, store this club for me, but be sure not to say, "Up, club!" or you'll be in danger! Listen to me carefully: don't you complain about Antuono again, for I won't put up with it and I'm making my bed beforehand.'

"The innkeeper, full of joy over this third stroke of luck, made sure Antuono was filled to the gills and shown the bottom of the jug, and as soon as he had dumped him onto a little cot he raced off to get the club and, calling his wife to the festivities, he said, 'Up, club!' The club began to search out the hold of the innkeepers' bodies,[21] and with a boom! here and a crash! there, it sounded like the round trip of a thunderbolt. Realizing that they were scantily and poorly protected, they ran off with that business following them and woke Antuono up, begging him for mercy. When he saw that the matter was going down just as it was supposed to, and that the macaroni was falling into the cheese and the broccoli into the lard, he said, 'There's no cure: you're going to die from the blows of this club unless you give me back my things.'

"The innkeeper, who at this point was beaten to a pulp, shouted, 'Take everything I have and get this backscratcher off me!' And to reassure Antuono, he brought out everything that he had pinched from him. Once it was all in hand Antuono said, 'Down, club!' and the club went and hunkered down in a corner of the room. Then he gathered up the donkey and the other things and left for his mother's house, where, after performing a royal trial on the donkey's ass and a thorough test on the tablecloth, he put together a good store of money, married off his sisters, and made his mother rich, proving the truth of the saying, *God helps madmen and children*."

---

20. One of dozens of musical metaphors in *The Tale of Tales*. This was a period of intense musical activity in Italy; for instance, the first modern operas were written in the academies and courts of early seventeenth-century Italy. As a court intellectual, Basile had a good deal of hands-on experience with musical culture, and several of his Italian works are musical dramas. Moreover, his sister Adriana was a renowned virtuosa of the time, collaborating with Claudio Monteverdi and singing for many years at the Mantuan court.

21. The comparison is between a ship's hold and the ribbed back of a person.

"Te', stipame sta mazza, ma vi' che no decisse 'auzate mazza'! ca passe pericolo! 'ntienneme buono, no te lamentare chiù d'Antuono, ca io me ne protesto e faccio lo lietto 'nante." ["Here, store this club for me, but be sure not to say, 'Up, club!' or you'll be in danger! Listen to me carefully: don't you complain about Antuono again, for I won't put up with it and I'm making my bed beforehand."]

2

THE MYRTLE

Second Entertainment of the First Day

A peasant from Miano gives birth to a myrtle bush. A prince falls in love with the myrtle and it turns into a beautiful fairy; he goes away and leaves the fairy in the myrtle with a little bell attached. Some wicked and jealous women enter the prince's bedroom, and when they touch the myrtle the fairy comes out and they kill her. The prince returns, discovers the carnage, and almost dies of sorrow, but when by a strange stroke of luck he gets the fairy back he has the courtesans put to death and takes the fairy for his wife.

No one was seen to utter a peep as long as Zeza continued her story, but once she had put an end to her talking a huge racket was heard, and none of those present could keep their mouths shut as they chattered about the ass's shit and the enchanted club, and someone said that if there were a wood of those clubs more than a few thieves would stop playing the cymbals[1] and more than a few others would get some sense into their heads, and asses would not outnumber beasts of burden, as is the case today. But after some discussion on the subject the lord ordered Cecca to continue the thread of the tales, and she spoke thus: "If man thought of how much damage, ruin, and destruction occur on account of the condemned women of this world, he would be more careful to flee from the path of a dishonest woman than from the sight of a serpent, and he would not consume his honor for the dregs of a bordello, his life for a hospital of ills, and all of his revenues for a public woman who's not worth three coppers,[2] since

---

AT 652A: The Myrtle. This tale bears some similarity to Grimm 76, "The Pink Flower," and has variants in Pitrè, *Fiabe, novelle e racconti popolari siciliani* 37 ("Rosemary"), and Pitrè, *Novelle popolari toscane* 6 ("The Apple"). Penzer notes that "tales in which a fairy or a dead woman lives in a flower, and assumes human form on certain occasions, are quite common in folk tales" (1:33).

1. I.e., would stop robbing.

2. *na pubreca . . . tre tornise* (Neap.): wordplay; "public woman" (prostitute) vs. *prubeca*, a copper coin worth one *tornise* (tournois) or six *cavalli*, emitted by Philip III of Spain in 1599 and on which was engraved *publica commoditas* (Rak 70). This is one of many currencies mentioned in *The Tale of Tales*. Often I do not translate the exact term, which would have little meaning for the modern reader, but do annotate when there is a play on words or otherwise significant use of the term.

the only thing she'll let you swallow are aggregate pills[3] of disgust and rage, as you will hear happened to a prince who put himself in the hands of that evil race.

"In the village of Miano[4] there lived a husband and a wife. Since they had not even the bud of a child, they desired with great longing to have an heir. And the wife, especially, was always saying, 'Oh, God, if only I could bring something into this world, I wouldn't care if it were a branch of myrtle!' And she repeated this song so often and bothered the heavens so much with these words that her belly became big and her womb round, and at the end of nine months, instead of delivering into the midwife's arms a little doll of a baby boy or a little fart of a baby girl, she cast out of the Elysian Fields of her womb a lovely branch of myrtle.[5] She planted it in a pot decorated with pretty grotesques, put it on a windowsill, and with great pleasure took care of it morning and evening, with more diligence than a farmer who tends to a broccoli patch from which he hopes to earn the rent on his garden.

"But when the king's son happened to pass by that house on his way to the hunt, he became infatuated beyond all measure with the lovely branch of myrtle, and he sent word to its owner that if she sold it to him, he would pay an eye for it. After a thousand no's and arguments, the woman was finally made greedy by the offers, pulled in by the promises, bewildered by the threats, and won over by the pleas, and gave him the pot, begging him to hold it dear to his heart, since she loved it more than a daughter and valued it as much as if it had come from her own loins.

"With the greatest joy in the world, the prince had the pot taken to his private bedroom and placed on a loggia, and he hoed and watered it with his own hands. Now it happened that one evening, when the prince had gone to bed and put out the candles, just as the world grew quiet and everyone was in their first sleep, he heard the sound of footsteps in the house, and then something groping its way toward his bed. He thought that it might be either a page who wanted to lift his wallet or else an imp[6] come to pull his covers off. But since he was a courageous man whom even the dreadful fires of hell could not frighten, he played the dead cat and waited to see how the deal would turn out. And when he felt that certain business drawing close and

---

3. Pills used for a variety of ailments (Croce 25).
4. Village outside of Naples.
5. "Ornamental plant of the Mediterranean. Symbol of love and erotic poetry and sacred to Venus for its ability to die and be reborn, it was subsequently used for decorative hedges in cemeteries. It is still used in Naples for funeral wreaths" (De Simone 47).
6. For the household imp, or *monaciello*, see tale 1.1 n19.

touched it, he realized what a smooth job it was; and where he imagined he would be squeezing hedgehog needles he found a little something that was more mellow and soft than Tunisian wool, more
yielding and pliable than the tail of a marten, more delicate and tender
than the feathers of a goldfinch. And so he flung himself from one side
of the bed to the other, and thinking that it might be a fairy (as in fact
it was) he wrapped himself around it like an octopus, and as they
played at 'Mute Sparrow,' they also tried out 'Stone in Your Lap.'[7]

"But—before the Sun came out like the chief physician to examine
the flowers that were ill and wilting—the guest got out of bed and
slipped away, leaving the prince full of sweetness, pregnant with curiosity, and laden with marvel. By the time this trafficking had gone
on for seven days, he was consumed by and melting with the desire to
know what sort of good luck was raining down on him from the stars
like this, and what sort of ship laden with Love's sweetness was coming to anchor in his bed. And so one night when the lovely girl was
sleeping, he tied one of her braids to his arm so that she could not slip
away, and then called a servant; and when the candles had been lit,
he saw the flower of all beauty, the marvel of all women, the mirror
and painted egg of Venus,[8] a beautiful little tidbit of Love. He saw a
baby doll, a gleaming dove, a Fata Morgana,[9] a banner, a golden spike
of wheat; he saw a stealer of hearts, a falcon's eye, a full moon, a little pigeon face, a morsel fit for a king, a jewel; he saw, in short, an
eye-popping spectacle.

"Gazing at all of this, he said, 'Now go jump in an oven, Cyprian
goddess![10] Wrap a cord around your neck, O Helen![11] Go back where
you came from, O Creusa and Fiorella,[12] for your beauties are rags

---

7. "Two children's games whose names are here used for their lewd connotations"
(Croce 26). "In Roman times the sparrow (*passer*) was regarded as the most lecherous of creatures" (Penzer 1:26). See also the introduction to day 2.
8. "G. B. Pino (in his *Ragionamento sovra del asino*, Naples c. 1530) says of Cupid:
'He was the dear son, he was the painted egg of his mother, little Venus.' It was the
custom to send eggs painted various colors as holiday gifts" (Croce 27).
9. "In *The Life of Merlin* (1150) by Geoffrey of Monmouth, Morgan le Fay is a sorceress who cures King Arthur's wounds on an enchanted island. In Celtic mythology
she may be either good or evil; in southern Italian culture *fata morgana* refers to a
mirage, usually in the strait of Messina" (Rak 71).
10. Venus, after the island best known for worship of the goddess and on which she
was born.
11. Helen of Troy, the mortal woman of Greek mythology whose beauty set off the
Trojan War.
12. The first is the Creusa of mythology, who was abducted and raped by Apollo and
bore the son Ion. The second is an "allusion to the story of Marco and Fiorella, two
famous lovers, which was very popular at one time. [. . .] Guillaume de Blois wrote a
Tragedy of Flaura and Marco around 1160" (Croce 542).

compared to this double-soled beauty, this complete, integral, seasoned, immense, well-built beauty! These arc graces to be whistled at, graces that rival those of Seville,[13] graces as loud as thunderbolts, first-rate, noble, lacking all defects and where there is no "z" to be found! O sleep; O sweet sleep, unload your poppies into the eyes of this lovely jewel, do not interrupt the pleasure of contemplating to my heart's content this triumph of beauty! O lovely braid that binds me; O lovely eyes that warm me; O lovely lips that refresh me; O lovely breast that comforts me; O lovely hand that pierces me; where, oh where, in which workshop of Nature's marvels[14] was this living statue created? From which India came the gold to forge this hair? From which Ethiopia the ivory to construct this forehead? From which Maremma[15] the carbuncles to set in these eyes? From which Tyre[16] the crimson to stain[17] this face? From which Orient the pearls to string these teeth? And from which mountains the snow to sprinkle on this breast—snow that betrays nature, that nourishes flowers and warms hearts?'

"While he was saying this he wound his arms around her like a vine, so as to comfort her life,[18] and as he squeezed her neck, she was freed from sleep and answered one of the enamored prince's sighs with a pretty little yawn. When he saw that she was awake, he said to her, 'O my precious, if I was already about to lose my senses when I saw this temple of Love without candles, what will be of my life now that you've lit two lamps in it? O lovely eyes, which with a triumph of light make the stars break the bank;[19] you and only you have pierced a hole in this heart, and only you, like fresh eggs, can make a poultice

---

13. "Many are the exquisite things of Seville: tobacco, stockings, women, and so forth" (Croce 27).

14. An allusion to "one of the *stanze* or chambers, very prevalent at the end of the century, in which the marvels of the century of voyages were collected and exhibited upon payment of an entrance ticket: embalmed animals, automatons, magic lanterns, and so forth" (Rak 71). These *Wunderkammern,* or "cabinets of curiosity," were the prototypes of the modern museum.

15. A region in southwestern Tuscany.

16. Tyre was an ancient Mediterranean port; Tyrian purple is a rich purple tinged with crimson.

17. *magriare* (Neap.): "to color red, to apply rouge; but *magriata* also referred to the act of smearing walls and doors with dirty substances to insult or scorn those who lived there" (Guarini and Burani 43). This could lead to feuds and bloodshed, and a number of laws were written prohibiting the practice, such as the one issued by the viceroy of Toledo in 1549. Basile's own sister, the famous singer Adriana, was the victim of a *magriata* (Croce 266).

18. Wordplay: *vite* (grapevine) vs. *vita* (life, or waist).

19. *trionfiello* and *banco felluto* (Neap.) were well-known card games, often played with tarots (Croce 28).

of tow to treat it.[20] My lovely doctor, be moved to pity for one so lovesick that the change of air from the dark of night to the light of this beauty has thrown him into a feverish state! Put your hand on this chest, take this pulse, write me a prescription! But why do I look for a prescription, my soul? Blow five bloodsuckers onto these lips with your lovely mouth! I want no other scrubbing down in this life than a caress from that dear little hand, for I'm certain that with the cordial water of your lovely grace and the root of that oxtongue, I will be free and healthy.'

"At these words the lovely fairy grew red as a flame of fire, and answered, 'Too much praise, lord prince. I am your servant, and to serve that face of a king I would go so far as to empty your chamber pot,[21] and I consider it a great fortune that from a myrtle branch planted in a clay pot I have been transformed into a laurel bough hung on the tavern of a heart of flesh and blood, a heart that contains such greatness and such virtue.' At these words the prince, melting away like a tallow candle, began to hug her again, and sealing his letter with a kiss he gave her his hand and said, 'You have my word: you will be my wife, you will be the mistress of my scepter, you will have the key to this heart just as you hold the rudder of this life.' And after these and a hundred other ceremonies and speeches, they got out of bed and checked to see that their intestines were healthy; and they followed this same routine for several days.

"But since Fortune is a game wrecker and marriage breaker, and always an obstacle to Love's footsteps, and a black dog that shits on the pleasures of those who love, it happened that the prince was called to hunt a great wild pig that was ravaging the town and had thus to leave his wife, or rather two-thirds of his heart. But since he loved her more than his own life and considered her more beautiful than all other beauteous things, from that love and that beauty sprung a third species of Love, which is a storm in the sea of amorous happiness, a shower on the laundry of Love's joys, and soot that falls into the greasy soup[22] of the pleasures of lovers; the sort of love, I mean, that is a serpent that bites and a woodworm that gnaws, bile that poisons, frost that numbs; the love because of which life always

---

20. "Tow soaked in egg, rose oil and turpentine, which was put on wounds" (Croce 28).

21. *lo necessario* (Neap.): lit., "the necessary." "The lack of hygienic services made it necessary for housewives to empty chamber pots in the sea, usually toward dusk, as many sources recount" (Rak 72).

22. *pignato grasso* (Neap.): "a soup made with cabbage, ham, lard, and other ingredients, and considered at this time the masterpiece of Neapolitan cuisine" (Croce 29).

hangs by a thread, minds are always unstable, hearts always full of suspicions.[23]

"And when he had called for the fairy, he said to her, 'I am forced, my heart, to stay away from home for two or three nights; God knows the pain I feel at tearing myself away from you, my own soul. Only the heavens know if before I even begin to trot I will run my last leg, but since to content my father I cannot avoid going, I must leave you. Therefore I beg you, in the name of all the love you feel for me, to go back into your pot and not come out until I return, which will be as soon as possible.' 'That I will do,' said the fairy, 'because I do not know how, I do not want, nor am I able to object to what pleases you. Go, then, with the mother of good luck, for I am here at your side to serve you. But do me a favor: leave a little bell on a silk thread attached to the top of the myrtle, and when you come, pull the thread and ring the bell, and I'll jump right out and say, "Here I am."'

"The prince did just that; indeed, he called a servant and said, 'Come, come here, you; open up your ears and listen carefully: prepare this bed every evening, as if I were going to sleep in it myself, and keep this pot watered. But mind you: I've counted the branches, and if I find one missing, I'll cut off your bread supply.' That said, he got on his horse and left, like a sheep being taken to slaughter, to chase after a pig.

"In the meantime seven women of vice who were kept by the prince, noticing that he had grown tepid and then cold in love and that he had given up working their fields, began to suspect that he had forgotten about his old friendship because of some new intrigue. And so, desirous of discovering the new land, they called a mason and with some good money got him to dig a tunnel that ran from under their house to the prince's bedroom. Then those wicked hospital cases[24] went in and looked around to see if a new resident, if another flirt had tricked them out of their hand and put a spell on their client. They opened the room, but found no one there, and when they saw the beautiful myrtle, each of them took a branch for herself; the youngest took the whole top of the plant, to which the bell was attached.

"The bell, barely touched, rang, and, thinking it was the prince, the fairy immediately came out. But as soon as the whorish nags saw that resplendent thing, they lay their paws on her, saying, 'You're the one who draws the water of our hopes to your mill? You're the one who took from our hands the lovely scraps of the prince's grace?

23. I.e., jealous love.
24. "Or, in other words, depraved and infected prostitutes" (Guarini and Burani 47).

You're that "madam Magnificence"[25] who has taken possession of the tender flesh that belonged to us? May you be welcome! Go on, you're on the draining board now![26] Oh, better if your mother had never shat you; go on, you're all set! You've taken Vaiano![27] This time you've really bumped into it! If you get out of this one, then I wasn't born in nine months!' Saying this, they hurled a stick at her head and immediately broke her into a hundred pieces. Then each of them took her share; only the youngest didn't want to have a hand in this cruel affair, and when she was invited by her sisters to do as they were doing, she wanted nothing more than a lock of that golden hair. When they were done, they cleared out, using the same tunnel.

"Meanwhile the servant arrived to prepare the bed and water the pot as his master had ordered, and when he found that fine disaster he had a fit and nearly died. Sinking his teeth into his hand, he picked up the bits of the flesh and bones that remained, and when he had scraped the blood off the floor, he piled everything back into the same pot, which he watered. He then prepared the bed, closed the door, locked it, and, putting the key under the door, took his old slippers far from that town.

"But then the prince returned from the hunt and pulled the silk thread and rang the bell. Go on, ring; you might catch some quails![28] Ring; the bishop might pass by! He could have tolled that bell over and over; the fairy was taking no heed. And so he went straight to his bedroom and, not having the patience to call his servant and ask for the key, he gave the door a kick, sent it flying open, entered, opened the window, and, seeing the branchless pot, began to beat himself on the chest and lament, shouting, shrieking, bawling, 'O bitter me; O desolate me; O miserable me; who has made me this beard of tow?[29] Who has given me the low card in *trionfo*? O ruined, devastated, shattered prince! O my branchless myrtle; O my lost fairy; O my wretched life! O my delights, you have gone up in smoke; O my pleasures, you have gone sour! What will you do, unlucky Cola Marchione?[30] What will

---

25. The character of a whore in the *Defennemiento della Vaiasseide* by Bartolomeo Zito (Rak 72).

26. "The inclined plane on which corpses were dried and their fluids drained off. The expression means, therefore, 'to be dead.' Even today the most atrocious of Neapolitan invectives, *pozze sculà!* ('may you drain off!') refers to this usage" (Guarini and Burani 47).

27. A town thirty kilometers from Naples vs. an impossible feat. "A very common expression used to indicate that things won't happen according to one's desires; Vaiano is a heavily populated town" (Rak 72).

28. "Allusion to the bells attached to quail nets" (Croce 31).

29. "Tow, or straw, beards were an accessory of buffoons and actors; the meaning is, therefore: 'who tricked me?'" (Guarini and Burani 48).

30. The name of the prince.

you do, unhappy one? Jump this ditch! Get out of this trouble! All that is good has expired for you, and you don't slit your throat? You've been relieved of every treasure, and you don't cut your veins? You've been treated like shit by life, and you don't beat it out of here? Where are you, where are you, my myrtle? And what sort of soul, harder than a bat's, has ruined this lovely pot of mine? O accursed hunt, you have hunted every joy of mine to its death! Alas, I'm done for, I'm fried, I've been sent to my doom, I've ended my days; I can't possibly attempt to survive in this life without my own dearest life; I'll be forced to stretch out my legs for the last time, since without my darling sleep will be torture, food poison, pleasure constipation, and life a bitter fruit.' The prince uttered these and other words fit to move the stones in the street, and after a long lament and a bitter dirge, full of anguish and fury, during which he never once closed his eyes to sleep nor opened his mouth to eat, he was so overcome by suffering that his face, which had once been of oriental minium,[31] now became like orpiment,[32] and the hams of his lips turned into rancid lard.

"When the fairy, who had begun to sprout anew from the remains placed in the pot, saw how her poor lover was tearing out his hair and throwing himself around, and how he had become a little pinch of a thing the color of a sick Spaniard,[33] a wormy lizard, cabbage juice, jaundice, a pear, the ass of a fig pecker, and a wolf's fart, she was moved to compassion and sprung out of the pot like the light of a candle comes out of a blind lantern.[34] She materialized before Cola Marchione and, squeezing him in her arms, said, 'Come on, cheer up, my prince, no more, no more! End that lament, dry those eyes, leave your anger behind, relax that long face! Here I am, alive and beautiful in spite of those old birds who, after they broke my head open, did to my flesh what Typhon[35] did to his poor brother!'

---

31. Or red lead; a poisonous oxide of lead used as a pigment.
32. *oro pimmiento* (Neap.): arsenic trisulphide, which has golden yellow crystals and is used as a dye or artist's pigment (*orpimento*) vs. "the false gold (*oro pimmiento*) obtained by an alloy of copper, zinc, and tin and that is used, in thin leaf, for gold-plating" (Guarini and Burani 49).
33. "The color of a sick Spaniard was proverbial. There was even a dye used for a certain fabric called 'sick Spaniard'" (Croce 32).
34. *lanterna a bota* (Neap.): "'A small oil lamp, invented by the Brescians, that allowed one to cover and uncover the light at will; today their use is prohibited almost everywhere,' says Tomaso Garzoni [in his *Piazza universale*]. In fact, only the police were permitted to use them" (Croce 32).
35. "Typhon [the Egyptian Seth, brother also of Isis] plotted against his brother Osiris, and tricked him into getting into a chest upon which the other co-plotters threw themselves, pushing the top closed, hammering it with nails, pouring molten lead into the holes, and finally throwing it to sea" (Croce 32). See Plutarch, *De Iside et Oside* 13.

"Seeing this when he least expected to, the prince came back to life, and as the color returned to his cheeks, the warmth to his blood, and the spirit to his breast, he gave her a thousand caresses and cuddles, smooches and squeezes,[36] and then wanted to know from beginning to end everything that had happened. When he heard that the servant was not at fault he summoned him, and then ordered a grand banquet, and with the benevolent consent of his father he married the fairy. And after he invited all the most important lords of the kingdom, he made sure that above all the seven hags who had butchered that suckling calf would be present.

"Once they had finished chewing, the prince asked each of his guests, one by one, 'What would someone who harmed this lovely girl deserve?' pointing to the fairy, who looked so beautiful that she pierced hearts like a missile, pulled souls to her like a winch, and dragged desire along like a sledge. Now then, everyone who was sitting at the table, starting with the king, had their say. One said that such a person would deserve the gallows; another that he would be worthy of the wheel; another, the pincers; another, to be thrown off a cliff; one mentioned this punishment and another that punishment. And then it was, finally, time for the seven grouper fish[37] to speak. Although they didn't like the tone of the conversation and were beginning to imagine the bad night ahead, nonetheless they answered—since truth always lies where wine has been plotting—that whoever had the courage even to touch that delectable morsel of Love's pleasures would deserve to be buried alive inside a sewer pipe.

"After this sentence was handed down from their own mouths, the prince said, 'You have brought suit against yourselves, you have signed the warrant yourselves. All that remains is for me to carry out your order, since you are the ones who, with the heart of Nero and the cruelty of Medea,[38] made an omelet out of this pretty little head and minced up these lovely limbs like meat for sausage. And so, quick, let's go, let no time be wasted! Have them thrown this very minute into a sewer main, where they may end their lives in misery.'

"This was effected at once, after which the prince married the youngest sister of those whores to his servant, giving her a good

---

36. *carizze, vierre, gnuoccole e vruoccole* (Neap.): *gnuoccole* are gnocchi and *vruoccole* broccoli, but both are also, metaphorically, caresses. "In Naples broccoli-vendors punningly call out 'Get your broccoli; they're good in bed!'" (Croce 33).
37. *cernie* (Neap.): "Metaphor used to indicate someone ugly, since the face of a grouper fish is horrible-looking; here in a moral sense" (Croce 33).
38. "Nero (37–68 AC) and Medea, the sorceress who stars in Euripides' homonymous tragedy (431 AC), were both current *exempla* of cruelty" (Rak 73).

dowry, and also gave the myrtle's mother and father enough to live on comfortably. He lived happily with the fairy, and the daughters of hell, concluding their lives in bitter torment, proved the truth of that proverb of the ancient sages: *The lame goat gets by if it finds none who block it.*"

3

PERUONTO

Third Entertainment of the First Day

Peruonto, a tried and true wretch, goes to the woods to gather some kindling, shows kindness to three boys who are sleeping in the sun, and receives an enchantment. When he is made fun of by the king's daughter he puts a curse on her, willing that she become pregnant by him, which happens. The king finds out that Peruonto is the father of the baby, puts him in a barrel with his wife and children, and throws it out to sea. But by virtue of the enchantment Peruonto frees himself from the dangerous situation and, after he turns into a handsome young man, becomes king.

They all showed signs of having felt great pleasure at the consolation that the poor prince had received, and at the punishment delivered upon those wicked women. But since Meneca needed to continue the conversation, an end was put to the others' chatter, and she began to tell of the fact that follows: "A good deed is never wasted; those who sow courtesy reap benefits, and those who plant kindness harvest affection. A favor granted to a grateful soul is never sterile, but generates gratitude and gives birth to rewards. One can find continual proof of this in the experiences of men; you will see one example in the tale that you are about to hear.

"An illustrious woman of Casoria[1] named Ceccarella had a son named Peruonto,[2] who was the most dismal creature, the greatest

---

AT 675: The Lazy Boy. Penzer points out the principal motifs of this tale: "The first is the 'gift of wishing,' in this case awarded for kindness. It is one of the varieties of the 'gratitude' motif. The second is the 'means of recognition,' consisting of tricks by which it is hoped to show up the culprit—in this case the father of the child of the unmarried Princess" (1:42). He notes similarities with tales by Straparola (*Le piacevoli notti* 3.1, "Crazy Peter"), Afanasev, and the many affinities with the "Hanns Dumm" type. The "means of recognition" motif also appears in the famous tale of Rhampsinitus in Herodotus and in Ser Giovanni's fourteenth-century rewriting of it, among others. Other variants of this tale can be found in Pitrè, *Fiabe, nov. e racc. siciliani* 188, "The Place of Raisins and Figs"; and Pitrè, *Nov. pop. toscane* 30, "The Tale of the Little Falcon." See also Marie-Catherine d'Aulnoy, "The Dolphin" (in Zipes, *Beauties, Beasts, and Enchantments*).
1. Town in a swampy area six kilometers northeast of Naples.
2. "Nickname that derives from the dialect term *peruontolo,* which in southern Italy has various meanings: a large fava bean, a bell clapper, or the phallus" (De Simone 65–67).

yokel, and the most solemn idiot[3] that Nature had ever created. On account of this his poor mother's heart was blacker than an old rag, and a thousand times a day she cursed the knees[4] that had held the door wide for a flycatcher who wasn't worth his weight in dog sperm. But the unfortunate woman could scream and open her mouth all she liked; the good-for-nothing wouldn't have gotten up from taking a shit to do her a damned service. Finally, after a thousand thunderous scoldings, a thousand juicy tirades, a thousand 'I'm telling you's' and 'I told you's,' and with a scream today and a shriek tomorrow, she sent him off to the woods for some kindling, saying, 'It's high time to choke on a morsel or two; run and get wood, don't lose your way, and come right back, for we need to drag a few broccoli stalks in a bit of oil so that we can drag this life of ours a little farther along.'

"That good-for-nothing Peruonto left like someone condemned to march between the Brothers of the White Justice;[5] he left and he walked as if he were treading on eggs, at a magpie's pace;[6] he counted his steps, moving off oh so slowly, advancing little by little, creeping ahead, poking lazily along the road to the woods, like the crow that flies off never to return again.

"And when he was in the middle of a meadow where a river ran—chattering and murmuring about the scant discretion of the stones that blocked its way—he came across three boys who had made a little mattress out of grass and a pillow out of flint and were sleeping like butchered animals under the blazing heat of the sun, which tormented them with its perpendicular rays. When Peruonto saw those poor boys, who looked like a fountain of water in a furnace of fire, he felt compassion for them, and with the hatchet he was carrying he cut a few branches from an oak tree and made a lovely bower over them. In the meantime the young men, who were the sons of a fairy, woke up, and when they saw how kind and loving Peruonto was they rewarded him with an enchantment: he might have everything he could wish for.

"After this, Peruonto set out on the road that led to the wood, where he gathered a bundle of kindling that was of such huge proportions that it would have taken a sledge to drag it along, and when he saw that try-

---

3. *sarchiopo . . . sarchiapone* (Neap.): "hoer (from the Latin *sarculus,* a small hoe used for weeding). The character of the boorish and dense peasant became proverbial with this same name of Sarchiapone" (Guarini and Burani 53).
4. "'To come out of the knee' was used euphemistically in place of 'to be born'" (Croce 36).
5. Men who assisted those condemned to death (Croce 36).
6. "That is, with the cautious pace of a magpie; or [according to another interpretation of the word *picca*] reluctantly, like a soldier condemned to 'pass down the pike line,' a torture introduced by the Swiss" (Guarini and Burani 54).

ing to carry it on his back was a lost cause, he got on and straddled it, saying, 'Oh my goodness, if this bundle of wood could only carry me, and trot like a horse!' And lo and behold, the bundle of wood began ambling along like a purebred Bisignano horse,[7] and when it reached the king's palace it twirled and executed curvets in astonishing fashion.

"The ladies-in-waiting were at a window, and at the sight of this marvel they ran to call Vastolla, the king's daughter. She looked out the window and as she watched the caracoles of a pile of kindling and the leaps of a bundle of firewood she burst out laughing, whereas due to her natural state of melancholy no one could remember her ever having laughed. When Peruonto raised his head and saw that he was being made fun of, he said, 'Go on, then, Vastolla; may you become pregnant by this fellow!' That said, he gave the bundle of kindling a good spur with his boots, and at a wooden gallop[8] he arrived home almost immediately, with so many little kids in tow taunting and shrieking at him that if his mother hadn't been quick to close the door behind him they would have killed him to the blows of citrons and broccoli.

"But after Vastolla stopped getting her period and started feeling certain cravings and palpitations of the heart, she realized that she had swallowed the dough.[9] She hid her pregnancy for as long as she could, but when her belly, which had swollen up like a little keg, could no longer be hidden, the king realized what was going on. He did things that were out of this world, then called his council and told them, 'You already know that the moon of my honor has given me horns;[10] you already know that my daughter has supplied me with

---

7. "The breed of horses raised by the Sanseverino family of Bisignano was esteemed and celebrated in all of Europe" (Croce 542).
8. Wordplay: kindling (*sarcena*) vs. *galoppo sarcinesco* (where *sarcinesco* may also mean "of a Saracen").
9. "The lump of sourdough used to make bread rise, or the rennet for fermenting cheese" (Guarini and Burani 55).
10. The topic of the "cornuto," the "horned one" or cuckold, is omnipresent in the Italian novella tradition. Rak cites B. Zito's more theoretical discussion of cuckoldry in his *Defennemiento della Vaiasseide*: "In Naples those whose wives spin them on crooked spindles are called billy goats, big sheep, or the horned. A billy goat is one who knows that his wife is betraying him and who eats and chats with the men she associates with, and this is in conformity with the nature of the animal, since, as Aristotle writes, the billy goat wants other billy goats to go, in his presence, with the she-goat that was his. A big sheep is one whose wife wrongs him without his being able to defend himself; this alludes to the fact that a sheep doesn't defend itself from wrongs committed by members of its own species. And horned is he who has a wife who shames him. This is not because he has horns on his head, but because the infamy and dishonor is public; and so in ancient times proclamations were publicly issued to the sound of a horn" (Rak 91). In Basile we find a number of cases of exaggerated preoccupation with "horns," though it is usually of a curiously misguided sort (as in this tale, where a father feels cuckolded by his daughter), as well as a good deal of punning on the subject.

ample material for the inkwell[11] that will be used to write the chronicles, or should I say hornicles of my disgrace; you already know that
she has laden her stomach in order to lade my forehead. And so tell
me what you think; counsel me. I would be of the mind to make her
deliver her soul before she gives birth to bad stock; I would be of the
mood to make her feel the pain of death before the pangs of birth; I
would be of the whim to cut off her buds and uproot her from this
world before she can bud and produce seeds.'

"The counselors, who had consumed more oil than wine, said,
'She truly deserves great punishment, and the horn that she has
planted on your forehead should be used to make the handle of the
knife that takes her life. But no; if we kill her now that she's pregnant, that reckless one will slip through the broken link: he, that is,
who has armed your right horn and your left so as to place you in the
middle of a battle of displeasures; he who has put before you a Cor-
nelius Tacitus so as to instruct you in the politics of Tiberius;[12] he
who has performed for you a dream of true infamy and made it exit
from the door of horn.[13] Let us wait, then, until she reaches port and
we are able to determine where the root of this shame lies, and then
we will reflect and decide, with a grain of salt, what we need to do.'
This advice set well with the king, who saw that they spoke in orderly
and proper fashion. And thus he stayed his hand and said, 'Let us
await the outcome of this business.'

"As the heavens willed, the hour of the birth arrived. With four
tiny little labor pains and at the first puff in the jar,[14] the first words
of the midwife, and the first cramping of her belly, Vastolla dumped
into the other woman's lap two hefty baby boys who looked like two
golden apples. The king, pregnant himself but with rage, called his
counselors so that he too could deliver, and said, 'All right, my child
has had her children; now it's time to help her along with a beating.'
'No,' said those old sages (and it was all to take as much time as possible), 'let us wait until the little darlings get bigger, so that we can
recognize their father's appearance in them.'

"The king would not produce a verse without the guidelines of his
council, out of fear of writing crooked, and so he shrugged his shoul-

---

11. "Horn was used to make inkwells" (Croce 38).
12. "An illusion to the contemporary debate regarding the passages from Tacitus on
Tiberius' political thought (*Annales* I–VI)" (Rak 91).
13. "One of the doors of Sleep in the Latin imaginary; see Virgil, *Aeneid* VI 893–
94" (Rak 91). From one door exited deceptive dreams and from the other truthful
ones; the latter was of horn.
14. "It was common for women in labor to blow hard into a flask, which helped in
the exertion of giving birth" (Croce 542).

"O Vastolla, và, che puozze deventare prena de sto fusto!"
["Go on, then, Vastolla; may you become pregnant by this fellow!"]

ders, kept calm, and waited until the boys were seven years old, at which time the counselors were once again encouraged to strike at the trunk and what was attached to it. One of them said, 'Since you haven't been able to get your daughter to take off her stockings and tell you with her own tongue who the counterfeiter is that used your image to tamper with your crown, we will now get rid of this stain. Order, then, that a great banquet be prepared and that every noble and gentleman of the city come. We will pay close attention and keep our eyes on the cutting board[15] so that we can see who the children, pushed by Nature, turn to most willingly, for he will without a doubt be their father, and we'll wipe him up like a bit of crow shit.'

"The king was pleased with this opinion. He ordered the banquet to be held and invited everyone who wore a cloak and was of any account, and when they had all eaten, he had them stand in a line, and the little boys passed before them. But the boys paid as much attention to them as Alexander's hound to rabbits,[16] so that the king stormed and bit his lips. And although there was no lack of footwear, the shoe was too tight for him and he stamped his feet on the ground in pain. But the counselors said to him, 'Calm down, your majesty, and listen to us: tomorrow we'll have another banquet, not for important people but for lower-class types. And since women always attach themselves to the worst, perhaps, seeing as we didn't find him among the gentlemen, we will find the seed of your rage among the cutlers, street vendors, and comb sellers.'

"This reasoning appealed to the king, and he commanded that a second banquet be held to which, as per proclamation, all the idiots, tramps, rogues, scoundrels, bad boys, thugs, good-for-nothings, ragamuffins, rascals, corpse strippers,[17] and everyone in the city who wore aprons and wooden shoes were to come. And when they were all seated like so many fine counts at a long, long table, they began to stuff themselves.

"Now Ceccarella, who had heard this proclamation, began to prod Peruonto, telling him that he, too, should go to the festivities. And she kept it up until he set off for the banquet, where he had barely arrived when those lovely little boys attached themselves to him like

---

15. "I.e., to make sure that no cats or dogs run off with the meat" (Penzer 1:37).
16. "The famous dog of Alexander [the Great], killed because it wouldn't fight with bears and boars, after which its donor sent the last of its breed to Alexander, with the warning that it not be allowed to fight unless with beasts of a strength equal to its own: elephants and lions" (Pliny, *Natural History* 8.61; Rak 91).
17. *spogliampise* (Neap.): these undressers of the hanged either stole the clothes right off the bodies, or bought the clothes from the executioners. Sellers of used clothing were also often called *spogliampise*.

ticks and showered him with hugs and kisses beyond all measure. When the king saw this he tore out his whole beard, for he realized that the bean in this cake,[18] the winning ticket in this lottery, had gone to a hideous monster the mere sight of whom brought on nausea and vomiting. Besides having a shaggy head, the eyes of an owl, the nose of a parrot, and the mouth of a grouper fish, he was barefoot and so ragged that even without reading Fioravante you could inspect his secret parts.[19]

"After a gloomy sigh, the king said, 'What did this sow of my daughter see that made her fancy this sea monster? What did she see that made her take to her heels with this hairy-foot? O shameless, blinded, false girl! What sort of metamorphoses are these? Becoming a cow on account of a pig so that I'm turned into a sheep? What are we waiting for? Why are we deliberating? Let her receive the punishment that she deserves; let her receive the penalty that you judge to be fit. Take her away from me, for I can't stomach her.' The counselors thus convened and concluded that she, together with the wrongdoer and their children, should be thrown into a barrel and cast out to sea so that their lives would come to an end without the king's having to dirty his hands with their blood.

"No sooner was this sentence issued than the barrel appeared, into which all four of them were stuffed. But before it was sealed some of Vastolla's ladies-in-waiting, crying and sobbing, placed a cask of raisins and dried figs in the barrel to keep them alive for a little while. And then, when it was closed, the barrel was taken and thrown into the sea, where it floated in whatever direction the wind carried it.

"In the meantime Vastolla, crying and making two torrential streams of her eyes, said to Peruonto, 'What a great misfortune to have Bacchus's cradle as our grave! Oh, if at least I knew who had trafficked with this body of mine so that it would be thrown into this container! Alas, I find my life tapped, without knowing why! Tell me, tell me, O cruel one, what sort of spell did you cast, and with what sort of wand, to close me inside the hoops of this barrel? Tell me, tell me, what sort of demon tempted you to put an invisible spigot in me, so that the only crack I have to look out of is this wretched hole?'

"Peruonto, who had been listening all the while with the ears of a

---

18. "The *copeta* is a pastry made of hazelnuts and honey, covered with sprinkles. On the day of Epiphany a sugar bean is put inside it, and whoever finds it is celebrated as 'king of the bean.' This custom still exists in many European countries" (Croce 543).
19. "The Bolognese Leonardo Fioravanti, doctor and charlatan of the sixteenth century, wrote, among other things, *Segreti medicinali* (Venice 1561) and *Compendio dei segreti razionali intorno alla medicina, chirurgia ed alchimia* (Venice 1564)" (Croce 543).

merchant, finally answered, 'If you want me to tell you give me raisins and figs.' Vastolla fed him a handful of one and the other so that she could get something out of him. And as soon as his gullet was full he told her, point by point, what had happened with the three young men, then with the bundle of kindling, and finally with her at the window, when she had treated him like a fat-bellied buffoon and gotten her own belly filled for it. Upon hearing this the poor young lady took heart and said to Peruonto, 'My brother, do we want our lives to burst inside this barrel? Why don't you turn this vessel into a lovely ship so that we can flee danger and sail to a secure port?' And Peruonto replied, 'Give me raisins and figs if you want me to do that.' Vastolla was all ready and immediately filled his throat so that he would open it wide, and like a fisherwoman at Carnival[20] she fished fresh words from his mouth with the raisins and dried figs.

"As soon as Peruonto had said what Vastolla wanted him to, the barrel turned into a boat, complete with all the riggings necessary to sail and all the sailors needed to service the vessel. And you could see one pulling the sheet, one rolling up the shrouds, one manning the helm, one tending to the sail, one climbing up to the crow's-nest, one shouting, 'Luff the helm!' and another, 'Bear up!' one playing a trumpet, one firing a battery, one doing one thing and one another.

"Vastolla was swimming in a sea of sweetness aboard the ship, and since it was already the hour when the Moon liked to play with the Sun at 'You Came and You Went, and Your Spot Is Spent,'[21] she said to Peruonto, 'My handsome young man, turn this ship into a beautiful palace, for we'll be safer that way. You know how the saying goes: "Praise the sea but stay on land."' And Peruonto answered, 'If you want me to do that give me raisins and figs.' She took care of the matter right away, and Peruonto, caught by his throat, asked for the favor, and the ship immediately landed and became a stupendous palace, elaborately decorated from top to bottom, and so full of furnishings and luxuries that nothing more could be desired.

"Whereas before Vastolla would have given up her life for three measly coins,[22] now she wouldn't have traded it with the most noble lady in the world, for she was given gifts and served like a queen. To seal all of her good fortune she had only to ask Peruonto to obtain the grace of becoming handsome and well groomed so that they

---

20. "During Carnival women masked as fisherwomen would throw out hooks with sweets hanging on them, and play other games" (Croce 42).

21. "Phrase from a children's game and, in general, used when someone takes a seat left empty by another person, and the first person comes back and finds it taken" (Croce 42).

22. *tre cavalle* (Neap.): see introduction to day 1 n22.

could enjoy everything together; for although the proverb says, 'Better to have a dirty little husband than an emperor for a friend,' nonetheless if he changed his face she would consider it the greatest fortune in the world. And, according to the terms of the usual deal, Peruonto answered, 'Give me raisins and figs if you want me to do that,' and Vastolla immediately found a remedy for the constipation of Peruonto's words with the laxative figs. No sooner had he spoken than he was transformed from a flycatcher into a goldfinch, from an ogre into a Narcissus,[23] from a grotesque mask into a lovely little doll. When Vastolla saw this she was in the seventh heaven of happiness, and, pressing him in her arms, she squeezed a juice of pleasure.

"At this same time the king, who had ever since the day the disaster occurred been up to his neck in 'leave-me-alones,' was taken hunting by his courtiers in an attempt to cheer him up. While they were out night came upon them, and when they saw an oil lamp shining in the window of that palace, the king sent a servant to see if they were willing to offer him lodging. He was answered that not only could he break a glass there but he could shatter a chamber pot as well. And so the king entered, and as he went up the stairs and passed through the rooms, he saw not a living soul except for those two little boys, who circled about him saying, 'Grandpa, Grandpa.'

"The king was stupefied, astonished, and dumbstruck, and stood there as if enchanted. And when he grew tired and sat down at a table, lo and behold! He saw tablecloths of Flanders linen invisibly spread and plates full of this and that carried to the table and then taken away again, and he ate and drank in a manner truly fit for a king. He was served by the two handsome boys, and the whole time he sat at the table music was played on the lute[24] and tambourine, and he felt its effect all the way down to the little bones of his feet. As soon as he finished eating there appeared a bed all frothy with gold where, when his boots had been taken off, he lay down to sleep, as did his entire court once they, too, had stuffed themselves at a hundred other tables set in the other rooms.

"When morning arrived and the king intended to leave, he wanted to bring the two little boys with him. But Vastolla came out with her husband and, throwing herself at his feet, asked for his pardon and

---

23. In Greek mythology, the boy, son of a river god and a nymph, who was insensitive to the desires of maidens and nymphs, among whom was Echo. Aphrodite punished Narcissus by making him fall in love with his own image reflected in the water of a fountain; he died as a result of this passion, and was later transformed into a flower.

24. *colascione* (Neap.): "A wide-necked lute with two or three strings, very popular in southern Italy in Basile's time" (Guarini and Burani 63).

told him of all her adventures. The king, who saw that he had acquired two grandsons who were two jewels and a son-in-law as handsome as a fairy,[25] embraced them all and carried them off to the city, where to celebrate these fine acquisitions he ordered grand festivities, which lasted for many days. And he had to confess, in spite of himself, that *man proposes, and God disposes*."

---

25. "The masculine of fairy, not infrequently used at this time. [. . .] In medieval Latin *fada* and *fadus* are used. In Sicilian folklore there are *fatuzzi* [little male fairies]" (Croce 543).

4

VARDIELLO

Fourth Entertainment of the First Day

After doing his mother a hundred bad services, Vardiello, who is a beast, loses a piece of her cloth. When he foolishly tries to get it back from a statue, he becomes rich.

When Meneca had finished her tale, which was judged to be no less wonderful than the others, packed as it had been with curious events that had kept her audience hanging by its tail right up until the end, Tolla, following the prince's command, followed. Without wasting time she spoke in this manner: "If Nature had given animals the need to clothe themselves and spend money for meals, the race of quadrupeds would without a doubt have been destroyed. But they are able to find food without a farmer having to pick it, a buyer to purchase it, a cook to prepare it, or a steward to carve it, and their own hide defends them from rain and snow without a merchant to give them fabric, a tailor to make them clothing, or an errand boy to ask for a tip. But Nature didn't think about giving man, who has intelligence, this convenience, because man knows how to procure what he needs by himself. That's the reason why it's normal to see the wise penniless and the beastly rich, as you'll be able to gather from the tale that I am about to tell you.

"Grannonia of Aprano[1] was a woman of great judgment, but she had a son named Vardiello who was the most good-for-nothing sim-

---

AT 1381: The Talkative Wife and the Discovered Treasure, and AT 1381B: The Sausage Rain (or Rain of figs, fishes, or milk). Penzer notes that "this is one of the well-known 'fool' or 'noodle' stories." Grimm 59 ("Freddy and Katy") follows it closely, and nos. 7, 32, and 185 contain some similar motifs. The motif of "the trick by which the fool is made to appear mad" also appears in the "Tale of Sinbad" in *Arabian Nights*. There are numerous Italian versions of similar fool tales; in southern Italy, especially Sicily, the fool often goes by the name of Giufà. "The closest to 'Vardiello' is Gonzenbach 37 ('Giufà'), where Giufà says, 'Don't you remember when I brought you home the pot, and in the night the Christ child rained figs and raisins from heaven into my mouth?' " (1:48). Croce also cites variants in Pitrè, *Fiabe, nove. e racc. siciliani* 190 ("Giufà") and *Nov. e legg. toscane* 32 ("Giucca"), G. Morlini, *Novellae, fabulae, comoedia* (1528) 49, and Giulio Cesare Croce's *Bertoldino* (Croce, *Lo cunto de li cunti*, 286).
1. A small town twenty kilometers from Naples, near Aversa.

pleton of the town. Even so, since a mother's eyes are bewitched and see things that aren't there, she had an unbounded love for him and brooded and preened him as if he were the most lovely creature in the world.

"Grannonia had a mother hen that was brooding her chicks, in whom she had placed all her expectations, hoping that it would be a good hatch from which she could squeeze a nice profit. And so when she had to go out on an errand, she called her son and said to him, 'Mommy's dear little boy, listen here: keep an eye on that hen, and if she gets up to peck, take care to make her get back into the nest, or else the eggs will get cold and then you won't have eggies or cheep-cheeps.' 'This fellow will take care of it,' said Vardiello, 'you're not talking to deaf ears.' 'One more thing,' replied his mother. 'Look, my blessed son: inside that cupboard there's a little jar of some poisonous stuff. Make sure not to commit the awful sin of touching it, or you'll stretch out your legs for the last time.' 'God forbid!' answered Vardiello. 'Poison won't get me; and you're a crazy-headed wise woman for warning me, since I might have bumped straight into it and then neither fishbones nor gristle could have blocked its way.'

"And so his mother left, and Vardiello was there by himself. So as not to waste any time he went out to the garden and set about making little ditches covered with twigs and earth for children to fall into. But right when he was in the middle of the job he realized that the hen was taking a walk outside her room, at which he began to say, 'Shoo, shoo, get out of here, get back in there.' But the hen didn't lift a foot and after the 'shoo shoo' Vardiello, seeing that the hen was behaving like an ass, began stamping his feet, and after stamping his feet he threw his cap, and after the cap he threw a rolling pin, which hit her squarely and caused her to stretch out her legs for the last time and croak.

"Upon seeing this terrible accident, Vardiello thought to find a remedy for the damage done, and, making virtue of necessity, he immediately pulled down his pants and sat on the nest so the eggs wouldn't get cold; but since he plopped down quite heavily, he made an omelet of them. Seeing that he had doubled his loss, he felt like banging his head against the wall; finally, since every sorrow ends in a mouthful,[2] when he felt his stomach rumbling he resolved to gobble up the hen. And thus, after plucking it and skewering it on a nice spit, he made an enormous fire and began to roast it. And so as to have everything ready in time, when it was almost done he spread a nice

---

2. "Allusion to the receptions and banquets that followed funerals" (Guarini and Burani 66).

freshly laundered towel on top of an old chest, and then got a jug and went down to the cellar to tap a little quarter cask[3] of wine.

"Right as he was in the middle of pouring the wine, he heard some noise, a racket, and an uproar in the house that sounded like armored horses. Terrified, he turned his eyes and saw that a huge cat had taken off with the hen together with the whole spit, and that another cat was running after it, screaming for its share. To make up for this damage Vardiello threw himself like an unchained lion on top of the cat and in his haste left the quarter cask uncorked, and after playing tag in every corner of the house he got the hen back, but all the wine had run out of the cask. When Vardiello came back and saw the mess he was in, he uncorked the barrel of his own soul through the spigots of his eyes. Helped, however, by his good sense, he made up for the damage so that his mother wouldn't notice the degree of destruction: he got a sack of flour that was chock-full, overstuffed, jam-packed, crammed to the top, and bulging, and sprinkled it on the wet area.

"Nonetheless, when he counted on his fingers the disasters that had occurred and considered that by kicking things to pieces like a real ass he had lost the contest for Grannonia's good graces, he resolved with all his heart not to let himself be found alive by his mother. And so he opened the little jar of cured nuts that his mother had told him were poisonous and didn't take his hands out until he could see the bottom of the jar, and when his belly was good and full he stuffed himself into the oven.

"In the meantime his mother came back. She knocked for a long time, but seeing that no one heard her she gave the door a kick, went in, and called for her son in a loud voice. When she saw that no one was answering she sensed that a bad day was ahead, and as her anguish grew, she shrieked even louder, 'Oh, Vardiello! Oh, Vardiello, are you deaf; why don't you hear me? Do you have arthritis; why don't you come running? Have you got the pip; why aren't you answering?[4] Where are you, gallows face? Where did you sneak off to, you bad seed? Oh, if only I had drowned you at the source, when I made you!'

"When Vardiello heard all this clamor he finally said, in the most pitiful little voice, 'Here I am. I'm in the oven and you'll never see me again, my dear mother.' 'Why not?' answered his poor mother. 'Because I've poisoned myself,' replied her son. 'Oh, dear,' added Grannonia, 'how did you do that? What reason did you have for committing

---

3. A quarter of a Neapolitan cask (eleven liters) (Rak 106).

4. *iorde* [. . .] *pipitola* (Neap.): "two animal diseases, the first of a horse's joints, the second of chicken's tongues" (Rak 106).

this crime? And who gave you the poison?' And, one after the other, Vardiello told her about all the nice ordeals he had been through, and how because of them he wanted to die so that he would have to put up with the trials of the world no longer.

"When his mother heard this she felt miserable, she felt bitter, and she had a lot to do and say before she could get this melancholy humor out of Vardiello's head, and since she loved him right down to the bottom of her heart, she gave him some kind of syrup that got the idea of the cured nuts out of his noggin, for they weren't poison but just a stomach tonic. And when she had convinced him with gentle words and offered him a thousand hugs, she pulled him out of the oven, and then she gave him a nice piece of cloth and told him to go sell it, warning him not to do business with people of too many words.

"'Great!' said Vardiello. 'Have no doubt, I'll serve you generously!' And taking the cloth, he went yelling through the city of Naples, which was where he had brought his merchandise, 'Cloth, cloth!' But to everyone who asked him, 'What kind of cloth is it?' he answered, 'You're not my type, you're a person of too many words.' And if someone else said, 'How much are you selling it for?' he called him a chatterbox and told him that he was taxing his brain and giving him a headache. Finally, he came across a plaster statue in the courtyard of a house that had been deserted on account of a house imp,[5] and the poor boy, foot-weary and tired of running around so much, sat down on a little wall. Not seeing any kind of traffic in that place, which looked like a pillaged farmhouse, he said to the statue, in a state of wonder, 'Tell me, pal, doesn't anyone live here?' And seeing that the statue wasn't answering, it seemed to him that this was a man of few words, and he said, 'Do you want to buy this cloth? I'll give you a good price!' And seeing that the statue remained silent, he said, 'I do declare, I've found what I was looking for! Take it, have it looked at, and give me whatever you want for it; tomorrow I'll be back for the dough.'

"That said, he left the cloth where he had been sitting, and the first mama's boy who went in there to pay a call to nature found his fortune and carried it off with him. When Vardiello returned to his mother without the cloth and told her how things had gone, she almost had a heart attack, and said to him, 'When are you going to get your head on straight? Look how many messes you've gotten me in! Just remember them all! But it's my own fault for having tender lungs; I didn't tan your hide the first time around and only now do I realize

---

5. See tale 1.1 n19.

that a merciful doctor makes for an incurable wound. You'll keep on making trouble for me until you get fixed up good, and then we'll settle our accounts once and for all.' As for Vardiello, he said, 'Hush, my dear mother, it won't be like you say! What more do you want than freshly minted coins? What do you think, that I'm from Ioio[6] and don't know my own business? Tomorrow is yet to come! It's not far from here to Belvedere,[7] and you'll see if I know how to put a handle on a shovel.'

"In the morning—when Night's shadows, chased by the Sun's cops, were evicted from the town—Vardiello took himself back to the courtyard where the statue was and said, 'Good day, sir; would it behoove you to give me those four little coins? Come on, now, pay me for the cloth.' But when he saw that the statue was mute, he picked up a stone and hurled it with all his might, hitting the statue smack in the middle of the chest, so that it burst a vein. And this was the salvation of his house, for several large chunks of plaster cracked off and inside he discovered a pot full of golden scudos.[8] He grabbed hold of it with both hands and ran home at breakneck speed, shouting, 'Mother, Mother, look at all these red beans, look at all of them, just look!'

"As soon as his mother saw the coins she realized that her son would make the matter public, and told him to wait on the doorstep for the ricotta seller to come by, since she wanted to buy a coin's worth of milk. Vardiello, who would eat anything up, sat right down in front of the door, and then for more than half an hour his mother, from the window above, sent down a hail shower of more than six rolls[9] of raisins and dried figs, which Vardiello gathered up, shouting, 'Oh, Mother, oh, Mother, get the basins, pull out the tubs, prepare the pails, for if this rain keeps up we're going to be rich!' And when his belly was good and full, he went upstairs to sleep.

"Now it happened that one day two workers, of the sort who hung around the courts, were arguing about who could claim a gold coin that had been found on the ground. Vardiello came along and said,

---

6. "Today Gioi, an area in the province of Salerno, near Vallo della Lucania. [. . .] It had come . . . to stand for the roughest, wildest, and most primitive part of southern Italy" (Croce 49, 544).

7. *bello vedere* (Neap.): Belvedere (a castle at a short distance from Pozzuoli, built by Frederick II) or, more in general, a balustrade on a high castle or fort that looks out over a panorama vs. "a fine sight."

8. Gold or silver coins introduced in the sixteenth century and current in many Italian states at Basile's time.

9. "The *ruotola*, or roll, was a measure of weight whose value differed in various Italian cities; in southern Italy it was about 900 grams" (Guarini and Burani 70).

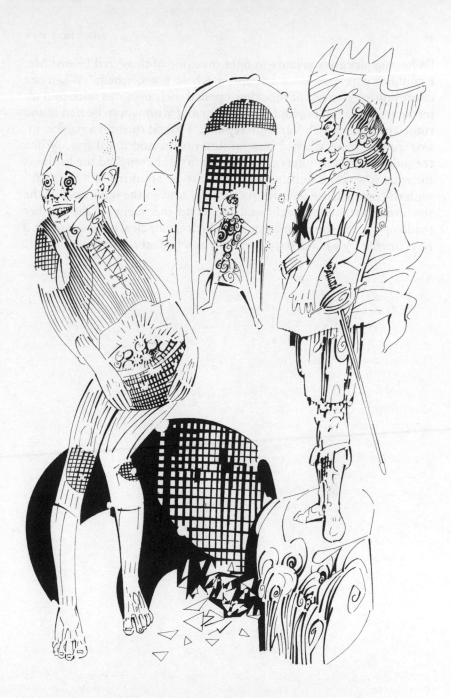

"Mamma, mamma, quanta lupine russe, quantane, quantane!"
["Mother, Mother, look at all of these red beans,
look at all of them, just look!"]

'What big jackasses you are to fight over one of those red beans! Me, I couldn't care less, since I found a whole pot of them.' When the court police got word of this, they opened their eyes this wide and interrogated him, asking him how, when, and with whom he had found those coins. To which Vardiello replied, 'I found them in a palace, inside a mute man, when it was raining raisins and dried figs.' When the judge heard this interval of a minor fifth[10] he smelled the business for what it was and sentenced Vardiello to be admitted to a hospital[11] with the competence to judge such cases. And so the ignorance of the son made the mother rich, and the good judgment of the mother made up for the son's asininity, for which it can clearly be seen that *a ship steered by a good skipper is only rarely dashed on the rocks.*"

---

10. "An interval unexpected to the ear (which would normally expect a 'perfect fifth'), just as Vardiello's answer was unexpected for the judge" (Croce 51).

11. "A hospital for the mentally and terminally ill, which in Naples was the Hospital of the Incurable" (Rak 106).

5

THE FLEA

Fifth Entertainment of the First Day

A king who does not have much to think about raises a flea until it becomes as big as a lamb, then has it skinned and offers his daughter as a reward to anyone who is able to recognize its skin. An ogre identifies it by smell and takes the princess, but she is freed by the seven sons of an old woman after seven trials.

The prince and the slave split their sides laughing over Vardiello's ignorance and praised his mother's good judgment, since she had been able to foresee his bestial behavior and find a remedy for it. When Popa was urged to start talking she waited for all the others to put their chatter under lock and key, and then began to speak: "Resolutions made without judgment always lead to ruin without remedy; he who behaves like a madman suffers like a wise man, as happened to the king of High Mountain, who on account of a four-soled mistake committed a high-heeled[1] folly and put his daughter and his honor in immeasurable danger.

"The king of High Mountain was once bitten by a flea, and when he had picked it off with great dexterity and saw how beautiful and solidly built it was, it seemed a shame to him to execute it on the block of his fingernail. And so he placed it in a carafe and, feeding it

---

AT 311: Rescue by the Sister, AT 513A: Six Go Through the Whole World, AT 621: The Louse-Skin, and AT 653: The Four Skillful Brothers. The tale consists of two distinct parts, each having many variants. The first, "the riddle as to what animal the skin belongs," can be found in Grimm (124 and 134) and Gonzenbach (22), among others. "The second part contains one of the most widely diffused motifs in folktales, that of pursuers being hindered by magical obstacles thrown in their path. In some cases safety is finally reached by means of the 'joint efforts' of various people endowed with wonderful gifts. Thus, in the present tale, out of the seven sons, numbers 2, 3, 4, and 5 produce 'magic obstacles,' while all seven form the 'joint efforts' motif as a whole. [. . .] [I]t will be noticed that the magic object resembles that which it forms. Thus spittle becomes a sea, a twig turns into a forest, and so on. This is merely the outcome of the belief in sympathetic magic" (Penzer 1:55). See also Grimm 71, Pitrè *Fiabe e legg. sic.* 2, Pitrè *Fiabe, nov. e racc. sic.* 21, Pitrè *Nov. tosc.* 10, and 5.7 of this collection.

1. *'n cordoana* (Neap.): "of high quality, like the leather used in the refined and ancient traditional leatherworking of Cordoba" (Rak 122).

"Chisso cuoiero è de l'arcefanfaro de li pulece."
["This hide belongs to the ringleader of all fleas."]

daily with blood from his own arm, it grew so quickly that at the end
of seven months, when he had to change its quarters, it was bigger
than a lamb. On seeing this, the king had it skinned, and when the
skin had been dressed he issued a proclamation: whoever was able to
recognize to which animal the hide belonged would be given his
daughter in marriage. After the notice was made public, flocks of
people came running, arriving from the asshole of the earth to be
present at this exam and try their luck. There was one who said it
was a monster cat, another a lynx, one a crocodile, one some animal
and another a different one; but they were all a hundred miles off and
not one was on the mark.

"Finally, an ogre presented himself at this anatomy exam, an ogre
who was the most horrible thing in the world and the mere sight of
whom brought tremors, diarrhea, worms, and chills to the boldest
young man in the world. Now as soon as he arrived the ogre started
buzzing around the skin and sniffing at it, and he hit the bull's-eye
straight on when he said, 'This hide belongs to the ringleader of all
fleas.'

"The king saw that the ogre had grafted onto the right tree[2] and summoned his daughter Porziella, who looked like she was made of nothing but milk and blood. Oh, my dear! She was a little spindle, so beautiful that you coddled her with your eyes. The king said to her, 'Daughter, you know the proclamation I issued and you know who I am. All things considered, I can't go back on my promise: either you're a king or you're poplar bark; I gave my word and now I have to keep it, even if it breaks my heart. Who could ever have imagined that an ogre would win this lottery? But since a leaf can't fall unless it's the will of the heavens, we have to believe that this marriage was arranged first of all up there and then down here. So be patient, and if you're a blessed daughter don't talk back to your daddy, for my heart tells me that you're going to be happy; a plain stone jar often houses treasures.'

"When Porziella heard this bitter decision her eyes grew dark, her face became yellow, her lips drooped, her legs trembled, and she was on the verge of sending the falcon of her soul off to pursue the quail of her suffering.[3] Finally, breaking out in tears and raising her voice, she said to her father, 'Just what kind of bad service have I performed in this house to receive such punishment? What sort of bad manners have I used with you to be delivered into the hands of this bogeyman? O miserable Porziella! Here you are, about to go into the throat of this toad of your own will, like a weasel; here you are, an unfortunate sheep about to be stolen away by a werewolf! Is this the affection you have for your own blood? Is this the love you show toward she whom you called the pupil of your soul? In this way you rip from your heart she who shares your own blood? In this way you remove from your sight she who is the apple of your eye? O father, cruel father, you could not possibly have been born of human flesh! Orcas gave you your blood, wild cats your milk![4] But why do I speak of sea and land animals? Every animal loves its offspring; you alone treat your own seed with a contrary heart and nausea, you alone cannot stomach your own daughter! Oh, better if my mother had suffocated me, if my cradle had been my deathbed, my wet nurse's tit a bladder of poison, my swaddling clothes nooses, and the little whistle they

---

2. Literally, "he had grafted it onto a lotus tree," or he had guessed it right. "This tree was once very common in Naples, and an alley near the Sedile di Porto and a point along the Materdei street take their name from it" (Croce 544).

3. "Terms from falconry, which had a great medieval tradition but was at this point in time in a phase of decadence due to the progressive improvements in firearms. There were, however, still numerous books on the subject" (Rak 122).

4. "[D]uris genuit te cautibus horrens Caucasus, Hycanaeque admorunt ubera tigres" (Virgil, *Aeneid* 4.366–67; cit. Croce 54).

tied round my neck a millstone, considering that this calamity was to befall me and that I was to find this accursed creature sitting right next to me and to feel myself caressed by a harpy's hand, embraced by two bear's shins, and kissed by two pig's tusks!'

"She was intending to say more, when the king, sending off smoke in every direction, said to her, 'Enough with the anger; sugar is expensive! Slow down there; your shields are made of poplar![5] Plug your mouth; it's spewing filth! Shut up, not a peep; you're a sharp-tongued, spiteful bigmouth! Whatever I do is done well! Don't try to teach a father how to have daughters! Cut it out; stick that tongue back in and take care the mustard doesn't reach my nose, since if I get my paws on you I won't leave a hair on your head, and I'll sow this earth with your teeth! Just look at this stink of my own ass who wants to play the man and lay down the law for her father! Since when does a girl whose mouth still reeks of milk have the right to question my will? Hurry up, give him your hand, and get off to his house this instant; I don't want to see your impudent and presumptuous face in front of my eyes for even another quarter of an hour.'

"Finding herself in these straits, poor Porziella had the face of one condemned to die, the eyes of one possessed by spirits, the mouth of one who has taken the Domini Agustini[6] laxative, and the heart of one whose head is between the blade and the stone.[7] She took the ogre's hand and was dragged by him, without company, into a wood—where the trees formed a palace for the meadow so that it wouldn't be discovered by the Sun, the rivers complained that when they flowed in the dark they tripped on stones, and the wild animals enjoyed their Benevento, not having to pay duty tax, and wandered safely through the thickets[8]—in which no one ever entered unless he had lost his way. In this place, dark as a clogged chimney and frightening as the facade of hell, stood the ogre's house, decorated and plastered all over with

---

5. "I.e., the defense is fragile: the *brocchiere* was a small wooden shield with a sharp spike (*brocco*) in the middle, used to wound the adversary in body-to-body combat" (Guarini and Burani 75).

6. The physician and philosopher Agostino Nifo da Sessa (1462–1538), the "inventor of that wonderful syrup without which it would seem to be impossible to make a perfect medicine, which is commonly called *syrupus Domini Agustini* by physicians and apothecaries" (Croce 544).

7. "In Naples and almost all of Italy capital punishment made use of the 'blade,' which fell from above and already had the form of a primitive and rough guillotine" (Croce 544).

8. "The right of *fida* [care] was paid by those who pastured their animals on land belonging to others, or on royal or communal land. Benevento was part of the pontifical state and was, therefore, a close and easy-to-reach 'land of exile' for Neapolitan outlaws" (Croce 55).

the bones of men he had eaten. Anyone who's a Christian can imagine
the tremors, the horror, the tightening of the heart, the runs, the
fright, the worms, and the diarrhea that the poor girl experienced:
let's just say that there wasn't a drop of blood left in her veins.

"But that was nothing, not even a dried fig, compared to the rest of
the change, since she had chickpeas for antipasto and fava beans for
dessert.[9] Indeed, the ogre returned home from hunting laden down
with quarters of slaughtered men and said to her, 'Now you can't
complain, my dear wife, that I don't take care of you! Here's a nice
supply of things to go with your bread; take them and enjoy them and
love me, for even if the sky were to fall I wouldn't deprive you of your
chow.' Poor Porziella, retching like a pregnant woman, turned her
face the other way. When the ogre saw this gesture he said, 'That's
what happens when you give sweets to pigs! But never mind: just
keep calm until tomorrow morning, for I've been invited to hunt wild
pigs. I'll bring a couple of them home for you, and then we can have
a first-rate wedding celebration with all our relatives and thus consume our relationship with even greater pleasure.'

"That said, he marched off into the woods. While Porziella was at
the window lamenting her fate, an old woman had the misfortune to
pass by the house. Feeling faint with hunger, she asked for some refreshment, to which the miserable girl answered, 'Oh, my good
woman, only God knows my heart. I am under the power of an infer-
nal creature who brings me nothing but quartered men and pieces of
slaughtered bodies, and I don't know how I even have the stomach to
look at such revolting things; indeed, my life is the most wretched
one a baptized soul has ever lived. And yet I'm a king's daughter, and
yet I was brought up on *pappardelle*,[10] and yet I've always lived in the
midst of plenty!'

"As she was saying this she started crying like a little girl whose
snack has been snatched away from her, so that the old woman's
heart softened, and she said, 'Cheer up, my lovely girl; don't consume
your beauty crying, for you have found your fortune and I am here to
help you mount any saddle I can. Now listen to me. I have seven sons
who are seven jewels, seven oak trees, seven giants—Mase, Nardo,
Cola, Micco, Petrullo, Ascadeo, and Ceccone—and they have more
virtues than rosemary.[11] In particular, each time Mase puts his ear to

---

9. "Chickpeas and dried fava beans were given to prisoners and to those condemned
to death" (Rak 123).

10. A long, wide noodle often prepared with game sauces.

11. "The science of herbalism attributed to rosemary legendary therapeutic powers;
it was a plant of purification and was associated with the dead and with fairies" (Rak
123). Rosemary is also an emblem of remembrance and fidelity.

the ground he hears and eavesdrops on everything that's happening up to thirty miles away; each time Nardo spits he makes a huge sea of soap; whenever Cola throws down a little piece of iron he makes a field of sharpened razors; every time Micco hurls a stick he makes a tangled wood; whenever Petrullo shakes a drop of water to the ground he makes a frightful river; each time Ascadeo throws a stone he makes a mighty tower spring up; and Ceccone shoots so straight with a crossbow that he can hit a chicken's eye from a mile away. Now with the help of these seven, all of whom are courteous and kind and will have compassion for your condition, I intend to try and get you out from under the claws of that ogre, for this lovely, tempting morsel is not fit for the gullet of that bogeyman.' 'There's never been a better time than now,' answered Porziella. 'That evil shadow of my husband has gone out and won't be back this evening, so we'll have time to throw up our heels and clear out of here.' 'It can't be this evening,' replied the old woman, 'because I live at some distance from here, but all right: tomorrow morning my sons and I will be here to put an end to your troubles.'

"That said, she left, and Porziella, with her heart completely at rest, slept through the night. And as soon as the birds shouted, 'Long live the Sun!' there was the old woman with her seven sons, and when Porziella had joined them they set off for the city. But they had gone no farther than half a mile when Mase, putting his ear to the ground, shouted, 'Look out! Hey! The fox is here! The ogre is back home already, and since he didn't find the girl he's coming after us with his hat under his armpit.' Upon hearing this, Nardo spit on the ground and made a sea of soap; when the ogre got there and saw the lather he ran home, got a sack of bran, and smeared great amounts of it all over his feet until, with great difficulty, he surpassed the obstacle.

"But when Mase put his ear to the ground again he said, 'Your turn, brother, here he comes.' Cola threw down his piece of iron, and a field of razor blades shot up. Finding his way blocked, the ogre ran back home again, dressed from head to toe in iron and, after he returned, stepped clear over the ditch. But Mase, when he stuck his ear to the ground once more, shouted, 'Come on, come on, grab your weapons; the ogre's going to fly in here at full speed any moment now!' And Micco quickly took his stick and made a terrifying wood spring up on the spot, a wood most difficult to penetrate. As soon as the ogre got to this impasse he grabbed a cleaver that he carried at his side and began to fell a poplar tree over here, an oak over there; on one side he sent a dogwood crashing, on another a service tree, so that with four or five blows he had beaten the wood to the ground and gotten out of the entanglement unharmed.

"Mase, who had the ears of a hare, started raising his voice again: 'Let's not stand here like we're about to shave; the ogre has sprouted wings, and in a minute he'll be at our backs.' When Petrullo heard this he took a sip of water from a little fountain that was trickling one drop at a time from a stone shell, spit it on the ground, and, lo and behold! there was a big river. When the ogre saw this new impediment and realized that for every hole he made the others found a plug, he stripped down stark naked and swam to the other side with his clothes on his head.

"Mase, who put his ear to every hole, heard the trampling of the ogre's feet and said, 'This business of ours is going badly, and the ogre is already beating his heels so hard that the heavens can tell you about it. So let's keep our wits about us and shelter ourselves from the storm; otherwise, we're done for.' 'Have no fear,' said Ascadeo, 'I'll show that ugly bum a thing or two now,' and as he said this he threw down a stone and made a tower appear, into which they immediately crowded, bolting the door behind them. But when the ogre got there and saw that they had escaped to safety he ran home, found a grape harvester's ladder and loaded it onto his back, and then ran back to the tower.

"Mase, whose ears were hanging, heard the ogre's arrival from afar and said, 'Our candle of hope is down to the quick, and our life's last refuge lies with Ceccone, since the ogre's coming back now. And is he ever furious! Oh, dear, my heart is beating and I predict it's going to be a bad day!' 'What a pants shitter you are!' answered Ceccone. 'Leave it to Menechiello here, and you'll see if my pellets hit the bull's-eye.' Just as he was saying this the ogre leaned the ladder against the tower and started to climb up; but Ceccone took aim and, after knocking out one of his orbs, sent the ogre falling to the ground like a pear. Then he left the tower and, with the knife that the ogre himself had been carrying, slit his throat as if it were ricotta.

"They carried the ogre off with great merriment to the king, who was overjoyed to get his daughter back, since he had repented a hundred times for having given her to an ogre. And after a few days he found her a lovely husband, and bestowed riches on the seven sons and their mother who had freed his daughter from such an unhappy life. He never stopped declaring himself a thousand times guilty to Porziella for having placed her in such danger on account of a mere whim, without a thought to how big a mistake is made by those who go looking for *wolves' eggs and fifteen-teethed combs*."[12]

---

12. "An expression of unclear derivation, used to indicate absurdities. . . . It is probably an allusion to carding combs, whose teeth were always fewer than 15; a comb with 15 teeth would be just as unnatural as a wolf's egg" (Croce 59).

6

THE CINDERELLA CAT

Sixth Entertainment of the First Day

Zezolla, incited by her teacher to kill her stepmother, believes that she will be held dear for having helped the teacher to marry her father; instead she ends up in the kitchen. But due to the power of some fairies, after numerous adventures she wins a king for her husband.

The audience looked like statues as they listened to the tale of the flea, and they gave a certificate of asininity to the boorish king, who had exposed his own flesh and blood and the succession of his state to such great risks, and all for a piddling matter. Once they had all corked their mouths, Antonella uncorked hers in the manner that follows: "In the sea of malice, envy always finds herself with a hernia[1] in the place of a bladder, and where she expects to see another drown, she finds herself either underwater or dashed against a reef, just as happened to certain envious girls that I have in mind to tell you about.

"You should know, then, that there once was a widowed prince who had a daughter so dear to him that he had eyes for no one else. He had taken on a first-rate sewing teacher for her, who taught her how to do the chain-stitch, openwork, fringes, and the hem-stitch, and showed her more affection than words can express. But the father had just remarried; he had taken a fiery, wicked, and demonic thing for his wife, and her stepdaughter soon began to make this accursed woman's stomach turn. She gave the girl sour looks, made

---

AT 510A: Cinderella. Basile's tale is the earliest literary version of Cinderella in Europe, preceding Perrault's "Cendrillon" (1697) by over sixty years. Penzer comments on two motifs that do not commonly appear in other versions: "The unusual incident of Cennerentola murdering her mother-in-law by letting the lid of a chest fall on her neck reminds us of Grimm 47 ['The Juniper Tree'], where the wicked step-mother shuts the lid of the apple-chest on the little boy as he stoops to get an apple." The other motif, "the stopping of the ship," appears also in tale 2.8, and in other folktales (Penzer 1:62). See also Grimm 21, Gonzenbach 32, Imbriani 11 and 21, Pitrè, *Fiabe, nov. e racc. sic.* 42 and 56, and Marie-Catherine d'Aulnoy, "Finette Cendron" (in Zipes, *Beauties, Beasts and Enchantment*).
1. "It was popular belief that hernias, and especially strangulated hernias, were caused by envy, since one can 'die' from both" (Guarini and Burani 81).

awful faces at her, and knitted her eyebrows in such a frightful manner that the poor little thing was always complaining to the teacher
of her stepmother's ill treatment, saying, 'Oh, God, couldn't you be
my little mommy, you who give me so many smooches and squeezes?'

"She chanted this so incessantly that she planted a wasp in the
teacher's ear, and one day, blinded by evil spirits, the teacher said to
her, 'If you follow the advice of this madcap, I'll become your mother
and you'll be as dear to me as the pupils of these eyes.' She was about
to go on speaking when Zezolla (for that was the girl's name) said,
'Forgive me if I take the words out of your mouth. I know you love
me dearly, so mum's the word, and *sufficit;* teach me the trade, for
I'm new in town; you write and I'll sign.' 'All right, then,' replied the
teacher, 'listen carefully; keep your ears open and your bread will
come out as white as flowers. As soon as your father leaves, tell your
stepmother you want one of those old dresses in the big chest in the
storeroom so that you can save the one you're wearing. Since she likes
to see you all patched up in rags, she'll open the chest and say, "Hold
the lid up." And as you're holding it while she rummages around inside, let it bang shut, and she'll break her neck. Once that's done, you
know that your father would coin counterfeit money to make you
happy, so when he caresses you, beg him to take me for his wife and,
lucky you, you'll become the mistress of my life.'

"After Zezolla heard this, every hour seemed like a thousand years
to her. She followed her teacher's instructions to a tee, and once the
mourning for the stepmother's accident was over, she began to play
her father's keys to the tune of marrying the teacher. At first the
prince thought it was a joke, but his daughter beat so hard that she
finally broke the door down, and in the end he yielded to Zezolla's
words. He took Carmosina, the teacher, for his wife, and held grand
festivities.

"Now while the newlyweds were off carrying on and Zezolla was
standing at one of the balconies[2] of the palace, a little dove flew down
onto the wall and said to her, 'If ever you should wish for something,
send your request to the dove of the fairies on the island of Sardinia,
and you will be immediately satisfied.'

"The new stepmother smoked Zezolla with caresses for five or six
days, seating her at the best place at the table, giving her the best
morsels, dressing her in the best clothes. But in no time at all she an-
nulled and completely forgot about the service rendered (oh, sad is
the soul housed in a wicked mistress!), and began to raise to all
heights six daughters of her own whom she had kept secret up until

---

2. *gaifo* (Neap.): "In Naples, a sort of small hanging terrace" (Croce 62).

then. And she worked her husband over so well that as his stepdaughters entered into his graces, his own daughter fell from his heart, and from one day to the next Zezolla ended up being demoted from the royal chamber to the kitchen and from a canopied bed to the hearth, from sumptuous silks and gold to rags, from the scepter to the spit. And not only did her status change, but her name as well, for she was no longer called Zezolla but Cinderella Cat.

"It happened that the prince had to go to Sardinia for affairs of state, and, one by one, he asked Imperia, Calamita, Shiorella, Diamante, Colombina, and Pascarella, who were the six stepdaughters, what they wanted him to bring them on his return. One asked for luxurious clothing, one for ornaments for her hair, one for rouges for her face, one for toys to pass the time, one for one thing, and one for another. Finally he asked his daughter, almost scornfully, 'And you, what would you like?' And she: 'Nothing, except that you give my regards to the dove of the fairies and tell her to send me something; and if you forget, may you be unable to go forward or backward. Keep in mind what I say: your arm, your sleeve.'[3]

"The prince departed, did his business in Sardinia, and bought what his stepdaughters had requested; Zezolla slipped his mind. But after he embarked on his vessel and it was about to set sail, the ship was unable to leave port, just as if it had been blocked by a sea lamprey.[4] The captain of the ship, close to desperation, fell asleep out of fatigue and in his dreams saw a fairy, who said to him, 'Do you know why you cannot remove the ship from port? Because the prince who is with you broke a promise he made to his daughter, remembering everyone except his own flesh and blood.' The captain awoke and told his dream to the prince, who, confused about his failing, went to the fairies' grotto and, after giving them his daughter's regards, asked that they send her something.

"And lo and behold, a lovely young woman who was a banner to beauty came out of the cavern and told him that she thanked his daughter for remembering her so kindly, and that Zezolla should be happy, as a tribute of love for the fairy. With these words, she gave him a date tree, a hoe, a golden pail, and a silk cloth, and told him that the date tree was for planting and the other things for cultivating it. The prince, astonished by these gifts, took leave of the fairy and returned to his land, where when he had given all of the stepdaugh-

---

3. "Proverbial way of saying: 'If you don't keep your word, all the worse for you'" (Croce 63).
4. *remmora* (Neap.): marine or sea lamprey, "which attaches itself, by a sort of suction cup, to other fish or to ships; according to popular lore the lamprey could prevent or hinder navigation (Pliny, *Natural History* IX 25)" (Rak 138).

ters what they had requested, he at last gave his daughter the gift sent by the fairy.

"Nearly bursting out of her skin with joy, Zezolla planted the date in a fine pot, hoed it, watered it, and dried it with the silk cloth every morning and evening, so that after four days, when the plant had grown as tall as a woman, a fairy came out and said to her, 'What is your wish?' Zezolla answered that she wished to leave the house now and then but didn't want her sisters to know. The fairy replied, 'Whenever you like, go to the pot and say,

> Golden date of mine
> I've weeded you with the little hoe of gold,
> I've watered you with the little pail of gold,
> I've dried you with the cloth of silk,
> Now strip yourself and dress me!

And when you want to undress, change the last verse to: "Strip me and dress yourself!"'

"Now then, a feast day arrived and the teacher's daughters went out, all flowery, bedecked, and painted; all ribbons, little bells, and baubles; all flowers, scents, rosies, and posies. Zezolla immediately ran to the pot, uttered the words the fairy had taught her, and found herself fixed up like a queen, after which she was placed on a white thoroughbred with twelve trim and elegant pages in tow. Then she went to the place her sisters had gone, and they drooled over the beauty of that splendid dove.

"As fate willed it, the king showed up there, too, and when he saw Zezolla's extraordinary beauty he immediately fell under its spell, and he asked his most trusted servant to find out how he could get more information about this phenomenon of beauty—who she was and where she lived. Without a moment's delay the servant went after her; but having discovered the ambush, she threw out a handful of golden coins obtained from the date tree for this purpose. When he caught sight of those gleaming coins the servant forgot about following the horse, preferring to fill his claws with small change, while Zezolla dashed back and slipped into the house. Once she had undressed the way the fairy had instructed her to, those harpies of her sisters arrived and, just to make her boil, told her of all the fine things they had seen. In the meantime the servant went back to the king and told him about the coins, at which the king erupted in a great rage and told him that for four shitty beans he had sold off his pleasure and that on the next feast day he was at all costs to make sure he found out who the beautiful girl was and where the lovely bird had its nest.

"The next feast day arrived, and after the sisters went out, all decorated and elegant, and left the despised Zezolla at the hearth, she immediately ran to the date tree. Once she had said the usual words, a band of damsels came out: one held a mirror, one a little bottle of squash water,[5] one a curling iron, one a rouge cloth, one a comb, one some brooches, one the clothes, and one pendants and necklaces. They made her as beautiful as a sun and then put her in a coach drawn by six horses and accompanied by footmen and pages in livery, so that upon reaching the same place where the other party had been held, she only compounded the astonishment in her sisters' hearts and the fire in the king's breast.

"But when she left again and the servant followed after her, she threw out a handful of pearls and jewels so that he would not catch up with her, and while that worthy fellow stopped to peck at them, since they were not to be wasted, she had time to drag herself back home and undress in the usual fashion. With a face this long, the servant returned to the king, who said, 'I vow on the soul of my ancestors that if you don't find her, you'll get a fine beating and a kick in the ass for every hair in your beard!'

"The next feast day arrived, and after the sisters went out, Zezolla returned to the date tree and repeated the enchanted song, at which she was magnificently dressed and placed in a golden coach accompanied by so many servants that she looked like a whore arrested in the public promenade and surrounded by police agents.[6] She went, made her sisters' mouths water, and then left, with the king's servant tailing the coach as if he were stitched to it by a double thread. When she saw that he was still stuck to her side she said, 'Use your whip, coachman!' and the coach rushed forth at breakneck speed. Indeed, it raced along so fast that she lost one of her pattens,[7] the prettiest little thing you ever did see. The servant, who wasn't able to reach the flying coach, picked the patten up from the ground and brought it to the king, telling him what had happened.

---

5. *acqua de cocozze* (Neap.): "cosmetic and medicinal oil extracted from squash" (Croce 65).
6. "Courtesans were prohibited from circulating in carriages in public streets or in gondolas along the Posillipo beach, the daily promenade of the viceroys and nobility. Those who transgressed the prohibition (and this was not infrequent) were apprehended and surrounded by police, and then taken to prison" (Croce 545).
7. *chianiello* (Neap.): "The *chianielli* were, at the time, more than simple mules: they were overshoes whose soles and heels—often of exaggerated height—were made of cork. When they were worn over ladies' shoes or slippers, they allowed their wearer to get out of a carriage and walk on the street without getting the hem of her dress dusty or muddy; during the sixteenth and seventeenth centuries in Naples, the use of *chianielli* also became popular among courtesans" (Guarini and Burani 87).

Non tanto priesto s'accostaie a lo pede de Zezolla, che se lanzaie da se stisso a lo pede de chella cuccopinto d'Ammore, comme lo fierro corre a la calamita. [No sooner was it drawn close to Zezolla's foot than it hurled itself with no help at all onto the foot of that painted egg of Love, just like iron runs to a magnet.]

"The king took the patten in his hand and said, 'If the foundations are so beautiful, what must the house be like? O lovely candlestick that held the candle that consumes me! O tripod of the charming cauldron in which my life is boiling! O beautiful corks, attached to the fishing line of Love used to catch this soul! There: I'll embrace and squeeze you; if I cannot reach the plant, I will adore its roots, and if I cannot have the capitals, I will kiss its base! You were once the memorial stone for a white foot, and now you are a snare for this black heart. You made the lady who tyrannizes this life a span and a half taller, and you make this life grow just as much in sweetness, as I contemplate and possess you.'

"As he was saying this the king called the scribe, summoned the trumpeter, and—toot toot toot!—issued a proclamation: all the women of the land were invited to come to the festivities and banquet that he had gotten the idea to hold. And when the appointed day came, oh, my goodness! What a spread, what merrymaking! Where did so many pastries and casseroles[8] come from? And the stews[9] and meatballs? And the macaroni and ravioli?[10] There was enough to feed an entire army!

"Once the women had all arrived—noble and common, rich and ragged, old and young, beautiful and ugly—and polished off their due, the king made a toast and then tried the patten on each of his guests, one by one, to see whom it would fit like a glove and as neatly as a pin, in the hope that he might recognize the one he was seeking from the fit of the patten. But when he couldn't find a foot to match it, he began to despair. Nonetheless, after he had requested silence, he said, 'Come back tomorrow to do penance with me again; but if I am dear to you, leave no woman at home, whoever she may be.' The prince said, 'I have a daughter, but she looks after the hearth and is an unworthy wretch and does not deserve to sit at the same table at which you eat.' The king said, 'Let her be at the top of the list, for that is my wish.' And so they left and all came back the next day, and along with Carmosina's daughters came Zezolla. As soon as the king saw her she seemed to him to be the one he wanted, although he pretended not to notice.

"After they finished working their jaws it was time to try the patten on. And no sooner was it drawn close to Zezolla's foot than it hurled itself with no help at all onto the foot of that painted egg of Love,[11] just like iron runs to a magnet. When the king saw this he raced to clamp her in the press of his arms, and when he had seated her under the royal canopy he put a crown on her head and commanded that all the women present curtsy and show her their veneration, for she was their new queen. Upon seeing this the sisters nearly died of anger, and, not having the stomach to stand this heartbreak, they quietly stole away to their mother's house, confessing in spite of themselves that *those who oppose the stars are crazy.*"

---

8. *pastiere e casatielle* (Neap.): "The *pastiera* is the famous Easter cake made with short pastry filled with ricotta, candied fruit, wheat berries, orange peel, and other flavorings. *Casatielli* are ring-shaped casseroles made with flour dough, lard, pepper, and unshelled hard-boiled eggs that decorate the borders; also an Easter dish" (Guarini and Burani 88).

9. *li sottestate* (Neap.): "*Sottestati* is composed of veal stewed in a sauce of plums, garlic, pine nuts, raisins, sugar, almonds, and cinnamon" (Guarini and Burani 88).

10. *li maccarune e graviuole* (Neap.): "That is, 'ravioli': not to be confused with 'gravioli,' which were a type of sweet made in monasteries"; "*Maccaruni* had not yet, at this time, come to take first place in Neapolitan cuisine; Neapolitans were not yet called 'maccaroni-eaters', but 'leaf-eaters' [because of their many vegetable dishes]. Macaroni are more often indicated as being Sicilian or Sardinian" (Croce 545).

11. Cupid, Venus's son (see tale 1.2 n8).

7

THE MERCHANT

Seventh Entertainment of the First Day

Cienzo breaks the head of a king's son, flees from his homeland, and, after freeing the daughter of the king of Lose-Your-Mind from a dragon and various other adventures, he marries her. A woman casts a spell on him and he is freed by his brother, whom he then kills out of jealousy, but when he discovers that he is innocent he brings him back to life with a certain herb.

It's impossible to imagine how much Zezolla's good fortune touched each of them right down to their marrow, and just as they praised the generosity the heavens had bestowed on the girl, they also passed judgment on the insufficient punishment of the stepmother's daughters, since there is no penalty too severe for arrogance and no ruin inappropriate for envy. But while the murmuring that followed this story could still be heard, prince Tadeo placed the index finger of his right hand across his lips and gave a signal to be quiet, at which their words suddenly curdled in their mouths[1] as if they had seen a wolf or were schoolboys who at the height of whispering unexpectedly see the teacher come in. And after he gave Ciulla the sign to unsheathe her arm, she began to speak in this manner: "More times than not troubles serve men as picks and shovels that pave the way for unimaginable good luck. And yet some curse the rain that wets their noggins, not knowing that it brings them an abundance capable of evicting hunger, as can be seen in the case of a young man that I will tell you about.

AT 300: The Dragon-Slayer, and AT 303: The Twins or Blood-Brothers. Croce notes that the motifs of the fight with a seven-headed dragon, the marriage to a princess, and the tricked villain all appear in a number of different sources (e.g., Straparola 10.3, "Cesarino de' Berni"), but that "Cienzo's motivation for departure appears to be an addition by Basile" (*Lo cunto de li cunti*, 287). Penzer highlights the similarities between this tale and Grimm 60, "The Two Brothers," and also comments on several minor motifs, such as "unintentional injuries," "women binding men with their hair," and "life-restoring plants" (1:76–77). See also Imbriani 28 and Pitrè, *Nov. e legg. tosc.* 1, 2, and 3. Another brother who sleeps with his sister-in-law without touching her appears in tale 1.9.

1. *'ncagliaro* (Neap.): lit., curdled; "like milk that curdles due to the acidity of the rennet added to make cheese. According to an ancient belief, even the milk in a mother's breast could curdle due to fright" (Guarini and Burani 90).

"It is said that there once was a very rich merchant named Antoniello who had two sons, Cienzo and Meo, so similar that you couldn't
tell one from the other. It happened that while Cienzo, the firstborn,
was throwing stones at the Arenaccia[2] with the son of the king of Naples, he broke the prince's noodle, for which Antoniello, furious, said
to him, 'Good boy, now you've really fixed things up nice! Write
home about it! Brag about it, you sack, or I'll rip out your seams!
Hoist it up on a pole! Go on, you broke what costs six coins![3] You
took apart the head of the king's son? What, didn't you have a ruler,[4]
you son of a billy goat? What's going to come of your business now?
I wouldn't put a price tag of three cents on you; you've cooked up a
mess, and even if you went back in where you came from I wouldn't
be able to keep you safe from the king's clutches, since, as you know,
their shinbones are long and they can reach wherever they like, and
he'll do things that stink.'

"After his father had talked and then talked some more Cienzo answered, 'My sir, I've always heard it said that it's better to have policemen in your house than a doctor. Wouldn't it have been worse if
he had beaned me? I was provoked, we're boys, we ended up in a
brawl, it's my first crime, the king is a sensible man; at the end, what
can he do to me a hundred years from now? If they don't want to give
me a mother, they can give me a daughter; if they don't want to give
it to me cooked, they can give it to me raw. It's the same the whole
world over: if you're afraid, you should become a cop.'

"'What can he do to you?' replied Antoniello. 'He can banish you
from this world, send you off for a change of air; he can treat you like
a schoolmaster, with a stick twenty-four spans[5] long that'll have you
racking the fish until they learn to speak;[6] he can send you off, with a
soap-starched collar three spans high, to take your pleasure with the

---

2. "Arenaccia is in the eastern part of Naples. It was not built up at Basile's time, as
it is today, and in the sixteenth and seventeenth centuries it was used as the playing
ground for Neapolitan stone throwers, who formed neighborhood teams that challenged each other. In these battles up to 2000 combatants were known to participate. . . . The viceroy, the duke of Alba, had thirty of the 'head stone throwers'
condemned to the galleys in 1625" (Croce 546). Rak notes that this practice continued until the late nineteenth century (162).
3. *chillo che va' sei rana* (Neap.): lit., "that which is worth six grains (a coin)." A reference to "the chamber pot, whose current price this was" (Croce 69).
4. *meza canna* (Neap.): a measurement commonly used in Naples, equivalent to four
spans; in this case Antoniello criticizes Cienzo for not using it to measure the distance between him and the king's son (Croce 69).
5. A unit of linear measure usually corresponding to the distance between the ends
of the thumb and little finger of a spread hand (approximately nine inches), though in
The Tale of Tales it often appears to refer to a shorter distance.
6. I.e., he can send you to row on the prison galleys (Croce 70).

widow,[7] where instead of touching your bride's hand you'll be touch
ing the hangman's feet.[8] And so don't just stand there with your hide
paying rent to both the cloth and the shearer, but start marching this
instant, and may none of your business, neither old nor new, be
known unless you want to get caught by the foot: better to be a country bird than a caged one. Here's some money; go get yourself one of
the two enchanted horses that I keep in my stable, and a bitch, who's
also enchanted. And don't wait any longer: better to kick up your
heels than to have someone dogging your every step; better to throw
your legs over your neck than to have your neck hanging between
your legs; better, ultimately, to walk a thousand feet than to end up
with three feet of rope around you. If you don't pack your bags, neither Baldus nor Bartolus[9] will be able to help you.'

"After asking for his blessing Cienzo mounted the horse, put the little bitch under his arm, and began to trot out of the city. But as soon
as he had gone through Porta Capuana,[10] he looked back and began to
say, 'Here I go, my beautiful Naples, I'm leaving you! Who knows if
I'll ever be able to see you again, bricks of sugar and walls of sweet
pastry, where the stones are manna in your stomach, the rafters are
sugarcane, the doors and windows puff pastry? Alas! Separating from
you, lovely Pennino,[11] is like walking behind a funeral pennant! Taking my leave of you, Piazza Larga,[12] my spirit is squeezed narrow! Removing myself from you, Piazza dell'Olmo,[13] I feel my soul split in
two! Parting from you, Lancieri,[14] is like being pierced by a Catalan

---

7. *la vedola* (Neap.): the gallows (cf. Fr. *la veuve*, the guillotine) (Croce 70).

8. "The hangman would get up onto the shoulders of the hanged man in order to finish him off more quickly" (Croce 70).

9. The two famous jurists, Baldus de Ubaldus (c. 1319–1400) and Bartolus of Saxo-
ferrato (1314–1357), both of whose works were reprinted many times in the course of
the sixteenth century (Rak 162). Wordplay with *bertole* (bags).

10. Porta Capuana is located in the eastern part of Naples; it was moved by King
Ferrante I of Aragon to where it still stands (Croce 546).

11. The Pennino, or Pendino, is "a neighborhood of Naples. Pun on *pennone*, a large
red pennant decorated with the royal arms, which was carried by a tribunal minister
as he accompanied, on horseback, the condemned to the scaffold" (Croce 546). Most
of the following place-names serve as the pretext for similar word play.

12. *Chiazza Larga* (Neap.): "a square near the church of San Pietro Martire" (Croce
546).

13. *Chiazza de l'Urmo* (Neap.): "later called via di Porto, it contained a large and
well-attended market" (Croce 547). Wordplay with *arma* (soul).

14. *Lanziere* (Neap.): "a street in the Porto area; at one time gunsmiths had their
shops there. In the seventeenth century, one could also find 'rich cloth of gold, finely-
woven fabrics, foreign wool, linens, veils, and other goods'" (Croce 547; Croce
quotes from Carlo Celano, *Notizie del bello, dell'antico e del curioso della città di
Napoli*).

lance! Where shall I find another Porto,[15] sweet port of all the world's riches? Tearing myself away from you, O Forcella,[16] my spirit tears itself away from the wishbone of my soul! Where is there another Gelsi,[17] where the silkworms of love weave never-ending cocoons of pleasure? Where another Pertuso,[18] resort to all virtuous men? Where another Loggia,[19] where plenty is lodged and pleasure is refined? Alas! My Lavinaro,[20] I cannot remove myself from you without a stream of tears flowing from my eyes! I cannot leave you, O Mercato,[21] without a load of grief as merchandise! Beautiful Chiaia,[22] I cannot part company with you without a thousand wounds tormenting my heart! Farewell, carrots and chard; farewell, fritters and cakes; farewell, broccoli and pickled tuna; farewell, tripe and giblets; farewell, stews and casseroles! Farewell, flower of cities, glory of Italy, painted egg of Europe, mirror of the world! Farewell, Naples, the *non plus ultra* where virtue has set her limits and grace her boundaries! I leave you to become a widower of your vegetable soups; driven out of this dear village, O my cabbage stalks, I must leave you behind!'

---

15. *Porto:* another neighborhood of Naples.
16. *Forcella:* "street that takes its name from the ancient *platea furcillensis*" (Croce 547). *Forcella* also means "wishbone."
17. *Ceuze* (Neap.): "[T]his area was called Gelsi ['the mulberries'] because until the beginning of the sixteenth century it was full of mulberry trees, and silkworms were kept there. People also went there for recreation: to drink and carouse. In the second half of the century houses began to be built, and Spanish soldiers established their quarters there" (Croce 547). Until they were made illegal in 1958, bordellos had proliferated in the area for several centuries. The area is still called the "Quartieri Spagnoli" and remains a center of both male and female prostitution (Guarini and Burani 94).
18. Lit., "hole." A place near the church of Montesano, it has this name because it was near a crack in the city walls, which was later replaced by a door. It was a frequent site for duels (Croce 547). Boccaccio also writes of an infamous area of Naples called Pertugio or Malpertugio in the novella of Andreuccio of Perugia (2.5) in his *Decameron*. It was near the Porto neighborhood and was home to pimps and prostitutes.
19. The "Loggia of Genoa," a famous food market that took its name from the Genoese merchants who frequented it (Croce 548).
20. The Lavinaro is a road that runs from Porta Nolana to the Carmine, down which the waters of the Bolla River used to run, forming a "lava," or torrential stream (Croce 548).
21. The Mercato is a large square in the south of Naples that hosted many dramatic historical events, such as Corradino of Swabia's decapitation in 1268 and the hanging of the Neapolitan Jacobins in 1799 (Croce 548).
22. Chiaia is located in the western part of Naples, along the gulf from Castel dell'Ovo to the lower slopes of Posillipo. Already in Basile's time this area had begun to fill up with luxurious waterfront palaces and villas, and it was favored by the nobility for strolls and recreation (Croce 548). "Chiaia" (Ital. "piaga") also means "wound."

"And while he was saying this he shed a winter of tears in a dog's day of sighs, and then walked so far that the first evening he arrived at a wood in the vicinity of Cascano[23]—a wood that kept its mule attended to outside its borders by the Sun, while it took its pleasure with the silence and shadows—where there stood an old house at the foot of a tower. He knocked at the tower, but since it was already night its owner was suspicious of bandits and didn't want to open the door, and so poor Cienzo was forced to stay in the ramshackle house. After putting his horse to pasture in a meadow, he threw himself onto some straw he found there, with the little dog at his side. But no sooner had he closed his eyes than he was awakened by the dog barking, and then he heard someone shuffling around in the room.

"Cienzo, who was brave and fearless, took hold of his carob pod[24] and began to slash right and left in the dark. But when he realized that he wasn't hitting anyone and that he was merely striking at the wind, he went and stretched out again. A little while later, though, he felt himself being pulled very slowly by the foot, so he took hold of his old saw and got up once more, saying, 'Hey, now you're really bugging me! What's the point of these little spying games? Show yourself, if you've got the guts to, and let's indulge our whims, for you've found the right foot for your shoe!'

"After uttering these words he heard side-splitting laughter and then a deep voice that said, 'Come down here, and I'll tell you who I am.' Without losing his nerve Cienzo answered, 'Wait, I'll be there in a minute,' and he groped around until he found a staircase that led to a cellar, and when he had gone down he found a little lit lantern and three creatures who looked like bogeymen. Engaged in a bitter lament, they were crying, 'My beautiful treasure, now I'm going to lose you!' When Cienzo saw this he, too, began to moan, in order to make conversation, and after they cried for a good while—until the Moon cut the fritter of the sky in half with its little hatchet of rays[25]— the three who were chanting the dirge told him, 'Now go and get the treasure; it is destined for you alone, and may you know how to take care of it.' That said, they vanished into thin air in the manner of He Who Never Shows Himself.

"Cienzo saw the sun through a hole and wanted to go back up, but he couldn't find the staircase, and he began to shout so loudly that

---

23. A village near Sessa Arunca.
24. *scioscella* (Neap.): a derogatory term for sword, from the form of the carob fruit (Croce 72).
25. "Basile alludes to a game consisting of the attempt to divide a fritter into equal parts; one player gives a blow to the fritter and the other player chooses ones of the halves, and so forth" (Croce 73).

the owner of the tower, who had come out to take a piss in the ram-shackle house, heard him. He asked him what he was doing, and when he learned what had happened he went to get a ladder, and upon reaching the bottom found a huge treasure. He wanted to give part of it to Cienzo, but the boy didn't want a thing and, taking the bitch, he got on the horse and set off.

"He then arrived in a solitary and deserted wood that was dark enough to make your mouth screw up, and on the bank of a river—which, to please the shade with whom she was in love, did caracoles in the meadows and curvets on the rocks—he came across a fairy surrounded by a gang of delinquents who were about to do away with her honor. Cienzo, who saw the evil things those rogues were up to, took hold of his blade and slaughtered them. When the fairy saw what had been done for her, she showered him with compliments and invited him to a palace not far from there, where she intended to pay him back for the service rendered. But Cienzo said to her, 'Don't mention it; a thousand thanks! You can do me a favor another time, since I'm in a hurry right now to take care of some important business.' Then he took his leave, and when he had walked another good distance, he came across the palace of a king that was draped all over in mourning, such that your heart grew dark at the sight of it.

"When Cienzo asked what the reason for the bereavement was, he was told that a seven-headed dragon had appeared in that land, the most terrible dragon ever seen in the world. It had the combs of a rooster, the heads of a cat, eyes of fire, the mouths of a Corsican hound, the wings of a bat, the paws of a bear, and the tails of a serpent. 'Now the dragon devours one soul a day, and since this business is still going on, today Menechella, the daughter of the king, has by chance pulled the winning ticket. And that's why they're tearing their hair out and stamping their feet in the royal house, for the love-liest creature in the land is going to be gobbled up and gulped down by a hideous animal.'

"After hearing this Cienzo moved off to one side and then saw Me-nechella arrive with her mourning train, accompanied by her ladies-in-waiting and by all the women of the land, who were beating their hands and pulling out their hair lock by lock and lamenting the bad fortune of this poor young lady with these words: 'Who could have ever told this miserable girl that she would have to assign the prop-erty of her life to the body of this evil beast? Who could have ever told this lovely goldfinch that a dragon's belly would be her cage? Who could have ever told this lovely silkworm that she would have to leave the seed of her stamen of life inside this black cocoon?'

"As they were saying this the dragon came out of a little cave. Oh,

dear mother, what a horrible face! Let's just say that the sun holed up
in the clouds from fear, and the sky grew dark; the hearts of all those
people were like mummies, and they were trembling so hard they
wouldn't have been able to take an enema made of a single pig's bristle.

"When Cienzo saw this he took hold of his blade and—whack!—
knocked one of the heads to the ground. But the dragon rubbed its
neck with some herb that grew not far from there and stuck its head
right back on, like a lizard that reattaches its tail. Upon seeing this,
Cienzo said, 'If you don't persevere, you won't deliver,' and he
clenched his teeth and then let fly a blow so powerful that all seven of
the heads were cut cleanly off, rolling from their necks like chickpeas
from a spoon. When he had ripped the tongues out and put them
away he hurled the heads a mile from the body, so that they couldn't
be put back together again. Then he picked a handful of that herb
that had glued the neck to the head of the dragon and sent Menechella to her father's house, and he went to rest at an inn.

"It's hard to imagine the joy the king felt when he saw his daughter, and after he heard how she had been freed he immediately issued
a proclamation announcing that whoever had killed the dragon
should come and take his daughter for his wife. When he heard this,
a sly peasant gathered up the heads of the dragon, went to the king,
and said, 'Thanks to this here fellow, Menechella is safe! These little
hands freed the land from such ruination! Here are the heads, witnesses to my valor! And so every promise is a debt!' Upon hearing
this the king took the crown off his head and placed it atop the peasant's noodle, which now looked like a bandit's head on the top of a
column.[26]

"The news of this event spread through the land until it reached
Cienzo's ears. He said to himself, 'I'm really a big nitwit; I had Fortune by the hair and I let her fall from my hands! One man wants to
give me half a treasure and I pay as much attention to it as a German
does to cool water![27] That other woman wants to grant me a favor in
her palace and I take as much notice of it as an ass does of music, and
now I'm called to the throne and I'm like a drunk woman in front of
a spindle, allowing a hairy-foot to step in front of me and a cheating,
thieving card player to take this lovely winning deal right out of my
hand!'

"As he was saying this he grabbed an inkwell, picked up a pen,

26. "When an outlaw or brigand was executed, his head would be exhibited in a
cage set on a column or hanging from a door, and often encircled by a mitre or gold
paper crown which had been put on as he was being led to his death" (Croce 75).
27. "The Germans' love of wine had already been proverbial for centuries, and there
were many witticisms on the subject" (Croce 75).

smoothed out some paper, and began to write: 'To the most beautiful jewel of women, Menechella, daughter of the king of Lose-Your-Mind. Having by the grace of the Sun in Leo[28] saved your life, I now hear that another man brags of my labors and claims as his own the service I rendered you. Since you were present during the incident, you can convince the king of the truth and make it impossible for another to earn a soldier's pension,[29] when I'm the one who spun my spoons. And this will be the proper demonstration of your refined queenly grace as well as the deserved reward for a hand as strong as Skanderbeg's.[30] In conclusion, I kiss your delicate little hands. From the Inn of the Urinal,[31] today, Sunday.'

"When he had written this letter and sealed it with chewed-up bread, he put it in the little bitch's mouth and said, 'Go, run as fast as you can and take this to the daughter of the king, and give it to no one else unless it is put directly into the hands of that face of silver.' The little bitch ran off, almost flying, to the royal palace, and when she went up the stairs she found the king still engaged in ceremonies with the bridegroom, who, upon seeing that little bitch with the letter in her mouth, ordered that it be taken from her. But the dog would not give it to just anyone, and jumping onto Menechella's lap, she placed the letter in her hands.

"Menechella got up from her chair and, bowing to the king, gave it to him so that he could read it, and after reading it he ordered that the little bitch be followed so that they could see where she went, and that her master be brought before him. And so two courtiers followed the dog and arrived at the inn and found Cienzo. They relayed the king's message to him and then carried him off to the palace, where he was asked in the royal presence why he was bragging that he had killed the dragon, if that man who was sitting next to the king with the crown on his head had brought the heads.

---

28. The "Sun in Leo" or *solleone* refers, of course, to the hottest period of summer. Its disruptive effects were well documented, as we see, e.g., in these verses by the sixteenth-century satirist Nelli: "Quando il sole è in quel segno, esce dal sesto / Ogni cervel; ma con diversi effetti, / Qual alquanto più tardi e qual più presto, / Secondo che quel sol trova i soggetti / Disposti" (cit. Croce 551).

29. *chiazza morta* (Neap.): a sort of military pension that had been instituted by the viceroy Pedro de Toledo, "which called for one place in each company of Spanish or Italian soldiers to be left empty in order to provide for the subsistence of three invalid soldiers. One was given the lodging of the 'absent' soldier, and the other two the salary" (Croce 76).

30. See tale 1.1 n8.

31. *Ostaria dell'Aurinale* (Neap.): "In *Topografia dell'agro napolitano* by Rizzi-Zannoni (1793), an 'Inn of the Urinal' is indicated on the road between Mugnano and Piscinola" (Croce 548).

"And Cienzo answered, 'That peasant would deserve a miter made from a royal decree of condemnation before he would a crown, since he's been so shameless as to try to pass off fireflies for lanterns. And to show you it's true that I was the one who performed this feat, and not this bearded billy goat, have the dragon heads be brought before us, and you will see that none of them can serve as proof since they do not have tongues, which, in order to convince you of the matter, I have brought to this judgment.' Saying this, he exhibited the tongues; the peasant stood there, stunned, not knowing what had happened to him, and even more so when Menechella added, 'He's the one! Ah, you dog of a peasant, you tricked me!'

"Upon hearing this, the king took the crown off the head of that dirty old lout-hide and put it on Cienzo, and when he wanted to send the peasant to jail Cienzo asked that he be pardoned, so as to pay back the other's indiscretion with his own courtesy. And once the tables had all been spread they had a meal fit for lords, after which the couple went off to a lovely bed smelling of fresh laundry, where Cienzo, raising the trophies won in his victory over the dragon, entered triumphantly into the Capitol of Love.

"But the next morning—when with both hands the Sun brandished its broadsword of light in the middle of the stars, shouting, 'Out of my way, scoundrels'!—as he was getting dressed in front of a window, Cienzo saw a beautiful young lady at the house opposite, and he turned to Menechella and said, 'What sort of lovely thing is that woman who lives across the way?' 'What business is that of yours?' answered his wife. 'Have you set your eyes on her? Are you in a bad mood, perhaps? Are you getting tired of rich food? Isn't the meat you get at home enough for you?'

"Lowering his head like a cat that has just caused some damage, Cienzo said nothing, but, pretending to go out on some business, he left the palace and slipped into the house of that young lady. And she truly was a delectable morsel: she looked like tender curds and whey, like sugar paste; she never turned the little buttons of her eyes without leaving hearts perforated by love; she never opened the basin of her lips without doing a little laundry of souls; she never moved the soles of her feet without pressing heavily on the shoulders of those hanging from the cord of hopes.[32] But besides so much spellbinding beauty, she had this power: whenever she wanted to she could enchant, bind, attach, knot, chain, and envelop men with her hair, as she did with Cienzo, who as soon as he set foot in her house remained tethered like a colt.

---

32. See note 8.

"In the meantime Meo, the younger brother, had received no news of Cienzo and got the whim to go searching for him. After asking his father for permission, he was given another horse and another little bitch, also enchanted, and he trotted off. When he arrived that evening at the tower where Cienzo had been, the owner, who thought he was his brother, showered him with all the kindness in the world and wanted to give him money, which Meo wouldn't take. Seeing what a fuss was being made he realized that his brother had been there and began to entertain the hope of finding him.

"As soon as the Moon, enemy of poets, turned its back on the Sun, he set out. When he arrived at the fairy's she thought he was Cienzo and flooded him with warm greetings, saying over and over again, 'May you be welcome, my young man, for you saved my life.' Thanking her for such kindness, Meo said, 'I apologize that I can't stay, but I'm in a hurry. I'll see you when I return.'

"And rejoicing to himself that he was continuing to find traces of his brother, he followed the road until he arrived at the king's palace, the very morning that Cienzo had been sequestered by the fairy's hair. When he entered he was received with great honor by the servants and embraced with great affection by the bride, who said to him, 'May my husband be welcome! He leaves in the morning, he's back in the evening! When all the birds are feeding, the owl comes home to roost! Why have you been gone so long, my Cienzo? How can you stay far from Menechella? You took me out of the dragon's mouth, but you throw me into the throat of suspicion if those eyes of yours are not always here to be my mirror!'

"Meo, who was a sly one, understood immediately that this was his brother's wife and, turning to Menechella, he apologized for being late; after he embraced her, they went to eat. But when the Moon, like a mother hen, called the stars to peck at the dew, they went to sleep, and Meo, who had respect for his brother's honor, divided up the sheets, so that they each had one and there wouldn't be any chance of him touching his sister-in-law.

"When she saw this new system Menechella grew brusque and, with a face like a mother-in-law, said, 'My darling, since when? What sort of game are we playing? What sort of jokes are these? What are we, the fields of feuding peasants, with these boundaries that you marked? What are we, enemy armies, with this trench that you made? What are we, wild horses, with this fence that you put up to separate us?' Meo, who knew how to count to thirteen, said, 'Don't complain about me, my darling, but about my doctor, who wants me to purge myself and has ordered that I go on a diet; besides, I'm so tired from hunting that I feel like I've lost my tail.' Menechella, who wasn't capable of muddying the waters, swallowed this whopper and fell asleep.

"But—when the Sun began to eavesdrop on the Night, who was given crepuscules of time to pack up its bundles[33]—as he was getting dressed at the same window where his brother had gotten dressed, Meo saw the same young lady who had ensnared Cienzo, and since he liked the looks of her very much, he said to Menechella, 'Who's that flirt at the window?' And all in a huff, she answered, 'So you're going to keep it up? If that's how it is, then we're all set! Yesterday, too, you tickled my pants with this grouper fish, and I'm afraid that the tongue goes where the tooth hurts! You should show some respect for me, though, since after all, I'm the daughter of a king and every piece of shit has its own smell! It was not without good reason, then, that last night you acted like the imperial eagle,[34] shoulder to shoulder! It was not without good reason that you retired on your revenues![35] Now I understand: you diet in my bed so you can have a banquet in the house of others! But if I see that happen, I intend to do crazy things and send sparks flying!'

"Meo, who had eaten bread from many ovens, calmed her down, and with kind words told and swore to her that he wouldn't trade his home for even the most beautiful whore in the world, and that she couldn't be dearer to his heart. Entirely comforted by these words, Menechella went into a little room to have her ladies-in-waiting smooth down her forehead with glass,[36] braid her hair, dye her eyelashes, rouge her face, and deck her all out so that she would look more beautiful for the one she believed to be her husband.

"In the meantime Meo had begun to suspect, from Menechella's words, that it was Cienzo who was at the young lady's house. He took the bitch, left the palace, and went into the other house. As soon as he arrived the lady said to him, 'Hair of mine, bind him!' And Meo, quick to do business, immediately answered, 'Little bitch of mine, eat her up!' And the bitch flung herself upon the lady and gulped her down like an egg yolk.

"When Meo went inside he found his brother, who appeared to be enchanted; but when he placed two of the bitch's hairs on him, it was as if he awoke from a long sleep. Meo told him everything that had

33. *a collegenno sarcinole* (Neap.): "parody of the juridical Latin *ad colligendum sarcinulas*" (Guarini and Burani 104).
34. "The two-headed eagle of the Hapsburg coat of arms" (Croce 80).
35. *le 'ntrate* (Neap.): "Noble families unable to maintain the high expense of living at court would retreat, with their revenues, to their country estates for periods of time" (Rak 164).
36. "Women of the time used a glass ball to smooth their foreheads" (Croce 80).

happened during the trip and, finally, at the palace, and how, when he had been mistaken for Cienzo, he had slept with Menechella; and he was planning to continue and tell him about the divided sheets, when Cienzo, tempted by the demon, grabbed his Spanish sword[37] and cut off Meo's head as if it were a cucumber.

"At the sound of this the king and his daughter came to the window, and when they saw that Cienzo had killed someone identical to himself they asked him why, and Cienzo said to them, 'Ask yourself, you who slept with my brother thinking you were sleeping with me; that's why I cut him down!' 'Ah, how many people are wrongly killed!' said Menechella. 'A fine job you did! You don't deserve this honorable brother! Because when he found himself in the same bed with me he divided the sheets with great modesty, and we each played on our own!'

"When he heard this, Cienzo regretted the gross error that had been son of a rash judgment and father of an asinine action, and he scratched off half of his face. But then he remembered the herb the dragon had shown him, and he rubbed it on his brother's neck, where it immediately took, and once the head was stuck back on, Meo was whole and alive again. And then Cienzo embraced him with great joy and asked to be pardoned for having been in too great of a hurry and poorly informed in his rush to rid the world of him, and the pair of them went to the palace. There they sent for Antoniello together with his whole household; Antoniello grew dear to the king, and in his son saw the verification of the proverb: *A crooked boat finds a straight port*."

---

37. *lopa vecchia* (Neap.): lit., "old wolf." "A Spanish sword whose blade was engraved with a wolf, mentioned also by other authors of this time" (Rak 164).

8

GOAT-FACE

Eighth Entertainment of the First Day

Due to a favor granted by a fairy, the daughter of a peasant be-
comes wife to a king. But when she shows herself ungrateful to the
one who had done her so much good, the fairy turns her face into
that of a goat. For this reason she is scorned by her husband and
receives a thousand abuses; but then through the intervention of a
kind old man she humbles herself and gets back her original face,
and thus enters once again into her husband's good graces.

When Ciulla had finished telling her sugary tale, Paola, whose turn it
was to enter the dance, began to speak: "All the evils committed by
man are colored in some way: either by disdain that provokes, or by
need that presses, or by love that blinds or fury that shatters; only ingratitude has no reason, either false or true, to which it can cling. Indeed, this vice is so terrible that it dries up the fountain of mercy, puts
out the fire of love, blocks the road to favors, and, in the person who
has been poorly recognized, gives rise to disgust and regret, as you
will see in the tale that you are about to hear.

"A peasant had twelve daughters, and one barely had the time to
hold the next in her arms, since every year that good lady of the
house Ceccuzza, their mother, gave birth to another little fart of a
girl. Every morning the poor husband went off to dig his day's worth
of earth so that his household might get by honorably, and it was
hard to know whether there was more of the sweat he dripped on the
ground or the spit he rubbed in his hands. In any case, with this little
bit of labor he kept all those frogs and urchins from dying of hunger.

"Now one day while he was digging at the foot of a mountain—a
spy for the other mountains, which kept its head above the clouds to
see what was going on in the air—he came across a grotto so deep
and dark that the Sun was afraid to enter, from which a green lizard
as big as a crocodile crawled out. The poor peasant was so terrified
that he didn't have the force to beat it out of there, and when the hideous animal opened its mouth he expected his days to come to a

---

AT 710: Our Lady's Child. See also Grimm 3 ("The Virgin Mary's Child") and
Gonzenbach 20.

close. But the lizard went over to him and said, 'Don't be afraid, my good man; I'm not here to do you any harm. I come only for your good.' When Masaniello heard this—for this was the name of the laborer—he got down on his knees in front of the animal and said, 'Madam what's-your-name, I am under your power. Behave like a decent person and have mercy on this poor fellow, who has twelve whiny brats to support.' 'That's why,' answered the lizard, 'I'm moved to help you. So then, tomorrow morning bring me the youngest of your daughters, for I want to raise her as my own, and I'll hold her as dear as life.'

"When he heard this, the miserable father was left more confused than a thief discovered with the stolen goods on him, for the fact that a lizard was asking him for one of his daughters, and the most tender of them besides, led him to conclude that this mantle was not without stiff hairs, and that the lizard wanted her as an aggregate pill[1] to evacuate his hunger. And he said to himself, 'If I give the animal my daughter, I give it my soul; if I deny it my daughter, it'll take this body of mine; if I allow it to take her, I'm deprived of the pupil of my eye; if I contradict it, it'll suck this blood of mine; if I give my consent, it will take away a part of my own self; if I refuse, it'll take the whole thing. How should I decide? What choice should I make? What expedient should I come up with? Oh, what a terrible day it's been! What a disaster has rained down on me from the heavens!' As he was saying this, the lizard said, 'Make up your mind soon to do what I have asked, or you'll be leaving your rags right here, for this is what I want and this is how it shall be!'

"After hearing this decree, Masaniello, who had no one to turn to, went home full of melancholy, so yellow in the face that he looked like he had jaundice, and Ceccuzza, when she saw him so dispirited, downcast, choked up, and out of sorts, said to him, 'What has happened to you, my husband? Did you have an argument with someone? Did someone send you a bill? Or did the ass die?' 'None of those things,' answered Masaniello. 'It was a horned lizard that shook me up, because it threatens to do abominable things if I don't bring it our youngest daughter, and my head is spinning like a wool winder and I don't know what to do! On the one hand I'm pressed by love, and on the other by the rent on this house! I love my Renzolla with all my heart, I love my own life with all my heart: if I don't weigh out this product of my loins for the lizard, it'll take the entire weight of my own poor body. So give me some advice, my dear Ceccuzza, or I'll be done for.'

---

1. See tale 1.2 n3.

"When she heard this his wife said to him, 'Who knows, my dear husband, that it won't be a two-tailed lizard[2] for our household? Who knows that this lizard won't bring an end to our miseries? You know, more times than not we bring down the hatchet on our own feet, and when we should have the eye of an eagle to recognize the good that presents itself, instead our eyes are too blurred and our hands too cramped to seize it. And so go, bring her to the lizard, for my heart tells me there's some good luck in store for that poor little girl.'

"These words convinced Masaniello, and the next morning—as soon as the Sun, with the paintbrush of its rays, whitewashed the sky, which was all black from Night's shadows—he took the little girl by the hand and led her to the grotto. The lizard was on the lookout for the peasant's arrival, and as soon as it caught sight of him it came out of its den. When it had taken the girl, it gave her father a big bag of small change[3] and said to him, 'Go, marry off your other daughters with these coppers and be happy, for Renzolla has found a mother and a father. Oh, lucky her, to have come across this good fortune!' Masaniello was full of joy, and he thanked the lizard and went skipping home to his wife. He told her what had happened and showed her the beans, which they used to marry off all the other daughters, and there was even enough relish[4] left for them to gulp down the hardships of life with pleasure.

"Once the lizard had Renzolla, it made a beautiful palace appear, and there it kept her, and brought her up on luxuries and gifts fit for a queen. Let's just say that there was no lack of ant's milk[5] and that she ate like a count, dressed like a prince, and had a hundred solicitous and experienced young ladies to serve her. And with all of this excellent treatment, in four snaps of a finger she grew as tall as an oak.

"Now it happened that while the king was hunting in those woods night fell upon him and, not knowing where to turn his head, he saw a candle glowing in the palace and sent a servant in to ask the master if he could offer him shelter. When the servant got there, the lizard appeared before him in the form of a splendid young lady, and when she heard the message she said that he would be welcome a thousand

2. "These were thought to bring good luck" (Croce 549).

3. *pataccune* (Neap.): "a coin equivalent to approximately 5 *carlini,* or little more than 2 lire" (Croce 85). These coins were silver and usually large; "by extension, any coin of large dimensions and little value" (Guarini and Burani 110).

4. *agresta* (Neap.): "a sauce made with the juice of sour grapes, and used on fish" (Croce 85).

5. "Anything rare and refined" (Guarini and Burani 110).

times over and that neither bread nor knives would be lacking. As soon as the king received the answer, he went and was received like a lord. A hundred pageboys came out to meet him with their torches aflame, so that it looked like an elaborate funeral rite for a rich man; a hundred other pageboys brought the food to the table, and they looked like the errand boys an apothecary sends to bring delicacies to the sick. But above all else, Renzolla poured the king's drink with such grace that he drank more love than wine.

"When the meal had ended and the tables had been cleared, the king went off to bed, and Renzolla herself pulled the socks off his feet and the heart from his breast, and in such a charming manner that the king felt love's poison rising up to infect his soul from the little bones of his feet touched by that lovely hand. And so in order to find a remedy for his death, he decided to procure himself the antidote to that beauty and, calling the fairy whose protection Renzolla was under, he asked to take her for his wife. The fairy wanted nothing more than the good of Renzolla and not only gave her to him freely but also supplied her with a dowry of seven million gold pieces.[6]

"The king was full of jubilation over his fortune and left with Renzolla, who, sullen and unthankful for what the fairy had done for her, took off with her husband without giving the fairy one accursed word of appreciation. And when the sorceress saw such ingratitude, she put a curse on Renzolla: her face would become like that of a goat. She had barely said these words when the girl's muzzle got longer and grew a span of beard, her jaws narrowed, her skin turned tough and her face hairy, and the braids wound around her head like a basket became pointed horns. When the poor king saw this, he shrank back and couldn't figure out what had happened and why a double-soled beauty had been transformed like that. And sighing and weeping a full meal of tears, he said, 'Where is the hair that bound me? Where are the eyes that transfixed me? Where is the mouth that was a snare for this soul, a trap for these spirits, and a noose for this heart? What is this? I should be the husband of a goat, and acquire the title of billy goat? I should be reduced in this fashion to paying my fees at Foggia?[7] Oh no, I don't want this heart of mine to croak because of a goat-face, a goat that will bring me war by shitting olives!'[8]

---

6. *cunte d'oro* (Neap.): from the Spanish *cuento* (million), a form of currency (Croce 86).

7. *fidareme a Foggia* (Neap.): for *fida*, see tale 1.5 n8. "The herds which came down from the Abruzzi for the winter gathered in Foggia, which lies at the center of the Apulia plain [in southeast Italy] and was home to the so-called customs-house for sheep. Therefore, 'to be in Foggia' meant 'to be horned' [a cuckold]" (Croce 87).

8. Form of goat feces; the olive (branch) is also the symbol of peace.

"Thus speaking he arrived at his palace, where he put Renzolla and a maid in the kitchen and gave them each four rolls[9] of flax to spin, setting the deadline of one week within which they were to finish the job. The maid obeyed the king and began to comb the flax, make the wicks, wind them on the distaffs, turn the spindle, roll the skeins, and labor like a bitch so that by Saturday evening the job was completed. But Renzolla thought she was the same person she had been at the fairy's house, since she hadn't looked at herself in the mirror, and she threw the flax out the window, saying, 'The king's wasting his time if he thinks he can give me these bothers! If he wants shirts he can buy them! And he better not believe he found me in a gutter stream![10] Let him remember that I brought seven million gold pieces to his house and that I'm his wife and not his servant; it seems to me that he's acting like an ass to treat me this way.'

"In spite of all this, when Saturday morning arrived and Renzolla saw that the maid had spun her whole share of flax, she became very afraid that she would get a good wool carding herself, and so she set off for the fairy's palace, where she told her of her misfortune. Embracing her with great affection, the fairy gave her a sack full of spun flax to give to the king and thus demonstrate that she had been an industrious wife and housekeeper. Renzolla took the sack without even saying 'many thanks' for the favor and went back to the royal palace, while the fairy threw rocks after her on account of the bad manners of this disaffected girl.

"Once the king had the spinning, he gave them two dogs, one to Renzolla and one to the maid, and told them to raise and take care of them. The maid raised hers on soft morsels of bread and treated it like a son, but Renzolla said, 'My grandpa bequeathed me this worry? Have the Turks[11] arrived? I have to comb dogs and take them out to shit?' And as she said this she hurled the dog out the window, quite another matter than getting it to jump through hoops.

"After several months the king asked for the dogs and Renzolla, spinning the fine thread of fear,[12] ran off again to the fairy, where she

___

9. *na decina* (Neap.): "according to the old Neapolitan system of measure, four rolls" (Croce 87).

10. *lava* (Neap.): "the *lave* were torrential streams that ran through many areas of Naples; fed primarily by rainwater, they swelled rapidly and ruinously, and in their wake it was possible to fish out all sorts of objects" (Rak 181). See also tale 1.7 n20.

11. "The incursions of Turks and Arabs, who would capture people for slaves, were at this time very frequent along the coasts of southern Italy, and even on the shores of Naples—as they were, in general, in the Mediterranean" (Croce 88).

12. *filanno male* (Neap.): wordplay; *filare* (to spin) vs. *filare male* (to get the runs out of fear). *Filatorio* is diarrhea (Guarini and Burani 114). This is a frequent pun in *The Tale of Tales*.

found a little old fellow, who was the doorman, at the door. He said to her, 'Who are you and what do you want?' When she heard this bizarre question, Renzolla said to him, 'Don't you know who I am, goat-beard?' 'You're coming at me with a knife?' answered the old man. 'The thief is chasing the cop! Stay away from me because you'll get me dirty, said the coppersmith! Duck if you don't want to get hit! Me, goat-beard? You're a goat-beard and a half, since you deserve this and even worse for your arrogance! You just wait, you insolent and arrogant girl, and I'll clear things up for you! You'll see where your haughtiness and presumption have driven you.'

"As he was saying this he ran into a little room, got a mirror, and placed it in front of Renzolla. When she saw that awful hairy face she came close to dying of anguish; not even Rinaldo's[13] torment when he looked at himself in the enchanted shield and saw how he had been transformed from his previous state was as great as the pain she felt at seeing herself so altered that she couldn't recognize herself.

"The old man said to her, 'You must remember, Renzolla, that you are the daughter of a peasant, and that the fairy treated you so well that she turned you into a queen. But you were an idiot, you were rude and ungrateful and gave her few thanks for so many favors; you left her in the middle room[14] without showing her a single sign of affection. And so take this and spend it, grab this and then come back for the rest! The deal went well for you; look at the face you've got, look at where you've ended up on account of your ingratitude: the fairy's curse has transformed not only your face, but also your state. But if you're willing to do what this white beard tells you, go in and find the fairy, throw yourself at her feet, pull out your hair, scratch your face, beat your chest, and beg her pardon for the bad behavior you showed her, and since she is of very tender lung she will be moved to pity you for your awful calamities.'

"Renzolla felt her keys being played and her nail hit on the head, and so she did things the old man's way. The fairy, hugging and kissing her, turned her back into her earlier form, and, after she gave her a dress heavy with gold, placed her in a marvelous carriage accompanied by a pack of servants and took her to the king. When he saw her like that, so beautiful and lavishly dressed, he held her as dear as his own life, and he beat his fists on his chest for all the agony he had

---

13. A character in Ludovico Ariosto's *Orlando furioso* and Torquato Tasso's *Gerusalemme liberata* (see 16.29–31).
14. *la cammara de miezo* (Neap.): the anus, or toilet; i.e., something of no value (Croce 89).

. . . quant'essa pigliaie dolore vedennose cossì stravisata che non canosceva se stessa. [. . . as great as the pain she felt at seeing herself so altered that she couldn't recognize herself.]

caused her to suffer and apologized that he had treated her like trash[15] because of that accursed goat-face. And so Renzolla lived happily, loving her husband, honoring the fairy, and showing her gratitude to the old man, since she had learned at her own expense that *it is always of use to be courteous*."

15. *l'aveva tenuta iusta li bene* (Neap.): a reference to "the ceremony of the *cedo bonis* of bankrupt merchants, during which they had to expose their behind and touch it to the column of the tribunal of the Vicaria three times" (Rak 182). The expression was also used for "old household objects that were sent off to be kept in country estates" (Guarini and Burani 115).

9

THE ENCHANTED DOE

Ninth Entertainment of the First Day

Fonzo and Canneloro[1] are born of a magic spell. Canneloro is envied by Fonzo's mother, the queen, who breaks his head. Canneloro departs, and when he becomes king a great danger befalls him. Through the power of a spring and a myrtle bush Fonzo comes to know of his troubles, and goes to free him.

Their mouths hung open listening to Paola's splendid tale, and they all concluded that a humble person is like a ball, since the harder you throw it to the ground the higher it bounces, or like a billy goat, since the farther it backs up the harder it butts its horns. But when Tadeo had signaled to Ciommetella to respect her place on the list, she set her tongue in motion as follows: "The strength of friendship is, without a doubt, great, and allows us to straddle all fatigue and perils in order to serve our friends. Worldly goods are considered a bit of straw, honor a little bug,[2] and life a mere trifle when we can spend them to help a friend. Fables are overflowing with proof of this, stories are full of it, and today I'm going to give you an example of one that grandma Semmonella (may her soul rest in peace) used to tell me, if you'll just close your mouths, let your ears hang low, and give me a little attention.

"There once was a certain king of Long Pergola named Iannone who had a great desire to have children and was always praying to the gods to make his wife's belly swell up. And in the hope that they would move fast to content him he was especially charitable with

---

AT 303: The Twins or Blood Brothers. Croce mentions a nearly identical tale from the Basilicata in Comparetti's collection ("Cannelora") and similarities with Imbriani 28 ("The Sorcerer with Seven Heads") (Croce, *Lo cunto de li cunti* 287). Penzer notes the resemblance to Grimm 60, "The Two Brothers," and discusses the motifs of the miraculous conception, the health index, and the sword of chastity (1:92). There is a similar episode in Lorenzo Lippi's burlesque epic *Il Malmantile racquistato* (1676). The latter part of this tale is also similar to tale 1.7.
1. "The second name derives from the medieval festival of the candles (*candelarum festum*), which later became the feast of the Purification of the Madonna, celebrated on February 2, when candles are blessed in churches" (Guarini and Burani 116).
2. "The *cufece* was a type of cricket that, salted and dressed, was eaten by Dalmatians and Arab pirates while at sea" (Croce 550).

wayfarers, to whom he would have given the pupils of his eyes. But finally, when he saw that things were taking a long time and there was no way they were going to sprout a bud, he hammered his door shut and shot at anyone who drew near.

"It happened that a great bearded sage came passing through that land, and not knowing that the king had changed his tune, or else knowing about it and wanting to find a cure for it, he went to see Iannone and begged to be received in his home. With a dark face and a terrible scowl, the king said to him, 'If this is the only candle you have, you can go to bed in the dark! The time is past for Berta to spin!³ The kittens have opened their eyes! There's no more mother now!' And when the old man asked about the reason for this transformation, the king answered, 'Out of my desire to have children, I spent and spread and threw away my belongings on all who came and went, and finally, when I saw that I couldn't get a clean shave, I pulled my hand out and took up the anchor.' 'If that's all there is,' replied the old man, 'calm down; I'll get her pregnant for you straightaway or you can have my ears.' 'If you do,' said the king, 'I give you my word that I'll reward you with half of my kingdom.'

"The other answered, 'Now listen carefully: if you want a good graft get the heart of a sea dragon and have it cooked by a young virgin who, at the mere odor coming from the pot, will find herself with swollen belly; when the heart is cooked, give it to the queen to eat, and you'll see that she'll immediately become pregnant, too, as if she were in her ninth month.' 'How can that be?' replied the king. 'To tell you the truth, it seems pretty hard to swallow.' 'No need to marvel,' said the old man, 'since if you read the myths you can find that after brushing against a flower while passing through the Olenian Fields Juno's belly blew up and she gave birth.'⁴ 'If that's how it is,' the king concluded, 'let the dragon's heart be found this very instant. After all, I've got nothing to lose.'

"And so he sent a hundred fishermen to sea, and they prepared

---

3. "An extrapolation taken from a famous song of the time by Velardiniello, and having its origin in a story of a peasant named Berta upon whom the Empress bestows her favors. The expression is used today to refer to the 'good old days,' remote and happier times" (Rak 196). See also the introduction to day 5 for a *villanella* (a popular pastoral ballad) containing a number of the same lines.

4. See Ovid, *Fasti* 5.251ff. "In the Olenian fields lay the garden of Flora, overflowing with flowers, some of which had been born from the blood of beautiful young boys wounded to their death, like Hyacinth and Adonis. In this garden Juno discovered the way to give birth without having any contact except with a flower, and it was in this way that Ares and his sister Eris were born" (Guarini and Burani 118). "Thus was Juno avenged upon Jove for the previous birth of Minerva without her aid" (Penzer 1:92).

Mese a lo fuoco lo core e . . . tutte li mobele de la casa 'ntorzaro e 'n capo de
poche iuorne figliattero. [She put the heart on the fire and . . .
all the furniture in the room began to swell up, and at the end of a few days
they were all delivered.]

harpoons, trawls, hooks, nets, traps, lines, and reels, and sailed around and searched far and wide until they finally caught a dragon. Then they ripped out its heart and brought it to the king, who gave it to a lovely lady-in-waiting to cook. She locked herself in a room, and no sooner had she put the heart on the fire and the vapor had started to rise from the stew than not only did the fair cook herself became pregnant but all the furniture in the room began to swell up, and at the end of a few days they were all delivered. The big canopy bed had a little bed, the strongbox a little chest, the big chairs little chairs, the big table a little table, and the chamber pot a little decorated chamber pot that was so pretty you could have eaten it. The cooked heart had barely been tasted by the queen before she felt her own belly growing large, and in four days she and her lady-in-waiting both gave birth at the same time to lovely strapping boys, the one such a spitting image of the other that you couldn't tell them apart. The two boys grew up together with such love that they became inseparable, and their fondness for each other was so intense that the queen began to feel a bit of envy, since her son showed greater affection for the son of one of her servants than for herself, and she couldn't figure out how to remove that speck from her eye.

"Now one day when the prince wanted to go hunting with his companion, he had a fire lit in the hearth in his room and began to melt down lead to make bullets, and since he was missing something or other, he went to look for it in person. In the meantime the queen came by to see what her son was doing, and when she found Canneloro, the son of the lady-in-waiting, alone in there, she thought that she would remove him from this world, and threw some red-hot bullet mold in his face. He ducked, but it hit him on the eyebrow and left him with an ugly gash; the queen was already about to send off a second charge when Fonzo, her son, arrived. Pretending that she had come to see how he was, she gave him a few insipid caresses and left.

"Canneloro pulled a hat down over his forehead so that Fonzo couldn't see what had happened, and he stood perfectly still even though he felt like he was frying with pain. And when he had finished rolling those balls[5] like a cockroach, he asked the prince's permission to leave town. Marveling at this sudden decision, Fonzo asked him what the reason was, to which Canneloro answered, 'Attempt to discover no more, my dear Fonzo. May it suffice you to know only that I am forced to leave, and the heavens know that as I leave you, heart

---

5. Wordplay: bullets vs. the pellets of feces that a certain type of beetle forms and rolls along the ground (Croce 93).

of mine, my soul plays tug-of-war with my breast, my spirit goes "row your boat" away from my body, my blood plays "beat it, Marco"[6] with my veins. But since there's nothing else to be done, take care of yourself and remember me.'

"After they embraced, Canneloro went off to his room in a state of despair. There he put on a suit of armor and a sword, to which another weapon had given birth when the heart was cooking, and, completely armed, he got a horse from the stable and was just about to put his feet in the stirrups when Fonzo came in crying and asked him if, seeing as he intended to abandon him, he could at least leave him some sign of his love so that Fonzo could reduce the anguish caused by the other's absence. At these words Canneloro took his dagger in hand and drove it into the ground, and, when a lovely spring gushed forth, he said to the prince, 'This is the best memento I can leave you, since from the course of this spring you will be able to tell the course of my life: if you see it run clear, you will know that my state is similarly clear and calm; if you see it muddy, you can imagine that I am in trouble; and if you find it dry (may the heavens will this not), you can assume that the oil of my lantern has burned off and that I will be where I have to pay my toll to nature.' That said, he put his hand on his sword and, striking the ground, caused a myrtle bush to sprout, saying, 'When you see that it is green, you will know that I am as green as garlic; if you see it withered, you can assume that my luck is not standing very tall; and if it becomes completely dry you can say a requiem of shoes and clogs[7] for your Canneloro.'

"That said, they embraced again and Canneloro left. He walked far and wide, and after the occurrence of many things that it would take a long time to recount, such as fights with coachmen, swindles by innkeepers, assassinations of customs officers, the dangers of treacherous roads, and the diarrhea caused by fear of thieves,[8] he finally arrived at Long Pergola[9] just when they were having a splendid joust, in which the daughter of the king was promised to the champion. Canneloro presented himself and performed so valorously that he proved a great bother to all the knights who had come from many different countries to earn themselves a name. And for his feats he

---

6. *Marco-sfila* (Neap.): "One of the nicknames of a famous bandit of the time, Marco Sciarra" (Rak 197).

7. *requie scarpe e zuoccole* (Neap.): "mangled form of '*reqiescat in pace*,' in which the syllable '*scat*' becomes '*scarpe*' and, in a logical conclusion of the associative enumeration, '*zoccoli*' [clogs] is added" (Croce 94).

8. "All common occurrences while traveling during Basile's time" (Croce 94).

9. Probably an oversight on Basile's part, since Long Pergola is Canneloro's own kingdom.

was given the king's daughter Fenizia for his wife, and great festivities were held.

"After living for a few months in blessed peace Canneloro got the melancholic urge to go hunting, and when he told the king, he in turn was told, 'Watch out for your legs,[10] my son-in-law, and see that Old Nick doesn't blind you! Keep your wits about you! Open your door, sir, for in those woods there's an ogre worse than the demon, who every day changes shape; now he appears as a wolf, now a lion, now a deer, now a donkey, and now one thing and now another, and with a thousand stratagems he drags the poor souls he encounters into a grotto where he eats them up. So, my son, don't put your health at risk, for you'll lose the rags off your back!'

"Canneloro, who had left all fear in his mother's belly, paid no heed to his father-in-law's advice and went off hunting as soon as the Sun had cleaned away the Night's soot with the straw broom of its rays. And when he got to the wood—where under the canopy of branches shadows congregated to form a monopoly and plot against the Sun— the ogre, who had seen him arrive, transformed himself into a lovely doe, which Canneloro began to pursue as soon as he saw it. The doe held him off and bounced him around from one place to another until it drove him to the heart of the wood, where it caused so much rain and snow to fall that it seemed like the sky was falling. And when Canneloro found himself in front of the ogre's grotto he went in to save himself, and since he was numb with cold he gathered up some wood he found there and, pulling his flint out of his pocket, lit a great fire.

"As he was standing there getting warm and drying his clothes, the doe appeared at the mouth of the grotto and said, 'Oh, sir knight, give me leave to warm up a little, for I'm frozen stiff.' Canneloro, who was courteous, said, 'Come closer, and may you be welcome.' 'I'll come,' answered the doe, 'but I'm afraid that you'll kill me.' 'Have no fear,' replied Canneloro. 'Come, on my word.' 'If you want me to come,' resumed the doe, 'tie up those dogs so they won't bother me, and secure that horse so it won't kick me.' And Canneloro tied up the dogs and tethered the horse. Then the doe said, 'Yes, now I feel almost reassured; but if you don't fasten your sword I won't come in, on the soul of my grandpa!' And Canneloro, who enjoyed familiarizing with the doe, fastened his sword like a farmer going to the city does, for fear of the police.[11] As soon as the ogre saw that Can-

---

10. "The shout of scorn or warning to an insolvent debtor before he was arrested" (Rak 197). Debtors were touched on the leg before being imprisoned (Croce 94).
11. "Countrymen entering the city had to keep their rifles unloaded, and probably their other arms in their sheaths" (Rak 197).

neloro was defenseless he took back his true shape, grabbed hold of him, lowered him into a ditch that was at the back of the grotto, and covered it with a rock so that he could eat him later.

"But when Fonzo, who morning and evening visited the myrtle bush and the spring for news of Canneloro, found the one withered and the other muddy, he immediately imagined that his friend was in trouble. Wanting to assist him, he got on his horse without asking leave of his father or mother, and, well armed and in the company of two enchanted dogs, he set off into the world. And he traveled and roamed in this direction and that until he finally arrived at Long Pergola.

"He found the kingdom completely draped in black for the presumed death of Canneloro, and no sooner had he arrived at court than every person there, believing that he was Canneloro because of his resemblance to him, ran to ask Fenizia for their reward. Throwing herself headlong down the stairs, she hugged Fonzo and said, 'My dear husband, my heart, where have you been all these days?' From this response Fonzo immediately suspected that Canneloro had come to this land and left it, and he decided to interrogate the princess very carefully in order to determine from her words where he might be. And, hearing it said that he had exposed himself to too great a danger in that accursed hunt, especially since he might have been discovered by the ogre, who was so terribly cruel with men, he immediately understood that that was what his friend had come up against. He feigned to know nothing about the matter, and when it was night he went off to bed.

"Pretending to have made a vow to Diana[12] not to touch his wife that night, he lay his unsheathed sword[13] between him and Fenizia like a stockade. In the morning he couldn't wait for the Sun to come out—and give some golden pills[14] to the heavens to make it shit its shadow—since as soon as he got out of bed he intended to go hunting, and neither Fenizia's pleas nor the king's orders could stop him.

"After mounting his horse he went to the woods with his enchanted dogs, and the same thing that had happened to Canneloro happened to him. He went into the grotto and saw Canneloro's weapons, dogs, and horse tied up, and he was then certain that that was where his friend had been snared. And when the doe told him to tie up his

---

12. In Roman mythology, the goddess of the moon, the hunt, and chastity.
13. "The motif of the sword that a knight, forced to go to bed with another knight's lady, puts between himself and the woman in order to protect their honor, derives from the legend of Tristan" (Guarini and Burani 124). The sword is also a metaphor for the phallus, here and elsewhere.
14. Purgative pills (Croce 550).

weapons, dogs, and horse, he sicced them on the doe and they tore it to shreds. As he was searching for some other trace of his friend, he heard moans coming from down in the ditch, and after lifting the rock he pulled out Canneloro along with all the others the ogre had been keeping there, buried alive, in order to fatten them up. And so they embraced with great rejoicing and went home, where upon seeing those two identical men Fenizia was not able to tell which of them was her husband. But when Canneloro lifted his hat she saw the scar and, recognizing him, she embraced him.

"After spending a month in amusements in that land, Fonzo wanted to return home and see his own nest again. With Fonzo as his messenger, Canneloro wrote to his mother to come and take part in his greatness, which she did, and from that time on he wanted nothing more to do with either dogs or hunting, always remembering the saying that goes, *Miserable is he who is punished at his own expense.*"

10

THE OLD WOMAN
WHO WAS SKINNED

Tenth Entertainment of the First Day

The king of Strong Fortress falls in love with the voice of an old woman, and after he is tricked with a sucked-on finger, he gets her to sleep with him. But upon discovering her old hide, he has her thrown out the window, and when she remains hanging on a tree she is enchanted by seven fairies, after which she becomes a splendid young woman and the king takes her for his wife. But the other sister is envious of her fortune, gets skinned to make herself more beautiful, and dies.

There wasn't one person who didn't like Ciommetella's tale, and they derived a double-soled pleasure from seeing Canneloro freed and the ogre, who had done such a butcher job on the poor hunters, punished. And when the order was given to Iacova to seal the next letter of entertainment with her coat of arms, she began to speak in this manner: "The accursed vice, embedded in us women, of wanting to look beautiful reduces us to the point where to gild the frame of our forehead we spoil the painting of our face, to whiten our old and wizened skin we ruin the bones of our teeth, and to put our limbs in a good light we darken our eyesight, so that before it is time to pay our

---

AT 877: The Old Woman Who Was Skinned. See Penzer's discussion of the appearance of a number of the motifs in this tale in legend, religious traditions, folklore, and the literary fairy tale tradition. These include a man marrying a hag who then turns into a beautiful lady ("The Weddynge of Syr Gawayne," the legend of Perceval); the "false sybarite" motif; and the flaying of the sister. With regard to the latter, he notes that the "terrible end of the other sister is rather surprising when we remember that the lucky sister had been given gifts by the fairies to make her beautiful, noble, and virtuous. Yet as soon as she is married, she proceeds to treat her less lucky sister in the most heartless and cruel way imaginable." The similarities with Hans Christian Andersen's "Little Claus and Big Claus" and Grimm 61, "Little Farmer," are also noted (1:103–04). Gonzenbach 73, "The King Who Wanted a Beautiful Wife," is in essence identical to "The Old Woman." Croce mentions a similar tale by Pitrè (6 in *Fiabe e legg. pop. sic.*) and cites corresponding Sicilian, Venetian, Abbruzzese, and Tyrolean versions (*Lo cunto de li cunti*, 287).

tribute to time we procure ourselves rheumy eyes, wrinkled faces, and rotten molars. But if a young girl who in her vanity gives in to such empty-headedness deserves reproach, even more worthy of punishment is an old woman who out of her desire to compete with young ladies becomes a laughingstock for others and the ruin of her own self, as I am about to tell you, if you will lend me a bit of your ears.[1]

"Two old women had retired to a garden facing the King of Strong Fortress's quarters. They were the summary of all misfortunes, the register of all deformities, the ledger of all ugliness: their tufts of hair were disheveled and spiked, their foreheads lined and lumpy, their eyelashes shaggy and bristly, their eyelids swollen and heavy, their eyes wizened and seedy-looking, their faces yellowed and wrinkled, their mouths drooly and crooked; in short, they had beards like a billy goat's, hairy chests, round-bellied shoulders, withered arms, lame and crippled legs, and hooked feet. And to prevent even the Sun from catching a glimpse of their hideous appearance, they stayed holed up in a few ground-level rooms[2] under the windows of that lord.

"The king was reduced to such a state that he couldn't even fart without causing those old pains in the neck to wrinkle their noses, for they grumbled and threw themselves about like squid over the smallest thing. First they said that a jasmine flower fallen from above had given one of them a lump on her head, then that a torn-up letter had dislocated one of their shoulders, and then that a pinch of dust had bruised one of their thighs.

"Upon hearing of this monster of delicacy, the king concluded that underneath him lived the quintessence of softness, the prime cut of the most delectable of meats, and the flower of all tenderness, by reason of which he was overcome by a craving all the way down to the little bones in his feet and a desire straight through to his bone marrow to see this marvel and to get a clearer idea of the matter. And so he began to send down sighs, to clear his throat when there was nothing to clear, and, finally, to speak more expeditiously and with greater

---

1. The introduction to the tale contains an antifeminist diatribe against the use of cosmetics and other instruments of false beautification that was common in disquisitions on the proper comportment of women, as well as in writings on rhetoric, where the celebration of what lies under the merely cosmetic—in body or words—was often linked to the topos of "naked truth." This passage, in particular, brings to mind the preamble to tale 1.10 of the *Decameron*, which criticizes the same female "vice."
2. *no vascio* (Neap.): street-level apartments were usually inhabited by members of the lower classes and were "at this time already a phenomenon connected to the growth in population and lack of housing" (Rak 218).

boldness, exclaiming, 'Where, oh where do you hide yourself, jewel, splendor, beautiful product of the world? "Come out, come out, Sun, warm up the emperor!"[3] Uncover those lovely graces, show those lamps of the shop of Love, stick out that dainty head, O counting house heaped with beauty's money! Don't be so stingy about letting yourself be seen! "Open your doors to the poor falcon!" "Give me an offering if you want to give me one!"[4] Let me see the instrument from which issues that sweet voice! Allow me to see the bell where that tinkling is formed! Let me catch a glimpse of that bird! Do not make me graze on absinthe like a sheep from Ponto[5] by refusing to allow me to look at and contemplate that beauty of all beauties!'

"The king said this and other words, but he might as well have been playing the Gloria, for the old women had stopped up their ears. This, however, only added wood to the king's fire: he felt himself heated up like an iron in the furnace of desire, squeezed by the tongs of deliberation, and pounded by the hammer of amorous torment, and all to forge a key that could open the little chest of jewels that was making him die of longing. And still he did not pull back, instead continuing to send forth entreaties and to strengthen his assaults, never taking a rest.

"The old women, who had begun to put on airs and grow cocky as a result of the king's offers and promises, resolved not to waste this opportunity to nab a bird that was about to fly into the snare all by himself. And so, one day when the king was ranting and raving[6] above their window, they told him through the keyhole in a tiny little voice that the greatest favor they could do would be to show him, in eight days, just one finger of their hand. The king, who as a practiced soldier knew that fortresses are won span by span, did not refuse this solution, hoping to conquer finger by finger the stronghold that he

---

3. A Neapolitan children's song, probably of ritual origin. The complete text of this song appears in the introduction to day 4, in which the company of tale-tellers and audience engages in song, dance, and merrymaking before the day's tales start. Recently (1976) this same song became the prologue to a musical based on Basile's "La gatta cenerentola" (Cinderella) created by Roberto de Simone and the Nuova Compagnia di Canto Popolare, a well-known group of Neapolitan "ethno-musicians."

4. Two more children's games: "Open the Doors" is a circle game, and "Give Me an Offering" is a song children sang on New Year's Eve as they went from door to door. See also Eclogue 1 n31.

5. For this belief on Pontine sheep, Basile refers to Pliny's *Natural History* (book 27): "Absinthi genera plura . . . Ponticum, e Ponto, ubi pecora pinguescunt illo, et ob id sine felle reperiuntur" (cit. Croce 100).

6. *faceva . . . lo sparpetuo* (Neap.): "playful deformation of the formula used in the mass for the dead: *lux perpetua eis; a sperpetua* is a whiny lament" (Guarini and Burani 129).

was keeping under siege, since he also knew that 'first take and then ask' was an ancient proverb. And thus, once he had accepted this ultimatum of the eighth day by which to see the eighth wonder of the world, the old women's sole activity became that of sucking their fingers like a pharmacist who has spilled some syrup, with the plan that when they reached the established day whoever had the smoothest finger would show it to the king.

"Meanwhile, the king was on tenterhooks as he waited for the agreed-upon hour to blunt his desire: he counted the days, he numbered the nights, he weighed the hours, he measured the moments, he made note of the seconds, and he probed the instants that had been meted out to him in anticipation of the desired good. Now he begged the Sun to take a shortcut through the celestial fields so that by gaining ground it would unhitch its fiery carriage and water its horses, tired after such a long trip, before the usual time; now he implored Night to sink the shadows so that he could see the light, which yet unseen was keeping him in the kiln of Love's flames; now he grew incensed with Time, who to spite him was wearing crutches and leaden shoes so as to delay the hour for liquidating the debt to the thing he loved and for respecting the contract stipulated between them.

"But as the Sun in Leo[7] would have it, the time came, and he went in person to the garden and knocked on the door, saying, 'Come out, come out, wherever you are!'[8] Then one of the two old women—the one most laden with years, since the touchstone had shown her finger to be of greater carats than her sister's—stuck her finger through the keyhole and showed it to the king.

"Now this was no mere finger, but a sharpened stick that pierced the king's heart. Or rather, it was no stick, but a cudgel that stunned him on the head. But what am I saying, stick and cudgel? It was a match struck on the tinder of his desires, a fuse lit from the powder magazine of his longings. But what am I saying, stick, cudgel, match, fuse? It was a thorn under the tail of his thoughts—indeed, a cure of laxative figs that made him eliminate the gas of amorous affect in a mess of sighs.

"And as he held that hand and kissed that finger, which had been transformed from a shoemaker's rasp to a goldsmith's burnisher, he began to say, 'O archive of sweetness, O rubric of joys, O register of Love's privileges, by reason of which I have become a store of troubles, a warehouse of anguish, and a customhouse of torment! Is it

---

7. See tale 1.7 n28.
8. Another children's game, of the hide-and-seek variety.

possible that you wish to appear so obstinate and hard that my laments cannot move you? I beg you, my fair heart, if you have shown me your tail through this hole, now show me your snout, and let us make a gelatin[9] of happiness! If you have shown me your shell, O sea of beauty, now show me your sweet flesh; uncover those eyes of a peregrine falcon and let them feed on this heart! Who keeps the treasure of that beautiful face sequestered in a shithouse? Who quarantines that fair merchandise in a hovel? Who imprisons the forces of Love in that pigsty?[10] Come out of that ditch, flee that stable, abandon that hole! "Jump, little snail, and give Cola your hand";[11] spend me for what I'm worth! You know, after all, that I'm a king and not any old cucumber; you know that I can do and undo as I like. But that impostor of a blind boy, son of a cripple and a whore, who has free rein over scepters, has willed that I be your subject and that I beg you for the grace of what I could seize however and whenever I please.[12] And furthermore, I know, as a certain someone said, that caresses, and not bravado, sweeten up Venus.'

"The old woman knew where the old devil kept his tail, since she was a master fox, a big old cat, a shrewd, astute, and wily one, and she reflected that it's precisely when a superior begs for something that he's actually issuing a command, and that a vassal's stubbornness gets the choleric humors of the master's intestines moving, which then burst forth in a dysentery of ruin. And so she decided to act accordingly, and with the little voice of a skinned cat she said, 'My lord, since you are inclined to put yourself beneath one who is under you, having deigned to descend from the scepter to the distaff, from the royal halls to the stable, from lavish robes to rags, from greatness to misery, from the terrace to the cellar, and from a steed to an ass, I cannot, nor ought not, nor want not to contradict the will of so great a king. And since you desire this alliance between prince and servant, this mosaic of ivory and poplar, this inlay of diamonds and glass, here I am, ready and prepared to do your will. I beg of you only one favor, as a first sign of the love that you bear me: that I be received in your bed at night and without a candle, since my heart could not bear the burden of being seen naked.' The king, gur-

---

9. Boiled pig snout, served in its own gelatin, was commonly sold by street vendors in Basile's time, as it still is today (Rak 218).

10. *mantrullo* (Neap.): "pigpen, also the cell of those condemned to death" (Guarini and Burani 131).

11. This is the first verse of a Neapolitan villanella.

12. Love or Cupid, the son of Venus and Vulcan, is "one of the recurrent figures of Greco-Roman mythology in these tales, in which sexual relationships are, directly or indirectly, a basic plot element" (Rak 219).

gling with delight, swore to her with one hand on the other that he would willingly do this. And so, after he sent a kiss of sugar to that fetid mouth, he left, and could hardly wait for the Sun to stop plowing and for the fields of the heavens to be sown with stars, so that he in turn could sow the field where he intended to harvest bushels of joy and heaps of delight.

"When Night arrived—and, finding itself surrounded by so many shop burglars and cloak thieves,[13] squirted out black ink like a squid—the old woman smoothed back all the wrinkles on her body and gathered them behind her shoulders in a knot, which she tied tightly with a piece of twine. A servant then led her by the hand in the darkness to the king's bedroom, where, once she had taken off her rags, she flung herself onto the bed. The king was more than ready to light the fuse on his artillery, and as soon as he heard her come and lie down he smeared himself all over with musk and civet and sprayed himself from head to toe with cologne water, and then raced to bed like a Corsican hound. And it was lucky for the old woman that the king was wearing so much perfume, on account of which he wasn't able to smell the fumes coming from her mouth, the stink of her little tickly areas, and the stench of that ugly thing.

"But no sooner had he lain down than, feeling around, he became aware of that business on the back of her neck and discovered the dried tripe and deflated bladders that the wretched old woman kept in the back of her shop. Keeping his composure, he decided not to say anything right then, since he needed to have a clearer idea on the matter. And so, pretending not to notice, he cast anchor at Mandracchio when he had believed he would be on the coast of Posillipo, and sailed forth on a barge when he had thought he would be charting his course on a Florentine galley.[14] But no sooner had the old woman dropped off into her first sleep than the king took a chamois bag containing a flint stone from his writing table of ebony and silver, and lit a little oil lamp. After conducting a search under the sheets and finding a harpy in the place of a nymph, a Fury in the place of a Grace, and a Gorgon in the place of a Cypriot, he flew into such a rage that he wanted to cut the towrope that had moored that ship. Snorting

---

13. Common crimes of the time, in which Spaniards were considered to have the greatest expertise (Croce 103).
14. Mandracchio was an area of ill repute near the Dogana (Customs) in the port of Naples; the famous Neapolitan hill of Posillipo was, since ancient times, the site of aristocratic pastimes. A *permonara* (barge) was an "old, discarded ship that was kept at wet dock to house the crew, to hold prisoners, or for other uses"; the elegant Florentine galleys were often, at this time, used to guard the Mediterranean coasts against pirates (Croce 104).

with fury, he yelled for all his servants, who when they heard the call to arms threw on their shirts[15] and came upstairs.

"Flailing about like an octopus, the king said to them, 'Look at the fine trick this old bogeyman's grandmother has played on me! I believed I was going to gobble up a milk-calf and instead I find myself with a buffalo placenta; I thought I had trapped a splendid dove and I end up with this owl in my hand; I imagined I had a morsel fit for a king and I find myself with this disgusting thing in my claws: taste it and spit it out! And yet when you buy a cat in the bag this and even worse happens! And yet it was she who arranged this affront, and it will be she who shits her penance! So go and get her right now, just as she is, and throw her out the window!'

"When the old woman heard this she began to defend herself with kicks and bites, saying that she appealed the sentence, since he was the one who had turned her like a winch until she came to his bed and that besides, she could call a hundred doctors to her defense along with, above all, the saying that goes, 'An old chicken makes a good broth,' and the other one, 'Don't leave the old road for the new.' But after all that they picked her straight up and hurled her down into the garden, and she had the luck not to break her neck, for she was left hanging by her hair on the branch of a fig tree.

"Early the next morning—before the Sun took possession of the territories it had been ceded by Night—some fairies came passing by the garden. Due to some irritation or other they had never spoken or laughed, and when they saw, hanging from the tree, the ugly shade who had caused the shadows to clear out before the usual time, they were overcome by such side-splitting laughter that they came close to getting a hernia, and once they set their tongues in motion they weren't able to close their mouths about that lovely spectacle for a good while. And such was their amusement and pleasure that in payment each of them cast a spell on her: one by one, they wished that she might become young, beautiful, rich, noble, virtuous, well loved, and blessed by good luck.

"When the fairies had left, the old woman found herself on the ground, sitting on a chair of rich velvet fringed in gold under the same tree as before, which had been transformed into a canopy of green velvet backed in gold. Her face had turned into that of a fifteen-year-old girl, so beautiful that by comparison all other beauties would have looked like worn-out house slippers alongside an elegant,

---

15. *fatto na 'ncammisata* (Neap.): according to Croce, a reference to how, "during night-time attacks, soldiers would put shirts over their armor so that they could recognize each other in the dark" (104–05).

perfect-fitting little pump; next to this enthroned grace all other graces would have been deemed worthy of Ferrivecchi or Lavinaro;[16] and where she played her chitchat and blandishments with a winning hand, all the others would have played a losing bank. And, furthermore, she was so primped up, fancified, and sumptuous that she looked like a royal majesty: her gold was blinding, her jewels dazzling, the bloom of her flowers stunning; and surrounding her were so many servants and ladies-in-waiting that it looked like the day of pardon.[17]

"In the meantime the king, who had thrown a blanket over his shoulders and a pair of old slippers on his feet, went to the window to see what had happened to the old woman. When he saw what he never would have imagined, he stood there with his mouth hanging open and looked that fine piece of a girl up and down from head to toe for a good long while, as if he were enchanted. Now he admired her hair, in part spread out over her shoulders and in part harnessed with a golden tie, which gave the Sun cause for envy; now he stared at her eyelashes, crossbows that took hearts as their targets; now he looked at her eyes, blind lanterns of Love's patrol;[18] now he contemplated her mouth, amorous winepress where the Graces squeezed out delight and obtained sweet Greco and savory Mangiaguerra wines.[19] He swung from side to side like a shaky rafter, and nearly went out of his mind when he saw the baubles and trinkets that were hanging at her neck and the magnificent clothes she was wearing. Talking to himself, he said, 'Am I asleep or am I awake? Am I in my right mind or am I going crazy? Am I myself or am I not myself? What kind of move[20] caused such a lovely ball to hit this king, so that I am sent to my ruin? I'll be done for, I'll be destroyed if I don't pull myself out of this! How has this sun risen? How has this flower blossomed? How was this bird hatched, so that she can pull my desires like a hook? What sort of boat brought her to these lands? What sort of cloud rained her down? What sort of torrents of beauty are carrying me straight to a sea of woes?'

---

16. *grazia de sieggio* (Neap.): "Neapolitan nobility was divided into those 'with a seat' (i.e., assigned to one of six noble seats), and those 'without a seat.' The first, and more ancient group was of much greater prestige" (Croce 552). Ferrivecchi and Lavinaro were among the poorest streets in Naples.

17. *la perdonanza* (Neap.): "processions for the purchase of indulgences" (Rak 219).

18. See tale 1.2 n34.

19. Two famous wines from the area around Naples.

20. *trucco* (Neap.): "a game in which small balls (*palle*) were thrown and hit" (Rak 220).

"As he was saying this he flew down the stairs and ran into the garden, where he went before the renovated old woman and, nearly wiping the ground, said to her, 'O my dear little pigeon-face; O little doll of the Graces, splendid dove of the carriage of Venus, triumphal cart of Love! If you have set your heart to soak in the Sarno River,[21] if cane seeds have not gotten into your ears and sparrow shit has not fallen into your eyes, I am sure that you can see and hear the pain and torment that, directly and on the rebound, those beauties of yours have cast into my chest. And if you cannot surmise from the ash cloth of this face the lye that boils inside this chest,[22] if you cannot imagine from the flames of these sighs the furnace that burns in these veins, then if you are sympathetic and of good judgment you can at least infer from that golden hair what sort of cord binds me, and from those black eyes what sort of coals roast me, and from the red arches of those lips what sort of arrow pierces me. Do not, then, bar the door of pity, do not lift the bridge of mercy, do not stop the duct of compassion! If you do not deem me worthy of obtaining a pardon from this lovely face, at least give me a safeguard of good words, a pass of a promise or two, and a pledge card of fair hopes, for otherwise I shall take my slippers far from here[23] and you shall never again see their shape.'

"These and a thousand other words issued forth from the depths of the king's heart and deeply moved the renovated old woman, who at the end accepted him as her husband. And so she rose from her seat and took him by the hand, and they went together to the royal palace, where in the wink of an eye a huge banquet was prepared. Since all the ladies of the land were invited, the old bride wanted her sister to be among them, but they had a lot to do and say before they were able to find her and drag her to the feast, because out of great fear she had gone and holed herself up and hidden away so that not a trace of her could be found. But God willed that she finally came, and once she was sitting next to her sister, whom it was no joke for her to recognize, they began the merrymaking.

"The wretched old woman had another hunger that was gnawing at her, though, since she was consumed with envy to see her sister's

---

21. Anything immersed in the waters of the Sarno River, it was said, would turn to stone; cane seeds were thought to have dangerous properties; sparrow feces was believed to cause blindness (as happened to Tobit in the Book of Tobit 2.17) (Croce 107).

22. The "ash cloth" (*cennerale*) was used to cover laundry basins in order to contain the ash therein (which was used as a detergent); lye is also a common detergent.

23. Neapolitan idiom meaning "to pass on to the other world."

coat shine, and every few minutes she would pull her by the sleeve
and say, 'What did you do, my sister, what did you do? "Lucky you,
you've got the chain!" '[24] And her sister would answer, 'Just think
about eating now, and we'll talk about it later.' The king kept on asking what was going on, and to cover things up his bride answered
that her sister wanted a little green sauce. And the king immediately
ordered that garlic paste, mustard, pepper sauce, and a thousand
other relishes that stimulate the appetite be brought.

"But the old woman, to whom the grape relish tasted like cow bile,
went back to nagging her sister, and asked her again, 'What did you
do, my sister, what did you do? Tell me, or I'll make you the fig under
my cloak.'[25] And her sister answered, 'Be quiet, for we have more
time than money; eat now, and may it go down the wrong way, and
then we'll talk.' The king, curious, asked what she wanted, and his
bride, who felt as tangled up as a chick in a pile of tow and would
have liked to do without that hammering at her temples, answered
that she wanted something sweet. And then there came a blizzard of
pastries, a bombardment of wafers and little doughnuts, a flood of
blancmange, and a downpour of honey brittle.[26]

"But the old woman, who was as agitated as a squid and had a bad
case of the runs, started up with the same music again until the bride
could no longer stand it, and to get her off her back she answered, 'I
skinned myself, sister.' When the envious sister heard this she said,
under her breath, 'All right then, your words don't fall on deaf ears! I
want to try my luck, too, for every spirit has a stomach, and if I come

24. Words of another children's game, here used as an augury.
25. *fare na fico* (Neap.): "A gesture of contempt, known in Italy, France, Germany,
Holland, England, etc., and consisting of placing the thumb between the index and
middle fingers. . . . [It] is held by some to be a sign-symbol of the vulva, and is used
for example in Italy, as both an insulting gesture and a counter to the evil eye (a wish
for good luck): one etymological theory holds that the expression originated in an
Italian word meaning both the fruit and the *pudendum muliebre*, thus making of the
gesture a punning symbol" (Leach and Fried 378). In this case, the potential ambiva-
lence of the gesture (insult or wish for good luck), as well as the pun, are fully ex-
ploited by Basile. See also Giuseppe Pitrè, *Biblioteca delle tradizioni popolari
siciliane* 17.244–45.
26. All traditional Neapolitan sweets. *Pastidelle* (pastries) were made with eggs,
sugar, and cinnamon; *neole* (wafers; from the Latin *nebulae*) from flour and boiled
must; *tarallucce* were small doughnut-shaped cookies (made with sugar) or crackers
(made with pepper, anise, or other spices); *iancomangiare* (blancmange) was another
sweet, a gelatinous pudding made with milk or almond milk, and produced in monasteries; *franfellicche* were little pieces of sweet brittle made with honey and syrup
(see Rak 220).

"Uh, chi bella vo' parere, pena vo' patere."
["Ugh, she who wants to appear beautiful must suffer."]

away with my hands full you won't be the only one having a good time. I want my part, too, right up to the fennel.'[27]

"As she was thus speaking, the tables were cleared. Pretending to go and satisfy a bodily need, she ran straight off to a barber's shop, where she found the master barber, took him aside in a back room, and said to him, 'Here are fifty ducats for you; skin me from head to toe.'[28] The barber, judging her to be crazy, answered, 'Go on, sister; you're talking funny and you're surely in need of someone to accompany you.'[29] And the old woman replied, with a face of marble, 'You're the one who's crazy, if you can't recognize your own good fortune. For if I win at a certain game, in addition to the fifty ducats I'll let you hold your basin under Fortune's beard. So, then, gather up your instruments and don't waste time; you're in for some good luck.'

"After arguing, fighting with her, and protesting for a good while, the barber was finally led by the nose, and behaved like the guy who 'ties up the ass wherever his master wants.' And when he had set her on a stool he started to hack away at that black bark, which drizzled and piddled blood all over and which every now and then, as steady as if he were giving her a shave, said, 'Ugh, she who wants to appear beautiful must suffer.' And as he continued to send her to her ruin and she repeated the same refrain, they kept up a counterpoint on the lute[30] of her body until he reached the rosette of her navel,[31] at which point her blood abandoned her and with it her strength, and she fired a departing shot from below, proving at her own risk the truth of Sannazaro's verse: *Envy, my son, destroys itself.*"[32]

---

27. Up to the very end; fennel is served at the end of the meal.
28. Barbers of the time performed multiple roles: "in barber shops one could have more or less complex surgical procedures done, such as teeth extraction, the application of leeches, and more" (Rak 220).
29. As patients at an insane asylum are accompanied by nurses (Croce 109).
30. *colascione* (Neap.): see tale 1.3 n24.
31. The *rosa* is the circular opening in the body of stringed instruments, from which derives the expression *contrapuntiare fi' a la rosa*, or to take a long time with something.
32. The reference is to these verses from Iacopo Sannazaro's *Arcadia* (6.4–6): "Nel mondo oggi gli amici non si trovano, / la fede è morta e regnano le invidie / e i mal costumi ognor più si rinovano." Rak comments that "envy was one of the most popular topics in court society, and was debated in numerous treatises" (220). One of the "authorities" frequently cited was Ovid, who in book 2 of the *Metamorphoses* describes Envy as an old hag not so dissimilar from Basile's old woman: "Eyes wild, teeth thick with mold, gall dripping green . . . / Envy is sleepless, her heart anxiety, / And at the sight of any man's success / She withers, is bitten, eats herself away" (Ovid 79).

This tale ended at the time of day when the Sun was given the deadline of one hour to vacate the quarters of the air, like a bothersome student.[33] Then the prince summoned Fabiello and Iacovuccio, one the linen valet and the other the steward of the house, to come and provide the day of telling with its dessert. And there they appeared, as quickly as cops, one dressed in trousers of black frieze with martingale straps and a bell-shaped jacket with buttons the size of antelope balls, and a flat cap that went down over his ears; the other with a beret the shape of a cutting board, a potbellied jacket, and breeches of white Taranta cloth. Coming out from behind a backdrop of myrtle bushes as if it were a set, they spoke in this manner:

---

33. "Allusion to the frequent eviction notices served to students residing in certain houses, or streets or neighborhoods." In 1505 King Ferdinand the Catholic issued a decree that students could live only in certain parts of the city. One of the many stone tablets banning "prostitutes, students, or similarly dishonest persons" can be found in the Museum of San Martino in Naples (Croce 552).

THE CRUCIBLE

Eclogue

Fabiello, Iacovuccio

FABIELLO: Where are you going so quickly? Where are you going in such a hurry, Iacovuccio?

IACOVUCCIO: To take this little thing home.

FAB.: Is it something nice?

IAC.: It sure is. Absolutely first-rate.

FAB.: Well, then?

IAC.: It's a crucible.

FAB.: What do you use it for?

IAC.: If you only knew.

FAB.: Hey, careful there. You get away from me!

IAC.: Why?

The four eclogues that divide the days are all recited by two characters, members of Tadeo's court but otherwise not involved in the tale-telling activities. The eclogues are in verse: an irregular alternation between hendecasyllable and seven-syllable lines (two of the most common in Italian verse) and a rhyme pattern that is also irregular, which I have translated in prose. Historically, the eclogue is a verse dialogue, often between shepherds, that treats pastoral themes (Virgil's are perhaps the best-known examples). Basile's intent appears ironic, since the actors in his eclogues are court servants and their topics of conversation are the social ills (specifically, the various hypocrisies) of urban civic society. Indeed, they have much in common with the tradition of satire in verse; after the Roman masters of this genre, one of the most important Renaissance satirists was Ludovico Ariosto, with whose *Satire* Basile was certainly familiar. With the choice of "staged" eclogues to divide the days of telling Basile also makes reference, although once again in a topsy-turvy sort of way, to the established tradition of *intermezzi,* or interludes, that were inserted between the acts (five) of a play. During the Renaissance these compositions could be pastoral or love poems (see, e.g., Machiavelli's *Mandragola*), though they could also be theatrical in form themselves (e.g., comic scenes), and in subject matter were generally extraneous (at least explicitly so) to the action in the principal play.

A *coppella* (Neap.) is "a type of porous crucible used for purifying or testing metals" (Rak 270).

FAB.: Who knows, maybe you've been blinded by the demon! Do you get what I'm saying?

IAC.: I hear you, but you're a hundred miles off.[1]

FAB.: What do I know, then?

IAC.: He who knows not is quiet and keeps his trap shut.

FAB.: I do know you're not a goldsmith, and you're not a distiller: draw your own conclusions!

IAC.: Let's move over to the side here, Fabiello. I want you to be amazed and stunned.

FAB.: We can go wherever you want.

IAC.: Let's go stand under that awning. I'm going to make you jump out of your clothes!

FAB.: Hurry up and get on with it, brother, you're making me pant.

IAC.: Take it easy, my brother! What a rush you're in! Tell me, did your mother make you in such a hurry? Take a good look at this contraption.

FAB.: I can see that it's a pot where you purify silver.

IAC.: You hit it on the head. You guessed it right off!

FAB.: Cover it up. Who knows, some copper might come by and we'll be taken off to the pen!

IAC.: What a pants shitter you are! But you can tremble in peace. This isn't one of those where you knead dough with all sorts of stratagems until three little coins[2] turn into three pieces of wood![3]

FAB.: Tell me, then, what do you use it for?

IAC.: To refine the things of this world, and to distinguish between garlic and figs.

FAB.: You've got a lot of linen to card! You'll get old in no time; in no time at all you'll have white hair!

IAC.: Look, there's not a man on earth who wouldn't pay an eye and a tooth to have a device like this one, which on the first try reveals every stain a person has inside him, the value of every art and every fortune! For inside here you can see if a noodle is empty or if it's got some sense, if something is adulterated or pure.

FAB.: What do you mean now?

IAC.: Listen to me straight through; calm down, and I'll explain my-

---

1. "Fabiello had thought that this crucible could be used to make counterfeit money, the most common crime in Naples at the time, and the most ruthlessly punished, with hangings and quarterings occurring on an almost daily basis, as the chronicles of the time document" (Croce 111).

2. *decinco* (Neap.): the *cinquina* was a coin of low value (Croce 112).

3. The gallows.

self better. Whatever by its outer aspect and on the face of things seems to be of value is all an illusion of the eye, a way to blind people, mere appearance. You can't just skim the surface or scratch the skin; you need to pierce a hole and go all the way in, for in this world he who does not fish deep is a fine blockhead! Use this crucible, and you'll be able to test whether the business is true or false, whether it's a sprouted onion or a pasty.

FAB.: It's a wondrous thing, on the life of Lanfusa![4]

IAC.: Hear me out, and then marvel. Let's move on. Take a deep breath, for you're going to hear of miracles! Listen now to an example. You die of envy, you swell up and get a hernia over a lord, count, or knight, because he travels in a carriage; you see him served and accompanied by so many small-fry, such riff-raff. There's one who screws up his face at him over here, one who bows to him over there, one who takes off his hat to him, one who says, "Your slave!" He reduces silk and gold to rags; when he eats, they fan him; and he even has a chamber pot of silver! But don't get pregnant on this pomp and appearance; don't sigh and let your mouth water. Put it all in this crucible, and you'll see just how many festering sores lie under the velvet saddle; you'll find out just how many snakes lie hiding in the flowers and the grass; if you uncover the commode, with its fringes and embroidery, and bullion and silks, you'll be able to tell if the business has to do with perfume or with stench! He has a gold basin, and he spits blood in it; he has choice morsels and they get stuck in his throat; and if you measure well, and observe even more carefully, what you think is a gift of fortune is a punishment from the heavens. All the crows he feeds bread to take out his eyes; all the dogs he keeps bark at him; he gives a salary to his enemies, who surround him, suck him up alive, and hoodwink him. Over here is one who sponges off him with grimaces and tall tales; over there is one who puffs him up with a bellows; one appears to be charitable right down to his asshole, a wolf in sheep's clothing with a lovely face and a horrible spleen, and induces him to commit wrongs and injustices; another plots machinations. That one is a "lemme tell you all about it" and turns his poor noggin upside down; this one betrays him and gives him dysentery, so

---

4. "In chivalric epics, Ferrau's oath on his mother's head (see, for example, Ludovico Ariosto, *Orlando Furioso* I.30). Here it is used with the meaning of swearing on the life of a stranger whose fate is of no interest" (Rak 270).

that he never sleeps restfully, eats with pleasure, or laughs with all his heart. If he eats, the noise drives him out of his mind; if he sleeps, his dreams terrify him; his haughtiness torments him, like Tityus's bird; his vanity is the water and fruit that surround him as he's dying of hunger; reason, lacking all reason, is Ixion's wheel, which gives him no peace; the plots and chimeras are the stones that Sisyphus drags up the mountain, from where they fall—boom!—back down to the bottom![5] He sits on a golden chair inlaid with ivory and studded with gold; under his feet he has cushions of brocade and taffeta and Turkish carpets. But above his noggin hangs a sharp-edged sword suspended by a single hair, so that he is ever with diarrhea, spinning the fine thread of fear and frozen with terror, ever with worms and the runs and in a fright and a state of dread. And, at the very end, this magnificence and grandeur are all shadows and trash, and a bit of earth in a narrow ditch covers rogues and kings alike.

FAB.: You're right, on the soul of you-know-who! I swear, it's even worse than you say, for the greater a lord is, the more massive his calamities are. And in short, that man from Trecchiena[6] who went around selling walnuts spoke well when he said, "All that glitters isn't gold!"

IAC.: Listen to this other one, and you'll become a lotus tree![7] Here's a man who praises war and puts it above all else, and when the time comes for a banner to be raised, for the rat-ta-tat-tat of a drum to be heard, he races off to enlist, pulled by the throat by four chips[8] thrown on a bench. He gets fresh money, he buys new clothes on the Giudecca,[9] he puts on his carob pod[10] and he looks like a pack mule, with his plume and sad-

---

5. All mythological figures condemned to punishment. Tityus, the giant son of Gaia, was punished by Apollo and Artemis for attempting to rape their mother, Leto, by being made eternally immobile while two vultures gnawed at his liver (recounted in book 11 of the *Odyssey*); Tantalus was punished with insatiable hunger and thirst as he sat in the middle of a lake with a fruit tree above him, both unattainable; Ixion was tied by Zeus with serpents to a fiery wheel in perpetual motion for having made sexual advances to Hera; and Sisyphus (founder of Corinth) was condemned for eternity to push a boulder up a hill, only to have it roll to the bottom again each time before it reached the top (Rak 270; Guarini and Burani 146–47).

6. Town in Basilicata (Trecchina), in the area around Lagonegro (Croce 117).

7. See tale 1.5 n2.

8. *iettarielle* (Neap.): "counters in the form of coins, used to mark points in a game" (Croce 117).

9. *Iodeca* (Neap.): "A street of Naples where Jews once lived. After they were expelled, the area was taken over by rag-sellers" (Croce 117).

10. A derogative term for sword, as in tale 1.7 n24.

dlecloth. If a friend asks him, "Where are we going?" he cheerfully answers, walking on air, "To war, to war!" He hangs out
in taverns, he triumphs on Mulberry Street,[11] he goes off to his
quarters, he sells his billets,[12] he makes noise and a racket, and
even Gradasso couldn't make him retreat![13] Poor fellow, if you
melt him down in this crucible! All that happiness, those airs,
and that strutting are transformed into tribulation and torment. Cold numbs him, heat puts an end to him, hunger gnaws
at him, fatigue massacres him, danger is always at his side,
and rewards are far away. Wounds come in cash, pay comes
on credit, suffering is long and sweetness short, life uncertain
and death sure. At the end, he's either exhausted by so many
torments and beats it out of there, and with three jumps is able
to verify whether the cord is a fuse or a halter,[14] or else he's
completely destroyed, or crippled, and he's got nothing left
other than the subsidy[15] of a pair of crutches, or a treatment
for scabies, or—and it's the lesser evil—a pension plan[16] in the
hospital.

FAB.: You've revealed everything rotten about it and there's nothing left to say; it's true and more than true, since a poor soldier spends the last drops of life either as a pauper or full of
holes!

IAC.: And what do you say about a man full of himself, who walks
on his tiptoes, struts like a peacock, and swells up and boasts
that he descends from the race and lineage of Achilles or Alexander: all day long he draws family trees, and he pulls the
branch of a holly oak from the trunk of a chestnut; all day
long he writes stories and Johnny-ologies of fathers who never
had children, and he would have it that a man who sells quarter barrels of oil is a quarter part noble. He adjusts privileges
on sheets of parchment and fumes them so that they'll look
old, thus feeding the fumes of vanity; he buys tombstones and

---

11. *Ceuze* (Neap.): see tale 1.7 n17.

12. *cartelle* (Neap.): "Soldiers received papers that authorized them to find lodging
in a private home, but it was common to give up this right in exchange for a payment
that the potential hosts often willingly paid, considering the difficulties involved in
living with soldiers" (Rak 271).

13. The Saracen king who appears in Boiardo's *Orlando innamorato* (1.4ff.) and
Ariosto's *Orlando furioso* (2.45ff.).

14. "That is, whether the rope with which he is hanged (for deserting) is thick or
thin" (Croce 118).

15. *aiuto de costa* (Neap.): from the Spanish "ayudo de costa," a subsidy given to
travelers when sent on missions (Croce 553).

16. *chiazza morta* (Neap.): see tale 1.7 n29.

attaches to them epitaphs made of a thousand nursery rhymes. He pays the Zazzeras[17] to dress up his shirttails, he spends at the Campaniles'[18] to tune his bells, and he spends an eye and a tooth at the di Pietris'[19] to lay down the foundations for a few crumbling houses. But when he is put to the test in the crucible, he who stretches himself out the longest, he who expects the best and talks through his nose and brags, still has calluses from his hoe!

FAB.: You're touching where it hurts and there's nothing left to say; you've hit the nail on the head! I remember, by the way (and keep these words in mind), that a wise man once said, "There's nothing worse than a peasant who's come up in the world."

IAC.: Now look: a vainglorious man, a perfume shitter, full of conceit, who has the presumption to hang a garland of cheese around his horse's neck, and goes off in a pique with great ostentation. He blows up balloons of air and blurts out nonsense, he spits out rotund words and swaggers about, twists and screws up his mouth, sucks his lips when he speaks, and measures his footsteps: try and guess who he thinks he is! He glories in himself and boasts, "Hey there, bring on the tawny horse, or the dapple! Call twenty of my men! See if my nephew the count wants to go for a little spin! When is our administrator going to bring me the carriage? Tell the master tailor that before evening I want the gold-embroidered breeches! Send an answer to that lady who suffers agonies for me and tell her that maybe, just maybe, I'll love her!" But as soon as he's tested in this crucible, there's not a coin left; it's all a straw fire, and the more he struts about the more he yawns with hunger: he's always talking of big money and he's without a cent, he puts on airs and has nothing to put in his mouth, he has a pleated collar and not a wrinkle in his purse, a nice belly but not a bit of cash. In conclusion, every beard of his turns

---

17. *le Zazzare* (Neap.): Francesco Zazzera was the author of *Della nobilità d'Italia* (Naples, 1610). "At this time Naples, as other places, had an abundance of writers, more or less venal and unreliable, of books on nobility" (Croce 120). Pun on *zazzere*, long shocks of hair that fell to the shoulders, in vogue among seventeenth-century men (Guarini and Burani 151).

18. *li Campanile* (Neap.): Filiberto Campanile, author of *Delle armi overo delle imprese dei nobili* (Naples, 1618), and *Historia della famiglia di Sangro* (Naples, 1615) (Croce 120). Pun on *campanili* (bell towers), which were often built by private families as a status symbol.

19. *le Prete* (Neap.): Francesco de Pietri, author of *Dell'Historia Napolitana* (Naples, 1634), of which a large part is dedicated to the history of noble families (Croce 120). Pun on *preta* (Neap.), rock.

out to be a sideburn, every pole a toothpick, every pie a boiled chestnut, and every bombard ends up shooting wind.

FAB.: May this tongue of yours be blessed! How well you've dissected it, how well you've investigated it! In short, it's an ancient saying that a vain man is like a bladder.

IAC.: He who follows the court is put under a spell by that ugly witch and swells up with wind, feeds on the smoke of the roast with his bladder full of hope, waits for bubbles of soap and lye that pop on the way before they ever get to him. With his mouth wide open he's amazed at such magnificent splendor, and for a used rag and the privilege of sopping up some broth with a hard piece of stale bread in the servants' quarters he sells his freedom, which has such a high price! If you pour some solvent on this false gold, you'll see labyrinths of fraud and betrayal; you'll find, my brother, abysses of deceit and simulation; you'll discover a large town of biting and cruel tongues. One minute he's raised high on the palm of the hand, the next he's thrown down to the bottom of the barrel; one minute he's in his master's favors, the next he makes him sick; now he's poor and now he's rich, now fat and tall, now small and thin. He offers his services, he labors, he makes sacrifices, he sweats like a dog; instead of walking he moves at a trot and even carries water on his ears. But he's wasting his time, his work, and his seed, since everything is done for the wind, everything is thrown to sea. You can do as much as you like, and it comes to nil; you can make plans and projects based on your hopes, your merits, and your sacrifices, but every little wind that blows in the wrong direction dashes all your labors to the ground. At the end, you find in front of you a buffoon, a spy, a Ganymede,[20] a wild and tough-skinned animal, or else one who makes houses with two doors[21] or a man with two faces.

FAB.: Brother, you're giving me new life! Believe me, I've learned more in this short time, and more in this one sitting, than I did in the many years that I spent in school! A council of doctors once decreed, "He who serves in court, dies on the haystack."

IAC.: You've heard what a courtier is; now hear about those who serve on a lower scale. Take a servant: handsome, polite and

20. In Greek mythology, the beautiful Trojan prince carried off to Olympus by Zeus to be cup bearer to the gods.
21. "Someone who acquires favor by means of his wife, who does not refuse her favors to the powerful (the husband comes in one door as his wife's lover goes out the other)" (Croce 554).

clean, and by all means well reared. He bows down a thousand times, he tidies up your house, pulls up water, cooks,
brushes your clothes, curries the mule, washes the dishes, and
if you send him to the town square he returns before a bit of
spittle has had the time to dry;[22] he's incapable of standing
with his hands by his side or being idle, he rinses glasses and
empties your chamber pot. But if you want proof and put him
to the royal test, you'll find that every novelty is pretty but that
a donkey can't run forever; when three days have gone by
you'll discover that he's a deceiver, a lifelong sluggard, a first-
rate panderer, a con man, a glutton, a bettor: if he spends, he
skims a bit off; if he gives the mule some fodder, he gives her
everything from the grape to the seed; he corrupts your maid;
he goes through your pockets; and finally, to round things off,
in one clean sweep[23] he rids you even of your dustpan and then
kicks up his heels! You see what happens when you tie up the
pigs next to the cucumbers!

FAB.: Those are words of substance, truly juicy! Oh, wretched and
unfortunate is he who meets up with a wily servant!

IAC.: Here we have a swashbuckler: he's the leader of the pack of
thugs, the master builder of swaggerers, the boss of bullies,
the head of the trade council of roughnecks, the true ringleader of blusterers, and the abbot of valiant men. He pre-
sumes to terrify people and takes pride in it, frightening you
with a turn of his eyes; he paces like a pike soldier, with his
cape thrown over his shoulder, his hat sitting low on his eyes,
his collar turned up, his moustache curled, his eyes crossed,
and his hand on his hip; he boasts, he stamps his feet, even a
speck of dust bothers him, and he would start a fight with
flies. He always travels with a gang, and you hear him talk of
nothing but "driving it in": one of his men pierces, another
perforates, does people in, guts them, takes them off the list,
pokes the air out of them; one breaks bones, another hands
out thrashings, breaks down all resistance, beats up, smashes,
rips apart, decapitates, chops to pieces; one tears out people's
stomachs or livers, another fills them with punches, leaves
them black and blue, puts dents in them, sticks it to them: if
you hear him bragging, earth, hold onto your life! One jots

22. "A popular custom; to urge a servant or boy to run an errand quickly, you spit
on the ground and told him to be back before the spit dried" (Croce 124).
23. *n'arravoglia-Cuosemo* (Neap.): lit., "a wrapping up of Cosimo"; a robbery in
which the booty is quickly taken care of (Guarini and Burani 156).

things down in his notebook, another removes people from the world, sends them off to their relatives, squeezes every last coin out of them, puts this one under salt and plants that one in the ground and makes mincemeat[24] of that other one, shoves them around and cuts them down by the hundred, and always in ruin and uproar, splitting skulls and chopping off legs.

But his sword, no matter how much strength and valor it shows, is a virgin to blood and a widow to honor! And this crucible will uncover the copper beneath, for the bravado of his mouth is in fact the trembling in his heart; the daggers in his eyes his feet in retreat; the thunder of his boasting the thin shit of fear; the thrusting of his sleep the blow he receives upon waking; the endless allowances[25] for outbursts the sequestration of his sword, which, like an honorable woman, is ashamed to show itself naked. If he looks bilious, he's always sick to his stomach with fear; if he gnaws on lions, he's shitting rabbits; if he issues challenges, he's sewed up and stuffed; if he threatens, he gets a lashing and then another one; if he plays the dice of swashbucklery, he always meets up with his match. In words he is brave but in effects brief; he grabs for his steel and then weighs anchor; he looks for a scuffle and then scuffles to get away. He is more volatile than valiant, always encountering those who trip him up and then make sure to clarify things, those who set his jacket straight on his shoulders, those who shake him up and give him his change, those who settle his accounts, card his wool, go after him with a belt, give him a beating, make his ears ring and his molars shake, ransack the hold of his body, tear out his tonsils, and make him foam with blood; or else take out an orb, give him a good combing, dress him up in his best finery, plane him down, tickle him with a club, deal him a hook, or let loose an uppercut or a haymaker, a jawbreaker, a backhander, a whack, a punch, a smack, a head butt, a roundhouse, a clobbering, a kick, a slug, a fusillade strong enough to close a shop, or go for the jugular and try to strangle him! Enough said: he gets struck by the point and wounded by the blade; he talks like a man and runs like a deer; he sows spit and reaps eggplant;[26] and just when you think he's going to butt you like a billy goat, get the best of an

---

24. *mesesca* (Neap.): chunks of salted meat (Croce 126).
25. *liberanze* (Neap.): "a part of a debtor's assets allotted to him by a judge for his personal expenses" (Petrini 722).
26. I.e., bruises.

entire army, start spinning his spoons[27]—day breaks, and it's a fine one. He looks like a horse returning home; he slinks away, he's out of there, he weighs anchor and beats it; he disappears, gives his notice, and goes off to pick violets. He decamps and sneaks off and sinks out of sight and fires a departing shot; he throws up his heels and tears off and races away; he grabs his saddlebags and says, "Help me, heels, I'm putting you on now!" His anklebones touch his shoulders, and he has the foot of a hare; he wields his broadsword standing on his two legs; like a big sluggard he hobbles along and then flees; he takes his blows and then goes to jail!

FAB.: The spitting image of those blustering cocks! Oh, it's so true to life! And don't forget to mention, on my word, that you won't find more than one of them who can break a chain with his tongue, and even he's no good as a quail dog!

IAC.: One minute a flatterer praises you and raises you up to the top of the moon; he follows wherever you lead, he offers you line and bait, he blows in your sails, nor does he ever contradict you. If you're an ogre or an Aesop he'll say that you're Narcissus, and if you have a scar on your face he'll swear that it's a mole and such a pretty thing. If you're a lazy bum he'll say that you're Hercules or Samson;[28] if you come from a lowly family he'll maintain that it's the lineage of a count; in short, he'll pet you and caress you. But see that you don't get too attached to the words of these gluttonous chatterboxes, and see that you don't found your hopes on them! Don't believe them for a second, don't think they're worth a cent, don't let yourself be led on, but put them to the test in this crucible, and you'll be able to touch with your own hand their two faces: one in front and one behind, with one thing on their tongues and another in their hearts. They're all face licking and feigning: they cheat you, put you in the middle, trick you, steal from you, deceive you, hoodwink you, slip you one and bamboozle you, and they swindle you and blind you and burn you! When they humor you, know that a storm is brewing; they bite with their giggles, they filthy you with their praise, they make your head swell and your bag deflate. Their whole goal is to pilfer and to sponge, and with the bloodhounds of their praise and nursery rhymes and tall tales they go hunting for dough in your heart,

---

27. I.e., his arms.
28. Two traditional symbols of strength, the first of Greek mythology and the second biblical.

and they'll sell you bladders for lanterns to scrounge up a few silver coins so that they can go to whores or taverns.

FAB.: May their seed be lost! Masked men, who live to pull the wool over our eyes: on the outside they're Narcissus and on the inside the demon himself!

IAC.: Now listen as I tell you of a woman who'll take whoever comes or goes. You see a little doll, a lovely and lavish thing, a dove, a mirror, a jewel, a painted egg, a Fata Morgana,[29] a round full moon; she's as pretty as a picture, you could drink her up in a glass of water, she's a morsel fit for a lord, a little lass who steals away hearts. She ties you up with her tresses, she takes you out of circulation with her eyes, she does you in with her voice. But when she's thrown into the crucible, oh, what fire you see! So many snares and traps, ambushes and trafficking, tangles and webs! She prepares a thousand birdlimes, she throws out a thousand nets, she invents a thousand ruses, a thousand traps and schemes, lures and stratagems, mines and countermines, and entanglements and disentanglements. She pulls like a hook, lets blood like a barber, swindles like a gypsy, and a thousand times you think she's bubbly wine when she's really infected meat! When she speaks she plots and when she walks she weaves; when she laughs she spins intrigue and when she touches you it stains. And even if she doesn't send you to the hospital, you're treated like a bird or an animal, since her accursed dagger leaves you either without feathers or without fur![30]

FAB.: If you put what you said on paper, you could sell this story[31] for six coins a copy,[32] for it offers a fine example of how men should take care to be on the lookout and not hand themselves over to those women of ill repute, since they're false coin and the ruin of both the meat and the sauce.

IAC.: If by chance you notice someone at a window who seems to be a fairy, with blond hair that looks like braids of *caciocavallo*,[33] a forehead like a mirror, eyes that speak to you, and you see,

---

29. See tale 1.2 n9.

30. "The effect of one of the diseases spread by prostitutes" (Rak 273).

31. "Allusion to the popular pamphlets, or chapbooks, sold in great quantities at fairs and markets, which offered news, description of extraordinary events, horoscopes, prayers, and more" (Rak 273).

32. *pubbreche* (Neap.): the word can both mean a coin and a "public woman," or prostitute. See also tale 1.2 n2.

33. *casocavalluccio* (Neap.): a type of cheese, still common in southern Italy, that is usually either pear shaped or braided.

in short, two lips like slices of prosciutto, a real bombshell of a girl, tall and as well displayed as a banner: no sooner have your eyes alit on her than you die into a faint, you suffer agonies and are done for! Idiot, good-for-nothing! Make sure you test her in the crucible, for you'll find that what looks like a lavish beauty is a painted-over crapper, a whitewashed wall, a mask from Ferrara,[34] since a true bride hangs out her tapestries:[35] her braids are fake, her eyelashes dyed with soot from the stove and her face reddened with more than one pot of minium, and limewater and varnish besides; she preens, makes herself up, decks herself out, paints herself, and smears the stuff all over! She's all gotten up and full of creams, all rags and little jars, powders and little bottles, so that with such an apparatus it looks like she's planning to medicate some wounds! How many, how very many defects are covered by her skirts and slips! And besides, if she takes off her pattens,[36] with their endless insoles and padding, you'll see a giant turn into a dwarf!

FAB.: My word, you're making yourself clearer by the minute! I'm about to turn into a mummy; I'm amazed, I'm beside myself! Every pronouncement, brother, that you spit out is worth a zillion scudos! You can beat on all those things you've said with a maul and you won't budge a hair from that ancient proverb that goes, "A woman is like a chestnut: beautiful on the outside, rotten on the inside."

IAC.: Let's move on to the merchant, who makes change and exchanges, insures sailing vessels and finds clients, who trafficks, plots, and swindles, bribes tax collectors, buys in lots and then rakes in the profits. He builds ships and constructs houses; he fills his sewers to the brim, decorates his house like a bride, puts on a display worthy of a count, rustles silk, and doles it out left and right, supporting manservants and free women; and everyone holds him in envy. Wretched soul, if he is put in the crucible! For his wealth hangs in the air, his fortune is founded on smoke, a glassy fortune exposed to a thousand winds and at the mercy of the waves! Lovely in appearance, but your eyes are deceived; and just when you see

---

34. The masks of Ferrara were renowned. Prostitutes would often dress up as "Ferrara nymphs" (Guarini and Burani 165).
35. "Girls about to be married would decorate their houses by hanging coverlets and ornate cloths at the windows" (Guarini and Burani 165). Here the expression is used in the sense of "reveals in outright fashion her true possessions."
36. See tale 1.6 n7.

him inundated by coins as shiny as a horse's harness,[37] he loses the whole game for a little mistake.

FAB.: I can count them by the thousands. They've destroyed entire houses, their riches vanish into thin air—now you see it, now you don't!—and what they do in this world, with no regard and entirely lacking in feeling for their third or fourth heirs, is to leave a full pot of soup and an empty will!

IAC.: Here we have the lover: he believes the hours he spends and squanders in the service of Love to be happy ones. The flames and chains are sweet to him; the arrow that pierces him because of a great beauty is dear to him. He confesses that he craves death and barely manages to live; he calls suffering joy, delirium and torment amusement, heartbreak and love-sickness pleasure. He eats no meal that brings him benefit, gets no sleep that is worth anything: half-baked sleep and meals without gusto. Though he earns no pay he patrols outside the beloved doors, though he is no architect he makes sketches and builds castles in the air, and though he is no executioner he tortures his own life without end. But in spite of all this he is overjoyed and grows fat, and the more that dart pricks and pokes him, the more lard he puts on; the more the fire cooks him, the more he parties and plays, and he considers it his most felicitous fortune to be knotted tight by a rope! But if you put him in the crucible, you'll realize there's a substratum of madness, a sort of consumption, a state ever uncertain between fear and hope, ever suspended between doubt and suspicion, a never-ending state like that of Mister Basile's cat,[38] who cries one minute and laughs the next! He walks with great difficulty and as if he's lost; he speaks in mumbles and stutters; he sends his brain out to pasture at all hours; and at every moment he has a heart like a rag, a face like a freshly laundered cloth, a heated breast, and a frozen soul. And even if he finally warms the ice and chips away at the stone of the one he loves, she who is nearest to him when she is farthest away, he no sooner tastes the sweetness than he repents!

FAB.: Oh, miserable is he who meets up with these headaches! Wretched he who gets his foot caught in this trap! For that

---

37. "The breast-plates of horses' harnesses were decorated with shiny studs and panels" (Guarini and Burani 166).
38. Perhaps an allusion to a beloved cat of the author.

Blind One sends pleasures by the handful and torments by the arm's length.

IAC.: And the poor poet sends out floods of octaves and mouthfuls of sonnets, and demolishes paper and ink; he dries up his brain and consumes his elbows and his time, and only because people in this world consider him an oracle. He walks around like one possessed, strained and in a daze, thinking of the conceits he kneads in his imagination; he talks to himself in the street, finding thousands and thousands of new turns of phrase: "towering pupils, liquid surmounting of flowers and fronds, funereal and stridulous waves, animated pyropes of lubricious hope," "oh, such immoderate presumption!"[39] But if he is put to the test of the crucible, everything goes up in smoke: "Oh, what a lovely composition!" and there it remains. "What a madrigal!" and it's all wasted breath. And when he is sounded, the more verses he produces, the smaller the cut. He praises those who despise him, exalts those who trouble him, stores up eternal memories of those who have forgotten about him, and gives his labors to those who never give him a crumb. This is how he dissipates his life: singing for glory and crying for misery.

FAB.: Indeed, the days of San Martino[40] are past, when poets were raised on high! In this dark age, Maecenases[41] are ground to bits; and in Naples, as elsewhere—and it makes me croak with pain—laurel comes after vegetable greens in line!

IAC.: The astrologer, too, gets many, so very many questions from all sides. One wants to know if he'll have a baby boy, another if it's the propitious time, another if he'll win the court case, and another if fate is working against him. One wants to know if his mistress is thinking of him; another if it's going to thunder or if there will be an eclipse. And so he tells his tall tales, so many that it would take a bar to ward them off, and he guesses half of one right and is wrong on a hundred others.

---

39. These lines in quotes are in Italian in the original text and are a parody of the language of the Petrarchan love lyric.

40. *chille sante Martine* (Neap.): San Martino falls on November 11 and is traditionally a harvest festival in which the new wine is tasted. The sense is, therefore, of "the good old days"; Rak notes that it was a common expression in Neapolitan literature (274).

41. C. C. Maecenas (62?–8 BC) was the protector and patron of a famous group of Latin writers (including Virgil, Propertius, and Horace). Wordplay: *Mecenate* (Maecenas) vs. *macenate* (ground).

But inside this crucible you can see whether he's powder or flour: he traces quadrants, but is long and wide; he draws houses, but has neither house nor fire. He shows his figures and uncovers ugly stories; he climbs up to the stars and finds himself with his ass on the ground; at last, in rags and tatters, all ribbons and shreds, his pants fall down and then you see the most genuine astrology of all, for he shows you his astrolabe[42] and its spheres!

FAB.: You make me laugh, brother, even if I'm not in the mood! But those who believe these people make me laugh even harder, until my sides split, since they presume to make predictions for others, and they can't even predict what's about to land on top of them: while they're gazing at the stars they fall into a ditch![43]

IAC.: Someone else thinks he's a big shot,[44] and he pulls the wrinkles out of his socks and measures his words and spits roundly, and thinks he's the best in the world. If you're dealing with poetry he takes a standing jump and passes Petrarch by; if it's philosophy he beats Aristotle by fifteen points and a foul;[45] in arithmetic, Cantone's no match for him; in the art of war, Cornazzano is fried; in architecture, Euclid go home! If it's music he finds fault with Venosa; if it's law he sends Farinaccio to his ruin; if it's language he doesn't give a shit about Boccaccio;[46] he strings together judgments and skewers suggestions even if he's not worth a thing at skittles. But if he's put to the

---

42. "An ancient instrument used to measure the height of the stars on the horizon, vs. the penis" (Rak 274).

43. "As did the Greek philosopher Thales of Miletus [c. 636–546 BC] who, according to legend, fell into a ditch as he was contemplating the stars" (Guarini and Burani 171).

44. *Patrasso* (Neap.): the *patres* of the Bible vs. the Greek city.

45. Terms taken from various games (Croce 139).

46. The poet Francesco Petrarca (1304–74) was one of the models for the European lyric tradition; Aristotle (384–322 BC) was the Greek philosopher whose works were an essential point of reference for early modern scientific research; Oberto Cantone was a Genoese mathematician whose *L'uso prattico dell'aritmetica* (1599) circulated widely at this time; Antonio Cornazzano of Piacenza wrote *De l'arte militar* (1493); Euclid, the mathematician of Alexandria (third century BC), is best known for his treatise on geometry, the *Stoicheia* (*Elements*), in which the basis of architecture in geometry is described; Carlo Gesualdo, prince of Venosa, was the most famous composer of madrigals of the time; the Roman Prospero Farinaccio (1544–1618) was one of the best-known penal lawyers of the time; Boccaccio (1313–75) was the author of the *Decameron,* the collection of *novelle* or short tales that became one of the narrative models for European prose (see Croce 555–56).

test it's found, in conclusion, that he's a ninny on a pile of books.

FAB.: Oh, how beastly it is to presume too much! A good student used to say, "He who thinks he knows the most is the most ignorant."

IAC.: Where does that leave alchemy and the alchemist? He already considers himself content and esteems himself happy, and he promises even greater things in twenty or thirty years; he tells of stupendous things that he has found while distilling with his alembic, which he hopes will make him rich. But once he's put in the crucible he's chewed to pieces, and then you can see if his art is adulterated and just how blinded he is: he who, greasy and full of smoke, has placed the columns of his hope upon jars of glass and all of his thoughts and plans amid smoke; he who, while he fans the flames with his bellows, at the same time uses his words to feed the desire of those who wait for something that will never come. He goes hunting for secrets and is proclaimed to be mad; in search of the prime matter he loses his own form; he thinks he can multiply gold and diminishes what he has; he imagines he can cure diseased metals and ends up at the hospital himself. And instead of making quicksilver coagulate, so that it can be spent and is worth something, he curdles his own life; and while he thinks he is transforming every metal into the most refined gold, he transforms himself from a man into a horse.[47]

FAB.: It is, without a doubt, madness to take on this enterprise! I've seen a hundred houses ruined, sunk to the bottom! Nothing ever comes of it, and desperate in his great hopes, he ever wanders, smoky and famished.

IAC.: But tell me: what else do you want for three coins?[48]

FAB.: Here I am with my mouth hanging open, ready to listen to you.

IAC.: And I'd carry on all the way to the rosette.[49]

FAB.: Keep on going then, now that you're in the mood.

IAC.: I would, if my soul weren't on edge, since dinner time has already passed! So let's beat it out of here, and come, if it pleases you, to my shop, and we'll get our choppers going, for "there's never a lack of crusts at a poor man's house."

47. *cavallo* (Neap.): horse vs. *callo*, a coin of little value (Croce 141).
48. Perhaps an allusion to the price of popular stories contained in chapbooks, which were sold, at this time, at fairs and markets (Rak 273, 275).
49. See tale 1.10 n31.

The words of this eclogue were accompanied by such graceful ges-
tures and lovely twists of the mouth that you could have pulled the
teeth of everyone who was listening.[50] *And since the crickets were*
calling the people to retire, the prince dismissed the women on the
condition that they come the next morning to continue their enter-
prise, and he and the slave retired into his chambers.

End of the first day.

---

50. Since everyone had their mouths open with laughter.

II

THE SECOND DAY

Dawn had come out to grease the wheels of the Sun's coach, and, after the effort of removing the grass from the hubs of the wheel with a stick, became as red as a summer apple. Then Tadeo got out of bed, and after a good long stretch he called the slave and they got dressed in four snaps and then went down to the garden, where they found that the ten women had already arrived. And after he had four fresh figs picked for each of them, figs that with their pauper's skin, hanged man's neck, and whore's tears[1] made everyone's mouth water, a thousand games[2] commenced so that the time left before eating might be deceived. And they overlooked neither Anca Nicola;[3] nor the Wheel of Kicks;[4] nor Watch Your Wife;[5] nor Covalera;[6] nor Buddy of Mine,

---

1. "The requisites for a ripe fig: the skin about to crack open, a long stem, and sticky discharge at the bottom" (Rak 280).
2. "Children's and society games have an important role in the structure of *Lo cunto*, a text destined for entertainment" (Rak 280). Besides this catalogue of thirty-one popular games, there are another fourteen mentioned at the start of day 4. Most of these, as well as others, also appear in Basile's letters published with Giulio Cesare Cortese's *Vaiasseide*. In M. A. Perillo's pastoral drama *La pescatrice* (1630), a similar catalogue can be found (Croce 145).
3. "One child bends down and puts his head on the lap of another sitting child, who then holds his hands over the eyes of the first. A third jumps onto the back of the first and sings 'Anca Nicola, you're beautiful and you're good, And you're married: How many horns do you have on your head?' as he puts a hand on the other's head and lifts up a certain number of fingers. The other guesses, and if he does not guess right, the round is repeated. The game and song are quite ancient, appearing, for example, in a scene painted at Herculaneum" (Ferdinando Galiani, *Del dialetto napoletano* 154–55; cit. Croce 556–57).
4. See frame tale n2.
5. Similar to the Sicilian game described by Pitrè: "One person kneels, and plays the part of the 'wife.' The 'mother' (game-leader) walks around him, just as the other players are doing, and defends the wife's head from their blows, which come in the form of punches, kicks, and shoves. If the mother, who has the role of 'wife watcher,' touches one of them, the touched person is 'it' and the previous wife becomes the game-leader" (*Giochi fanciulleschi* no. 168, 290–91; cit. Guarini and Burani 176–77).
6. A variant of hide-and-seek, "the game of the brooding hen [*covalera* means 'she who broods'] is played in Naples by older girls in this way: eight or ten gather together and first play at *tocco* [a sort of finger game to determine who takes the first

I'm Wounded;[7] nor Proclamation and Command;[8] nor the Master Is Welcome;[9] nor Little Swallow, My Little Swallow;[10] nor Empty the Cask;[11] nor Jump a Palm's-Length;[12] nor Stone in Your Lap;[13] nor Fish in the Sea, Go After Him;[14] nor Anola Tranola, Pizza Fontanola;[15] nor King Macebearer;[16] nor Blinded Cat;[17] nor Lamp to Lamp;[18] nor

---

turn] to see who will be the brooding hen. The one to whom it falls must swear not to look where the others are going to hide; when they have hidden they call out to the brooding hen: 'Come out! Come out!' The brooding hen gets up and starts looking for the others; when she finds one she embraces her, saying 'Bird, bird!' and the one caught becomes the brooding hen" (B. Zito, *Defennemiento della Vaiasseide* 68; cit. Croce 557).

7. Similar to the Sicilian game described by Pitrè: "Two children lie face-down on the ground, head to head, and cover themselves completely, so they can neither see nor be seen; the person assisting them is called the 'mother.' The other players stand and hit, one at a time, the two who are covered. The one hit says to the other: 'Buddy of mine, I'm wounded,' and the other: 'Who was it?' If the answer is correct, the player who guessed gets out from under cover and takes the place of the hitter, who goes down" (*Giochi fanciulleschi* no. 110, 200–201; cit. Guarini and Burani 177–78).

8. "Game whose words were modeled on the ritualistic formulas used in public proclamations" (Croce 558).

9. Also the name of a dance (Guarini and Burani 177).

10. "One girl kneels, others put their hands on her head, and another runs around the circle singing 'My little swallow, my swallow, get up and dance.' 'What do I need to get up and dance for?' 'Your father wants you, for he intends for you to marry,' etc. When the song ends, the girl singing takes one of the other girls and starts again, until all of the girls are 'taken,' with the exception of the girl in the middle" (Corazzini, *I componimenti minori della letteratura popolare italiana* [1877]; cit. Croce 558).

11. "A child sits on the knees of an adult, who bounces him in imitation of a horse trotting and chants: 'Piripirotta, empty the cask, Piripirino, empty the wine.' On the last verse, the adult opens his knees so that the child falls through them" (Luigi Molinaro del Chiaro, *Giambattista Basile* [a journal] 3.45; cit. Croce 558).

12. Described in a sonnet in Sgruttendio's *Tiorba a taccone* (1.37) (Croce 558).

13. One child goes around to others with an object (a rock, a ring, etc.) closed in her fist, and pretends to let it slip into each of their hands or lap. She then asks one of them who she has really given the object to (Pitrè, *Giochi* 97–98; cit. Croce 558).

14. *'ncagnarlo* (Neap.): lit., to throw oneself onto someone like a rabid dog.

15. In tale 5.3 these words are one of the magic formulas that Betta uses.

16. The macebearer (*mazziere*) was an employee of the tribunal or a confraternity who proceeded processions with a long club (Croce 559); also a card dealer.

17. A variation of blindman's bluff.

18. "Not so much a game as a common beginning for games. One child puts his index finger on the palm of another's hand, and sings: 'To the lamp, to the lamp, some will die and others survive; to Salvatore's parish, and whoever is left goes to prison'. The second child closes his hand, and if he is able to grab the other's finger, the first 'goes under'" (Corazzini, *I componimenti* 108–09; cit. Croce 559).

Hang My Curtain;[19] nor Butt and Drum;[20] nor Long Beam;[21] nor the Little Hens; nor the Old Man Hasn't Come;[22] nor Empty the Barrel;[23] nor Mammara and Hazelnut;[24] nor Seesaw; nor the Outlaws;[25] nor Argue the Case, Court Clerk;[26] nor Come Out, Come Out;[27] nor What's in Your Hand, the Needle and Thread?;[28] nor Bird, Bird, Sleeve of Iron;[29] nor Greco Wine or Vinegar;[30] nor Open the Door for the Poor Falcon.[31]

---

19. "A number of children stand in a line, holding hands. As the game leader says: 'Hang, hang my curtain' the children stretch out their arms as far as they can, and answer: 'I've hung it.' Then, when they hear: 'Make a knot,' the whole line goes under the arms of the first and second in line, and answer: 'I've made it.' The arms of the second child are now crossed on her chest. This sequence is repeated until everyone is in this position. The game usually ends with everyone rolling around on the ground" (E. Rocco, *Giambattista Basile* 7.6–7; cit. Croce 559).

20. A variation on blindman's bluff. Pitrè describes a game that is probably the same, "A tafara e tafaruni": "A good number of children make a circle without holding hands. One of them, blindfolded, is put in the middle. The others take turns touching and pinching him on various parts of his body. The next to last to do this pinches his behind and says: 'Tafara'; the last slaps him and adds 'Tafaruni.' The blindfolded child has to guess the identity of the last to touch him, who is then blindfolded for the next game" (*Giochi* nos. 109, 200; cit. Guarini and Burani 179). In tale 5.3 this expression appears as another of the enchanted formulas.

21. A version of leapfrog (Guarini and Burani 179).

22. Both of these are mentioned, but not described, by Pitrè.

23. "A game in which two children stand back to back, lock arms, and then take turns lifting each other off the ground" (Guarini and Burani 179).

24. "Two children hold hands and stretch out their arms, forming a hollow like a chair and clasping their hands as if pledging their faith. Then another child sits on the 'chair,' and they carry her through the house, singing: 'A sack of kicks for Mammara and hazelnuts; your mother did so bad that she broke the cauldron'" (Zito, *Defennemiento* 85; cit. Croce 560).

25. "A game similar to Cops and Robbers, Soldiers and Bandits, etc." (Guarini and Burani 179).

26. "The game imitated, in some ways, judiciary proceedings" (Guarini and Burani 179).

27. Variant of Covalera (Croce 560).

28. Possibly a variant of Stone in Your Lap (Guarini and Burani 179).

29. Another variant of Covalera (Croce 560).

30. Greco is a wine produced near Naples.

31. "Everyone holds hands and moves around in a circle, leaving one in the middle who has to try to escape by passing under the arms of one of the couples. When she has sung 'Open the door for the poor falcon,' all of the others lift their arms as high as they can and reply: 'The doors are open, if the falcon wants to come in.' If in that moment the one in the middle is able to escape through one of the openings before being stopped by the joined hands, which quickly lower to block her way, she wins; if not, she goes back and the game continues. . . . The name of falcon is given to the one in the middle, as if she were in a cage" (Galiani, *Del dialetto* 146; cit. Croce 561).

But when the hour had arrived for them to fill their bellies[32] they sat down at the table, and when they had eaten, the prince told Zeza to act the part of the valiant woman and start her tale. She had so many of them in her head that they were overflowing, and calling them all to order she chose the best one, which I'll now tell you.

---

32. *'nchire lo stefano* (Neap.): *stefano* is stomach. Stefano and Trinculo (the term *trincole* is also used in tale 1.10) were the two Neapolitans in Shakespeare's *The Tempest* (Croce 561).

I

PETROSINELLA

First Entertainment of the Second Day

A pregnant woman eats some parsley from an ogress's garden, is caught in the act, and promises the ogress the offspring she is about to bear. She gives birth to Petrosinella, and the ogress takes her and locks her in a tower. A prince steals her away and with the help of three acorns they are able to flee from the danger of the ogress, and after Petrosinella is brought to her lover's house she becomes a princess.

"My desire to keep the princess happy is so great that all last night, when not a thing could be heard high or low, I did nothing but rummage in the old chests of my mind and search all the closets of my memory, choosing from among the things that the good soul of madam Chiarella Vusciolo, my uncle's grandmother, used to tell—may she rest in God's glory, and to your health!—the tales that seemed most appropriate to distribute to you one a day, those that, if I haven't put my eyes on backward, I imagine will please you. And if they prove not to be squadrons that send the sorrows of your heart to certain defeat, they will at least be trumpets that give these fellow storytellers of mine a wake-up call to enter the battlefield with more transport than my poor forces allow me, so that the riches of their minds may compensate for the lackings of my own words.

"There once was a pregnant woman named Pascadozia who, while sitting at a window that overlooked an ogress's garden, noticed a lovely bed of parsley, for which she got such a craving that she felt she would faint. And so, not being able to resist, she kept close watch until the ogress went out, and then she picked a handful of it. But after the ogress came back home and wanted to make a sauce, she realized that a sickle had been at work and said, 'May my neck snap if I don't collar

---

AT 310: The Maiden in the Tower, and AT 313: The Girl as Helper in the Hero's Flight. Croce mentions versions from Pitrè (*Fiabe, nov. e racc. siciliani* 20, "The Old Woman in the Garden," as well as 13 and 18) and Imbriani (16, "Prezzemolina"). Readers will also, of course, recognize the tale as a predecessor of Grimm 12, "Rapunzel." A variant closer to Basile's time can be found in Charlotte-Rose Caumont de la Force's "Persinette" (in Zipes, ed., *The Great Fairy Tale Tradition*).

this thief and make him repent, so that he may learn to eat from his own cutting board and not to dip his spoon into the pot of others.'

"But the poor pregnant woman continued to go down to the garden, until one morning she was caught by the ogress who, all angry and livid, said to her, 'I've got you, you swindling thief! What, you think you pay rent on this garden, so that you can come with so little discretion and pinch my herbs? On my word, I'll send you to Rome for your penance!'[1] The unfortunate Pascadozia started to apologize, explaining that it wasn't because she was a glutton or ravenous that the demon had blinded her and made her commit this sin, but because she was pregnant and afraid that the face of her newborn would be sown with parsley; in fact, the ogress should be grateful that Pascadozia hadn't sent her a sty or two.[2] 'The bride wants more than just words!' answered the ogress. 'This chatter is no bait for me! You're finished with the job of life if you don't promise to give me the baby you're going to have, and it matters not whether it's a boy or a girl.' To escape the dangerous situation in which she found herself, poor Pascadozia swore to this with one hand on the other, and the ogress let her go free.

"When it came time to give birth Pascadozia bore a daughter so beautiful that she was a joy to behold, and she named her Petrosinella on account of the lovely little clump of parsley on her chest.[3] Petrosinella grew a span every day, and when she was seven her mother sent her to a teacher. And whenever she was on the road and ran into the ogress, the ogress would say to her, 'Tell your mother to remember the promise!' And she bothered her about it so many times that one day the poor mother, who couldn't bear to listen to this music any longer, said to her daughter, 'If you run into the old woman again and she asks you about that damned promise, you answer her, "Take her!" '

"When Petrosinella, who knew nothing about the matter, next encountered the ogress, she repeated the usual proposition, to which Petrosinella innocently answered what her mother had told her to say.

---

1. "A pilgrimage to the sacred sites of Rome was a common penance" (Rak 294).

2. "According to popular belief, if someone fails to satisfy a pregnant woman's cravings, he or she will be punished with a sty, resulting in red and swollen eyelids" (Croce 148).

3. *Petrosinella*: lit., "little parsley." Here, as in the frame tale, we find an allusion to another, much more widespread popular belief regarding a pregnant woman's craving: that if it is not satisfied and the woman touches a part of her own body, the shape of whatever was craved will appear on the newborn's body in that same spot. Birthmarks are, in fact, called *voglie*: "longings" or "fancies." Penzer notes, "The peasantry are convinced of the necessity of gratifying the longings of a pregnant woman. Should this be impossible, charms and spells are resorted to so as to prevent miscarriage and other evils" (1:140).

"Dì a mammata che se allecorde de la 'mprommessa!"
["Tell your mother to remember the promise!"]

At that, the ogress grabbed her by the hair, took her to a wood—where the Sun's horses never entered, so as not to pay rent on those pastures of shadow—and locked her in a tower that she had created with a spell. This tower was without doors or stairs; it had just one little window through which the ogress climbed up and down on Petrosinella's hair, which was very long, like a ship boy uses shrouds to climb the masts.

"Now it happened one day that while the ogress was away from the tower, Petrosinella stuck her head out of the hole and spread her braids in the sun.[4] The son of a prince passed by, and when he saw those two golden banners summoning souls to enlist in the ranks of Love and noticed that heart-enchanting face of a Siren[5] amid those precious waves, he became hopelessly infatuated with such beauty. And after sending her a memorial of sighs, it was decreed that the stronghold should be surrendered to his grace. The negotiations went so well that the prince received nods of the head in exchange for kisses sent on his hands, winks of the eye in exchange for bows, thanks in exchange for offers, hopes for promises, and kind words for salaams. When this had gone on for many days they became so friendly that they made an appointment to meet, which had to take place at night—when the moon played 'Mute Sparrow'[6] with the stars—at which time Petrosinella would give the ogress a sleeping potion and then hoist the prince up on her hair.

"And so they remained. The appointed hour came and the prince arrived at the tower. He gave a whistle and Petrosinella lowered her braids, which he grabbed with both hands, saying, 'Heave ho!' And when he had been pulled up, he threw himself through the little window of the room and made himself a meal of that parsley of the sauce of Love, and then—before the Sun taught its horses to jump through the circle of the zodiac—lowered himself down on the same golden ladder and went off to look after his affairs.

"Since they continued to do this often, one of the ogress's neighbors caught on, and, troubling herself about it like Rosso,[7] she decided to stick her face in the shit. She told the ogress to take heed, for

---

4. "Women of the time would dye their hair blonde by smearing it with a certain substance and then letting it dry in the sun for many hours. While doing this they circled their foreheads with a straw visor" (Croce 561).
5. "The sirens were among the most popular mythological icons in Campania" (Rak 294).
6. A children's game; *passara* (sparrow) is also a euphemism for the female genitals.
7. "Rosso, a thief, was being taken to the gallows, and when the carriage he was in jolted him due to the broken pavestones, he begged his guard to tell the appropriate magistrate to repair the street, since it was a disgrace that those passing along it on their way to be hanged had to feel their insides being shaken up. The expression 'Rosso's troubles' is Florentine in origin" (Croce 562).

Petrosinella was making love with a certain young man and she suspected that things might have gone even farther because she could see
the buzz of activity and trafficking, and feared that once they had
made a clean sweep, they would vacate the house before May.[8] The
ogress thanked her neighbor for the helpful warning and told her that
she would take care of blocking Petrosinella's way, and that besides,
she couldn't possibly escape because she had put a spell on her. If she
didn't have three acorns in her hand, which were hidden in one of the
rafters in the kitchen, trying to slip out of there was a lost cause.

"While they were engaged in this talk Petrosinella, who had kept
her ears pricked since she was a bit suspicious of the neighbor, heard
the whole conversation, and—as soon as Night shook out its black
clothes so they wouldn't be eaten by moths—when the prince arrived
in the usual manner she got him to climb up into the rafters. They
found the acorns, which Petrosinella knew how to use because she
had been enchanted by the ogress, made a ladder of string down
which they both went, and then threw up their heels and took off in
the direction of the city.

"But as they were leaving they were seen by the neighbor, who
began to scream and call for the ogress, and her screams were so loud
that she woke her up. When the ogress heard that Petrosinella had escaped she went down that same ladder, which was still tied to the little window, and began to race after the lovers. They saw her coming
after them faster than an unreined horse, and thought they were lost;
but then Petrosinella remembered the three acorns and immediately
threw one of them on the ground. Out sprung a Corsican hound; and
was it terrifying, oh, dear mother! With its mouth hanging open it
ran toward the ogress, barking, intending to eat her up in one bite.
But since she was slyer than Old Nick himself, she reached into her
little sack, pulled out a loaf of bread, and gave it to the dog, which
made its tail lower and its fury subside.

"The ogress returned to running after the fleeing ones, and Petrosinella, seeing her draw close, threw down the second acorn. Out
came a ferocious lion, which, beating its tail on the ground and shaking its mane, opened its gaping jaws two spans wide and prepared to
crush the ogress between them. The ogress backed off, skinned a
donkey that she found grazing in a field, put on its skin, and ran back
to confront the lion, which thought she really was a donkey and was
so scared that it's still running.

8. "That is, before May 4, which is still, in Naples, the day designated for moving
and changing residence," and was established as such by the viceroy Count of Lemos
(1610–16) (Croce 150).

"Having jumped this second ditch, the ogress returned to chasing after those poor youngsters. When they heard the footfalls and saw the cloud of dust that rose up to the sky, they concluded that the ogress was back again. Since she suspected that the lion might still be after her, the ogress had not taken off the donkey skin, and when Petrosinella threw down the third acorn, out came a wolf, which—without giving the ogress time to find another solution—gobbled her up as if she really were a donkey. Now that the lovers were freed from their predicament, they set off at a leisurely pace to the prince's kingdom, where, with the kind permission of his father, the prince took Petrosinella for his wife. And thus they proved, after so many tempests of travail, that *just one hour in a safe harbor, and a hundred years of bad fortune are forgotten.*"

2

GREEN MEADOW

Second Entertainment of the Second Day

Nella is loved by a prince, who by means of a glass tunnel goes often to take his pleasure with her. But when the passageway is broken by Nella's envious sisters, he gets all cut up and comes close to death. By a strange twist of fate Nella hears of a possible remedy for his ills, administers it to the sick man, cures him, and takes him for her husband.

Oh, my dear, they listened to Zeza's tale right up until the end with such pleasure that if it had lasted another hour it would have seemed like a moment to them! And since it was now Cecca's turn, she carried on with the speaking in this manner: "It is truly a strange thing, if you think about it, that from the same piece of wood may be carved statues of gods and gallows beams, emperors' thrones and covers for chamber pots; just as it is also curious that from the same rag is made paper which, after it is used for love letters, may receive a fair lady's kisses or wipe an ugly asshole: and this would make the best astrologer in the world lose his mind. The same thing can be said about a single mother from whom is born a good daughter and a ruinous one, one full of gas and one a hard worker, one beautiful and one ugly, one envious and one loving, one a chaste Diana and one a ducky little Catherine,[1] one who encounters misfortune and one who has good luck. Because according to reason we're all of the same stock and should all have the same nature. But let's leave this topic to those who know more about it. I'll merely give you an example of what I've

---

AT 432: The Prince as Bird. Croce mentions popular versions of this tale from Pitrè and Imbriani. The name "Verde Prato" (Green Meadow) does not appear in the tale itself (perhaps Basile had intended to use it for the prince), but a possible source is M. A. Biondo's *Angitia cortigiana de natura del Cortigiano* (1550), in which "It happened that a gentleman by the name of Green Feather came to die because of a female friend of his. He had fallen in love with a very noble and courtly lady by the name of Lucente, and since he had no other way to enter into where she lived [. . .] he had a tunnel of crystal made" (cit. Rak 308). See also Pitrè, *Fiabe, nov. e racc. sic.* 38, "The Magic Balls," and Gonzenbach 27, "The Green Bird."

1. *na Caterina papara* (Neap.): "A woman famous at this time for her dissolute and criminal life. The family name 'Paparo' [duck] existed in Naples" (Croce 153).

been referring to with a tale of three daughters of the same mother, in which you'll see the difference in behavior that brought the wicked ones to their grave and the honorable girl to the top of the wheel of Fortune.

"There once was a mother who had three daughters, two of whom were so unlucky that nothing ever turned out right for them; all their plans went awry and all their hopes ended up in crumbs. But the youngest, Nella, took her good fortune with her when she left her mother's belly, and I do believe that when she was born everything was orchestrated so that she would be given the very best possible: the heavens gave her the zenith of its light, Venus the prime cut of beauty, Amor the first cream of his strength, Nature the most perfect of comportments. She offered no service that was not done flawlessly; she began no enterprise that was not completed in exemplary fashion; she joined no dance without leaving it with honor. For this reason she was less envied by those hernia-bound sisters of hers than she was loved and held dear by everyone else, and her sisters' desire to bury her underground was not as strong as the desire of other people to raise her up high on the palms of their hands.

"In that land there was an enchanted prince who sailed on the sea of her beauty, and he threw the hook of amorous servitude to that bream so many times that he finally stuck her in the gills of her affection and made her his. And in order to take their pleasure without causing any suspicion on the part of her mother, who was a wicked little demon, the prince gave her a special powder, and he constructed a crystal tunnel that ran from the royal palace to right up under Nella's bed, even though it was eight miles away. And he said to her, 'Whenever you want to feed me like a sparrow on your lovely grace put a little bit of this powder in the fire, and I'll immediately come through the tunnel and respond to your call, running down a road of crystal so that I can enjoy that face of silver.'

"Once things were thus arranged, there wasn't a night that the prince didn't do in-and-out and come-and-go through the tunnel. Finally the sisters, who were spying on Nella's affairs, discovered the dirty business and decided to make her choke on her tasty morsel. And so they went and broke the tunnel at various points in order to tangle up the thread of those amours; and when the poor girl threw the powder in the fire to give her lover the signal to come, he who usually came racing in a naked frenzy battered himself up so badly on the shards of crystal that he was a sorry sight. Not being able to proceed, he turned back, all sliced up like a pair of

German breeches,[2] and then put himself to bed and summoned all the doctors of the city.

"But since the crystal was enchanted, his wounds were so fatal that no human remedy was of any use. For this reason the king, seeing that his son's situation was desperate, had a proclamation issued: whoever found a remedy for his son's illness would be given his son for a husband, if a woman, and half of his kingdom, if a man. When Nella, who was madly in love with the prince, heard this she colored her face, disguised herself, and, unbeknownst to her sisters, left home to go see him before he died.

"Since by that time the golden balls with which the Sun plays in the celestial courts had taken a downward turn to the West, night overtook Nella in a wood close to the house of an ogre where, in order to flee danger, she climbed up a tree. The ogre and his wife were at the table, and they had the windows open to let in some fresh air. When they had finished emptying jugs and putting out lamps,[3] they began to chat about this and that, and since she was as close to them as a nose is to a mouth, Nella could hear every word. Among other things, the ogress said to her husband, 'My hairy darling, what have you been hearing? What are people talking about in the world?' And he answered, 'Let's just say that there's not a corner that's clean, and everything is topsy-turvy and all awry.' 'All right, but what about it?' replied his wife. And the ogre: 'I could go on and on about the deceits perpetrated; you hear of things that would make you jump out of your clothes: buffoons rewarded, scoundrels esteemed, lazybones honored, assassins protected, counterfeiters[4] defended, and respectable men barely appreciated or esteemed. But since it's enough to make you explode, I'll tell you only about what happened to the king's son, who built a crystal road on which he traveled, naked, to take his pleasure with a lovely wench. I don't know how but the passageway was broken, and when he tried to go through it he got himself shredded up so badly that before he plugs up all those holes, the drainpipe of his life is going to come completely unclogged. And although the king has had a proclamation issued that promises great things to whoever heals him, it's a wasted effort, and he might as well

---

2. "Heavily decorated velvet breeches, cut in long strips up to the knee, that German lords of the time wore" (Croce 155).

3. "*Lampa* is both a lamp and a measure (2 carafes) used for wine in some areas of the Kingdom of Naples" (Croce 156).

4. *zannettarie* (Neap.): "money-clippers, especially of half-carlin coins, which took on the name of *zannette*" (Croce 156).

pick his teeth with it; the best he can do is get the mourning clothes ready and prepare the funeral.'

"Upon hearing the cause of the prince's illness Nella, heaving with great sobs, said to herself, 'Who was that accursed soul who broke the duct where my splendid bird passed, so that the pipe where my own spirits pass is about to shatter?' But since the ogress had started talking again, Nella grew silent and mute, and listened. She was saying, 'And is it possible that the world is lost for this poor lord? And that no cure for his illness can be found? Go tell medicine to stick itself in the oven! Go tell the doctors to wrap a cord around their necks! Go tell Galen and Mesua[5] to give the master back his money, since they're not capable of finding the right prescriptions for the health of this prince!' 'Listen, my little drooler,' answered the ogre, 'doctors aren't obliged to find cures that go beyond Nature's own limits. This is not a passing colic, where all you need is a bath of oil; it's not flatulence, which you get rid of with suppositories of laxative figs and mouse shit; it's not a fever, which goes away with medicine and diets; nor are they ordinary wounds that call for tow plasters or oil of hypericum.[6] The spell put on the broken glass has the same effect that onion juice[7] has on an arrow tip: it makes the wound incurable. There's only one thing that could save his life, but don't make me say what, for it is of some weight.' 'Tell me, my tusky,' replied the ogress, 'tell me what it is, if you don't want to see me dead!'

"And the ogre: 'I'll tell you, but you must promise not to share it with a living soul, for it would mean the destruction of our family and the ruin of our life.' 'Have no doubt, my dear, darling little husband,' answered the ogress, 'you'll see pigs with horns, monkeys with tails, and moles with eyes before a word of it ever escapes my mouth!' And when she had sworn to it with one hand on the other, the ogre said to her, 'Now you should know that there's not one thing under the heavens and on the earth that could save the prince from the thugs of Death except for our own fat,[8] which, if used to lubricate his wounds, would result in the sequestration of the soul that presently wants to vacate the house of his body.'

"Nella heard this little conversation and let things take their own

---

5. Galen (c. AD 129–200) was a Greek physician and writer whose works constituted one of the main foundations of medieval medical knowledge in the West. Mesua (Yaḳya ibn Māsawaih.) was "an Arab physician (c. mid-9th century) whose works were translated and printed in Italian until the late 16th century" (Rak 309).
6. Hypericum perforatum, or St. John's wort, a medicinal plant with astringent properties.
7. "The juice of onion was, according to popular belief, an irritant" (Rak 309).
8. "The fat of various animals was said to have therapeutic qualities" (Rak 309).

course. She waited until they had finished chatting, and then climbed down the tree, gathered up her courage, and knocked on the ogre's door, shouting, 'Pray, my most ogrish lord and lady, a bit of charity, some alms, a sign of your compassion, a little mercy for a poor wretch, a miserable girl who has been ruined by fortune and is far from her homeland, stripped of all human aid, whom Night has come upon in these woods, and who is dying of hunger!' And then again, knock knock! At this headache the ogress wanted to throw out half a loaf of bread and send her away. But the ogre, who was greedier for Christian flesh than a siskin is for walnuts, a bear for honey, a cat for little fish, a sheep for salt, and a donkey for bran mash, said to his wife, 'Let the poor thing come in, for if she sleeps outside in the fields she might be torn apart by some wolf.' And he kept at it for so long that his wife opened the door and the ogre, with his hairy charity, devised a plan to make four mouthfuls out of her.

"But the glutton calculates one bill and the innkeeper another. After the ogre had gotten good and drunk and put himself to sleep, Nella took a knife from a cupboard and did a butcher job on him. Then she put all the fat in a jar and set off in the direction of the court, where she presented herself to the king and offered to heal the prince.

"With great happiness the king let her into his son's room, where she lubricated him thoroughly with the fat, and—no sooner said than done—his wounds immediately closed up, as if she had thrown water onto fire, and he became as healthy as a fish. When the king saw this he told his son that the good woman deserved the reward promised in the proclamation and that he should take her for his wife. But upon hearing this the prince answered, 'From this moment on she can content herself with a toothpick, for my body does not contain a pantry of hearts that I can hand out to so many women. My heart has already been given in down payment, and another lady is its owner.'

"When Nella heard this she answered, 'You should not dwell on the one who was the cause of all of your troubles!' 'Her sisters were the cause of my troubles,' replied the prince, 'and they will have to shit their penance!' 'You love her that much?' Nella went on. And the prince answered, 'More than the pupils of these eyes!' 'Well, then,' Nella continued, 'hug me and squeeze me tight, for I am the fire of your heart!' But the prince, seeing her with such a dark face, answered, 'It's more likely that you're coal than fire! So move away, or you'll get me dirty!' When Nella saw that he didn't recognize her she asked for a basin of fresh water and washed her face; as soon as she had gotten rid of that cloud of soot the sun came out, and once she was recognized by the prince he held her tight as a squid. And when he had taken her for his wife, he had her sisters walled inside a fireplace so that, like leeches, they would purge themselves of the contaminated blood of envy in the ashes,[9] proving the truth of the saying: *No evil has ever gone unpunished.*"

---

9. "Leeches are put in the ashes after they have performed their job, so that they expel the sucked blood" (Croce 157).

3

VIOLA

Third Entertainment of the Second Day

Viola is envied by her sisters, and after playing many jokes on a prince and having as many played on her, she becomes his wife to spite them.

Those who heard that tale felt its effects all the way down to the little bones in their feet, and they blessed a thousand times over the prince who had given Nella's sisters a dressing-down, and praised to the stars the unbounded love of the girl who had managed to merit the prince's love in the midst of so many difficulties. But then Tadeo signaled them all to be quiet and ordered Meneca to do her duty, and she paid her debt in this manner: "Envy is a wind that blows so strongly that it brings down the stays of the glory of worthy men and destroys the fertile fields of good fortune. But quite often, as a heavenly punishment, just when it looks like this wind is going to knock you flat on your face, instead it pushes you even faster to reach the happiness awaiting you, as you will hear in the tale that I want to tell you.

"There once was a good and respectable man by the name of Colaniello, who had three daughters: Rosa, Garofano, and Viola.[1] The last of the three was so beautiful that she prepared syrups of desire to purge hearts of their every torment, and for this reason Ciullone, the king's son, was smoldering and burning for her, and every time he passed by the room on the street[2] where the three sisters worked, he would take off his hat and say, 'Good day, good day to you, Viola.' And she would answer, 'Son of the king, good day. I know more than you, hey!'

"At these words the other sisters would swell up with rage and grumble, saying, 'You're an ill-bred girl and you're going to tick the

---

AT 879: The Basil Maiden. Croce notes similarities with Italian tales from Pitrè (*Fiabe, nov. e racc. sic.* 58 ["The Pot of Basil"] and *Fiabe e legg. tosc.* 13 ["The Teacher"]), Imbriani ("The Star of Diana"), and others (*Lo cunti de li cunti* 288). See also Gonzenbach 35, "The Daughter of Prince Cirimimminu."

1. Rose, Carnation, and Violet.
2. See tale 1.10 n2.

prince off in a bad way!' But Viola just left her sisters' words in the dust. And so to spite her they did her the bad service of going to their father and telling him that she was too fresh and presumptuous, and that she answered the prince without respect, as if she and he were the same thing, and that one day he was going to fly off the handle and give the sinner her just punishment.

"Colaniello was a man of good judgment, and in order to avoid such a situation he sent Viola to stay with an aunt of hers, named Cucevannella, so that she could teach the girl to work. But when the prince passed by the house and no longer saw the target of his desires, for a number of days he acted like a nightingale that finds the nest emptied of her children and hops from branch to branch complaining of her loss. And he spent so much time with his ears pressed to keyholes that he got wind of the place where Viola was staying, and he went to see the aunt and said, 'My dear madam, you know who I am and what I'm capable and worthy of, and so, between us, let's be quiet and keep our mouths shut; do me this favor and then fleece me for whatever sum you desire.' 'In whatever I can,' answered the old woman, 'I am entirely at your command.' And the prince: 'I want nothing more from you but that you allow me to kiss Viola, and you may have the pupils of these eyes.' And the old woman replied, 'I can do no more to serve you than hold your clothes while you're out swimming; but I don't want her to catch on that I'm playing the handle to this pitcher and that I have a hand in this shameful business, or else at the end of my days I'll earn the reputation of a blacksmith's boy who manages the bellows. So the favor I can do for you is to hide you in the ground-floor room off the garden, where I'll send you Viola after inventing some excuse. And if you've got the cloth and scissors in your hand and don't know how to use them, then it'll be your fault.'

"Upon hearing this, the prince thanked her for her great kindness, and without wasting any more time he hid himself away in the room. With the excuse that she wanted to cut some piece of cloth or other, the old woman said to her niece, 'Oh, Viola, if you love me go downstairs and get me the measure.' When Viola entered the room to do her aunt this service, she became aware of the ambush, and once she had gotten the measure she leapt from the room as nimbly as a cat, leaving the prince long-nosed with shame and swollen with rage. The old woman, who saw her come back at such a run, suspected that the prince's wiles hadn't caught fire, and a short time later said to the girl, 'Go, my niece, to the room downstairs and get me the ball of Brescia thread that's on top of that little chest.' Viola ran and got the thread, and then slithered through the prince's hands like an eel.

Se lassaie scappare no vernacchio cossì spotestato e co tanto remmore e strepeto che Viola, pe la paura, strillava, "Oh, mamma mia, aiutame!" [He let out a fart that was so colossal and that made such a noise and uproar that Viola, out of fear, started shrieking, "Oh, dear mother, help me!"]

"But it wasn't long before the old woman went back to saying, 'Viola, my dear, if you don't go downstairs and get me the scissors, it'll be the end of me.' And when Viola went down she received the third assault, but with the strength of a dog she got out of the trap, and when she was back upstairs she cut off her aunt's ears with those very scissors, saying to her, 'Here's a generous tip for your match-making. Every job deserves a reward: for honor disfigured, ears damaged; and if I don't cut off your nose as well it's only so you can smell the stench of your reputation, you go-between, panderer, chicken carrier, eat-it-all-up, baby spoiler.'[3] And speaking in this manner she hopped back home, leaving her aunt short on ears and the prince full of leave-me-alones.

"The prince returned to passing by Viola's father's house, and when he saw her sitting in the same place as always, he resumed the usual music: 'Good day, good day to you, Viola.' And she answered immediately, just like a good deacon, 'Son of the king, good day. I know more than you, hey!' The sisters, who could no longer bear this meddler, agreed among themselves to get rid of her. And since they had a window that overlooked the garden of an ogre, they thought they would throw the coins in that direction. So they dropped a skein of thread they were using to make a curtain for the queen down into the garden, and said, 'Oh, poor us! We're ruined and we won't be able to finish the job in time unless Viola, who is the smallest and lightest of us, lets us lower her with a rope so she can get our thread!' And Viola, not wanting to see them so afflicted, offered at once to go. When they had tied her to the rope they lowered her down, and after lowering her they let go of the rope.

"At that same moment the ogre came out to take a look at his garden, and since he had grown quite damp from the contact with the earth, he let out a fart that was so colossal and that made such a noise and uproar that Viola, out of fear, started shrieking, 'Oh, dear mother, help me!' The ogre turned around and saw this pretty girl behind him, and remembering that he had once heard from some students that Spanish mares are impregnated by the wind,[4] he thought that the air from his fart had fecundated one of the trees and that this splendid creature had come out. And so he embraced her with great love and said, 'Daughter, my daughter, part and parcel of this body, breath of this spirit, who would ever have thought that a bit of flatulence could have given this lovely face its form? Who would ever have

3. "All of these epithets refer to match-makers" (Guarini and Burani 199).
4. The story of horses impregnated by the wind can be found in Pliny (*Natural History* 8.67) and Virgil (*Georgics* 3.271–79), among others.

thought that the effect of a chill could generate this fire of Love?' And after saying these and other tender and doting words, he put her in the care of three fairies and ordered them to look after her and raise her on cherries.

"When the prince no longer saw Viola and heard nothing new or old about her he became so upset that he got bags as big as hernias under his eyes, his face took on a deathly hue, his lips grew ashen, and there was no morsel that tasted juicy to him and no sleep that brought him peace. Finally, by means of inquiries and the promise of rewards, he spied so hard that he found out where she was. He then had the ogre summoned and told him that he was ill, as the ogre could see for himself, and that he must do him the favor of allowing him to stay just one day and one night in his garden, for all he needed was a room to get his spirits back up. The ogre, who was a vassal of his father's, couldn't refuse him this small favor and offered him, as if one weren't enough, all of his rooms and his very life. The prince thanked him and had himself assigned a room that, as luck would have it, was near the room where the ogre slept in the same bed with Viola.

"And—as soon as Night came out to play Hang My Curtain[5] with the stars—when the prince found the ogre's door open, since it was summer and this was a safe place and the ogre liked a little cool air, he went in very quietly and, after feeling around on Viola's side, gave her two pinches. Waking up, she began to cry, 'Oh, Daddy, so many fleas!' The ogre immediately had the girl move to another bed, but the prince began to do the same thing again and Viola to scream in the same manner, so that the ogre had to keep on changing first her mattress and then her sheets, and they spent the whole night bustling about—until Dawn brought the news that the Sun had been found alive, and the sky shed its mourning clothes.

"But as soon as it was day in that house and the prince saw the girl by the door, he said to her, as usual, 'Good day, good day to you, Viola,' and when Viola answered, 'Son of the king, good day. I know more than you, hey!' the prince replied, 'Oh, Daddy, so many fleas!' When she heard that shot Viola immediately realized that all of that bother the night before had been a trick on the part of the prince, and she went to visit the fairies to tell them about it. 'If that's the case,' said the fairies, 'we'll fight pirates with pirates and galley slaves with sailors and if that dog bit you, we'll see that we get his coat sheared; he played one on you and we'll play one and a half on him! Now ask the ogre to make you a pair of slippers covered with bells, and then let us do the rest, for we intend to pay him back in fine coin!'

---

5. A children's game; see introduction to day 2 n19.

"Desirous of revenge, Viola immediately had the ogre make her the slippers, and then—after waiting until the sky, like a Genoese lady, had veiled its face with black taffeta[6]—the four of them went off together to the prince's house, where the fairies and Viola entered his bedroom without being seen. As soon as the prince's eyes grew heavy, the fairies made a huge commotion and Viola started to stamp her feet so loudly that, what with the noise of the feet and the clamor of the bells, the prince woke up in a great fright and yelled, 'Oh, Mommy, Mommy, help me!' And when this had been repeated two or three times they stole off back to their house.

"The next morning, after he had taken some lemon juice and wormwood seeds[7] for his fear, the prince went for a walk in the garden, since he couldn't live a moment without the sight of that Viola, who was the perfect match for his carnations,[8] and when he saw her in front of the door he said, 'Good day, good day to you, Viola,' and Viola to him, 'Son of the king, good day. I know more than you, hey!' and the prince: 'Oh, Daddy, so many fleas!' and she: 'Oh, Mommy, Mommy, help me!'

"When the prince heard this he said, 'You've got me; the game is yours! I give up and you win, and now that I truly realize that you know more than I do, I want you without further ado for my wife!' And so the ogre was summoned and the prince asked for her hand. But the ogre didn't want to touch someone else's harvest, since that very morning he had learned that Viola was Colaniello's daughter and that his rear eye had been deceived into thinking that this fragrant vision was born from a fetid breeze. And so he called Viola's father and informed him of the good fortune awaiting his daughter, and amid great joy the festivities were held, demonstrating the truth of the saying: *A pretty girl gets married in the square.*"

---

6. "Genoese women, like Venetian women, would cover their faces with a half-mask when they went out" (Croce 165).
7. "A seed given to children as a cure for worms" (Croce 165).
8. A vulgar allusion?

4

CAGLIUSO

Fourth Entertainment of the Second Day

Due to the industry of a cat left to him by his father, Cagliuso becomes a gentleman. But when he shows signs of being ungrateful to the cat, it reproaches him for his ingratitude.

It is impossible to describe the great pleasure that everyone felt at the good fortune of Viola, who used her wits to construct such a fine destiny in spite of the vexations caused her by her sisters, enemies of their own flesh and blood, who tried so many times to trip her and break her neck. But since it was time for Tolla to pay the rent she owed, she coughed up the golden coins of lovely words and paid her debt in the following manner: "Ingratitude, my lords, is a rusty nail that when driven into the tree of courtesy causes it to dry up; it is a broken sewer that turns the foundations of affection into a sponge; it is a bit of soot that, falling into the pot of friendship, takes away its aroma and taste. And this can be formally seen and proved; you'll see a rough sketch of it in the tale that I am about to tell you.

"There once was, in my city of Naples, an old, wretchedly poor man, who was so full of withouts, so destitute, hungry, miserable, gaunt, and lacking even the smallest wrinkle in his purse, that he

---

AT 545B: Puss in Boots. This is, of course, the tale that will become better known in Charles Perrault's version, "The Master Cat, or Puss in Boots." Basile had a predecessor in Straparola (*Le piacevoli notti* 11.1, "Costantino Fortunato"), and popular variants can be found in Pitrè (*Fiabe, nov. e racc. sic.* 88, "Don Giuseppi Birnbaum" and *Nov. tosc.* 12, "The Fox") and Imbriani 10 ("King Messemèmi-gli-bocca-'l-fumo"). A version of this tale (largely derived from Perrault) also appeared in the 1812 edition of the Grimms' tales, though was later removed. Penzer comments that "Perrault was troubled about the ending to the tale and affixes a moral that is quite inapplicable. It has been repeatedly pointed out that the cat is an unscrupulous adventurer who indulges in a series of mean frauds to benefit a worthless youth who usually plays a very passive part in the tale [. . .] we are still ignorant whence Straparola and Basile derived their tale—a curious tale that never seemed to have a satisfactory end. [. . .] Thus in some cases the cat turns into a human being, in others he becomes prime minister" (1:158). The end of Basile's tale differs notably from Straparola's, since in the latter the cat merely disappears from the tale once its important work as a helper is done. Another notable difference between Straparola and Basile's and later versions is that the cat in the first two is female.

went around as naked as a louse. When he was about to shake out the sacks of his life he called Oraziello and Pippo, his sons, and said to them, 'I have already been convened according to contract for the debt I owe Nature. And believe me, if you are Christians, that it would be my great pleasure to sail out of this Mandracchio[1] of sorrows and escape from this pigsty of suffering, if it weren't for the fact that I'll be leaving you impoverished, as penniless as Saint Chiara,[2] stranded on the five roads of Melito[3] without a coin, as clean as a barber's basin, as light on your feet as a sergeant, and as dry as a prune pit. For you own as much as a fly can carry on its foot, and if you run for a hundred miles you won't drop a cent,[4] since my luck has driven me to where the three dogs shit;[5] life is no longer mine to have, and what you see is what you can write about, because I have always, as you know, been one for yawns and little crosses,[6] and I've always gone to bed without a candle. But despite all of this, I still want to leave you a sign of my love when I die; so you, Oraziello, my first-born, take that sieve that's hanging on the wall, with which you'll be able to earn your bread; and you, Pippo, the nest shitter, take the cat. And remember your daddy.' As he was saying this he burst into tears, and a short while later he said, 'Farewell, night has come!'

"Oraziello had his father buried with the help of some charity, and then took his sieve and went running around from here to there trying to make a living, and the more he sifted the more he earned. But Pippo, upon taking the cat, said, 'Just look what a pathetic inheritance my father has left me! I don't know how to provide for myself and now I have to shop for two! Who ever heard of such a wretched legacy? Better if it had never been!' The cat, who heard this moaning, said to him, 'You complain too much! You've got more luck than brains, though you don't know your own luck, for I can make you rich if I try.' When he heard this Pippo thanked Her Royal Catness, petted her three or four times on the back, and warmly entrusted himself to her care. And then the cat, feeling sorry for poor Cagliuso,[7]

---

1. See tale 1.10 n14.
2. As poor as Saint Chiara (Claire), the founder of the order of the Clarisse, with its ideal of absolute poverty; "alternately, the reference might be to the church of Santa Chiara, one of the biggest in Naples, built by Robert of Anjou" (Rak 334).
3. "In Melito, on the road from Naples to Aversa, there is an area called 'the five roads,' where, in a spot called 'Fascenaro,' there are always great numbers of beggars" (Croce 564).
4. *na maglia* (Neap.): "ancient name for a coin of very low value" (Croce 168).
5. "I.e., in miserable conditions; the origin of the expression is unknown" (Croce 168).
6. "Made on the mouth to prevent evil spirits from taking advantage of that moment [the yawn] to enter into the body" (Croce 564).
7. At this point in the text Pippo's name changes to Cagliuso.

showed up every morning—when the Sun went fishing for Night's shadows with its golden hook and bait of light—at either the Chiaia beach or the Rock of Fish,[8] and when she spotted a big mullet or a nice bream she grabbed it and brought it to the king, saying, 'Lord Cagliuso, slave to Your Highness from the ground floor up to the terrace, sends you this fish with his respect and says, "Great lord, small gift."' The king, with the happy face usually awarded to those who bring goods, answered the cat, 'Tell this lord whom I don't know that I send him infinite thanks.'

"Other times the cat would run off to the hunting grounds, either the swamps or the Astroni,[9] and when the hunters shot down an oriole or a great tit or a blackcap, she collected them and presented them to the king with the same message. And she employed this stratagem so often that one morning the king said to her, 'I feel so obliged to this lord Cagliuso that I would like to meet him in order to reciprocate the affection that he has shown toward me.' To which the cat answered, 'Lord Cagliuso's desire is to give his life and blood for your crown; and tomorrow morning—when the Sun sets the stubble of the aerial fields on fire—he will, without a doubt, come to pay homage to you.'

"And so when morning came, the cat went to the king and said to him, 'My lord, Lord Cagliuso sends his apologies, for he cannot come. Last night some servants of his ran off, and they didn't even leave him the shirt on his back.' Upon hearing this the king immediately had an armful of clothes and undergarments taken from his wardrobe and sent them to Cagliuso. And before two hours had gone by, Cagliuso, led by the cat, came to the palace, where he received a thousand compliments from the king, and after sitting him at his side the king gave orders that a magnificent banquet be prepared.

"But as everyone was eating, every now and then Cagliuso would turn to the cat and say to her, 'My little kitty, keep an eye on those rags of mine, for I wouldn't want anything bad to happen to them.' And the cat answered, 'Be quiet, shut your trap, don't talk about such trifles!' When the king wanted to know what Cagliuso needed, the cat answered that he had gotten the craving for a little lemon, and the king immediately sent someone to the garden to get a basket of them. And Cagliuso kept up with the same music about his tatters and

---

8. "Place where fish was distributed to fishmongers by the wholesale buyers, on via della Marina. There were 'fish stones' at Santa Lucia and Chiaia as well" (Croce 564).
9. "Hunting grounds, the Paduli (Ital. 'marshes') are in the eastern part of Naples; the Astroni are near the Agnano lake." The latter were a royal hunting reserve (Croce 564).

"Stà zitto, appila, non parlare de ste pezzenterie!"
["Be quiet, shut your trap, don't talk about such trifles!"]

shirttails and the cat kept on telling him to plug up his mouth and the king asked him again what he needed and the cat invented another excuse to make up for Cagliuso's pettiness.

"Finally, after having eaten and chatted for a long time about this and that, Cagliuso took his leave. But that fox of a cat stayed with the king and described to him Cagliuso's valor, brains, good judgment, and above all his great riches in the countryside outside of Rome and in Lombardy, for which he would deserve to marry into the family of a crowned king. When the king asked what exactly there was, the cat answered that it was impossible to keep track of the furniture, buildings, and other furnishings of that moneybags, since even he did not know how much he had, and that if the king wanted to find out more about it he could send his people outside the kingdom with her, and they could see with their own eyes that his riches were without equal in the world.

"The king summoned some of his faithful men and ordered them to obtain detailed information on the matter, and they followed in the cat's footsteps. As soon as they had gotten beyond the borders of the kingdom the cat, with the excuse that she had to find refreshment for them along the way, at every turn ran ahead and for every flock of sheep, herd of cattle, stable of horses, and drift of pigs she came across, she said to the shepherds and guardians, 'Hey there, take heed! A bunch of bandits intends to sack everything they find in this land! But if you want to escape their fury and make sure your goods go unharmed, just say they belong to Lord Cagliuso, and no one will touch a hair on your head.' She said the same thing at the farms along the way, so that wherever the king's men arrived, they found a bagpipe tuned to the same key: everything they encountered was said to belong to Lord Cagliuso. And so, tired of asking, they returned to the king and praised Lord Cagliuso's riches from the sky to the sea. When the king heard this, he promised the cat a nice reward if she arranged the marriage between Cagliuso and his daughter, and the cat, shuttling back and forth, finally pulled off the deal.

"When Cagliuso arrived, the king delivered him a great dowry and his daughter, and after a month of festivities Cagliuso said that he wanted to take his bride to his estates. The king accompanied them to the border of his kingdom, and they set off for Lombardy, where, on the cat's recommendation, Cagliuso bought some properties and land, and became a baron.

"Cagliuso now found himself rolling in wealth, and he thanked the cat over and over again, saying that he owed his life to her and his greatness to her good offices, that a cat's devices had done him more good than his father's wits, and that she should therefore feel free to

do and undo whatever she thought fit and pleased her with his possessions and his life. Finally, he gave her his word that as soon as she
died—a hundred years from then!—he would have her stuffed and
placed inside a golden cage in his own bedroom, so that he might always keep the memory of her before his eyes.

"The cat listened to this show of braggadocio, and before three
days had gone by she pretended to be dead and stretched herself
straight out in the garden. When Cagliuso's wife saw this she shouted,
'Oh, my husband, what a great tragedy! The cat is dead!' 'And may
every evil accompany her,' answered Cagliuso. 'Better her than us.'
'What shall we do?' replied the wife. And he: 'Take her by her foot
and throw her out the window!'

"Hearing of this fine reward when she would have least imagined
it, the cat began to say, 'This is the great gratitude for the fleas that I
picked off your neck? These are the thousand thanks for those rags I
got you to throw away, so worn out that you could have hung them
on spindles? This is what I get back, after having dressed you as elegantly as a spider and fed you when you were hungry, miserable, and
threadbare? When you were in tatters, covered with shreds, all
patched up, and coming apart at the seams, you corpse stripper? This
is the fate of those who try to wash an ass's head! Get lost, and may
everything I've done for you be damned; your throat doesn't deserve
to be spit in![10] What a lovely golden cage you've prepared for me,
what a fine burial you've planned for me! There you have it: you offer
your services, you make sacrifices, you labor, you sweat, and all for
this nice prize! Oh, miserable is he who fills up his pot with the hopes
of someone else! That philosopher was right when he said, "If you go
to bed an ass, you'll wake up one!" In short, the more you do, the less
you should expect. Good words and wicked actions deceive only the
wise and the mad.'

"So speaking and shaking her head, she headed out of there, and
however much Cagliuso tried to lick her down with the lung[11] of hu-
mility, nothing could get her to come back. And as she ran off without once turning her head, she said, *May God save you from the rich
who become poor and from the beggar who has worked his way up.*"

---

10. "Reference to the popular custom of spitting in a newborn's mouth as a first sign
of recognition and affection" (Guarini and Burani 209).
11. "Cat food that a street vendor, called a *polmonaro* [lung seller] would bring to
the houses of Naples in the morning; all the cats in the neighborhood would become
agitated and meow as they heard their benefactor getting closer" (Croce 172).

5

THE SERPENT

Fifth Entertainment of the Second Day

The king of Long Acres marries his daughter to a serpent, and when the king discovers that he is a handsome young man he burns his skin. The young man tries to break a glass window to escape and instead breaks his head, for which he can find no remedy. The king's daughter leaves the house of her father, and after she learns the secret for healing her lover from a fox, she kills the fox with a ruse. Then with the fat of the fox and various birds she lubricates the wounded young man, who is the son of a king, and he becomes her husband.

The poor cat was pitied beyond measure for having been so badly compensated, even if one person said that there was at least something about which she could be consoled, since she was not alone. For nowadays ingratitude has become a domestic ill, like the French disease[1] or the wheeze,[2] and people who have done and undone, consumed their property, and ruined their lives to serve that race of ingrates find themselves destined to a common burial at the hospital just when they thought they had their hands on much more than golden cages. Meanwhile, seeing that Popa was prepared to speak, they became silent, and she said, "Those who are too curious to know the business of others have always brought the ax down on their own feet, as the king of Long Acres can testify. Because he stuck his nose in a certain business, he tangled his daughter's spinning and

---

AT 425A: The Monster (Animal) as Bridegroom, AT 432: The Prince as Bird, and AT 433: The Prince as Serpent. Croce mentions similar tales from Pitrè. The tale also bears a resemblance to Grimm 108, "Hans My Hedgehog," and to other variants of the "beast as bridegroom" type. The principal motifs include "tasks," "Cupid and Psyche," "helpful animals," and "overhearing" (Penzer 1:168). See also Straparola 2.1, "The Pig King," Pitrè, *Fiabe, nov. e racc. sic.* 56 ("The Serpents"), Imbriani 12 ("King Pig"), Gonzenbach 43 ("The Story of Prince Scursuni"), and tales 1.2 and 2.2 of this collection.
1. Syphilis. "Venereal disease was widespread in Europe from the 16th century on" (Rak 354).
2. *lo crastone* (Neap.): "an epidemic catarrhal fever that had assumed vast proportions in 1580. Basile himself probably died of it during the epidemic of 1632" (Croce 173).

ruined his poor son-in-law, who tried shattering a window with his head but ended up with a shattered head himself.

"Now it is said there once was a countrywoman who longed for a child more than a litigant longs for a sentence in his favor, a sick person cool water, and an innkeeper the passing of a guarded caravan.[3] But although her husband labored daily with his hoe, she never managed to see the fertility she desired.

"One day the poor man went into the mountains to collect a bundle of firewood, and upon opening it at home he found a lovely little serpent in among the branches. When Sapatella, for this was the name of the countrywoman, saw this, she let out a great sigh and said, 'There you have it: even serpents have little serpents, and I was born to this world unlucky, with a hernia of a husband who isn't a good enough gardener to give me a graft.' To these words the serpent answered, 'Since you cannot have children, take me; you'll be making a good deal and I'll love you more than I love my own mother.' When she heard a serpent talking Sapatella nearly died of fear, but then she took courage and said, 'If for nothing else, because of this loving nature of yours I'll be glad to accept you as if you had come out of my own knee.'[4] And so she gave him a little hole in the house for his cradle and fed him what she had with the greatest affection in the world.

"Day by day he grew, and when he was a big little thing he said to Cola Matteo, the countryman he considered his father and master, 'Oh, Daddy, I want to get married.' 'Well, then,' said Cola Matteo, 'we'll find another serpent like you and we'll make a shopkeeper's agreement.' 'What do you mean, a serpent?' answered the little serpent. 'So we're one and the same with vipers and grass snakes? It's quite clear that you're an Antuono[5] and that you can't tell the wheat from the chaff! I want the daughter of the king! You go this very instant and ask the king for his daughter and say that a serpent wants her.'

"Cola Matteo, who was an unsophisticated man and didn't know too much about these games of Empty the Barrel,[6] simply went to the king and brought him the message, saying, 'Don't blame the messenger, or he'll get as many blows as there are grains of sand. Now you should know that a serpent wants your daughter for his wife; and so

3. *percaccio* (Neap.): "These were guards who guided and protected travelers' caravans with the help of soldiers stationed along the main routes of communication. This made possible a reduction of the danger of bandits after the mid-16th century" (Rak 354). A passing caravan thus meant a significant increase in business for an innkeeper.

4. See tale 1.3 n4.

5. I.e., someone stupid (like the protagonist of tale 1.1, who has this name).

6. See introduction to day 2 n23.

I come, in my capacity as gardener, to see if we can graft a serpent with a little dove.' The king's nose told him that Cola Matteo was a blockhead, and to get him off his back he said, 'Go tell this serpent that if he turns all of the fruit in my park to gold I will give him my daughter,' and after he had a good laugh he dismissed him. But when Cola Matteo gave this answer to the serpent, the serpent said, 'To-morrow morning go and gather all the fruit pits you find in the city and sow them in the park, and you'll see pearls strung on rush stems.'

"Cola Matteo, who was a bit off, was able neither to reply nor to disagree, and—as soon as the Sun swept away the rubbish of the shadows from Dawn's damp fields with its golden brooms—he went with a basket on his arm from square to square gathering up all the pits he could find, peach pits and apricot pits and wild prune pits and cherry pits, and all the nuts and seeds he found on the roads. And then he went to the park and sowed them as the serpent had told him to do, and—no sooner said than done—they sprouted and grew trunks, leaves, and fruits, all of glittering gold, and when the king saw this he went into an ecstasy of amazement and was overcome with delight.

"But then Cola Matteo was sent by the serpent to ask the king about his promise. 'Don't hit so hard,' said the king, 'for if he wants my daughter I want something else. He must turn all the walls and the grounds of the park into precious stones.' When this was reported by the farmer to the serpent he answered, 'Tomorrow morning go and gather all the pieces of things you find on the ground and throw them onto the roads and walls of the park, for we intend to catch up with this cripple.'

"And—as soon as Night was exiled for having stooged for swin-dlers, and started gathering up its bundles of twilight from the sky—Cola Matteo put a basket on his arm and began to go around gathering fragments of jars, pieces of lids and lidlets, bottoms of clay pots and pans, rims of basins, handles of pitchers, lips of chamber pots; and he collected as many broken lamps, smashed flower pots, cracked jugs, and fragments of crockery as he was able to find in the streets. And when he had done what the serpent had told him to do, the park was paved with emeralds and chalcedonies and plastered with rubies and carbuncles, and its splendor sequestered vision in the warehouses of eyes and planted marvel in the provinces of hearts.

"At this spectacle the king was dumbfounded and couldn't under-stand what had happened; but when the serpent sent the message once again to keep his word, the king answered, 'What has been done is a trifle unless he transforms this palace into solid gold.' And after Cola Matteo reported this other whim of the king to the serpent, the serpent said to him, 'Go get a bunch of mixed greens and lubricate the foundation of the palace with them, and we'll see if we can satisfy this crybaby.' That very instant Cola Matteo put together a big bundle of chard, turnip greens, garlic chives, purslane, arugula, and chervil, and when he had lubricated the base of the palace, it immediately began to shine all over like a gilded pill that could have made a hundred houses constipated by ill fortune evacuate their poverty.

"And when the countryman returned on behalf of the serpent and presented the request for his wife, the king, seeing every road cut off, summoned his daughter and said, 'My dear Grannonia, in order to trick someone who wanted to be your husband I proposed terms that I thought would be impossible to respect. But now that I see I have been caught up with and am under an obligation—and I know not how!—I beg you, if you are a blessed daughter, to allow me to keep my word and to content yourself with what the heavens will and I am forced to do.' 'Do what you please, my lord daddy,' answered Grannonia, 'for I will not veer one iota from your wishes.'

"When he heard this the king told Cola Matteo to have the serpent come, and, hearing the call, the serpent came to court in a carriage made of solid gold and pulled by four golden elephants. But wherever he passed the people fled, terrified at the sight of such a large and frightening serpent out for a ride in the city. When he arrived at the palace all of the courtiers trembled like rushes and then cleared out, until not even the scullery boys were left, and the king and queen, frozen with fear, holed themselves up in a room. Only Grannonia stayed put and didn't budge, and although her father and mother shouted, 'Run for it! Get out of here, Grannonia! Save yourself, Rienzo!'[7] she wouldn't move a hair and said, 'Why should I run from the husband that you have given me?'

"When the serpent entered the room he grabbed Grannonia around her middle with his tail and gave her a bunch of kisses; the king shat a quarter bushel of worms, and if you had bled him no blood would have come out. Then the serpent took her into another room, locked the door, and, shaking his skin to the floor, became a splendid young man who had a head covered with golden curls and eyes that cast a spell on you. And after embracing his bride, he picked the first fruits of his love.

"The king, who saw the serpent hole up with his daughter and then

---

7. "From a popular saying, deriving probably from an anecdote in which a certain Renzo was in serious danger" (Guarini and Burani 216); possibly the Roman patriot Cola di Rienzo, who was murdered by a mob in 1354 and whose fame was widespread (Penzer 1:169).

close the door, said to his wife, 'May the heavens send that good soul of my daughter to rest in peace, for there's no question that she's gone; that accursed serpent has probably gulped her down like an egg yolk.' And he put his eye to the keyhole so that he could see what had become of her. But when he saw the incredible grace of the young man and the skin that he had left on the ground, he gave the door a kick and went in, and then took the skin and threw it on the fire, where it burned up.

"At the sight of this the young man cried, 'Ah, you renegade dogs, you've got me!' and transformed into a dove. As he tried to escape he flew into the glass panes of the windows and banged his head so many times that at the end he broke the window. But he emerged so badly battered that there wasn't one whole piece of his noggin left. Grannonia, who found herself happy and wretched, full of joy and ill fated, rich and penniless, and all in the same moment, clawed at her face and lamented to her mother and father that her pleasure had been muddied, her sweetness poisoned, and her good fortune sent down the wrong path. They apologized, saying that they hadn't intended to cause any harm.

"But she kept on moaning until Night came out to light the cata-falque[8] of the Heavens for the Sun's funeral procession, and when she saw that everyone had gone to bed, she took all her jewels, which she kept in a writing desk, and left through a secret door, intending to search until she found the goods that she had lost. After she left the city, guided by the light of the moon, she met a fox, who asked her if she wanted company. Grannonia answered, 'You'd be doing me a favor, sister, since I'm not too familiar with these parts.'

"And so they walked along until they came to a wood—where the trees, playing like children, made little houses to hide the shadows in—and since by then they were tired of walking and wanted to rest, they retired under the cover of the leafy branches, where a fountain played at carnival with the cool grass, pouring down pitcherfuls of water.[9] And after lying down on a mattress of tender young grass, they paid the duty of rest that they owed to Nature for the merchandise of life, and they didn't awake until the Sun, with its usual fire, gave sailors and couriers the signal to continue their journeys.

"Upon awakening they stayed on a good deal longer listening to the songs of various birds, since it was a great pleasure for Grannonia

---

8. "Funeral catafalques were magnificent in this century of magnificence" (Croce 178).

9. "At Carnival time, people would squirt each other with fragrant waters (usually contained in eggs)" (Croce 568).

to hear their twittering. When the fox saw this she said, 'You'd feel even more pleasure if you understood what they're saying, as I do.' Since by nature women are just as prone to curiosity as they are to chatter, when she heard these words Grannonia begged the fox to tell her what she had heard in bird language. The fox let Grannonia beg for a good long time, so as to stimulate even greater curiosity for what she was about to say, and then told her that the birds were conversing among themselves about a misfortune that had befallen the king's son, who was as handsome as a fairy. Since he had refused to satisfy the unreined desires of an accursed ogress, he had been put under a curse: he would be transformed into a serpent for seven years. He was already close to finishing this time when, after falling in love with the daughter of a king, he was with his new bride in a room and left his skin on the floor. The mother and father of the bride, however, were too curious, and they burned the skin. Escaping in the form of a dove, he broke some glass trying to fly out of the window and smashed himself up so badly that as far as the doctors were considered he was a desperate case.

"When Grannonia heard her own business being discussed, she asked first off whose son this prince was and then if there was any hope that a cure might be found for his condition. The fox answered that the birds had said that his father was the king of Wide Ravine, and that there was no other secret for plugging the holes in his head— so that his soul wouldn't leave him—than to lubricate his wounds with the blood of the very birds that had told this story. At these words Grannonia knelt before the fox, begging her to do the service of catching those birds so that she could remove their blood, and then they would split the earnings like two good friends. 'Slow down,' said the fox. 'Let's wait until night, and when the birds go to roost just leave it to your mommy here; I'll climb up the tree and cut them down one by one.'

"And so they passed the whole day talking first of the young man's beauty, and then of the mistake made by the father of the bride, and then of the accident that had occurred, and as they chatted about this and that the day came to an end, and the Earth spread out a big piece of black cardboard to collect the wax from the torches of Night.[10] As soon as the fox saw the birds getting drowsy amid the branches she climbed stealthily up and, one by one, plucked out every oriole, goldfinch, wren, chaffinch, woodcock, owl, hoopoe, skylark, finch,

---

10. "A technique commonly used for gathering wax or preventing the oil that dripped from torches to spread; permission to collect wax and oil during public ceremonies was often given to the poor or reserved for certain people" (Rak 355).

"Autro tanto piacere senterrisse 'ntennenno chello che diceno,
comme lo 'ntenno io." ["You'd feel even more pleasure if you
understood what they're saying, as I do."]

screech owl, and flycatcher in the tree, and when she had killed them she put their blood in a little flask she carried with her on her travels for refreshment. Grannonia was walking on air with joy, but the fox said to her, 'Oh, you're dreaming this happiness, my girl! You've done nothing if you don't also have my blood to mix with the birds'!' That said, she ran away.

"Grannonia, who saw her hopes dashed to the ground, took recourse in the woman's art of craftiness and flattery, and said to the fox, 'Fox, my dear, you would be right to save your skin if I were not so indebted to you and if there were no other foxes in the world. But since you know how much I owe you and, furthermore, that there is no lack of the likes of you in this countryside, you can rest assured of my word and not act like the cow that kicks the pail right when it's full of milk. You've done so much, and now you're going to miss the best part! Stop right there; believe me, and accompany me to the city of this king, and I'll be like a bought slave to you.' The fox, who would never have believed that the quintessence of foxiness could be found, found herself outfoxed by a woman, for once she started walking at Grannonia's side they had not gone fifty paces before the girl planted a blow with the club she was carrying and hit the fox's noodle so hard that she was able to get the blood straightaway and add it to the little flask.

"Then she began to get her feet moving, and she arrived at Wide Ravine, where she headed for the royal palace and had word sent to the king that she had come to heal the prince. The king ordered her to be brought before him and marveled at seeing a girl promise what the best physicians in his kingdom hadn't been able to do. Even so, since there's no harm in trying he said that it would give him great pleasure to witness the experiment. But Grannonia replied, 'If I am to produce the effect that you desire, I want you to promise to give me the prince for my husband.' The king, who considered his son dead, answered her, 'If you give him back to me free and healthy, I'll give him to you free and healthy, for it's no big thing to give a husband to someone who gives me a son!'

"And so they went to the prince's room, and no sooner had she lubricated him with the blood than it was as if he had never been wounded. When Grannonia saw the prince strong and vigorous she told the king to keep his word and the king, turning to his son, said, 'My son, you've just seen yourself close to death and now I see you alive and I can hardly believe it. But since I promised this young lady that if she healed you you would be her husband, now that the heavens have bestowed this grace upon you allow me, out of all the love you have for me, to grant what I promised, since my gratitude obliges me to pay this debt.'

"To these words the prince answered, 'My lord, I would like to have such liberty with my own desires, so as to be able to give you as much satisfaction as I have love for you. But since I have given my word to another woman, I believe neither that you will consent that I break my promise nor that this young lady will advise me that I do this wrong to the one I love, nor that I will be able to change my mind.' When Grannonia heard this she felt an indescribably profound pleasure as she realized that she was still alive in the prince's memory. And, her face turning crimson, she said, 'If I made it so that this young lady loved by you were content to let me win the game, would you not yield to my desires?' 'It will never happen,' answered the prince, 'that I banish the lovely image of my beloved from this breast! Whether she makes preserves of her love or gives me a dose of senna to purge it with, I will always have the same longing and the same determination, and even if I found myself in danger of losing the game at the card table of life I would never trip things up like that or play such a trick!'

"Grannonia could no longer keep herself in the shackles of deception, and she revealed herself for who she was, since the room had been kept closed and dark on account of the prince's head wounds and the fact that she was disguised had caused the prince not to recognize her. But when he did recognize her he immediately embraced her, dizzy with jubilation, and told his father who she was and what she had suffered and done for him. And then they sent for the king and queen of Long Acres and, by common consent, celebrated their marriage, and above all they derived great amusement from the trick played on the fox, concluding at the very end that *Love's pleasures are always seasoned with pain*."

THE SHE-BEAR

Sixth Entertainment of the Second Day

*The king of Dry Rock wants to take his daughter for his wife.
Thanks to the trickery of an old woman, the girl changes into a
bear and flees to the woods. She falls into the hands of a prince,
and he sees her in her true form in a garden where she is arranging
her hair and falls in love with her. After various adventures she is
revealed to be a woman and becomes his wife.*

The entire tale that Popa told had the women shaking with laughter,
but when the subject turned to their own cunning, which could trick
even a fox, they really split their sides. And women truly have so
many different forms of cunning that you could thread them by the
hundred on each hair of their head, like little chips of garnet.[1] Fraud
is their mother, falsehood their wet nurse, flattery their teacher, du-
plicity their counselor, and deceit their constant companion; and they
twist and turn men in whatever manner they please. But let's return
to Antonella, who was getting frisky as she waited for her turn to
speak. After seeming lost in thought for a while, as if she were re-
viewing her thoughts, she spoke in this manner: "That wise man
spoke well when he said that a bitter command cannot be sweetly
obeyed. Man must command things of the right measure in order to
obtain obedience of a corresponding weight; from inappropriate orders is born resistance that cannot be overcome, as, in fact, happened
to the king of Dry Rock, who asked his daughter for something that
was not due him, thus giving her cause to flee and risking the loss of
honor and life.

"Now it is said that there once lived a king, the king of Dry Rock,
who had a wife who was the mother of beauty itself. Right at the fast-
est point in her race of years she fell from the horse of health and

---

AT 510B: The Dress of Gold, of Silver, and of Stars (Cap o' Rushes). The two best-
known later versions of this tale are Perrault's "Donkey-Skin" and Grimm 65, "All-
Fur." Croce mentions Sicilian (Pitrè, *Fiabe, nov. e racc. sic.* 43, "Little Furry," and
Gonzenbach 38, "Betta the Furry") and Sardinian variants. The first part of the tale
resembles somewhat Straparola 1.4, "Tebaldo."
1. "The combs and hair pins with which Neapolitan ladies adorned their hair were
covered with little pieces of garnet" (Guarini and Burani 222).

broke her life; but before the candle of her life was put out at the auc-
tion of years[2] she called her husband and said to him, 'I know that
you've always loved me with all your heart; therefore, in the dregs of
my years show me the froth of your love and promise me that you
will never marry unless you find another woman as beautiful as I
once was. Otherwise I will leave you with a curse squeezed from
these tits,[3] and I will hate you even when I'm in the world beyond.'

"The king, who loved her from here all the way up to the terrace,
burst into tears when he heard this last wish of hers, and for a long
time was not able to answer even one accursed word. Finally, when
he had stopped sobbing he said to her, 'If I ever want to hear anything about a wife again, may I first be struck by gout; may I first be
hit by a Catalan spear; may I first be treated like Starace.[4] Get this
out of your mind, my darling; don't even dream that I could love another woman! You were the beginning of my affection, and you will
take with you the rags of my desires.' While he was saying these
words, the poor young woman, who already had the death rattle,
rolled her eyes and stretched out her legs for the last time.

"When the king saw that Patria had been unplugged,[5] he unplugged the spigots of his eyes and made such a racket banging
around and shrieking that his whole court came running. And as he
called that good soul by name, he cursed the bad fortune that had
taken her away from him and, tearing at his beard, rebuked the stars
that had sent him this disaster.

"But then he decided to act according to that saying that goes, 'The
pain of a sore elbow and the pain of a lost wife both hurt a lot but go
away soon,' or that second one, 'One in the grave and another between your thighs.' And Night had not yet come out onto the drill
ground of the heavens to review the bats when he started to count on
his fingers: 'My wife has gone and died on me and now I'm a widower and miserable, with no hope of seeing anyone but this poor
daughter that she has left me. And so I'll need to find some way to

---

2. "In public auctions a candle was kept lit" (Croce 184).
3. "According to an ancient popular belief, squeezing one's breast with the nipples
pointed toward the person being cursed gave greater power to the accompanying
words of ill omen" (Guarini and Burani 223).
4. "During a famine in 1585 the Elected of the People [Eletto del Popolo] Giovan
Vincenzo Starace, although he alone opposed proposals to lower the weight of bread
and increase its price, was instead accused of being the author of this plan, odious to
the common people; and on May 9 he was taken by popular force from the convent
of Santa Maria la Nuova and tortured, then killed and torn into pieces, some of
which were even eaten by the raging crowd" (Croce 565).
5. "In November the mouth of the Patria lake near Naples was opened, and hunting
and fishing allowed; in the other months it was a hunting reserve" (Rak 370).

have a male child. But where do I start pecking? Where do I find a
woman whose beauty is identical to my wife's, if every other woman
looks like a harpy when compared to her? I want you back here, now!
How do you find another one, with a stick? How do you look for another one, with a bell? Nature made Nardella—may she rest in
glory—and then broke the mold![6] Alas, what a labyrinth she's put me
in, what a cage the promise that I made her has become! But what am
I saying? I haven't seen the wolf yet and I'm running away? Let's take
a look, let's see, let's try to understand. Is it possible that there's no
other ass in Nardella's stable? Is it possible that the world must be
lost for me? Is there perhaps a shortage of women; are they becoming
extinct? Or has the seed for them been lost?'

"Thus speaking he immediately had a proclamation and an order
issued by Master Iommiento:[7] all the beautiful women in the world
were to come to be judged at the touchstone of beauty, for he intended to take the most beautiful for his wife and endow her with his
kingdom. Word of this spread everywhere, and there was not a
woman in the universe who did not come to try her luck. There was
not a hag, no matter how deformed, who did not join the mix, since
when the subject of beauty is broached there's not a witch who ad-
mits to defeat, there's not an orca that gives up: every single one of
them puffs up with pride, every single one of them wants the best!
And if the mirror tells her the truth, she blames the glass that does
not show her as she really is and the quicksilver that was applied in-
correctly.[8]

"Now at this point the land was full of women, and the king put
them in line and began to walk among them like the Grand Turk[9]
when he enters his seraglio to choose the best Genoese whetstone on
which to sharpen his Damascus knife.[10] And as he came and went up
and down their ranks like a monkey that is never still, and peered at
this one and that one and looked them over from head to toe, one
seemed to him to have a crooked forehead, one a long nose, one a
wide mouth, one thick lips; this one was as tall as a beanpole, that

6. See Ariosto, *Orlando furioso* 10.84: "Natura il fece e poi roppe la stampa" (cit.
Croce 185).

7. "A 'false' rhyme with the opening formula of bans, *banno e commannamiento*,
also used in many works in which official proclamations were satirized" (Rak 370).

8. "The images reflected by the mirrors of the time were distorted, due to the imper-
fect surface of the glass and its metallic face" (Guarini and Burani 226).

9. "One of the frequent references to the closest region of the Middle East, with
which Italy was engaged in wars and commerce" (Rak 370).

10. The Genoese whetstone was "a blackish stone rich in quartz, used to sharpen
bladed weapons." The famous Damascus knives were inlaid with gold and silver;
here it is used as a phallic metaphor (Rak 370–71).

one short and deformed, one too swollen, and one excessively frail; the Spanish woman displeased him because of her sallow color, the Neapolitan was not to his taste because of the platform heels she walked on,[11] the German seemed to him cold and icy, the French-woman too featherbrained, and the Venetian looked like a distaff of flax with her bleached hair.

"At the very end he sent them all away with one hand in front of him and the other behind, one for one reason and one for another. And seeing as so many beautiful faces had all come to naught, he had decided to strangle himself when he happened to bump into his own daughter, and he said, 'Why am I looking for Maria in Ravenna[12] if my daughter Preziosa was made in the same mold as her mother? I have this lovely face in my own house and I go to the asshole of the world looking for another one?' But when he made his intentions clear to his daughter, she flew off the handle and gave him a piece of her tongue, and I'll let the heavens tell you about it in my place. Enraged, the king said to her, 'Lower that voice and stuff that tongue back in there, and make up your mind to tie this marriage knot tonight or else the biggest piece left of you will be your ear!'

"When Preziosa heard this decision she withdrew to her room to wail over her bad fortune, and she left not a tuft of hair on her head. In the midst of these dismal laments, an old woman who often supplied her with makeup came passing by, and when she found her closer to the world beyond than to this one and heard the cause of her sorrow, she said, 'Keep your spirits up, my dear girl; don't despair, for every ailment has its remedy, apart from death. Now listen: tonight, when your father wants to behave like a stallion—though he has more in common with an ass—put this stick in your mouth, and you'll immediately become a bear. And then clear out, for in his fear he'll let you escape, and go straight to the woods, where the heavens have preserved a good destiny for you. And when you want to look like a woman, which you are and always will be, take the stick out of your mouth and you'll return to your original form.'

"Preziosa embraced the old woman and ordered that she be given a nice apronful of flour and some slices of ham and lard, and then she sent her off. And as the Sun, like an unsuccessful whore, began to change quarters, the king had musicians brought in and invited all of his lord vassals to great festivities. Following five or six hours of

---

11. *stanfelle* (Neap.): the platform shoes popular in Neapolitan fashion at the time (see Cennerentola's *chianiello* in tale 1.6 n7). The traits attributed to the women of various countries represent common stereotypes.

12. "Proverbial expression used to signify a fruitless and superfluous search for something" (Croce 186).

Moorish dancing[13] they sat down at the tables, and after they ate beyond all measure the king went off to bed. But when he called the bride to bring him the register in which to settle their amorous accounts, she put the stick in her mouth and took the shape of a terrifying bear, and then went in to him. Terrified by this marvel, he rolled himself up in the mattress and wouldn't stick out his noggin even when it was morning.

"In the meantime Preziosa left and set off in the direction of a wood—where the shadows conspired to see if they could, at dusk, cause the Sun some affront—where she lived in sweet conversation with other animals, until one day the son of the king of Running Water came to that land to hunt. He set eyes on the bear and almost died of fright, but when the animal started circling him, crouched close to the ground and wagging its tail like a puppy, he took courage. Caressing it and saying 'oink oink, meow meow, cheep cheep, coo coo, grunt grunt, and snort snort,' he brought it home and ordered that it be taken care of as if it were he in person, and he had it put in a garden next to the royal palace so that he could see it whenever he wanted to from his window.

"Now when everyone else had gone out and the prince was all alone in the house, he went to the window to look at the bear and saw that Preziosa had taken the stick out of her mouth so that she could arrange her hair, and was combing out her golden braids. At the sight of this beauty beyond all imagination, he was stunned with wonder, and, throwing himself down the stairs, he ran into the garden. But Preziosa, who had become aware of the ambush, thrust the stick into her mouth and turned back into what she had been before. When the prince got down there and didn't find what he had seen from above, he was so bewildered by the deception that a great melancholy came over him, and in four days he fell ill, repeating over and over again, 'My dear bear, my dear bear!' When his mother heard this lament she imagined that the bear had treated him badly in some way, and ordered it to be killed. But the servants had become enamored of the tame nature of the bear, who made even the stones in the street love her, and since they were too compassionate to slaughter her, they brought her to the wood and told the queen that they had done away with her.

"When word of this reached the prince's ears he did unbelievable

---

13. *catubba* (Neap.): "The Sfessania and Lucia dances, in which the words 'tubba catubba' appear" (Croce 187). See introduction to day 1 n6. De Simone maintains that the "catubba" had a particular relation to childbirth and was thus performed at weddings and as an augury for a newborn baby (7).

things, and as soon as he got out of bed he wanted to make the servants into stew. But when he heard from them what had really happened, he got on his horse, half dead, and rode all over and searched so hard that he finally found the bear. Then he brought her back home, put her in a room, and said to her, 'O, lovely morsel fit for a king, holed up in that skin! O, candle of love, shut inside that hairy lantern! Why all this tenderness with me? So that you can watch me writhe in agony and take leave of me, hair by hair? I'm dying of longing, consumed and spent on account of this beauty, and you can see the clear proof of it: I'm reduced to a third of what I was, like boiled wine; I'm nothing but skin and bones; and I've got a fever that's double-stitched to these veins of mine. And so lift the curtain of that stinking hide and let me see the stage set of your beauties; remove, oh, remove the branches from that basket and let me take a look at your lovely fruit; lift that drapery from your door and let these eyes come in and see the pomp of your marvels! Who put such a sleek piece of work in a jail woven of fur? Who locked such a lovely treasure in a strongbox made of hide? Let me see this monster of grace, and take my every desire as your payment, my darling, for only the fat of this bear can cure my twitching nerves!'

"But after repeating these things over and over again he saw that he was throwing away his words. And so he went back and flung himself into bed, and he came down with such a terrible illness that the doctors gave these affairs of his a bad prognosis. His mother, who had no other pleasure in the world but him, sat at the side of his bed and said, 'My son, whence is born all this heartbreak? What sort of melancholic humor has gotten hold of you? You're young, you're well loved, you're great, you're rich; what are you missing, my son? Tell me, for "the shamefaced pauper always has empty pockets." If you want a wife, you choose and I'll put down the deposit; you take and I'll pay. Don't you see that your pain is my pain? Your pulse is throbbing, as is my heart; you have a fever in your blood and I have an ailment in my head, for there is no other bastion of my old age but you. And so be cheerful; you'll cheer up this heart of mine and avoid seeing this kingdom go to ruin, this house crumble to the ground, and this mother shave off all her hair.'[14] When the prince heard these words he said, 'Nothing can comfort me but the sight of the bear. Therefore, if you want to see me healthy allow her to stay in this

---

14. I.e., as a widow would do. "The custom of a woman shaving her hair off on her husband's death and burying it with the corpse, tied to its hands, and then not marrying again until the hair had grown back, was still in use in some parts of the Kingdom of Naples" (Croce 190).

room, and I want no one but her to take care of me, make my bed, and cook for me. And, without a doubt, the pleasure I derive will make me healthy in four snaps.'

"Even though his mother thought it a mistake to have the bear act as cook and maid and suspected that her son was raving, all the same, to content him, she had the bear come. As soon as the bear arrived at the prince's bed she lifted her paw and felt the patient's pulse, which frightened the queen, who thought that from one moment to the next she might tear off his nose. But when the prince said to the bear, 'My dear Chiappino,[15] don't you want to cook for me and feed me and take care of me?' she lowered her head, indicating that she accepted the proposition. And so his mother had an armful of chickens brought in, and the fire was lit in a fireplace right there in the bedroom, and water put to boil; and the bear, taking a chicken in her hand, scalded it, plucked it expertly, and when she had gutted it stuck part of it on a spit and with the rest made a nice gratin. The prince, who hadn't been able to keep even sugar down, was now licking his fingers, and when he had finished stuffing himself she gave him something to drink with such grace that the queen wanted to kiss her on the forehead.

"After that the prince went downstairs to provide the touchstone of all doctors' judgments,[16] and the bear immediately made the bed and, running out to the garden, picked a pretty bunch of roses and orange blossoms and scattered them on top of the bedclothes, so that the queen said that this bear was worth a fortune and that her son had a chamber pot of good reasons to hold her dear.

"At the sight of this lovely service, tinder was added to the prince's fire, and if before he had consumed himself by the dram, now he was destroying himself by the quintal, and he said to the queen, 'Mother, my lady, if I don't give this bear a kiss, my last breath will leave me!' The queen, who saw that he was about to faint, said, 'Kiss him, kiss him, my lovely animal, don't let me see this poor son of mine perish!' The bear went over to him, and the prince grabbed her cheeks and couldn't get enough of kissing her, and as they stood there muzzle to muzzle, I don't know how but the stick fell out of Preziosa's mouth and the most beautiful thing in the world was left standing there in the arms of the prince. Squeezing her with the amorous pincers of his arms, he said to her, 'You fell into the trap, my finch, and now you won't get away from me again without good reason!'

"Adding the color of her embarrassment to the canvas of her natu-

---

15. "A name given to trained bears" (Croce 190).
16. I.e., to give a urine sample.

ral beauty, Preziosa said to him, 'I am already in your hands. I beg you to respect my honor, and you may chop and weigh and turn me whichever way you like.' When the queen asked who this beautiful young lady was and what had forced her into this savage life, Preziosa told the story of her misadventures, leaving out nothing, at which the queen, praising her as a good and honorable girl, told her son that she would be content if she became his wife. And the prince, who desired nothing else in life, immediately gave her his word. His mother blessed the couple, and this lovely union was celebrated with great festivities and light displays, and on the scale of human judgment Preziosa was able to verify that *those who do good may always expect good*."

7

THE DOVE

Seventh Entertainment of the Second Day

Because of an evil spell cast on him by an old woman, a prince undergoes many hardships, which are made even worse by the curse of an ogress. Finally, due to the industry of the ogress's daughter he overcomes all dangers, and they marry.

When this tale of Antonella's had reached its "z"[1] and had been vociferously praised for being lovely and charming as well as a wonderful example for a girl of honor, Ciulla, whose lot it was to continue the tale-telling, spoke in this manner: "He who is born a prince must not behave like a scoundrel. A great man must not give a bad example to those beneath him, for it is from the big ass that the little one learns to eat straw. Otherwise, it's no wonder if the heavens send him misfortunes by the bushelful, like what happened to a prince who had a gadfly[2] up his ass and made trouble for a poor little woman, on account of which he came close to losing his life in disastrous fashion.

"There once was, eight miles outside of Naples in the direction of the Astroni, a wood of fig trees and poplars where the Sun's arrows struck but were not able to penetrate. In this wood there was a little, half-ruined house inhabited by an old woman who was as unburdened with teeth as she was laden by years, and whose hump was as high as her fortunes were low. She had a thousand wrinkles on her face but not a single one in her purse, and although her head was laden with silver she couldn't find half a penny[3] to restore her spirits,

AT 313C: The Girl as Helper in the Hero's Flight, followed by the episode of the Forgotten Fiancée. Croce mentions similarities with tales from Pitrè (*Fiabe, nov. e racc. sic.* 13) and Imbriani. See also Grimm 56, "Sweetheart Roland" and 113, "The Two Kings' Children," and Gonzenbach 13 and 15.

1. *rumme e busse* (Neap.): "At the end of old primers the four abbreviations *et, cum, rum,* and *bus* would be listed; schoolchildren of long ago had a playful saying that went: 'Et con rum e busso, / Quando cade, te rumpe 'u musso' [Et, con, rum, and bus, / When you fall down you'll break your puss]" (Croce 193).
2. *li cruosche* (Neap.): "Intestinal worms that make horses excitable and sometimes uncontrollable" (Croce 193).
3. *uno de ciento vinte a carrino* (Neap.): see introduction to day 1 n22.

and she was always going around to the huts in the area, begging for some charity to keep her alive.

"Nowadays, however, people would more willingly give a fat bag of coins to a greedy spy than three measly coins to a needy pauper, and so she labored for an entire threshing season just to get a bowl of beans, at a time when there was such abundance in those parts that there were few houses that did not have bushels of them. But 'An old cauldron has either dents or holes,' and 'God sends flies to a scrawny horse,' and 'A fallen tree gets a nice hatchet job.' And when the poor old woman had come back with the beans she cleaned them, threw them into a pot, put the pot on the windowsill, and then went to the woods to look for a few little sticks so that she could cook them. But between the time she left and returned Nardo Aniello, the son of the king, came passing by those parts on his way to the hunt. Seeing the pot on the windowsill, he got the urge to take a nice shot, and he made a bet with his servants as to who could aim the straightest, and hit it smack in the middle with a rock. They thus began to bombard that innocent pot, and after three or four throws the prince hit the bull's-eye and smashed it to pieces.

"By the time the old woman got back they had left, and when she found that cruel disaster she began to do terrible things and to yell, 'Tell the Foggia billy goat[4] that butted horns with this pot that he can flex his muscles and go bragging! That son of a witch has dug a ditch for his own flesh; that lout of a dirty peasant has sowed my beans in the wrong season! Even if he didn't have a drop of compassion for my misery, he should have had some respect for his own interests and not thrown the coat of arms of his own house to the ground, nor caused what is kept on the head to end up underfoot. But go on! I pray to the heavens with my knees bared[5] and with all my heart that he may fall in love with the daughter of some ogress who will make him boil and cook in the worst way, and that his mother-in-law may whip him so badly that he sees that he is alive but cries to be dead and that, when he finds himself tethered by the daughter's beauties and the mother's enchantments, he may never be able to pack his bags but always, even if he should croak, be subject to the torments of that ugly harpy. And may she order him to do anything she wants and send him his bread on a crossbow,[6] so that he sighs more than a few times over those beans of mine that he threw away.'

---

4. "An ancient proverb, referred to below (and based on the similar shape of beans and horns) went: 'He who sows beans, sprouts horns'" (Guarini and Burani 235). For Foggia, see tale 1.8 n7.

5. "A solemn oath" (Guarini and Burani 235).

6. I.e., "unwillingly and rudely" (Guarini and Burani 238).

"The old woman's curses put on wings and immediately rose to the sky so that, although the proverbs say, 'You can sow a woman's curses in your asshole' and 'A cursed horse's coat shines,' they nonetheless hit the prince right between the eyes and almost caused him to lose his hide. For before two hours had gone by he was separated from the rest of his men and lost his way in the woods, where he encountered a most beautiful girl who was walking around gathering snails and saying, to amuse herself, 'Come out, come out, horns, or mommy will break them off! She'll break them off on the terrace, and then have a baby boy!'[7] When the prince saw before him this writing desk full of Nature's most precious possessions, this bank of the heavens' richest deposits, and this arsenal of Love's most almighty forces, he did not know what had happened to him, and the rays of her eyes, passing through that round crystal face until they reached the bait of his heart, lit him up to such a degree that he became a furnace that fired the stones of the plans for the construction of the house of his hopes.

"Filadoro, for that was the young lady's name, did not waste her time peeling medlars. The prince was a nice hunk of a young man, and her heart was immediately pierced through and through, so that each of them used their eyes to beg the other for mercy, and even if their tongues had the pip, their gazes were trumpets of the Vicaria crier[8] that rendered public the secrets of their souls. And when both one and the other had stood there for a long time with sand in their gullets, unable to squeeze out one accursed word, at last the prince, unclogging the pipe of his voice, spoke to her in this manner: 'In which meadow has this flower of beauty blossomed? From which sky has this dew of grace rained? From which mine has this treasure of beauteous things come? O happy forests, O fortunate woods, inhabited by this magnificence, illuminated by this light display[9] of Love's festivities! O woods and forests, where not handles for brooms are cut, nor crossbeams for gallows, nor lids for chamber pots, but doors for the temple of beauty, rafters for the house of the Graces, and shafts from which to make Love's arrows!'

"'Keep your hands down, my dear knight,' answered Filadoro, 'you're far too kind, for the epitaph of praise that you have given me refers to your virtues and not my merits. I am a woman who knows how to take her own measure, and I do not need others to serve as my

7. "A children's song used to try to get a snail to stick out its horns. It is also found in other countries of Europe" (Croce 566).
8. See tale 1.1 n18.
9. "The art of fireworks and night illumination is one of the most sophisticated semiotic traditions of the Baroque" (Rak 394).

ruler. But whatever I am, beautiful or ugly, dark or light, disfigured or stocky, quick or lazy, a grouper fish or a fairy, a little doll or a swollen toad, I'm entirely at your command. This lovely cut of a man has filleted my heart; this handsome face of a lord has run me through from back to front; and I give myself to you like a little slave girl in chains,[10] now and forever after.'

"These were not words, but the blast of a trumpet that called the prince with a 'Dinner's ready!' to the table of amorous delights; indeed, words that roused him with an 'Everyone on your horses!' to the battle of Love. And seeing himself given a finger of tenderness, he took the whole hand, and kissed the ivory hook that had snagged his heart. At this princely ceremony Filadoro put on the face of a marquise;[11] indeed, she put on a face like a painter's palette, where you could see a blend of the minium of embarrassment, the cerise of fear, the verdigris of hope, and the cinnabar of desire.

"But right when Nardo Aniello was intending to continue in this fashion, his words were cut off, since in this wretched life there is no wine of satisfaction without the dregs of disappointment, and no rich broth of happiness without the foam of misfortune. For just as he was at the best part there suddenly appeared Filadoro's mother, an ogress so ugly that Nature had fashioned her as a model for all monstrosity. Her hair was like a broom made of dry branches, not to sweep dust and cobwebs from houses but to blacken and smoke out hearts; her forehead was made of Genoese stone, to whet the knife of fear that rips open chests; her eyes were comets that predicted shaky legs, wormy hearts, frozen spirits, diarrhea of the soul, and evacuation of the intestines, for she wore terror on her face, fear in her gaze, thunder in her footsteps, and dysentery in her words. Her mouth was tusked like a pig's and as big as a scorpion fish's, twisted like those who suffer from convulsions, and as drooly as a mule's. In short, from head to toe you saw a distillate of ugliness and a hospital of deformities, so that if the prince didn't breathe his last at that sight, he must certainly have been carrying a story of Marco and Fiorella[12] sewn in his jacket.

"The ogress grabbed Nardo Aniello's doublet and said, 'Hands up! Police! Birdy, birdy, sleeve of iron!'[13] 'Be my witnesses!'[14] answered the prince. 'Back off, scoundrel!' and he was about to lay hand on his

---

10. "A formula used in signing letters" (Croce 567).
11. *marchesa* (Neap.): marquise vs. menstruation (Croce 197).
12. See tale 1.2 n12.
13. One of the children's games mentioned in the opening to day 2.
14. "Another formula used to invoke the testimony of bystanders present at the scene of an insult or injury" (Croce 198).

sword, which was an old she-wolf,[15] when instead he ended up like a sheep that has just seen a wolf: he could neither move nor utter a peep. In this state he was dragged like an ass by its halter to the ogress's house, where, as soon as they arrived, she said to him, 'Take good care to work like a dog, if you don't want to die like a pig. For your first job, make sure that the plot of land[16] outside this room is hoed and planted by the end of the day, and mind you, if I come back this evening and don't find the work done, I'll eat you right up!' And after she told her daughter to take care of the house, she left to visit with the other ogresses in the wood.

"When he saw himself reduced to this awful situation Nardo Aniello's chest began to flood with tears, and he cursed the ill fortune that had dragged him to this treacherous passage. Filadoro, on the other hand, comforted him and told him that he needed to keep his spirits up, for she would give her own blood to help him, and that he shouldn't say that it was wicked fate that had led him to that house, where he was so passionately loved by her, and that he was showing very little reciprocation of her love by being so desperate about what had happened to him. To which the prince answered, 'I don't mind that I've gotten off the horse and onto the ass, nor that I've traded a royal palace for this hole, sumptuously laid tables for a crust of bread, a court of servants for having to serve up piecework, a scepter for a hoe, terrifying armies with seeing myself terrified by an ugly skunk; I consider all my misfortunes luck if I am here and able to gaze at you with these eyes. But what pierces my heart is that I must use a hoe and spit in my hands a hundred times, whereas before I didn't deign to spit on a boil. And even worse, I have so much to do that a whole day with a pair of oxen wouldn't be enough, and if I don't get this dirty business done by tonight I'll be gobbled up by your mother, and I won't suffer as much for having to tear myself away from this wretched body as I will for having to separate myself from your lovely person!' As he said this he sent forth sobs by the basketful and tears by the quintal.

"But Filadoro, drying his eyes, said, 'Do not believe, my dear heart, that you have any land to work other than the garden of Love; nor should you fear that my mother will touch even one hair on your body. There's no need to doubt, for you have Filadoro: in case you don't know, I'm enchanted; I can make water curdle and the sun grow dark. But that's enough; that will do! Be happy, for by this eve-

---

15. See tale 1.7 n37.

16. *muoio* (Neap.): "The *moggio* was an ancient land measure equal to approximately one third of a hectare" (Guarini and Burani 239).

"Testemmonia vosta!" . . . ma restaie comm'a na pecora quanno ha visto lo lupo. ["Be my witnesses!" . . . when instead he ended up like a sheep that has just seen a wolf.]

ning the land will be hoed and planted without your having to lift a finger.' When Nardo Aniello heard this he said, 'If you're a fairy, as you say you are, O beauty of the world, why don't we vacate this town, since I want to keep you like a queen at my father's house?' And Filadoro answered, 'A certain conjunction of the stars is an obstacle to this game, but the influence will pass shortly and then we shall be happy.'

"The day went by in these and a thousand other sweet discussions, and when the ogress came back home she called her daughter from the road, saying, 'Filadoro, let down your hair,' since the house didn't have stairs and she always went up on her daughter's locks. When Filadoro heard her mother's voice she shook out her hair and lowered it, making a ladder of gold for a heart of iron. After climbing up the ogress immediately ran to the garden, and when she found it tended to, she nearly jumped out of her clothes with amazement, as it seemed impossible to her that a delicate young man could have done this dog's labor.

"But no sooner had the Sun come out the next morning to hang itself out to dry after catching the damp in the river of India[17] than the old woman went out again, leaving Nardo Aniello the message that by evening he was to split six piles of logs that were in a big room into four pieces each, or else she would mince him up like lard and make spiced meat[18] of him for their meal that evening. When the poor prince heard the injunction of this decree he was about to die of agony, and Filadoro, seeing him pale and listless, said to him, 'What a pants shitter you are! Bless the new year! You'd shit at the sight of your own shadow!' 'What, it seems like nothing to you,' answered Nardo Aniello, 'to have to split six piles of logs into four pieces each between now and this evening? Alas, before that happens I myself will be split in half so that I can fit into that wretched old woman's gullet!' 'Don't worry,' replied Filadoro, 'the wood will find itself all nice and split without a bit of effort on your part; but in the meantime be a little more pleasant and don't split this soul of mine with so much complaining.'

"But when the Sun closed the shop of its rays so that it wouldn't have to sell light to the shadows, the old woman came back, and after asking for the usual ladder to be lowered, she climbed up, and when she found the wood split she began to suspect that her daughter had checkmated her. And on the third day, for the third test she told him

---

17. The Ganges.
18. *piccatiglio* (Neap.): "From the Spanish *picadillo*, meat cut into small pieces and seasoned with spices and beaten egg" (Croce 200).

to clean out a cistern that contained a thousand barrels of water be-cause she wanted to fill it up again, and to make sure it was done by evening or else she would make escabeche[19] or stew out of him.

"When the old woman had left, Nardo Aniello started moaning again and Filadoro, seeing that his labor pains were growing ever-more frequent and that the old woman was an ass to want to load the poor man with so many troubles and hardships, said to him, 'Be quiet; the conjunction of the stars that had kept my art sequestered is past, and we're going to say "take care" to this house before the Sun says "I take my leave of you."[20] Enough said; by evening my mother will find this town deserted, and I intend to come with you dead or alive.' When he heard this news the prince simmered down, whereas he had been about to croak, and, embracing Filadoro, said, 'You are the north wind of this troubled boat, my soul; you are the bastion of my hopes!'

"It was almost evening by then, and Filadoro dug a hole under the garden, where there ran a big tunnel, and they left, heading in the di-rection of Naples. But as soon as they arrived at the Pozzuoli grotto,[21] Nardo Aniello said to Filadoro, 'My darling, it's not a good idea to have you come to the palace on foot and dressed that way. Wait in this inn, and I'll be back right away with horses, carriages, servants, clothes, and other nice trifles.' And so while Filadoro stayed there he headed for the city. In the meantime the ogress returned home, and when Filadoro didn't answer the usual calls she became suspicious and ran to the woods, where she cut a long pole that she leaned against the window, and, scrambling up like a cat, she climbed into the house. She looked everywhere, inside and outside, upstairs and downstairs, and when she found no one she noticed the hole; after she saw that it led to the square, she left not a single tuft of hair on her head, cursing her daughter and the prince and praying to the heavens that at the first kiss her daughter's lover received he would forget her.

"But let's leave the old woman to her savage paternosters and go back to the prince. After he arrived at the palace, where he was sup-posed dead, the whole house was thrown into a state of commotion, with everyone rushing to see him and saying, 'It's about time; wel-

---

19. "A marinade (vinegar, basil, garlic, mint) for seasoning fish and vegetables that have already been cooked" (Croce 201).

20. *m'arrequaquiglio* (Neap.): "Literally, 'I'm going back into my shell'; also used at the end of letters" (Croce 201).

21. "The tunnel in the Posillipo hill, constructed at the time of Augustus by the ar-chitect Cocceius, for the new road that ran from Pozzuoli to Naples. In the Middle Ages it was attributed to the magical arts of Virgil" (Croce 567).

come back! Here he is, safe and sound! How handsome you look now that you're back in these parts!' and a thousand other loving words. He went upstairs and met his mother halfway there, and she hugged him and kissed him, saying, 'My son, my jewel, pupil of my eye; oh, where have you been? Why did you take so long, and make us all suffer so?' The prince didn't know what to answer, and he would have told of his misadventures, but no sooner had his mother kissed him with her lips of poppy than, because of the ogress's curse, everything that had happened to him left his memory. And then the queen went on to say that in order to eliminate the cause for hunting and consuming his life in the woods, she intended to marry him off, and the prince responded, 'And it won't be soon enough! Here I am, ready and waiting to do everything that my lady mother desires.' 'That's how blessed children act,' replied the queen. And so they agreed that in four days' time they would bring the bride to the house; she was a lady of great nobility who had come to that city from the parts of Flanders.

"And hence they ordered grand festivities and banquets. But meanwhile, Filadoro saw that her husband was taking too long, and her ears started buzzing—I don't know how—with the news of the festivities that everyone was talking about. And one evening, after she made sure that she had seen the innkeeper's errand boy go to bed, she took his clothes from the head of his mattress and left her own there. Thus disguised as a man she went off to the king's court, where the cooks, who were in need of help because of all they had to do, took her on as a scullery boy.

"The morning of the event arrived—when, on the counter of the sky, the Sun displayed its privileges, granted by Nature and sealed by light, and sold secrets to sharpen the eyes[22]—and the bride arrived to the sound of shawms and cornets. The table was set and everyone seated, and the food began to come out thick and fast, and as the steward was cutting a large English pie[23] that Filadoro had made with her own hands, out flew a dove so beautiful that the guests forgot about eating and gazed with wonder at this beauteous thing. And with the most pitiful voice in the world it said to the prince, 'Have you eaten cat's brain,[24] O prince, that has made you forget in word and deed Filadoro's affection? This is how the services you received have left your memory, O thankless one? This is how you pay back

22. "Like charlatans and tooth-extractors, who exhibited the 'privileges' [licenses] they had obtained, as well as various other certificates" (Croce 203).
23. *'mpanata 'ngrese* (Neap.): "A meat pudding also called 'English pie'" (Rak 395).
24. "According to popular belief, eating cat's brain led to loss of memory" (Croce 567).

the favors that she did for you, O ingrate? Saving you from the ogress's clutches? Giving you her life and all of herself? Is this the compensation you give to that unlucky girl for the passionate love she showed you? You tell her to turn around and get out of here; you tell her to gnaw on a bone until the roast comes! Oh, wretched is the woman that lets herself be impregnated by the words of men, who always accompany their words with ingratitude, their favors with thanklessness, and their debts with forgetfulness! There you have it, the poor thing imagined she would be making pizza with you according to the rules of Donatus,[25] and now she finds herself playing cut-the-cake; she believed she would be doing "close the ranks" with you, and now you're yelling, "Escape, escape"![26] She thought she would be able to break a glass with you, and now she's broken the chamber pot! Go on, never you mind, deadbeat-face, for if the heart-felt curses that this wretched soul is sending you hit their target, you'll realize how much it costs to trick a little girl, to dupe a young lady, and to hoodwink a poor innocent by taking a dirty shot at her,[27] wearing her on your back cover while she wore you on her frontis-piece, putting her under your tailbone while she carried you on her head, and while she gave you her complete servitude keeping her where enemas are served! But if the heavens have not put on a blind-fold and if the gods have not plugged their ears, they'll see the wrong you have done her and, when you least expect it, you'll get the holi-day and its eve, thunder and lightning, fever and diarrhea! But enough said. Take care to eat well; amuse yourself as you will; wallow and triumph with the new bride; and poor Filadoro, as she spins her thin threads of grief, will break the thread of her life and leave the field open for you to enjoy your new wife.' Having said these words she flew out the window and the wind bore her away.

"When the prince heard this dovish grumbling he stood there, stiff as a board, for a long time. At last he asked where the pie had come from, and when he heard from the steward that a kitchen boy hired for the occasion had made it, he had the boy brought before him. When she arrived she threw herself at Nardo Aniello's feet and, cry-ing a stream of tears, she could say nothing but, 'What did I do to you, filthy dog? What did I do to you?' Due to the power of Filadoro's beauty and the force of her enchantment, the prince began to remem-

---

25. "Aelius Donatus' Latin grammar [fourth century AD] was used for centuries; this is perhaps an allusion to a student's joke" (Croce 203).
26. "Shouts during mass riots" (Croce 204).
27. *trucco mucco* (Neap.): "A shot in the game of *trucco* in which the opponent's ball is knocked out of its position, which one's own comes to occupy" (Croce 204). For the game of *trucco*, similar to bocce, see tale 1.10 n20.

ber the obligations he had stipulated before her in the tribunal of
Love, and he immediately had her rise and sit next to him. Then he
told his mother of the great debt he owed this beautiful young
woman, of all that she had done for him, and of the promise he had
made her, which he needed to keep.

"His mother, who had no pleasure other than this son, said to him,
'Do what you like, as long as you respect the honor and desire of this
little miss whom you took for your wife.' 'Don't bother yourselves,'
answered the bride, 'for if you really want to know the truth, I would
have been reluctant to stay in this land. But since the heavens have
treated me well, with your kind permission I would like to return to
my Flanders so that I can find the grandparents of the glasses[28] that
are used in Naples, where, when I thought I would be lighting the
lamp the right way,[29] the lantern of this life almost went out.'

"With great happiness the prince offered her a vessel and servants,
and after Filadoro was dressed like a princess and the tables were
cleared the musicians came in and the dancing began and lasted until
evening. But then—when the Earth was covered in mourning clothes
for the funeral rites of the Sun—torches were brought out, and on the
stairs there was suddenly heard a loud jangling of bells, at which the
prince said to his mother, 'This must be a nice masquerade[30] of some
sort, to honor the festivities. My word, Neapolitan gentlemen are certainly refined, and when they have to they squander the raw and the
cooked.'

"While they were passing this judgment, in the middle of the hall
there appeared a hideous mask, no taller than three spans but wider
than a barrel. When it was before the prince, it said, 'You should
know, Nard'Aniello, that your jokes and bad deeds have been the
cause of all of the misfortunes you have encountered. I am the shadow
of that old woman whose pot you broke, immediately after which I
died of hunger. I put a curse on you so that you would fall victim to
the torments of an ogress, and my prayers were granted, but due to
the power of this lovely fairy you fled those troubles. Then you received another curse from the ogress, that at the first kiss you were
given you would forget Filadoro. Your mother kissed you and Fila-

---

28. "Large wine mugs that were used in Flanders and Germany" (Croce 568). I.e.,
"the models for the glasses used in Naples, an allusion to the crystal-makers of these
countries but also to the capacity of the glasses, quite different from those used in
Naples" (Rak 396).

29. Vs. drinking a few carafes. See tale 2.2 n3.

30. "Basile himself organized the masquerade held in the Royal Palace of Naples in
October 1630 for the arrival of Queen Maria of Hungary, who was to marry Arch-
duke Ferdinand of Austria" (Croce 568).

doro passed from your mind, but due to her art you now find her at your side. I've returned, though, to put yet another curse on you: in remembrance of the harm you did me, may the beans that you threw always appear before you, and may the proverb "He who sows beans sprouts horns" come true.' That said, she slipped away like quicksilver, leaving not a wisp of smoke behind her.

"The fairy, who saw that the prince had grown pale at these words, cheered him up by saying, 'Have no fear, my husband. *Sciatola* and *matola*:[31] if it is a spell may it not be valid; I'll get you out of the fire!' When this was said and the festivities had ended, they went to bed, and to authenticate the contract of their newly promised loyalty the prince had his two witnesses[32] sign it. And the past hardships made the present pleasures more tasty, since it can be seen in the crucible of all that happens in the world that *he who stumbles and does not fall advances in his journey*."

---

31. "Magic formula; perhaps *matola* comes from the Calabrese *matula*, in vain" (Guarini and Burani 248).
32. Vs. testicles. E.g., Plautus, *Curculio* 1.1 31 (Rak 396).

8

THE LITTLE SLAVE GIRL

Eighth Entertainment of the Second Day

Lisa is born from a rose petal and then dies because of a fairy's curse. Her mother puts her in a room and gives her brother instructions not to open it. But his jealous wife wants to see what is in there, finds Lisa alive, and, after dressing her as a slave, makes her suffer a thousand torments. She is finally recognized by her uncle, who drives his wife away and arranges the richest of marriages for his niece.

"Truly," said the prince, "every man must practice his own trade: the lord that of the lord, the groom that of the groom, and the cop that of the cop. For just as the boy who wants to act like a prince makes himself ridiculous, so the prince who acts like a boy loses his reputation." Saying this, he turned to Paola and told her that she could let herself go. After sucking her lips at length and scratching her head, she began in this manner: "If it's worth anything to tell the truth, jealousy is a terrible little demon, a vertigo that makes your head spin, a fever that heats up your veins, a calamity that chills your limbs, a dysentery that makes your intestines churn, and, finally, a sickness that takes your sleep away, makes your food bitter, disturbs your peace, and cuts your life in half; it's a serpent that bites, a woodworm that gnaws, bile that poisons, snow that numbs, a nail that perforates, a marriage breaker of the delights of Love, a wrecker[1] of amorous joys, and a constant tempest in the sea of Venus's pleasures, from which nothing of good has ever sprung, as you will confess with your own tongues upon hearing the tale that follows.

"There once was a baron, the baron of Dark Wood, who had a maiden sister who always went with other young ladies her age to frolic in a garden. And on one of these occasions they found a lovely,

---

AT 410: Sleeping Beauty, and AT 894: The Ghoulish Schoolmaster and the Stone of Pity. Penzer mentions a Turkish tale similar to this one. The tale also shares motifs with Grimm 89, "The Goose Girl" (where the heroine recounts her sorrows to an iron stove), and 54, "Snow White" (the comb and the glass coffin), as well as with Gonzenbach 11 and tale 5.5 of this collection.

1. *scazzellacane* (Neap.): "literally, someone who separates mating dogs" (Croce 207).

overblown rosebush, and pledged that whoever jumped clean over it without touching a leaf would win something.

"A number of the girls jumped, straddling their legs, but they all brushed against it, and none of them got clear over. But then it was the turn of Lilla, the baron's sister, and she took a little running start and then raced off so fast that she jumped clear over the rose. She did cause one petal to fall, but she was so quick and agile that she picked it up in a flash from the ground, swallowed it, and won the prize.

"But before three days had gone by she felt pregnant and nearly died of grief, since she knew for certain that she hadn't been up to any tricks or dirty business, and couldn't figure out how her belly had swollen up. And so she ran off to some fairies who were friends of hers, who told her not to fear, for it was the rose petal that she had swallowed. When Lilla heard this she tried to hide her belly as best she could, and when it came time to unload the weight she gave birth in secret to a lovely daughter whom she named Lisa. She sent the girl to the fairies, who each gave her a charm, but as the last one came running to see the baby girl she twisted her foot so dreadfully that in her pain she put a curse on her: when she was seven years old, her mother would comb her hair and forget the comb on her head, where it would remain stuck and cause her to die.

"When the time arrived, all of this occurred. The poor mother, desperate over this misfortune, first lamented bitterly and then enclosed Lisa in seven crystal caskets, each contained within the other, and put her in the last room of the palace, keeping the key for herself. But since the pain caused by this matter had reduced her to the last drops[2] of her life, she called her brother and said to him, 'My brother, I feel myself being pulled, bit by bit, by Death's hook, and thus I leave you all my trinkets, and may you be lord and master of them. I ask only that you give me your word that you will never open the last room of the house, and that you hide this key in the writing desk.' Her brother, who loved her with all his heart, gave her his word in the same instant that she said, 'Farewell; the pods are full.'

"Within a year,[3] after he had married, the lord was invited to a hunting party and left the house in his wife's hands, begging her above all not to open the room whose key he kept in the writing desk. But no sooner had he turned his back than she, pulled by suspicion,

---

2. *scolatura* (Neap.): see tale 1.2 n26.
3. Possibly an error on Basile's part, since Lisa, who died when she was seven, couldn't have grown to be a woman in one year.

driven by jealousy, and choked by curiosity, which is the prime endowment of women, took the key and opened the room. When she opened the caskets, through which she could see the girl shining, what she found seemed to be asleep; the girl had grown just like any other woman, and the caskets, too, had increased in size at the same rate as she had grown.

"When she saw this beautiful creature the jealous woman immediately said, 'Good boy! For the life of me! "Key on the belt and Martin inside!"[4] That's the reason for all this diligence about not opening the room, so that no one would see the Mohammed[5] that he was worshiping in the caskets!' Saying this she grabbed the girl by the hair and pulled her out, and as she did so the comb fell to the ground and the girl came to her senses, screaming, 'Oh, dear mother! Oh, dear mother!' 'Come on, I'll give you mommy and daddy!' answered the baroness and, as full of bile as a slave, as angry as a bitch that has just pupped, and as full of poison as a serpent, she immediately cut off Lisa's hair, gave her a juicy beating, put her in a ragged dress, and every day unloaded lumps on her head, eggplants on her eyes, brands on her face, and gave her a mouth that looked like she had eaten raw pigeons.

"Upon his return her husband saw this girl who was being treated so badly, and asked who she was; his wife answered that she was a slave his aunt had sent, and that she was always fishing for a beating and needed to be harnessed all the time. And when the lord had occasion to go to a fair he asked everyone in the house, even the cats, what they wanted him to buy for them; some asked for one thing and some for another, and he finally came to the little slave girl. His wife behaved like no Christian when she said, 'Go ahead, put this thick-lipped slave in the same bag as us; let's have one rule for everyone, and then we'll all want to piss in the same chamber pot. Leave her alone, damn it, and let's not award so much importance to an ugly animal like her!' The lord, who was a courteous man, wanted at all costs that the little slave girl ask for something, and she said, 'I want nothing more than a doll, a knife, and a pumice stone. And if you

---

4. I.e., "even with the house key in one's pocket it's possible to be betrayed" (Rak 408). "In the south of Italy cuckolded husbands are called 'martini' . . . and Saint Martino was considered the protector of cuckolded husbands, who, it was imagined, on the feast day of this saint walked in processions." See, e.g., Basile's own *Muse napolitane* 6.149.

5. "Mohammed's body, according to a legend common in Europe, was preserved in Medina in a coffin that was suspended in the air by the force of a magnet" (Croce 209).

forget, may it be impossible for you to cross the first river you find on your way.'

"When the baron had purchased everything except what his niece had asked him for, he came to a river—that carried stones and trees from the mountains to the seacoast to pour foundations of fear and raise walls of marvel—across which it was impossible for him to pass. And so he remembered the curse of the little slave girl and went back and bought every last thing, and when he returned home he distributed, one by one, the things he had bought.[6]

"After Lisa had her little things she went into the kitchen and, putting the doll in front of her, began to cry and wail, telling that bundle of rags the whole story of her troubles as if she were speaking to a living person, and when she saw that the doll was not answering, she took the knife, sharpened it on the pumice stone, and said, 'You'll see; if you don't answer me I'm going to stick myself, and the party will be over!' And the doll, swelling up slowly like a bagpipe when it's blown into, finally answered, 'Yes, I heard you, and better than a deaf person!'

"Now this music lasted a few days, and it happened once that the baron, who had a little room that shared a wall with the kitchen, heard the usual dirge and stuck his eyes to the keyhole of the door. He saw Lisa telling the doll about how her mother had jumped over the rose, eaten the petal, and given birth; about the spell that had been cast on her, the fairy's curse, how the comb had stayed in her hair, her death, how she had been shut in the seven caskets and hidden in the room; about her mother's death, the key left to her brother, the hunting trip, the wife's jealousy, her entrance into the room where Lisa lay against the brother's order; about how her hair had been cut and she had been treated like a slave, and the so very many torments to which she had been subjected. As she was recounting all this and weeping, she cried, 'Answer me, doll, or I'll kill myself with this knife!' But while she was sharpening it on the pumice stone with the intention of stabbing herself, the baron gave the door a kick and took the knife from her hand. When he had heard the story in greater detail he embraced her as his niece and removed her from the house, putting her in the care of a relative of his so that she could recover a little, for she had become half of what she had once been due to the bad treatment received from that heart of Medea.

"Within a few months, when she had grown as beautiful as a goddess, he had her brought to his house, saying that she was a niece of

---

6. This part of the tale recalls the similar events of "The Cinderella Cat" (1.6).

his, and after they had a great banquet and the tables had been cleared, he asked Lisa to tell the story of the suffering she had undergone and the cruelty of his wife, which made all the guests cry. And then he kicked out his wife, banishing her to the house of some relatives, and gave a nice husband to his niece, just as her heart desired. And thus Lisa touched with her own hands the fact that *when you least expect it, the heavens rain down their graces.*"

9

THE PADLOCK

Ninth Entertainment of the Second Day

Lucia goes to get some water at a fountain and finds a slave who puts her in a splendid palace, where she is treated like a queen. But she is advised by her envious sisters to look at the person with whom she sleeps at night, and when she discovers that it is a handsome young man she loses favor with him and is sent away. After wandering through the world for several years, pregnant and big-bellied, she reaches her lover's house and gives birth to a son. Following various incidents they make peace and she becomes his wife.

Everyone's heart was moved to great compassion by all the misfortunes that poor little Lisa had undergone, and more than a few of them displayed red eyes welled up with tears, for there is nothing that arouses pity more than seeing someone suffer innocently. But since it was Ciommetella's turn to work the spinning wheel, she spoke in this manner: "Advice given in envy has always been the father of misfortune, because under the mask of goodwill hides the face of ruin, and a person who finds his hands in Fortune's hair must imagine that at any moment there will be a hundred other people who stretch cords in front of his feet to make him trip and fall. That is what happened to a poor girl who, because of the bad advice of her sisters, fell from the top of the ladder of happiness, and it was only by the mercy of the heavens that she didn't break her neck.

"There once was a mother who had three daughters, and because of the great poverty that had stepped foot into her house, which was a sewer pipe where streams of misfortunes flowed, she sent them out

---

AT 425: The Search for the Lost Husband, and AT 425E: Enchanted Husband Sings Lullaby. This is one of a number of stories in *The Tale of Tales* that share their motifs with the Cupid and Psyche story. Croce makes reference to Italian variants, as well as Grimm 88 ("The Singing, Springing Lark") (*Lo cunto de li cunti* clxv–vi). Penzer discusses a very similar Greek tale and hypothesizes that Basile may have derived his from it. There are also variants from Turkey and Crete, and Basile could have heard one of these while in Venice or Crete (where he was stationed during 1604–07), though it does not seem that he knew either Turkish or modern Greek (1:200–01). See also Gonzenbach 15 and 43, Pitrè, *Fiabe, nov. e racc. sic.* 32.

to beg so that they could scrape by. One morning she found some cabbage leaves that had been thrown away by a cook in a palace and, wanting to cook them, she told each of her daughters to go get a little water at the fountain. They batted it back and forth between them like a cat giving orders to its tail[1] until the poor mother said, 'Give orders, but do it yourself,' and, taking the jug, she intended to go do the chore in person even if she could barely drag her legs on account of her advanced old age.

"But Luciella, the youngest, said, 'Give that to me, my dear mother, for although I don't have all the strength I might need, I still want to relieve you of this labor.' And she took the jug and went outside the city, where there stood a fountain—that when it saw the flowers pale with fear of the night threw water in their faces—at which she encountered a handsome slave, who said to her, 'My lovely girl, if you want to come with me to a grotto not far from here, I'll give you a lot of nice little things.' Luciella, always dying for a favor, answered him, 'Let me bring this bit of water to my mother, who is waiting for me, and then I'll come right back.' She brought the jug home, then returned to the fountain with the excuse of going to look for a splinter or two of wood; there she found the slave again and set off with him. She was taken through a grotto of tufa decorated with maidenhair and ivy and then into a splendid underground palace, all aglitter with gold, where a fabulous table was immediately set for her. In the meantime two lovely pieces of servant girls came out, took off the few rags she was wearing, and dressed her to perfection, and in the evening they put her to sleep in a bed embroidered all over in pearls and gold, where, as soon as the candles were put out, someone came and lay down beside her.

"This went on for a number of days until eventually the girl got a craving to see her mother, and told the slave. He entered into a room and spoke with I don't know who, came back out, and gave her a large sack of money, telling her to give it to her mother. Then he reminded her not to get lost on the way and to return soon, and to tell no one where she was coming from or where she was staying.

"Now when the girl arrived and her sisters saw how well dressed and well treated she looked, they almost died of envy. And when Luciella wanted to go back, her mother and sisters wanted to accompany her. But she refused their company and returned to the same palace through the same grotto, and after staying there peacefully for another few months she finally got the same longing again,

---

1. "Proverbial expression alluding to the unwillingness to perform some action, even if the pretense of doing it is there" (Croce 214).

and with the usual warning and the usual gifts was sent to her mother.

"After this happened three or four more times, always adding a new sirocco gale of envy to the sisters' hernia, those ugly harpies poked around so hard that they finally found out everything that was going on from an ogress, and when Luciella came home to them the next time they said to her, 'Although you didn't want to tell us anything of your pleasures, you should know that we know everything. Since every night you're given a sleeping potion, you can't be aware of the fact that a splendid young man is sleeping with you. But your happiness will always be incomplete unless you resolve to follow the advice of those who love you; at the end, you're our blood, and we only desire what is profitable and pleasing for you. And so when you go to bed in the evening and the slave comes with the mouthwash, tell him to get you a napkin to clean your mouth, and carefully pour out the wine from the glass so that you'll be able to stay awake during the night. As soon as you see that your husband has fallen asleep, open this padlock, and in spite of anything he may do, the spell will have to be broken, and you will become the happiest woman in the world.'

"Poor Luciella, who didn't know that under the saddle of velvet there was a festering wound, amid the flowers a serpent, and in the golden basin poison, believed the words of her sisters. And after returning to the grotto, night came and she did what those wily girls had told her to. When everything was quiet and silent she lit a candle with a flint and saw next to her a flower of beauty, a young man who was all lilies and roses.

"At the sight of such a beauteous thing she said, 'My word, now he'll never escape from my clutches!' and she took the padlock, opened it, and saw a group of women carrying quantities of fine yarn on their heads. One of them dropped a skein, and Luciella, who was a fountain of charity, didn't remember where she was and raised her voice, crying, 'Pick up the skein, madam!' The young man awoke at this shout and felt such displeasure at having been discovered that in that same instant he called a slave, had Luciella's original rags put on her back, and sent her away. And with the color of someone who has just gotten out of the hospital she returned to her sisters, who then kicked her out with wicked words and even worse actions.

"Luciella then set off to beg her way through the world, and after a thousand torments and when the poor soul was pregnant and big-bellied, she arrived at the city of Tall Tower and went to the royal palace, where she asked for a little straw on which to rest. A lady-in-waiting of the court, who was a good person, took her in, and when it was time to unload her belly she gave birth to a son as beautiful as a golden ear of wheat.

"The first night after he was born, while everyone was sleeping, a handsome young man entered the chambers and said, 'O lovely son of mine: if my mother only knew, she would wash you in a basin of gold and swaddle you in layers of gold, and if the rooster never sang, I would never part from you!' While saying this, he slipped away like quicksilver at the first song of the rooster.

"The lady-in-waiting discovered what was going on, and when she saw that every night the same person was coming to make the same music, she told the queen, who—as soon as the Sun, like a physician, discharged all the stars from the hospital of the sky—had a most cruel proclamation issued: all the roosters of the city were to be killed, causing every hen there to be widowed and scalped[2] in one fell swoop. And when the same young man returned that evening the queen, who was ready with her weapon and wasn't wasting her time sorting lentils, realized that it was her son, and embraced him tightly. Since the curse put on him by an ogress had stipulated that he would always wander far from home until his mother embraced him and the rooster stopped crowing, as soon as he was in his mother's arms the spell was broken and the evil influence ended.

"And thus his mother found that she had acquired a jewel of a grandson; Luciella found herself with a fairy of a husband; and her sisters, when they got the news of her good fortune, came to see her with brazen faces. But they were given pizza for pasty[3] and received payment in the same coin, discovering with great anger in their souls that *the son of envy is heartache.*"[4]

---

2. *carose* (Neap.): see tale 2.6 n14.
3. *tortano* (Neap.): "A ring-shaped yeast bread made with lard and a lot of pepper, and stuffed with cracklings and, sometimes, small pieces of salami, cheese, and hard-boiled eggs" (Guarini and Burani 260).
4. *antecore* (Neap.): "Literally, a stomachache accompanied by nausea and faintness" (Croce 217).

10

THE BUDDY

Tenth Entertainment of the Second Day

Cola Iacovo Aggrancato has a scoundrel of a buddy who sucks him out of everything, and since he's unable to get him off his back with tricks and stratagems, he pulls his head out of the bag and banishes him from his house with rude words.

The tale was truly wonderful and was told with grace and listened to with attention, so that a thousand things contributed to give it the juice necessary to provide pleasure. But since every little bit of time that put itself between one tale and the next kept the slave jerking about as if she had a cord around her neck,[1] Iacova was urged to take her turn at the lathe. She put her hands into the barrel of nursery stories to refresh the thirst of the audience and spoke in this manner: "Lack of discretion, ladies and gentlemen, causes the merchant's measure of good judgment to fall from his hands, the architect's compass of manners to lose accuracy, and the mariner's needle of reason to go awry. And when it takes root in the soil of ignorance, it produces no fruit but shame and humiliation. You can see this happen every day, and in particular it befell a certain bald-faced buddy, as I'm about to tell you.

"There was a certain Cola Iacovo Aggrancato of Pomigliano,[2] husband of Masella Cernecchia of Resina[3] and a man as rich as the sea who didn't even know what he owned, since his pigs were in the pen and he had enough straw to last him till morning.[4] With all of this,

---

This tale, devoid of fairy-tale elements, is in the mold of the Boccaccian novella. Both of the main characters are also variations of stock characters familiar to the repertoire of comic theater from Plautus on—the parasite with the bottomless stomach and his miserly host. Penzer gives variants from a number of collections of Italian popular tales; Grimm 61, "Little Farmer," has some of the same motifs.

1. *li deve li butte* (Neap.): lit., "that gave her the jerks"; "inflicted upon those condemned to torture by the rope, which caused painful sprains and dislocations" (Rak 432).

2. Pomigliano d'Arco, between Naples and Nola. Cola Iacovo's surname (Aggrancato) means "stingy" in Neapolitan.

3. "Outside of Naples, it was built over the ancient city of Herculaneum" (Croce 568).

4. "Burlesque ways of indicating an abundance of goods" (Croce 219).

and in spite of the fact that he had neither children nor troubles and that he weighed his brass by the bushel, he could have run a hundred miles without dropping half a cent[5] and, subjecting himself to every sort of deprivation, he led the miserable life of a dog, and all so that he could save up and accumulate.

"Nevertheless, every time he sat down to eat barely enough to keep alive, it was just his misfortune that a bad-day buddy of his would turn up and refuse to leave him alone for a moment; as if there were a clock in his body and an hourglass between his teeth he presented himself at feeding time so that he could join them and, unabashed, he stuck to them like a tick, and they couldn't have driven him off with a pickax. He counted the bites that went into their mouths and came out with quips and beat with a stick until he was told, 'Please, help yourself.' At which point, without having to be begged too hard, he would throw himself between husband and wife and, as if overcome with cravings, dying of hunger, sharp as a razor, fierce as a hound sent to sic, and with a wolfish craving in his belly and lightning speed—'where are you coming from, the mill?'[6]—he would wave his hands around like a piper, roll his eyes like a wild cat, and work his teeth like a grindstone. He swallowed things whole, not allowing one mouthful to wait for the next, and when his cheeks were good and full, his tummy loaded and his belly like a drum, when he had seen the bottom of the plates and swept up the whole town, without even saying 'take care' he would grab a jug of wine and suck it up, empty it dry, siphon it off, glug it down, and drain it all in one breath until you could see the bottom. And then he would be off on his way to tend to his business, leaving Cola Iacovo and Masella with long faces.

"When they saw this lack of discretion on the part of their buddy, who like a ripped bag gobbled up, guzzled, devoured, gulped down, shoveled in, emptied, ripped off, stole away, lifted, porked down, razed to the ground, polished off, sent down his hatch, demolished, and cleared out everything on the table, they didn't know how to remove this bloodsucker, this poultice on their chest, this infection between their legs, this August cure,[7] this horsefly, this greedy tick, this tourniquet, this splint, this high rent, this perpetual lease, this octopus, this subjection,[8] this weight, this headache; and they could

---

5. See introduction to day 1 n22.
6. "Popular saying that refers to the voracity of gluttons" (Guarini and Burani 263).
7. The heat of the August sun (the *solleone* or "Sun in Leo" mentioned in other passages).
8. *sasina* (Neap.): "Small opening or slit in a house that, looking into a neighboring house, causes the neighbors annoyance" (Croce 220).

barely wait for the time when, at least once, they could relax and eat without this attendant at their side, this grease on their corks.

"One morning, having learned that his buddy had gone out of town to assist some official, Cola Iacovo said, 'Oh, may the Sun in Leo be praised; for once in a hundred years we'll be able to work our chops, unrein our jaws, and stick our noses in without always having that itch up our ass! And so if the Court[9] wants to ruin me, I'll be ruined! In this shithole of a world you get as much as you're able to tear off with your teeth; hurry and light the fire, for now that we've got a time-out[10] when we can have a nice feast, let's give ourselves the satisfaction of eating something tasty, some juicy morsels!' As he was saying this he ran off to buy a fine Pantano[11] eel, a bag of superfine flour, and a good flask of Mangiaguerra wine. After he got back home his wife busied herself preparing a nice pizza while he fried the eel, and when everything was ready they sat down at the table.

"But no sooner were they seated than their sponge of a buddy came knocking at the door. When Masella looked out and saw the party pooper of their happiness, she said to her husband, 'My dear Cola Iacovo, there's never been a roast in the butcher shop of human delights that didn't come with the bone of displeasure; one never sleeps between the white sheets of satisfaction without a few bedbugs of travail; a laundry of pleasure has never been done without some rain of dissatisfaction falling on it! Here we are with this bitter mouthful that has gone down the wrong way; here we are with this shit of a meal stuck in our throats!' To which Cola Iacovo answered, 'Put away those things on the table, get rid of them, hide them, cover them up so you can't see them, and then open the door; maybe if he finds the village sacked he'll have the discretion to leave quickly and give us the chance to gobble up this little bit of poison!' While their buddy was ringing the alarm and chiming the Gloria, Masella stuck the eel behind a cupboard, the flask of wine under the bed, and the pizza between the mattresses, and Cola Iacovo dove down under the table and kept a lookout through a hole in the tablecloth, which hung down to the ground.

"The buddy saw all this traffic through the keyhole, and as soon as the door was opened for him, he went in brazen faced, pretending to

---

9. "A reference to the Neapolitan barons who, summoned from their lands to the prince's court, would spend large amounts of money in pomp and luxuries, and often came to financial ruin because of it" (Croce 220).

10. *mazzafranca* (Neap.): "An allusion to the game called *mazza e piuzo*, in which the suspension of play can be requested with the words 'free club'" (Croce 220).

11. "A place near Naples in whose marshy lake eels were fished" (Guarini and Burani 264).

be all bewildered and frightened, and when Masella asked him what had happened, he said, 'While you were making me suffer with such tribulation and worry outside the door and I was waiting for you to open as if for the urge to go or for the crow to come home, a snake slithered by my feet, and oh, dear mother, what a huge and hideous thing! Let's just say that it was as big as the eel you put in the cupboard. When I found myself in that tight spot I started trembling like a rush; my body began to spin the fine thread of terror; I was wormy with fear and shaking with shock. Then I picked up a rock from the ground, which was as big as that flask under the bed, and boom! I threw it at the snake's head and made a pizza out of it, just like the one between the mattresses! And as it was dying and writhing in pain, I could see that it was looking at me, like my buddy under the table. I don't have a drop of blood left in my body; I'm scared stiff and terrified!'

"No longer able to keep still at those words, Cola Iacovo, who couldn't swallow this sugar, stuck his head out from behind the tablecloth, like Trastullo[12] when he comes onto the stage, and said, 'If that's how it is, we're in a mess! Now we've really filled the spindle! Look, now we've baked the bread! Look, now we've won the case! Look, if we owe you something report us to the Bagliva court;[13] if we insulted you register a complaint at the Zecca![14] If you feel offended hog-tie me; if you've got a fancy use an enema tip to get rid of it; if you expect something from us chase us with a fox's tail[15] or hit us on the nose in Naples![16] What are these terms; what kind of way to proceed is this? You act like an occupying soldier[17] who wants to scare us out of our possessions! A finger should have been enough, but you took the whole hand, and at this point it's clear that you intend to kick us out of our house with all this commotion! He who lacks discretion owns the whole world, but he who will not measure his actions is measured by others, and if you have nothing to measure with, we have reels and rolling pins! And finally, you know what they say: "A nice

---

12. "Famous mask of the *commedia dell'arte,* already popular in Naples by the end of the 16th century" (Croce 222).
13. "Tribunal which heard cases regarding damages to rural properties and all other cases in which the value in question was no more than three ducats. Its jurisdiction included Naples and its outlying villages" (Croce 568).
14. "Another tribunal that heard cases having to do with currency, weights, and measures, and cases of fraud in sales and purchases" (Croce 569).
15. "As children do, chasing a cat or other animal around the house with a duster" (Croce 222).
16. A reference to the ritual for treatment of insolvent debtors (see tale 1.8 n15).
17. "Reference to the disturbances created by soldiers when they lodged in private houses" (Croce 222).

face deserves a nice pounding"! And so each bit of straw to its mattress, and leave us with our own misfortunes. From today on, if you
think you can keep on playing this music you're wasting your footsteps and you won't get a crumb out of it; you'll lose your every adorn-
ment and nothing will go right for you. If you think you can keep on
sleeping in this soft bed, you've got a good time coming, you really do!
You've taken the March cure![18] You can go find a toothpick if you
think this inn is open for your rotten gullet! Look how you run to slip
it on the ring![19] Forget it, get it out of your head; it's wasted effort, it's
thrown to the wind, and there's no more bait or trimmings for you!
You set your eyes on the suckers and the pigeons, you spotted the
featherbrains, you sounded out the jackasses, you found the Land of
Plenty! And now you can just go back where you came from; nothing
is going to be done for you any longer and you can call this house a
feather,[20] for you won't be drawing any more water from my well!
And if you're a dinner spy, a bread gobbler, a table cleaner, a kitchen
sweeper, a pot licker, a bowl shiner, a glutton, a sewer pipe; if you're
ravenous and have a wolf's appetite, if your intestines flood open and
crash in so that you could teach an ass a few things, then empty a ship,
bolt down the prince's bear,[21] do away with the Holy Grail,[22] drink
your fill in the Tiber or the Angravio,[23] and eat up Mariaccio's trousers,[24] and then go to some other parish, go pull up the trawl net, go
pick rags from the garbage dump, go look for nails in the street gul-
lies,[25] go collect wax from funeral candles, and go unplug latrine pipes
so you can fill your gorge. May this house be like fire to you, for everyone has their own problems, everyone knows what they've got under
their clothes and what their stomach can take. We have no need for
these bankrupt firms, these unsuccessful clients, these broken lances!
He who can save himself is saved; we've got to wean you from this
titty, you idler of a bird, useless thing, good-for-nothing! Go to work;
go to work, learn a trade, find yourself a master!'

"When he heard himself given this straight-talking lecture, this

---

18. Another allusion to the ailments associated with the month of March.
19. "An allusion to the game of the ring (or 'sortija,' as it is called in Spanish), which
consisted in trying to 'tilt' or slip a pole in a ring while running" (Croce 223).
20. "Said for things that were difficult to find" (Guarini and Burani 267).
21. "Allusion to the pet bears that nobles kept in their palaces and parks" (Guarini
and Burani 268).
22. "The Saint-Graal of *Perceval* and other romances of the Breton cycle: the precious chalice in which Joseph of Arimathaea had gathered Christ's blood" (Croce
223).
23. "Another river, perhaps the Arno" (Guarini and Burani 268).
24. Proverbial character and expression.
25. See tale 1.8 n10.

bursting abscess, this carding without a reed, the hapless buddy grew all cold and icy, like a thief caught in the act, a pilgrim who has lost his way, a sailor who has wrecked his boat, a whore who has lost her client, or a little girl who has dirtied her bed. And with his tongue between his teeth, his head bowed low, his beard stuck to his chest, his eyes teary, his nose moldy, his teeth icy, his hands empty, his heart heavy, and his tail between his legs, he gathered up his things and left very quietly, cautiously, slowly, and deliberately, silently and without a word. Not once did he turn his head back, and he was reminded of that honorable saying: *A dog not invited to the wedding should not go, or it will get a beating.*"

They all laughed so hard at the humiliation of the shameless buddy that they didn't realize the Sun had been too extravagant with its light and gone bankrupt and, after putting its golden keys under the door, escaped to safety. But then Cola Ambruoso and Marchionno came out with their thigh pieces and their jackets of fringed twill to recite the second motif, and everyone's ears perked up when they heard the epitaph of the eclogue that follows.

THE DYE

Eclogue

Cola Ambruoso and Marchionno

COLA AMBRUOSO: Of all the trades, Marchionno, dyeing must be given first prize and first place, as was noted by someone, whether he was a scullery boy or a cook I don't know.

MARCHIONNO: I oppose that conclusion, Cola Ambruoso, because it's a filthy art; your hands are always covered with gallnut,[1] vitriol, and alum, just like the varnish on a Moor.

COLA: On the contrary, it's the cleanest of all practices; one, in fact, of a man who wants to appear clean even if he is full of grease.

MAR.: You'll have me believe that it's like being a perfumer or an embroiderer! Go on, get out of here, you're wrong!

COLA: I want to prove to you, and even put it to the test of the oven, that the art of the dyer is a noble thing. Nowadays it's used by everyone; with its help man is able to survive and is held in high esteem; whether you have deceit in your belly or vice in your breast, with the dye you can cover any defect.

MAR.: What do the vices of life have to do with dyeing wool or second-rate silk?

COLA: How clear it is that you don't have a clue! You think I'm talking about dyeing socks and old rags! The dye I'm talking about is quite a different thing from indigo or sappanwood;[2] it's a dye that makes the color of myrtle appear like flesh to people!

MAR.: I'm tied in a sack; I don't understand a speck of this; this talk of yours leaves me all tangled up and in the dark!

---

1. A swelling on a plant, from which is derived gallic acid, used to make dyes and inks.
2. Derived from the *Caesalpina sappan* tree, from whose wood a red colorant is extracted (Rak 454).

COLA: Look, if you listen to me I'll teach you how to be a dyer, or else how to recognize those who dye, and you'll get great pleasure out of learning this new art, this art which is the latest thing among the shrewdest of people, an art that can take a cockroach and make it look just like a cat! Listen: someone may be a three-alarm scoundrel, who sweeps away whatever he runs into and whatever he eyes, lifts whatever he sees, and makes off with whatever he finds. Now those who know this dye do not give him the vile name of pilfering thief or sly rogue but will say that he makes good use of his judgment and that his money comes from underground, that he earns a living and would be able to survive even in the woods, that he takes good advantage and is a good knave, a sea bream that knows its way around the port, an ingenious guy, a pirate who knows how to use the crucible, one who never loses his hat in a crowd. And, in short, with this dye, so lovely and gallant, a scoundrel goes by the name of a judicious man!

MAR.: Gosh, you're making yourself clearer by the minute! This is an amazing art! An art, though, that doesn't work for poor fellows, but only for certain ringleaders who come from afar and who are permitted to call—as dryly as can be—their booties comforts and their thefts fruits!

COLA: Take a lazy turncoat, a pants-shitting Jew,[3] a hen, a weak-spirited little fellow with the heart of a chick. He's frightened, terrified, frozen stiff, on the verge of a heart attack; he trembles like a reed, is always spinning the fine thread of fear, always full of vermin and with diarrhea in his bowels, and is afraid of his own shadow. If someone eyes him the wrong way, out comes a quarter bushel of worms; if someone threatens him, he looks likes a plucked quail, he becomes pale and lifeless, he's without words, and he immediately gets the runs. And if that someone puts his hand on his sheath, he pulls up anchor and beats it out of there. But with this noble dye, people take him for a person who is prudent, composed, and respectable, one who makes his way with a plumb line and a compass, who never grabs flying shit, nor buys lawsuits in cold cash. He doesn't hang around courts; he minds his

---

3. Proverbial expression referring to the state of fear Jews lived in due to the centuries-long persecutions and hatred to which they were subjected. Croce maintains that Basile's contacts with Jews must have been in Venice and Candia, not in Naples, where there was no longer a community during his time (569).

own business; he's calm and measured. And in this way, my son, a rabbit is taken for a fox!

MAR.: It seems to me that those who save their own skin have the right idea, for once I read in a story, I don't remember if handwritten or printed, that "a beautiful flight can save a whole life."[4]

COLA: But then, someplace else, you see a man all of a piece, a man who takes risks, a man of courage who's not a crumb less worthy than Rodomonte,[5] who could exchange blows with Orlando and trade punches with Hector,[6] who doesn't allow a fly to pass by his nose and sees to facts before words, who keeps every bully and gang leader tight in his fist and with their two feet in one shoe. He works his hands well, he has a lion's heart, he duels with Death; nor does he ever take a step backward, and he's always butting like a ram. But if he is treated with this dye, he's taken by everyone for an impertinent breakneck, an insolent daredevil, a touchy madman fragile as glass, a demon, a house-consuming fire; one who makes sure you trip on every stone, who looks for fights with a stick; a man without reason, a person without control and without rein for whom there's not a day without a brawl, who makes his neighbors anxious and provokes the stones on the street. In short, the man who we saw to be worthy of verses is now deemed worthy of the oar![7]

MAR.: You be quiet! They're right; a wise and well-adjusted person is one who makes himself respected without a sword!

COLA: Now here we have a miser, a penniless wretch, a belt tightener, a bag closer, a tinker's pincer, a constipated dry shitter, a nail gnawer, a Sienese horse, a juiceless citron, a greasy cork, a prune pit, a sorb ant, a skinflint; the mother of misery, poor little thing, who like a frisky horse will show you a pair of buns[8] before he gives you a hair from his tail. Mean and tight-fisted, he'll run a hundred miles but won't drop a cent; he'll take a hundred bites of a bean; he'll tie a hundred

---

4. Parody of the verse "un bel morir tutta la vita onora," from Petrarch, *Rerum* 1.16.13 (Croce 229).

5. The Saracen warrior of the two best-known Italian chivalric epics, M. M. Boiardo's *Orlando innamorato* and L. Ariosto's *Orlando furioso;* a symbol of brute force (Rak 454).

6. The heroic defender of Troy in Greek mythology and Homer's *Iliad*.

7. I.e., of the galleys.

8. I.e., give you a kick.

knots around a half-penny;[9] and he never shits so he won't have to eat. But this dye immediately puts things right, and it's said that he's a man who saves, who doesn't throw away or waste what he has, who doesn't allow his possessions to be thrown out with the water, who's a good man around the house and doesn't let a crumb of bread fall on the ground. At the end, he's called (but only by certain rabble) a man as meticulous as a compass, when he's a pincer!

MAR.: Oh, may this race, who keep their hearts inside their money, vanish! They follow diets unprescribed by doctors, they wear a hundred rags, you always see them afflicted; they treat themselves like beggars and servants, and then die, all dried up, amid richness!

COLA: But on the other side of the coin is he who spends and squanders: he would empty a ship, he would consume a mint; like a sack coming apart at the seams he scatters whatever he has and pays no attention to the things he possesses. He's surrounded by a hundred spongers and scoundrels, all without a single virtue, and heaps compensation on them. He dissipates without judgment, throws away without reason, gives to dogs and pigs and sends himself up in smoke. But with this dye he acquires the reputation of a generous spirit, courteous, magnanimous, and kind, who would give the pupils of his eyes and is the friend of all friends; a man who has the stink of a king about him and never says no to anyone who asks him; and with this fine face he empties chests and sends his house to ruin!

MAR.: Whoever calls one of these men generous is lying through the teeth: a generous man is one who gives at the right time and place and doesn't throw worthless coins to buffoons and people without honor, but distributes his money to the poor and honorable man of virtue.

COLA: You see a pimp, a full pot, a wooly sheep, a ram,[10] a billy goat, a jump-and-butt, a house with two doors, a shoehorn that comes from Corneto and lives in Forcella, a procurer, a bullock who is the original painting of infamy and the spitting image of excess. And when he, too, is dyed, they call him a calm, respectable man, a gentleman who minds his own

---

9. *de cinco* (Neap.): a coin of little value.

10. *martino* (Neap): see tale 2.8 n4. The geographical names that follow indicate concrete locales (Forcella is an area of Naples, Corneto in Abruzzo) and continues the series of puns on having "horns," or being a cuckold.

business and gets along with everyone; he is courteous with all, his house is open to friends, he is not one for ceremonies nor piques, he's as good as bread, as sweet as honey, you can do with him what you like. And meanwhile, without even blushing, he trades in meat and saves the bones!

MAR.: Nowadays these types live richly; they can even see when they go out at night to the tavern, since they've got a lantern that shines from between their bones.[11]

COLA: A man lives in seclusion, has nothing to do with rascals and thieves; he avoids conversation, he wants neither headaches nor to be accountable to the third or fourth in line. He lives a peaceful life; he is master of himself and has no one who wakes him when he is sleeping or counts the mouthfuls when he is eating. But there are those who use the dye on him and call him wild and woodsy; hawk shit that smells neither fragrant nor fetid; a bitter, insipid, rustic lout; a man without flavor and without love; wretched, beastly, a good-for-nothing; macaroni without salt.

MAR.: Oh, happy is he who lives in the desert, for he neither sees nor has cause for anger! Let them say what they will: but I find well proven the saying that goes, "Better alone than badly accompanied."

COLA: But then, on the other hand, you find a conversational type, who's like flesh and blood with his friends, a good pal, affable, who treats you without any fuss. But with this dye—who would believe it?—he discovers those who cut him to pieces and tear him to shreds, sew him up and then take out the stitches, rub him the wrong way, and bring a case against him behind his back, calling him impudent, nosy, a pants farter, a punch face, a broken shoelace, insolent, parsley for every sauce, one who would salt whatever he sees and stick his nose in everything he smells, a busybody, arrogant, a big pain in the neck: take this and spend it, you poor little thing!

MAR.: There's this, and even worse! It was well understood by that Spaniard who said, a long time ago, "La mucha aqueja es causa de desprecio."[12]

COLA: If by chance a man is clear of speech, chats and converses and makes a display of wit and eloquence, and however you touch him and turn him round you find that he's knowledge-

---

11. Possibly an expression used for husbands who turn a blind eye to their wives' illicit activities (Rak 454).

12. "Too much complaining is cause for disdain."

able and answers you by the rule, this dye reduces him to where he's given the mortarboard of a jabbering bigmouth, a sewer throat, one who would have a thing or two to teach crickets, who's wordier than a magpie and makes your ears ring and your head ache with such nonsense, so many nursery rhymes and ogre tales,[13] and so much complaining and psst-pssting that, when he puts that tongue in motion, with his mouth like a chicken's ass, he infects you, stuns you, and deafens you.

MAR.: In this age of jackasses, you try as hard as you can but you're always going to be wrong!

COLA: But if someone else is silent and mute, all clammed up, with his trap shut and plugged, and if he saves his mouth for eating figs and you don't hear one peep out of him, this dye changes his color so that he is called an Antuono, a baboon, a retard, a blockhead, a ninny, a log good for burning in hell, always cold and frozen, like the bride who came against her will. I see no possibility of a north wind for this gulf: if you speak, poor you, and if you don't speak, even worse!

MAR.: That's the truth; nowadays you don't know how to behave, you don't know where to fish, there's no beaten road to walk on: lucky are those who are able to guess it right in this world!

COLA: But who could ever describe from A to Z the effects of this dye? It would take a thousand years, without a doubt, nor would a tongue of metal suffice! Do with it what you will, treat it as you like; in any case it will change your color, and the buffoon is called humorous and entertaining; the spy, one who knows the map of the ways of the world; the scoundrel, an ingenious man and a bream who knows his waters; the lazybones, a calm man; the glutton, a man who knows how to live the good life; the flatterer, an able courtier who pays attention to his master's moods and knows how to please him; the whore, courteous and of noble bearing; the ignoramus, a simple and respectable man. And so, you go on and on discussing and then . . . enough! It's no marvel if at court the mean man gurgles with delight and the good man laments his lot, because their true colors are concealed from the lords by this dye, and they mistake and exchange this one for that one, as has always been the case, leaving the good man for the bad.

---

13. *cunte de l'uerco* (Neap.): The first tale of *The Tale of Tales* is "Lo cunto de l'uerco."

MAR.: Wretched is he who serves! Oh, better if his mother had delivered him dead! A storm is always brewing, and he can
never hope to find port.

COLA: The court is made solely for people of vice, who keep good as
far from them as possible, kicking, pushing, and throwing it
away. But let us leave these tales, for if I scratched wherever it
itches I would finish neither tomorrow nor the day after. So
let's cut it short and leave our labors, now that the Sun is
playing hide-and-seek,[14] and we can cover the rest another
evening!

*At the same time that Cola Ambruoso closed his mouth the Sun
closed the day; and thus, after agreeing to return the next morning
with a new arsenal of tales, they all went off to their houses, full of
words and loaded down with appetite.*

End of the second day.

---

14. *covalera* (Neap.): see introduction to day 2 n6.

III

THE THIRD DAY

No sooner were all of the shadows that had been imprisoned by the tribunal of Night liberated by the Sun's visit than the prince and his wife, together with the women, returned to the usual place. And in order to pass in merry fashion the hours that had placed themselves between morning and the time to eat, they had musicians brought in and they began to dance with great pleasure. They did the Ruggiero, the Villanella, the Tale of the Ogre, the Sfessania, the Beaten Peasant, All Day Long with That Little Dove, the Stupefaction, the Nymph's Basso, the Gypsy, the Capricious, My Clear Star, My Sweet Fire of Love, What I'm Looking For, the Charmer and Little Charmer, the Go-Between, Short Lady, Tall Lady, the Chiarantana, Stick Your Foot Out, Look Who I've Gone and Fallen in Love With, Open Up 'Cuz It's a Good Idea, Clouds Floating Up in the Air, the Devil in a Shirt, Living on Hope, Change Hands, the Cascarda, and the Little Spanish Girl; and they closed the dancing with the Lucia Canazza, to please the slave.[1] And thus time raced by faster than they realized, and the hour to work their jaws arrived and brought with it all of the heavens' riches, and, indeed, they're still eating. And when the tables had been cleared, Zeza, who had sharpened herself like a razor to tell her tale, spoke in this manner:

1. "Many of the dances remembered here are described in *Nuove inventioni di balli* (Milan, 1604) by the Milanese Cesare Negri, called 'The Trombone,' famous and excellent professor of dance, and in *Ballarino* (Venice, 1631), by Fabritio Caroso de Sermoneta. Del Tufo, in his *Ritratto di Napoli*, also mentions many of the same dances" (Croce 570). The Sfessania and the Lucia (the last dance mentioned) were similar. In Sgruttendio's *Tiorba a taccone* (9, "La catubba") the dances are described. See also introduction to day 1 n6.

I

CANNETELLA

First Entertainment of the Third Day

Cannetella is unable to find a husband to her liking, and her sin causes her to fall into the hands of an ogre, where she is given an awful life; finally a sewer cleaner who is a vassal of her father's frees her.

"It is a bad thing, ladies and gentlemen, to look for bread better than that made from wheat,[1] because you end up desiring what you've thrown away. One should be content with what is honest, for those who want everything lose everything and those who walk on treetops have just as much madness in their noggins as danger under their heels, as was the case with a king's daughter, who will be the subject of the tale that I'm about to tell you.

"There once was a king, the king of Lovely Knoll, who had a greater desire to breed than porters have the desire for funerals to be held so that they can gather the melted wax. He even made a vow to the goddess Syrinx:[2] if she gave him a child he would call her Cannetella, in memory of how the goddess had transformed into a reed. And he prayed and prayed so hard and long that he received the grace, and with his wife Renzolla had a lovely little fart of a baby girl to whom he gave the promised name.

"She grew by leaps and bounds, and when she was as tall as a pole the king said to her, 'My daughter, you've already grown as big— may the heavens bless you!—as an oak tree, and it's the right time for you to pair up with a little husband who's deserving of that lovely face, so that we can maintain our family line. And so, since I love you like the pupils of my eyes and desire your happiness, I'd like to

---

ATT 311: Rescue by the Sister. "The name Cannetella existed in Neapolitan dialect, as a diminutive of Canneta, or Candida" (Croce 243). Here it is also a diminutive of *canna*, or reed. Penzer notes similarities between this tale and Gonzenbach 10, as well as a tale by Luigi Alamanni (1:231); see also Gonzenbach 22.

1. "Probably a common saying to indicate a difficult and useless endeavor" (Rak 476).

2. "The nymph desired by Pan, who was unable to reach her before she transformed into a reed, from which the multi-reeded flute (syrinx), or 'Pan-pipes,' was subsequently made (Ovid, *Metamorphoses* I 690–712), vs. the penis" (Rak 476).

know what breed of a husband you would like. What sort of man
suits your fancy? Do you want a man of letters or a swashbuckler? A
young boy or a mature man? Dark, white, or red? Tall and lanky or
a little twig? Narrow-waisted or round as an ox? You choose and I'll
sign off on it.'

"When Cannetella heard these generous offers, she thanked her father and told him that she had dedicated her virginity to Diana and
that under no circumstance did she want to glut herself on a husband.
But in spite of all this, after the king begged and pleaded with her, she
said, 'So as not to reveal myself indifferent to so much love I will be
content to do your wishes, as long as I am given a man who has no
equal in the world.' Upon hearing this, her father sat with great joy
from morning till evening at the window, studying, measuring, and
examining everyone who passed through the square. And when a
nice-looking man passed by, the king said to his daughter, 'Run, look
out the window, Cannetella, and see if this one measures up to your
liking!' And she had him come up, and they prepared a splendid banquet for him, where there was everything that one could possibly desire. As they were eating, an almond fell out of the young man's
mouth, and he bent over and picked it up from the ground expertly,
pushing it under the tablecloth. And when the meal was over, he left.
The king said to Cannetella, 'How do you like the young man, my
dear heart?' And she: 'Keep that worthless fellow away from me, because a great big man like him shouldn't have let an almond fall out
of his mouth!'

"When the king heard this he went back to the window again, and
when another man of the right sort passed by he called his daughter
to see if this other one pleased her. Cannetella answered that he
should come in, and he was called up and another feast prepared.
After they finished eating and the man left, the king asked his daughter if she liked him. She said, 'What am I supposed to do with that
wretched soul? He should have at least brought a couple of servants
with him to take off his cape.' 'If that's how it is, we're in trouble,'
said the king. 'These are the excuses of someone who doesn't want to
pay, and you're looking for lint so you won't have to do me this favor.
But resolve yourself, for I want to marry you off and find a root
strong enough to make my line of succession regerminate.' At these
heated words Cannetella answered, 'If, Lord Daddy, you want me to
speak frankly and tell you how I really feel, you're hoeing in the sea
and counting things wrong on your fingers, since I'll never subjugate
myself to any man alive unless he has a head and teeth of gold.' The
hapless king saw that his daughter had a hard head and issued a proclamation: if there was anyone in his kingdom who fulfilled his daugh-

ter's requirements he should come forward, and the king would give him his daughter and his kingdom.

"This king had a great enemy named Fioravante, whom he couldn't even stand to see painted on a wall. When Fioravante, who was an expert necromancer, heard of this proclamation, he summoned a number of those expelled by God and ordered them to make him a head and teeth of gold immediately. They answered that they would be able to do him this service only with great effort because it was a most extravagant thing for this world, and that it would be easier for them to give him golden horns,[3] which was a more usual thing nowadays. But in spite of all this they were forced by charms and spells to do what he desired.

"When he had his head and teeth of twenty-four carats, Fioravante passed by under the windows of the king, who, when he saw exactly what he was looking for, called his daughter. As soon as she saw him she said, 'Now this is the one; he couldn't be any better if I had molded him with my own hands!' And as Fioravante was getting up to leave, the king said to him, 'Wait a minute, brother, your back is really burning! You're acting like you're at the Jew's with something to pawn,[4] like you've got mercury at your backside and a stick under your tail! Slow down; I'm going to give you baggage and people to accompany you and my daughter, whom I want to be your wife.' 'I thank you,' said Fioravante, 'but there's no need. A horse will be more than enough; I'll just throw her on its back, and once we get to my house there will be as many servants and furnishings as grains of sand.' After arguing for a while Fioravante finally won, and he put her on the horse's back and left.

"In the evening—when the red horses were led away from the waterwheel of the sky and the white oxen yoked up—they arrived at a stable where some horses were feeding. Fioravante brought Cannetella in and said to her, 'Take heed: I have to race back home, and it takes seven years to get there; make sure you wait for me in this stable, and don't go out or let yourself be seen by a living soul or I'll make you remember it for as long as you're alive and healthy.' To which Cannetella answered, 'I am your subject and will do what you command, right down to the fennel. I would only ask to know what you're going to leave me to live on during this time.' And Fioravante replied, 'What's left in those horses' feedbags will be enough for you.'

"Now consider the state of poor Cannetella's heart; she cursed the

3. "A Neapolitan proverb goes 'Horns of a sister, horns of gold; horns of a wife, horns for real.' Perhaps Basile was thinking of this or a similar saying" (Croce 571).
4. "The Jewish community had control of pawnshops" (Rak 476).

hour and the moment she had mentioned any of this. Cold and icy, she made meals of tears as often as she lacked food; she damned her fate and blamed the stars for demoting her from the royal palace to the stable, from perfumes to the stink of manure, from mattresses of Barbary wool to straw, and from delicious, mouth-watering morsels to horses' leftovers. Several months of this life of hardships passed; the horses were given their feed to eat—you couldn't see by whom—and she subsisted on the scraps from their table.

"After much time had gone by, she was looking out through a hole when she saw a splendid garden with so many espaliers of bitter orange trees, so many grottos full of citron trees, and so many flower beds and fruit trees and grape pergolas that it was a joy to behold. And she got a craving for a lovely bunch of Ansonic[5] grapes that she had caught a glimpse of, and said to herself, 'I'll go out very, very quietly and snitch some of those grapes, and whatever happens will happen, even if the sky falls. What can it possibly matter a hundred years from now? Who would want to tell my husband? And even if by accident he found out, what would he do to me, after all? These are Ansonic, not horned grapes!' And so she went out and revived her spirits, which had grown thin with hunger.

"But a short while later, before the appointed time, her husband came back and one of the horses accused Cannetella of having taken the grapes, so that Fioravante became indignant and took a knife out of his pants, intending to kill her. But she kneeled on the ground and begged him to still his hand, since hunger had driven the wolf from the woods, and she talked at such length that Fioravante said to her, 'I'll forgive you this time and I'll give you your life in alms, but if the evil spirit tempts you again and I find out that you've seen the light of day, I'll make a stew of your life! So take heed of what I say: I'm going away again and I really will be there for seven years. You'd better toe the line or you won't ever get an even deal again and I'll make you pay for the old and the new!'

"That said, he left. Cannetella wept a river of tears, and slapping her hands, pounding her breast, and pulling out her hair, she said, 'Oh, if only I had never been born into this world, seeing that I was to have this bitter fate! Oh, my father, how you've drowned me! But why am I complaining about my father if I did the harm myself, if I am the one who fabricated this bad fortune? There you have it: I wanted a head of gold so that I could fall like a piece of lead and die in the irons! Oh, this is what I deserve: I wanted teeth of gold, and

---

5. "A large, sweet grape of oblong shape, either white or dark-colored. Two best friends are referred to as *'nzolia e muscateddu* [Ansonic and muscatel]" (Croce 571).

now my own tooth is turning gold![6] This is a punishment from the heavens, for I should have done my father's wishes and not had so many whims and tantrums! Those who do not listen to mother and father take a road unknown!' There wasn't a day when she didn't repeat this refrain, and her eyes had turned into two fountains and her face had become so gaunt and yellow that it inspired pity. Where were those sparkling eyes? Where were those rosy apples? Where was that mouth's little laugh? Her own father wouldn't have recognized her.

"Now after a year had gone by, the king's sewer cleaner chanced to pass by the stable and was recognized by Cannetella. She called him over and came out, but the poor girl was so transformed that when he heard himself called by name he didn't recognize her and was dumbfounded. But once he heard who she was and the reason why she had changed so much from her previous state, in part out of pity for the girl and in part to earn the king's graces, he put her in an empty barrel that he was carrying on his beast of burden and trotted off toward Lovely Knoll, where he reached the king's palace at four o'clock in the morning. He knocked at the door and the servants came out, and when they realized it was the sewer cleaner they gave him a double-soled scolding, calling him an animal with no discretion for coming at that hour to ruin everyone's sleep, and telling him that he was getting a good deal if they didn't bean him with rocks and boulders.[7]

"The king heard the noise and was told by a valet who it was, and immediately had the sewer cleaner let in, thinking that if he was taking this liberty at such an unusual hour something important must have happened. Once he had unloaded his beast of burden, the sewer cleaner split open the barrel and out came Cannetella, though it took more than words for her father to recognize her; if it hadn't been for a wart that she had on her right arm she would have had to get right back in. But as soon as he was certain of the fact, he hugged her and kissed her a thousand times and immediately had her drawn a hot bath, and when she was all clean and tidied up he had her served breakfast, for she was faint with hunger.

"And then he said to her, 'Who would ever have thought, my daughter, that I would see you like this? What happened to your face? Who has reduced you to this miserable state?' And she answered, 'This is how it went, my dear lord. That Barbary Turk made me suffer torments fit for a dog; I found myself with my spirit between my

---

6. Perhaps from lack of use.
7. *mazzacano* (Neap.): lit., "dog killers."

teeth at every moment. But I don't want to tell you everything I went through, because just as it surpassed human endurance, so it goes beyond the belief of common man. Enough: I'm here, my father, and I never want to leave your feet again. I'd rather be a servant in your house than a queen in someone else's; I'd rather be a rag where you are than a gold cloak far from you; I'd rather turn a spit in your kitchen than hold a scepter under the royal canopy of another.'

"Meanwhile, Fioravante had come back from his travels and was told by the horses that the sewer cleaner had stolen Cannetella away inside a barrel. When he heard this he was humiliated by shame and boiled with rage, and ran off to Lovely Knoll, where he encountered an old woman who lived across from the king's palace, to whom he said, 'How much will you charge, madam, to let me see the king's daughter?' She asked him for a hundred ducats, and Fioravante put his hand in his bag and counted them right out for her, one after the other. When she had taken the sum she led him up to the terrace, from which he could see Cannetella out on a loggia drying her hair. As if her heart had spoken to her, she turned in his direction and became aware of the ambush; hurling herself down the stairs, she ran to her father, shouting, 'My lord, if you don't make me a room with seven doors of iron right this instant, I'm done for!' 'I should lose you for so little?' said the king. 'Even if it costs me an eye, may this lovely daughter of mine be contented!' and—no sooner said than done—the doors were immediately forged.

"When Fioravante found out about this he went back to the old woman and said to her, 'Tell me what else you want from me, and go to the king's house with the excuse of selling a pot or two of rouge, and when you go in to where his daughter is, carefully stick this little piece of paper between the mattresses. As you're putting it there say, under your breath, "May everyone fall asleep, and only Cannetella stay awake!"' The old woman agreed to do this for another hundred ducats, and then she served him a fine relish. Oh, wretched are those who open their houses to those ugly skunks, who with the excuse of bringing makeup tan your honor and your life until it's as dark as cordovan leather! Now when the old woman had done him this nice service, everyone in the house fell into such an extraordinarily deep sleep that they looked like they had all been massacred. Only Cannetella still had her eyes open, and it was for this reason that when she heard the doors being broken down, she began to shriek as if she were being cooked on an open fire. But there was no one to come running at her cries and Fioravante was able to knock down all seven doors, and when he entered the room he grabbed Cannetella with all of her mattresses and made as if to take her away.

"But as her fate would have it, the little paper that the old woman had put there fell out, and when the powder spilled the whole house woke up. Hearing Cannetella's shrieks, everyone came running, even the dogs and the cats, and when they had gotten hold of the ogre they made salami[8] out of him. And thus he fell into the same trap that he had prepared for the unfortunate Cannetella, proving at his own expense that *there is no worse suffering than being killed by one's own weapons.*"

---

8. *tonnina* (Neap.): a sort of salami made from tuna (Guarini and Burani 294).

2

PENTA WITH THE CHOPPED-OFF HANDS

Second Entertainment of the Third Day

Penta disdains marriage with her brother, and she cuts off her hands and sends them to him as a present. He has her thrown to sea in a chest, and when she ends up on a beach a sailor brings her to his home, where his jealous wife throws her back into the sea in the same chest. She is found by a king and marries him, but because of the trickery of that same wicked woman she is driven out of the kingdom. After undergoing many hardships she is found by her husband and her brother, and they all end up happy and satisfied.[1]

After hearing Zeza's tale they were all of the opinion that Cannetella had deserved this and even worse for having split hairs like that. Nonetheless, they were greatly comforted to see her extricated from such suffering, and they reflected on how although all men stunk to her she was reduced to bowing down before a sewer cleaner so that he would remove her from such great hardship. But when Tadeo signaled to Cecca to set her tale free she did not hesitate to speak and began in this manner: "In times of trouble virtue is put to the test; the candle of goodness shines brightest where it is darkest; hard labor gives birth to merit, and merit has honor attached to its navel. Those who triumph do not stand around with their hands at their sides but spin their spoons, as the daughter of the king of Dry Rock did when she built the house of her happiness by sweating blood and putting herself in mortal danger. And I've got it in my noggin to tell you the tale of her good fortune.

AT 706: The Maiden without Hands. Penzer discusses the two parts of the tale, "the drastic way the sister puts a stop to her brother's advances, and . . . the well-known 'letter of death' motif." Of the first, he comments, "The use of self-mutilation to preserve virginity or to keep religious vows has been a favorite theme in both East and West," from Buddhist to Christian hagiology (see also Grimm 31, "The Maiden without Hands" and Gonzenbach 24). For the letter of death motif, Penzer recalls the stories of Uriah (2 Sam. 11), Bellerophon (*Iliad* 6.155ff.), and Mutalammis (in Islamic tradition) (1:241).

1. *contiente e conzolate* (Neap.): this expression, which frequently appears as a concluding formula, is the rough equivalent in sense to "happily ever after."

"Seeing as the king of Dry Rock had remained a widower and without wife, a little demon put it into his head to take Penta, his own sister, for his wife. For this reason he called her one day and, when they were alone, said to her, 'It is not the act of a judicious man, my sister, to let what is of value leave his house, and, moreover, you do not know how it will turn out if you let strangers set foot there. Thus, after chewing this matter over thoroughly, I have decided to take you for my wife, since you're of the same breath that I am and I know your character. Be content, then, to make this inlay, this shopkeepers' agreement, this *uniantur acta,*[2] this *misce et fiat potum,*[3] and both of us will see good days.'

"When Penta heard this minor fifth she was beside herself, and one color left her face as another entered it, for she never would have thought that her brother could be subject to these sudden changes in mood and that he would try to give her a couple of rotten eggs while he himself was in need of a hundred fresh ones.[4] After remaining silent for a long time while she thought about how she should answer such an impertinent and inappropriate demand, at last she unloaded the beast of burden of her patience and said to him, 'Even if you have lost your mind, I don't want to lose my modesty! I'm amazed at you, that you allow those words to come out of your mouth! If they're in jest they're worthy of an ass, and if they're in earnest they stink like a billy goat. I'm sorry that you have the tongue to say those ugly and shameful things, and that I have the ears to hear them. Me, your wife? Who did this to you? What kind of trap is this?[5] Since when have people made these blends?[6] Since when these stews? These mixtures? And where are we, at Ioio?[7] Am I your sister or cheese cooked in oil?[8] Get your head on straight, for the life of you, and don't let any more of those words slip out of your mouth or else I'll do things

---

2. "As in trials, when the proceedings of two or more cases are combined" (Croce 252).

3. "Formula taken from medical prescriptions" (Croce 252).

4. "That is, he had gone mad. The cure that at Basile's time the insane of the Hospital of the Incurables were given consisted in turning the waterwheel to get water from a well; eating a hundred eggs, since they were considered nourishing and light; and receiving periodic beatings" (Croce 252).

5. The meaning of the textual "Chi fatto a tene? Che nasa faise?" is unclear. Guarini and Burani comment that "it could be one of those expressions that characters of *The Tale of Tales* sometimes use to imitate 'high' language by deforming it, or dialect by 'refining' it" (297).

6. *crapiate* (Neap.): "blend of white and red wine; cf. Spanish 'calabriada'" (Croce 253).

7. See tale 1.4 n6.

8. The expression refers to the incestuous relationship Penta's brother is proposing, since cheese and oil are two ingredients that do not mix well (Guarini and Burani 297).

you wouldn't believe, and if you no longer respect me as your sister then I won't consider you for what you are to me!'

"As she was saying this she slipped away into another room, barred the door behind her, and didn't see her brother's face for more than a month, leaving the miserable king, who had gone off with a face like a maul to slow down the balls,[9] as humiliated as a little boy who has broken a jug and as confused as a servant girl whose meat has been stolen by the cat. But after many days, when she was summoned anew by the king to pay the tax[10] of his unreined desires, she decided to find out down to the very last detail what it was about her that the king had taken a fancy to, and, leaving her room, she went to find him and said, 'My brother, I have looked long and hard at myself in the mirror, and I have found nothing in this face that could merit your love, since I am not such a delectable morsel that I send people into fits.'

"And the king said to her, 'My Penta, all of you is beautiful and flawless, from your head to your toes, but your hand, more than anything else, is what makes me swoon: your hand, serving fork that pulls my entrails out of the pot of this chest; your hand, hook that lifts the bucket of my soul from the well of this life; your hand, vise that grips my spirit while Love files it! O hand, o lovely hand, ladle that dishes out sweetness, pincer that tears out my desires, stick that sends this heart spinning!'[11] He was intending to say more when Penta answered, 'All right, I heard you! Wait, don't move a hair, I'll be back in a minute!' And she went back to her room and called for a slave who didn't have much of a brain, handed him a large knife and a handful of old coins, and said, 'My dear Ali, you cut my hands, me want make nice formula and get more white!'[12] The slave, thinking he was doing her a favor, cut them clean off with two blows. She had them placed on a Faenza platter[13] and sent them, covered with a silk cloth, to her brother, with the message that he should enjoy what he most desired, along with good health and baby boys.

"When the king saw how he had been betrayed, he was so infuriated that he flew into a frenzy and immediately had a tarred chest made into which he stuffed his sister and had her thrown to sea. Car-

---

9. "Metaphor taken from soccer" (Croce 253), as well as a bawdy reference to the king's sexual frustration.

10. "Allusion to the tax paid by prostitutes" (Guarini and Burani 298).

11. *paletta che da bolee a sto core* (Neap.): "The *bolea* was a risky move in a ball game" (Guarini and Burani 298).

12. "Another example of 'Turkish' speech" (Rak 498).

13. Faenza was famous for its highly decorated majolica, which had been manufactured at least since the twelfth century.

[E]d essa, fattole mettere a no vacile de Faienza, le mannaie . . . a lo frate, co na 'masciata che se gaudesse chello che chiù desiderava co sanetate e figlie mascole. [She had them placed on a Faenza platter and sent them . . . to her brother, with the message that he should enjoy what he most desired, along with good health and baby boys.]

ried forth by the waves, the chest ended up on a beach, where it was pulled in by some sailors who were casting their nets, and when they opened it they found Penta, much more beautiful than the moon when it looks like it's spent Lent in Taranto.[14] And so Masiello, who was the one in charge and the ringleader of the men, took her home with him, telling his wife Nuccia to treat her kindly. But no sooner had her husband gone out than Nuccia, who was the mother of suspicion and jealousy, put Penta back in the chest and threw her to sea again.

"Tossed by the waves, the chest drifted here and there for so long that it finally crossed the path of a vessel in which the king of Green Earth was traveling. When he saw this thing floating amid the waves, he had the sails lowered and a dinghy thrown into sea. His men retrieved the chest and opened it, and upon discovering the wretched girl the king, who saw a living beauty inside a coffin, believed he had found a great treasure, even if his heart wept for the fact that a writing box full of so many amorous joys had been found without handles. And he took Penta to his kingdom and gave her to the queen as a lady-in-waiting, and she did every imaginable job with her feet, even sewing, threading a needle, starching collars, and combing the queen's hair, and for this she was held as dear as a daughter.

"But after several months the queen was issued a summons to appear at the bank of the Parcae[15] to pay her debt to nature, and she called the king to her and said, 'My soul has only a little longer to wait before it dissolves the marriage knot between itself and my body. And so take care of yourself, my dear husband, and let's be sure to write; but if you love me and want me to go happily to the world beyond, you must do me a favor.' 'I'm at your command, my pretty little face,' said the king, 'and even if I cannot give you the double testimony[16] of my love while you're alive, I will give you a sign of the affection that I have for you when you're dead.' 'All right then,' replied the queen, 'since this is your promise, I beg you with all my heart: after I've closed my eyes in the dust, you must wed Penta who, even if we know neither who she is nor where she comes from, reveals that she is a thoroughbred horse from the brand of her good manners.'[17] 'May you live for another hundred years,' answered the king,

---

14. I.e., like a full moon. "Since Taranto [in Puglia, the southeastern tip of the peninsula] boasts an abundance of exquisite fish and crustaceans, one could spend the meatless period of Lent there and still satisfy one's appetite and grow big and fat" (Croce 254).

15. The fates, in Roman mythology.

16. *li testimmonie* (Neap.): testimony (or witness) vs. testicles, as elsewhere.

17. "Thoroughbred horses raised in the stables of noble families were branded on their haunches with the initials of the family" (Guarini and Burani 300).

'but if by chance you have to say good night and my day turns bad, I swear to you that I will take her for my wife. And it does not matter to me that she is scrawny and without hands, for one should always take only a small amount of the unpleasant.'[18] But he mumbled these last words under his breath so that his wife wouldn't hear them, and when the queen had snuffed out the candle of her days he took Penta for his wife, and on the first night he grafted a baby boy onto her.

"But since the king needed to go on another sailing trip to the kingdom of High Cliff, he took his leave of Penta and pulled up anchor. Nine months later Penta gave birth to a lovely little baby boy; the whole city was decorated with light displays, and the council immediately sent off a sloop for the express purpose of notifying the king. The boat met up with a storm, though, so that first it found itself thrown onto the mantle[19] of the waves and bounced up to the stars, then rolled down to the bottom of the sea, and at last, as the heavens willed it, it landed on the shore where Penta had been rescued by the compassion of a man and cast out by the cruelty of a woman. And there the captain of the sloop had the misfortune to encounter that same Nuccia, who was washing her son's diapers. Curious to hear of other people's business, as is women's nature, she asked him where he was coming from, where he was headed, and who had sent him. And the captain said, 'I come from Green Earth and I'm going to High Cliff to find the king of my land and give him a letter. It is for this that I have been sent; I believe it is his wife who writes to him, but I could not tell you precisely what it is about.' 'And who is the wife of this king?' replied Nuccia. The captain answered, 'From what I understand they say that she is a very beautiful young woman named Penta with the Chopped-Off Hands, on account of her hands, which are both missing. I hear that she was found floating in the sea in a chest and had the good luck to become the wife of this king, and I don't know what she is writing to him about with such urgency that I need to rush at full sail[20] to get there quickly.'

"Upon hearing this, that Jew Nuccia invited the captain to have a drink, and when she had poured him full right up to his ears she took the letter out of his pocket and had it read to her, nearly dying of

---

18. "A saying echoing others that go back to ancient times" (Croce 255). The "unpleasant" here refers to women in general.
19. *mantiata* (Neap.): "From the Spanish 'mantear,' to put someone on a blanket held at its corners by four people, who then throw him into the air and catch him again; a joke played among pages and buffoons, and also with Sancho Panza [in *Don Quijote*]" (Croce 256).
20. *lo triego* (Neap.): "the first of the three sails: the biggest, square one on the main mast" (Rak 499).

envy and letting out a sigh at every syllable. And then she had the same student who had read her the letter, a client of hers, write in a forged hand that the queen had given birth to a wolf dog and that they were awaiting orders about what to do. After it was written and sealed she put it in the pocket of the sailor, who, when he awoke and saw that the weather had cleared, luffed up with a southwesterly at his stern. He got to the king and gave him the letter, and the king answered that they should keep the queen in good spirits and that she should not have a dram of displeasure, since these things happened by license of the heavens and a respectable man must not try to rearrange the stars.

"After he was sent off, the captain arrived two evenings later at the place where Nuccia lived. She made a big fuss over him and crammed him full of food; he ended up with his legs in the air again so that finally, stuffed and in a daze, he went to sleep, and Nuccia put her hand in his thigh piece and found the answer. She had it read to her and immediately had another false letter written to the council of Green Earth, which ordered that they burn mother and son without a moment's delay.

"As soon as the captain had sobered up he left, and upon arriving at Green Earth he presented the letter. When it was opened there was much whispering among those old sages and, after spending a good deal of time discussing the matter, they concluded that the king had either gone crazy or was under a spell, since he had a wife who was a pearl and an heir who was a jewel, and he wanted to grind them into powder for Death's teeth. For this reason they were of the opinion that they should take the middle road and send the young woman and her son off to wander through the world, so that no one would ever be able to hear anything new or old about them. And so they gave them a handful of little coins to help them get by and removed a treasure from the royal house, a shining lantern from the city, and two bastions of hope from the husband.

"Poor Penta, finding herself evicted though she was neither an immoral woman nor the relative of a bandit nor a bothersome student,[21] took her little cucumber in her arms and, bathing him with milk and tears, set out in the direction of Torbid Lake, where the ruler was a sorcerer. When he saw this lovely cripple who crippled hearts and waged a fiercer war with the stumps of her arms than Briareus[22] with

---

21. "Three categories of people who were commonly removed from their place of residence or exiled from the Kingdom of Naples" (Croce 258). See also tale 1.10 n33.
22. "The giant with a hundred hands and fifty heads who helped Zeus in the battle against the Titans; another common emblem of brute strength. See Homer, *Iliad* I, 527–29" (Rak 499).

his hundred arms, he wanted to hear the whole story of the misfortunes that had befallen her: from when her brother was denied a meal of meat and wanted to make a meal of fish out of her, up to the day that she had set foot in his kingdom.

"Upon hearing this bitter tale the sorcerer shed tears without reserve, and the compassion that entered through the holes of his ears was exhaled in sighs through the crack of his mouth. Finally, comforting her with kind words, he said, 'Cheer up, my girl, for no matter how badly the house of a soul has rotted, it can remain standing with the support of hope. So don't let your spirits leak away, for the heavens sometimes drag human misfortunes to the verge of ruin in order to render the ultimate success more marvelous. Have no fear; you have found mother and father and I will help you with my own blood.' Poor Penta thanked him and said, 'I don't care a fig if the heavens shower me with misfortunes and send me hailstones of ruin, now that I am under the canopy of your grace, you who have power and valor; and the lovely sight of you alone is enough to satisfy me.' And after a thousand words of courtesy on the one hand and thanks on the other, the sorcerer gave her a beautiful apartment in his palace and had her taken care of like a daughter. The next morning he issued a proclamation: anyone who came to his court and told of a misfortune would be given a golden crown and scepter worth more than a kingdom.

"This news spread all through Europe, and more people came to that court to earn those riches than caterpillars. And one told how he had served in court his entire life, and after losing lye and soap, youth and health, was paid with a little piece of cheese; one said that he had been unjustly treated by a superior and couldn't take offense but had to swallow the pill without evacuating his anger; one lamented that he had put all his belongings in a ship, and a little wind blowing the wrong way had robbed him of every last thing; another complained that he had spent all his years wielding a pen without it bringing him a profit of even one quill, and despaired more than anything that his efforts with the pen had brought him so little fortune, while the material used to make inkwells[23] encountered such good luck in this world.

"In the meantime the king of Green Earth returned, and upon discovering that fine syrup of things at home he behaved like an unchained lion, and he would have had the councilors' skin removed if they hadn't shown him his letter. And when he saw the falsified writing he summoned the courier, and after getting him to tell what he

---

23. I.e., horn.

had done during the trip he realized that Masiello's wife had done him this harm, and he immediately rigged a galley and set sail himself for that shore. When he found the woman he used nice manners to get her to spit out her deceit, and after hearing that the cause of it had been jealousy he gave orders that she be covered in wax. And when she was thoroughly waxed and tallowed he placed her on a huge pile of dry wood and set her on fire, and as soon as he saw that the fire, with its bright red tongue of flames, had devoured the wretched woman, he hoisted his sails.

"On the high sea he ran into a ship carrying the king of Dry Rock, who, after a thousand formalities, told the king of Green Earth that he was sailing in the direction of Torbid Lake for the proclamation issued by the king of that kingdom and that he was going to try his luck, since his misfortunes were second not even to those of the most afflicted man in the world. 'If that's the issue,' answered the king of Green Earth, 'I can outrun you with my feet tied together and beat the most unfortunate person who ever was by fifteen and bust. While others measure their pain in teaspoons, I measure mine in bushels. And so I want to come with you, and we'll behave like gentlemen: whoever wins shares the winnings like a good sport, right down to the fennel.' 'Most willingly,' said the king of Dry Rock, and they gave each other their word and went of one accord to Torbid Lake, where they landed and presented themselves to the sorcerer. He received them with the grand ceremony fit for crowned heads, had them seated under his royal canopy, and told them that they were welcome a thousand times over. And when the sorcerer heard that they had come for the contest of the miserable men, he wanted to know what load of pain rendered them subject to the sirocco winds of sighs.

"The king of Dry Rock began to tell of the love that he had directed toward his own blood, of the way his sister had acted like an honorable woman, of the dog's heart he had revealed when he locked her up in the tarred chest and threw her to sea; of how on the one hand the conscience of his own errors pierced him and on the other the pain of losing his sister stung him; of how he was tormented here by the shame and there by the damage done, so that if all the suffering of the most terribly anguished souls of hell were distilled it wouldn't amount to the quintessence of affliction that his heart felt.

"When this king had finished speaking, the other one began. 'Alas, your sufferings are sugar cookies, sweetmeats, and bits of honey[24] compared to the pain that I feel. After I found Penta with the

---

24. *strufole* (Neap.): "Neapolitan Christmas sweets made with a flour and egg dough and fried in small rounds and then covered with honey and sprinkles" (Croce 261).

Chopped-Off Hands, looking like a Venetian wax torch,[25] in a chest destined to become the casket of my own funeral rite, and took her for my wife and was given a lovely baby boy by her, the one and the other came close to being set on fire due to the wickedness of an old hag! And what's even worse—O nail in my heart! O sorrow that gives me no peace!—they banished both of them and sent them from my kingdom, and I, unburdened of every pleasure, do not know why the ass of my life does not fall to the ground under the load of so much suffering!'

"When the sorcerer had heard the one and the other he knew by scent that one of them was the brother and the other the husband of Penta, and he called for Nofriello, the son, and said to him, 'Go and kiss the feet of your lord daddy!' The little boy obeyed the sorcerer, and his father, seeing the good manners and grace of the little bruiser, threw a lovely golden chain around his neck. After this the sorcerer continued, 'Kiss your uncle's hand, my lovely boy,' and the darling babe immediately obeyed. His uncle was amazed at the high spirits of this frisky little fellow and gave him a nice jewel, asking the sorcerer if the boy was his son, to which the sorcerer replied that he should ask the boy's mother.

"Having heard the whole conversation from behind the door, Penta now came out. And, like a little dog that has been lost for many days and then finds her master and barks, licks, wags her tail, and gives him a thousand other signs of her happiness, so she ran first to her brother and then to her husband, first pulled by the affection for the one and then by the blood ties to the other, and she embraced first this one and then that one with such jubilation that it's impossible to imagine: let's just say that they put on a three-part concert of truncated words and interrupted sighs.

"But when there came a pause in this music they went back to caressing the boy, and first his father, then his uncle took turns squeezing and kissing him until they were nearly in ecstasy. And after things had been said and done on this side and that, the sorcerer brought things to an end with these words: 'The heavens know how delighted this heart is to see lady Penta comforted. She deserves to be raised high for her good qualities, and it was for her that I labored so hard to bring her husband and her brother to this kingdom, so that I could give myself to the one and the other like a slave in chains. But since man is bound by his words and oxen by their horns, and the promise of a respectable man is a contract, and since, in my judgment, the king of Green Earth truly came close to bursting with sorrow, I want

25. "Bright-colored wax was produced in Venice" (Rak 499).

to keep my word. And so I will give him not only the crown and scepter mentioned in the proclamation, but also my kingdom, and because I have neither children nor preoccupations of that sort, with your permission I would like to take this lovely couple of husband and wife for my adoptive children, and they will be as dear to me as the pupils of my eyes. And so that there remains nothing left to desire for Penta's happiness, let her put the stumps under her apron, and she'll pull out hands that are more beautiful than they were before.'

"This was done, with the results the sorcerer had predicted, and the happiness that followed cannot be described: let's just say that everyone was gurgling with joy, and in particular Penta's husband, who considered this good fortune far greater than the other kingdom given to him by the sorcerer. And after they spent a handful of days in great festivities, the king of Dry Rock returned to his kingdom, and the king of Green Earth, having sent the permit for the rule of his state to his younger brother, stayed on with the sorcerer, paying off fingers of suffering with arm's lengths of delight, and testifying to the world that *you cannot find sweetness dear if you have not first known bitterness.*"

3

FACE

Third Entertainment of the Third Day

Renza is enclosed in a tower by her father, since it was predicted that she would die from a big bone. She falls in love with a prince and, with a bone brought to her by a dog, makes a hole in the wall and flees. But when she later sees her beloved kiss the bride he has since married, she dies of a broken heart, and out of sorrow the prince kills himself.

While Cecca was telling her tale to great effect, you could see a stew[1] of pleasure and disgust, of comfort and affliction, of laughter and tears cooking. They cried at Penta's misfortune, they laughed at how her hardships came to an end, they were afflicted to see her in so much danger, it was a comfort to them that she was saved so honorably, they were disgusted by the betrayals of which she was a victim, and they felt pleasure at the vendetta that followed. In the meantime Meneca, who was about to light the fuse of her chatter, took her weapons in hand and said, "It often happens that just when someone thinks he has escaped a misfortune he runs right into one. For this reason a wise man should put all of his affairs in the hands of the heavens and not go searching for magicians' circles or astrologers' eyeholes, since if he tries to foresee dangers in a prudent manner he falls to his ruin like a beast. Listen, and you will find that it is true.

"There once was a king, the king of Narrow Ditch, who had a beautiful daughter. Since he wanted to know what sort of destiny was written for her in the book of the stars, he summoned all the necromancers, astrologers, and gypsies of the land. They came to the royal court, and when some had examined the lines of her hand, others the signs on her face, and others the birthmarks on Renza's body,

---

AT 313: The Girl as Helper in the Hero's Flight, and AT 410: Sleeping Beauty. This tale stands out for its unhappy ending (one of the only ones in *The Tale of Tales*) and its theme of irrevocable fate. Penzer believes that "the fact that Basile has not altered it is an additional proof of the contention that he wrote down the tales as he heard them" (1:250). There are similarities with Gonzenbach 26–28.

1. *oglia potrita* (Neap.): "The famous Spanish dish [*olla podrida*], a stew made with various types of meat, sausage, lard, cabbage, and legumes . . . the Spanish version of the Neapolitan *pignata maritata* [or *grassa*]" (De Simone 435). See also tale 1.2 n22.

for this was her name, each of them spoke their opinion; and the majority of them concluded that she was in danger of tapping the sewer main of her life because of a big bone.[2] When the king heard this he decided to duck so that he wouldn't get hit, and he had a lovely tower built where he enclosed his daughter together with twelve ladies-in-waiting and a governess to serve her, and gave the order that, under penalty of death, they were always to bring her meat without bones so as to bypass that unlucky planet.

"Renza grew like a moon, and one day, as she was at a window covered by an iron railing, Cecio, the son of the queen of Wide Vineyard, passed by the tower. At the sight of such a beautiful thing he immediately got all heated up, and when he saw that his greeting was returned and that a little laugh filled her mouth, he took heart, moved closer to the window, and said, 'Hello, register of all of nature's privileges! Hello, archive of all of the heavens' concessions! Hello, universal table of all of the titles of beauty!' Hearing this praise bestowed upon her, Renza became more beautiful in her embarrassment, and as she threw wood onto Cecio's fire she poured, as someone once said, boiling water on his burns. And since she didn't want Cecio to outdo her in courtesy, she answered, 'May you be welcome, O larder of the Graces' provisions, O warehouse of Virtue's merchandise, O customshouse of Love's commerce!'

"Cecio replied, 'How can the castle of Cupid's forces be shut up in that tower? How can the prison of souls be thus jailed? How can there be a golden apple behind that iron railing?' And when Renza explained the situation to him, Cecio told her that he was the son of a queen but the vassal of her beauty, and that if it were her pleasure to steal away to his kingdom, he would put a crown on her head. Renza was feeling musty inside those four walls and couldn't wait to air out her life, and so she accepted the proposal and told him to come back in the morning—when Dawn would call the birds as witnesses to the filth Aurora smeared her with[3]—and they would sneak out together. And after she threw him a kiss from the window, she went back in and the prince returned to his lodgings.

"Now while Renza was thinking of how she could slip out of there and fool her ladies-in-waiting, a Corsican hound, which the king kept to guard the tower, came into her room with a big bone in its mouth, and as the dog was gnawing on it under the bed Renza put her head down and saw the goings-on. Since all this seemed to have been sent by fortune for her very needs, she kicked the dog out and

2. *uosso mastro* (Neap.): "The femur of animals" (Croce 265).
3. *magriata* (Neap): see tale 1.2 n17.

took the bone, and when she had made it clear to her ladies-in-waiting that her head hurt and they should therefore leave her to rest without bothering her, she set a prop against the door and began, with this bone, to put in a day's work.

"Chipping at a stone in the wall, she worked until she pried it away and took enough of the wall out to be able to get through it without hardship. Then she ripped up a couple of sheets and knotted them together like a rope, and—as soon as the curtain of shadows had been raised on the stage of the heavens so that Aurora might come out and recite the prologue to Night's tragedy—when she heard Cecio whistle she attached the end of the sheets to a doorpost and lowered herself down to the street below where, once Cecio had embraced her and put her on a donkey covered by a rug, they set off for Wide Vineyard.

"That evening they arrived in a certain place called Face and found a splendid palace there, where Cecio planted his stakes in the lovely farmland and marked off his amorous property. But since Fortune always has the bad habit of tangling the yarn, putting an end to games, and slamming the door on the nose of all the fine plans that lovers may have, just as their pleasure reached its highest point a courier arrived with a letter from Cecio's mother, in which she wrote that if he did not race home that very instant to see her he would not find her alive, since she was carrying on as best she could but was close to reaching the 'z'[4] of the alphabet of life.

"Upon hearing this bad news Cecio said to Renza, 'My heart, this business is of great importance, and I'll need to run off posthaste in order to arrive in time. So stay for five or six days in this palace, and then I'll either return or send someone to get you.' And when Renza heard this bitter news, she burst into tears and answered, 'O, hapless is my fate! How quickly the barrel of my pleasures has been drained to its dregs, the pot of my good times scraped to its very bottom, the basket of my delights filled with mere scraps! Poor me; my hopes are thrown away with the water, my plans turn to bran, and every satisfaction I have goes up in smoke! I have only just brought this royal sauce to my lips and already it's caught in my throat, I have only just put my mouth to this fountain of sweetness and already my pleasure has muddied, I have only just seen the sun rise and I can already say, "Good night, uncle mattress!" '

"These and other words were coming out from under the Turkish arches of those lips to pierce Cecio's soul, when he said to her, 'Quiet, O lovely support of my life,[5] O bright lantern of these eyes, O cura-

---

4. *rummo e busse* (Neap.): see tale 2.7 n1.
5. *vita* (Neap.): life vs. grapevine.

tive hyacinth[6] of this heart. I will soon be back, and the miles of distance cannot separate me one span from this lovely body, nor can the force of time knock the memory of you from this noggin! Calm down, rest that head, dry those eyes, and keep me in your heart!' And as he said this he got on his horse and began to gallop toward his kingdom.

"Renza, who saw herself ditched like a cucumber seed, set out to follow Cecio's tracks, and after untying a horse that she found grazing in the middle of a field, she raced off on his trail. When she encountered a hermit's errand boy she got off her horse and gave him her clothes, which were all trimmed with gold, and had him give her the sack and cord that he was wearing. She put it over her head and tied it with the rope—she who tied up souls with the lasso of Love—and then got back on her horse, spurring the animal so hard that in a short time she reached Cecio, and said to him, 'Good to see you, my dear gentleman!' And Cecio answered her, 'Welcome, my little monk! Where are you coming from? And where are you headed?' And Renza answered,

> I come from a place where there is
> A woman ever in tears, who cries, "O white face,
> Alas, who has taken you from my side?"

When he heard this, Cecio said to what he thought was a boy, 'O my lovely young man, how dear your company is to me! Do me a favor and take the pupils of my eyes. Never leave my side, and every now and then repeat those verses, which really tickle my heart!'

"And so, cooling themselves with the fan of chatter[7] to relieve themselves from the heat of the road, they arrived at Wide Vineyard, where they found that the queen had arranged a marriage for Cecio, having sent for him with a ruse, and that the bride was ready and waiting. When Cecio arrived, he begged his mother to keep the boy who had accompanied him in their house and to treat him as if he were a brother of his, and since his mother was happy with this she

---

6. "The hyacinth stone, a reddish-brown variety of zircon, was set in rings and considered to have health-restoring powers; it brought happiness, strengthened the heart, and favored sleep" (Rak 518).

7. Croce cites from Pietro Aretino (*Ragionamenti* 1, day 2): "it being time to get rid of the heat with the fan of chatter" (573). This and other passages drawn from Aretino make it clear that Basile was an attentive reader of the burlesque, or anticlassicist, tradition, which included such authors as Cecco Angiolieri, Francesco Berni, Teofilo Folengo, Ruzante, and others and which often drew on the resources of the various dialect traditions.

made sure the boy was always at his side and ate at the table where he
and his bride sat.

"Now consider how poor Renza's heart felt, and whether she was
able to swallow this nux vomica![8] Nonetheless, every now and then
she repeated the verses that Cecio liked so much. But when the tables
had been cleared and the newlyweds retired to a little room so that
they could talk in private, the field was open for Renza to pour out
her heart's passion in solitude. She went into a garden outside the hall
and retired under a mulberry tree, where she began to lament in this
manner, 'Alas, cruel Cecio, is this your thousand thanks for the love
I bear you? Is this the deposit on the fondness I feel for you? Is this
the reward for the affection I show you? There you have it: I dumped
my father, left my home, trampled on my honor, and let myself fall
under the power of a rabid dog, and all so that I can see my steps
stayed, the door slammed in my face, and the bridge raised, and just
when I believed I would take possession of this lovely fortress! So
that I can see myself put on the tax list of your ingratitude, when I
thought I would live quietly at the Duchesca[9] of your graces! So that
I can see myself made to play Master Iommiento Proclaims and Orders, when I imagined I'd be playing Anca Nicola[10] with you! I sowed
hope, and now I'm harvesting bits of cheese![11] I threw out nets of desire, and now I'm pulling in sands of ingratitude! I built castles in the
air, and now my body is knocked—boom!—to the ground! So this is
what I get in exchange! This is the trade-off I'm given! This is the
payment I've gotten out of all this! I lowered the bucket into the well
of amorous longing and I'm left with the handle in my hand; I hung
out the laundry of my plans and out of the blue it started to rain; I
put the pot of my thoughts on the fire of desire and the soot of disgrace fell in! But who would have thought, you turncoat, that your
words[12] would reveal themselves to be copper? That the barrel of
your promises would be drained to its dregs? That the bread of your
goodness would turn moldy? Nice manners for a respectable man,
nice example for an honorable person, nice habits for a king's son to

---

8. "The seed of a plant of Asian origin (strychnus nux vomica), from which strych-
nine is extracted" (Rak 519).
9. "An area in Naples (near the main train station) where, in about 1487, the duke of
Calabria, Alfonso of Aragon, built a palace and garden. [. . .] These were later torn
down and houses built on the same site, and the alleyways of the new 'Duchesca' became a meeting-place for prostitutes and criminals" (Croce 269, 573).
10. Children's games. For the first (Master Iommiento Proclaims and Orders), see
tale 2.6 n7; for the second (Anca Nicola), see the introduction to day 2 n3.
11. I.e., "a small profit or a gift worth no more than a piece of cheese" (Croce 269).
12. *fede* (Neap.): word, faith, or wedding band. Copper was the metal most often
used for counterfeit coins, to which was applied a patina of gold or silver (Rak 519).

have! You tricked me, you hoodwinked me, you gave me a stomachache, you cut me a wide cape only to leave me with a jacket that's too
short, you promised me the sea and the mountains only to hurl me
into a ditch, you washed my face clean only to leave me with a black
heart! O promises of wind! O words of bran! O oaths of sautéed
spleen![13] There you have it: I said "four" before it was in the bag;[14]
I'm a hundred miles away when I thought I'd reached the baron's
house! It seems quite clear that evening words are carried off by the
wind! Alas, I thought I'd be flesh and blood with this cruel man, but
we'll be like cat and dog; I imagined I'd be bowl and spoon with this
rabid mutt, but we'll be like snake and toad, since I can't bear that
with a fifty-five of good fortune someone else will take the winning
primero of hopes from my hand,[15] and I can't stand that I'll be checkmated! O misguided Renza, see what trust brings you, see what happens when you let men's words impregnate you! Men without law,
without faith; poor is the woman who mixes with them, sorry is the
woman who grows attached to them, wretched is the woman who
gets into the wide bed they're in the habit of preparing for you! But
not to worry: you know that he who tricks children dies like a cricket;
you know that in the bank of the heavens there are no swindling
clerks to fiddle with the papers![16] And when you least expect it your
day will come! You worked this sleight of hand on one who gave herself to you on credit, only to receive this bad service in cash! But don't
I realize that I'm telling my reasons to the wind, that I'm sighing into
the void? I'm sighing at a net loss; I'm lamenting to myself! This evening he'll settle his accounts with the bride and collect his ransom,
while I balance my accounts with Death and pay my debt to Nature;
he'll lie in a white bed that smells of fresh laundry, and I'll be in a
dark coffin that stinks of the freshly killed; he'll play Empty the Barrel with that good-luck bride, while I do I'm Wounded, My Friend[17]
and pierce my loins with a pointed stick to prove my mastery over
life!'

   "After these and other words spoken in rage, it was by then time
for everyone to get their teeth moving, and Renza was called to the
table, where the gratins and the stews were arsenic and euphorbia to

13. I.e., of little worth.
14. I.e., I declared myself a winner too soon.
15. Metaphors taken from the card game of *primero*.
16. "Satirical treatment of clerks, those low officials of courts and other places of
public administration, and of their tricks and venality, are abundant in Neapolitan
dialect literature" (Croce 573). See also the eclogue "The Hook" at the end of day 4.
17. "Two more games, with sexual allusions to the gesture of the male 'emptying'
and the female being 'wounded' on her marriage night" (Rak 519–20).

her, since she had other things in her head than the desire to eat, and other things in her stomach than an appetite for filling it. When Cecio saw her so lost in thought and downhearted he said to her, 'What does it mean that you're not doing honor to these dishes? What's the matter? What are you thinking? How do you feel?' 'I don't feel at all well,' answered Renza, 'nor do I know whether it's indigestion or vertigo.' 'You're right to skip a meal,' replied Cecio, 'for a diet is the best tobacco[18] for every ill. But if you need a physician we can send for the urine doctor,[19] who can recognize people's illnesses by merely looking at their face, without even taking a pulse.' 'This is not an ailment that can be cured by prescription,' answered Renza, 'for no one knows the troubles of the pot like the serving spoon.' 'Go out for a bit and get some air,' said Cecio. And Renza: 'The more I see, the more my heart breaks.'

"As they continued talking, the eating came to an end and it was time to go to sleep. Cecio wanted Renza to sleep on a sofa in the same room where he was going to sleep with the bride, so that he could always hear her song, and every now and then he called her over and had her repeat the usual words, which were daggers in Renza's heart and a headache for the bride, who, after sitting there for a while, finally burst out, 'You've broken my ass with this white face! What kind of dark music is this? It's been going on for so long now that it's nothing short of diarrhea! That's enough, for heaven's sake! What, are your brains falling out, so that you repeat the same thing over and over again? I thought I was getting into bed with you to hear the music of instruments, not a lament for voices, but just look how you stoop down and always play the same note! By your good graces, no more of this, my husband. And you shut up, since you stink of garlic, and let us rest a little!' 'Be quiet, my wife,' answered Cecio, 'we're going to break the thread of our talk now!' And saying this, he gave her a kiss so loud you could hear it a mile away. The sound of their lips was thunder in Renza's breast, and she felt such pain that when all of her spirits raced to aid her heart it happened just as the proverb says—'Too much breaks the lid'—for the rush of blood was such and so much that it suffocated her, and she stretched out her feet for the last time.

"After Cecio had given the bride four little pats he called Renza under his breath, so that she would repeat those words that he liked

18. "In this period tobacco was entering into general use, and was considered a cure for many illnesses" (Croce 573). Basile's contemporary Francesco Zucchi exalts it as a panacea in his work of 1636, *La tabaccheide, scherzo estivo sopra il tabacco.*
19. "At this time a distinction was made between 'urine doctors,' general physicians, and 'wound doctors,' surgeons" (Croce 574).

so much. Not hearing her answer as he wished, he started begging her again to do him this little favor, but when he saw that she was not saying a word he got up very quietly and pulled her by the arm. When she didn't respond even then, he put his hand on her face, and when he touched her freezing nose he realized that the fire of that body's natural heat had gone out.

"This dismayed and terrified him, and he had candles brought in; Renza was uncovered, and he recognized her by a lovely mole she had in the middle of her chest. His shrieks rising to the sky, he began to cry, 'What do you see, O wretched Cecio? What has happened to you, unlucky one? What sort of spectacle is before your eyes? What sort of ruin falls on your joints? O my flower, who has picked you? O my lantern, who has put you out? O pot of Love's delights, how did you overflow? Who has demolished you, O lovely house of my joys? Who has torn you up, O permit of all my pleasures? Who has sunk you, O lovely ship of the pastimes of this heart? O my darling, when those beautiful eyes closed, the shop of beauty went bankrupt, the business of the Graces came to a halt, and Love went to throw bones off the bridge.[20] With the departure of this beautiful soul the seed of all beautiful women has been lost and the mold of all charming women broken, nor will the compass for the sea of amorous sweetness ever be found again! O damage without repair, O agony without comparison, O ruin without measure! Go flex your muscles, my dear mother, for you've been quite successful at strangling me until I lost this lovely treasure! What will I do, hapless, devoid of every pleasure, cleaned out of every consolation, lightened of every joy, deprived of every satisfaction, stripped of every amusement, emptied of all happiness? Do not believe, O dear heart, that I intend to continue weighing on this world without you, for I intend to follow you and lay siege to wherever you may go. And in spite of Death's grip we will be united; if I took you on to do service as a bedside companion, now I will be your partner in the grave, and one and the same epitaph will tell of the misfortunes of us both!'

"As he said this he took hold of a nail and gave himself a devigorating treatment under his left tittie, and his life gushed out all at once, leaving his bride cold and freezing. As soon as she was able to untie her tongue and unleash her voice she called the queen, who at all the noise came running with the whole court. And when she saw the dismal end of her son and Renza and heard the reason for this disaster,

---

20. "The bones of the executed and suicides, as well as carcasses of horses and other animals, were thrown from the Ricciardo or Maddalena bridges in Naples into the Sebeto River" (Croce 273).

she left not a lock of hair on her noodle, and, heaving herself this way and that like a fish out of water, she accused the cruel stars that had caused so much ill luck to rain down on her house and cursed her sad old age that had preserved her for so much ruin. And after she screamed, knocked herself around, pulled her hair out, and moaned and groaned, she had the two of them thrown into a ditch and atop it written the whole bitter story of their fortune.

"At that same time Renza's father, the king, arrived. While roaming the world in search of his runaway daughter, he had encountered the hermit's servant selling Renza's clothes; he had told the king what had happened and how Renza was following the king of Wide Vineyard. And the king got there at the very moment when Death had finished harvesting the spikes of their years and they were about to be buried in the ditch.[21] He saw her and recognized her and cried for her and sighed for her, and then cursed the bone that had fattened up the soup of his ruin, for he had found it in his daughter's room and recognized it as the instrument of her bitter tragedy. And this abomination thus verified for him, in general and in particular, the gloomy omen of those mountebanks who had said that she would die from a big bone, in clear demonstration of the fact that *when calamity intends to strike, it enters through the cracks in the door*."

---

21. "Allusion to the municipal ditches in which wheat was stored" (Croce 274).

4

SAPIA LICCARDA

Fourth Entertainment of the Third Day

Through her ingenuity Sapia remains virtuous during the absence of her father, in spite of the bad example set by her sisters. She plays a trick on her suitor, and when she foresees the danger she is in she manages to protect herself, and at the end the king's son takes her for his wife.

All of the pleasure of the past tales was muddied by the miserable story of those poor lovers, and for a good while everyone looked like a baby girl had just been born. When the king saw this, he told Tolla to tell something pleasant in order to temper the affliction felt at the death of Renza and Cecio. Upon receiving this command Tolla let herself loose in the manner that follows: "In the night of the world's woes the good judgment of men is a shining lantern that allows ditches to be jumped without danger and treacherous passages to be crossed without fear. It is thus much better to have brains than coins, since the latter come and go, whereas you can spend the former whenever you need to. You will see a great example of this in the character of Sapia Liccarda, who with the steady north wind of her good judgment sails from a vast gulf only to land at a safe port.

"There once was a very rich merchant named Marcone, who had three beautiful daughters: Bella, Cenzolla, and Sapia Liccarda. One day he had to leave town on some business, and knowing well that the two older daughters were window-mounting mares, he nailed shut all the windows and left them each a ring set with certain stones that became spotted all over if whoever wore it on her finger performed shameful acts. And then he left.

"But no sooner was he away from Open Villa, which was the name of the town, than the two daughters began to scale the windows and

---

AT 879: The Basil Maiden. In Italian *sapia* means "wise"; Liccarda is a verson of the female name Riccarda. "Savia Riccarda (or Leccarda) was also the bowl made of copper or other material that was placed under a spit to catch the grease dripping from roasts" (Guarini and Burani 322). Penzer offers a long list of variants of the "envious sister" tale type (1:256). See also Marie-Jeanne Lhéritier, "The Discreet Princess; or, The Adventures of Finette" (in *Beauties, Beasts and Enchantments*).

peek out from behind the shutters, even if Sapia Liccarda, who was the youngest, was beside herself and shouted that their house was neither the Gelsi nor the Duchesca nor the Cetrangelo warehouse nor Pisciaturo,[1] and that they shouldn't be joking and flirting with the neighbors.

"In front of their house stood the palace of the king, who had three sons: Ceccariello, Grazullo, and Tore. Once they caught sight of those good-looking young ladies, they began to wink at them, and then from winks they progressed to blown kisses, from blown kisses to words, from words to promises, and from promises to actions, until they made a date for one evening—when the Sun retired with its earnings so as not to compete with the Night[2]—and all three of them climbed up the side of the sisters' house. The two older brothers came to an agreement with the older sisters, but when Tore tried to get his hands on Sapia Liccarda she slithered away like an eel into another room, barricading herself so that it was impossible to get the door open. And the poor little boy was thus forced to count his brothers' morsels, and while the two of them loaded the sacks for the mill he had to hold the mule. But then morning came—when the birds, trumpeters of the Dawn, played 'Everyone on their horses!' to get the hours of the day into their saddles—and they left, the first two full of happiness over the pleasure they had received and the other one full of gloom over the awful night he had spent. And before long the two sisters were pregnant.

"An unpleasant pregnancy it was, though, with all that Sapia Liccarda had to say to them, for just as they swelled up from one day to the next, she blew up at them from one hour to the next, always concluding that their lizard's bellies[3] would bring them war and ruin and that, as soon as their father came back from his travels, there would be some fine sheep dancing.

"In the meantime, Tore's desire grew, in part because of Sapia Liccarda's beauty and in part because it seemed to him that he had received an affront and been tricked. And so he plotted with the older sisters to get her to fall into a trap when she least expected it, arranging for them to induce her to go and look for him in his own house. And so one day they called Sapia and said to her, 'My sister, what's done is done; if you had to pay for advice it would either cost more or

---

1. "All neighborhoods of ill repute in Naples, home to prostitutes and lowlifes" (Croce 276).
2. "Like the nobles who retired to their country estates when they were unable to afford the expensive life at court" (Rak 534). See also tale 1.7 n35.
3. "Other writers of the time use the expression 'lizard-eye' to describe a flirtatious and seductive woman" (Croce 277).

be more respected. If we had listened to you properly we wouldn't have deflated the honor of this house, nor would we have inflated our bellies the way you see us now. What can we do, though? The knife is in up to the hilt; things are too far along; the goose already has its beak. But we can't imagine that your anger would devastate you to the point of wanting to see us taken from this world. So we hope, if not for us at least for these poor creatures we carry in our bellies, that you will have some compassion for our state.'

"'The heavens know,' answered Sapia Liccarda, 'how my heart weeps for this mistake of yours, when I think of the present shame and of the trouble awaiting you when my father returns and finds this failing in his own house; and I would give a finger of my hand for this business never to have happened. But since the demon blinded you, let me know what I can do, just as long as my honor doesn't enter into it. For you can't make cream from blood and at the very end flesh calls, and the pity I have for your situation tickles me so that I would offer my own life to find a solution to this matter.' When Sapia had finished speaking her sisters answered, 'We desire no other sign of your affection than that you go and get a bit of the bread the king eats, for we've developed such a craving that if we don't satisfy it the babies risk being born with little rolls on their noses. So if you're a good Christian, tomorrow morning when it's still dark do us this favor, and we'll lower you down from the window where the king's sons climbed up and dress you as a beggar so you won't be recognized.'

"Sapia Liccarda, full of compassion for those poor unborn creatures, put on some ragged clothes, slung a flax comb over her shoulder, and—when the Sun lifted high the trophies of light won in victory against the Night—went to the king's palace asking for a few crumbs of bread. Tore, who had been waiting cunningly for this occasion, recognized her immediately and, when after obtaining her alms she wanted to leave, attempted to grab her. But she suddenly turned her back, with the result that his hands ended up on the comb, and he scratched himself so badly that for several days he was out of commission.

"The sisters got their bread, but poor Tore's hunger only grew. And so they started plotting again, and after another two days the pregnant women went back to complaining to Sapia that they had a craving for a couple of pears from the king's garden. Their poor sister put on a different outfit and went to the royal garden, where she found Tore, who as soon as he caught sight of the beggar and heard that she was asking for pears, insisted on climbing a tree himself. When he had thrown a handful of pears into Sapia's lap and was intending to come down and grab her, she took the ladder away and left him up in the arbor shouting at the crows, and if a gardener hadn't happened to come by to pick a few heads of romaine lettuce and helped him down, he would have been there all night. At this he bit his hands in rage and threatened to take fierce revenge.

"Now as the heavens willed it, after the two sisters gave birth to two lovely cherubs they said to Sapia, 'We'll be completely ruined, my dear girl, if you don't make up your mind to help us, since it can't be long before our master comes back, and when he finds this bad service in the house, the largest piece of us left will be our ears. So go downstairs; we'll pass these babies out to you in a basket and you take them to their fathers, who can worry about them.' Sapia Liccarda was full of love, and although this seemed like a heavy load to bear for the asininity of her sisters, she nonetheless let herself be convinced to go downstairs. The babies were lowered and she brought them to their fathers' chambers; finding no one there, she put each of them in the proper father's bed, using information she had expertly obtained. Then she went into Tore's chambers, put a large stone in his bed, and returned home. When the princes came back to their chambers and found those lovely boys with the names of their fathers written on little tags sewn to their chests, they felt great joy. But Tore went to bed with a lump in his throat, since he was the only one who had not been worthy of continuing his race, and when he threw himself on the bed he hit his head on the stone so hard that he got a big bump.

"In the meantime the merchant returned from his travels. After he looked at his daughters' rings and found that those of the two older girls were all spotted, he did terrible things and was already thinking of putting them in irons and torturing and beating them until he discovered what had happened, when the king's sons came to ask him for his daughters' hands in marriage. The merchant didn't know what was going on and at first thought they were playing a joke on him. Finally, when he heard how they had conducted business with his daughters and of the children who had been born, he considered himself happy with his good luck. And so they agreed to hold the wedding that evening.

"Sapia rubbed her stomach and remembered the way she had tormented Tore, and although she saw herself pursued with so much insistence, she imagined nonetheless that all grass is not mint and that the coat was not without bristles. For this reason she immediately made a lovely statue of sugar paste, put it in a large basket, and covered it up with some clothes. And after they danced and celebrated all evening, Sapia made up the excuse that she was having palpitations and went off to bed before everyone else. Then, with the excuse that she had to get changed, she had the basket brought in, tucked the statue under the sheets, and hid behind a curtain to await the results of this business.

"When the time came for the newlyweds to go to sleep and Tore arrived at his bed he said, believing that Sapia was lying there, 'Now you're going to pay, bitch, for the grief you caused me! Now you'll see what happens to a cricket that wants to compete with an elephant! Now you're going to suffer for everything! And I want to remind you of the linen comb, the ladder you pulled away from the tree, and all the other disturbances you caused me.' As he was saying this he grabbed a dagger and ran it through her from front to back, and, not content even with this, said to her, 'And now I want to suck your blood, too!' When he took the dagger out of the statue's chest and licked it, he tasted the sweetness and the fragrance of musk, so strong that it stunned him. At this he regretted having impaled such a sugary and fragrant girl, and began to lament his fury, uttering words that would have moved stones to pity and crying that his heart must have been full of bile and his sword full of poison to have offended such a sweet and suave creature. And after wailing at length he let himself be pulled into the noose of desperation and he lifted his hand, which still held the dagger, with the intention of cutting his own veins.

"But Sapia quickly came out from where she was, stayed his hand, and said to him, 'Stop, Tore, lower that hand; here's a piece of what you're crying for! Here I am, healthy and alive and able to see that you, too, are alive and green. Do not think that I was as obstinate as an old ram if I tormented you and caused you some displeasure, since it was only to test and probe your constancy and faithfulness.' And she told him that she had orchestrated this final trick as a remedy for the rage of a scornful heart, and that therefore she begged his pardon for everything that had happened. The bridegroom, full of love, hugged her and had her lie down next to him, and then made peace with her. And when it had been proved to him that pleasure is sweeter after much suffering, he respected the bit of reluctance on his wife's part much more than the excessive readiness of his sisters-in-law, since, as that poet said, *neither naked Cythera*[4] *nor bundled Cynthia:*[5] *the middle way has always been the most esteemed.*"

4. Aphrodite (or Venus), the goddess of love; "derived either from Cythera in Crete or from the island of Cythera, where the goddess is said to have first landed" (Penzer 1:255).
5. Cynthia, or Artemis (or Diana), goddess of the moon and chastity; "derived from Mt. Cynthos in the island of Delos. Being a virgin, she is taken as the opposite of Aphrodite" (Penzer 1:255).

5

THE COCKROACH, THE MOUSE, AND THE CRICKET

Fifth Entertainment of the Third Day

Nardiello is sent three times to market by his father, each time with a hundred ducats. The first time he buys a mouse, and then a cockroach and a cricket. His father kicks him out of the house and he ends up in a place where he cures the daughter of a king by means of the animals, and after various other adventures he becomes her husband.

The prince and the slave heartily praised Sapia Liccarda's wisdom, but they praised Tolla even more for her ability to present the story so well that everyone hearing it had seemed to be present. And since, following the order of the list, it was Popa's turn to speak, she behaved like Orlando and began telling her tale in this fashion: "Fortune is a stubborn woman who avoids the faces of learned men because they pay more attention to the turning of pages than to the rotation of a wheel. For this reason she more willingly associates with ignorant and paltry people and—in order to receive plebeian glory—does not worry about dividing her goods among the big birds, as I will tell you about in the tale that follows.[1]

"There once was, on the Vomero hill,[2] a very rich farmer named Miccone, who had a son named Nardiello, the most wretched blockhead you could ever find on any ship of fools.[3] The poor father was embittered and miserable, for he knew of no way or means of

---

AT 554: The Grateful Animals, and AT 559: The Dungbeetle. Besides the "grateful animals" motif, this tale also features one of the many foolish protagonists of *The Tale of Tales* (others appear in 1.1, 1.3, 1.4, 2.4, 3.8, 4.4), and yet another "princess who would not laugh."

1. The theme of Fortune's supposed predilection for the weak—in this case, the dim-witted—reiterates the Aristotelian affirmation, much quoted in these centuries, that those who have the fewest rational means for looking after themselves receive compensation in the form of better luck.

2. "A hilly area near Naples, in which at this time villas and country houses were beginning to appear" (Croce 574).

3. *permonara* (Neap.): "an old ship [kept at wet dock] that was used as a hospital" (Croce 282).

inducing his son to lead a level-headed and useful life. If Nardiello went to the tavern to guzzle with his buddies he was cheated by crooks; if he associated with women of ill repute he was given the worst meat for the top price; if he played in gambling dens they kneaded him like a pizza and took him out when he was nice and hot. And so, in one way or another, he had dissipated half of his father's wealth.

"For this reason Miccone was always armed and ready to defend his castle and would shout and threaten, saying, 'What do you think you're doing, spendthrift? Can't you see that my wealth is trickling away like water at low tide? Leave, leave those damned taverns,[4] which start with the name of the enemy and end up signifying evil! Leave them, for they're migraines to your head, dropsy to your throat, and diarrhea to your wallet! Leave, leave that godless gambling, which puts your life at risk and gnaws away at my fortune, which repels happiness and eats up cash, where the dice reduce you to zero and the words whittle you down to a peg![5] Leave, leave your bordello commerce with that evil race of the daughters of ugly sin, where you squander and spend! You consume pouches of money for a perch[6] and you suffer agonies and reduce yourself to picking at a bone for a piece of rotten meat; they are not meretrices, but a Thracian sea[7] where you are captured by the Turks! Keep away from the occasion, and you'll give up the vice; if the cause is remote, said that fellow, the effect will be removed. So here are a hundred ducats: go to the Salerno fair[8] and buy as many steer so that in three or four years we'll have as many oxen; once we've got the oxen we'll work the fields; once we've worked the fields we'll start dealing in wheat, and if we meet up with a good famine we'll weigh our coins by the bushel and at the very least I'll buy the title on some friend's land and then you'll be titled, too,[9] like

---

4. *ostarie* (Neap.): One of the many burlesque etymologies that we find in Basile. The origin of *oste* is posed as *ostis* (Latin; enemy) and that of *rie, rio* (wicked).
5. *pirolo* (Neap.): "the peg on a violin for screwing up the strings" (Croce 283).
6. Wordplay: *perchia* (perch or, metaphorically, women of ill repute) vs. *purchie* (large amounts of money).
7. Another facetious etymology, which plays on the phonetic similarity between *meretrice* (meretrix) and *mare trace* (Thracian sea).
8. The Salerno fair was one of the most important fairs of the time. "'It lasted eight days, beginning on the eve of St. Matthew's Day': people came to it 'from very far away,' and 'animals and every sort of goods' were exhibited" (Croce 574, who cites the 1703 work by Pacichelli, *Il regno di Napoli in prospettiva*).
9. *sarrai tu puro tritolato* (Neap.): a play on words between *titolato* (titled) and *tritolato* (ruined, destroyed, torn to shreds).

so many others.[10] So be careful, my son, everything has a head; he who does not begin, cannot continue.'

" 'Leave it to this fellow,' answered Nardiello. 'I know how to do my calculations now, and I've learned the rules for every situation!' 'That's what I want to hear,' answered his father, and when he had forked out the money, Nardiello started off to the fair. But he had not yet reached the waters of the Sarno when he came upon a lovely little elm wood where, at the foot of a rock that had surrounded itself with fronds of ivy so as to cure its perpetual wound of cool water, he saw a fairy frolicking with a cockroach, and the cockroach was playing a tiny guitar so beautifully that a Spaniard would have said that it was a superb and grandiose thing.[11] When Nardiello saw this he stopped to listen as if enchanted, and said that he would give one of his eyes to have such a talented animal. The fairy told him that if he paid a hundred ducats she would give it to him. 'There's never been a better time than this,' Nardiello answered, 'since I have the money ready and waiting!' Saying this he threw the hundred ducats in her lap, then took the cockroach away in a little box and ran back to his father with a joy that went from the little bones of his feet up, and said to him, 'Now you'll really get to see, my sir, if I'm a man of ingenuity and know how to go about my business, for without tiring myself by going all the way to the fair I found my fortune when I was halfway there, and for a hundred ducats I got this jewel!'

"Upon hearing these words and seeing the little box, his father was certain that his son had bought a diamond necklace or something of the sort, but when he opened it and saw the cockroach, the humiliation of being tricked and the pain of losing his money were a set of bellows that made him swell up like a toad. And while Nardiello would have liked to tell him all about the virtues of the cockroach, he wasn't allowed to say a word, for his father went on and on, saying, 'Shut up, plug it, close that mouth, cork it; not a peep, you mule, you horse brain, you ass head! Take the cockroach back this very instant to whoever sold it to you, and with these other hundred ducats that I'm giving you buy just as many steer. And come back right away and take care the Wicked One doesn't blind you or I'll make you eat your hands with your own teeth!'

---

10. "The Venetian ambassador Lippomano noted, in 1575, the ease with which merchants of the kingdom of Naples bought, from one day to the next, fiefs, estates, and houses" (Croce 574). The buying and selling of noble titles was, in the first half of the seventeenth century, a thriving business.

11. "A reference to the hyperbolic mode of expression that Italians often noted in Spaniards" (Croce 284).

"Nardiello took the money and set off toward the Tower of Sarno,[12] and when he had reached the same place as before he came upon another fairy playing with a mouse, which was executing the loveliest dance steps you ever did see. For some time Nardiello watched with amazement the fawn steps,[13] twirls, caprioles, point dancing, and leaps of this animal, until he was beside himself with wonder and told the fairy that if she was willing to sell it to him he would give her a hundred ducats. The fairy accepted these terms, and after taking his coins she gave him the mouse in a box. When Nardiello went back home and showed poor Miccone the fine purchase he had made, Miccone made an awful scene, slamming himself around like a beaten octopus and snorting like a skittish horse. Indeed, if it hadn't been for a neighbor of his who happened to appear in the middle of all this uproar, he would truly have taken the measure of Nardiello's shoulders. Finally Miccone, boiling with anger, took a hundred more ducats and said to Nardiello, 'I'm warning you, don't try another one of your tricks because the third time it won't work. Go to Salerno and buy the steer, and I swear on the souls of my ancestors that if you slip up this time, woe to the mother who gave birth to you!'

"With his head hanging, Nardiello made off in the direction of Salerno. When he arrived at the same place as before he came upon another fairy, who was amusing herself with a cricket that sang so sweetly that it lulled people to sleep. Upon hearing this new breed of nightingale Nardiello immediately felt the desire to do business, and once they had agreed on a hundred ducats, he put it in a tiny cage made of a long hollowed squash covered with sticks and went back to his father. When he saw the third bad service his son had performed for him, Miccone lost his patience and, grabbing a club, fixed Nardiello up so well that even Rodomonte[14] couldn't have done better.

"Nardiello escaped from Miccone's clutches as soon as he could; he took all three animals, moved out of that town, and set off in the direction of Lombardy, where there lived a great lord named Cenzone who had an only daughter whose name was Milla. On account of a certain illness Milla had become so melancholy that no one had seen her laugh for seven years straight, so that her father, after having attempted a thousand remedies and spent money in every direction,

---

12. "The castle of Scafati, on the left bank of the river Sarno" (Rak 554).
13. *dainette* (Neap.): the name of a well-known dance step of the time. Some of the other terms used in translation were coined only later to describe the moves in question.
14. See eclogue 2 ("The Dye") n5.

Nardiello cavaie da la sctaola li tre animale, li quale sonaro, ballaro e cantaro co tanta grazia e co tante squasenzie che la regina scappaie a ridere. [Nardiello took the three animals out of the box. They played, danced, and sang with such grace and such charm that the queen burst into laughter.]

issued a proclamation announcing that whoever made her laugh would receive her for his wife.

"Nardiello heard of this proclamation and fancied that he would try his fortune, and he went before Cenzone and offered to make Milla laugh. To which the lord responded, 'Be mindful, my friend, that if you do not succeed your hood will lose its shape!'[15] 'Both my hood and my shoe can lose their shape, for all I care,' replied Nardiello, 'for I want to try my luck, and whatever happens will happen!' The king summoned his daughter to come sit with him under a canopy, and Nardiello took the three animals out of the box. They played, danced, and sang with such grace and such charm that the queen burst into laughter, whereas the prince's[16] heart wept, for, according to the terms of the proclamation, he was now forced to give a jewel of a woman to a scum of a man. But since he was not able to go back on his promise he said to Nardiello, 'I will give you my daughter, and my state as dowry, but with the agreement that if you do not consummate the marriage in three days I will feed you to the lions.' 'I have no fear,' said Nardiello, 'since in that time I'm man enough not only to consummate the marriage but to consume your daughter and your whole house as well!' And the king: 'Slow down, we'll get to that, as Carcariello[17] said; you can't know a good watermelon until you've seen its flesh.'[18]

"After the festivities were held and evening fell—when the Sun, like a thief, was taken off to the prison of the West with a cape over its head—the bride and bridegroom went to bed. But since the malicious king had arranged for a sleeping draught to be given to Nardiello, he did nothing but snore all night. After the same thing happened on the second and the third days the king had him thrown into the lion pit, where Nardiello, realizing he was nearing his end, opened the animals' box and said, 'Since my fate has dragged me with a bitter towline to this wretched impasse, and since I have nothing else to leave to you, O lovely animals of mine, I will free you, so that you can go where best you please.' As soon as they were let out, the ani-

---

15. I.e., of the head inside it.
16. It would have to be the other way around—i.e., the princess laughed, and the king's heart wept—since Milla is Cenzone's daughter. This is not the only inconsistency of this sort in *The Tale of Tales* and should probably be attributed to the lack of a final editing.
17. Carcariello was "an authority of the burlesque tradition" (Rak 554).
18. *la prova* (Neap.): "Watermelons were sold 'with a proof': that is, with a piece cut out of their rind, to offer proof of their redness and consequently of their flavor" (Croce 287).

mals began to exhibit themselves in so many little capers and games that the lions became as still as statues. In the meantime the mouse addressed Nardiello, whose spirit was already in his mouth, saying to him, 'Cheer up, master, for even if you've given us our freedom we want more than ever to be your slaves, seeing that you've nourished us with so much love and cured us with so much affection and that at the end you gave us a sign of your great devotion by setting us free. Have no doubts: he who does good may expect good; do good and then forget about it. But you should know that we are enchanted, and if you want to see what we are capable and worthy of, follow us, and you'll free yourself of this danger.'

"With Nardiello behind them, the mouse soon made a hole in the wall big enough for a man, through which, after going up a staircase, they led him to the top, where it was safe. There they put him in a hut and told him to order them to do whatever he wished, for they would leave nothing undone which might bring him pleasure. 'My desire would be,' responded Nardiello, 'that if the king has given Milla another husband, you do me the favor of not allowing the marriage to be consummated, because it would bring about the consummation of my own miserable life.' 'That and nothing are but the same thing,' answered the animals. 'Keep your spirits up and wait for us in this shack, for we'll clean up the mess without delay!'

"They set off for the court, and found that the king had married his daughter to a great German lord and that that very evening the cask was to be uncorked. Once the animals had skillfully entered the chamber of the newlyweds, they waited until the banquet was over and evening came—when the Moon came out to feed the Pleiades[19] with dew—and the couple went to bed. And since the bridegroom had loaded his crossbow and taken one too many cards,[20] as soon as he had holed himself up under the sheets he immediately fell asleep and lay there as if his throat had just been cut. When the cockroach heard the bridegroom's snoring, it crawled very quietly up the foot of the bed, made its way under the covers, and nimbly slipped into the bridegroom's asshole, serving him a suppository that uncorked his body in such a way that one might have said, with Petrarch: 'love drew from him a subtle liquid.' The bride, who heard the rumbling of this dysentery—'the breeze and the fragrance and the coolness and

---

19. *gallinelle* (Neap.): lit., the little hens. The Pleiades were, in myth, the seven sisters pursued by Orion and his two dogs, Sirius and Procyon, and then turned into a constellation that marks the seasons and the time for sowing and planting.
20. "One of the many expressions used to signify 'to get drunk,' which the bridegroom, living up to the fame of Germans, had not failed to do" (Croce 288).

the shade'[21]—woke her husband up. When he saw the sort of perfume he had incensed his idol with, he nearly died of shame and croaked with rage, and once he had gotten out of bed and his whole body had been laundered, he sent for the doctors, who attributed the cause for this disgrace to the excesses of the banquet the day before.

"When the next evening arrived and he asked his servants' advice, they were all of the opinion that he should swathe himself with sturdy cloths so as to avoid another mishap; he did this and then went to bed. But after once again he fell asleep and the cockroach returned to play a second trick on him, it found the passageway blocked. And so it went back unhappily to its companions and told them how the bridegroom had prepared shields of bandages, dikes of diapers, and trenches of rags. Upon hearing this the mouse said, 'Come with me and you'll see whether I'm a good enough sapper to clear you a way!' When the mouse arrived in sight of the place in question, it started to gnaw the cloth and make a hole at the same level as that other one; the cockroach then went in and administered another one of its medicinal cures, so that a sea of liquid topaz flowed forth and the Arabian fumes infected the palace. This caused the befouled bride to awaken, and when, by the light of the lamp, she saw the citron-colored flood that had turned the Dutch bed linens into yellow-rippled Venetian moiré,[22] she plugged her nose and flew into her damsels' room. The wretched bridegroom called his valets, and complained at length of the disgrace of having begun to construct the grandeur of his house on such a slippery foundation.

"His servants comforted him and advised him to keep his wits about him the third night, telling him the tale of the gassy patient and the sharp-tongued doctor who, when his patient let loose a fart, put on erudite airs and said to him, 'Sanitatibus!' When another fart followed he added, 'Ventositatibus!' But when a third proceeded, he opened his mouth wide and said, 'Asinitatibus!' Consequently, if the first mosaic work that had decorated the nuptial bed could be blamed on excessive eating and the second on the bad state of his stomach, which had upset his whole body, the third would be imputed to a shitty nature and he would be driven away in stink and shame. 'Have no doubt,' said the bridegroom, 'because tonight, even if I have to die for it, I intend to stay awake the whole time and not let sleep win me over. And furthermore, we'll think of some remedy for plugging the

---

21. The verses from Petrarch can be found in his *Rime sparse* (or *Rerum*) nos. 185 and 327 (following the numbering in Robert M. Durling's 1976 translation). The *Rime* was one of the most important models for the Italian lyric tradition.
22. *tabiò de Venezia* (Neap.): a heavy watered silk, similar to taffeta (Guarini and Burani 337–38).

main pipe, so that no one can say to me, "Three times he fell and the third time he lay still!" [23]

"That agreed, when the next night arrived and the bridegroom moved to a different room and bed, he summoned his friends and asked them for advice on how to stop up his body so that it wouldn't play a third trick on him; as for staying awake, all the poppies in the world couldn't have put him to sleep. Among his servants there was a young man who dabbled in the bombardier's art; and, since everyone is most interested in his own trade, he advised the bridegroom to have himself a wooden stopper made, like the ones used for firecrackers. It was prepared without delay, and after the German positioned it in the right manner, he went to bed—neither touching the bride, for fear that his exertions might ruin the creation, nor closing his eyes, so that he could be ready for any movement that his intestines might make.

"The cockroach, who saw that the bridegroom wasn't falling asleep, said to its companions, 'Alas! This time they've shown us up; our skills aren't of any use, since the bridegroom isn't sleeping and won't give me a chance to carry on my business!' 'Just a minute,' said the cricket, 'I'll take care of this for you now!' and, starting to sing sweetly, it put the bridegroom to sleep. When the cockroach saw this it raced forth to apply its usual syringe, but upon finding the door closed and the road barricaded, it went back to its companions in desperation and confusion, and told them what had happened. The mouse, who had no other goal than to serve and to please Nardiello, went off to the larder that very instant, and after sniffing in jar after jar, came across a pot of mustard. It rubbed his tail in it and then ran to the bridegroom's bed and lubricated the nostrils of the wretched German, who began to sneeze so hard that the stopper flew out with such fury that, since he had his back to the bride, it hit her in the chest so violently that it almost killed her.

"At the bride's shrieks the king came running, and when he asked what the matter was, she told him that a firecracker had been shot at her chest. The king marveled at this absurdity, and at the fact that she could even speak with a firecracker in her chest. But then he lifted the covers and the sheets and found the explosion of bran and the stopper to the firecracker, which had given the bride a nice eggplant-colored bruise, although I'm not sure if the stink of the fire powder or the blow of the cannonball caused her more harm. Upon seeing this revolting scene and hearing that it was the bridegroom's third attempt at liquidating the deed, the king threw him out of his kingdom,

---

23. This verse from Virgil's *Aeneid* is found at the end of book 4.

and when he considered that this whole misfortune had been caused by the cruelty shown toward poor Nardiello, he began to beat his fists on his chest. And while, repentant for what he had done, he was wailing, the cockroach appeared before him and said, 'Do not despair, since Nardiello is alive, and for his fine qualities deserves to be the son-in-law of Your Highness, and if it pleases you that he come we will send for him immediately.' 'Oh, be welcome, you who bring me this news worthy of a reward, my dear animal! You have given me life, you have rescued me from a sea of woes, since I felt such pain in my heart for the way I did that poor young man wrong! And so have him come, for I want to embrace him like a son and give him my daughter for his wife.'

"When it heard this, the cricket went hopping away to the shack where Nardiello was and told him of everything that had happened. Then it brought him to the royal palace, where, once the king had met and embraced him, he was given Milla's hand. The animals cast a spell on Nardiello so that he became a handsome young man, after which he sent for his father from the Vomero. And they all lived together, happy and content, proving after a thousand hardships and a thousand woes that *more happens in one hour than in a hundred years.*"

6

THE GARLIC PATCH

Sixth Entertainment of the Third Day

Because she obeys her father by doing his pleasure and conducts herself shrewdly in what she has been ordered to do, Belluccia, daughter of Ambruoso of Barra, is most richly married to Narduccio, the firstborn of Biasillo Guallecchia, which results in her poor sisters being supplied with dowries and given as wives to his other sons.

The wretched bridegroom didn't shit all over himself nearly as much as the listeners pissed in their pants laughing when they heard of the trick the mouse had played. And the laughter would have lasted until the next morning had the prince not done a little something to make them lend an ear to lady Antonella, who was all ready to chatter and began to reason in this manner: "Obedience is secure merchandise that brings earnings without risk and the sort of property that yields fruit in every season. The daughter of a poor peasant will prove it to you: by showing her obedience to her father not only did she open the road of good fortune to herself but also to her sisters, who, thanks to her, married into riches.

"There once was, in the village of Barra,[1] a rustic man named Ambruoso, who had seven daughters, and all that he had to support them honorably in the world was a garlic patch. This respectable man had a great friendship with Biasillo Guallecchia,[2] a man of Resina

---

AT 879: The Basil Maiden, and AT 884: The Forsaken Fiancée: Service as Menial. The title seems unrelated to the characters and actions of the tale. Croce changes it to "Belluccia." Penzer recalls similar attempts to determine the true sex: "Grimm 67 ('The Twelve Huntsmen'), chapter 11 of *Huckleberry Finn,* an episode in Benvenuto Cellini's autobiography, as well as the most classic example, the Homeric tale of the discovery of Achilles among the daughters of the King of Scyros by Odysseus, who disguised himself as a peddler bringing dress and weapons. The real maidens admired the robes, but Achilles seized the shield and spear" (1:270). See also Gonzenbach 12 and 17.

1. "At this time, 'royal village' of Naples, famous for the palace and villa the Flemish merchant Gaspare Roomer had built, where he received Queen Maria of Hungary in 1630" (Croce 575).

2. As a common noun or adjective *guallecchia* also means "good-for-nothing" (Guarini and Burani 341).

who was rolling in money and had seven sons. One day Narduccio, the firstborn and his father's right eye, fell ill, and although the purse was always open no cure could be found for his illness.

"Ambruoso went to visit him, and was asked by Biasillo how many children he had. Ashamed to tell him how he had grafted so many little farts, he said, 'I have four sons and three daughters.' 'If that's the case,' replied Biasillo, 'send one of those sons of yours to keep my son company, and you'll be doing me a big favor.' Ambruoso, who found himself taken at his word, didn't know how to answer except by nodding his head, and when he got back to Barra he was overcome with such melancholy that he thought he would die, for he didn't know how to content his friend. He finally called his daughters to him one at a time, from the oldest to the youngest, and asked which of them would be willing to cut her hair, put on man's dress, and pretend to be a boy so as to keep Biasillo's son, who was sick, company.

"At these words the oldest daughter, Annuccia, answered, 'Since when has my father died and I need to cut off all my hair?' Nora, the second, answered, 'I'm not even married yet and you want me to cut off all my hair, like a widow?'[3] Sapatina,[4] the third, said, 'I've always heard it said that girls shouldn't wear pants.' Rosa, the fourth, answered, 'Forget it! You're not going to find me going around looking for something that apothecaries don't have, just to amuse an invalid!' Cianna, the fifth, said, 'Tell that sick fellow to take a cure and try some bloodletting, because I wouldn't give a hair off my head for a hundred life threads of a man!' The sixth, Lella, said, 'I was born a woman, I live a woman's life, and I want to die a woman. I don't want to lose the reputation of a good woman by disguising myself as a fake man.' When the last little nest shitter, Belluccia, saw that at each of her sisters' answers her father heaved a sigh, she answered, 'If disguising myself as a man is not enough to serve you, I'll become an animal, I'll shrink down to nothing to make you happy!' 'Oh, bless you!' said Ambruoso. 'You're giving me your life in exchange for the blood that I gave you! Now come on, let's not waste time; we need to strike while the iron is hot.'[5] He cut her locks, which were little golden ropes of the policemen of Love, and when he had found a few shreds of men's clothes for her, he brought her to Resina. Ambruoso was received by Biasillo and his son, who was in bed, with the greatest ca-

---

3. See tale 2.6 n14.
4. "From Sabatina, which in turn derives from 'sabato' [Saturday], it may also mean sly or crafty, since those born on Saturday are considered such" (Guarini and Burani 343).
5. Lit., "tops are made at the lathe." Wooden tops of the time often had a metal tip.

resses in the world, and when he returned home he left Belluccia to
serve Narduccio, the invalid.

"At the sight of such astonishing beauty shining through the rags,
Narduccio gazed at her, feasted his eyes on her, and examined every
bit of her, and then said to himself, 'If I don't have warts in my eyes,
this has got to be a woman: the softness of her face betrays it, her
speech confirms it, her walk attests to it; my heart tells me so and
Love reveals it to me. She is without a doubt a woman, and she must
have come with this ruse of dressing like a man so she could set an
ambush for this heart.' And as he became completely immersed in
this thought, his melancholy increased so greatly that his fever went
up and the doctors thought that he was close to the end.

"For this reason his mother, who burned all over with love for
him, began to say, 'My son, blind lantern of these eyes of mine,
crutch and tongs of my old age, what is it supposed to mean that instead of gaining in vigor you're losing your health, and instead of
advancing you're retreating farther and farther back, like a pork
rind on the coals?[6] Is it possible that you want to keep your mommy
in such a dejected state, without telling her the cause of your illness
so that she can find a remedy? So speak, my jewel, blurt it out, unload your heart, blow off some steam, tell me exactly what you need
and what you would like, and let Cola take care of things, for I
won't neglect to provide you with all the pleasures in the world!'
Encouraged by these pretty words, Narduccio let himself go and
poured out the passion of his heart, telling her how he was certain
that that son of Ambruoso's was a woman, and that if she weren't
given to him for his wife he was fully resolved to cut off the course
of his life.

" 'Slow down!' said his mother. 'If we want to put your mind to
rest we'll first need to perform a few tests to discover if this is a
woman or a man, flat or hilly countryside. Let's have him go down to
the stable and mount one of the colts, the wildest one there; if she's a
woman you'll see her spin the thin thread of fear, since women don't
have much courage, and then we'll check which way those weights
fall.'[7] Her son liked the idea, and Belluccia was sent down to the stable, where they gave her a little demon of a colt. After saddling it she
got on, and with the courage of a lion began to perform amazing
promenades, astounding prances, marvelous caracoles, wondrous
jumps, curvets that were out of this world, and gallops to make you

---

6. I.e., "you're being consumed."

7. *sti pise* (Neap.): lit., "these weights"; euphemistically (as elsewhere in the text),
testicles.

jump out of your clothes. And so Narduccio's mother said to him, 'Get this frenzy out of your noodle, my son. Look, you can see that this boy is steadier on his horse than the oldest saddle shitter of Porta Reale!'[8]

"But Narduccio still wouldn't change his course, and continued to say that any way you looked at it she was a woman, and not even Skanderbeg[9] could have dispelled the idea from his noggin. To help him get rid of this craving his mother said to him, 'Slow down, black-bird,[10] now we'll perform a second test and we'll clear everything up.' And she had a musket brought to them and called Belluccia over, tell-ing her to load and shoot it. Taking the weapon in hand, Belluccia packed the barrel with gunpowder and Narduccio's body with itchy powder,[11] lit the fuse of her weapon and the fire of the invalid's heart, and, emptying the musket, filled the chest of that wretched soul with amorous desires. His mother, who saw the grace, skill, and elegance with which the boy shot, said to Narduccio, 'Get rid of that head-ache; you must realize that a woman could never do that!' But Nar-duccio still argued and was not able to resign himself, and would have bet his life that this lovely rose had no stalk. He said to his mother, 'Believe me, my mother, if this beautiful tree of Love's graces produces a fig for this invalid, this invalid will make the doctor the fig.[12] And so let's try in every way possible to know for sure, since if we don't it will be my ruin, and if I don't find the way to a hole I'll end up in a ditch!'

"His poor mother, who saw that he was more stubborn than ever and that he was digging in his heels and rattling on, said to him, 'You want to clear up your doubts? Take him swimming with you and then we'll see if he's a Happy Arch[13] or the Baia Cauldron,[14] Wide

---

8. "That is, an expert horseman. The ancient Porta Reale had been moved by the viceroy Pietro di Toledo to the beginning of the via Toledo, and was later torn down, in 1775. It was a congregating spot for couriers and coachmen" (Croce 575).

9. See tale 1.1 n8.

10. "A saying that continues: 'for the way is difficult'" (Croce 297).

11. *porvere de Zanne* (Neap.): "The 'itch powder' that the *zanni* [zanies, or jesters] of the *commedia dell'arte* used on stage or in street theater" (Rak 568). Its properties were also reputed to be magical and aphrodisiac (Guarini and Burani 346).

12. See tale 1.10 n25.

13. *Arco Felice:* "the large arch on the road from Pozzuoli to Cuma, through Monte Grillo" (Croce 575).

14. *'Ntruglio de Vaia:* "the people of Baia use this expression for the so-called tem-ples of Venus, Mercury, and Diana, large round structures that were used as baths. It may be that the word is a corrupted form of 'trullo' (from Byzantine Greek), in use in some parts of southern Italy to designate rural stone structures with a round shape and cupola roof" (Croce 575).

Square or Forked Way,[15] Circus Maximus[16] or Trajan's Column.'[17] 'Very good!' answered Narduccio. 'There's no doubt about it, you've cooked it to perfection. Today we'll see if he's a spit or a frying pan, a rolling pin or a sieve, a distaff or a bobbin bowl.'[18] But Belluccia got a whiff of the scheme and immediately sent for one of the father's errand boys, who was quite sly and cunning, and instructed him that when he saw that she was about to get undressed on the beach, he should bring her the news that her father was close to kicking the bucket and wanted to see her before the top of his life stopped spinning. As soon as the boy saw Narduccio and Belluccia arrive at the seashore and start to get undressed, he did as agreed and, with mandate in hand, served her the choice cut. Upon hearing the news, she took her leave of Narduccio and set off for Barra.

"The invalid returned to his mother with his head bowed, his eyes popping out of his head, his face a sickly yellow, and his lips pale, and told her that the deal had gone in the wrong direction and that due to the misfortune that had occurred he hadn't been able to perform the final test. 'Don't despair,' answered his mother. 'If you want to catch the hare you'll have to send a cart for it.[19] You'll turn up suddenly at Ambruoso's house, and when he calls his son you'll be able to tell if there's a trap and uncover the scheme by seeing whether he comes down right away or takes his time.'

"At these words Narduccio's cheeks, which had grown white, became rosy again, and the next morning—when the Sun took hold of its rays and kicked out the stars—he went straight off to Ambruoso's house, where he called him out and said that he wanted to speak to his son about something important. Feeling short and tall in the same instant, Ambruoso told him to wait a bit, and he would have his son come down without delay. Belluccia, so as not to be found with material evidence of the crime, took off her skirt and bodice, put on man's dress, and then raced downstairs. Her hurry was so great, though, that she forgot the little rings in her ears. When Narduccio saw this he received the signal of the calm that he desired from Belluccia's ears, just as you can predict bad weather from an ass's ears,

---

15. *Chiazza Larga e Forcella:* see tale 1.7 nn12, 16.
16. "The circus built between the Palatine and Aventine hills in Rome and restructured between 366 and 31 BC; one of the best-known emblems of classical culture" (Rak 569).
17. Trajan's Column, in the Forum of Trajan in Rome, was dedicated in AD 112–13.
18. *vosseta* (Neap.): "a wooden bowl in the middle of which turns the end of a small iron rod with a wooden cover, used to spool silk" (Croce 298). All of the above monuments and objects allude euphemistically to male or female genitalia.
19. "To conduct things with reflection and calm" (Croce 298).

. . . dove se fece na festa de sette a levare, che le museche e li suoni iero fi' a le sette celeste. [. . . where they played "seven up" at the festivities, and the music and noise went straight up to seventh heaven.]

and grabbing her like a Corsican hound he said, 'I want you to be my wife, in spite of envy, in defiance of Fortune, even against Death's will!' Ambruoso, who saw Narduccio's good intentions, said, 'As long as your father is happy with this, one hand of his and a hundred of mine.'

"And so together they all went to Biasillo's house, where Narduccio's mother and father, seeing their son healthy and happy, welcomed their daughter-in-law with enormous pleasure. And when they wanted to know why he had played this little game of sending her dressed as a man, and heard that it was so that it would not be discovered that he was a good-for-nothing who had produced seven girls, Biasillo said, 'Since the heavens gave you so many girls, and me so many boys, on my word, let's perform seven services in one trip! Go, then, and bring them to this house; I want to give them all dowries since, praise the heavens, I have enough sauce for the whole fish-fry.' When Ambruoso heard this he put on wings and went to get his other daughters and then brought them to Biasillo's house, where they played 'seven up' at the festivities, and the music and noise went straight up to seventh heaven. And now that all of them were happy it could be seen quite clearly that *divine graces are never long in coming.*"

7

CORVETTO

Seventh Entertainment of the Third Day

Corvetto is envied by the king's courtiers because of his virtuous qualities and is sent to face many dangers. When he pulls through with great honor he is given the princess for his wife, and his enemies' ire is thus further fed.

The listeners had been so transported by Belluccia's adventures that when they saw her married they were as happy and jubilant as if she had been born from their own loins. But the desire to hear Ciulla gave pause to their applause, and their ears hung upon the movement of her lips, which spoke in this manner: "I once heard it said that Juno, in her search for lies, went to Candia.[1] But if I were asked where one could really find feigning and fraud, I could indicate no better place than the court, where everyone dons a mask, and where Trastullo's gossip, Graziano's backbiting, Zanni's betrayals, and Pulcinella's[2] roguery thrive, where at one and the same time people snip and sew, sting and salve, break and glue. And I'll show you just a scrap of all of this in the tale that you're about to hear.

"There once was, in the service of the king of Wide River, a most respectable young man named Corvetto. His admirable behavior had earned him a place in his master's heart, and for this reason he inspired hate and nausea in all of the king's courtiers, who were bats of ignorance and thus incapable of beholding the shining virtue of Corvetto, who with the cash of his good actions bought the grace of his

---

AT 328: The Boy Steals the Giant's Treasure, and AT 1525: Master Thief. Penzer comments, "This tale includes the favorite 'tasks' motif which occurs several times in the present collection (III.5 and 7, IV.5, and V.4), but the kind of tasks imposed are closely allied to the 'Master Thief' tricks, while the jealousy of the favorite reminds us of Grimms 126" ("Faithful Ferdinand and Unfaithful Ferdinand") (1:277). Penzer lists a number of variants; in Pitrè, *Fiabe, nov. e racc. sic.* 33 (also in Crane's *Italian Popular Tales*), the hero uses his wits to steal an ogre's coverlet, horse, and bolster, and then brings back the ogre himself, locked in a chest.
1. "An invention that derives from a saying of Epimenides, preserved by St. Paul in the First Epistle to Titus 12: 'Cretenses semper mendaces, malae bestiae, ventre pigri'" (Croce 575). Basile spent some time in Candia (Crete) when he was in the service of Venice.
2. *Trastullo . . . Pulcinella*: well-known masks of the commedia dell'arte.

master. Indeed, the breezes of favor that the king blew on him were siroccos to the hernias of those envy-bitten souls, who did nothing but gather in every corner of the palace at all hours to murmur, gossip, whisper, gripe, and cut the poor man to pieces, saying, 'What sort of spell has this muttonhead cast on the king, who loves him so dearly? What kind of luck does he have that not even a day goes by without his receiving some new favor, while we are ever going backward, like rope makers, moving down to lower and lower rungs? And yet we serve him like dogs, and yet we sweat like fieldworkers and run like deer to make certain that the king's every fancy is perfectly satisfied! How true it is that in this world you've got to be born lucky, and that if you lack good fortune you might as well throw yourself in the sea! At the end all you can do is watch it all and drop dead!'

"These and other words shot out of the bows of their mouths, and they were poisoned arrows directed at the target of Corvetto's ruin. Oh, hapless is he who is condemned to live in that hell that goes by the name of court, where flattery is sold by the basket, malice and bad services measured by the quintal, and deceit and betrayal weighed by the bushel! And who can say how many melon rinds were put under his feet to make him slip?[3] Who can describe the soap of falsehood used to lubricate the steps to the king's ears so that Corvetto would tumble down and break his neck? Who can tell of the ditches of deceit dug in his master's brain and then covered with the light branches of zeal so that he would fall in?

"But Corvetto was enchanted, and he took notice of the traps and uncovered the treachery and recognized the fraud and sensed the intrigue, ambushes, mousetraps, snares, plotting, and tricks of his enemies. He always kept his ears pricked up and his eyes wide open so as not to lose his thread, for he knew that the courtier's fortune is made of glass. But the more this young man continued to rise, the steeper the others' descent and the more evident their writhing grew until finally, not knowing how to get him out from under their feet, since when they talked badly of him they were not believed, they decided to throw him off a cliff along the road of praise (an art invented in hell and perfected in court). And they attempted this in the manner that follows.

"Ten miles from Scotland, where this king's realm lay, there lived an ogre, the most ferocious and wild one that had ever existed in Ogredom. Since he was persecuted by the king, he had built a fortress for himself on top of a mountain in a solitary wood where not even birds flew, a wood so intricate that it never received the visit of the

---

3. "As happened, and still happens, on the streets of Naples in the summertime" (Croce 301).

sun. This ogre had a splendid horse that was as pretty as a picture, and among its other merits it lacked not even the power of speech, since it was enchanted and could talk like the rest of us. Now the courtiers, who knew how wicked the ogre was, how harsh the wood was, how high the mountain was, and how difficult it was to reach this horse, went to the king and described to him in minute detail the perfection of the animal, telling him that it was fit for a king and that he should try in every way and by every means to deliver it from the ogre's claws, and that Corvetto would be the right one to put his hand to it, since he was a talented young man who could pass through fire. The king, who did not know that under the flower of those words lay a serpent, called Corvetto at once and said to him, 'If you love me, you must attempt in every way possible to obtain my enemy the ogre's horse, and you will find yourself happy beyond measure and glad to have done this service for me.'

"Although he realized that this drum was being beaten by those who wished him evil, Corvetto nevertheless obeyed the king and set out on the road to the mountain. After silently entering the ogre's stable he saddled the horse, jumped onto its back with his feet firmly in the stirrups, and started toward the door. But when the horse saw that it was being spurred out of the palace, it shouted, 'Look out, Corvetto's taking me away!' At the sound of this the ogre came out, together with all the animals that served him: over here was a bogey cat, over there a prince's bear, on this side a lion, on that side a werewolf, and all of them ready to butcher Corvetto to pieces. But the youth cracked his whip well and was able to distance himself from the mountain and proceed at a gallop toward the city. When he arrived at court he presented the horse to the king and was embraced more warmly than a son, after which the king got out a bag and filled Corvetto's hands with coins.

"And so a good dose of starch was added to the courtiers' suit of rage, and whereas before they had blown up as if inflated by a straw, they now exploded like the blast of a bellows when they saw that the picks with which they had planned to demolish Corvetto's good luck were being used to clear the way to his advantage. Still, knowing that a wall is not brought down the first time it's hit by a war machine, they decided on a second attempt, and said to the king, 'That lovely horse, which will truly be the honor of the royal stable, is most welcome here. Now if you only had the ogre's tapestries, which are a thing of unspeakable beauty, your fame could become the talk of the fairs. And there's no one who would be able to add these riches to your treasure better than Corvetto, who has an expert hand when it comes to this sort of job.' The king, who danced to every music and ate only the skin of those bitter but sugar-covered fruits, called Corvetto and begged him to get the ogre's tapestries for him.

"Not replying a word, in the wink of an eye Corvetto was back at the ogre's mountain. Unseen he entered the room where the ogre was sleeping, hid himself under the bed, and waited there, crouching, until Night, to make the stars laugh, wrote a Carnival book[4] on the face of the sky. When the ogre and his wife had gone to bed, he cleaned out the room in perfect silence and, wanting to take the coverlet off the bed, too, he started to pull on it, very slowly. But the ogre woke up and told his wife not to pull so hard because she was uncovering him and he'd get a bellyache. 'Actually, you're the one who's uncovering me,' answered the ogress. 'I've got nothing left on me!' 'Where the devil is the blanket?' replied the ogre, and putting his hand on the floor, he touched Corvetto's face and began to shout, 'An imp, an imp![5] Help, bring candles, hurry!' At the sound of those screams the entire household was pitched into a state of turmoil. But Corvetto, who had thrown the pieces of cloth out the window, dropped down on top of them and, after making a nice bundle, headed off in the direction of the city. And no one can describe the caresses bestowed on him by the king and the burns suffered by the courtiers, who were bursting their sides with rage.

"They thus decided to attack Corvetto with the rearguard of roguery, and when they found the king all agurgle with pleasure over the tapestries—which, apart from being of silk and embroidered with gold, were decorated with thousands of devices[6] representing various whims and thoughts, among which there was, if I remember correctly, a rooster singing to the breaking dawn,[7] accompanied by a motto in Tuscan that read 'I am the sole one to gaze upon you,'[8] as well as a wilted heliotrope with the Tuscan motto 'As the sun sets,'[9]

---

4. "A probable allusion to the immensely popular *Contrasto di Carnevale e Quaresima* of this period" (Croce 576).

5. See tale 1.1 n19.

6. "Emblems or devices, accompanied by mottos, were still quite in vogue at this time, and there were many books on the topic, among which the most exhaustive is perhaps Picinelli's *Mondo simbolico* (Venice 1678)" (Croce 576). The most important Renaissance book of emblems was Andrea Alciato's *Emblemata* of 1531.

7. *l'Arba* (Neap.): "An homage to the duke of Alba, don Antonio Alvarez of Toledo, who was viceroy of Naples from 1622 to 1629, the period in which Basile wrote his book. In 1627 Basile dedicated the complete collection of his *Odi* to him" (Croce 576).

8. "Sol ch'io te miri" can also be translated as "Sun, I gaze upon you."

9. "In this second device, Basile perhaps alludes to himself and to his lack of fortune at the end of his life" (Croce 304). The "Tuscan" mentioned—that of Dante, Petrarch, and Boccaccio—was the literary Italian of the time.

"Lo monaciello, lo monaciello! Gente, cannele, corrite!"
["An imp, an imp! Help, bring candles, hurry!"]

and so many others that it would take more memory and time than I
have to describe them all—and when they found the king, as I was
saying, all happy and jubilant, they said to him, 'Since Corvetto has
accomplished so very much in your service, wouldn't it be a wonderful thing if he did you the special favor of obtaining the ogre's palace,
which is fit for an emperor? Indeed, it has so many rooms inside and
out that you could put a whole army in there, and you wouldn't believe its courtyards, porticoes, loggias, terraces, spiral latrines, and
tubed chimneys, and the architecture is such that art takes pride in it,
nature bows before it, and astonishment wallows in it.' The king,
who had a fertile brain that was easily impregnated, called Corvetto
and told him that he had a craving for the ogre's palace and that if he
added this leftover to the plate of pleasures he had already given the
king, the king would write his name with the charcoal of obligation
on the walls of the tavern of his memory.[10]

"Corvetto, who was a lit match and could run a hundred miles an
hour, threw his legs over his shoulder, and when he arrived at the
ogre's palace he discovered that the ogress had just given birth to a
lovely little ogrelet. Her husband had gone to invite all their relatives
to a party, and the new mother was already out of bed, all busy lay-
ing out the feast. Corvetto entered, brazen faced, and said, 'Nice to
see you, illustrious woman, lovely lady of the house! Why are you
tormenting yourself like this? Yesterday you gave birth and now
you're working so hard. Have you no mercy for your own flesh?'
'What do you want me to do,' answered the ogress, 'if there's no one
to help me?' 'I'm here,' replied Corvetto, 'to help you with kicks and
bites!' 'Well, then, you're welcome,' said the ogress. 'And seeing as
you offer your services so kindly, help me chop these four pieces of
wood.' 'With pleasure,' replied Corvetto, 'and if four aren't enough
let them be five!' He picked up a freshly sharpened hatchet, and instead of giving the wood a blow he used it on the ogress's neck and
sent her to falling to the ground like a pear. After that he ran to the
doorstep, dug a very deep ditch, and when he had covered it with
branches and earth took up a lookout post behind the door. Upon
seeing the ogre and the relatives arrive, he ran into the courtyard and
started shouting, 'May you be my witnesses: watch that piece of
shit,[11] and long live the king of Wide River!' When he heard this bit
of bravado, the ogre ran like lightning toward Corvetto with the in-

10. "A reference to the graffiti in charcoal with which idle customers would fill the
walls of taverns" (Croce 576).
11. "Parody of a formula already derided in II.7 (n15). Here, the addition of 'piece of
shit' agrees well with the other meaning of *testemmonia* (testicles)" (Guarini and Burani 356).

tention of tearing him to shreds. But as all the ogres rushed under the portico, their feet trampled the ditch and they tumbled down into it. Corvetto then bombarded them with rocks until he made a pizza of them, after which he locked the door and brought the keys to the king.

"When the king saw how the valor and ingenuity of this young man had survived in the face of Fortune's teasing, envy's spite, and the courtiers' plotting, he married Corvetto to his daughter. Indeed, the rafters of envy were, for Corvetto, the posts[12] that allowed him to launch the boat of his life in the sea of greatness, and his enemies, confused and consumed with rage, went off to shit without a candle, since *the punishment of a wicked man may be delayed, but it never fails to arrive.*"

---

12. *falanghe* (Neap.): "hollowed-out blocks of greased wood, still used to beach or to launch boats" (Rak 583).

8

THE IGNORAMUS

Eighth Entertainment of the Third Day

Moscione's father sends him to do business in Cairo to get him out
from under his own roof, where he behaves worse than a jackass.
At every turn of the road he meets up with men of exceptional
powers whom he takes with him; thanks to them he returns home
weighed down and laden with silver and gold.

There was no lack of courtiers around the prince who would have
made evident the anger they felt at being touched on their sore point,
if their art had not been precisely that of dissimulation. Nor could
one say whether the affront of seeing their own deceit thrown back in
their faces or the envy in hearing of Corvetto's happiness irritated
them more. But as she began to speak, Paola drew their hearts out of
the well of their self-love with the hook of these words: "An ignoramus who frequents virtuous men has always been praised much more
than a wise man who associates with worthless people, because just
as the ignoramus may earn comfort and greatness thanks to the former, the wise man may lose his goods and honor by the fault of the
latter. And if you can tell that a ham is good by testing it with a
stick,[1] you will be able to tell if what I have proposed to you is true
from the case that I will tell you about.

"There once was a father as rich as the sea, but since perfect happiness is not possible in this world, he had a son who was so wretched
and worthless that he couldn't tell a carob pod from a cucumber. No
longer able to digest his idiocy, the father gave him a nice handful of
scudos and sent him in the direction of the Orient[2] to do business,
since he knew that seeing diverse countries and associating with dif-

---

AT 513: The Extraordinary Companions, and AT 513A: Six Go Through the Whole
World. This tale bears some similarity to the latter part of tale 1.5. The "joint efforts" motif is a common one and can be found in Grimm 71 ("How Six Made Their
Way in the World") and 134, and other variants.
1. "The quality of a ham was ascertained by making a hole in it with a stick, which
revealed, by smell, any internal rancidity" (Guarini and Burani 358).
2. "The privileged route to arrive at the mythical Orient, full of spices and riches,
was Venice, and then Cairo" (Rak 596).

ferent people awakens wits, sharpens reason, and makes a man clever.

"Moscione, for this was the name of the boy, got on his horse and started to walk off in the direction of Venice, arsenal of the world's marvels,[3] from which place he intended to embark on a vessel that went to Cairo. When he had traveled a good day he came across a man standing at the foot of a poplar tree, to whom he said, 'What do they call you, my young man? Where are you from? And what's your trade?' And the other answered, 'My name is Flash, I come from Thunderbolt, and I can run as fast as lightning.' 'I'd like to see proof of that,' replied Moscione. And Flash said, 'Wait a minute, and you'll see if it's dust or flour!' They stood there for a while, and then a deer passed through the countryside and Flash, after letting it get a bit ahead so that it would have the advantage, began to run at such an excessive speed and with such a fleet foot that he could have passed over a field of flour without leaving a footprint, and in four leaps he reached the deer. When he saw this, Moscione was full of marvel and told Flash that if he wanted to stay with him he would pay him handsomely. Flash agreed, and they set off together.

"But they had walked no farther than four miles when they met another young man, to whom Moscione said, 'What's your name, pal? What town are you from and what trade do you practice?' And the other answered, 'My name is Hare's-Ear, I'm from Curious Valley, and when I put my ear to the ground I can hear what's going on all over the world without moving a hair. I can hear artisans putting together monopolies and intrigues to alter the price of their goods, courtiers plotting bad actions, go-betweens offering woeful advice, lovers on their dates, thieves dealing, servants complaining, spies giving their reports, old women psss-psssting, sailors cursing; not even Lucian's rooster or Franco's lamp[4] could see as much as these ears of mine do.' 'If that is the truth,' answered Moscione, 'tell me: what are they talking about at my house?' Hare's-Ear put his ear to the ground and said, 'An old man is talking with his wife, and he's saying, "May the Sun in Leo be praised! I managed to get that Moscione out from under my eyes, that face like an old robe, that nail in my heart; at least if he travels around the world he'll become a man and won't be such a brutish ass, cretin, and slacker!"' 'No more! No more!' said Moscione. 'You're telling the truth and I believe you! Come along

---

3. Venice is praised even more lavishly in tale 4.9.
4. The references are to Lucian's famous dialogue *The Rooster, or The Dream,* and to two of Niccolò Franco's *Pistole volgari* (Venice 1538) titled "Alla lucerna" and "Risposta de la lucerna," which satirize human conditions and professions (Croce 309).

with me, then, for you've found your fortune.' 'I'm coming,' said the young man.

"And so they set off together, and after another ten miles they met another young man, to whom Moscione said, 'What name do you go by, my respectable man? Where were you born and what can you do in this world?' And the other answered, 'My name is Sharpshooter, I come from Surefire Castle, and I can hit a target with my crossbow with enough precision to split a jujube in two.' 'I'd like to see proof of that,' replied Moscione, and Sharpshooter took up his crossbow, aimed, and hit a chickpea that was sitting on a stone. When he saw this, Moscione took him on as he had the others in his company.

"After walking for another day they met some men who were building a fine mole under a sun that blazed so strong that they might have said, with good reason, 'Parrella, add some water to the wine, for my heart is burning.'[5] Moscione felt so sorry for them that he said, 'And how is it, O masters, that you can bear to stay in this oven, where it's hot enough to cook a buffalo placenta?' One of them answered, 'We're as fresh as a rose because we have a young man who breathes so hard on us from behind that it seems like the west wind is blowing.' And Moscione said, 'Let me see him, and may God watch over you!' The masons called the young man, and Moscione said to him, 'What name do you go by, on the life of my father? What land are you from? What is your profession?' And the other answered, 'My name is Blowboy, I'm from Windy Land, and I can do all the winds with my mouth. If you want a breeze I'll give you one that'll send you to seventh heaven; if you want something stronger I can blow down houses.' 'I won't believe it unless I see it,' said Moscione. And Blowboy started to blow, at first so gently that it seemed like the wind that wafts through Posillipo in the evening, but then he suddenly turned toward some trees and blew such a furious wind that he uprooted a whole row of oaks. When Moscione saw this, he took him on as a companion.

"After they walked for another day he met another young man, to whom he said, 'Don't think I'm ordering you around, but what's your name? Where are you from, if one may know? And what's your trade, if that's a fair question?' And the other answered, 'My name is Strongback, I'm from Valentino, and I'm so powerful that I can throw a mountain on my back and it feels like a feather.' 'If that's the case,' said Moscione, 'you would deserve to be the king of customs[6] and

---

5. "Probably words of a popular song. [. . .] Parella was a name given to masonry laborers" (Croce 310).
6. "The king, or head, of the customs-house porters" (Croce 310).

you would be chosen to carry the banner on May Day,[7] but I'd like to see proof.' And Strongback began to load himself up with boulders, tree trunks, and so many other types of weights that a thousand big carts couldn't have carried it all. When Moscione saw this, they made a deal that Strongback would stay with him.

"And after walking some more they arrived at Bel Flower, where there lived a king who had a daughter who ran like the wind and could have run through a field of broccoli in flower without bending their tops. The king had issued a proclamation that he would give her in marriage to the man able to beat her in a race, but that he who remained behind would have his throat cut. Upon arriving in this land and hearing of the contest, Moscione went to the king and offered to race against his daughter, and when they had come to a fine agreement—either he kicked up his heels or left his noodle—he sent word to the king the following morning that he had come down with a sudden illness and, since he couldn't run in person, would send another young man in his place. 'Let whoever wants to come, come,' answered Ciannetella, the king's daughter. 'I don't give a hoot and there's enough for everyone.'

"And so when the square was full of people eager to see the race—men were crowded at windows like ants and the balconies were as full as eggs—Flash appeared and positioned himself in one corner of the square to wait for the starting signal. And then Ciannetella came out, with her skirt tucked halfway up her legs and wearing a lovely little close-fitting, single-soled slipper, no bigger than a size ten.[8] They lined up shoulder to shoulder and when the 'ta-ta-ta-ta' and 'toot toot' of the trumpet had sounded, they started running so fast that their heels touched their shoulders. Let's just say that they looked like hares chased by greyhounds, horses escaped from their stalls, dogs with bladders on their tails,[9] donkeys with clubs up their behinds. But Flash, who was just that in name and in fact, left her more than a span behind, and when they reached the finish line you should have heard the shouts, the racket, the uproar, the shrieks, the whis-

---

7. "On the first of May in Naples, especially in the street that took the name 'Maio di Porto,' 'a festival was held, and everything was decorated with broom flowers . . . a long ship's mast was planted in the ground and at the top of it various prizes were hung, which went to those who had the strength and dexterity to climb up the pole, and this game still has the name of Maio today' " (Carlo Celano, *Notizie* 4.292; cit. Croce 576). Apparently the winner would receive a banner. This sort of contest is akin to those common in Naples during Basile's time.

8. *dece punte* (Neap.): lit., ten points. "Shoe and glove sizes were measured in points" (Guarini and Burani 362).

9. "Bladders blown up like balloons, which children would tie to the tails of dogs and cats as a prank" (Guarini and Burani 362).

tles, the hand clapping and foot stomping of the people, who yelled, 'Long live the foreigner!' And Ciannetella's face turned the color of a schoolboy's ass after a good spanking, so humiliated and offended she was at having been beaten. Since the race had to be run twice, though, she decided that she would avenge herself of this affront, and as soon as she got home she cast a spell on a ring so that the legs of whoever wore it on his finger would fall asleep until he could no longer walk, let alone run. And she sent the ring as a gift to Flash, asking him to wear it on his finger out of love for her.

"Hare's-Ear, who heard daughter and father thus conspiring, kept quiet and waited for the deal to be closed, and when—as to the sound of the birds' trumpeting the Sun whipped the Night, who rode the donkey of shadows[10]—they took the field again, the usual starting signal was given, and they began to shake their heels. But if Ciannetella looked like a new Atalanta,[11] Flash had become a feeble donkey and a hollow-flanked horse unable to take even one step. When Sharpshooter saw what danger his friend was in and heard from Hare's-Ear how they had been tricked, he took his crossbow in hand, shot a pellet, and hit Flash's finger with great precision, causing the stone, wherein lay the power of the spell, to break off the ring. And so Flash's knotted-up legs came untied, and in four goat leaps he passed Ciannetella and won the race.

"Upon seeing that the victory had gone to a booby head, the palm to a featherbrain, and the triumph to a big sheep, the king thought long and hard about giving his daughter to Moscione. He called the wise men of his court to council, and they told him that Ciannetella was not a morsel for the teeth of a scoundrel and a good-for-nothing birdbrain, and that without the stain of going against his word he could commute the promise of his daughter into a monetary gift, which would satisfy this big ugly ragamuffin more than all the women in the world. The king liked this suggestion, and when Moscione was asked how much money he wanted in exchange for the wife that had been promised to him, he consulted the others and then answered, 'I want as much gold and silver as my friend is able to carry on his back.' The king agreed, and they brought in Strongback and began to load him up with piles of trunks of gold ducats, sacks of brass coins,

10. "It was common to see thieves or prostitutes or other delinquents led through the city on a donkey and whipped" (Croce 312).
11. The mythological nymph who challenged her suitors to a footrace, with the agreement that if they won they could marry her but if they lost they would die. Hippomenes was the only one to beat her, helped by three golden apples given to him by Aphrodite, which he threw down during the race to distract Atalanta (Ovid, *Metamorphoses* 10.560ff.).

huge bags of scudos, barrels of coppers, and jewelry boxes full of necklaces and rings. But the more they loaded on the more firmly Strongback stood there, like a tower, and since the stores of the treasury, banks, usurers, and money changers of the city were not sufficient, the king sent all his knights off to ask for loans of chandeliers, basins, jugs, saucers, dishes, trays, baskets, and even silver chamber pots, and all of that still wasn't enough to bring up the weight. Finally, not entirely laden but satisfied and restless to go, they left.

"But when the king's counselors saw the bottomless treasure that that company of scoundrels was carrying off, they told the king that it was pure asininity to allow the very backbone of his kingdom to be carted away, and that therefore it would be a good idea to send his men after them to lighten the great load of that Atlantis[12] who carried on his shoulders a sky of treasures. The king submitted to this counsel and immediately dispatched a bunch of armed men, on feet and on horse, to go and find them. Hare's-Ear, who had heard them in counsel, warned his companions, and while the pounding of the feet of those who were coming to unload their rich burden sent clouds of dust into the sky, Blowboy, who saw that things were going badly, began to blow so hard that not only did he cause all of their enemies to fall flat on their faces, but he sent them flying for more than a mile, as the north winds do to people walking in the country.

"And so without encountering other obstacles they arrived at the father's house, and after Moscione divided the earnings up among his companions—since, as the saying goes, 'When someone helps you win a cake, you give him a piece'—he sent them off, satisfied and content, and lived the rest of his days with his father, rolling in money. And thus he found that he had become a gold-laden ass, proving that the following saying is not a lie: *God sends biscuits to those who have no teeth*."

---

12. In myth, the Titan who was father to Calypso and condemned by Jove to hold up the sky on columns resting on his own body or hands (Homer, *Odyssey* 1.52ff.; Ovid, *Metamorphoses* 4.645–62).

9

ROSELLA

Ninth Entertainment of the Third Day

The Grand Turk has a prince captured so that he can bathe in a lord's blood. His daughter falls in love with the prince and they run away, but the girl's mother comes after them and her hands are cut off by the prince. The Grand Turk dies of a broken heart; when his daughter is put under a curse by her mother the prince forgets about her. But after the girl performs some trickery, she returns to her husband's memory and they live happily ever after.

They listened to Paola's tale with great satisfaction, and everyone said that the father was right to want a son who knew something, even if in this case the cuckoo had sung for him,[1] since if the others had kneaded the pasta he had taken off with the macaroni. But then it was Ciommetella's turn to have her say and she began speaking in this manner: "Those who live badly cannot die well, and whoever eludes this sentence is a white crow, for those who sow rye grass cannot reap wheat, and those who plant spurge cannot pick broccoli florets. The tale with which I now come to you will prove that I am not a liar. I beg you to pay me for it by allowing your ears to fly wide open and your mouths to hang while I make all efforts to satisfy you.

"There once was a Grand Turk who had leprosy and could find no cure for it. His doctors were unable to find an expedient to get this patient, with his insistent requests, off their back, and decided to propose something impossible to him, telling him that it was necessary to bathe in the blood of a great prince.[2]

"The Grand Turk wanted his health back, and when he heard this savage prescription he immediately sent a large fleet to sea, commanding them to scour every corner of the earth and with spies and the promise of great rewards to try to get their hands on a prince.

AT 313C: The Forgotten Fiancée. This tale bears similarity to Gonzenbach 55 as well as to the novella "Filenia" in Francesco Bello's 1509 collection *Mambriano*.

1. "The song of the cuckoo was held to be a good omen, at least by Neapolitan dialect authors; in popular belief, it is generally considered the opposite" (Croce 314).

2. Penzer notes that "the blood-bath as a cure for leprosy was recognized from the time of the ancient Egyptians in the Middle Ages" and that "the belief that bathing in a child's blood will produce offspring to the barren is well known" (1:291).

And as they sailed along the coast of Clear Fountain they ran into a little pleasure boat that was carrying Paoluccio, son of the king of that land, whom they stole away and carried off to Constantinople.

"When the doctors saw him they acted not so much out of compassion for the poor prince as in their own interest, for since the bath was not to bring any improvement, they would be the ones to shit their penance. Intending to play for time and draw the matter out as long as they could, they explained to the Grand Turk that this prince was angry about the freedom he had lost playing at *tressette,* and that his torpid blood would cause more harm than benefits; it was therefore necessary to suspend the cure until the melancholy humor had left the prince and to keep him happy and feed him hearty food that would enrich his blood. When the Grand Turk heard this, he decided to make him live happily by closing him in a beautiful garden on which spring had a perpetual lease and where the fountains competed with the birds and the cool breezes to see which could gurgle and murmur the best. He also put his daughter Rosella in there, so as to have the prince believe that he intended to give her to him for his wife. As soon as Rosella saw the beauty of the prince, she was tied tight to the towrope of love and, making a lovely inlay of her longings with those of Paoluccio, they were both set in the ring of the same desire.

"But when the time came for cats to be in heat and the Sun to have fun playing billy goat with the heavenly sheep,[3] Rosella discovered that since it was spring, when blood is of better quality, the doctors had decided to cut Paoluccio's throat and make the bath for the Grand Turk. For although her father had kept it hidden from her, she nonetheless knew about the treachery being plotted against her beloved, since she had been enchanted by her mother. And so she gave him a fine sword and said to him, 'My darling face, if you want to save your freedom, which is so dear, and your life, which is so sweet, waste no time; with the feet of a hare go to the seashore, where you'll find a boat. Get in and wait for me, and by the power of this enchanted sword you will be received by the sailors with the honor you deserve, as if you were an emperor.' When Paoluccio saw such a fine road to his salvation opening up he took the sword and set off for the seashore, where he found the boat and was welcomed with great deference by those manning it. In the meantime Rosella cast a certain spell on a piece of paper and then, without being seen or heard, slipped it into the pocket of her mother, who immediately fell into a sleep so deep she could feel nothing from head to toe. When this was

---

3. "The constellation of Aries, which the sun enters on March 21" (Croce 316).

done she took a bundle of jewels and ran off to the boat, and they set sail.

"Meanwhile, the Grand Turk went into the garden and, finding neither his daughter nor the prince, put the whole world in a state of alarm. And when he ran to look for his wife and could wake her neither by screaming nor by pulling her nose, he thought that some sort of sudden indisposition had caused her to lose her senses and, calling her ladies-in-waiting, he had her undressed. Once her skirt was taken off, though, the spell ended and she woke up, yelling, 'Alas, that traitor of your daughter has put one over on us and run away with the prince! But don't you worry; I'll fix her legs and shorten her steps!' Saying this, she rushed off to the seashore, where she threw a tree branch into the sea; it became a light felucca[4] in which she began to race after the young fugitives. Although her mother followed them invisibly, Rosella, whose eyes were touched by magic and thus saw the ruin that was about to befall them, said to Paoluccio, 'Hurry, my heart, put this blade in your hand; don't move from the stern, and as soon as you hear the sound of chains and hooks being thrown onto the boat, fire with a pig's eye;[5] and whoever you hit you hit, and too bad for the loser! Otherwise we're lost and our escape will be blocked!'

"Since his own hide was at stake, the prince heeded the warning, and as soon as the sloop pulled up alongside the boat and the Grand Turkess threw out the hooked chains, he gave a huge backhand swipe of his sword, which fortunately for him cut off the sultaness's hands in one blow. Shrieking like a damned soul, she put a curse on her daughter: after the first step the prince took in his land, he would forget her. She then rushed back to Turkey and presented herself to her husband with blood dripping from her stumps, and after she showed him this sorrowful spectacle she said to him, 'There you have it, my husband: you and I have gambled ourselves away at the table of fortune; you your health and me my life!' As she was saying this her spirit and her last breath left her, and she went off to recompense the master who had taught her the art. The Grand Turk, diving like a billy goat after her into the sea of desperation, followed after his wife's footsteps and left, as cold as snow, for the house of flames.

"When Paoluccio arrived at Clear Fountain he told Rosella to wait for him in the boat, because he was going to get people and carriages

4. A small sailing boat used in the Mediterranean and on the Nile with curved triangular sails.
5. "'Attack blindly, with closed eyes'; pigs' eyes are half-buried in their flesh" (Guarini and Burani 368).

to bring her triumphantly to his home. But no sooner had he put his foot on the ground than Rosella left his mind, and when he arrived at the royal palace he was received by his father and his mother with more caresses than it is possible to imagine, and there were festivities and light displays that would have astounded the whole world. After she spent three days waiting in vain for Paoluccio, Rosella remembered the curse and bit her lips for not having thought of finding an antidote. And so, like a desperate woman, as soon as she landed she took a palace facing the king's house to see if in some way she could make the prince's obligation to her return to his memory.

"When the lords of the court, eager to put their noses everywhere, caught sight of the new bird who had come to live in that house and contemplated her beauty, which surpassed all limits, went beyond every measure, crossed every boundary, reached nine[6] on the scale of marvel, was a full house in the deck of astonishment, and an 'out' in the game of amazement, they began to buzz around her like gnats, and not a day went by without them promenading around and performing curvets in front of her house. Sonnets arrived in a frenzy, messages in floods, musical compositions in stupefying quantities, and there was enough hand kissing to make your asshole itch. And since not one of them knew of the others, they all aimed at the same target and they all tried, drunk on love, to tap that lovely barrel. Rosella, who knew where to moor the boat, showed a pleasant face to them all, treated them all well, and kept all their hopes up.

"But finally, when she wanted to squeeze the sacks shut, she came to a secret agreement with a gentleman of high rank: if he gave her a thousand ducats and an elegant outfit of clothes, when night came she would refund the deposit of his affection. The poor window impregnator,[7] blindfolded by passion, immediately borrowed the money and, going into debt with a merchant, procured a rich cut of double-piled decorated brocade; and he couldn't wait for the sun to change places with the moon so that he could pick the fruit of his desires. When night came he went in secret to Rosella's house, where he found her lying in a lovely bed like a Venus in a field of flowers. Full of charm, she told him not to come to bed without first closing the door. It seemed to the gentleman that this was a small thing to do to serve such a beautiful jewel, and he went to close the door, which, how-

---

6. In esoteric numerology, the number 9 has great powers. "On the mystical significance of the number 9 and other numbers, Pietro Bongo's *Numerorum mysteria* (Bergamo 1599) was widely read at this time" (Croce 577).

7. *'mprena-fenestre* (Neap.): "He who makes love by walking under the windows of the woman he desires in order to see if she'll look out, and if she does, communicating with her from the street to the window by means of looks and signs" (Croce 577).

ever, as many times as it was closed opened wide again. He pushed and the door opened, so that he played this game of seesaw[8] and waged this tug-of-war all night—until the Sun sowed with its golden light the fields that Aurora had plowed. And thus he fought for a night, in all of its length and breadth, with an accursed door, without having been able to use his key; and as an addendum to this commission he got a good tongue-lashing from Rosella, who called him a pathetic thing who hadn't been up to closing a door but expected to open the chest of Love's pleasures. Finally the unfortunate fellow, tricked, confused, and put to shame, went off with a hot head and a cold tail to attend to his business.

"The second evening Rosella made an appointment with another baron, asking him for another thousand ducats and another outfit of clothes, and this one pawned all his silver and gold at the Jews'[9] to satisfy a desire that would transform regret into the heights of pleasure. And—as soon as Night, like a shamefaced pauper,[10] had covered its face with a cloak to beg the alms of silence—he presented himself at Rosella's house, where she had already retired; she told him to put out the candle and then come to bed. The gentleman took off his cloak and sword and began to blow on the candle, but the more he huffed and puffed the brighter it became, so that the wind emanating from his mouth had the same effect as a bellows on a blacksmith's fire. And he spent the whole night blowing like that and consumed himself like a candle in order to put out a candle. But—when Night hid itself so as not to have to see the various follies of men—the poor fellow, derided with another syrup of insults, went off like the first one.

"When the third night arrived a third lover came forward with another thousand ducats borrowed on usury and an outfit of clothes he had scrounged up, and when he had gone up on the quiet to Rosella's, she said to him, 'I do not intend to go to bed unless I comb my hair

---

8. *sto seca-molleca* (Neap.): "This is also the beginning of a children's nursery-rhyme ('Seca molleca / E le donne di Gaeta . . .') that wet-nurses sing with children on their knees, pulling them forward with their hands and then pushing them back" (Croce 577).

9. "There were no longer any Jews in Naples, since they had been driven out in 1541 by the viceroy Toledo. After their departure, a chronicler deplored that poor people were worse off and that, with respect to loans on pawned goods, 'Christians were beginning to be worse than Jews ever were'" (Castaldo, *Historia* 66; cit. Croce 577).

10. "The clothes of the 'disgraced poor' were worn, with due license, by those who had fallen into a state of need due to bad fortune, and are described by Vecellio (in *Habiti antichi e moderni* 176) as 'a sack or robe of old and patched black cloth, which represented their poverty, and a hood that they wore on their heads'" (Croce 577).

first.' 'Let me do it,' answered the gentleman, and he had her sit with her head in his lap. Thinking that it was a matter of smoothing out French cloth, he began to untangle her hair with the ivory comb, but the more he tried to get the knots out of that disheveled head the more he entangled the terrain, so that he dangled there all night without doing one thing right, and for having tried to neaten a head he put his own head into such a state of disorder that he was about to bang it on the wall. And—when the Sun came out to hear the lesson recited by the birds and with the whip of its rays beat the crickets that had infected the school of the fields—with another generous scolding he left the house, all cold and icy.

"Finding himself in conversation in the king's antechamber, where things are cut and sewn, where every mother who keeps a daughter there is to be pitied, where the bellows of adulation blow, the canvases of deception are woven, the keys of gossip are played, and ignorance is sliced like a melon so that it may be tasted,[11] this last gentleman recounted everything that had happened to him and told of the trick played on him. To this the second gentleman answered, saying, 'You be quiet, for if Africa cried,[12] Italy did not laugh! I've passed through this eye of the needle myself; a shared tribulation is half a jubilation.' To which the third one answered, 'You see, we're all stained by the same tar and we can shake hands without envy on anyone's part, for this traitoress has rubbed us all the wrong way! But it won't do to swallow the pill without resentment. We're not men to be deceived and put in a bag! So let's make her repent, this freeloader who fleeces little kids!'

"After they came to an agreement, they went to the king and told him the whole story. He immediately sent for Rosella and said to her, 'Where did you learn to trick my courtiers like this? Don't think I won't have you put on the tax lists,[13] you perch, you little slut, you ragged ass!' And Rosella, without changing color a bit, answered him, 'What I did was for the purpose of avenging myself on a member of your court for a wrong done me, even though nothing in the world would be enough to compensate for the affront that I have received!' And when she was ordered by the king to tell of the offense that had been done her, she recounted in third person how much she had done to serve the prince, how she had removed him from slavery, freed him from death, rescued him from the dangers of a sorceress, and brought him back safe and sound to his land, only to be paid

11. See tale 3.5 n18.
12. See Petrarch, *Trionfi d'amore* 2.83.
13. See introduction to day 1 n12.

with a turn of the back and a piece of cheese, which was hardly appropriate for her status, since she was a woman of great blood and the daughter of one who commanded kingdoms.

"When he heard this the king immediately had her seated at a place of great honor and begged her to reveal who the indifferent one was, the ingrate who had played this fine joke on her. Taking a ring off her finger, she said, 'Whomever this ring goes to is the unfaithful traitor that tricked me!' And when she threw down the ring, it went and slipped onto the finger of the prince, who was standing there like a doorpost. The ring's power immediately entered his brain and his lost memory returned, his eyes opened, his blood began to circulate again, and his spirits woke back up. He ran to embrace Rosella, and could neither get his fill of pulling tight the chain of her soul nor tire of kissing the vase of his happiness.

"And when he begged her pardon for the displeasure he had given her, she answered, 'There's no use begging pardon for those mistakes not generated by will. I know why you forgot your Rosella, since the curse that the lost soul of my mother put on you has not left my mind, and for this reason I forgive you and sympathize with you.' And as a thousand words of love thus passed between them, the king heard of Rosella's lineage and the debt he owed her for the good that she had done his son, and he was delighted that they should unite. And after Rosella was made a Christian the king gave her to his son for his wife, and they were more satisfied than anyone who has ever borne the yoke of matrimony, at the end realizing that *given time and straw, you can see that medlars always ripen.*"

10

THE THREE FAIRIES

Tenth Entertainment of the Third Day

Cicella, badly treated by her stepmother, receives gifts from three fairies. The envious stepmother then sends them her own daughter, who receives only humiliation. For this reason the stepmother sends Cicella to look after pigs, and a great lord falls in love with her. But with a ruse the stepmother gives him her ugly daughter instead, and leaves her stepdaughter in a barrel with the intention of boiling her to death. The lord discovers the foul play and puts the daughter in the barrel; the stepmother arrives and boils her own daughter's flesh off with hot water. When she discovers her mistake, she kills herself.

Ciommetella's tale was judged to be one of the best told so far, so that when Iacova saw that everyone was struck with amazement she said, "If it were not for the prince and princess's order, which is the winch that hoists me up and the towline that pulls me, I would put an end to my chatter, for it seems like too much of a stretch to compare the busted lute[1] of my mouth to the arch-viola[2] of Ciommetella's words. But since it is my lord's wish, I will force myself to play for you a little composition[3] on the punishment of an envious woman who, although she wanted to sink her stepdaughter, instead led her up to the stars.

"In the village of Marcianise[4] there was a widow named Cara-

AT 403: The Black and the White Bride, and AT 480: The Spinning-Woman by the Spring and the Kind and the Unkind Girls. This tale bears some similarity to the latter part of 1.5. The "joint efforts" motif is a common one and can be found in Grimm 71 ("How Six Made Their Way in the World"). See also Grimm 13 ("The Three Little Gnomes in the Forest"), 24 ("Mother Holle"), 89 ("The Goose Girl"), 130 ("One-Eye, Two-Eyes, and Three-Eyes"), Perrault's "The Fairies," Marie-Jeanne Lhéritier's "The Enchantments of Eloquence; or, The Effects of Sweetness," and Jeanne-Marie Leprince de Beaumont's "Aurore and Aimée" (the last two in *The Great Fairy Tale Tradition*).
1. See tale 1.3 n24.
2. "A type of large viola that Basile lists among the 'modern musical instruments' in the ninth eclogue of the *Muse napolitane*" (Croce 323).
3. *recercatella* (Neap.): a short *recercata*; see tale 1.1 n17.
4. "Commune in the province of Caserta, at Basile's time in the territory of Capua, 27 km. north of Naples" (Croce 323).

donia, who was the mother of all envy. She could never see anything go well for a neighbor without getting a lump in her throat; she could never hear of the good fortune of an acquaintance without it going down the wrong way; nor could she see any woman or man happy without getting the hiccups.

"This woman had a daughter named Grannizia, who was the quintessence of all cankers, the prime cut of all sea orcas, and the cream of all cracked barrels. Her head was full of nits, her hair a ratty mess, her temples plucked, her forehead like a hammer, her eyes like a hernia, her nose a knotty bump, her teeth full of tartar, and her mouth like a grouper's; she had the beard of a goat, the throat of a magpie, tits like saddlebags, shoulders like cellar vaults, arms like a reel, hooked legs, and heels like cabbages. In short, she was from head to toe a lovely hag, a fine spot of plague, an unsightly bit of rot, and above all she was a midget, an ugly goose, and a snot nose. But in spite of all this, the little cockroach looked like a beauty to her mother!

"Now it happened that one day this good widow married a certain Micco Antuono, a very wealthy farmer from Panecuocolo[5] who had twice been bailiff and mayor of that village and was much esteemed by all the Panecuocolese, who set great store by him. Micco Antuono had a daughter, too, by the name of Cicella, who was the most marvelous and beauteous creature in the world: her twinkling eyes cast a spell on you, her little mouth made for kissing put you in a state of ecstasy, and her cream-colored throat sent you into spasms. She was, in short, so charming, savory, gay, and mouth watering, and she possessed so many little graces, lovely airs, dainty little mannerisms, and so much allure and appeal that she stole hearts from their breasts. But what's the use of all these 'let me tell you's' and 'I told you's'! May it suffice to say that she was as pretty as a picture and you couldn't find the slightest defect in her.

"When Caradonia saw that her daughter, compared to Cicella, looked like a kitchen rag next to a cushion of the finest velvet, the bottom of a greasy pan in front of a Venetian mirror, a harpy face-to-face with a Fata Morgana, she began to scowl at her and have trouble keeping her down. Nor did the matter end there; spitting out the abscess that had formed in her heart and no longer able to stay hanging,[6] Caradonia began to torment the poor girl with an open show of

---

5. "In ancient times Cuculum, then Panicocoli, today Villaricca, a commune in the province of Naples in the Casoria district. Since the name Panicocoli was the object of derision among people of nearby towns, it was changed to Villaricca in the early 1800s" (Croce 578).

6. Reference to the torture of the ropes (Rak 634).

her cards. She dressed her daughter in a little twill skirt with a fringed hem and a gauzy top, and the poor stepdaughter in the worst rags and tatters in the house; she gave her daughter bread as white as flowers, and her stepdaughter hard and moldy crusts; she let her daughter stand around like the ampulla of the Savior, and forced her stepdaughter to rush to and fro like the shuttle on a loom and to sweep the house, wash the dishes, make the beds, do the laundry, feed the pig, take care of the donkey, and empty the chamber pot, all of which the good girl, always eager and able, did in most timely fashion, saving herself no effort in order to make her evil stepmother happy.

"But as her good fortune would have it, the poor girl was on her way to dump the trash off a large cliff near the house when her basket fell, and while she was trying to figure out how she could fish it out of that precipice, all of a sudden—what's this? what's this?—she saw a monster so horrible that it was hard to say whether he was the original of Aesop[7] or a copy of Old Horny. He was an ogre who had hair like the blackest of pig bristles that reached down to the little bones in his feet; a wrinkled brow, on which every fold looked like a plowed furrow; stiff and hairy eyelashes; shriveled and sunken eyes full of what's-it-called that looked like two filthy workshops under the wide awnings of his eyelids; a twisted and drooling mouth that sprouted two tusks like those of a wild boar; and a warty chest that was such a forest of hair you could have stuffed a mattress with it. And above all, he had a tall hump, a round belly, thin legs, and crooked feet, and he made your mouth twist with fear.

"But even if Cicella had in front of her an evil shadow that would have spooked anyone, she summoned up all her courage and said to him, 'My good man, hand me that basket that fell, and may you find yourself richly married!' The ogre answered, 'Come down, my dear girl, and get it yourself.' Grabbing onto roots and grasping at stones, the dear little girl tried her hardest until she finally got down there, where, incredibly, she found three fairies, one more beautiful than the other. They had hair of spun gold, faces like full moons, eyes that spoke to you, and mouths that petitioned, according to the terms of the contract, to be satisfied with sugary kisses. What else? Tender throats, delicate breasts, soft hands, dainty feet, and, in short, a grace that was the honorable frame of all that beauty.

"Cicella received more caresses and kindness from the fairies than can be imagined, and they took her by the hand and led her to a house located underneath the precipice, which could have accommodated a ruling king. When they arrived, they sat down on Turkish

---

7. The ugliness of the fabulist Aesop was proverbial.

carpets and cushions of smooth velvet tied with wool and moleskin bows, and the sorceresses then put their heads in Cicella's lap and had her comb their hair. And while she most delicately performed her task with a comb of gleaming buffalo horn, the fairies asked her, 'My lovely girl, what are you finding on this little head?' And she answered, with great politeness, "I'm finding little nits, tiny lice, and pearls and garnets!' The fairies were ever so pleased with Cicella's fine manners, and once their disheveled hair was all arranged those great ladies took her with them around the enchanted palace, showing her, bit by bit, all the extraordinary beauty it had to offer. There were splendidly carved writing desks of chestnut and hornbeam topped by boxes covered with horse skin and decorated in tin plate, walnut tables in which you could see your reflection, pantries with batteries of pots and pans so shiny they blinded you, draperies of flowered green cloth, leather chairs with backrests, and so many other lavish things that anyone else would have been in a stupor at the mere sight of it all. But, as if it had nothing to do with her, Cicella admired the grandeur of the house without marveling or letting her mouth hang open like a bumpkin.

"At the end they brought her into a wardrobe stuffed with sumptuous clothing, and they showed her petticoats of Spanish cloth; dresses of velvet gold-cloth, with leg-of-mutton sleeves; coverlets of thick silk trimmed with little enamel pendants; delicate shifts of bias-cut taffeta; tiaras made of real little flowers; baubles of oak leaves, seashells, half-moons, and serpent tongues; collars decorated with blue and white glass and ears of wheat; lilies and plumes to be worn on the head; chips of enamel set in silver; and a thousand other tidbits and doodads to wear around your neck. And they told the girl to choose whatever she liked and to take as many of those things as she wanted.

"Cicella, who was as humble as oil, ignored the most valuable things and decided on a tattered little skirt that wasn't worth three cents. When the fairies saw this they said, 'From which door would you like to leave, my little sweetie?' Bowing down so low that she almost dragged herself in the dirt, the girl said, 'Going out through the stable is good enough for me.' Then the fairies, hugging and kissing her a thousand times, dressed her in a magnificent gown embroidered all over in gold and did her hair in Scottish fashion, with braids that circled her head and so many ribbons and frills that it looked like a meadow of flowers. And with her padded rooster's crest[8] and her rolled braids, they accompanied her to the door, which was made of

---

8. "Hair knotted on top of the head, with a little tail hanging off it, which might have recalled the crest of parrots (from the Spanish *periquito*)" (Rak 635).

solid gold and had a frame inlaid with carbuncles, and said to her, 'Go, my dear Cicella, and may you find yourself well married! Go, and when you're out the door, lift your eyes and see what's above you!' The girl paid her proper respects and left, and when she was under the door she lifted her head and a golden star fell onto her forehead, and it was a beauteous thing to behold. And so, star-marked like a horse, she returned to her stepmother all neat and shiny, and told her what had happened from the beginning to the end.

"This was no fairy tale but a beating for the gouty woman, who was not able to find peace until she had gotten directions to where the fairies lived and sent her grouper fish of a daughter there. When the second girl arrived at the enchanted palace and found those three jewels, they first and above all had her look in their hair, and when they asked her what she had found, she said, 'Every louse is as big as a chickpea and every nit as big as a spoon.' The fairies were outraged and felt a lump in their throats at the coarse manners of this ugly lout, but they feigned indifference and recognized the bad day from the morning. In fact, when they took her to the room of sumptuous clothing and told her to pick out the best things, Grannizia, seeing herself offered a finger, took the whole hand and grabbed the most beautiful cloak that the wardrobes held. The sorceresses saw that the matter was getting out of hand and were taken aback; nevertheless, they wanted to see how far she would go and said to her, 'From which door would you like to leave, O lovely girl of mine, the golden door or the garden door?' And she answered brazenly, 'From the best there is!' When they saw how presumptuous that little ragamuffin was, the fairies gave her not one grain of salt and sent her away with these words: 'When you're under the stable door, lift your face to the sky and see what you get.' After the girl passed through the manure and went out, she lifted up her head, and a donkey's testicle fell onto her forehead, where it stuck to her skin and looked like a birthmark caused by a pregnant mother's cravings. And with this nice reward she returned, ever so slowly, to Caradonia.

"Foaming at the mouth like a bitch that's just given birth, Caradonia made Cicella get undressed, threw a filthy rag on her bare ass, and sent her to look after some pigs, after which she decked out her own daughter in Cicella's clothes. And with great calm and a patience worthy of Orlando, Cicella tolerated that wretched life. Oh, the cruelty! It was enough to move the stones in the street! That mouth, worthy of pronouncing amorous conceits, was forced to play a conch horn⁹ and to shout, 'Here, oinky, oinky, here, oinky'; that

---

9. "A shell used to call animals, especially pigs, from the fields" (Rak 635).

beauty, which should have attracted the noblest of suitors, was relegated to the pigs; that hand, which deserved to halter a hundred souls, prodded along a hundred sows with a stick. And damn a thousand times over the wickedness of the person who ordered her to those woods, where under the canopy of the shadows fear and silence found refuge from the Sun!

"But the heavens, which trample the arrogant and raise the humble up high, sent a most noble lord named Cuosemo to those parts. When he saw that jewel in the mud, that phoenix among pigs, and that lovely sun in the broken clouds of those rags, he became so infatuated with her that after he asked who she was and where she lived, without wasting a minute he went to talk with her stepmother and requested her for his wife, promising that he would give her a counter-dowry of thousands of ducats. But Caradonia set her eyes on him for her own daughter, and told him to come back that night since she wanted to invite the relatives. Full of joy, Cuosemo left, and it seemed like every hour was a thousand years until the Sun retired to the silvery bed prepared by the river of India[10] and he could in his turn retire with the Sun that inflamed his heart. In the meantime Caradonia threw Cicella into a barrel and sealed it up, with the intention of giving her a nice hot scalding: since she had abandoned the pigs, she wanted to skin her like a pig in boiling water.

"The air had already grown dark and the sky like a wolf's mouth when Cuosemo, who was having convulsions and dying of the desire to expand his impassioned heart by squeezing the beauties of his beloved, set off with great joy, saying, 'The hour has finally come to tap the tree that Love has planted in this breast so that it may send forth the sap of amorous sweetness; the hour has finally come to go and dig for the treasure that Fortune has promised me. And so waste no time, Cuosemo; when you've been promised a suckling pig go running with your rope! O night, O happy night, O friend of lovers, O body and soul, O ladle and pot; O Love, run, run head over heels, so that under the tent of your shadows I may find relief from the heat that is consuming me!'

"As he was saying this he arrived at Caradonia's house and found Grannizia instead of Cicella—an owl in the place of a goldfinch, a weed in the place of an overblown rose. For although she had put on Cicella's clothes and you could have said, 'Dress Darin and he'll look like a baron,'[11] she still looked like a cockroach wrapped in golden

---

10. The Ganges.

11. *vieste Cippone ca pare barone* (Neap.): Cippone was evidently the name of a proverbial character.

cloth. Neither the rouge, nor the other makeup, nor the poultices, nor the smoothing down administered by her mother could remove the dandruff from her hair, the bleariness from her eyes, the freckles from her face, the tartar from her teeth, the warts from her throat, the pustule from her chest, and the grit from her heels; you could smell the stench of bilge a mile away. When the bridegroom saw this fairy of a girl, he couldn't understand what had happened, and backing away as if the Old Serpent himself had materialized before him, he said to himself, 'Am I awake, or did I put my eyes on backward? Am I myself or not? What do you see, poor Cuosemo? Have you shit in your pants? This is not the face that yesterday morning caught me by my throat; this is not the image that was painted in my heart! What can this be, O Fortune? Where, where is the beauty, the hook that caught me, the winch that pulled me, the arrow that pierced me? I knew that neither women nor canvases could be seen well by candlelight, but I bagged this one in sunlight! Alas, this morning's gold has revealed itself to be copper, its diamonds to be glass, and my beard to be little more than sideburns!'

"Although he muttered and grumbled these and other words under his breath, at the end he was forced by need to give Grannizia a kiss. But as if he were kissing an ancient vase, he brought his lips close and then pulled them away more than three times before he touched the bride's mouth, and when he drew near to her it was like finding himself at the Chiaia marina in the evening, when those illustrious women offer the sea a tribute quite different from Arabian perfume.[12] But since the sky had dyed its white beard black to appear younger and his lands were quite distant, that night Cuosemo was forced to bring her to a house at a short distance from the Panecuocolo border, where after a straw mattress was laid upon two chests he went to bed with his bride.

"Who can tell of the awful night spent by the two of them, which, even if it was summer and lasted barely eight hours, seemed like the longest night of winter? On one side of the bed the restless bride spat, coughed, gave a kick now and then, sighed, and with silent words went in search of the rent on the house she had leased out. Cuosemo, on the other hand, pretended to snore, and he had moved so far over to the edge of the bed in order not to touch Grannizia that he fell

---

12. "In the neighborhood of Chiaia, on the waterfront, houses were built at sea level and there was no space in which to place cesspits or sewer pipes. Household sewage was therefore dumped into the sea, usually in the evening hours, which were called the 'dumping hours' or the 'stinky hours,' and the first hour of night also took the name of 'the evil Chiaia hour,' and is so designated even in legislative proceedings" (Croce 578).

right off the mattress and ended up on top of a chamber pot, and the whole thing came to a stinky and embarrassing conclusion. Oh, how many times the bridegroom damned the ancestors of the Sun,[13] which was taking its sweet time so that it could keep him in that tight spot for as long as possible! How often he prayed that Night might break its neck and the stars fall from the sky so that he could remove that bad day from his side with the arrival of the new one! And no sooner had Dawn come out to shoo away the Pleiades[14] and awaken the roosters than Cuosemo jumped out of bed and, barely fastening his trousers, raced off to Caradonia's house to repudiate her daughter and pay her for the sample taste with a broom handle.

"He entered the house but didn't find her, since she had gone to the woods for some firewood to scald the water for her stepdaughter, who was corked up in Bacchus's tomb even if she deserved to stretch out in Love's cradle. Looking for Caradonia and finding that she had disappeared, Cuosemo began to shout, 'Hey, where are you?' And a tabby cat that had been sleeping in the ashes came out with these unexpected words, 'Meow, meow, your wife is plugged up inside the barrel—meow!' When Cuosemo went over to the barrel and heard a certain faint and suffocated moaning, he took a hatchet from near the hearth and smashed it, and as the staves dropped away it looked like a backdrop being lowered for a scene where a goddess recites the prologue.[15] I don't know how it was that the bridegroom didn't drop dead before all that splendor; he stood there for a long time, staring at her like someone who has just seen a house imp. Then, when he was himself again, he ran to embrace her, saying: 'Who put you in this dreadful place, O jewel of my heart? Who hid you from me, O hope of my life? What is the meaning of this—a splendid dove in this hooped cage and a griffin vulture at my side? What's going on? Speak, my pretty face; comfort my spirits; let this breast be relieved!'

"At those words Cicella answered by telling him the whole story, without leaving out a single word, of everything she had had to bear in her stepmother's house from the moment she first stepped foot

---

13. "According to popular custom in Naples [and southern Italy in general], imprecations are not addressed directly to the person one wishes to offend, but to his immediate family (mother, sister, etc.) and to the 'dead ones' whose memory he reveres" (Croce 578).

14. See tale 3.5 n19.

15. "At Basile's time stage curtains were usually not raised, but lowered. In his own theatrical work *Monte di Parnaso* (Naples 1630), one can read: 'The first things one sees, when the wide curtain is lowered, is a spatious theater in the largest hall of the Royal Palace, which shows a woodland scene'" (Croce 332). A similar *scena boscareccia* appears in the frame tale, in the form of an old hag's private parts.

there to when Bacchus turned off her spigot by burying her in a barrel. After Cuosemo heard this he had her squat down and hide behind the door, and when he had put the barrel back together again he
summoned Grannizia and stuffed her into it, saying, 'Stay in here for
a bit, just long enough for me to have an enchantment made that will
protect you from the evil eye.' And then he corked the barrel tightly,
embraced his wife, and threw her onto a horse and took her straight
to Pascarola, which was his land.

"After Caradonia came back with a great bundle of sticks, she
made a big fire and put on a large cauldron of water. As soon as it
started to boil she poured the water into the hole in the barrel and
stewed all of the flesh off her daughter, who was grinding her teeth as
if she had taken a bite of the sardonic herb[16] and shedding her skin
like a serpent leaving its slough. When it seemed to her that Cicella
was most likely drenched to the bone and had stretched out her feet
for the last time, she broke open the barrel and saw—oh, what a
sight!—her own daughter, cooked by her crude mother. And tearing
her hair out, scratching at her face, pounding her breast, slapping her
hands together, beating her head on the wall, and stamping her feet,
she made so much noise and such a racket that the whole village came
running. After she did and said incredible things, for there were no
words comforting enough to console her and no advice that could
calm her, she raced off to a well and—splash!—jumped headfirst in
and broke her neck, proving the truth of the saying that *when you
spit into the sky it falls back on your face*."

*This tale had barely ended when, following the order given by the
prince, Giallaise and Cola Iacovo, one of them a cook and the
other the court cellar master, sprung out before them dressed in
the style of old Neapolitans, and recited the eclogue that follows.*

---

16. See introduction to day 1 n8.

THE STOVE

Eclogue

Giallaise and Cola Iacovo

GIALLAISE: Nice to see you, Cola Iacovo!

COLA IACOVO: You're the welcome one, Giallaise! Tell me, where are you coming from?

GIALL.: From the stoves.

COLA: The stoves in this heat?

GIALL.: The hotter the better!

COLA: And don't you croak in there?

GIALL.: I'd croak, brother, if I didn't go!

COLA: What sort of pleasure do you get out of it?

GIALL.: The pleasure of tempering the pain of this world, where you have no choice but to get angry, since these days everything goes the wrong way.

COLA: I believe you're making fun of me. Do you think I'm a blockhead, and that I'm not capable of fishing down deep? What do stoves have to do with the world?

GIALL.: You think you're fishing deep, but you're not fishing at all! Do you think I'm talking about the sort of stove where you're shut up in a little room and just sit there without moving until you suffocate and die of heat? No, no. I'm

---

"The use of hot baths, called *stufe* or stoves, with steam or thermal waters, was widespread in the area of Naples" (Rak 652). "They were managed by *stufaroli* [bath keepers] . . . and had small chambers in which after their baths ladies and gentlemen could also rinse their mouths, sip beverages brought to them by their servants, and rest on beds" (Del Tufo, *Ritratto* f. 79; cit. Guarini and Burani 388). Tomaso Garzoni, in his *Piazza universale*, comments that "there are few of them [bath keepers] who are not pimps and who do not rent out their rooms, thus mixing outer cleanliness with inner filth in those baths, which are a refuge for a thousand shameful and immodest acts of carnal lust" (cit. Croce 579). But here *stufa* (from the verb *stufare*, to bore or to make weary) is above all used to refer to the tedium that results from any type of worldly experience, however stimulating.

talking about that other thing at the mere thought of which every pain in this anguished life is cut in half; and what I see makes that thing of mine swell up!

COLA: This is all news to me. You astound me! On my word, you're not such an ass as you seem!

GIALL.: Well, then, you should know that there's another stove in this world into which both good and evil trickle. You may have joy and pleasure by the barrel and grandeur the size of a horse's chest, and yet everything ends in tedium and is wearisome. And to prove that this is true, open up your ears and listen, and in the meantime take comfort, for every human joy and amusement follows this track.

COLA: You truly deserve a nice gift! Go ahead, speak. I'm listening to you with my mouth hanging.

GIALL.: You see, for instance, a fine young girl. You take a liking to her, you send for the matchmaker, you arrange the marriage, you enter into agreement, you call the notary so that he can draw up the vows; you go up and kiss the bride, who is full of pomp and frills; you, too, wrap yourself up in a new suit, like a prince; the musicians are called; the banquet takes place, people dance. In short, that one night is anticipated with more desire than a sailor has for wind, a scribe for lawsuits, a thief for crowds, and a doctor for illness. And then night falls, that night of ill omens, and it wears mourning clothes, poor wretch, because freedom—miserable fellow!—is dead! Your wife squeezes you in her arms, and you know not that they are galley chains! The blandishments and caresses, the little charms and tenderness last for three days, but before the fourth arrives you already feel tedium, you curse ever having made mention of any of it, and damn a thousand times those who were its cause. If the poor girl speaks, you take it the wrong way and scowl and glare at her; when you're in bed you're like a two-headed eagle;[1] you writhe if she kisses you; and there will never again be anything good in that house.

COLA: He who marries is an unlucky gardener! He sows happily for just one night, then reaps a thousand days of torments.

GIALL.: Now a father sees his little baby born. Oh, what delight, oh, what fun! Right away he has him wrapped in buntings of silk and cotton wool; he polishes him like a pestle and

---

1. See tale 1.7 n34.

hangs all sorts of things on his shoulders:[2] wolves' teeth, figs, half-moons, and coral and amulets and little pigs, so that he's the spitting image of a street vendor! He finds him a wet nurse; he has eyes for no one else; he talks to him in cutesy talk: "How is pretty little baby? Me love you so much! You dada's little sweetheart! Mama's little yum-yum!" And while he's sitting there absorbed, with his mouth hanging open, listening to "caca" and "din-din," everything that squirts out ends up on his lap! In the mean-time the boy grows like a weed and flowers like broccoli; the father sends him to school and spends the pupils of his eyes for him. And right when he had counted on seeing him become a doctor the boy gets out of hand; he takes the wrong track; he mixes with sluts, deals with crooks, and hangs out with gangs and young hoods; he receives and hands out blows, and argues with barbers and scribes. And thus his fa-ther, weary of him, either kicks him out or curses him or, to get his sad head back on straight, has him taken prisoner and thrown into a castle.[3]

COLA: What do you expect if not prison? A wicked son who's as changeable as the moon grows up to take either an oar in the galleys or his place on the rope.

GIALL.: You want some more? Even eating, which is a necessity of life, grows tedious. You stuff your belly full, devour, swal-low, engorge, raze, rake, ingurgitate, pork down, move your jaws, shovel it in under your nose; you fill up your cheeks with the sweet and the sour, the lean and the fatty, and send your chops trotting; you spend your time at ban-quets and bazaars. And at the very end, when you find that your stomach is full of indigestion and your farts reek of sulfur and your burps of rotting eggs, you lose your appe-tite, and your tedium grows so great that meat stinks, fish makes you sick, sweets become absinthe and bile, wine your enemy, and you barely keep yourself alive with a little sip of broth.

COLA: If only it weren't true that lack of moderation, more than anything else, makes you shit blood, and every ill enters through the throat!

---

2. "The amulets with which the clothes and cradle of a newborn were immediately decorated; the first days following birth were considered to be of great importance for the destiny of the newborn, as is seen by the numerous mentions, in *The Tale of Tales,* of midwives, the calculations of astrologers, and fairies' gifts" (Rak 652).
3. "By request of parents, unruly children were placed in castle dungeons" (Croce 338).

GIALL.: If you play cards, dice, marbles, skittles, the Cedrangolo game,[4] chess, tiles; if you spend your time, risk your soul, and compromise your honor on this, you leave your money behind and lose your friendships, and can't sleep soundly or ever eat a whole morsel. Your mind is always on this accursed vice, where two agree to put you in the middle and divide the earnings in half; and yet when you realize you've fallen for it and you've been conned, your losses become tedious to you, and when you see a game it's as if it were fire and plague.

COLA: Blessed are those who flee from it! May it stay far from me, watch out for your legs![5] You lose your days even if you don't lose your money.

GIALL.: And entertainments,[6] which are not as risky and provide more pleasure, are also cause for bother: farces, comedies, and mountebanks; the woman who jumps rope, the other with a beard, and the other still who sews with her feet; jugglers with their bagatelles; the goat that walks on reels. In short, all amusements become tedious: buffoons and jokes, fools and madmen.

COLA: That's why Compar Biondo[7] used to sing, "There's no lasting pleasure in this world!"

GIALL.: Music is something you feel all the way down to the little bones in your feet, with its many varieties of graces and modes, trills, fugues, flights and warbles, and falsetto pieces and retropoints and passacaglias; with voices that are melancholy or cheerful, low or soaring, that sing in arias or in the part of a bass or a falsetto or a tenor; with keyboard or wind instruments, or with strings made of cord or metal. And yet it all grows tedious, and if you're not in the proper mood, your lungs swell the wrong way and you could smash both theorbo and lute.[8]

COLA: When you're not in your right mind, anyone—even Stella

---

4. "Perhaps a game of chance played in the taverns of Cedrangolo, one of the most ill-reputed streets of the city" (Guarini and Burani 393).

5. See tale 1.9 n10.

6. "These entertainments took place in Naples, in Piazza or Largo del Castello, today Piazza Municipio" (Croce 579).

7. See the introduction to day 1 n21.

8. *teorbie e colasciune* (Neap.): both stringed instruments belonging to the lute family and popular in seventeenth-century music.

and Giammacco[9]—can sing and warble, and a symphony[10]
will still sound worse than a dirge.

GIALL.: I won't say a thing to you about dancing: you see round
leaps and trick jumps, cabrioles and fawn steps, chasses
and curtsies. For a bit you like it and it gives you pleasure,
but then it becomes an August cure: you find even four
steps tedious, and you can't wait for the torch dance or the
fan dance[11] to start and the party to end so that you can
beat it out of there, your feet tired and your head in pieces.

COLA: Without a doubt it's a waste of time; hopping around consumes you, and you don't gain a thing from it.

GIALL.: Conversations and business meetings, amusements and get-
togethers with one's friends, drinking and reveling in taverns and hanging out at the Gelsi bordellos, turning the
town square upside down with your rusty blades and latrine
covers, never having a moment of peace, your head spinning, your heart reeling. And once the flower of your years,
when your blood is hot, is past, you find all of this more tedious than anything and, lowering your head and hanging
your carob pod[12] over the fireplace, you withdraw to mind
your own affairs and feel only tedium for those years that
gave you the shadows of pleasure and the reality of sorrow.

COLA: All that pleases man is like a straw fire; it passes and is destroyed, it collapses and melts away!

GIALL.: There's no sense in our head that is without whimsy: the eye
soon grows weary of contemplating resplendent and lovely
things, magnificence, beauties, paintings, spectacles, gardens, statues, and buildings; the nose of smelling carnations, violets, roses and lilies, amber, musk, civet, seasoned
broth, and roasts; the hand of touching soft and tender
things; the mouth of tasting juicy mouthfuls and the choicest of morsels; the ears of hearing fresh news and gazettes.
In short, if you count it up on your fingers, all that you do,
see, and hear, both amusements and hardships, becomes, at
the end, nauseating.

COLA: Man, who is made solely for the heavens, would become
too attached to the earth if in this world he found complete

9. Two other famous singers of the time (Rak 653).
10. In Basile's time, a *sinfonia* was usually a piece for an instrumental ensemble such
as, for example, the overture to an opera.
11. Dances typically performed at the end of festivities (Rak 653).
12. I.e., sword.

satisfaction; that's why baskets of sorrow are thrown into our mouths, whereas pleasures are rationed out.

GIALL.: There is only one thing that never grows tedious but always restores you and leaves you happy and comforted: and that is knowledge joined with wealth. For this reason that Greek poet said to Jove with warm and heartfelt prayers, "Give me, my lord, coins and virtue!"

COLA: You've got a chamber pot and a half of reasons to think that, for you never get your fill of one or the other. He who has both relish and salt is made great by his gold and immortal by his virtue!

The eclogue was so tasty that the audience, enchanted by pleasure, with great reluctance recognized that the Sun, tired of doing the Canary dance[13] *all day in the fields of the heavens, had sent out the stars to do the torch dance and had itself retired to change its shirt. And so, when they saw that the air had grown dim, the usual order to return was given and everyone retired to their own houses.*

End of the third day.

---

13. One of the most famous dances of the time (Rak 653).

IV

THE FOURTH DAY

Dawn had just come out to take its cut from the laborers,[1] since the Sun would be rising at any time, when the white prince and black princess met at their place of appointment; the ten women had also just arrived, after filling their bellies with red mulberries that left their faces looking like a dyer's hand. And together they all went and sat next to a fountain, which served as a mirror to some citron trees that were braiding their hair so as to blind the Sun. Deciding to pass in some way the hours until it was time to get their jaws moving, to please Tadeo and Lucia they began to discuss if they should play Saw the Brick,[2] Head or Tails, Full or Just Wind,[3] Bat and Stick,[4] Morra,[5] Odds or Evens, Bell,[6] Norchie,[7] Little Castles,[8] Get Near the Ball,[9] Put Them Together or Di-

---

1. Reference to a practice common among agricultural laborers. "Still today, in many parts of the South, day laborers meet before dawn at a central gathering place in the hope of being chosen by the 'foremen' who distribute the daily work. In exchange for giving them work, the laborers must give the foremen a percentage of their pay" (De Simone 585).
2. Mentioned in Del Tufo, *Ritratto* f. 101 (Croce 580).
3. "One player has to guess which of his adversary's closed fists contains something" (Guarini and Burani 400).
4. "This game consists in making the *piuzo*, a wooden cylinder with pointed ends, jump in the air, hitting it and keeping it up with a bat" (Guarini and Burani 153–54).
5. The well-known game, played with two people, the object of which is to predict the number of fingers the other player will hold up (usually by shouting out a number at exactly the same time as the other player shows her fingers). It is often used to decide who will be "it" or go first in a game.
6. A variation on hopscotch. "On the ground, a semi-circle is drawn with chalk, then a square with its diagonals, and then three rectangles, so that a bell-shaped figure of eight parts is formed. Players take turns throwing a key, tile, or other small object into the sections, after which they hop on one foot to the object and try to kick it out of the bell. If the object or foot touches a line, the player loses" (Rocco, *Vocabolario napoletano*; cit. Croce 580).
7. A card game (Croce 580).
8. "Players try to hit and knock down little piles of walnuts, chestnuts and the like by throwing another walnut or chestnut at them" (De Bourcard, *Usi e costumi di Napoli* 1.299; Pitrè, *Giochi* no. 66; cit. Croce 580).
9. A primitive form of bocce in which "a ball is thrown, and then players take turns

vide Them Up,[10] Touch,[11] ball, or skittles. But the prince, annoyed by
so many games, ordered that some instruments be brought in and that
in the meantime there be singing. And right away a group of servants
who knew how to play rushed out with lutes, tambourines, cithers,
harps, pipes, fire throwers, cro-cros, Jew's harps, and zuche-zuche,[12]
and after they performed a nice symphony and played "The Tenor of
the Abbot," "Zephyr," "Cuccara Giammartino," and "The Dance of
Florence," they sang a handful of songs from the good old times[13] that
are easier to pine for than to find today, and among others they sang

> Shoo, get out of here, Margaritella,
> you're too much of a scandal for this fellow,
> since for any trifling bit of dirt
> first you want a pretty little skirt.
> Shoo, get out of here, Margaritella.

And that other one:

> I would like, O cruel one, to become
> a patten, so that I could be under that foot;
> but if you knew about it,
> you would run all the time, just to torture me.

---

throwing the others, trying to make them go as close as possible to the first" (De
Bourcard, *Usi* 1.302; cit. Croce 580).

10. A variation on Odds and Evens (Croce 581).

11. "A variation on *morra*, used to determine whose turn it is for something (and in
particular, to drink wine, and therefore much used in wine-cellars)" (Croce 581).

12. For the *colascione* (lute), see tale 1.3 n24; "the *chiuchiero* (pipes) was a rustic
wind instrument similar to bagpipes; the *vottafuoche* (fire-throwers), mentioned a
number of times in *The Tale of Tales*, were also wind instruments; the *cro-cro* (also
called *zerre-zerre*) consisted of a stick with a toothed wheel attached to it, which
when shook and turned struck a reed and produced a sound; the *scacciapensieri* is a
sort of Jew's harp; and the *zuche-zuche* a form of violin. These were all popular and
ancient instruments that Basile contrasted to modern instruments in the ninth eclogue of his *Muse napoletane*, praising them and inveighing against the person who
first ruined them" (Croce 581).

13. In the ninth eclogue of the *Muse* Basile also laments the disappearance of songs,
especially *villanelle*, from "the good old days, where the memory of gentle Naples
was preserved, sweet as honey," and lists various types of *villanelle*, transcribing one
in its entirety. "*Villanelle*, in fact, began to disappear in the first decades of the 17th
century, while madrigals endured for some time still" (Croce 582). See, for example,
G. M. Monti, *Le villanelle napoletane e l'antica lirica dialettale* (Città di Castello,
1925), and Elena Barassi, *Costume e pratica musicale in Napoli al tempo di Giambattista Basile* (Firenze: Olschki, 1967). The Flemish musician and composer Orlando di Lasso's collection of villanelle from the mid-sixteenth century is an
important testimony of this tradition and one that Basile was most probably familiar
with.

And then they followed with

> Come out, come out, sun,[14]
> warm up the Emperor!
> Little silver bench
> that's worth four hundred,
> or a hundred and fifty,
> it sings the whole night;
> Viola's singing,
> The schoolmaster, too,
> Oh master, master,
> Send us off soon,
> For master Tiesto is coming down
> With lances and swords
> Accompanied by birds.
> Play, play, little bagpipe,
> And I'll buy you a pretty little skirt,
> A skirt of scarlet cloth,
> But if you don't play I'll break your head.

Nor did they fail to play that other one:

> Don't rain, don't rain,[15]
> I want to go and dig!
> To dig the wheat
> Of master Giuliano.
> Master Giuliano,
> lend me your lance,
> I want to go to France,
> from France to Lombardy,
> where madam Lucia is![16]

Right when they were at the best part of their singing the victuals were brought to the table, and when they had eaten until their bellies were about to burst Tadeo told Zeza to head things off by beginning the day with her tale. Following the prince's command, she thus spoke:

---

14. *Iesce, iesce Sole* (Neap.): see tale 1.10 n3. "This is a nursery rhyme, many variants of which may be found in Luigi Molinaro del Chiaro, *Canti popolari raccolti in Napoli* (Naples 1916)" (Croce 583).
15. Possibly a song of fourteenth-century origin (Croce 583).
16. These compositions are all in rhyme, and often the meaning (in many cases, not clear) seems to be subordinate to the meter.

THE ROOSTER'S STONE

First Entertainment of the Fourth Day

Mineco Aniello becomes young and rich due to the powers of a stone found in a rooster's head, but when he is tricked out of it by two necromancers he goes back to being old and penniless. As he is wandering through the world he receives news of his ring in the Kingdom of the Mice, and with the help of two mice he gets it back, returns to his previous state, and takes revenge on the thieves.

"The thief's wife does not always laugh; he who weaves fraud works on the loom of ruin; there is no deceit that cannot be discovered, nor are there betrayals that never come to light; the walls spy on scoundrels; and thievery and whoring make the earth split open and tell about it, as you shall now hear, if you keep your ears where they should be.

"There once was, in the city of Black Grotto, a certain Mineco Aniello, who was so indebted to his misfortune that all of his property and possessions, from top to bottom, consisted of a miniature rooster[1] that he had raised on bread crumbs. But one morning he found himself consumed by appetite, and since hunger drives the wolf from the woods he decided that he would try to make some small change off of it. He took it to market, where he met two bird-brain necromancers with whom he made a deal, and after they freed him of the rooster for half a coin they told him to bring it to their house and they would count him out his brass.

"When the sorcerers had set off with Mineco Aniello behind them, he heard that they were speaking to each other in thieves' cant, saying, 'Who could ever have told us we'd have this fine encounter, Iennarone? There's no doubt that this rooster will make us a fortune with the stone that, as you know, it's got inside its noggin.[2] We'll have it

---

AT 560: The Magic Ring.

1. *gallo patano* (Neap.): "a small breed, with short legs" (Croce 351).

2. "Perhaps Basile was thinking of the *alettoria* or 'rooster's stone' that could be found under certain conditions, not in the head but in the ventricle of the rooster, and to which were attributed many powers. See Pliny, *Natural History* XXXVII, 54, as well as medieval lapidaries" (Croce 583).

set immediately in a ring, and then we'll get everything we're able to ask for.' Iennarone answered, 'Shut your mouth, Iacovuccio. I already see myself rich and I can hardly believe it. I can't wait to chop this rooster's head off and give poverty a kick in the face and smooth out my stockings,[3] for in this world virtue without money is the same as a patch for a shoe, and whatever you look like, that's how you're judged.'

"Mineco Aniello, who had traveled in many lands and eaten bread from many ovens, finished listening to their argot, and as soon as he came to a little path he careened off in another direction and made the dust fly, and after racing home he wrung the rooster's neck and opened its head, where he found the stone. He immediately had it set in a brass ring and, wanting to see proof of its power, said, 'I would like to become an eighteen-year-old boy!' He had barely said these words when his blood flowed more briskly, his nerves grew stronger, his legs more solid, his complexion fresher, and his eyes more lively. His silver hair became golden; his mouth, which had been a ransacked farmhouse, was now populated with teeth; and his beard, which had been a hunting reserve, became a field fit for seed.

"In short, once he had become a most handsome young fellow, he started up again: 'My desire would be to have a magnificent palace, and to become the relative of a king!' And right before his eyes there sprung forth a palace of incredible beauty, full of marvelous statues, amazing columns, astounding paintings; it was overflowing with silver, you walked on gold wherever you set foot, jewels blazed in your face, there were swarms of servants, and the number of horses and carriages couldn't be counted. In short, he put on such a show of richness that the king set his sights on him and was all too pleased to give him his daughter, Natalizia.

"In the meantime, when the necromancers discovered Mineco Aniello's great fortune they decided to remove this good luck from his hands. They made a beautiful little doll that played music and danced by means of counterweights,[4] and then dressed up as merchants and went off to find Pentella, the daughter of Mineco Aniello, with the excuse of selling it to her. When she saw that lovely thing, she asked what price they were asking, and they answered that no amount of money could buy it but that she could become its owner merely by

---

3. "Tight socks were a particular of the dress of the upper classes" (Rak 674). The expression thus means to change social status, or to put on airs.

4. "Movable wooden dolls, animated by a system of weights and counterweights, were at this time very popular, and occupied an important place among the attractions taken around to town squares by traveling peddlers of toys and knick-knacks" (Guarini and Burani 405).

doing them a favor, which was to let them see how her father's ring was made so that they could copy the model and make another one like it, and then they would give her the doll without any kind of payment. After listening to this offer, Pentella, who had never heard the proverb 'Think twice if it's a steal,' immediately accepted the arrangement and told them to return the next morning and she would get her father to lend her the ring. When the sorcerers had left and her father came home, she said so many sweet words and used so many charms that, with the excuse that she felt melancholy and wanted to cheer herself up a little, she convinced him to lend her the ring.

"But the next day—when the Sun's street cleaner had the litter of the shadows swept from the squares of the sky—the sorcerers came back, and no sooner did they have the ring in their hands than they cleared out like the Dickens without leaving a trace of smoke behind them, and poor Pentella almost died of anguish. When the sorcerers reached a wood where some of the tree branches were doing the flower dance[5] and others were playing hot bread,[6] they told the ring to ruin everything that the rejuvenated old man had created. No sooner said than done: Mineco Aniello, who at that moment found himself before the king, saw his hair turn shaggy and white, his forehead become lined and his eyelashes bristly, his eyes glaze over, his face grow creased, his mouth lose its teeth, his beard reforest itself, his hump rise back up, his legs tremble, and, above all, his flashy clothes return once more to rags and patches. At the sight of that miserable vagabond sitting there chatting with him, the king immediately had him thrown out to the tune of stick beating and vulgar words.

"When he saw himself fall plumb down like that, Mineco Aniello went home to his daughter in tears and, looking for the ring so that he could find a remedy for this disaster, he heard of the trick the false merchants had played on her. And then he nearly threw himself out the window, cursing a thousand times the ignorance of his daughter, who on account of a wretched doll had caused him to end up like an old bogeyman,[7] and on account of a bunch of rags had reduced him

5. "A dance in which poles or clubs decorated with flowers were held, replacing the swords previously used. During Carnival people danced in masks under the windows of fair ladies or nobles, who would throw money to the dancers" (Croce 583).
6. "Four children gather around a big fire, and another four go off to hide. The first four each throw a rock into the fire shouting 'Hot bread!' and the ones who hid come out and run toward the 'oven.' The 'bakers' run away and try not to get caught. Whoever is caught has to carry his captor piggyback to the oven" (Croce 583).
7. Wordplay: *pipata* (doll) vs. *paputo* (bogeyman).

to running himself ragged, since he had resolved to roam far and wide, like bad money, until he got news of those merchants.

"As he was saying this he put an old cloak[8] on his shoulders, some rough boots[9] on his feet, a knapsack on his back, and a club in his hand and, leaving his daughter cold and icy, he began walking in desperation. And he walked so far that he arrived at the kingdom of Dark Hole, which was inhabited by mice, where he was mistaken for a spy sent by the cats and was immediately taken before Rosecone, the king. When asked who he was, where he came from, and what he was doing in those parts, Mineco Aniello first gave the king a pork rind as a sign of tribute. Then he told him, one by one, of all his misfortunes, concluding that he intended to consume that black bark of his body until he got news of those damned souls who had tricked him out of a joy so dear to him and taken from him all at once the flower of his youth, the fountain of his wealth, and the bastion of his honor.

"At these words Rosecone felt pity gnawing at him and, wanting to give the poor man some consolation, he called the oldest mice to council and asked them for their opinion on Mineco Aniello's misfortune, ordering them to conduct an investigation to see if they might perhaps obtain some news about those disguised merchants. Among these were, by chance, Rudolo and Sautariello, mice well versed in worldly matters who had spent nearly six years at an inn on one of the thoroughfares. They said, 'Keep your spirits up, friend, for things will go better than you think. Now you should know that one day when we found ourselves in a room at the Inn of the Horn,[10] where the most esteemed men in the world find lodging and revel in happiness, two men of Hooked Castle passed through. After they ate and reached the bottom of the wine jug, they started discussing a trick they had played on some old man from Black Grotto: how they had robbed him of a stone that had great powers, which, said one of them whose name was Iennarone, he would never take off his finger so as not to chance losing it like the daughter of the old man did.' When Mineco Aniello heard this he told the two mice that if they were willing to accompany him to the town of those thieves and get the ring back for him, he would give them a load of cheese and salted meat, which they could enjoy together with the lord their king. Since it involved greasing their hands, the mice offered to travel across seas and

8. *no capopuorpo* (Neap.): lit., octopus head. "A sort of pilgrim's cloak, which has this name because it hangs in frayed shreds that recall the tentacles of the octopus" (Guarini and Burani 407).
9. *calantrielle* (Neap.): heavy pigskin boots (Guarini and Burani 407).
10. Evidently frequented by cuckolds.

Lo quale co chiù allegrezza che non ha lo 'mpiso quanno l'arriva la grazia,
fece subeto deventare dui asene li nigromante, sopra l'uno de li quale stiso lo
ferraivolo se accravaccaie . . . e, carrecato l'autro de lardo e caso, toccaie a la
vota de Pertuso Futo. [With greater joy than a man condemned to hanging
feels when he is granted a pardon, Mineco Aniello immediately turned the
two necromancers into asses, and, spreading his cloak over
one of them . . . he straddled it. Then he loaded the other one with lard
and cheese and set off toward Dark Hole.]

over mountains for him, and when they had gotten permission from the crowned head of mousedom, they left.

"After a long journey they arrived at Hooked Castle, where the mice had Mineco Aniello stop and wait for them under some trees on the shore of a river that, like a bloodsucker, took the blood of day laborers and threw it out to sea. Once they found the sorcerers' house, they observed that Iennarone never took the ring off his finger; for this reason they decided to attempt to win their victory by means of a stratagem. They waited—until Night dyed the face of the sky with ink, since it had been burned by the Sun[11]—and as soon as Iennarone had gone and stretched himself out to sleep, Rudolo began to gnaw on his ring finger. Iennarone felt something hurting him, and took the ring off and placed it on a table at the head of the bed. When he saw this happen, Sautariello put it in his mouth and in four hops they were back with Mineco Aniello. With greater joy than a man condemned to hanging feels when he is granted a pardon,[12] Mineco Aniello immediately turned the two necromancers into asses, and, spreading his cloak over one of them, like a fine count he straddled it. Then he loaded the other one with lard and cheese and set off toward Dark Hole, where he presented the gifts to the king and the counselors and thanked them for all the good he had received thanks to them, praying to the heavens that they might never be caught in a trap, never be bothered by a cat, and never be afflicted by arsenic.

"He left that town and arrived at Black Grotto, where he became even more handsome than before and was received by the king and his daughter with the most tender caresses in the world. And after he had the asses thrown off a mountaintop, he enjoyed himself with his wife, never taking the ring off his finger so as not to cause another calamity, for *a dog scorched by hot water becomes afraid of cold water, too*."

---

11. "An application of ink was a popular remedy for burns" (Croce 356).
12. "Receiving a last-minute pardon was not uncommon for those condemned to death" (Rak 675).

2

THE TWO BROTHERS

Second Entertainment of the Fourth Day

*Marcuccio and Parmiero are brothers, one rich and full of vices
and the other virtuous and penniless. After various adventures the
poor brother is turned out by his rich brother and becomes a
baron, and the rich one falls into misery and is taken to the gallows. But when he is recognized as innocent, he receives from his
brother a portion of his riches.*

The story of Mineco Aniello gave great satisfaction to the prince and
his wife, and they blessed the mice a thousand times for having
caused the poor man to recover his stone and the sorcerers to recover
the measure of their ring finger with a broken neck.[1] But Cecca was
prepared to chatter, and when everyone had barricaded the door of
their words with a bar of silence, she began to speak in this manner:
"There is no greater parapet against the assaults of Fortune than Virtue, which is an antidote to misfortune, a bastion against ruin, and a
port in a sea of troubles; it drags you out of the mud, saves you from
storms, protects you from terrible disasters, consoles you in despair,
aids you in need, and defends you against Death, as you will hear
from the tale that I have on the tip of my tongue, all ready to tell you.

"There once was a father who had two sons, Marcuccio and Parmiero. When he was about to settle his accounts with Nature and tear
up the register of his life, he called them to the side of his bed and
said to them, 'My blessed sons, the cops of Time will not take much
longer before they come to break down the door of my years and con-
fiscate, even if it is against the law of the kingdom,[2] the dotal goods
of this life as payment for the debts I owe to the earth. And therefore,
since I love you like the pupils of my eyes, I cannot depart from you
without leaving you with a few good memories, so that you will be
able to sail with the north wind of good advice in this gulf of troubles

---

AT 613: The Two Travelers, and AT 910D: The Treasure of the Hanging Man. Penzer
notes some resemblance to Grimm 107 and refers to Eastern and Western variants of
the motif of "the intended suicide's luck" (2:20). See also Straparola 1.1, "Salardo."
1. *na rotta de cuollo* (Neap.): "a miscalculated jump through the hoop" (Rak 696).
2. Justinian law, which was at this time used in the kingdom of Naples (Croce 584).

and reach a safe port. So open your ears, for even if what I'm giving you seems like nothing, you should know that it is a treasure that will never be stolen by thieves, a house that will never be demolished by earthquakes, and a field that will never be consumed by earthworms.

" 'Now[3] in the first place and above all, be fearing of the heavens, for everything comes from up there and if you lose your way you'll end up with a fried liver. Do not let yourselves be butchered by idleness, growing up like pigs at their troughs, for just because someone grooms his own horse does not mean he can be called a stable hand. You've got to help yourself by kicking and biting; he who works for another eats for himself.

" 'Save when you have something to save, for he who saves earns; big money is made coin by coin; he who lays by comes by; he who has the means dresses a good salad; if you store up you eat; don't fritter your things away, for friends and relatives are fine but the house where there is nothing is a gloomy one; he who has money builds, and he who has wind sails, and he who has no money is a bogeyman and an ass, prey to agony at every moment. And so, my kind friend, you make your purchases based on your earnings; have as much ass as you can cover and as much land as you can smell; a small kitchen makes for a big house.

" 'Do not be too much of a chitchat, for though the tongue is without bones it can break a back; listen, look, and keep quiet if you wish to live in peace; whatever you see, you see; whatever you hear, you hear; eat little and speak little; the warmth of clothes never hurt anyone; he who speaks too much often errs.

" 'Content yourselves with little, for broad beans that last are better than confections that run out; small enjoyments are better than large tribulations; he who cannot have meat may drink broth; he who has no other options may sleep with his wife; *cot cot autem,*[4] patch things up as you can; he who cannot have the pulp may gnaw on the bone.

" 'Always associate with those better than you and do their shopping for them: tell me who you go around with and I'll tell you what sort of man you are. He who associates with a cripple will be limping by the end of the year; he who sleeps with the dog won't get up without fleas; give a wicked man your things and let him be on his way, for bad company leads a man to the gallows.

---

3. "What follows is a 'decalogue' of the emerging 'popolo civile' [urban middle class], situated between the nobility and the lower classes. Advice of this sort was widely circulated at the time in booklets" (Rak 696).

4. Deformed citation of the first words of a passage from the Gospel of John (1.12) that reads, "Quotquot autem receperunt eum" (cit. Rak 696).

"'Think and then act, for it's a bad thing to close the stable once the oxen have gone out; when the barrel is full, plug it immediately, since when it's empty there is nothing to plug; first chew and then swallow, for out of haste the cat gave birth to blind kittens; he who walks slowly has a good day.

"'Flee from disputes and quarrels, and do not step on every stone, for he who jumps over too many poles ends up getting one stuck in his behind; a horse that bucks gets more kicks than it gives; he who wounds by scratching dies by the switchblade; the jug goes to the well so often that it finally leaves its handle there; the gallows is made for the unfortunate.

"'Do not let yourselves get heated up with pride, for you need more than a white tablecloth to make a table; bow down and adapt; the house that sent off smoke was never a good one; the good alchemist puts his distillate in the ashes so that it will not fill with smoke, and the respectable man must remind himself to reduce his proud thoughts to ash in order not to be smoked by arrogance.

"'Do not take on Rosso's[5] way of thinking, for he who meddles ends up in a muddle; only a fool tries to fix the prices of cucumbers[6] and the salt that goes in stewpots.

"'Do not get mixed up with noblemen, and go more readily to draw fishnets than to serve at court; a lord's love and wine in a flask are good in the morning but bad by nightfall, and you get nothing but nice words and rotten apples from them; at court your services are fruitless, your plans spoiled, your hopes broken; you sweat mercilessly, run without pause, sleep without peace, shit without a candle, and eat without appetite.[7]

"'Keep clear of the rich man who has become poor and the peasant who has made his way up, of the desperate pauper, the cunning servant, the ignorant prince, the self-serving judge, the jealous woman and the "tomorrow" man, those who hang around courts of justice, the hairless man and the bearded woman, calm rivers, smoky chimneys, bad neighbors, whiny children, and envious men.

"'Finally, make an effort to realize that he who has a trade has a place in the world and he who has some sense in his noggin can survive in the woods and has gotten his wisdom teeth and shed his first ears; a good horse lacks not a saddle.

"'I'd like to tell you a thousand more things, but Death's agonies

---

5. See tale 2.1 n7.

6. Since cucumbers were of little value, there was no point in fixing their price (Rak 696).

7. See the end of tale 2.4, and the eclogue "The Crucible," for similar reflections on serving noblemen or in court.

are upon me and I lack breath.' As he said this he barely had the strength to raise his hand and bless them before the sails of his life were lowered and he entered into the port of all the troubles of this world.

"When their father had departed, Marcuccio, who had sculpted his words inside his heart, dedicated himself to studying at school, circulating among the academies, debating with students,[8] and discussing noble things, so that in the wink of an eye he became the top man of letters in that town. But since poverty is a tick that feeds on virtue, and the waters of good fortune slide off the man anointed with the oil of Minerva,[9] the poor man was always penniless, always dry, always singing 'Cruel Heart and Harsh Desire,'[10] and more often than not he found himself fed up with emptying texts and longing instead to lick frying pans, tired of studying court decisions and needy of legal assistance himself, hard at work on the *Indigestion*[11] and always obliged to fast.

"Parmiero, on the other hand, had given himself up to a careless and extravagant way of life, spending his time either gaming or tavern hopping, and he grew big and tall and was without any virtue in the world. But even so, in one way or another he was able to fill his mattress with good straw. When Marcuccio saw this he proclaimed that he regretted that because of his father's advice he had lost his way, since the Donatus grammar[12] had not donated him a thing, the Cornucopia[13] had reduced him to a state of dire need, and Bartolus had put nothing in his bags,[14] whereas by entertaining himself with the bones of dice[15] Parmiero was able to eat good meat and by amusing himself with his hands he was able to keep his gullet full.

"Finally, no longer able to resist the itch of need, Marcuccio went

---

8. *a fare accepe cappiello co li studiante* (Neap.): "In scholastic debates the winner wore a laurel wreath, while the loser took his hat and left, and it was said to him: 'Accipe pileum pro corona' (quote from E. Rocco's *Vocabolario*)" (Croce 360).

9. "The goddess of wisdom was also the creator of the olive and, therefore, of the lamp oil that wise men use in order to continue their studies into the night, consuming 'more oil than wine'" (Rak 697).

10. "Jocose citation of a verse of a song, used proverbially to indicate a desperate situation" (Guarini and Burani 414).

11. *l'Indigeste* (Neap.): jocose reference to the *Digesta*, the anthology of sentences of the most celebrated Roman jurists that is part of the *Corpus Juris Civilis*, or Code of Justinian (Rak 697).

12. The grammar of Aelius Donatus was still used in schools at this time. See also tale 2.7 n25.

13. Another well-known grammar of the time, N. Perrotti da Sassoferrato's *Cornucopia linguae latinae* (1489) (Rak 697).

14. See tale 1.7 n9.

15. Dice were made from bones.

to see his brother and begged him, seeing that fortune had made him the son of a white chicken,[16] to remember that they were of the same blood and had both come out of the same hole. Parmiero, who with all the stimulation of wealth had become constipated, said to him, 'You, who wanted to pursue your studies because of your father's advice and have always reproached me for the company I keep and for my gaming, go gnaw on your books and leave me alone with my misfortunes, for I wouldn't give you a pinch of salt, considering how hard I toil for these few coins that I have! You're of age, you have common sense. He who does not know how to live must suffer the consequences; each man for himself and God for all! If you don't have money, play hearts![17] If you're hungry, take a bite of your legs; if you're thirsty, take a bite of your fingers!' And after saying these and other words he turned his back on him.

"Marcuccio, who saw himself treated with such cruelty by his own brother, became so desperate that he resolved with a firm heart to separate the gold of his soul from the soil of his body with the acid of desperation,[18] and he set off in the direction of a very high mountain, which, like a spy for the earth, wanted to see what was happening up in the air; or, like a Grand Turk of all the mountains, with its turban of clouds rose up into the sky to pierce the moon and affix it to its forehead.[19]

"Marcuccio climbed the mountain, scrambling up as best he could on a very narrow road that ran between crags and sheer cliffs, and when he had reached the top, which looked out over a steep precipice, he opened the faucet of the fountain of his eyes, and at the end of a long lament he was intending to throw himself down headfirst when a lovely woman, dressed in green with a garland of laurel atop her hair of spun gold, grabbed him by the arm and said, 'What are you doing, poor man? Where are you letting yourself be dragged by such a bad state of mind? You are that virtuous man who has burnt so much oil and lost so much sleep studying? You are the one who in order to send your fame to sea like a well-greased sailing vessel has

16. I.e., fortune's favorite; not of the common lot (used ironically here). Popular saying also present in the Latin tradition: "gallinae filius albae" (Juvenal, *Satires* 13.141; cit. Croce 361).
17. Money (coins) and hearts, along with clubs and swords, are the suits of Neapolitan cards. The meaning is "play whatever you have." "Playing cards were used for predicting the future and as a mnemonic device for learning" (Rak 697).
18. Reference to the work of a goldsmith, who purifies gold with nitric acid (Guarini and Burani 416).
19. The crescent moon was the emblem of the emperor of Turkey.

spent so much time under the lash?[20] And now, right at the best part
you get lost and you don't make use of the arms that you tempered at
the forge of your studies to combat misery and bad fortune? Don't
you know that virtue is an antidote against the poison of poverty, a
tobacco[21] against the catarrh of envy, a prescription against the infir-
mity of time? Don't you know that virtue is a compass for gaining
your bearings amid the winds of adversity, a windproof torch for
walking in the darkness of displeasure, an unshakable arch for resist-
ing the earthquakes of torments? Come back, you poor soul, come
back to your senses and do not turn your back on those who can give
you courage in times of danger, strength in times of trouble, and calm
in times of desperation. And know that the heavens sent you to this
mountain, so difficult to climb and where Virtue herself resides, so
that she in person, so wrongly accused, could rid you of the bad intentions that were blinding you. Wake up, then, be comforted and
change your mind, and to help you see that virtue is always good,
worthy, and useful, here, take this little paper full of powder and go
to the kingdom of Wide Field, where you will find them reciting the
Confitemini[22] for the daughter of the king, who can find no cure for
her ailment. Have her take this powder inside a fresh egg, and you'll
immediately serve her illness an eviction notice—the illness that, like
a soldier who demands lodging, is sucking away her life. And you'll
receive such a great reward that you'll be able to cast off your poverty
and live as one like you deserves to live, without needing anything
from anyone.'

"At the first whiff Marcuccio had recognized her, and he threw
himself at her feet and begged her to pardon him for the mistake that
he had been about to make, saying, 'Now I am able to lift the veil
from my eyes and recognize from your appearance that you are the
Virtue praised by all and followed by few, the Virtue that causes in-
tellects to stand up erect, minds to grow bold, judgment to sharpen,
honorable labor to be embraced, and wings for flying to seventh
heaven to be donned! I recognize you, and declare myself repentant
for having improperly used the arms you gave me, and promise you
that from this day on I'll make such good use of your antidote that
even March thunder won't be able to touch me!' And as he was about
to kiss her feet she vanished before his eyes, leaving him greatly com-

---

20. *sparmata* (Neap.): greased vs. lash.
21. See tale 3.3 n18.
22. "The beginning of the psalm 'Confitemini Domino quoniam bonus' (117), which
in the Roman rite was the first of the psalms to be used at the bedside of the dying"
(Rak 697).

forted, like a poor sick man who, after getting through the moment of crisis, is given a bit of root[23] in cool water to drink.

"He slid down the mountain and set off toward Wide Field, and when he arrived at the royal palace he immediately had the king informed that he intended to cure his daughter's ailment. The king received him with the greatest honors and then took him to the princess's room, where he found the unfortunate girl lying in a perforated bed,[24] so consumed and worn that there was nothing left of her but skin and bones. Her eyes had caved in, so that you would have needed Galileo's glass[25] to see her pupils; her nose was so pointy that it could have taken over the job of an enema tube; her cheeks were so hollow that she looked like the Death of Sorrento;[26] her bottom lip hung down to her wattle; her chest looked a magpie's; and her arms were like legs of lamb that had been picked clean. In short, she was so haggard that she toasted compassion with the glass of pity.

"When Marcuccio saw her in this terrible state, tears welled up in his eyes, and he considered how the weakness of our nature is subject to the ravages of time, changes in constitution, and the maladies of life. But then he asked for the fresh egg of a spring chicken, and after barely warming it up a little, he sprinkled the powder in. He forced the princess to sip it down, and covered her with four blankets. And Night had not yet reached its port and set up tent when the invalid called her ladies-in-waiting and asked them to change her bed, which was soaked with sweat. Once she had been dried off and given clean clothes she asked for some refreshment, a word that in the seven years of her illness had never once come out of her mouth. They took hope from this and gave her a sip of broth, and with each hour she won back more strength and with each day her appetite advanced, so that before a week had passed she was completely and entirely better and got out of bed. For this the king honored Marcuccio as if he were the

---

23. One of the roots used in potions in medical practice of the time (Croce 364).

24. A bed for paralytics or others forced to stay in bed, perforated to allow for hygienic functions.

25. Galileo's telescope was new (1609–10), and in Naples other books and experiments had immediately followed, such as N. Stelliola's *Del telescopio overo ispecchio celeste* (1627) (Rak 698).

26. "In the representation of Carnival and Lent that was performed in Sorrento and elsewhere, on the last night of Carnival, one of the characters was a gigantic skeleton of wood and cardboard, armed with a sickle, which represented Death and reaped the life of Carnival" (Croce 584). Carnival, too, was an enormous, big-bellied figure that sat on a float and was surrounded by delicacies. When Carnival was killed, the crowds threw themselves on the bounty, and its members were burned in a bonfire, while Lent, personified as a lurid and wasted old woman, entered the city in triumph on another float (Rak 698).

god of medicine, making him not only baron of vast lands but also the first of his court counselors, and he married him to the richest lady in the kingdom.

"In the meantime Parmiero was stripped of all he had, since gambled money goes as easily as it comes and a gambler's luck falls as often as it rises. And thus, finding himself poor and disgraced, he decided to walk either until the change of place brought him a change of fortune, or until his place on the roster of life was freed. And he walked so far that after six months of twists and turns he reached Wide Field, with his tail dragging and in such a state of exhaustion that he couldn't stand on his feet. When he saw that it was impossible to find a place to drop dead and that his hunger was increasing proportionately and that his clothes were falling off of him in shreds, he was so overcome by desperation that as soon as he found an old house outside the city walls, he took the strings, which were made of yarn and cotton wool, out of his socks, and knotted them together to make a nice noose, which he attached to one of the rafters. Then he climbed onto a little hill of stones that he had piled up himself, and pushed off. But fate willed it that the rafter was worm-eaten and rotten, and when it was jerked like that it split in half and the living hanged man banged his side on those stones so hard that he was sore for quite a few days.

"Now when the rafter split, a handful of golden chains, necklaces, and rings fell out onto the ground; they had been stuffed into the cavity made by the worms and, among the other things, there was a bag of Cordovan leather with a bunch of money in it. Parmiero saw how he had jumped the ditch of poverty with a hanged man's jump, and if before he had been hanging by a thread of desperation, now he was suspended by happiness, so that his feet didn't touch the ground. And he took this gift of fortune and raced off to a tavern to get his spirits back up, since they had almost left him.

"Two days earlier some thieves had lifted that same money from the very tavern keeper where Parmiero went to eat, and they had hidden it in the rafter, which they were familiar with, so that later on they could change it and spend it little by little. So when Parmiero had filled his stomach to capacity and pulled out the bag to pay, the tavern keeper recognized it and called over some guards who were customers of the tavern, and they collared him and with great ceremony brought him before the judge. The judge had him searched, and once the material evidence was found and compared with the tavern keeper's goods, he was declared guilty and condemned to play the game of three,[27] where his feet would spin like the blades of a mill.

---

27. I.e., to be hung from the two posts and crossbeam of the gallows.

"The wretched fellow saw that he was under the hammer, and when he realized that the eve of sock strings would be followed by the feast of the rope, and that after the dress rehearsal of the rotten rafter would come the tournament of the crossbeam on a brand-new gallows, he began to thrash about and shriek that he was innocent and intended to appeal the sentence. And as he was shouting and howling in the street that there was no justice, that no one listened to poor people, and that judgments were handed out as if it were a game of smash-the-top,[28] and that since he hadn't greased the judge's hand, sweetened up the scribe's mouth, tipped the clerk, and made a deposit in the name of the attorney, he had been sent to the widowed teacher to do openwork,[29] he happened to run into his brother, who, since he was counselor and head of the tribunal,[30] had the procession stopped so that he could hear Parmiero's explanation.

"When he had recounted everything that had happened, Marcuccio answered, 'You keep quiet, for you don't know how lucky you are; there's no doubt that if on the first try you found a chain that was three spans long, on the second you'll find another that measures three strides! Go, and be cheerful, for the gallows are your blood sisters, and where others evacuate their lives you will fill your bag!' Parmiero, who felt himself being pulled by the leg, said to him, 'I come for justice, not to be made fun of! And you should know that regarding this matter of which I've been accused, my hands are clean, and although you see me ragged and in tatters like this I'm an honorable man, for clothes don't make a monk. But because I didn't listen to my father Marchionne and my brother Marcuccio I'll have to deal with the proceedings, and it won't be long before I sing a three-part madrigal[31] under the hangman's feet.'"

"When he heard his father's and his own name mentioned, Marcuccio felt his blood stir, and, staring fixedly at Parmiero, he seemed to recognize him. Finally, when he discovered that it was his brother, he found himself torn between shame and affection, flesh and honor, justice and mercy. He was ashamed to reveal himself as the brother of

---

28. A game in which one top is spun violently against another top that is already spinning on the ground, until it breaks. By association, "at random" or "by chance" (Croce 584).

29. The gallows, here compared to a sewing mistress who orders the hanged to do the hem-stitch with his dangling feet (which make the same rapid movements as the hands of a seamstress) (Guarini and Burani 421; Rak 698).

30. *capo de la Rota* (Neap.): "The tribunal of the Vicaria in Naples was divided into four sections, or *ruote,* two civil and two criminal, and each was headed by a councilor (*caporota*)" (Croce 366).

31. Again, the three posts of the gallows.

one who had the face of a hanged man; he was tormented to see his own blood end up like that; and if his flesh pulled him like a hook to find a remedy for this matter, his honor pushed him back so as not to disgrace himself before the king over a brother condemned for *menatione uncini*.[32] Justice willed that he satisfy the offended party; pity searched for a way to procure the salvation of his own brother.

"As his brain was weighing this out and his noggin was thus divided, in ran a messenger sent by the judge, his tongue hanging down to his chin, and shouted, 'Stop, stop the execution! Don't move, don't move! Wait!' 'What's the matter?' asked the counselor. And the other answered, 'Something incredible has happened, luckily for this young man. Two thieves went to get some money and gold that they had hidden in a rafter of an old house, and when they couldn't find it each of them thought that his buddy had pulled one over on him, and they came to blows and fatally wounded each other. The judge arrived, and they immediately confessed what they had done, and now that the innocence of this poor man is established, he sends me to prevent the execution and free this man, who bears no guilt.'

"Upon hearing this Parmiero grew a span taller, whereas he had been afraid, before, to extend himself an arm's length, and Marcuccio, who saw his brother's reputation return, took off his mask and allowed himself to be recognized, saying to Parmiero, 'My brother, if you have met your ruin through vice and gaming, meet in the same way life's pleasures and goodness through virtue. Come now, of your own free will, to my house, where you and I will together enjoy the fruits of the virtue you so despised, for I have forgotten the scorn you showed me and I will hold you as dear as the pupils of my eyes.' As he was saying this he embraced him, took him home, dressed him from head to toe, and showed him, after all the evidence was in, how everything else is wind, since *virtue alone makes for a blissful man*."

---

32. Macaronic Latin for "throwing out a hook" (i.e., stealing) (Croce 367).

3

THE THREE ANIMAL KINGS

Third Entertainment of the Fourth Day

Tittone, son of the king of Green Knoll, goes in search of his three blood sisters, who are married to a falcon, a stag, and a dolphin. After a long journey he finds them, and while returning home he encounters the daughter of a king, who is kept prisoner in a tower by a dragon. Tittone uses a signal given to him by his brothers-in-law, and all three of them appear to help him. Together they kill the dragon and free the princess, after which Tittone takes her for his wife and returns to his kingdom with his brothers-in-law and sisters.

More than a few of the listeners were moved by the mercy shown by Marcuccio to Parmiero, and they all acknowledged that virtue is an unfailing wealth that time cannot consume, storms cannot blow away, and woodworms cannot gnaw to dust, unlike other forms of wealth in this life that come and go, and that what is acquired dishonestly never reaches the third generation. Finally Meneca seasoned the episode that had just been told by bringing the following tale to the table of nursery stories.

"There once was a king, the king of Green Knoll, who had three daughters who were three jewels. These daughters were ardently loved by the three sons of the king of Lovely Meadow, who due to the curse of a fairy had all been turned into animals, for which reason the king of Green Knoll did not want to give them his daughters in marriage.

AT 552A: Three Animals as Brothers-in-Law. Penzer comments, "This tale of the animal princes is a great favorite, and is found, in some form or other, in all the most important collections." In Grimm it is no. 197 ("The Crystal Ball"), and in Italy variants can be found in Crane, Pitrè (*Fiabe, nov. e racc. sic.* 16 and *Nov. tosc.* 11), and Gonzenbach (29), among others. Penzer also discusses the "ring of recognition" motif, common in folktales the world over and present, in Italy, in tale 10.9 of Boccaccio's Decameron. "It is one of the accepted methods of 'declaring presence,' and becomes a most useful *deus ex machina* to introduce at critical moments. In some cases the ring is merely handed by one person to another, but more often it is slipped unawares into a cup of wine by the lover or husband in disguise. In some cases the ring is broken and each person keeps half" (2:26).

"And thus the first of them, a beautiful falcon and enchanted as well, summoned all the birds to an assembly, to which chaffinches, wrens, orioles, siskins, flycatchers, screech owls, hoopoes, larks, cuckoos, magpies, and other members of the feathered species came. When they had responded to his call, the falcon sent them all to demolish the choicest trees of Green Knoll so that neither flower nor leaf was left. The second of them, a stag, summoned the deer, rabbits, hares, porcupines, and all the other animals of that land, and ordered them to devastate the farmlands so that not even a blade of grass was left. The third, a dolphin, plotted with a hundred sea monsters and unleashed such a storm on the shores of that land that not one boat remained whole.

"When the king saw that things were going worse and worse and he couldn't remedy the damage that these three beastly lovers were causing him, he decided to put an end to the predicament and consented to give them his daughters in marriage. And the three grooms, wanting neither festivities nor music making, took their brides and left the kingdom. Upon the brides' departure Grazolla, the queen, gave three similar rings to each of her daughters and told them that if they ever had to separate and after some time needed to find each other or someone of their own blood again, they could be recognized by means of these rings.

"And so, after saying good-bye they took their leave. The falcon carried Fabiella, the first sister, to the top of a mountain so terribly high that its dry head rose above the border of clouds to a place where it never rains, and there he showed her to a splendid palace, where he kept her like a queen. The stag carried off Vasta, the second of the daughters, to a wood so entangled that when they were summoned by Night the shadows that lived there didn't know how to find their way out to go pay her court. And there, in a marvelous house with a garden that was the most beautiful thing in the world, he had her live as his equal. The dolphin swam away with Rita, the third daughter, on his shoulders until he got to the middle of the sea, where he showed her to a house atop a lovely reef that was fit for three crowned kings.

"In the meantime Grazolla gave birth to a beautiful baby boy, whom she named Tittone. Since he had always heard his mother lament her three daughters, who were married to three animals and about whom she had never received a bit of news, when he was fifteen he got it into his head to roam the world until he found some sign of them. After bothering his father and mother about it to no end, the queen gave him another ring similar to the ones she had given her daughters and they sent him on his way, making sure he took with him all the equipment and companions that were necessary and fitting for a prince of his station.

"He left no hole unexplored in Italy, no cave in France nor corner of Spain unsearched, and when he had passed through England and covered Flanders and seen Poland and, in short, traveled through East and West, at last, having left all his servants behind in either taverns or hospitals and without a penny in his pocket, he found himself atop the mountain where Fabiella and the falcon lived. And as he was standing there, his eyes popping out of his head in contemplation of the beauty of the palace, which had jambs of porphyry, walls of alabaster, windows of gold, and roof tiles of silver, he was seen by his sister, who called him over and asked him who he was, from whence he came, and what circumstance had brought him to that land. Tittone told her the name of his land, who his father and mother were, as well as his own name, and Fabiella recognized him as her brother, which was confirmed when she compared the ring that he wore on his finger to the one her mother had given her. She embraced him with the greatest joy, but then, out of fear that her husband might be displeased by his arrival, made him hide. And when the hawk returned from outside, Fabiella began saying that she had a longing to see her relatives, to which he responded, 'Just let it pass, my wife; that won't be possible until I'm in the mood to let you go.' 'At least,' said Fabiella, 'let me have the comfort of having one of my relatives sent for.' And the hawk replied, 'And who would want to travel so far to see you?' 'But if someone did come,' Fabiella resumed, 'would that displease you?' 'And why should that displease me?' answered the hawk. 'Anyone who shares your blood will be the apple of my eye.' When Fabiella heard that she cheered up, called out her brother, and showed him to the hawk, who said, 'Five and five makes ten;[1] love passes through gloves[2] and water through boots! May you be welcome, for you are the master of this house; your wish is my command; make yourself at home!' And he ordered that Tittone be honored and served in the same way that he himself was.

"But after he was on that mountain for fifteen days, Tittone thought that he would go and look for the other sisters. When he asked his sister and brother-in-law if he could take leave of them, the hawk gave him one of his feathers, saying, 'Take this with you, Tit-

---

1. "A formula used when shaking hands" (Rak 714).
2. "When someone loves it can be felt even through a gloved handshake" (Croce 372), or "a formula used to apologize for not taking off one's glove before shaking hands" (Rak 914).

tone, and hold it dear, for you may find yourself in a situation in which you'll deem it a treasure. Enough said; take good care of it and if you need something, throw it on the ground and say, "Come out, come out," and you will sing my praises.' Tittone wrapped up the feather in a piece of paper, put it in a little bag, and with a thousand ceremonies left, and after a devastating walk he reached the wood where the stag and Vasta lived. Devoured by hunger, he went into their garden to pick a few pieces of fruit, and was seen by his sister. When she recognized him in the same way that Fabiella had, she introduced him to her husband, who gave him a warm reception and treated him as he would a prince. After another fifteen days Tittone wanted to leave in search of the other sister, and the stag gave him one of his hairs, with the same words that the hawk had used for his feather.

"And so he set out with a handful of coins that the hawk had given him, and just as many that he had received from the stag, and he walked so far that he reached the end of the earth, where, unable to proceed because of the sea, he engaged a ship, with the plan that he would search all the islands for news of his sister. He set his sails to the wind and traveled so far that he was carried to the island where the dolphin lived with Rita. As soon as he landed he was seen by his sister, who recognized him in the same way that the others had, and he received a thousand caresses from his brother-in-law. And when he wanted to leave to go back to see his mother and father after such a long time, the dolphin gave him one of his scales and told him the same things, at which he took a horse and began to trot.

"But before he was half a mile from the seashore, he entered a wood—free port for fear and shadows, where a nonstop fair of darkness and fright was held—and there he found a great tower in the middle of a lake that kissed the feet of the trees so that they wouldn't reveal its ugliness to the Sun, and at one of the windows he saw a most beautiful young woman at the feet of an awful dragon, which was asleep. When she saw Tittone she said, speaking softly in a voice that inspired great compassion, 'O my handsome young man, sent perchance by the heavens to comfort my miseries in this place where never a Christian face is seen, take me from the clutches of this tyrannical serpent that stole me away from the king of Clear Valley, my father, and confined me to this wretched tower, where I have nearly perished and turned rancid!' 'Alas,' said Tittone, 'what can I do to serve you, my fair lady? Who can cross this lake? Who can climb that tower? Who can approach that awful dragon that terrifies you with his stare, sows fear, and generates diarrhea? But hold on, wait a minute, let's see if we can get rid of that serpent by using someone else's sleeve. "Step by step," said Gradasso![3] Now we'll see if this fist is empty or full!'[4]

"That said, he threw down, at the same time, the feather, the hair, and the scale that his brothers-in-law had given him and said, 'Come out, come out!' As soon as they hit the ground, the falcon, the stag, and the dolphin all appeared in the same way that drops of summer water give birth to frogs, and all together they shouted, 'Here we are, what is your command?' When Tittone saw this he said, with great happiness, 'I want nothing more than to remove this poor young woman from the claws of that dragon, to get her away from that tower, to destroy everything, and then to take her home with me as my lovely wife.' 'Hush,' answered the hawk, 'the bean sprouts where you least think it will. We'll make the dragon spin on a coin,[5] and you'll see that there'll be a shortage of earth beneath his feet.' 'Let's waste no time,' replied the stag. 'Troubles and macaroni are best when they're hot.'

"As he was saying this, the hawk summoned a troop of griffins that flew up to the window of the tower, stole the girl, and carried her away from the lake to where Tittone and his brothers-in-law were. And if from afar she had looked like a moon to him, up close she was so beautiful that he found her to be a sun. But while he was hugging her and uttering sweet words to her, the dragon woke up, hurled itself out the window, and was swimming toward Tittone with the intention of devouring him when the stag conjured up a team of lions, tigers, panthers, bears, and bogeys that attacked the dragon and tore it to pieces with their claws. When this was done Tittone wanted to leave, but the dolphin said, 'I intend to do something to help you, too,' and so as not to leave even the memory of such an accursed and wretched place, he made the sea rise so high that it overflowed its bounds and smashed the tower with such fury that it was uprooted from its very foundations.

"When Tittone saw this, he thanked his brothers-in-law as best he could and told his future bride to do the same, since it was due to them that they had escaped such a great danger. But the animals answered, 'On the contrary, we are the ones who should be thanking this lovely lady, for she is the reason we will return to our original state. Because of our mother's unkindness to a fairy we have been since birth under a curse that forced us to remain in this animal form

---

3. See eclogue 1 ("The Crucible") n13.
4. A game consisting in getting an adversary to guess if one's closed fist has something in it or not (as in the introduction to day 4) (Rak 714).
5. Expression used to describe horses that make turns in a very small space (Croce 374).

until we freed the daughter of a king from some great trouble. And now the moment we so desired has arrived! Now the string of berries has ripened! We already feel a new spirit in our lungs and new blood in our veins!' As they were saying this they became three splendidly handsome young men, who one after the other tightly embraced their brother-in-law and squeezed the hand of their new relative, who had gone into raptures of happiness. When Tittone saw this he said, with a great sigh, 'O lord God, why can't my mommy and daddy take part in this joy? They would melt to bits if they discovered they had such charming and handsome sons-in-law!' 'It's not night yet!' answered the brothers-in-law. 'The shame of seeing ourselves disguised like that had induced us to flee the sight of men, but now, thank heavens, that we can appear among people we all want to be together under one roof with our dear little wives, and live our lives happily. Let's soon be on our way, then, so that before the Sun unpacks the merchandise of its rays at the customshouse of the East tomorrow morning, our wives will be with us.'

"That said, to avoid going on foot—since they had nothing but the frayed nag that had carried Tittone there—they made a splendid carriage pulled by six lions appear, and all five of them got inside. They traveled all day, and in the evening found themselves at a tavern, where as they were getting ready to work their teeth they passed the time reading the many testimonials of ignorance of the men who had left their mark on those walls.[6]

"Finally, when the others had eaten and put themselves to sleep the three young men, pretending to go to bed, busied themselves all night so that in the morning—when the stars, bashful as maidens, refused to be seen by the Sun—they were reunited with their wives at the tavern. After many rounds of hugs and a joy that cannot be imagined, all eight of them got into the same carriage and at the end of a long journey reached Green Knoll, where the king and queen received them with incredible caresses, since they had recovered their capital of the four children whom they had considered lost, and through usury had gained three sons-in-law and a daughter-in-law who were four columns of the temple of beauty.

"And when the kings of Lovely Field and Clear Valley were informed about what had happened to their children they both came to the festivities, adding the fat of joy to the soup of happiness and putting an end to all of the past anguish, for *an hour of happiness makes a thousand years of torment be forgotten*."

---

6. Tavern graffiti are also mentioned in tale 3.7.

4

THE SEVEN LITTLE
PORK RINDS

Fourth Entertainment of the Fourth Day

*An impoverished old woman beats her gluttonous daughter, who
has eaten seven pork rinds, and when she makes a merchant believe that she did it because the girl had worked too hard filling
seven spindles, he takes her for his wife. But the girl does not want
to work, and it is thanks to the help of a fairy that her husband returns from a trip and finds the cloth spun. After another of his
wife's tricks he resolves to make her work no longer, so that she
will not fall ill.*

Everyone blessed Meneca's mouth for having told the tale with so
much gusto that she was able to bring before the eyes of her listeners
things that had happened so far away. This stirred up Tolla's envy,
and she was overcome by a desire to jump clear past Meneca that
rose from the little bones in her feet. And so first she cleared her
throat and then she said, "Every word that is uttered is either half or
whole; and thus whoever said, 'crooked face, straight fortune' knew
something about how things go in this world, and perhaps had read
the story of Antuono and Parmiero:[1] 'Good luck, Antuono, and don't
bat an eye, for you can catch fig peckers without a trap!' For experience teaches us that this world is a spitting image of the land of Cock-
aigne,[2] where those who work most earn least, and those who live

---

AT 501: The Three Old Women Helpers. The tale as a whole is quite similar to
Grimm 14 ("The Three Spinners"), and also recalls 55 ("Rumpelstiltskin") and 128
("The Lazy Spinners"). See also Pitrè, *Fiabe, nov. e racc. sic.* 93, and Marie-Jeanne
Lhéritier, "Ricdin-Ricdon" (in *The Great Fairy Tale Tradition*).
1. *Il lamento de Ianni, Antuoni e Parmieri de le lor disgrazie alla Napolitana* was a
popular booklet that was widely circulated at this time (Rak 48).
2. Numerous chapbooks used by mountebanks and others had the land of Cock-
aigne as their subject. This was a utopian land of plenty in which the entire landscape
offered itself up to be eaten. See, for example, the land of Bengodi described by Boccaccio in *Decameron* 8.3, in which "vines are tied with sausages and you could get a
goose and a duck besides for a half penny, and there was a mountain entirely made of
grated Parmesan cheese, on top of which there were people who did nothing but
make macaroni and ravioli and cook them in capon broth, and then they rolled them

best take life as it comes and let the macaroni fall into their mouths; and you can touch with your hand the fact that the feet and clothes of Fortune are earned with broken-down boats and not with oiled ships, as you shall now hear.

"There once was a miserable old woman who, with distaff in hand, went spitting on people in the street and begging alms from door to door, and since 'with craft and deceit you can live half the year,'[3] she made some tender-lunged little women who fell for anything believe that she wanted to make I don't know what kind of rich dish for her emaciated daughter, and thus managed to get hold of seven little pork rinds. She brought them home with a nice armful of sticks that she had gathered from the ground and gave them to her daughter, telling her to put them on the fire to cook while she went back out to beg some farmers for a few greens that she could use to make a little soup.

"Saporita, the daughter, took the rinds and burned off the bristles, and then put them in a little pot and started to cook them. But they boiled in the pot less vigorously than they boiled in her own gullet, for the aroma that came out of the pot was a lethal challenge on the battlefield of her appetite and a credit check in the bank of her throat. Finally, no matter how hard she tried to resist, she was provoked by the odor from the pot, pulled by her own natural gluttony, and strangled by the hunger that was gnawing at her, and she let herself go and tried a little bit, which tasted so good that she said to herself, 'If you're afraid, you should become a cop! Since I happen to be right here, let's eat up! And may thunder and rain come falling down on me! What is it but a pork rind? Is that such a big deal? I have enough hide on my back to pay for these rinds!' As she was saying this she swallowed the first one, and when she felt her stomach cramp up even harder with hunger, she reached for the second one, then she snatched the third one, until piece by piece, one after the other, she had done away with all seven of them. But once she had messed things up like that, she began to think about her mistake and imagine that the rinds were going to stick in her throat, and she decided to pull the wool over her mother's eyes; she found an old shoe, cut its sole into seven parts, and put them in the pot.

---

down the mountain, and whoever grabbed the most, had the most; and down at the bottom there was a little river of the best Vernaccia wine that was ever drunk, without a drop of water in it" (908). See also Penzer's extensive discussion of this topos, in which he offers examples of how it can be used "to describe abundance, plenty, peaceful ease and laziness; [or] as synonymous with what is impossible or nonexistent" (2:32), and Giuseppe Cocchiara's classic *Il paese di Cuccagna*.

3. The proverb continues: "and by deceit and craft the rest of the time" (Croce 378).

"In the meantime Saporita's mother came back with a little bunch of cabbages, which she minced up, stalks included so as not to lose a crumb, and as soon as she saw that the pot was boiling at full steam she threw the vegetables in and added a bit of grease a coachman had given her in alms, left over from oiling a carriage. Then she spread a cloth over a little chest of old poplar wood, pulled two crusts of stale bread out of her sack, took a wooden cutting board from the dish rack, broke the bread into tiny bits, and ladled the vegetables and the pieces of hide over it. But when the old woman started to eat she immediately realized that her teeth were not those of a shoemaker and that the pork rinds, as if by a new Ovidian metamorphosis, had become buffalo tripe. She turned to her daughter and said, 'You did me in, you damned sow! What sort of crap did you put in the soup? What, you think my stomach has become an old shoe that needs resoling? Confess right now what's going on or you'll regret the day you were born, for I won't leave a single bone of yours in one piece!' Saporita began to deny everything, but as the old woman's pained cries gained force, the girl finally blamed the steam of the pot for having blinded her to the point of committing this bad act. When it became clear to the old woman that her meal had been poisoned, she grabbed hold of a broom handle and began to work it like a lathe, so that she caught the girl and then let her go more than seven times, beating her wherever she was able to.

"At Saporita's shrieks a merchant who happened to be passing by entered the house, and when he saw how cruelly the old woman was treating her, he took the club from her hand and said, 'What did this poor girl do for you to want to kill her? Is this a way to punish her, or to get rid of her? Could it be that you caught her throwing spears or breaking money banks?[4] Aren't you ashamed to be treating a poor little girl this way?' 'You don't know what she did to me,' answered the old woman. 'This shameless girl sees that I'm without a penny and pays no attention; she wants me to be ruined by doctors and pharmacists. Now that it's hot outside I ordered her to stop working so hard so that she won't fall ill, because I haven't the means to cure her. And this morning that self-centered thing insisted on filling seven spindles just to spite me, even though she risks weakening her heart and spending a couple of months in the depths of her bed.'

"When the merchant heard this, he thought that such an industrious girl could become the fairy of his household, and he said to the old woman, 'Put your anger aside, for I want to relieve your home of this danger by taking this daughter of yours for my wife and bringing

---

4. Metaphors for the sexual act.

her home with me, where I will have her live like a princess, since, thanks be to the heavens, I raise hens, fatten pigs, and keep pigeons, and I can't even turn around in my house, it's so full! May the heavens bless me and the evil eye stay far from me; I have barrels of wheat, crates of flour, jugs of oil, pots and bladders of grease, beams hanging with lard, dish racks full of crockery, piles of wood, heaps of coal, a chest of bed linens, and a bridegroom's bed, and, above all, with my rents and other revenues I'm able to live like a lord. Besides, I'm going to invest a few dozen ducats at the fairs, which if all goes well will make me an even richer man.' The old woman, who saw this good fortune rain down on her when she least expected it, took Saporita by the hand and handed her over to him, as is the use and custom in Naples,[5] saying, 'Here she is: may she be yours for now and for many fine years, and may you be healthy and have beautiful heirs!'

"The merchant put his arms around her neck and then took her home, and he could barely wait until it was market day to make some purchases. When Monday arrived he got up early in the morning and went off to where the countrymen sold their wares, and bought eighty rolls of flax.[6] Then he brought them to Saporita and said, 'Now you can spin as much as you like. You don't need to be afraid of meeting up with another raging madwoman like your mother, who broke your bones because you filled up spindles, since for every ten spindles you fill I intend to give you ten kisses, and for every wick[7] you prepare I'll give you this heart! So work cheerfully, and when I get back from market, which will be in twenty days, have these eighty rolls of flax spun, for I intend to have a nice pair of sleeves made for you, of red cloth trimmed with green velvet!'

" 'Get out of here, and make it snappy!' answered Saporita under her breath. 'Now you've really filled the spindle! Just look how you're running to slip it in the ring![8] If you expect shirts from my hands, you can start stocking up on scrap paper! You think you've found it? You think I drank the milk of a black goat[9] and can spin eighty rolls of flax in twenty days? Damn the boat that brought you to this town! Go on, you've got time; you'll find your flax spun when livers have hair and monkeys have tails!' In the meantime her husband left and Saporita, who was as gluttonous as she was lazy, had been waiting for nothing better than to take out packages of flour and cruets of oil

---

5. The mother of the bride held out her daughter's finger for the wedding ring to be slipped on (Croce 584).

6. *vinte decina* (Neap.): a *decina* was the equivalent of four rolls, or bolts.

7. *corinola* (Neap.): wordplay with *core* (heart).

8. See tale 2.10 n19.

9. A devil, witch, or the like (Croce 381).

and make fritters and fried pizzas, which she nibbled like a mouse and devoured like a pig from morning till night.

"But when the date of her husband's return arrived, she began to spin the fine thread of fear[10] thinking about the uproar and racket that was bound to occur when the merchant found the flax in exactly the same state as he had left it and his chests and jars empty. And so she took a very long pole and wound twenty rolls of the flax onto it, with all the tow and hards, and after sticking an Indian gourd with a large hairpin and tying the pole to the parapet of the terrace, she began to lower this abbot of all spindles from the terrace down to the ground, using a large pot of macaroni broth as her moistening dish.[11] And while she was spinning thread that was as thin as a ship's cables and squirting the passersby every time she wet her finger, just like at carnival, some fairies happened to pass by and were so amused at this hideous vision that they almost died laughing, and for this gave her an enchantment: all the flax she had at home would not only be immediately spun but also made into cloth and bleached. This was instantly done, and Saporita began to swim in the grease of joy when she realized that this good fortune had rained down from the sky upon her.

"But to make sure her husband would never again bother her about such a matter, she put herself to bed on top of a pile of hazelnuts, and when he arrived she began to complain, and turning this way and that she made the hazelnuts crack so that it seemed like her bones were breaking. And when her husband asked how she was feeling, she answered in a pained and miserable little voice, 'I couldn't be worse, dear husband, for I haven't one whole bone left in me! What, does spinning eighty rolls of flax in twenty days and making cloth out of it besides seem like gathering a bit of grass for the sheep to you? Go on, husband, you forgot to pay the midwife, and the ass has eaten up all your discretion! When I'm dead my mother won't be making any more of me, so you're not going to catch me at these labors fit for a dog again; I don't intend to empty the spindle of my life because I've filled too many spindles!' Caressing her, the husband said, 'Stay healthy, my dear wife, for I'm more concerned about this lovely loom of love than I am about all the cloth in the world! Now I realize that your mother was right to punish you for working so hard, since it makes you lose your health. But take heart, for I intend to spend an eye and a tooth to get you well again; just wait, I'm going

10. I.e., to get diarrhea.
11. For wetting one's fingers while spinning.

E però, pigliato na perteca longa longa. . . . vennereo passanno certe fate.
[And so she took a very long pole. . . . [S]ome fairies happened to pass by.]

for the doctor right now.' And as he was saying this he ran off to get master Catruopolo.[12]

"In the meantime, Saporita gulped down the hazelnuts and threw the shells out the window. The doctor arrived, and after taking her pulse, observing her face, examining her urine, and sniffing at the chamber pot, he concluded, along the lines of Hippocrates and Galen, that her illness consisted of too much blood and too little work. The merchant, to whom this sounded like utter nonsense, put a coin in his hand and sent him off all warm and smelly,[13] and when he was about to go off in search of another doctor Saporita told him that there was no need for that, since the mere sight of the first one had cured her. And so her husband, embracing her, told her that from then on she was to conduct her life without working, since it's impossible to grow grapes and cabbages,[14] or to have *a full barrel and a drunken slave girl.*"

---

12. The doctor. For Galen (below), see tale 2.2 n5. The Greek physician Hippocrates of Cos lived from circa 460 to 370 BC.
13. Like fresh feces (Guarini and Burani 438).
14. Since the land where cabbages are grown cannot be used for cultivation of the precious *grieco* wine (Croce 383).

5

THE DRAGON

Fifth Entertainment of the Fourth Day

Due to the actions of a queen, Miuccio is sent off to face various dangers, and he manages to overcome all of them honorably with the help of an enchanted bird. The queen finally dies, and when it is discovered that Miuccio is the king's son he frees his mother, who becomes the wife of that king.

The tale of the seven little pork rinds fattened up the soup of the prince's pleasure to such a degree that it was dripping with oil as he tasted the ignorant malice and the malicious ignorance of Saporita, which had been ladled out with so much gusto by Tolla. But Popa, not wanting to do a crumb worse than Tolla, sailed off on the sea of nursery stories with the tale that follows: "Those who try to harm others encounter their own demise, and those who go looking to ensnare a third or even fourth person with betrayals and deceit often remain ensnared in the traps that they themselves have prepared, as you will hear about in the tale of a queen who with her own hands built the trap where her foot got caught.

"It is said that there once was a king, the king of High Marina. Due to the cruelty and tyranny that he practiced, one day, when he had gone to enjoy himself with his wife at a little castle far from the city, his royal seat was occupied by a sorceress. For this reason he prayed to a wooden statue that gave certain answers in code, and the statue answered that he would recover his kingdom only when the sorceress lost her sight. Seeing as the sorceress was well guarded but could also detect the scent of the people he dispatched to cause her trouble, whom she then executed like dogs, he fell into a state of despair, and to spite the sorceress took the honor and with the

---

"In the critical appendix to the *Kinder- und Hausmärchen* (3rd ed., 1856), Jacob Grimm noted a number of analogies between this tale and the saga of Siegfried: the secret birth of the hero, his humble first job, the bird's advice and help, the enemy queen who instigated the hero to confront the dragon (who is her brother and whose life is tied to hers), and finally, the regenerative power of the dragon's blood" (Guarini and Burani 450).

honor the lives of all the women of the land that he could get his hands on.[1]

"After hundreds of women were led there by their bad fortune and saw the bottoms knocked out of their reputations and their days smashed to smithereens, among the others arrived a girl named Porziella. She was the most resplendent thing you could find on the whole earth: her hair was a set of handcuffs for the cops of Love, her forehead a tablet on which was written the price list for the shop of the Graces of amorous pleasures, her eyes two lighthouses that signaled the vessels of desire to turn their prow toward the port of joys, her mouth a honeycomb amid two rose hedges. When she fell into the king's hands and it was her turn at roll call,[2] he intended to kill her like the others, but right when he was lifting his dagger a bird dropped some sort of root on his arm, and he began to tremble so hard that the weapon fell from his hand. This bird was a fairy who, while she had been asleep a few days earlier in a wood—where under the tent of shadows heat refreshed itself on the galley of fright—was approached by a certain satyr that wanted to do some bad things to her; she had, however, been awakened by Porziella, whose footsteps she now followed in order to reciprocate the favor.

"Now when the king saw what had happened, he thought that the beauty of that face had sequestered his arm and mandated his dagger not to impale her as he had done with so many others. And so he decided that one madman per house was enough and that he would not bathe the tool of death with blood as he had done with the instrument of life, but instead wall her up in an attic of his palace until she died. And he did just that: he closed the poor and embittered girl behind four walls without leaving her anything to eat or drink, so that she would take her departure as quickly as possible.

"When the bird saw her in this predicament, it consoled her with human words and told her to keep her spirits up, since to pay her adequate thanks for the favor she had done, the bird would be willing to help her with its own blood. And as much as Porziella pleaded with the bird, it would never say who it was, only that it was indebted to her and would leave nothing undone to serve her. And seeing as the poor girl was weak with hunger, it went for a fly outside and came back immediately with a sharp knife lifted from the king's pantry and told her to make, a little at a time, a hole in a corner of the

---

1. The motif of the vengeful slaying of hundreds of women after their rape brings to mind the actions of King Shahriyar in the frame story of the *Arabian Nights*.
2. *a rollo* (Neap.): "As in IV.2, to go down the list of the victims? Or in the sense of having made her pass through the cylinder (Span. *rulo*), or penis?" (Rak 750).

attic that would open onto the kitchen, where the bird would always be able to get something to keep her alive. Porziella thus exerted herself for a good while and dug until she made a path for the bird, which, after ascertaining that the cook had gone to get a bucket of water at the fountain, went down through the hole and carried off a lovely spring chicken that was warming and brought it back to Porziella. To remedy her thirst, since it didn't know how to bring her something to drink, the bird flew to the larder, where there were a lot of grapes hanging, and brought her a lovely bunch, and that's how she fared for a number of days.

"In the meantime Porziella, who was pregnant, gave birth to a lovely son, whom she nursed and brought up with the continual help of the bird. But when he got bigger his mother was advised by the fairy that she should enlarge the hole and remove as many planks from the attic walls as were needed to allow Miuccio (for that was the name of the son) to go through, and after lowering him with some little cords that the bird had brought, put the planks back in place so that it couldn't be seen where he had gone down. Porziella did as the bird told her to, and ordered her son never to say where he came from nor whose son he was, and then lowered him down when the cook was out. When the cook came back and saw such a lovely boy, he asked him who he was, how he had entered, and what he had come for. Miuccio, keeping his mother's advice in mind, said that he had lost his way and was looking for a master. During this exchange the steward arrived, and upon seeing a young lad of such high spirits, he thought that he would be a good page for the king. He brought him to the royal chambers, and when the king saw this boy who was as handsome and charming as a jewel, he immediately took a liking to him. He kept him in his service as a page and in his heart as a son and had him given all of the training appropriate for a gentleman, so that he grew up to be the most virtuous member of the court, and the king loved him far more than he did his own stepson.

"For this reason the queen began to hold the boy in distaste and even hate him. And the more her envy and malevolence gained ground, the more the favors and kindness the king bestowed on Miuccio smoothed the boy's way, until the queen got it into her head to soap the staircase of his fortune so well that he would slide straight down from the top.

"After tuning their instruments together one evening, the king and the queen were playing the music of conversation when the queen told the king that Miuccio had bragged that he could make three castles in the air. Both because he was curious and to please his wife, as soon as it was morning—when the Moon, schoolmistress of shadows, gave its pupils a holiday for the festival of the Sun—the king sent for Miuccio and ordered him to make three castles in the air as he had promised, or else the king would make him jump in the air himself.[3]

"When Miuccio heard this he went to his room and began to utter a bitter lament, for he saw how fragile the grace of princes was and how the favors they granted were so short-lived. But as he was crying and shedding copious tears, all of a sudden the bird arrived and said to him, 'Take heart, O Miuccio, and have no fear as long as you've got me here, for I can pull you from the fire.' After saying this, it ordered him to get a quantity of cardboard and glue and with it to make three big castles. Then the bird brought in three large griffins and tied one to each castle.[4] Once they were flying in the air Miuccio called the king, who at such a spectacle came running with his whole court, and this proof of Miuccio's ingenuity only caused the king to feel an even greater affection for him and to shower him with the most extraordinary blandishments. And thus snow was added to the queen's envy and fire to her contempt, since she saw that nothing was going as she wished, and she was never awake during the day without thinking of the way nor asleep at night without dreaming of the means to remove this speck from her eye. After a few more days she said to the king, 'My husband, it is now time to return to our past greatness and to the pleasures of a year ago, for Miuccio has offered to blind the fairy and with an outlay of eyes allow you to buy back your lost kingdom.'

"The king felt himself touched where it hurt, and called Miuccio to him that very instant and said, 'I'm quite amazed, considering how much I love you and that you have the ability to place me back on the throne from which I have tumbled, that you go around in such light-hearted fashion and don't attempt to remove me from the miserable state in which I find myself: demoted, as you can see, from a kingdom to the woods, from a city to a poor little castle, and from commanding a great number of people to being barely served by a few starving servants[5] able to do nothing more than cut bread and pour out broth.

---

3. I.e., hang him.
4. Penzer notes how the motif of building castles in the air is renowned in Arabia, Syria, and the Near East and was familiar to the author of the books of Tobit and perhaps Daniel. It was known to Mohammed, is mentioned in the Koran, and appears in the *Arabian Nights*. Miuccio's approach to the problem, however, differs from many other versions of the motif in that "by a cunning device [he] conformed to the words of the command, if not to its intended meaning" (2:41).
5. *da quatto pane a parte* (Neap.): "of the sort who get four loaves of bread each." "This would seem to be related to the name of *settepanelle* [seven little loaves of bread] that was given to servants. Here it is used to mean that due to the state of need to which the king was reduced, his servants each received 4, not 7, loaves of bread a week" (Croce 388).

. . . l'ordenaie . . . e fattone tre gran castielle e, facenno venire tre gruosee grifune, ne pose legato uno pe castiello, li quale volanno pe coppa l'aiero Miuccio chiammaie lo re. [. . . it ordered him . . . to make three big castles. Then the bird brought in three large griffins and tied one to each castle. Once they were flying in the air Miuccio called the king.]

Therefore, if you do not wish me ill fortune, run at once and go blind the eyes of the fairy who has my possessions, because when you close her shops you'll open the warehouse of my greatness, and when you put out those lanterns you'll light the lamps of my honor, which are now dark and sooty.' Upon hearing this proposal Miuccio intended to answer that the king was badly informed and had mistaken him for someone else, since he was neither a crow that dug out eyes nor a latrine cleaner who unclogged holes, but the king continued, 'Not another word; that's how I want it and that's how it will be! Let's just say that I've prepared the scales in the mint of this brain of mine: on this plate there's a reward, if you do what you are supposed to; and on this other one there's a punishment, if you do not do what I order you to.'

"Miuccio, who couldn't butt horns with a rock and was dealing with a man that would make any mother who gave him her daughter miserable, went off to a corner to despair. Then the bird arrived and said to him, 'Is it possible, Miuccio, that you always drown in a glass of water? And if I had been killed, would you have held forth with such a dirge? Don't you know that I worry about your life more than my own? So don't lose heart. Follow me and you'll see what Moniello is capable of!'[6] And the bird flew off. Then it stopped in a wood, where it began to chirp and was surrounded by a flock of birds, to whom it announced that those with the wherewithal to take out the sorceress's eyes would receive a safeguard against the talons of sparrow hawks and goshawks and a pass against muskets, bows and arrows, crossbows, and hunters' birdlime.

"Among these was a swallow that had made its nest in a rafter of the royal palace; it hated the sorceress since she had kicked it out of her room a number of times with the suffumigations that were part of her accursed spells. For this reason, in part out of its desire for revenge and in part to win the prize the bird was promising, it offered to do the job. And when it had flown off like lightning to the city and entered the palace, it found the fairy lying on a sofa, where she was being cooled with a fan by two ladies-in-waiting. The swallow dived straight down into the fairy's eyes and, shitting into them, took away her sight, and when she saw night at noon and realized that with this closing of her customshouse the merchandise of her kingdom was exhausted, she gave up her scepter shrieking like a damned soul. Then she holed up in some grottos where, beating her head on the wall in continuation, she ended her days.

---

6. "Probably a popular saying that meant 'what a skilled person like me is capable of' " (Croce 389).

"Once the sorceress was gone the counselors sent off ambassadors to the king to tell him that he could come back and enjoy his home, since the blinding of the sorceress had made it possible for him to see this lovely day. And at the same time they arrived Miuccio did, too, and, egged on by the bird, said to the king, 'I have served you in good coin: the sorceress has been blinded, the kingdom is yours. And if therefore I deserve any payment for this service, I want nothing more than to be left alone with my troubles without being put in such danger again.' The king embraced the boy with great affection and had him put on his hat[7] and sit at his side, and only heaven knows how the queen swelled up with rage—so much so that from the spectrum of colors that showed on her face you could recognize the wind of ruin that she was plotting in her heart against poor Miuccio.

"Not very far from the castle lived a frightfully fierce dragon that had been born from the same womb as the queen; when her father had summoned the astrologers to utter some prediction on the matter, they had said that his daughter would live for as long as the dragon lived, and that when one of them died the other would necessarily die, too. Only one thing could resuscitate the queen, and this was if her temples, her breastbone, her nostrils, and her wrists were lubricated with the blood of the same dragon.[8]

"Now then, the queen, being well familiar with the fury and the strength of this animal, decided to send Miuccio right into its claws, since she was sure of the fact that the dragon would make a nice mouthful of him and that he would be like a strawberry in the throat of a bear. Turning to the king, she said, 'My word, Miuccio is truly the treasure of your house, and you would be an ingrate if you did not love him, all the more so because he has let it be known that he would like to kill the dragon, which, even if it is my brother, is such an enemy of yours that I prefer one hair of my husband to a hundred brothers.' The king, who hated this dragon to death and had no idea how to get it out of his sight, immediately called Miuccio and said, 'I know that you've got a good handle on things, and so, after doing so

---

7. "As only some noblemen could do in the presence of the king, according to the dress code of the time" (Rak 750).
8. See Penzer on the motifs of the "external soul" and the dragon's blood. Regarding the first, he notes that it "occurs twice in our tale, but in two very different forms. Of these the first is the most curious: the life of the sorceress depending on her eyesight. It rather reminds us of the heel of Achilles. The second is the more usual form: when the dragon is slain, the Queen must die. However, the most usual form of all is where an individual hides his 'soul' in some object in an inaccessible place" (2:41).

very much for me, you're going to have to do me one more favor, after which you can spin me any way you wish. Get going this instant and kill the dragon. You'll do me a signal service for which I will reward you well.'

"At these words Miuccio nearly lost his senses, and when he was able to articulate a few words he said to the king, 'This is getting to be a headache! Now you're really starting to rub me the wrong way! Is my life like the milk of a black sheep, for you to wreak such havoc on it? This is no peeled pear that glides smoothly down your throat; this is a dragon that can tear you up with its claws, break your bones with its head, smash you to pieces with its tail, rip you to shreds with its teeth, poison you with its eyes, and kill you with its breath! So how is it that you want to send me to my death? This is the pension[9] I get for having given you a kingdom? Who is the accursed soul that has thrown this die on the table? Who is the son of hell that is jerking you around like this and has impregnated you with these words?' The king, who was as light as a ball when it came to being tossed around but heavier than a rock when it came to holding fast to what he had once said, dug in his heels and said, 'You've done this and you've done that, and now you're losing your way right at the best part! But not another word: go and remove this plague from my kingdom, unless you want your own life to be removed!'

"Miuccio, poor soul, saw himself offered first a favor and then a threat, first a caress on the face and then a kick in the ass, first a warm one and then a cold one. He pondered over how changeable fortunes are in court, and he would have liked to have his stomach more than empty of the acquaintance of the king. But since he knew that talking back to great and beastly men is akin to shaving a lion's beard, he went off into a corner to curse his fate, which had reduced him to the court in order to cut short the hours of his life. And as he was sitting on a doorstep with his face between his knees, washing his shoes with his tears and warming his balls[10] with his sighs, the bird appeared before him with an herb in its beak and, throwing it into his lap, said, 'Get up, Miuccio, and rest assured that you won't be playing "unload the ass" with your days, but "rout the enemy"[11] with the dragon's life. Take this herb, and when you get to the grotto of that hideous animal toss it in, and the dragon will immediately become so terribly drowsy that it will fall into a deep sleep. And right

---

9. See tale 1.7 n29.
10. *contrapise* (Neap.): lit., counterweights.
11. Card games.

away throw it a party with a nice big knife in its backside[12] and then come back here, where things will go much better than you think. Enough said: I know what I've got down here; we have more time than money; and he who has time has life.'

"After the bird had thus spoken Miuccio got up, stuck a large knife under his clothes, took the herb, and set off for the dragon's grotto, which was under a mountain so well grown that the three mountains that served as steps to the Giants[13] wouldn't have reached its waist. When he arrived he threw the herb into the cavern, and as soon as he put the dragon to sleep Miuccio began to chop away. As he was mincing up the animal the queen felt her own heart being minced; and when she saw herself in this trouble she recognized her mistake, for she had bought her death in hard cash. She called her husband and told him what the astrologers had predicted and how her life hung on the dragon's, and that she suspected Miuccio had killed the dragon, since she felt her life slipping away from her bit by bit.

"To which the king answered, 'If you knew that the dragon's life was the bastion of your own life and the root of your own days, why did you make me send Miuccio? Whose fault is it? You caused this harm to yourself and now you can cry over it; you broke the mug and now you can pay for it!' The queen answered, 'I would never have believed that a mere runt could have the skill and strength to bring down an animal that had little consideration for an army, and I was convinced that he would leave his rags there. But since I calculated my bill without the innkeeper, and the boat of my plans has sunk, do me a favor, if I am dear to you. As soon as I am dead take a sponge soaked in the dragon's blood and lubricate all the extremities of my body before I am buried.' 'That is a small thing to do, considering the love I have for you,' answered the king, 'and if the dragon's blood is not enough, I'll add mine to satisfy you!' But just as the queen was intending to thank him her spirit and with it her words left her, because at that very moment Miuccio had finished butchering the dragon.

"As soon as Miuccio appeared before the king to give him the news of what had happened, the king ordered him to go and get the dragon's blood. But since the king was curious to see the feat that Miuccio had accomplished with his own hands, he followed him. As the boy was going out of the palace door the bird came out to meet him and

---

12. *fra nacca e pacca* (Neap.): an expression taken from the chorus of a tarantella from Salerno that goes "fra nacca e pacca e nierve de vacca" (between the hip and the buttocks and the nerves of a cow) (Guarini and Burani 447).
13. The mythological Giants Otus and Ephialtes attempted to climb mounts Olympus, Ossa, and Pelion, which were piled one on top of the other, in order to overthrow the gods (see Homer, *Odyssey* 11.305–20, among others; cit. Rak 750).

said, 'Where are you going?' to which Miuccio answered, 'I'm going where the king sends me; he spins me like a shuttle and can't leave me still for an hour.' 'To do what?' said the bird. And Miuccio: 'To get the dragon's blood.' The bird replied: 'Oh, poor you! The dragon's blood will be bull's blood[14] for you; it will explode inside you and revive that bad seed that's at the root of all your troubles, for it is she who keeps putting you in new perils so that you may lose your life. And the king, who lets himself be harnessed by an ugly old hag, throws you like a die to risk your life, even if you are of his own blood, even if you are broccoli off his same plant! But I forgive him, for he does not know who you are. And yet his intrinsic affection should give him some inkling of the relationship, so that the services you have rendered this gentleman and the reward he reaps in acquiring such a lovely heir might have the strength to make that unlucky soul, your mother Porziella, enter into his graces, for it's fourteen years now that she's been buried alive up in a garret, where she looks like a temple of beauty built inside a closet!'

"As the fairy was saying this the king, who had heard everything, came forward so that he could understand the matter more clearly. And after hearing that Miuccio was the son of Porziella, whom he had made pregnant, and that Porziella was still alive in that room, he immediately ordered that she be unwalled and brought before him. When he saw that she was more beautiful than ever, thanks to the bird's good care, he embraced her with great love and could not get his fill of squeezing first the mother and then the son, at the same time begging the mother's pardon for the bad way he had treated her and the son's pardon for the dangers he had exposed him to. And then he had her dressed in the dead queen's most sumptuous clothing and took her for his wife.

"Finally, when he learned that Porziella had survived and his son had emerged unharmed from such danger all because the bird had kept the one fed and the other well advised, he offered the bird his state and his life. The bird said that it wanted no reward for all the services other than Miuccio for its husband, and as it was saying this it transformed into a splendid young lady, who, to the great pleasure of the king and Porziella, was given to Miuccio for his wife. And at the same time that the dead queen was being thrown into her grave, the pair of newlyweds began to reap bushels[15] of happiness and set

---

14. On the poisonous effects of bull's blood, see, e.g., Pliny, *Natural History* 11.90, 28.41 (cit. Croce 393).

15. Wordplay: *tumolo* (grave) vs. *tommola* (a measure roughly equivalent to a bushel).

off for their kingdom for even grander festivities, where they were
awaited with great pleasure. And they recognized that all the good
fortune bestowed upon them by the fairy had been a result of the
favor that Porziella did for her, since at the very end, *a good deed is
never wasted.*"

6

THE THREE CROWNS

Sixth Entertainment of the Fourth Day

*Marchetta is abducted by the wind and carried off to the house of
an ogress, from whom, after various events, she receives a slap.
She departs, dressed as a man, and ends up in the house of a king,
where the queen falls in love with her and, resentful that her love
is not returned, accuses her in front of her husband of attempting
to disgrace her. Marchetta is condemned to hang, but due to the
power of a ring given to her by the ogress she is freed, and when
her accuser is killed she becomes queen.*

Popa's tale gave them extreme pleasure, and there was no one who
did not savor Porziella's good fortune. But there was also no one who
envied her a fate that had been bought with so much hardship, since
in order to reach the status of royalty she had almost lost her status as
a person. When Antonella saw that Porziella's troubles had darkened
the hearts of the prince and his wife, she wished to lift their spirits a
little and began to speak in this manner: "Truth, my lords, always
rises to the surface like oil, and a lie is a fire that cannot remain hidden; indeed, it is a modern-day musket that kills the person shooting
it,[1] and it is not without reason that we call those who are not faithful
to their words liars, for they burn[2] and scorch not only all the virtues
and goodness they carry inside their breasts but the lie itself where
these words are preserved, as I will make you confess upon hearing
the following tale.

Penzer discusses the motifs of longing for a child (also found in tales 1.2, 1.9, and
2.5), escaping one's fate, a woman disguised as a man, and the forbidden door. The
last motif often derives from a ritual or tribal taboo, and the imposer of the taboo is
typically either a Bluebeard type, in which case the ending is most likely tragic, or a
generic magic power, in which case the fatal curiosity may result in hardship but ultimately leads to a happy ending (2:52). For similar motifs, see Straparola 4.1 ("Cos-
tanza and Costanzo"); Marie-Catherine d'Aulnoy, "Belle-belle; or, "The Chevalier
Fortuné"; Henriette Julie de Murat, "The Savage" (the last two in *The Great Fairy
Tale Tradition*), Gonzenbach 9; and Pitrè, *Fiabe, nov. e racc. sic.* 75.

1. "Allusion to the shoddy way that 'modern' harquebuses, or rifles, were constructed" (Croce 395). Basile served time as a soldier on Crete and thus had firsthand
experience with firearms.

2. Wordplay: *busciardo* (liar) vs. *abruscia* (burn).

"There once was a king, the king of Shaken Valley, who since he could not have children would say at every hour of the day and wherever he happened to be, 'O heavens, send me an heir to my state so that my house will not be left desolate!' And on one of the occasions that he was thus lamenting he found himself in a garden, and as he uttered the usual words with loud cries, he heard a voice issue from inside the branches, which said,

> King, which do you prefer?
> A daughter who flees from you,
> Or a son who destroys you?

"The king was confused by this proposal, and could not decide how to answer. Thinking that he would consult the wise men of his court, he immediately went off to his chambers, and when he had summoned his counselors he ordered them to discuss the matter. One answered that he should set greater store by his honor than by his life; another that he should value his life more, since it was an intrinsic good, whereas honor was extrinsic and therefore to be considered of lesser value; one said that the price of losing life was small, since it is water that passes, and so too for worldly goods, which are the columns of life set on the glass wheel of fortune, whereas honor, which is lasting and leaves tracks of fame and signs of glory, must be guarded jealously and taken care of lovingly; another argued that life, by which the species is preserved, and worldly goods, by which the greatness of one's house is maintained, must be considered dearer than honor, since honor is an opinion that derives from virtue, and losing a daughter due to fortune and not to one's own defect did not compromise a father's virtue or dirty the honor of the family. But above all, there were some others who concluded that honor was not to be found in a woman's apron strings and that, besides, a just prince should pay more attention to the common good than to particular interests, and, since a fugitive daughter brings only a little shame to her father's house, whereas a wicked son sets fire to his own house and the whole kingdom, that, therefore, seeing as the king wanted children and these two alternatives had been proposed, he should ask for a girl, since she would not put his life and his state in danger.

"This opinion pleased the king. He returned to the garden and cried out as he was used to doing; when he heard the same voice as before, he answered, 'A girl, a girl.' Upon returning home that evening—when the Sun invited the hours of the day to take a look at the pygmies of the Antipodes[3]—he went to bed with his wife, and after nine months he had a beautiful daughter, whom he immediately had locked in a strong and well-guarded palace so as not to neglect, on his part, any possible attention that might remedy her sad destiny. She was brought up to have all the virtues appropriate to a kingly race, and when she was nice and big he began negotiations for a marriage with the king of Lose-Your-Mind.

"Once the marriage had been arranged and the girl was turned out of her house, which she had never before left, to be sent to her husband, there came such a big gust of wind that she was swept off her feet and seen no more. The wind carried her along in the air for a while and then put her down in front of an ogress's house, which was in a wood that had banished the Sun like a plague victim for having killed the infected Python.[4] There she found a little old woman whom the ogress had left to guard her things, who said to her, 'Oh, bitter is your life; where do you set foot? Unlucky you, if the ogress who is mistress of this house comes back! Your hide would not be worth three coins to her; she feeds on nothing but human flesh, and my own life is safe only to the extent that her need for my services holds her back, and she turns up her fangs at this poor old bark of mine, full of syncopes, palpitations, gas, and stones. But you know what you need to do? Here's the key to the house: go in, tidy up the rooms, and clean every last thing, and as soon as the ogress comes in, hide so she can't see you. I won't leave you lacking in what you need to stay alive. In the meantime, who knows? The heavens may assist; time may bring great things. Enough said: have good sense and patience, and you'll pass through every gulf and overcome every storm.'

"Marchetta, for this was the girl's name, made virtue out of necessity and took the key, and when she entered the ogress's rooms the first thing she did was get her hands on a broom, and she made the house so clean you could eat macaroni off the floor. Then she took a bit of pork rind and polished the chests of walnut, and she shone them so brightly you could see yourself in them. And after she made the bed, she heard the ogress coming and hid inside a barrel where wheat had been kept.

"When the ogress found this unusual state of things, she was most pleased and called the old woman and asked her, 'Who tidied things

---

3. "Probably an allusion to the pygmy populations that were thought to exist in the Americas" (Croce 585).
4. "The myth of Python, the serpent that infected the earth with his fumes and was killed by Apollo's arrow, also symbolized the victory of the Sun over the winter (Ovid, *Metamorphoses* I, 434–47)" (Guarini and Burani 454).

up so nicely?' The old woman answered that it had been her, and the ogress replied, 'Those who do what they usually do not have either already tricked you or intend to! Truly, you can put a stick in the hole today; you've done something out of the ordinary and you deserve a rich soup.' Saying this, she ate, and the next time she went out she found, upon returning, all the cobwebs removed from the rafters, all the copperware polished and hung prettily on the wall, and all the dirty clothes washed in hot water. She was knocked out with pleasure and blessed the old woman a thousand times, saying, 'May the heavens always fecundate your fortune, my dear madam Pentarosa, may you always prosper and get ahead, for you cheer my heart with the wonderful way you tidy up and deliver me a house fit for a doll and a bed fit for a bride.'

"The old woman was in seventh heaven with this new reputation she had earned, and she was always passing tasty morsels on to Marchetta and filling her up like a stuffed capon. And when the ogress went out again the old woman said to Marchetta, 'Keep quiet; we're going to catch up with this cripple and try your luck. Make something delicious with your own hands, something that appeals to the ogress, and if she swears on the seven heavens don't believe her, but if by chance she swears on her three crowns you can show yourself, for it will be smooth sailing from then on and you'll see that I've given you a mother's advice.'

"Upon hearing this Marchetta slaughtered a nice duck, made a lovely stew out of its extremities, and after stuffing it well with lard, oregano, and garlic, put it on a spit. Then she kneaded a few gnocchi[5] on an upside-down basket and prepared the ogress's table, decorating it with roses and branches of bitter orange. When the ogress came back and found this display, she nearly jumped out of her clothes, and she called the old woman and asked her, 'Who did me this wonderful service?' 'Eat,' answered the old woman, 'and ask no more; it is enough that you have someone who serves you and gives you satisfaction.' While the ogress was eating and those delicious morsels were going all the way down to the little bones of her feet, she began to say, 'I swear on the three words of Naples[6] that if I knew who the cook is I would give her the pupils of my eyes.' Then she continued, 'I swear on three bows and three arrows that if I can find out who it is,

---

5. *strangolaprievete* (Neap.): "Today called *strozzapreti* [priest stranglers], this is a small, short pasta, similar in form to gnocchi, with a hollow pressed in the middle; it is cooked and treated like macaroni" (Croce 399).
6. "Perhaps epithets that were given to Naples, such as the three of the expression 'Gentile, Sirena e Sacra.' Or, perhaps, an allusion to the proverb 'Those who stay in Naples need three things: broccoli, wooden shoes, and traps'" (Croce 586).

I intend to keep her inside this heart of mine; I swear on the three candles that are lit when a contract is signed at night; on the three witnesses necessary for a man to be hanged; on the three spans of rope wrapped around the hanged man; on three things that drive a man from his home: stench, smoke, and a wicked woman; on three things that a house consumes: fritters, warm bread, and macaroni; on the three women and a duck that make a market; on the three Fs of fish: fried, frosty, and fresh; on the three principal singers of Naples: Giovanni della Carriola, Compare Biondo, and the King of Music;[7] on the three Ss a lover must be: solitary, solicitous, and secret; on the three things a merchant needs: credit, courage, and good fortune; on the three sorts of people a whore takes to: swashbucklers, handsome young men, and dimwits; on the three things important for a thief: eyes for spotting, claws for grabbing, feet for beating it; on three things that ruin youth: gambling, women, and taverns; on the three greatest virtues of a cop: staking out, chasing, and catching; on three things useful to a courtier: dissimulation, phlegm, and luck; on three things that a procurer should have: a big heart, a lot of hot air, and little shame; on the three things a doctor checks: the pulse, the face, and the chamber pot.' But she might as well have talked from today until tomorrow, for Marchetta, who had been warned, didn't say a peep.

"But when she finally heard her say, 'On my three crowns, if I find out who the good housekeeper is who did all these wonderful services for me, I intend to give her more caresses and squeezes than she could ever imagine,' Marchetta came out and said, 'Here I am!' Seeing her, the ogress answered, 'I could kick myself; you were one up on me! You did a master's job, and you saved yourself a nice bake inside this belly. But since you've been capable of doing so much and have given me pleasure, I intend to treat you even better than a daughter. And so here are the keys to my chambers, and may you be mistress and ruler of them. Only one thing will I withhold from you: you must not under any circumstance open the last room, which this key opens, for it would be like mustard under my nose. Take care to serve me well, and—lucky you!—I promise, on my three crowns, that I will arrange a very rich marriage for you.' Marchetta kissed her hand in thanks for so much grace and promised to serve her better than a slave.

---

7. For the last two, see the frame tale (introduction to day 1 n21). "The first was called 'of the wheelbarrow' due perhaps to the cart that he either pushed or rode in because he was crippled or paralytic. Three chapbooks authored by Giovanni were reprinted without interruption until the 19th century: a *Dialogo del povero e del ricco*, a *contrasto*, *Sdegno d'amanti*, and the *Istoria di Marzia Basile*, the account of a murderess who was executed in 1603 [no relation to Giambattista]" (Croce 586).

"When the ogress left, however, Marchetta felt terribly tickled by the curiosity to see what was inside that forbidden chamber, and when she opened it she found three girls, all dressed in gold and seated on three imperial thrones, who appeared to be sleeping. These girls were all daughters of a fairy who had been put under a spell by their mother because she knew that they would meet with great danger if the daughter of a king did not come to awaken them, and she had enclosed them there so as to remove them from the perils threatened by the stars.

"Now when Marchetta went in, the noise she made with her feet brought the girls back to consciousness, as if they were awakening, and they asked for something to eat. She immediately got them three eggs apiece, cooked the eggs under the ashes, and gave them to the girls. As soon as they had gotten back their breath, they wanted to go get some air outside the room. In the meantime, however, the ogress returned and was so incensed that she gave Marchetta a nice big slap on the face, which offended her so greatly that before a moment had passed she asked the ogress for permission to leave and wander through the world in search of her fortune. And however much the ogress tried to soothe her with nice words, saying that she had been joking and wouldn't do it again, it was not possible to get her to change her mind, until she was finally forced to let her leave. She gave the girl a ring and told her to wear it with the stone on the inside of her hand and never to look at it unless she found herself in great danger and heard her name repeated as an echo;[8] she also gave her a fine suit of men's clothes, which Marchetta had requested.

"So dressed, Marchetta set off on her way. When she arrived at a wood—where Night went to collect wood to warm itself from the recent frost—she ran into a king on his way to the hunt, who, when he saw this handsome young man (for this is how she appeared), asked him where he was coming from and what he was doing. She answered that she was the son of a merchant, that her mother had died, and that she had fled because of the torments of her stepmother.

"The king was pleased with Marchetta's quickness and good manners and took her on as a page. He brought her to his palace, and as soon as the queen saw her she felt all her longings blown up by a bomb of graces, and although she tried for a few days, in part out of fear and in part out of pride—always a companion to beauty—to dissimulate the flame and disguise the bites of love under the tail of her

---

8. The echo was a favorite device in the poetry of the time, especially in pastoral dramas. Basile's own marine pastoral, *Le avventurose disavventure*, has an echo scene (4.2).

desire, she was, nevertheless, short at the heel and unable to stand up under the impact of those unreined longings. And so one day she called Marchetta aside and began to reveal her suffering and tell of the weight of affliction with which she had been burdened since she had seen his beauty, and that if he did not make up his mind to water the field of her desires, without a doubt not only her hopes but also her life would wither away. She praised, on the one hand, the beauteous things of his face, and put before his eyes the fact that he would be acting like a bad student in the school of Love if he left an inkblot of cruelty inside the book of so many graces, and that, moreover, he would get a nice ruler of regret on his knuckles. To the praises she added prayers, beseeching him in the name of all seven heavens not to desire that someone who kept his lovely image on the signboard of the shop of her thoughts find herself inside a furnace of sighs and in the middle of a puddle of tears. Next came offers: she promised to pay for each finger of pleasure with a span of benefits and to keep the warehouse of her gratitude open for the satisfaction of every request from such a handsome client. Finally, she reminded him that she was queen, and that since she was already in the boat he should not leave her unassisted in the middle of that gulf, or else she would crash into the rocks and he would have to pay for it.

"When Marchetta heard these caresses and stings, these promises and threats, this washing of the face and lifting of the cape, she would have liked to say that she was missing the key needed to open the door of the queen's happiness; she would have liked to explain that she was not Mercury, with his caduceus,[9] and therefore could not give her the peace that she desired. But, not wanting to unmask herself, she answered that she could not believe that the queen wanted to plant crooked spindles[10] on such a worthy king as her husband, and that, moreover, even if the queen was willing to disregard the reputation of her lineage, she herself could not and would not wrong a master who loved her so much. When the queen heard this first replication to the injunction of her longing, she said to Marchetta, 'Come now, consider this carefully and keep your plow straight, for when my peers beg for something, it's a command, and it's when they kneel that they kick you in the neck! So do your calculations well, and you'll see what a good deal this merchandise can be for you! But enough said, and *sufficit*. Before I leave let me tell you one more thing, and that is: when a woman of my quality is scorned, she does her best to remove the stain from her face by washing it with the

9. The winged staff entwined by two serpents that is carried by Mercury.
10. Horns; i.e., to cuckold.

blood of he who offended her.' And saying this, she turned her back
on the girl with a forbidding scowl, leaving poor Marchetta confused
and gelid.

"But after the queen continued her assault on the lovely fortress for
a number of days and finally saw that her labors were a waste of time
and her efforts thrown to the wind, and that she was sweating without making a spot by throwing her words to the wind and her sighs
into the void, she switched register and changed love into hate and
the longing to enjoy the beloved object into a desire for vendetta. And
thus, pretending to have tears welling up in her eyes, she went to her
husband and said, 'Who could ever have told us, my husband, that a
serpent was growing in our sleeve? Who could ever have imagined
that a puny little wretch would be so bold? But it's all because of the
excessive kindness you showed him: if you give a peasant a finger
he'll take the whole hand! In short, we all want to piss in the urinal;
but if you don't give him the punishment he deserves, I'm going back
to my father's house, and I won't want to see you or ever hear your
name again!' 'What did he do to you?' asked the king. And the queen
replied, 'Oh, nothing at all! The little scoundrel wanted to be the tax
collector of the matrimonial debt that I have with you, and without a
bit of respect or fear or shame he had the nerve to appear before me
and the tongue to ask for free access to the field that is sown with
your honor.' When he heard this, the king asked for no further testimony so as not to compromise the word and the authority of his wife,
and immediately had Marchetta collared by the cops. And in the heat
of the moment, without giving her any way to defend herself, he condemned her to see how much weight the executioner's scales could
hold.

"While she was being carried off to the place of torture, Marchetta, who neither knew what had happened nor realized she had
done anything wrong, began to shout, 'O heavens, what have I done
to deserve the funeral of this poor neck before the last rites of this
wretched body are celebrated? Who could have told me that, without
enlisting under the colors of thieves and delinquents, I would be
mounting guard at this palace of Death with three lengths of rope
round my gullet? Alas, who will comfort me during this extreme passage? Who will help me in such danger? Who will free me from this
haltering?' 'Ring,' answered the echo,[11] and when Marchetta heard
this manner of reply she remembered the ring she was wearing on her
finger and the words the ogress had said to her when she left and,

---

11. The original reads: "Chi mi libera da sta forca?" ("Who will free me from these
gallows?"), to which the echo answers: "Orca" ("ogress").

turning her eyes to the stone that she had not yet looked at, she suddenly heard a voice in the air repeat three times, 'Let her go, she's a woman!'

"This voice was so terrifying that there wasn't a single cop or rag seller who remained near the chef of justice,[12] and when the king heard these words, which shook the palace down to its very foundations, he had Marchetta brought before him and ordered her to tell the truth about who she was and how she had ended up in that land. Forced by necessity, she told of everything that had happened during her life: how she was born, shut up inside that palace, and carried off by the wind; how she ended up at the ogress's house and wanted to leave; what the ogress said and gave to her; what happened with the queen, and how, not knowing what she had done wrong, she found herself in danger of having to use her feet to row the three-beamed galley.

"When the king heard this story and compared it with what he had once spoken about with his friend, the king of Shaken Valley, he recognized Marchetta for who she was and at the same time became aware of the wickedness of his wife, who had given her this bad reputation. He thus ordered his wife to be thrown without delay into the sea with a millstone round her neck, and after inviting Marchetta's father and mother to be his guests he took her for his wife, she who gave clear proof that: *God finds a port for a desperate boat.*"

12. I.e., the executioner.

7

THE TWO LITTLE PIZZAS

Seventh Entertainment of the Fourth Day

Marziella is enchanted after she shows kindness to an old woman, but her aunt, envious of her good fortune, throws her to sea, where a siren keeps her in chains for a long time. Finally, she is freed by her brother and becomes queen, and her aunt is punished for her wrongdoing.

The prince and his lady would surely have affirmed that Antonella's tale beat all of the others that had been told, had they not feared that Ciulla's spirits might be dampened. And so, after placing the lance of her tongue in its rest,[1] Ciulla aimed at Tadeo and his wife's ring of pleasure in the following manner: "I have always heard it said that those who do favors find favor; the Manfredonia bell says 'give to me and I'll give to you';[2] and those who do not put the bait of courtesy on the hook of affection will never catch the fish of benefits. And if you want to learn the meaning of this listen to this tale, and then you'll tell me who has always lost the most, the stingy or the generous.

"Now it is said that there once were two blood sisters, Luceta and Troccola, who had two daughters, Marziella and Puccia. Marziella's heart was as beautiful as her face; conversely, the heart and face of Puccia were, following the same rule, like the face of illness and the heart of plague. Indeed, she resembled her parents, for Troccola, her mother, was a harpy on the inside and an old hide on the outside.

"Now it happened that Luceta needed to warm up a few carrots to fry in green sauce, and she said to her daughter, 'My dear Marziella, go, darling, to the fountain, and fetch me a pitcher of water.' 'With

---

AT 403: The Black and the White Bride, and AT 480: The Spinning-Women by the Spring and the Kind and the Unkind Girls (2:60). Penzer offers a number of variants of the "true bride" motif, both in Italian and non-Italian sources, and notes the resemblance to Grimm 135 ("The White Bride and the Black Bride") and 24 ("Mother Holle") (2:60). See also Straparola 3.3 ("Biancabella"), Perrault, "The Fairies," Gonzenbach 33 and 34, Pitrè, *Fiabe, nov. e racc. sic.* 60, and Imbriani 25.

1. "The *resta* was the hook found on armor that was used as support for the lance in the course of tournaments or battles. Here, the reference is to a ring contest" (Rak 786).

2. *damme e dotte* (Neap.): "Perhaps in imitation of the sound of bells" (Croce 586).

pleasure, dear mother,' answered her daughter, 'but if you care for me give me a little pizza, which I'd like to eat with some of that fresh water.' 'Gladly,' said her mother, and she went to a bread sack that was hanging on a hook and took from it a lovely little pizza—the day before she had baked bread—and gave it to the girl. Marziella put the pitcher on a head ring and went off to the fountain, which, like a charlatan performing on a marble counter to the music of the falling water, sold secrets for quenching thirst.

"As Marziella stood filling the pitcher, there arrived an old woman who on the stage of a large hump was acting out the tragedy of Time. Noticing that lovely pizza right when Marziella was about to take a bite out of it, she said, 'My lovely girl, may the heavens bless you with good fortune if you give me a little of that pizza.' Marziella, who had the stink of a queen about her, said, 'Here, you can have the whole thing, my noble woman, and I'm sorry it's not made of sugar and almonds, in which case I'd still give it to you with all of my heart.' When the old woman saw how loving Marziella was, she said to her, 'Go, and may the heavens always make you prosper for the generous love that you've shown me! I pray to all the stars that you may always be happy and content, and that when you breathe roses and jasmines may come out of your mouth, when you comb your hair pearls and garnets may fall from your head, and when you put your foot to the earth lilies and violets may spring forth.'

"The girl thanked her and returned home, where after her mother finished cooking they paid their natural debt to their bodies. And when that day was over—as soon as morning came and in the market of the celestial fields the Sun spread out the luminous wares that it had brought from the Orient—Marziella was combing her hair when she began to see pearls and garnets rain down upon her lap. With great joy she called her mother and they put the jewels in a chest, and then Luceta went off to a money changer, who was a friend of hers, to dispose of a good quantity of them. At the same time Troccola stopped by to see her sister, and when she found Marziella bustling around and all busy with those pearls, she asked her how, when, and where she had gotten them. The girl was incapable of muddying the waters, and perhaps had not heard the proverb that goes, 'Do less than you can, eat less than you will, spend less than you have, and say less than you know,' and she told her aunt about the whole business. Troccola didn't even bother to wait for her sister, since each hour until she returned home seemed like a thousand years to her. Once she got there she gave a little pizza to her daughter and sent her to get water at the fountain.

"The girl encountered the same old woman, and when the woman asked her for a little bit of her pizza the girl, who was very bad-tempered, answered, 'As if I have nothing better to do than give my pizza to you! What, you think you made my donkey pregnant and I should give you my stuff? Get out of here; teeth are closer than relatives!' As she was saying this she gulped down the pizza in four bites, making the old woman's mouth water. And when she saw that the last bite was gone and her hopes had been buried along with the pizza, the old woman flew into a rage and said to her, 'Go, and when you breathe may you foam at the mouth like a doctor's mule,[3] when you comb your hair may mounds of lice fall from your head, and wherever you touch your foot to the ground may ferns and thistles grow!' After Puccia got the water and returned home, her mother couldn't wait to comb her hair; she spread a fine tablecloth on her lap, pulled down her daughter's head, and as she started to comb, the stream of alchemical animals that flowed forth was strong enough to stop quicksilver.[4] When her mother saw this, the snow of envy was joined by the fire of anger, so that she breathed flames and smoke from her nose and mouth.

"Now after some time had gone by, Ciommo, Marziella's brother, found himself at the court of King Chiunzo.[5] As the court was conversing about the beauty of various women, Ciommo came forward without being asked and affirmed that if his sister were to appear there, all other beautiful women could go throw their bones off the Ricciardo Bridge,[6] since apart from her physical beauty, which played counterpoint to the plainchant of her lovely soul, she also had in her hair, her mouth, and her feet the powers that the fairy had given her. When he heard this praise the king told Ciommo to have her come, and that if he found her to be as exceptional as Ciommo boasted she was he would take her for his wife. This did not seem to Ciommo like a chance to be missed, and he immediately dispatched a courier with a message for his mother, in which he told her what had happened and begged her to come at once with her daughter, so as not to lose this good fortune.

"Luceta, however, was very ill and, putting the sheep in the wolf's

---

3. "Doctors would travel by mule, accompanied by their assistants on foot" (Croce 408).
4. "Mercury was used to treat lice. But they are so copious in this case that they would counter mercury and, as if by alchemy, stop its actions" (Croce 409).
5. "In the first eclogue of the *Muse napolitane* Basile calls someone who thinks he's great the 'mayor of Chiunzo.' The Chiunzo was a mountain near Tramonti (on the Amalfi coast), and its name appears in various proverbial sayings" (Croce 587). Today *chiunzo* or *chionzo* means "idiot" (Guarini and Burani 466).
6. See tale 3.3 n20.

care, she begged her sister to do her the favor of accompanying Mar-ziella to the Chiunzo court for this and that matter. When Troccola saw that this business was growing in her hands, she promised her sister that she would deliver the girl safe and sound to her brother, and she set off on a boat with Marziella and Puccia. But as soon as they were in the middle of the sea and the sailors were all asleep, Troccola threw Marziella into the water, where, just as she was about to do a duck dive down to the bottom, a splendid mermaid appeared, gathered her up in her arms, and carried her off.

"Now when Troccola arrived at Chiunzo, Ciommo received Puccia as if she were Marziella, for he had not see her for such a long time that he no longer recognized her, and he immediately brought her be-fore the king. The king had her comb her hair, from which began to rain down those animals that are such enemies of truth that they never fail to offend the witnesses.[7] When he looked closely at her face he saw that she was breathing quite heavily after the effort of the journey, and that her mouth was so lathered up that it looked like a washbasin, and when he turned his eyes to the ground he saw a meadow of fetid weeds the sight of which made his stomach turn.

"And so he banished Puccia and her mother and, out of irritation, sent Ciommo to guard the court ducks. In a state of desperation over all of this and not understanding what had happened, Ciommo took the ducks into the countryside and, leaving them to wander as they liked on the seashore, went off to sit in a straw hut where he wept over his bad fortune until evening, when it was time to go home. But while the ducks ran on the shore every day, Marziella came out of the water and gave them royal almond paste[8] to eat and rose water to drink, until they grew as big as lambs and could barely keep their eyes open in all that fat. And when they returned in the evening to a little garden under the king's window, they began to sing:

> Quack, quack, quack
> the sun is beautiful, and so is the moon,
> but she who takes care of us is more beautiful still.

"After hearing this ducky music evening after evening, the king called for Ciommo and demanded to know where, how, and what he was feeding his ducks. Ciommo said to him, 'I feed them nothing but

---

7. Lice offend—*offendono* (but also bite) the witnesses—*testimoni* (but also testi-cles) (Rak 786).
8. A type of almond paste made in Naples, especially during the Christmas period (Rak 786).

fresh country grass.' The king, to whom this answer didn't sound right, sent one of his faithful servants after him so that he could see where he was taking the ducks. The servant followed in his footsteps and saw Ciommo go into the straw hut and leave the ducks on their own. The ducks headed in the direction of the seashore, and when they arrived, Marziella came out of the sea, and I don't believe that even the mother of that blind boy[9]—he who, as that poet said, wants no other alms but tears—was as beautiful when she emerged from the waves. When the king's servant saw this he was dumbfounded and beside himself, and ran back to his master to tell him of the lovely spectacle he had seen on the stage of the sea.

"The king's curiosity was given a jolt by this man's words, which instilled in him the desire to go see this lovely sight in person. And so the next morning—when the rooster, rabble-rouser[10] of the birds, incited them to arm all living beings against the Night—Ciommo went with the ducks to the usual place with the king following behind, never letting him out of his sight. The ducks arrived at the sea without Ciommo, who stopped at the same place as always, and the king saw Marziella come out and give the ducks a little basket of fancy cakes to eat and a little pot of rose water to drink. When she was done she seated herself on a rock and began to comb her hair, from which pearls and garnets fell by the handful, while in the meantime a cloud of flowers came out of her mouth and under her feet an Arabian carpet of lilies and violets took shape. Upon seeing this, the king sent for Ciommo and showed him Marziella, asking him if he knew this lovely girl. Ciommo recognized her and rushed over to embrace her and then, in the presence of the king, heard the whole story of Troccola's betrayal and how the envy of that hideous scourge had reduced this lovely fire of love to living in the waters of the sea.

"It's impossible to describe the pleasure the king felt upon acquiring such a beautiful jewel; he turned to Marziella's brother and told him that he had been perfectly right to heap praise on her and that he himself found that two-thirds or more of what Ciommo had told him was true, and that he thus considered her more than worthy of becoming his wife, if she were content to receive the scepter of his kingdom. 'Oh, if only the Sun in Leo willed it,' answered Marziella, 'and

9. Venus, mother of the blindfolded Cupid.

10. *capopuopolo* (Neap.): "The 'leaders of the people' who incited the lower classes were familiar to Neapolitans, who might remember, among others, Fucillo, whom the viceroy Pedro de Toledo had had strangled and exhibited to the rioters. More recent *capipopolo* took part in demonstrations at the time of the viceroy Ossuna, and were the predecessors of Masaniello [who would attempt to orchestrate a full-scale popular revolt in 1647]" (Croce 587).

I could come and pay homage to your crown as a servant girl! But can't you see this golden chain that I wear on my foot, by which the sorceress keeps me a prisoner? When I take too much air or stay too long on the seashore, she pulls me back in. And so she keeps me in rich servitude, enchained by gold.' 'What kind of solution might there be,' asked the king, 'to free you from the claws of that siren?' 'The solution would be,' said Marziella, 'to saw through this chain with a silent file and beat it out of here.' 'Wait for me tomorrow morning,' replied the king, 'for I plan to take care of this matter without delay and bring you home with me, where you'll be my right eye, the pupil of my heart, and the entrails of my soul.'

"After they exchanged a down payment on their love with a touch of their hands, Marziella went off into the water and he into the fire of his passion, and such a fire it was that it did not allow him an hour of rest the whole day. And when that black Moor of a Night came out to play *tubba catubba*[11] with the stars, he still was not able to close an eye, and he went about ruminating with the jaws of his memory on Marziella's beauty and debating with his thoughts on the marvels of her hair, the miracles of her mouth, and the wonders of her feet, and when he tested the gold of her graces on the touch-stone of his wisdom, he found that they measured twenty-four carats. He cursed the Night for being so slow to finish its embroidery work of stars, and he cursed the Sun for not arriving soon enough with its coach of light to enrich his home with the goods he desired and bring to his chambers a mine of gold that sent forth pearls and a shell of pearls that sent forth flowers.

"But as he was out at sea thinking of she who was in the sea, the Sun's sappers[12] began to clear the way for the passage of the army of its rays, and after he got dressed the king set off with Ciommo to the shore. When they found Marziella, the king took out the file they had brought and with his own hands sawed the chain off the foot of his loved one, at the same time, however, fabricating another, even stronger chain in his own heart. He then hoisted she who rode astride his heart to the saddle and spurred the horse on to the royal palace, where he had ordered that Marziella find all of the loveliest ladies of the town waiting to receive her and honor her as their mistress.

"They got married with great festivities, and the king requested that, along with the numerous barrels[13] that were burned in the light

11. Another dance similar to the Sfessania (see introduction to day 1 n6).
12. Sappers were regular members of armies.
13. "Incendiary barrels were among the most popular spectacles in nocturnal light shows" (Rak 787).

displays, Troccola herself be included in a little cask, as payment for the trick she had played on Marziella. He then sent for Luceta and gave her and Ciommo everything they needed to live a lord's life. Puccia was banished from the kingdom and spent the rest of her life begging; for not having sowed a little piece of pizza she had for the rest of her life a dearth of bread. For it is the will of the heavens that *those who lack compassion will never find it*."

8

THE SEVEN LITTLE DOVES

Eighth Entertainment of the Fourth Day

Seven brothers leave their home because their mother does not give birth to a daughter. She finally has one, and while they are awaiting the news and the sign, the midwife sends the wrong signal, on account of which they go wandering through the world. The sister grows up, searches for her brothers, finds them, and after various adventures they all return home rich.

The tale of the two little pizzas was truly a stuffed pizza, which everyone savored so much that they're still licking their fingers. But Paola was prepared to tell her tale, and the prince's command was like the eye of a wolf that took the words out of everyone's mouth, and so she began to speak in this manner: "When you do a favor you always find one; benevolence is the hook of friendship and the spike of love; if you don't sow you can't reap. Ciulla has given you an antipasto of an example, and I'll give you another as an after-dinner treat, as long as you remember what Cato said: 'Talk little at table.'[1] Thus do me the courtesy of lending me your ears, and may the heavens make them always grow, so that you can hear satisfying and pleasing things.

"There once was, in the town of Arzano,[2] a good woman who unloaded a son every year, until they got to be seven and you might have taken them for a seven-piped syrinx of the god Pan, each pipe bigger than the next. Once they lost their baby ears[3] the boys said to their mother, Iannetella, who was pregnant again, 'You should know, my dear mother, that if you do not have a girl, after so many boys, we've

---

AT 451: The Maiden Who Seeks Her Brother. Penzer notes similarities with a Bolognese story, as well as with Grimm 9 ("The Twelve Brothers"), 25 ("The Seven Ravens"), and 29 ("The Devil with the Three Golden Hairs") (2:71).

1. Cato Dionysius, *Disticha* 3.20: "In conversations among table companions make sure you keep a moderate tone; / do not be too chatty if you want your speech to be elegant and urbane" (cit. Croce 414).

2. A village, and now commune, in the province of Naples, district of Casoria (8.5 kilometers from Naples).

3. "A playful expression; as if children lost their ears as they do their teeth" (Croce 415).

made a firm resolution to leave this house to go out into the world and wander far and wide like a blackbird's children.' When the mother heard this bad news, she begged the heavens to strip her sons of this desire and to prevent her from losing seven such jewels. And when the hour of the delivery arrived, the sons said to Iannetella, 'We're going to retire up to that crag, the cliff right across from here. If you give birth to a boy put an inkstand and a pen on the window-sill, and if you give birth to a girl put a serving spoon and a distaff there, and if we see the signal for a girl we'll come home and spend the rest of our lives under your wings, but if we see the signal for a boy you can forget about us and give us the name of feathers!'

"Her sons left, and the heavens willed it that Iannetella gave birth to a lovely little daughter. But when the midwife was told to give the sign to the brothers, she was such a scatterbrain and a dolt that she put out the inkwell and the pen. At the sight of that, the seven broth-ers threw up their heels and walked so far that after three years of traveling they reached a wood—where the trees did a flower dance[4] to the sound of a river that played in counterpoint on the stones—in which there lived an ogre. Because this ogre's eyes had once been torn out by a woman when he was sleeping, he was such an enemy of the female sex that he ate up every one of them that he could get.

"When the young men reached the ogre's house, tired from their travels and weak with hunger, they asked him if he would have the compassion to give them a few bites of bread. The ogre answered that he would give them enough to live on if they were willing to serve him, and they wouldn't have to do anything but lead him around, one of them each day, like a little puppy. When the young men heard this, they felt like they had found a mother and a father, and they agreed to the terms and remained in the service of the ogre, who, once he had memorized their names, now called for Giangrazio, now Cecchitiello, now Pascale, now Nuccio, now Pone, now Pezillo, and now Carcavecchia, for these were the brothers' names. And he gave them a room on the ground floor of his house and supplied them with what they needed to stay alive.

"But in the meantime their sister had grown up, and, upon hearing that seven brothers of hers had left to go wandering through the world because of the midwife's forgetfulness and that no one had re-ceived any news of them since, she got a whim to go searching for them. And she did and said so much that her mother, in a daze after all those pleas, dressed the girl as a wayfarer and gave her permission to leave.

---

4. See tale 4.1 n5.

"She walked and walked, always asking everywhere she went if anyone had seen seven brothers, and she traveled through so many towns that she finally received news of them in a tavern, and after getting directions to the wood, one morning—when with the penknife of its rays the Sun was erasing the inkblots that Night had made on the paper of the sky—she found herself in that very place, where she was recognized with great joy by her brothers, who cursed the inkwell and the pen that had forged so many of their misfortunes. Once they had showered her with a thousand caresses, they warned her to stay locked up in a certain room so the ogre wouldn't see her and, moreover, to give a part of anything to eat that she happened to get hold of to a cat that lived in the room, or else it would harm her in some way. Cianna, for this was the sister's name, wrote this advice in the notebook of her heart, and she shared everything she had with the cat, always cutting fairly, always saying 'this is for me, this is for you, and this is for the daughter of the king,' always giving the cat its part right down to the fennel.

"Now it happened that the brothers had gone hunting on behalf of the ogre, and they left a basket of chickpeas for her to cook. While picking through them she had the bad luck to find a hazelnut, which wreaked havoc on her peace, for after she put it in her mouth without giving half of it to the cat, to spite her the animal ran to the hearth and peed on the fire until it went out. When Cianna saw this, she didn't know what to do, and she left the chambers against her brothers' orders and went into the ogre's apartment to ask for a little fire. When he heard the voice of a woman the ogre said, 'The master is always welcome![5] Wait just a moment, for you've found what you're looking for!' That said, he took a whetstone, greased it with oil, and began to sharpen his fangs. Cianna, who saw that the cart was off to a bad start, grabbed some embers, ran into her room, and propped the door shut, making sure to push bars, chairs, bedroom benches, little chests, rocks, and everything that was in the room against it.

"As soon as the ogre's teeth were sharpened he ran to the room, and, finding the door locked, he began to kick it and try to knock it down. At the sound of this the seven brothers arrived, and when they found themselves in the middle of this uproar and heard themselves accused by the ogre of being traitors because their room had become the Benevento[6] of his female enemies, Giangrazio, who was the oldest and had more good sense than the others, saw that the deal was about to go under and said to the ogre, 'We know nothing about this

---

5. Words of a game. See also introduction to day 2.
6. Traditional land of exile. See tale 1.5 n8.

matter, and it might just be that this accursed girl came into the room by mistake while we were out hunting. But since she has barricaded herself behind the door, come with me and I'll take you to a place where we can attack her without giving her any way to defend herself.' And he took the ogre by the hand and led him to a deep, deep ditch where they gave him a push and sent him crashing to the bottom. Then they grabbed a shovel that they found on the ground, covered him with earth, and, after getting their sister to open up, chewed her out for the mistake she had made and the danger she had placed herself in, and told her to use her head more wisely in the future and to take care not to pick grass around the place where the ogre was buried or else they would all become seven little doves. 'Heaven forbid,' answered Cianna, 'that I would do you this harm!' And after they took possession of the ogre's things and became masters of the whole house, they spent their time happily waiting for the winter to go by—for the Sun to give the Earth the present of a green skirt embroidered with flowers, for having taken possession of the house of Taurus[7]—so that they could set off on their journey to return home.

"It happened that while her brothers were gathering wood on the mountain to protect themselves from the cold that was increasing daily, a poor wayfarer arrived in that wood. Because he had made fun of a bogeyman sitting in a pine tree, the bogeyman had thrown down one of the fruits of the tree and hit him on the noodle, and he had a bump so enormous that the poor thing was screaming like a damned soul. Cianna came out when she heard the noise and felt pity for his suffering. She immediately picked a rosemary sprig from a bush that had grown on the ogre's grave and, with some chewed-up bread and salt, made him a plaster, and after giving him a little meal sent him on his way.

"While Cianna was setting the table as she waited for her brothers, in flew seven little doves, who said to her, 'O you who are the cause of all our ills, better if your hands had been paralyzed before you picked that damned rosemary, which will force us to fly off to the seashore! What did you do, eat cat's brain,[8] my sister, so that our warning slipped your mind? Here we are, turned into birds and exposed to the talons of kites, sparrow hawks, and goshawks; here we are, turned into companions to bee eaters, blackcaps, goldfinches, screech owls, lady finches, owls, magpies, crows, wheatears, titmice, wild capons, shrikes, larks, water hens, woodcocks, siskins, golden orioles, chaffinches, wrens, great tits, butcher birds, wrynecks, sky-

7. The sun enters the constellation of Taurus on April 20.
8. See tale 2.7 n24.

larks, greenfinches, flycatchers, hoopoes, scissortails, little grebes, sedge warblers, herons, wagtails, garganeys, tufted ducks, goslings, linnets, and woodpeckers! You've fixed things nice! We come back to our town to find nets and birdlime waiting for us! You treat the head of a wayfarer but break the heads of your seven brothers, and there will be no remedy for our ailment unless you go find the mother of Time,[9] who will teach you the way to rid us of our troubles.'

"Cianna felt like a skinned quail because of the mistake she had made and asked her brothers' pardon, offering to travel all over the world until she found the house of that old woman. She begged them to stay in the house at all times so that nothing bad might happen before she got back, and then she began to walk. And she never grew tired, and although she was on foot the desire to help her brothers carried her along like a pack mule, and she covered three miles an hour.

"When she had arrived at a shore—where the sea, with a smack of its waves, beat the rocks that wouldn't give the answers to the Latin exercises they had been assigned—she saw a large whale, which said to her, 'My dear young lady, what are you doing?' And she: 'I'm looking for the house of the mother of Time.' 'You know what you need to do?' replied the whale. 'Keep going straight down this coast, and at the first river you reach go upstream and you'll find someone who'll show you how to get there. But do me a favor: as soon as you find that kind old woman, ask her if she would do me the pleasure of coming up with a solution for swimming safely without hitting the rocks and ending up on the sand so often.' 'Just leave it to me,' said Cianna, and she thanked the whale for showing her the way and began to trot along the beach, and after a long journey she arrived at the river, which like a tax commissioner was pouring silver coins into the bank of the sea, and then took the path that went upstream. She came to a lovely countryside, where the meadow aped the sky with its green mantle starred with flowers; there she encountered a mouse that said to her, 'Where are you going all alone like that, lovely lady?' And she: 'I'm looking for the mother of Time.' 'You have too far to walk,' the mouse went on, 'but don't lose heart, for everything has an end. Just keep walking toward those mountains, which as the free lords of these fields ask that they be addressed by the title of "your highness," and you'll always have better news than what you're looking for. But do me a favor: as soon as you've reached the house you want, get that nice little old woman to tell you what kind of solution we might find for freeing ourselves from the tyranny of cats, and then command me as you wish, since I'll be your bought slave.'

---

9. Gaea (or Gea, or Gaia), Earth, was the mother of Cronus and the other Titans.

"After she promised him she would do this favor, Cianna set off toward the mountains, which although they looked close took forever to get to. Nonetheless, after she got there as well as she could she sat down, tired, on a stone, and noticed an army of ants carrying a large supply of wheat. One of them, turning to Cianna, said to her, 'Who are you? And where are you going?' Cianna, who was polite with everyone, said, 'I am an unfortunate girl, who because of something very important to me is looking for the house of the mother of Time.' 'Keep on walking,' said the ant, 'and when those mountains open out onto a large plain you'll get some new information. But do me a big favor: see that you find out from that old woman what we ants can do to live longer, for it seems to me that one of the crazy things about earthly affairs is that we acquire and accumulate so much to eat for such a short life, which, like an auctioneer's candle, is put out at the best bid that the years make.' 'Don't worry,' said Cianna, 'for I intend to repay you for the kindness you've shown me.'

"And when she had gone over those mountains, she found herself on a lovely plain across which she walked for quite a while until she came to a large oak tree[10]—witness to antiquity, bonbon[11] of a once-happy bride, morsel given by Time to the present century, so bitter over lost sweetness. The tree, forming lips from its bark and a tongue from its pith, said to Cianna, 'Where, oh where are you going all breathless like that, my girl? Come under my shade and rest yourself.' And she, giving it her many thanks, excused herself and explained that she was in a hurry to find the mother of Time. When the oak heard this it said, 'You're not very far away; before you walk for another day you'll see a house on top of a mountain where you'll find what you're looking for. But if you have as much kindness as you have beauty, try to discover what I might do to get back my lost honor, for I've gone from being the nourishment of great men to food for pigs.' 'Leave this matter to Cianna,' she answered. 'I'll see that I serve you well.'

"That said, she left and walked on without ever taking a rest until she reached the foot of a spoilsport of a mountain that went around with its head in the clouds just to bother them. There she found a little

---

10. The oak is worshiped worldwide; according to Virgil, e.g., the human race originated from it. It is also a symbol of strength and triumph, characteristics that Basile sees as sorely lacking in his own time.

11. *confiette* (Neap.): not paper confetti, but white sugared almonds, distributed (and sometimes thrown) at weddings in Italy. "Plaster imitations were used at Carnival, being known by the name of *coriandoli*. As time went on these *coriandoli* gave place to the bits of colored paper that we, quite erroneously, still call confetti. Our word 'confectionary,' however, preserves the original meaning" (Penzer 2:66).

old man who, tired of walking, had gone to sleep in the middle of some hay. When he saw Cianna he immediately recognized her as the one who had medicated his bump; and when he heard what the girl was looking for he told her that he was bringing Time the rent on the land that he had cultivated, and that Time was a tyrant who had usurped everything in the world and wanted taxes from everyone, in particular from men of his age. And since he had received a favor from Cianna's hand, he wanted to pay her back a hundred times over by offering her a few good words of caution having to do with her ascent of this mountain. He was sorry not to be able to accompany her there, but his age, condemned to descend more readily than to climb, forced him to remain on the lower slopes of those mountains where he would settle his accounts with the clerks of Time, which are the troubles, misfortunes, and infirmities of life, and pay his debt to Nature.

"And so he said to her, 'Now listen carefully, my dear, innocent girl: you must know that on top of that mountain you'll find a crumbling house that was built before anyone remembers. The walls are cracking, the foundation rotting, the doors worm-eaten, the furniture moldy: in short, everything is consumed and destroyed. On one side you can see broken columns, on the other shattered statues; nothing remains intact but a quartered coat of arms over the door, where you can see a serpent biting its tail, a stag, a crow, and a phoenix.[12] Upon entering you'll see silent files, saws, scythes, and pruning hooks on the ground, and hundreds and hundreds of cauldrons full of ashes, labeled like apothecary jars with names such as Corinth, Saguntum, Carthage, Troy, and a thousand other cities[13] gone bad whose ashes are kept by Time in memory of his exploits. Now as soon as you get near the house, hide somewhere until you see Time come out, and when he leaves, you slip in. In the house you'll find a very old woman whose beard touches the ground and whose hump reaches the sky; her hair, like the tail of a dapple-gray horse, covers her heels, and her face is like a lettuce-leaf collar,[14] the folds stiff with the starch of the years. She will be sitting on a clock that's fastened to the wall, and since her eyelids are so heavy that they bury her eyes she won't be able to see you. Once you're inside, take off the clock's weights right away, then call the old woman and beg her to grant you what you wish. She will immediately call her son and tell him to eat you, but since the clock his mother is sitting on is missing its weights

---

12. "Symbols of return, speed, and rebirth" (Croce 422).
13. "All of the great cities of antiquity, whose power was consumed by Time" (Rak 812).
14. From the Spanish *cuello de lechuguillas* (Rak 812).

he won't be able to walk, and she'll be forced to give you what you want. But don't believe any of the oaths that she swears to unless she swears on the wings of her son. In that case you can believe her; do what she tells you to do, and you'll be satisfied.'

"As he was saying this the poor little soul disintegrated like a corpse in a crypt when it sees the light of day. Cianna took the ashes and mixed them with a small measure of tears, made a grave, and buried them, praying to the heavens that they might find peace and rest. And after climbing the mountain, which left her out of breath, she waited until Time came out of the house.

"He was an old man with a very long beard, and he wore an ancient cloak that was covered with little sewn-on labels bearing the names of this person and that; he had large wings and ran so fast that she lost sight of him at once. When she entered his mother's house she was frightened by the sight of the old woman's black bark and, immediately grabbing the weights, she told the old woman what she wanted. The woman emitted a shriek and called her son, but Cianna told her, 'You can hit your head against these walls all you like, but it's certain that you won't see your son while I'm holding these weights!' The old woman saw that her way was blocked, and to lure her in began saying, 'Let go of them, my darling, don't stop my son's journey, something that no living man in the world has ever done! Let go of them, may God help you, and I promise you, on the acid that my son uses to corrode all things, that I will not harm you.' 'You're wasting your time,' answered Cianna. 'You'll have to do better than that if you want me to let them go.' 'I swear to you, on those teeth that gnaw on all mortal things, that I will let you know whatever you want.' 'You're not going to get a crumb out of me,' replied Cianna. 'I know you're tricking me!' And the old woman: 'All right, then! I swear to you, on those wings that fly everywhere, that I want to do you a bigger favor than you can imagine!' Cianna let go of the weights and kissed the old woman's hand, which smelled of mold and stank of must. Seeing the good manners of the girl, the old woman said to her, 'Hide behind that door, and when Time arrives I'll get him to say what you want to know. And as soon as he goes out again—since he never stays still in one place—you can slip out. But don't let him hear you, for he is so greedy that he spares not even his own children, and when he has nothing else he eats himself and then regerminates.'

"After Cianna did what the old woman told her to, Time arrived, light and agile, and very quickly nibbled at everything he could get his hands on, even the plaster on the walls. When he was about to leave his mother told him everything that she had heard from Cianna, begging him, in exchange for the milk that she had given him, to answer, point by point, all the questions that were asked of him. After a thousand entreaties her son answered, 'You may tell the tree that it can never be dear to people while it keeps treasures buried under its roots; the mouse that they will never be safe from cats unless they attach a little bell to the cats' legs so that they can hear them when they come; the ant that they will live for a hundred years if they can do without flying, for when an ant wants to die it puts on wings; the whale to keep its spirits up and count among its friends the sea mouse,[15] which will always be its guide and keep it from going the wrong way; and the little doves that when they build a nest on top of the column of richness they will return to their previous state.'

"That said, Time began to run his usual course and Cianna, taking leave of the old woman, went down the mountain at the same moment that the seven doves arrived, following in the footsteps of their sister. Tired from such a long flight, they went and perched on the horns of a dead ox, and no sooner had they put their feet down than they became the handsome young men they had been before and, marveling over this fact, they heard the answer Time had given and understood that the horns, as the symbol of the goat, were the column of richness referred to by Time. And after celebrating their happiness with their sister, they set out on the same road that Cianna had traveled.

"When they found the oak tree and told it what they had heard from Time, the tree begged them to take the treasure out from under it, since this was why its acorns had lost their reputation. The seven brothers found a hoe in a nearby garden and dug until they found a large jar full of gold coins, which they divided in eight parts among themselves and their sister in order to carry them more easily. But then, since they were tired from their journey and from the weight, they went to sleep next to a hedge. And when a bunch of bandits[16] passed by and saw those poor souls sleeping with their heads on the bundles of coins, they tied their hands and feet to some trees and took off with the beans, leaving them to lament not only the wealth that had no sooner been found than had slipped through their hands but their life itself, since without the hope of help they ran the risk of being consumed by either their own hunger or the hunger of some wild beast. And while they were wailing over their unfortunate

---

15. "Pliny (*Natural History* IX, 88), discussing animal fiends and enemies, writes of the 'exemplary friendship' between the whale and the mouse" (cit. Croce 587).

16. "There was a fresh outbreak of banditry in the Kingdom of Naples during the last decades of the 16th century, and stories of banditry circulated widely in chapbooks of the time" (Rak 813).

. . . e compresero che lo cuorno, comme simmolo de la capra, fosse la colonna de la ricchezza azzennata da lo Tiempo. [. . . and they understood that the horns, as the symbol of the goat, were the column of richness referred to by Time.]

plight, along came the mouse, and when it heard Time's answer, out of gratitude for the service done it gnawed through the ropes that bound them and set them free.

"After walking for a good while longer they met up with the ant in the road, who, once it had heard Time's advice, asked Cianna why she was so out of spirits and wan. When Cianna told of the troubles they had had and the way they had been swindled by the thieves, the ant answered, 'Hush, for now I have the opportunity to pay you back for the favor I received from you! You should know that while I was carrying a load of wheat underground I saw a place where those murderous dogs stash their spoils. They've made a number of cavities under an old building, where they stow all their stolen goods, and now that they've gone off for some more loot I want to accompany you and show you where it is so you can get back what is yours.' That said, it set off on a road that led to some dilapidated houses, where it showed the seven brothers the entrance to one of the ditches. They lowered Giangrazio down, since he was more courageous than the others; he found all the money that had been stolen from them, brought it out, and then they set off toward the seashore.

"There they found the whale and told it of the good suggestions offered by Time, the father of all advice, and while they were going on about their travels and everything that had happened to them, the rogues suddenly sprang out before them, armed to the teeth, for they had followed in the trail of their footsteps. At the sight of this Cianna and her brothers said, 'Alas, this time there's not going to be a hair left of these hapless souls; here come the bandits now, arms in hand, and they'll skin us alive!' 'Have no fear,' answered the whale. 'I'd pull you out of fire to pay you back for the loving kindness you showed me! Get on my back and I'll take you right off to a safe place.'

"The poor things, who saw their enemies at their back and the water up to their necks, got on the whale, which swam away from the rocks and brought them to within sight of Naples. Not feeling safe about putting them ashore for fear of getting beached, the whale said, 'Where do you want me to leave you, along the Amalfi coast?' And Giangrazio answered, 'See if we can avoid doing that, my lovely fish, because I wouldn't willingly get off in any of those places; in Massa they say "offer your greeting and move on," in Sorrento "clench your teeth," in Vico "take some bread with you," in Castellamare "neither friends nor buddies." '[17]

"And so to please him the whale changed course and went off in

---

17. "Playful proverbs, still in existence today, referring to the various towns of the Sorrento peninsula" (Croce 426).

the direction of the Salt Rock,[18] where it left them, and when the first boat of fishermen came by they asked to be brought to land. They then returned to their town healthy, beautiful, and rich, and were a comfort to their mother and father; and they enjoyed, thanks to Cianna's goodness, a happy life, which demonstrated the authenticity of the ancient saying: *Do good whenever you can, and then forget about it.*"

---

18. "Off the cape of Posillipo various maps of the 18th century indicate a rock with the name of 'Pietra salata,' probably the one Basile is thinking of. Basile himself seems to have been born in Posillipo, since in his *Avventurose disavventure*, which is set in Posillipo, he says: 'I first opened my eyes to daylight on this very shore'" (Croce 587).

9

THE CROW

Ninth Entertainment of the Fourth Day

*To please Milluccio, the king of Shady Thicket, his brother Ien-
nariello takes a long journey, and when he brings his brother back
what he had desired and frees him from death, he is condemned to
death himself. But in order to prove his innocence he becomes a
marble statue, and then due to a strange incident he returns to his
former state and lives happily.*

If I had a hundred reeds in my throat, a bronze chest, and a thousand
tongues of steel,[1] I would not be able to describe how much Paola's
tale was appreciated when it was heard how none of the good deeds
that Cianna performed had gone unrewarded. And so they had to increase the dose of entreaties to Ciommetella so that she would tell her
tale, since she had lost her confidence about pulling the cart of the
prince's orders as well as the others did. Even so, she had no choice
but to obey, and in order not to ruin the game she began to speak in
this manner: "The proverb that says 'we see crooked and judge
straight' is truly a great one, but so difficult to put to use that few
men have good enough judgment to hit the nail on the head. On the
contrary: in the sea of human affairs most are freshwater fishermen
who catch only crabs, and those who think they can take more accurate measure of what passes through their heads are the ones most
likely to be mistaken. And so it happens that people dash around
wildly, labor away blindly, think upside down, act rashly, judge as if
it were a game of smash-the-top,[2] and, most of the time, with a bad
tumble from a good resolution to a gross mistake, buy themselves a
commonsense repentance, as did the king of Shady Thicket, about

AT 516: Faithful John. This tale bears similarities to Grimm 6 ("Faithful Johannes"),
has variants in Eastern collections (see Penzer 2:81), and was the source of Carlo
Gozzi's *Il corvo*, a theatrical fairy tale first performed in Venice in 1761.
  1. Parody of the verses pronounced by Tisiphone, one of the Furies and the virgin
soothsayer appointed by Hecate to guard Avernus: "If I had a hundred tongues and a
hundred mouths, / and an iron voice, I would not be able to describe all the types of
misdeeds there are, / nor to number all the kinds of suffering" (*Aeneid* 6.625–27; cit.
Guarini and Burani 485).
  2. See tale 4.2 n28.

whose adventures you'll hear if you use the doorbell of courtesy to call me from inside the revolving door of modesty, and then lend me your ear for a bit.

"Now it is said that there once was a king of Shady Thicket named Milluccio, who was so taken by hunting that he neglected the most vital things in his state and his home so that he could follow the tracks of a hare or the flight of a lark. And he continued down this road so far that one day fortune took him to a wood that had put together a tightly serried squadron of land and trees to keep the horses of the Sun from breaking through. Here, on top of a splendid piece of marble, he found a freshly killed crow.

"When the king saw the bright red blood that had spattered the brilliant white stone, he heaved a great sigh and said, 'O heavens, couldn't I have a wife as white and red as that stone, with hair and eyelashes as black as the feathers of this crow?'[3] And he became so immersed in this thought that for a good while he acted out *The Menaechmi*[4] with the stone, and he looked like a marble statue that was making love with that other marble. And as he drove this dismal whim into his head and fed it with the pap of desire, at the snap of a finger he went from a toothpick to a bean pole, a jujube to an Indian squash, a barber's warming pan to a glassblower's furnace, and a dwarf to a giant, so that he thought of nothing else but the image of that thing set in his heart like a stone in stone.[5] Wherever he turned his eyes he always found the same form that he carried in his breast and, forgetting all his other business, he had nothing but that marble in his head. He had grown so thin over the stone that he was dwindling down hair by hair, since the stone was the mill that ground his life, the porphyry[6] where the colors of his days were mixed, the flint where the match of his soul was lit, the magnet that attracted him, and, lastly, the stone that had taken root in his gall bladder and gave him no rest.

"When Iennariello, his brother, saw him so waxen and sallow, he said, 'My brother, what has come over you? Your pain is lodged in your eyes and your desperation seated atop the pallid signboard of your face! What has happened to you? Talk, open your heart to your brother! The stink of coal in a closed room infects those within; pow-

---

3. The motif of desiring another person (usually a spouse or child) as red, white, and black as certain elements that appear in a character's surroundings (blood, animals, rocks, and so forth) also appears in 5.9, as well as in Chrétien de Troyes's story of Perceval and the Grimms' "Snow White," among others.

4. Plautus's comedy. See introduction to day 1 n17.

5. "As in inlay work" (Croce 428).

6. The stone used by painters to grind their pigments.

der compressed inside a mountain sends fragments of rock flying through the air; scabies shut up inside veins makes the blood rot; wind held inside the body generates flatulence and bad colics. So then, open your mouth and tell me what you're feeling, and at the end you can rest assured that wherever I can I'll put a thousand lives on the line if I can be of use to you.'

"Chewing on words and sighs, Milluccio thanked him for his kind love and told him that he had no doubts about his affection, but that there was no cure for his illness since it was born of a stone on which he had sown his desires without the hope of any fruit, a stone from which he could not hope for even one mushroom of happiness, a stone of Sisyphus[7] that pushed his plans up a mountain and, once it got to the top, sent them rolling down—crash!—to the bottom. Finally, after a thousand prayers he told him everything about his love.

"When Iennariello heard the matter, he comforted him as best he could and told him to cheer up and not be dragged down by that melancholic humor, for to content him he was determined to travel through the world until he found a woman who was the original of that stone. And he immediately armed a large ship full of merchandise, dressed himself as a merchant, and set off in the direction of Venice[8]—mirror of Italy, shelter of virtuous men, ledger of the marvels of Art and Nature—where he had a pass prepared that would allow him to travel to the East. Then he set sail in the direction of Cairo, and when he entered the city and saw a man carrying a beautiful falcon, he immediately bought it to take back to his brother, who was a hunter. A little while later he encountered someone else with a marvelous horse, and he bought this, too, and then went to a tavern to refresh himself from the labors he had undergone at sea.

"But the next morning—when the army of stars was charged by the general of light and removed its tents from the stockade of the sky, abandoning its post—Iennariello began to walk around the city, setting his eyes on everything like a lynx and looking at this woman and that, to see if by chance he might find the resemblance with a stone on a face of flesh. And as he wandered here and there without direction, always turning and looking around like a thief afraid of cops, he came across a tramp wearing a hospital of plasters and a junk shop of rags, who said to him, 'My good man, what's wrong? Why do you look so bewildered?' 'I should tell you my business?' an-

7. See eclogue 1 ("The Crucible") n5.
8. Venice is also praised in 3.8 and was often the subject of similar literary accolades. Basile was quite familiar with the city since as a young man he had spent a number of years there and served as a soldier in its territories.

swered Iennariello. 'Now I've really baked my bread, if I start telling my side of things to cops!' 'Just a minute, my handsome young man,' replied the tramp. 'Human flesh is not sold by weight! If Darius had not told his troubles to a stable boy, he would not have become master of Persia.[9] So then, it wouldn't be such a strange thing if you told a poor tramp your business, for there's no stick so thin it can't be used to clean your teeth.' Iennariello, who heard the poor little fellow speaking in such a well-ordered and sensible manner, told him what had brought him to that town and what he was so diligently searching for. When the tramp had listened to this, he answered, 'Now you see, my son, how you need to take every person into account! For although I'm trash I'll still be good for fertilizing the garden of your hopes. Now listen: with the excuse of begging for alms I'll go knock on the door of a beautiful young woman, the daughter of a necromancer. Open your eyes wide; look at her, contemplate her, study her, consider her, take her measure, and you'll find the image of the woman your brother desires.'

"Saying this, he knocked on the door of a house not far from there, where a girl named Liviella came out and threw him a piece of bread, and as soon as Iennariello saw her it seemed to him that this was a building made according to the plan given to him by Milluccio. He gave the tramp a nice offering and sent him off, and went back to the tavern and disguised himself as a vendor of notions. Then he took two little cases filled with all the world's bounty and walked by Liviella's house hawking his wares until she called him over. And after taking a look at all the beautiful hairnets, veils, ribbons, headkerchiefs, laces and patches, linens, buckles, pins, pots of rouge, and bonnets he had, and inspecting all the merchandise and then inspecting it again, she finally told him to show her some other beautiful thing, and he answered, 'My lady, in this case I have ordinary and low-priced things, but if you deigned to come to my ship I would show you things that are out of this world, for I have beautiful treasures worthy of a great lord.' Liviella did not lack in curiosity, and so as not to compromise the nature of women she said to him, 'Upon my word, if my father weren't away I'd like to stop by.' 'Even more reason for coming,' replied Iennariello, 'since he might not grant you this pleasure. I promise I'll show you things so lavish they'll drive you mad. Such necklaces and earrings; such belts and corsets; such combs, bracelets, and lacework! In short, I intend to make your eyes pop out of your head.'

---

9. The story of Darius, king of Persia from 521 to 486 BC, and his groom Oebares is told by Herodotus (*Histories* 3.85–87; cit. Croce 430).

"Upon hearing of this grand display, Liviella called for a friend to accompany her and set off for the ship. Once she was aboard, Iennariello kept her enchanted by showing her the many beautiful things he had brought with him, at the same time that he cleverly had the anchor pulled and the sails unfurled, and before Liviella lifted her eyes from the merchandise and saw that they were far from land, the ship had already traveled several miles. When she became aware of the deceit it was too late, and she began to act like Olympia,[10] but the other way around, since if the latter lamented that she had been left on a rock Liviella lamented that she had left the rocks.

"But then Iennariello told her who he was, where he was taking her, and of the fortune that awaited her, and, moreover, described to her Milluccio's beauty, valor, virtue, and, finally, the love with which he would receive her. And he did and said so much that she quieted down and even begged the wind to take her quickly to see the colors of the drawing that Iennariello had sketched for her. But as they were thus sailing cheerfully on, they suddenly heard the waves whispering under the ship, and although they were speaking in a low voice, the ship's captain, who could understand, shouted, 'Everyone on the alert; there's a storm coming, and let's pray to God that it spares us!' At these words the testimony of a gust of wind was added, and then the sky was covered with clouds and the sea filled with breakers. And since the waves were curious to know everyone else's business, they came aboard the ship without being invited to the wedding. One of the men tried to bail the water out with a ladle and a little tub, one tried to evict it with a pump, and while all the sailors, seeing as it was a matter of their lives, either took the helm or worked the sails or the sheets, Iennariello climbed up to the crow's nest with a long-distance glass to see if he could catch sight of some land where they might set anchor.

"And as he was measuring the distance of a hundred miles with the two spans of the glass, he saw a male and a female dove fly by, and when they landed on the lateen mast the male said, 'Coo coo,' and the female answered, 'What's the matter, my husband, why are you complaining?' The male dove said, 'This poor prince bought a falcon, but as soon as it is in the hands of his brother it will take out his eyes; and whoever does not bring it to him or warns him will turn into a piece of marble!' That said, he went back to crying 'coo coo,' and the female dove said to him again, 'You're still complaining? Is

---

10. The reference is to the tears of Olimpia, abandoned by Bireno, in Ludovico's *Orlando furioso* (10.25–33). The source here is, however, Giambattista della Porta's *L'Olimpia* (1589) (Rak 836).

there some other news?' And the male dove: 'There is one more little matter: he also bought a horse, and the first time his brother rides it he will break his neck; and whoever does not bring it to him or warns him will turn into a piece of marble. Coo coo!' 'Oh, dear, so many coo coos!' the female dove began saying again. 'What else do we have on the cutting board?' And the male dove said, 'He's bringing his brother a beautiful wife, but the first night he goes to bed with her they will both be eaten up by a terrible dragon; and whoever does not bring her to him or warns him will turn into a piece of marble!'

"That said, the storm ended and the sea's ill temper and the wind's anger passed, but a much larger tempest began to rise in Iennariello's breast on account of what he had heard, and more than a few times he wanted to throw all those things into the sea so that he wouldn't be carrying the cause of his brother's ruin. But on the other hand he thought of himself, and of how the first cause of it all originated with him, and he was afraid that if he didn't bring those things to his brother or if he warned him, he would turn into marble. And so he decided to pay more attention to his proper name than to his family name, since his shirt was tighter than his jacket.

"Upon his arrival at the port of Shady Thicket his brother, having seen the ship return, was waiting for him on the shore with great joy. And when he saw that he had brought the woman he held in his heart and compared one face with the other and saw that there wasn't a hair of difference, he felt such joy that that the excessive load of happiness nearly killed him under its burden. Embracing his brother with great delight, he said to him, 'What is this falcon you have on your fist?' And Iennariello said to him, 'I bought it to give to you.' And Milluccio answered, 'It truly appears that you love me, for you attempt to humor my every whim; if you had brought me a treasure you certainly couldn't have pleased me more than with this falcon!' And as he was about to take it in his hand, Iennariello quickly chopped its head off with a big knife he carried at his side. At this action the king remained stunned and considered the brother of his who had committed this rash act to be crazy, but so as not to disturb the happiness of his return he said not a word.

"When he saw the horse and asked whose it was, he heard that it was his, and had the desire to ride it; but as the stirrups were being held for him, Iennariello cut its legs clean off with a cleaver. This made the king fume, since it seemed to him that his brother had done it out of spite, and his guts began to churn. But it seemed to be the wrong time to be resentful about it, for he didn't want to put a bad taste in the bride's mouth right from the start, she whom he never tired of gazing at and holding by the hand. When they arrived at the royal palace he invited all the lords and ladies of the city to a lovely feast, where in the main hall could be seen a veritable school of cavalry performing curvets and caracoles, and a group of fillies dressed to look like women. And when the dance was over and they had polished off a huge banquet, they went to bed.

"Iennariello had no thought in his head but to save his brother's life, and he hid behind the couple's bed and waited vigilantly to see when the dragon would come. And at midnight a hideous dragon did indeed enter the room, sending out flames from its eyes and smoke from its mouth; it would have made a good middleman for the sale of apothecary's wormwood,[11] so great was the terror the sight of it inspired. When Iennariello saw this, he began to thrash about and deliver blows right and left with a Damascus blade that he had put under his clothes, and among the other blows, he landed one so powerful that it cut one of the columns of the king's bed in two.[12] At the sound of this his brother awoke and the dragon disappeared.

"When Milluccio saw the knife in Iennariello's hand and the halved column he began to shout, 'Hey men, hey people, hallo there, help! Help, this brother of mine is a traitor! He's come to kill me!' At these cries a number of assistants who had been sleeping in the antechamber came running, and when Iennariello had been tied up, the king sent him straight off to prison, and the next morning—as soon as the Sun opened its bank to pay out the deposit of light to the creditors of the day—he summoned his council and told them what had happened, which was consistent with the malevolence demonstrated when Iennariello had killed the falcon and the horse to spite him. They sentenced him to death, and even Liviella's prayers were not strong enough to soften the heart of the king, who said, 'You do not love me, my wife, since you have more esteem for your brother-in-law than for my life! You saw that dog of an assassin with your own eyes when he came to make mincemeat of me with a blade that could have split a hair in two, and if that column of the bed hadn't protected me—column of my life!—you would be a bald widow[13] by this time!'

"Thus speaking, he ordered the sentence to be executed. When Iennariello heard the decree served and saw himself reduced to such a terrible state for having done good, he knew not what to think of his affairs: if he said nothing it was bad; if he said something it was worse. It's awful to get scabies but worse to get ringworm, and no

---

11. A plant used as a remedy for intestinal worms (Rak 836).

12. "One of the columns that would have supported the canopy of a typical Neapolitan bed of this period" (Rak 836).

13. I.e., with a shaved head. See tale 2.6 n14.

No bruttissemo dragone . . . lo quale sarria stato buono de sanzaro a fare vennere tutta la semmentella de li speziale, pe lo terrore che portava a la vista. [A hideous dragon . . . it would have made a good middleman for the sale of apothecary's wormwood, so great was the terror the sight of it inspired.]

matter what he did it was like falling from a tree into a wolf's mouth: if he remained silent he would lose his neck under a sword; if he talked he would end his days inside a stone. Finally, after various squalls of consultations with himself, he decided to reveal the whole business to his brother, for since he had to die in any case, he thought it a better solution to inform him of the truth and end his days with the title of innocent than to keep the truth to himself and be banished from the world as a traitor.

"And so Iennariello sent word to the king that he wanted to speak with him about something important for the well-being of the state, and was brought to his presence. He began with a long preamble on the love that he had always had for him, then went on to the trick played on Liviella in order to satisfy his brother's desires, then to what he had heard from the doves about the falcon, and how, therefore, he had brought it to him so that he would not turn into a piece of marble himself, and how he had killed it without revealing the secret so that he wouldn't have to see his brother without eyes. As he was saying this he felt his legs hardening and becoming marble, and when he went on in the same manner to tell of the horse, you could see him turning to stone up to his waist and growing miserably rigid,[14] something for which he would have paid cold cash at another time; now, instead, his heart was crying. He finally got to the part about the dragon, at which he turned completely to stone and remained standing there in the middle of the hall like a statue. When the king saw this, he blamed his own error and the rash judgment he had passed on a brother who was so good and loving; he remained in mourning for more than a year, and whenever he thought of him he cried a river of tears.

"In the meantime Liviella gave birth to two sons who were two of the most beauteous things in the world. After a few months, one day the queen had gone out to amuse herself in the countryside and the king found himself with the children in the middle of that same hall. As he was gazing with piddling eyes upon the statue, reminder of his own foolishness that had taken the flower of all men away from him, a big old man came into the hall. His mane of hair covered his shoulders and his beard blanketed his chest, and bowing to the king he said, 'How much would your royal Highness pay if this fine brother of yours were to return to his previous state?' And the king answered, 'I would pay my entire kingdom!' 'This is not something,' replied the old man, 'that requires a payment in riches, but since it is a matter of life it must be paid for with another life.'

---

14. I.e., he had an erection. For a similar motif, see Giambattista Marino's poem "Amori notturni" (in the *Lira* collection; cit. Croce 436).

"In part out of the love he had for Iennariello, in part because he felt guilty for the harm that had been done him, the king answered, "Believe me, my good sir, I would exchange my life for his life, and as long as he comes out from inside that stone, I would be happy to be stuck inside a stone myself.' When the old man heard this he said, 'Without putting your life to such a test, since it takes so much hard work to grow a man, the blood of these children of yours smeared on the marble would be enough to revive him immediately.' At these words the king said, 'You can always make more children! As long as the mold for these little dolls still exists, more can be made, but let me have my brother back, for I can never hope to have another!'[15] Saying this, he made a miserable sacrifice of two innocent kids before an idol of stone, and after he smeared the statue with their blood it immediately came to life and was embraced by the king, and there was more rejoicing than can be described.

"At the very moment those poor creatures were being put into a casket so that they could be buried with the honor they deserved, the queen returned home. The king had his brother hide, and said to his wife, 'What would you pay, my heart, to have my brother return to life?' 'I would pay,' answered Liviella, 'this whole kingdom.' And the king replied, 'Would you give the blood of your children?' 'Not that,' answered the queen. 'I would not be so cruel as to tear out the pupils of my eyes with my own hands!' 'Alas,' resumed the king, 'I slaughtered the children so that I could see my brother alive! That was, you see, the price of Iennariello's life!' As he said this he showed her the children in the casket, and when she saw that bitter spectacle she screamed like a crazy woman and said, 'O my children; O staffs of this life; O eyes of this heart; O fountains of my blood! Who filthied the windows of the Sun in this way? Who bled the principal vein of my life without a physician's license? Alas, my children; my children, my cracked hope, clouded light, poisoned sweetness, lost support! You were pierced by the iron, and I am run through by pain! You suffocate in blood; I drown in tears! Alas, you have killed a mother to give life to an uncle, for I can no longer weave the canvas of my days without you, lovely counterweights on the loom of this black life! The organ of my voice will crack now that the bellows have been removed! O children, O children, why don't you answer your mommy, who once put her blood in your bodies and is now pouring it out to

15. Penzer notes that the choice of a brother to survive, over a husband or a child, is found in Greek and Indian classics: the episode of Intaphernes in Herodotus, *Histories* 3.19; Antigone's explanation of her actions at her brother's death (Sophocles, *Antigone* 909ff.); and so forth (2:81–82).

you from her eyes? But since my fate indicates that the fountain of my amusements is dry, there is no longer any reason for me to live in this world, and I will follow in your footsteps and come looking for you!'

"As she was saying this she ran to a window and was about to jump out when at that very moment her father entered through the same window in a cloud, and said to her, 'Stop, Liviella, for after taking a journey and performing three services I have had my revenge on Iennariello, who came to my home to steal my daughter from me, by forcing him to stay inside a stone for so many months like a date mussel.[16] I have been repaid for the bad act you committed, when you allowed a ship to lead you astray without any respect for me, by having you see two children, or rather two jewels, slaughtered by their own father; and I have mortified the king for falling victim to a pregnant woman's whim by making him first the criminal judge of his brother and then the executioner of his children. But since I wanted to shave you, not flay you, I intend for all the poison to turn back into marzipan. So go get your children, and my grandchildren, who are more beautiful than ever, and you, Milluccio, embrace me, for I accept you as my son-in-law and as my son, and I forgive Iennariello his offenses, since he did what he did to serve such a worthy brother.'

"That said, the children came in, and their grandfather couldn't get his fill of hugging and kissing them. Iennariello partook in this happiness, too, as a third party, since after jumping through so many hoops he was now swimming in macaroni broth. But even with all the pleasures that he experienced in life, the dangers he had been through never left his mind; he reflected on his brother's mistake and on how careful one must be in order not to fall into a ditch, since *every human judgment is false and twisted*."

---

16. "The *pholas dactilu,* or lithophagous mollusk" (Croce 438).

10

PRIDE PUNISHED

Tenth Entertainment of the Fourth Day

The king of Lovely Land is spurned by Cinziella, daughter of the king of Long Furrow. After he avenges himself fiercely, reducing her to a miserable condition, he takes her for his wife.

If Ciommetella hadn't made the wizard appear quickly to throw water on the fire, everyone's spirits would have been squeezed so tightly by pity for Liviella that it would have been hard for them to breathe. But they were all comforted by the poor girl's comfort, and once their souls were put to rest they waited for Iacova to enter the field with the livery of her tale. And she raced with this lance toward the target of their desire:[1] "Those who pull too hard on something break it, and those who look for trouble find trouble and misfortune; if you go to the top of a mountain and fall off, it's your own fault, as you will hear from the story of a woman who, as a result of her distaste for crowns and scepters, came to be in need of a stable. Even so, the concussions sent by the heavens always come with a poultice, since there has never been a punishment without a caress, nor a club without a piece of bread.[2]

"It is said that there once was a king, the king of Long Furrow, who had a daughter named Cinziella. She was as beautiful as a moon, but she hadn't a dram of beauty that wasn't counterbalanced by a pound of pride,[3] so that she gave heed to no one, and it was impossible for her poor father, who wanted to get her settled, to find a

---

AT 900: King Thrushbeard. This tale is quite similar to Grimm 52 ("King Thrushbeard"); see also Straparola 1.4 ("Tebaldo and Doralice") and 9.1 ("Galafro, King of Spain"), and Gonzenbach 18.

1. A contest similar to that of the ring. See tale 2.10 n19. The target mentioned here (*vastaso*) is that of the *quintana*, "a joust of medieval origin in which the competitors, armed with lances, galloped on horseback towards a revolving silhouette dressed like a Saracen and tried to hit its shield without getting knocked off their horses by the club attached to the other hand of the figure" (Guarini and Burani 498).

2. Allusion to the proverb "Clubs and bread make children nice; bread without clubs make them crazy" (Croce 440).

3. Two measures of weight in use at the time in various European countries. The dram was the eighth part of an ounce, the pound slightly over 300 grams (Rak 852).

husband, no matter how good or great he might be, that could satisfy her.

"Among the many princes that had come to ask for her hand in marriage was the king of Lovely Land, who left nothing undone in his attempts to earn Cinziella's affection. But the more he weighed the scales of his servitude in her favor, the more she measured out crooked rewards; the more he offered her his love at a good price, the more there was a shortage of desire at her end; the more generous of soul he was, the more stingy of heart was she. And not a day went by without the poor man exclaiming, 'When, O cruel lady, after so many melons of hope that I've found to be white as squash, will I be able to taste a red one? When, O cruel bitch, will the tempests of your cruelty calm? When will I have a favorable wind and be able to direct the rudder of my plans into this lovely port? When, after I have besieged you with entreaties and pleas, will I be able to plant the banner of my amorous desires atop the walls of this lovely fortress?'

"But all of his words were thrown to the wind; although she had eyes that could bore holes in rocks, she did not have ears to hear the laments of he who lay wounded and moaning. On the contrary: she gave him dirty looks, as if he had cut her grapevine. This went on until the poor lord, well aware of the brutality of Cinziella, who paid as much attention to him as the demon does to crooks, retreated with all his revenues and an angry face, saying, 'I quit the fire of Love!' But he solemnly swore to take a revenge on that dark Saracen that would force her to repent for having so tormented him.

"He left town and let his beard grow and put I don't know what kind of makeup on his face, and after a few months he returned to Long Furrow disguised as a peasant, where he bribed his way into becoming the king's gardener. And there he attempted to work as best he could, until one day he spread an imperial-style gown studded with gold and diamonds under Cinziella's windows. When her ladies-in-waiting saw it they immediately informed their mistress, who had one of them ask the gardener if he was willing to sell it. He answered that he was not a merchant or a dealer in used clothes, but that he would gladly give it to her on the condition that they let him sleep for one night in the princess's waiting room. When the ladies-in-waiting heard this they said to Cinziella, 'What do you lose, our lady, by giving the gardener this satisfaction, if you can make off with this gown that is fit for a queen?' Cinziella let herself be caught by a hook used for fishing quite a different sort of blenny and agreed to it, and after she took the gown she granted the gardener his favor.

"But the following morning he spread out a similarly made skirt in the same place, and when Cinziella saw it she had someone tell him that if he was willing to sell it she would give him whatever he wanted. The gardener answered that he wasn't selling, but that he would give it to her for nothing if they let him sleep in the princess's antechamber. And Cinziella let herself be pulled by the neck so that she could complete her outfit, and contented him.

"When the third morning arrived—before the Sun showed up to strike the flint to the fuse of the fields—in the same spot he spread out a splendid jacket that matched the rest of the outfit. When Cinziella saw it she said, just as she had for the others, 'If I don't have that jacket I'll never be happy!' She had someone call the gardener, and she said to him, 'My good man, I need you to sell me that jacket I saw in the garden, and you can take my heart as payment!' 'I am not selling it, my lady, but if it pleases you I will give you the jacket and a diamond necklace as well, if you let me sleep in your bedroom for a night.' 'Now you're really being a boor!' said Cinziella. 'It wasn't enough to sleep in my waiting room and then in my antechamber; now you want the bedroom! Sooner or later you'll probably even want to get into my bed!' The gardener answered, 'My lady, I'll keep my jacket, and you your bedroom! If you feel like whistling for me, you know where to find me. I'd be happy to sleep on the floor, something you wouldn't deny a Turk; and if you saw the necklace I intend to give you perhaps you'd offer me a better deal.'

"The princess was in part fleeced by her own greediness and in part urged on by her ladies-in-waiting, who were helping the dogs to climb up, and she let herself be convinced to content him. And that evening— when Night, like a leather dresser, threw tanning water onto the hide of the sky so that it turned black—the gardener took the necklace and the jacket and went to the princess's apartment. When he had given her these things she let him enter her bedroom, where she had him sit in a corner, and she said, 'Now freeze right there and don't move, if my favor means anything to you!' Then she traced a line on the floor with some charcoal and added, 'If you try to cross this line, you'll leave your ass on it!' That said, she pulled the curtain on the canopy until it was closed and went to bed.

"As soon as the gardener king saw that she was asleep, it seemed to him that it was time to work the fields of Love; he got into bed next to her, and before the owner of the land could awaken he had picked the amorous fruits. When she did awaken and saw what had happened, she didn't want to turn one mistake into two and ruin the garden by sending the gardener to his ruin. And so, making vice of necessity, she contented herself with the disorder and took pleasure from the mistake, and whereas before she had disdained crowned heads, now it didn't bother her to subjugate herself to a hairy foot, since that's what the king looked like and that's what Cinziella thought he was.

"This practice continued, and Cinziella became pregnant. Seeing how her belly was growing day by day, she told the gardener that she imagined she would be ruined if her father realized what was going on and that they would have to think of a way to avoid this danger. The king answered her that he could think of no other solution for their predicament apart from leaving, and that he would take her to the house of an old employer of his who would supply her with what she needed to give birth. Cinziella, who saw how low she had sunk and how she had been pulled by the sin of her pride, which was dragging her from one reef to the next, let herself be moved by the king's words and left her home, placing herself at the will of Fortune. After a long journey the king brought her to his own house, where he told his mother about the whole matter and begged her to go along with the disguise, for he wanted to pay Cinziella back for her haughtiness. And so he set her up in a little stable in the palace and left her to live miserably, sending bread to her on a crossbow.[4]

"Now when the king's servant girls were making bread, he ordered them to call Cinziella to help them, and at the same time told her to try to snitch a roll or two so that they could take care of their hunger. As she was taking the bread out of the oven, poor Cinziella, disregarding all the eyes upon her, snatched up a roll and stuck it in her pocket. But at that very moment the king arrived, dressed as who he really was, and said to the servant girls, 'Who told you to let this little beggar woman into the house? Can't you see from her face that she's a thief? And if you want proof that it's true, put your hand in her pocket and you'll find the evidence!' They searched her, and when they found the goods they chewed her out so badly that the jeers and uproar lasted the whole day.

"But then the king put his disguise back on and, finding her humiliated and melancholic on account of the affront she had received, told her not to be so afflicted by what had happened, since need is the tyrant of men, and, as that Tuscan poet said, 'A wretch who is starving sometimes commits actions which, in a better state, he would have blamed on someone else.'[5] And therefore, seeing as hunger draws the wolf from the woods, she could be forgiven for doing what it would be wrong for someone else to do. Thus she should go upstairs, where the lady was cutting some cloth, and, offering to help, see if she could

---

4. See tale 2.7 n6.
5. Verses from Petrarch, *Rime sparse* 207 ("Ben mi credea passar mio tempo omai"), following the Durling edition.

steal a few pieces, since she was close to giving birth and there were a thousand things they needed. Cinziella didn't know how to contradict her husband (for she considered him such) and went upstairs. After she joined the ladies-in-waiting in cutting a quantity of swaddling cloths, sashes, little caps, and diapers, she lifted a bundle of them and put them under her clothes. But then the king arrived and there was another outburst, as there had been with the bread. He had her searched, and when the stolen goods were found on her she received another flood of insults, as if she had been found with a whole load of laundry on her. And after that she went down to the stable.

"The king disguised himself again and ran downstairs, and when he found her there, desperate, he told her not to give in to her melancholy, since everything in the world was an opinion, and to try a third time to get hold of some little thing, since she was close to giving birth and the time was right for making a profit: 'Your mistress has wed her son to a foreign lady and wants to send her a few dresses of brocade and golden cloth, all nice and ready to wear; she says the bride is just your size, and so she wants to cut them using your body as a model. Now it's very likely that a pretty scrap or two will pass through your hands: put them in your bag[6] and then we'll sell them and survive a bit longer.' Cinziella did what her husband had ordered her to, and had just tucked away a fine piece of looped brocade when the king arrived. Making a big scene, he had Cinziella searched, and when he found the stolen goods he sent her away covered in shame; then he disguised himself again as the gardener and ran downstairs to comfort her. For if with one hand he stung her, out of the love he felt for her it gratified him to grease her up with the other, so that she would not be driven to despair. But, out of anguish for what had happened, poor Cinziella thought that it was all a punishment sent from the heavens for the arrogance and pride she had demonstrated, that because she had used so many princes and kings like foot wrappings now she herself was being treated like a little rag, and that because her father's advice had been met with a hard heart she was now blushing at the servant girls' braying. And out of the anger, as I was saying, that came over her due to this humiliation, her labor pains began.

"When the queen was notified, she had the girl brought upstairs and, showing compassion for her state, put her in a bed embroidered all over with gold and pearls, in a room whose walls were covered with golden cloth. This bewildered Cinziella, for she found herself

---

6. *corbona* (Neap.): literally, the bag in which offerings are collected in places of worship (Croce 445).

taken from a stable to a royal chamber and from a dunghill to such a precious bed, and she could not understand what had happened. And she was immediately given choice broths and cakes so that she would be more vigorous when it came time to deliver.

"As the heavens willed it, without too much suffering she gave birth to two beautiful baby boys, the most splendid things you ever could see. But no sooner had she been delivered than the king came in, saying to his mother, 'Where has your good judgment gone? You put a fancy saddlecloth on an ass? You think this is a bed fit for a filthy whore? Quick, beat her till she jumps out of that bed and then fumigate the room with rosemary to get rid of the stench!'[7] When the queen heard this she said, 'No more, no more, my son! Enough, enough of the torments you've already given this poor girl! By now you should be sated, since you've boiled her so thoroughly that she's shrunk to little more than a nightcap! If you don't feel avenged for the disdain she showed you at her father's court, then let these two beautiful jewels she has given you serve as payment for her debt!'

"As she was saying this she had the babies brought in, who were the most beauteous things in the world. When the king saw those pretty little dolls, his heart grew tender and, embracing Cinziella, he revealed himself for who he was, telling her that everything he had done had been the result of his indignation at seeing a king of his level held in such low consideration, but that from now on he would raise her up higher than his own head. And with the queen embracing her, in the meantime, as her daughter-in-law and child, she was given such a good reward for her sons that this moment of consolation seemed far sweeter to her than all of her past suffering, even if she always made sure to keep her sails lowered, ever remembering that *the daughter of pride is ruin.*"

> When the tales given out as piecework for that day had been completed, so as to rid his spirit of some of the melancholy that Cinziella's travails had given him the prince called Cicco Antuono and Narduccio to do their part. Wearing wide-brimmed hats, black thigh pieces with knee bands, and jackets fringed with lace, they came out from behind a garden bed to recite the eclogue that follows.

---

7. Rosemary was used to purify the air in contaminated rooms (Rak 852).

THE HOOK

Eclogue

Narduccio, Cicco Antuono

NARDUCCIO: Hey, Cicco Antuono, lend me a coin, and take something in pledge.

CICCO ANTUONO: On my word, I'd gladly lend you one if I hadn't made a substantial purchase just this morning.

NARD.: Bad luck for me; what did you buy?

CICCO: I got a good deal on a new hook, and even if they had wanted thousands of scudos for it, I would have spent it!

NARD.: You're rash when it comes to spending! The most a hook can be worth is two cents.

CICCO: Sure, my dear Narduccio! You don't know a thing about it; get out of here, sweetheart! Don't you know that hooks have risen in value? They were once used to fish for buckets, but now they fish for money!

NARD.: What do you mean, they fish for money? I don't get it.

CICCO: I'm sorry, but you're a jackass. You're like someone arriving in the world for the first time! Don't you know that there's not a man who doesn't hold a hook in his hand? He earns a living and revels with it, he flaunts his stuff and grows fat with it, he puts good straw under his behind, he fills his pen with pigs, he shines and stuffs himself to the brim; in short, he dominates the world with it!

NARD.: You astound me; I'm in ecstasy! I'll bet you got it into your noggin to show me the moon in the well, and to make me swallow the idea that a hook is a rare thing, a philosopher's stone!

CICCO: That's exactly what it is; it's a stone straight out of the alembic of an ingenious mind!

A *vorpora* (Neap.) is "a hook with one or more sharp, curved prongs used to remove buckets which have fallen into a well" (Croce 448).

NARD.: I've got to tell you, brother, that I've eaten bread from many ovens and I've never heard it mentioned. Either I'm a feather-brain or you're trying to pull the wool over my eyes.

CICCO: Open your ears and learn something, for you're a simpleton. Few people call it a hook, since at first glance that would give a bad impression. And so the best minds have changed its name, since in this age everything wears a mask. The prince gives it the name of a "present" or "donation"; the judge has assigned it the name of a "nice bonus" or "softener-up" or "hand greaser" or "morsel"; the scribe calls it a "straight fee" and heaven only knows that it's more crooked than a dog's haunch. For the merchant it's "earnings," for the artisan "a certain matter," for the shopkeeper "busi-ness," for the thief "ingenuity" or a "slap," for the cop a "touch of the hand," for the bandit "an arrangement,"[1] for the soldier "a redemption,"[2] for the spy "the fact," for the whore a "gift," for the procurer "income" or "a glove liner," for the matchmaker "a tip," and the commissioner calls it a "provision." In short, the pirate gives it the color of "spoils," the captain of "peaceful living," and if it's not peaceful he returns to bring havoc and ruin, and I assure you, on my word, that he wages greater war with his hook than with his sword! Do you want more? The poet strips all the books that find their way into his hands of their conceits and words—those by Aratus and Ovid and Masaro[3] and Big-nose[4]—and gives it the name of "imitation!"[5]

NARD.: I do declare, I get what you're saying, by God! On my word, it seems to me that you're a fine knave, a member of the trade council, familiar with the crucible, a wily old fox, a sly

---

1. *composta* (Neap.): "Bandits or brigands would sometimes constitute themselves as a group; that is, they came to a compromise with the governing authorities whereby they would receive pensions or military offices" (Croce 450).

2. As explained in eclogue 1, "The Crucible," n12, the exchange of lodging cards for cash.

3. It is not clear who this is.

4. *Nasone* (Neap.): one of Ovid's nicknames.

5. The questions of literary imitation and plagiary were widely debated in the seven-teenth century. See, e.g., Giambattista Marino's letter to Claudio Achillini, which prefaces Marino's *Sampogna* (1621). Marino comments that he " 'learned to read with a hook always present, drawing to himself everything that served *his* purpose, entering it into *his* notebook, and making use of it in *his* own time.' . . . He also pro-tests, however, against 'certain little harpies with hooked talons who go around stealing the ideas of others' " (cit. Croce 588).

boots; you're a crafty fellow, cunning and slick as a Saturday child. You're telling me they all wield a grapnel?

CICCO: A grapnel and a hook are the same thing! Enough said:
there's not a man who doesn't carry one on his belt—some
gold, others silver, copper, iron or wood, according to the
quality of the person. How should I say it? That great man[6]
who conquered the world used one made of gold and set
with carbuncles and diamonds to fish his kingdoms; he who
helped Cicero salt so many sow tits[7] carried one of silver;
others, according to their judgment and power, make them
as they can. The important thing is that everyone fishes, and
that's why this fishing has various names: clutching, relieving, wrapping up, lightening and lifting, scratching off and
neatening up, shearing, blowing away, tearing off, defraud-
ing, scraping, cleaning out and pinching, swiping and pulling off a coup, ripping off,[8] cleaning out the dustpan,
robbing the abbot, playing the cymbals, shaking up the
purse, and wielding the iron.

NARD.: You can say all of that with just one word: playing the game
of triumph,[9] robbing and assassinating!

CICCO: You have a short memory! I told you that nowadays the
world gives evil the title of good, and minds are sharpened
for no other reason than to set this hook in action, this
hook that pulls and is not seen, clasps and is not heard,
grabs and is not touched, and always takes and snatches
and claws.

NARD.: I am, my brother, without envy, for everything is eventually
thrown out with the water. What is acquired in a bad way is
never enjoyed by the third heir; people with bottomless
riches sink to the bottom and see their houses crumble, and
their families destroyed and reduced to rags and wandering
far and wide like vagabonds. A schoolmaster expressed it
well: "the millstone grinds it all out."

CICCO: These days the crooked necked[10] are hanged by their hunger; he who robs not, has not; he who takes not, has no

---

6. Alexander the Great.
7. *verrinie* (Neap.): the breast of a sow vs. Cicero's *Verrine*.
8. *fare arravoglia-Cuosemo* (Neap.): "corrupted form of *arravoglia quaesumus*. It
was pretended that there was an oration of the breviary that began in this manner,
since many of them begin with a word followed by *quaesumus* [. . .] it also means a
theft" (Galiani, *Vocabolario;* cit. Rak 874).
9. See tale 1.2 n19.
10. I.e., the pious.

straw; he who catches not, always has anguish in his soul;
and he who fishes not, never celebrates Easter![11]

NARD.: But at payback time give me three lashings![12] Besides the
fact that quite often a three-alarm scoundrel, greedy to
snatch dough, is sentenced to ride on a jackass like a baboon. He receives from the court a paper miter; he finds
himself marked in the market square;[13] he becomes infamous so that he won't famish; he loses his honor so that he
can revel for an hour; for a little copper he gets himself an
oar; the best of relishes tastes like seawater to him; he earns
three pieces of wood for clawing with his nails; his plumes
become a black pennant.[14] What's the use of so much bread,
so much tin, so many berries and rocks, chips and coins,
and pennies and half-pennies if, as it has been seen from so
many, so very many examples and tests, those who have the
most cash never cash in on happiness?

CICCO: If you try the hook once, you'll never part with it. It's like
the mange: the more you scratch the more you itch. Let's
take a spin among the trades and professions of this world,
and you'll see that everyone uses it. We'll start first, and
above all, with he who keeps vassals. He catches sight of
and spots a farmer who has filled his pen with pigs. Today
he asks him for a loan of many scudos, which he'll return to
him when it rains raisins and dried figs;[15] tomorrow he
sends for a load of barley, which he'll pay back at harvest
time; now he orders that he give him a donkey, or some
oxen, with the excuse that he needs them for his court. And
this annoyance lasts so long, this bitter siege continues at
such length, that the farmer, desperate, insults the bailiff in
some way, or gets a little too free with his hands. Oh, unfortunate fellow, better if your mama had not shat you, bet-

---

11. Each of the phrases in this speech contains alliterative punning: i.e., *chi no ar-*
robba non ha robba (the second phrase), *chi non piglia non ha paglia* (the third), and
so forth.

12. *tre cavalle* (Neap.): play on the two meanings of *cavallo*: a coin (*caallo*) vs. a
beating inflicted on schoolchildren (Guarini and Burani 512).

13. I.e., Piazza del Mercato in Naples. "Like Piazza Greve, capital executions were
carried out here. In a 1566 map of Naples there is a drawing of the scaffold and gallows in this square" (Croce 454). See also tale 1.7 n21.

14. Here, too, puns abound: *rimmo* (oar) vs. *ramma* (copper); *legna* (wood) vs.
l'ogna (fingernail); *pennone* (the banner that accompanied those condemned to
death) vs. *penne* (plumes).

15. The literalization of this figure of speech, connoting an impossible situation, appears in tale 1.4, "Vardiello."

ter if you had broken your neck! There, he's carried off and thrown into a ditch with shackles on his feet, irons around his neck, cuffs on his hands, and an epitaph hanging on the gate: "Proclamation and command: hey you, get out of here! He who speaks to this man pays six ducats!" In short, he can shout as much as he likes, send out memorials, and spend all his means, but he'll never be freed unless after so many bitter agonies and torments, expenses and suffering, he strikes a deal. When the cravings of this wolf are finally quenched and satisfied, his assassin ways go by the name of pardon![16]

NARD.: O accursed hook! May the shameless forge where you were hammered and tempered be damned!

CICCO: Listen. As the calf learns from the full-grown ox to pull the plow, so you can see the captain or the magistrate's clerk suborn witnesses, mix up the papers, rent out sentences, hide documents, and jail without cause, and there the hook is worth seven.[17] And whereas he should be dragged away, he earns the title of a man practiced at his affairs, or a go-getter and a man of good judgment!

NARD.: That is more than true, and if a respectable man comes home with a purse as clean as his conscience—something that has happened to me maybe twelve times—everyone says he'd better stay out of it, it's not a job for him, and it's a shame to give him a license to practice,[18] since he's a good-for-nothing who reaps no profits.

CICCO: The doctor, if he is a bad fellow, draws out the illness and divvies it up with the apothecary. Even if he's a good one, he makes it clear that apart from all his prescriptions he also knows the secret of holding his hand out behind him.[19]

NARD.: You can't say anything bad about this hook, for it is modest and honorable. In fact, you can call it a reward of fate: the one who makes you shit is paid off behind!

---

16. "Basile served a number of times (below he says 'about twelve') as baronial governor in the fiefs of the Kingdom of Naples, and he knew from experience that cases like the one he describes here and below were frequent" (Croce 456).

17. "Like in those card games in which a seven, especially of *denari* [coins; one of the suits in the Neapolitan deck], has a higher value than the other cards" (Guarini and Burani 514).

18. *patiente* (Neap.): "licenses, or the office itself, of a governor or captain" (Croce 457).

19. "A dignified way to receive the fee for a medical visit without seeming to receive payment like just any vendor of goods or services" (Croce 457).

CICCO: The merchant doesn't lose his cap in the crowd: he hands out musty goods; he puts glue on the interface to bring the weight up; he swears, he vows, he affirms that what is rotten is new, that what is falling apart is first-rate, and with pretty words and ugly actions he hoodwinks you and pretends it's white when it's black, though you always find some flaw in the merchandise; and when it comes time to measure, with elegant ostentation he stretches the fabric so that later you find that it's too short.

NARD.: No wonder, then, that the heavens turn against him and because of one error he loses his catch.

CICCO: The butcher sells you an old, sickly billy goat for the finest of mutton, an ancient ox for a heifer, and he displays all of it covered with gold leaf and flowers so that your mouth waters; he sells bones for flesh, and he doesn't respect the official price list, and always adds more than a little something[20] to what you've got, and when it's time to weigh, may God help you! He plays games with his fingers, and the scales go down.

NARD.: It's enough to make your lungs explode! That's why they look like barons on feast days.

CICCO: The oil seller tries to blind you when he's measuring out; and to show you that he's pouring your oil right to the top, all the way to the mark, he presses the bottom of the measuring cup in, and pushes it up so that it's higher than the hump on his back. He always mixes flour with his oil, which gives it body and color: you see a golden foam, and only when you fill a nice oil cruet do you find the dregs; in fact, you find a mixture of water and sludge which, when placed in a poor dark lamp, farts and fires.

NARD.: There's not a span that's clean; everything good is past: corrupt world, how you've changed!

CICCO: The tavern keeper's carafes are half empty; he trafficks about all night, and if he finds a barrel that has a touch of sourness or mold, he treats it with a poultice of egg whites. But above all, he cuts the good wine with the bad, he turns vinegar into Asprinio[21] and even water into wine, and he covers the spout of the carafe with his fingers and blocks

---

20. *lo ruotolo* (Neap.): about 900 grams.
21. A white wine of Campania (Aversa).

your vision so that you never see the sorry way he's measuring.

NARD.: Oh, wretched are those who meet up with him, for they
need a stomach of iron and a gullet of gold!

CICCO: The tailor skims from the cloth, and with every cut sees if
there's a cut for himself. He uses yarn in place of silk, and if
you take him along when you go to make purchases, he
wears a needle on his chest[22] and after coming to a generous
agreement with you goes back to the merchant for his own
business. But this is nothing yet: he cheats you on the list of
expenses so that when you read the bill you curse the unfortunate moment you decided to dress well.

NARD.: O blessed, O happy animals, who can go naked through
forests, valleys, plains, and mountains, and who do not live
subject to this ruination!

CICCO: Now hear about the rag sellers at the Giudecca.[23] If you get
the whim to sell something, there you'll find a whole gang in
cahoots who'll seize you by your throat. If you buy a piece
of clothing, as soon as you put it on you'll find it in pieces;
it'll last from Christmas to Saint Stephen's,[24] and with injury
and scorn, you go from elegant to disdained in the same day.
But why play so many keys? It would take a ream of paper
to list all the trades that render honor to this hook, and all
the gaunt and impoverished people who have used it to become fat and rich!

NARD.: Accursed invention that poisons honor and because of
which truth is darkened and trust blackened!

CICCO: Say what you like, but everyone makes use of it! May I die
strangled by a rope if I don't buy one myself today!

NARD.: Oh, better if you had a heart attack! If you use the hook in
this world, the hook will pull you straight down to the
bottom.

*I couldn't say if the head or tail of the delicious gelatin of this day
was more pleasing, since if one was tasty, the enjoyment caused by
the other went all the way down to the bone marrow, and the
prince's delight was so great that, to show that he was truly as*

---

22. "A signal of recognition to the merchant, who would understand that the price
of the goods was to be made higher so that the tailor could be paid his part" (Rak
875).
23. See eclogue 1 ("The Crucible") n9.
24. December 26.

*kind and generous as a lord, he called the head of his wardrobe
and ordered that the actors be given the lining from an old hat that
had been his grandfather's. And since the Sun had been called in a
hurry to the other pole to assist its states, which had been occupied by shadows, they all got up and set off down the road to their
pallets, with the charge to return in the morning to the usual place
for the same appointment.*

End of the fourth day.

V

THE FIFTH DAY

The birds were already reporting to the ambassador of the Sun on all the tricks and traps that had been prepared during the night when prince Tadeo and princess Lucia delivered themselves bright and early to the usual place, where, at a whistle, nine of the ten women arrived. Seeing this, the prince asked why Iacova had not come, and when he was told that she had fallen seriously ill—to her health!—he ordered that another woman be found to take the place of the missing one. And so as not to go too far abroad they summoned Zoza, who lived across from the royal palace. She was received by Tadeo with great regard due both to his obligations and to the affection he felt for her.

Then she and the others picked flowered calamint, lavender, five-leafed rue, and some of this and some of that; one of them made a garland, as if she were to recite a farce, another made a little nosegay, another affixed an overblown rose to her breast, and another put a flecked carnation in her mouth.

But since there were still nearly four hours before the day would be split in half, to help ripen the time before they stuffed themselves the prince ordered that some games be played as entertainment for his wife. He gave the task to Cola Iacovo the steward, a man of great ingenuity, and as if his pockets were full of invention he found one right away, saying, "Those tastes that are without some element of advantage, my ladies, have always been insipid. For this reason entertainments and evening gatherings were not devised for worthless pleasure but also for tasty profit, for such manner of games serve not only to pass the time but also awaken and quicken the wits for making decisions and answering what is asked of one, precisely as happens in the game of games[1]

---

1. This was a sort of truth-telling society game, also called the "game of blunders." See, e.g., Lorenzo Lippi, *Il Malmantile racquistato* 2.47. The "game of solitude" mentioned in Stefano Guazzo's *La civil conversatione* has a similar structure (Rak 886). The concept of gaming as a hermeneutic tool is present in countless Renaissance texts, especially those, like Baldassar Castiglione's *Il Cortegiano*, that have as their subject social and intellectual life at court. See also Michelangelo Picone, ed., *Passare il tempo: La letteratura del gioco e dell'intrattenimento dal XII al XVI secolo* (Rome: Salerno Editrice, 1993).

that I thought we would play, which goes like this: I'll propose to one
of these women here a sort of game, and she, without thinking about
it, will immediately have to tell me that she does not like it and the
reason why it is not to her liking; and whoever takes too long to answer or does not answer to the point must pay a penalty, which will
be whatever penance our lady the princess commands. And so, to
begin the game, I would like to play *trionfiello*[2] with madam Zeza,
for half a penny!" And Zeza immediately answered, "I don't want to
play, because I'm not a thief!" "Well done!" said Tadeo, "for those
who rob and kill are the ones who triumph!"

"If that's how it is," replied Cola Iacovo, "I've got a coin worth
four and a half that I'd like to use to play break-the-bank with madam
Cecca." "You're not getting me," answered Cecca, "for I'm no merchant!" "She's right," said Tadeo, "because this game is made for
them."

"At least, madam Meneca," continued Cola Iacovo, "let's spend a
couple of hours playing malcontent." "I'm sorry, but that's a game
for courtiers!" answered Meneca. "She hit the nail on the head,"
said Tadeo. "That breed of people never does anything with good
humor!"

"I know," Cola Iacovo resumed, "that madam Tolla will play four
corners with me for six old coins."[3] "Heaven save me!" answered
Tolla, "that's a game for husbands who have bad wives." "You
couldn't have answered better," answered Tadeo. "This game is made
for them, since so very often they butt horns like billy goats."

"At least, madam Popa," replied Cola Iacovo, "let's play twenty
figures, and I'll give you my hand." "I wouldn't think of it," answered
Popa. "That's a game for flatterers!" "She has spoken like Orlando,"
said Tadeo, "for flatterers make twenty or thirty different figures for
themselves and transform whenever they want so that they can swindle a poor prince."

Continuing, Cola Iacovo said, "On your life, Madam Antonella,
let's not waste our time, but let's play 'taxes' for a nice plate of fritters."
"You've really hit on it!" answered Antonella. "It's a good thing you're
treating me like a mercenary woman!" "She's not wrong," said Tadeo,
"for that breed of women often ends up being taxed."[4]

---

2. Lit., "little triumph." These and the following are names of card games, here used
as pretext for wordplay.
3. *pubreche* (Neap.): see tale 1.2 n2. Once again, play on *pubreca*: coin vs. "public
woman" or prostitute.
4. Play on *gabella*: in general, tax, but also a special tax imposed on prostitutes vs.
the name of a game.

"Go get her, Evil One!" continued Cola Iacovo. "I'm beginning to imagine that the hour will go by without my having any amusement, if madam Ciulla doesn't play summons for a measure of lupins." "What, you think I've become a cop?" answered Ciulla. And Tadeo immediately added, "She has given a truly royal response, since it's the duty of bailiffs and cops to issue summons to the court."

"Come over here, madam Paola," Cola Iacovo went on, "and let's play picket for three times five." "You've missed the mark," answered Paola, "for I'm not a court gossip!" "This one here has a doctorate," answered the prince, "for there is no place where honor is more piqued than in our homes."

"Without a doubt," resumed Cola Iacovo, "madam Ciommetella will be content to play pushcart with me." "Fiddledeedee!" answered Ciommetella. "A fine schoolmaster's game you've found for me!" "This one has to pay the penalty," said Cola Iacovo, "since the proposal has nothing to do with the answer." "Go get your money back from the master!" answered the prince. "The answer is a marvelous fit, since pedants play so well at pushcart that even if they lose five points, they put it down as a game won."

But Cola Iacovo, turning to the last of the women, said, "I can't believe that madam Zoza[5] would refuse an invitation as the others have done; and so she will give me the pleasure of playing take-off-your-pants with me for a silver coin."[6] "Watch out for your legs,"[7] answered Zoza, "that's a child's game." "Now this one does have to do the penance," concluded Tadeo, "because even old people play this game; and so, madam Lucia, it's up to you to give her the penalty."

And Zoza got up and went and knelt before the princess, who as penance ordered that she sing a Neapolitan villanella. When a tambourine had been brought and as the prince's coachman played a cither, she sang this song:[8]

---

5. The text reads "Iacova," an apparent error, since Iacova is absent from this day of telling due to illness (as specified at the beginning of the day), and Zoza will take her place as the teller of the last tale of the day.

6. *cianfrone* (Neap.): originally worth a ducat, and later a *patacca* (a coin of little value) (Croce 468).

7. See tale 1.9 n10.

8. "This villanella contains many proverbial sayings, most of which have already been referred to, and in its general sense expresses a disdainful farewell to a person who was once loved but from whose yoke the lover now feels himself freed" (Croce 469).

If you thought you could hammer on me
and I would get the runs
just because you put on airs and wrinkle your nose,
go on, my girl, for March has ruined you!

The time is past when Berta spun
And the bird ploughed,
And I feel neither the arrow nor the flame of Love:
Patria has opened up; there's no more mother now!

Go on, even the kittens have opened their eyes,
And the crickets are now awake;
If you give no hope to this beauty,
Be on the watch for misfortunes, wherever you run and stick it!

I've cut my wisdom teeth,
And I move to your nod no more,
And by now I can tell the figs from the garlic!
Get it out of your head: there'll be no more cuts for you!

   The song and the pleasure of all those listening to it ended at the same time the tables were set, and if what they gobbled down was good, what they drank was even better. But when their stomachs had been sealed and the tables removed, Zeza was ordered to give the start to the tales. And even though she was tipsy and her tongue had grown quite thick and her ears quite small, at the end she paid her debt, speaking in this manner:

THE GOOSE

First Entertainment of the Fifth Day

Lilla and Lolla buy a coin-shitting goose at the market. A neighbor asks to borrow it, and when she sees that it's the opposite of what it should be, she kills it and throws it out the window. The goose attaches itself to a prince's ass while he's relieving himself, and no one but Lolla can remove it; for this reason the prince takes her for his wife.

"That great and respectable man emitted a great sentence when he said that an artisan envies other artisans, a toilet cleaner other toilet cleaners, a musician other musicians, a neighbor other neighbors, and a pauper the penniless,[1] since there's not a hole in the edifice of the world where the accursed spider of envy does not weave its web. For envy feeds on nothing other than the ruins of our fellow creatures, of which you'll hear more particularly in the tale that I'm about to tell you.

"There once were two sisters who were so flat on their face that they managed to survive only by spitting on their fingers from morning till night so that they could spin a little yarn to sell. But in spite of this miserable life, the ball of need wasn't able to hit the ball of honor[2] and send it off the table. And so the heavens, which are as open-handed when they compensate for good as they are tight-fisted when they punish evil, put into these poor girls' heads the idea of going to market to sell a few skeins of yarn and, with what little they got for it, buying a goose. When they had done this and brought the goose home, they grew to love it so much that they treated it as if it were another sister, even letting it sleep in their bed.

"And when morning breaks it's a nice day, for the good goose began to shit hard cash until, shitload upon shitload, they had filled up a whole chest. There was so much shit, in fact, that the two sisters began

---

AT 571: All Stick Together, and AT 571C: The Biting Doll. This tale is quite similar to Straparola 5.2 ("Adamantina"), and recalls Grimm 64 ("The Golden Goose"). See also Pitrè, *Fiabe, nov. e racc. sic.* 25, 288.

1. Hesiod, *Opera et dies* 25–26 (Croce 471).
2. Metaphor deriving from the game of billiards.

to raise their heads and see their fur shine, so that one day when they had gathered to gossip, certain neighbors of theirs said to themselves, 'Have you noticed, sister Vasta, how Lilla and Lolla, who just a few days ago didn't have a place to die in, have now polished themselves up so fine that they're parading around like ladies? Do you see their windows, always full of chickens and pieces of meat that they display in front of our noses? What can have happened? Either those two have opened the barrel of their honor or else they've found a treasure!' 'I felt like a mummy when I saw them,' answered Perna. 'They used to drag themselves around half dead before, and now they're at the top of the pole and back in the running, and it all seems like a dream to me.'

"They said these things and others, and spurred on by their envy they made a hole between the wall of their house and the rooms of the two girls so that they could keep a secret watch on them and give their curiosity a meal or two. And they played spy for so long that one evening—when the Sun beat the boats of the Indian Sea with the whip of its rays so that the hours of the day might have a holiday—they saw Lilla and Lolla spread a sheet on the ground and put the goose on it. When the women at the hole saw the goose begin to squirt out streams of coins, their pupils almost popped out of their eyes at the same time as their gullets nearly flew out of their mouths.

"And in the morning—when Apollo, with his golden rod, implored the shadows to retire—Pasca, one of the women, went to see the girls, and after chattering and shilly-shallying around, with a thousand twists and turns she came to the point and begged the girls to lend her the goose for a couple of hours, since she had bought a few goslings of her own and thought that their goose might make them feel more at home. And she spoke and begged with such skill that, in part because they were good-hearted and didn't know how to say no, in part because they didn't want their neighbor to grow suspicious, those two simple-minded sisters lent it to her, with the agreement that she would bring it back right away.

"The woman went to find the other neighbors, and then without delay they spread a sheet on the ground and put the goose on it. But instead of revealing in its foundations a mint that coined new currency, the goose opened up a latrine pipe that decorated the linens of those poor women with a yellow soil whose smell wafted through the whole neighborhood the way that on Sundays you can smell the stews cooking. When they saw this the women thought that if they treated it well it might work better than a philosopher's stone[3] to sat-

---

3. The miraculous stone, the object of medieval alchemists' quest and central to the alchemical *opera*, which was believed could transform metals into gold.

isfy their desires, and so they fed it everything that they managed to stuff down its throat. Then they put it on another clean sheet, but if at first the goose had revealed itself to be of lubricious intestines, it now gave evidence of having dysentery, since it had all that food to digest. At this, the indignant neighbors became so enraged that they wrung the goose's neck and threw it out of the window into a little back alley where no one ever stopped but where everyone threw their garbage.

"But as fate, which sends up beans where you least expect it, would have it, a king's son was passing by those parts on his way to the hunt, and his intestines began to rumble so badly that he gave his sword and horse to a servant and entered into that little alley to unload his belly. When he had completed the service, he couldn't find any paper in his pocket with which to wipe himself and, seeing the freshly killed goose, he used it as a rag.[4] The goose, however, was not dead, and it grabbed hold of the poor prince's flesh with its beak. The prince started to shout, at which all his servants came running and tried to pry it off his flesh, but this was not possible because it had attached itself like a feathery Salmacis to a hairy Hermaphrodites.[5] And so the prince, not able to stand the pain and seeing that the efforts of his servants were thrown to the wind, ordered that they carry him in their arms to the royal palace. There he summoned all the doctors, and after they conducted an on-the-spot inspection they made every sort of attempt to find a remedy for this mishap by applying unguents, employing pincers, and sprinkling powders. But when he saw that the goose was a tick that quicksilver could not detach[6] and a leech that vinegar could not remove, the prince issued a proclamation: whoever was able to remove that pain in his ass would be given half his kingdom, if a man; if a woman, she would be made his wife.

"You should have seen the flocks of people who came to stick their noses in that affair! The more they tried to find a remedy, though, the more the goose held on tight and nipped at the poor prince, so that it seemed like all the prescriptions of Galen, the aphorisms of Hippocrates, and the remedies of Mesua had ganged up against the *Posteri-*

---

4. Croce does not see a direct descendance from the famous episode in Rabelais (*Gargantua* 13); others (Guarini and Burani) think it possible. In the passage in question, Gargantua concludes, after listing various ways of cleaning oneself, that "there is no ass-wiper like a fluffy goose" (37).

5. "The nymph Salmacis fell in love with Hermaphrodites and, wrapping herself around him, she implored the gods never to be separated from him, forming a single body" (Ovid, *Metamorphoses* 4.361–76; Guarini and Burani 529).

6. "Mercury dissolves gold and other metals" (Guarini and Burani 529).

. . . e, volennola sciccare da la carne, non fu possebele, che s'era attaccato
comme na Sarmace de penne a n'Ermafrodito de pilo. [. . . and tried to pry it
off his flesh, but this was not possible, since it had attached itself like a
feathery Salmacis to a hairy Hermaphrodites.]

ora of Aristotle[7] to torment the wretched man. But, as fate had it, among the many who came to attempt the trial was Lolla, the younger of the two sisters. As soon as she saw the goose she recognized it and started shouting, 'Chubbikins, my little chubbikins!' Hearing the voice of the one who loved it, the goose immediately let go and ran to Lolla's lap, where it cuddled up to her and kissed her, not worrying that it was trading a prince's ass for a peasant's mouth.

"The prince, who witnessed this marvel, wanted to know what was going on, and after being informed of the neighbors' prank, he had them whipped in the streets and sent into exile. And then he took Lolla for his wife and the goose, which shat a hundred treasures, as dowry, and he gave Lilla an exceedingly rich husband. And they were thus the most satisfied people in the world, in spite of the neighbors, who, in their attempt to block off the road leading to the riches that Lolla had been sent by the heavens, opened up another one that led to her becoming queen, ultimately realizing that *obstacles often work to one's advantage.*"

---

7. All are authorities of ancient medicine. For Mesua, see tale 2.2 n5. The full title of Aristotle's work, here burlesqued, is *Analytica posteriora.*

2

THE MONTHS

Second Entertainment of the Fifth Day

Cianne and Lise are brothers, one rich and one poor. Lise, since he is poor and not helped at all by his rich brother, leaves home and encounters such good fortune that he becomes immensely rich. Out of envy, the other brother pursues the same fate, but everything goes wrong and he is unable to save himself from great misfortune without the help of his brother.

The laughter that came over the company when they heard of the prince's misfortune was so excessive that every one of them nearly got a hernia, and they would have kept on laughing in counterpoint right up to the rosette of their navels[1] had Cecca not signaled that she was ready to spit out her tale. And so she sequestered the mouths of them all, and began to speak: "A proverb that should be written in letters big enough for a catafalque[2] says that keeping quiet never hurt anyone. So pay no attention to the tongues of those certain gossips who never say anything kind and are always cutting and sewing, snipping and pricking; they get what they have coming to them, for when it's time to empty the sacks, it has and always will be seen that while kind words buy love and opportunity, bad words earn enemies and ruin. Listen how, and you'll agree that I have a chamber pot's worth of reasons for saying so.

"It is said that there once were two brothers: Cianne, who lived as comfortably as a count; and Lise, who was barely in possession of his life. But the one was as poor in fortune as the other was miserable in spirit, to the point where he wouldn't have gotten up from shitting to breathe life back into his brother. And so poor Lise left home in desperation and set himself to walking through the world.

AT 480: The Kind and the Unkind Girls, and AT 563: The Table, the Ass, and the Stick. Penzer mentions Grimm 13 ("The Three Little Gnomes in the Forest") and other tales, for the moral of "always be polite"; and Grimm 7 ("The Good Bargain") for the equivocation regarding the whip lashes (2:113). See also Grimm 24 ("Mother Holle").

1. See tale 1.10 n31.
2. I.e., "letters as large as those used to write the names of the defunct on funeral catafalques, at this time often grandiose and full of pomp" (Guarini and Burani 531).

"And he walked so far that one evening he arrived at a tavern, where he found twelve young men sitting around the fire. When they saw poor Lise all numb and nearly frozen stiff from the cold—due both to the season, which was harsh, and his clothes, which were threadbare—they asked him to sit beside them at the fireplace. He accepted their invitation, since he needed to very badly, and began to warm himself up. And as he was warming himself he was asked by one of those young men, who was covered all over with hair and had such a surly face that it was frightening to look at, 'What do you think, friend, of this weather?'

"'What am I supposed to think?' said Lise. 'I think all the months of the year do their duty, and we, on the other hand, are the ones who don't know what we ask for. We want to dictate laws to the heavens, and since we desire things our way we don't fish down too deep to see if what we get a whim for is good or evil, or useful or dangerous, so that when it rains in the winter we wish for the dog days of summer, and in August for downpours from the clouds, never thinking that if this were the case the seasons would be topsy-turvy, seeds would be lost, harvests would go to ruin, our bodies would be eaten by worms, and Nature would have her legs kicked out from under her. So let's allow the heavens to follow their own course, since their trees have been made for this purpose: to temper winter's cold with their wood and summer's heat with their branches.'

"'You speak like Samson,'[3] said the young man, 'but you cannot deny that this month of March, that we're in now, is a bit too impertinent: with all its frosts and rains, snow and hail, winds, flurries, fogs, storms, and other trifles, it makes us grow tedious of life.' 'You speak badly of this poor month,' answered Lise, 'but you did not say anything about its usefulness, for by issuing in spring it gives rise to the generation of all things, and if it were for nothing else it causes the Sun to feel the happiness of the present time, since March lets it into the house of the Ram.'[4]

"The young man listened to Lise's words with great pleasure, because he himself was that very month of March, who with his other eleven brothers had happened to stop at the tavern. To repay Lise's kindness of not finding a bad word to say about a month that is so dismal that not even shepherds like to name it, he gave him a pretty little chest and said, 'Take this little chest and ask it for whatever you

---

3. Samson was the judge of the tribe of Dan, which was at war with the Philistines. The source of his incredible strength was his hair (Rak 908). See eclogue 1 ("The Crucible") n28.

4. "Yet another satirical reference to having 'horns'" (Croce 477). The sun enters into the constellation of Aries on March 21.

need, and when you open it you will find it before you.' With words
of great regard Lise thanked the young man and, putting the chest
under his head like a pillow, he fell asleep, and then—no sooner had
the Sun come to whitewash the Night's shadows with the brushes of
its rays—he took his leave of the young men and went on his way.

"Before he had taken fifty steps from the tavern he opened the little
chest and said, 'Oh, my dear, couldn't I have a litter lined with wool,
with a bit of a fire in it, so that I could travel nice and warmly through
this snow?' No sooner had he finished saying this than there appeared
a litter with some litter bearers, who lifted him right up and placed
him inside it, after which Lise told them to start walking in the direction of his house. And when it was time to start working their jaws,
he opened the little chest and said, 'Come out, things to eat!' and
then and there all sorts of good things poured down from the sky,
and the spread was so grand that it could have fed ten crowned kings.

"One evening Lise arrived in a wood—which denied the Sun entrance since it was coming from suspicious places[5]—and he opened
the little chest, saying, 'I would like to rest in this lovely place tonight, where the river plays counterpoint on the stones to accompany
the plainsong of the cool breezes.' Then and there a bed canopied in
fine scarlet cloth sprung forth, with feather mattresses, Spanish coverlets, and sheets as light as a breath of air, all under a waxed tent.
And when he asked for something to eat, a silver credenza worthy of
a prince was immediately prepared, and under another tent a table
was spread with food whose aroma could be smelled from a hundred
miles away.

"He ate, went to sleep, and then—when the rooster, who is the
Sun's spy, informed its master that the shadows were weak and tired
and that it was the right time, as an experienced soldier knows, to get
on their tail and turn them into pulp—he opened the chest and said,
'I would like some fine clothes, because today my brother is to see me
and I'd like to make his mouth water.' No sooner said than done: he
found himself dressed like a gentleman in a suit of the finest black
velvet, with a collar of red camel's hair and beautiful lacework cover-
ing the lining of yellow felt, so that it looked like a field of flowers.
And once Lise was dressed he got into the litter and arrived home.

"Seeing him arrive in such pomp and with all those luxuries, Cianne wanted to know what sort of fortune he had encountered. His

---

5. *che non deva prattica* (Neap.): "Reference to the pratique that was or was not
granted to vessels in arrival, and to the quarantines to which suspicious ships were
subject" (Croce 477). In this case the "suspicious place" is the East, from which
Turks and Barbary pirates hailed (Rak 908).

brother told him about the young men he had met at the tavern and about the presents they had given him, but he kept the conversation he had had with the young man between his teeth. Cianne couldn't wait to take his leave of Lise, and with the excuse that he was going to rest since he was tired, he immediately set off on his way.

"He arrived at the tavern, where he met the same young men. He began to chat with them, and when he was asked the same question about what he thought of the month of March he opened his mouth wide and began to say, 'Oh, may God confound that accursed month, enemy of those with the French disease,[6] hated by shepherds, disturber of the humors, wrecker of all bodies! The month cited when you want to announce ruination to someone: "You're in for it, since March has got you!" The month cited when you want to tell someone he's more than conceited: "You're a real March cure!"[7] In short, it's a month that would bring good fortune to the world, good luck to the earth, and riches to all men if its position in the ranks of its brothers were eliminated.'

"The month of March listened to Cianne dressing him down like that, but until the next morning acted as if nothing had happened, with the idea that he would make him suck that nice outburst back up. And when Cianne was about to leave he gave him a handsome flail[8] and said to him, 'Whenever you wish for something, just say, "Flail, give me a hundred of them!" and you'll see rushes strung with pearls.' Cianne thanked the young man and began to work his spurs, and he didn't want to try out the flail until he got back home, where as soon as his foot hit the ground he went into a secret chamber to store away the money he hoped to get from the flail, to which he said, 'Flail, give me a hundred of them!' And if the flail didn't give all of them to him, tell him to come back for the rest! It played a composer's counterpoint on his legs and on his face, so that at the screams Lise came running. When he saw that the flail couldn't be stopped, since it was acting like a wild horse, he opened the little chest and made it stop.

"He asked Cianne what had happened and, after listening to his story, told him that he had nothing to complain about but himself, since like a thrush he had shat his troubles on his own, and that he had acted like the camel that out of its desire to have horns lost its ears. And that he should learn, if it ever happened again, to rein in his

---

6. "Since those suffering from syphilis (the 'French disease') suffer more in March" (Croce 478).

7. "Current sayings on the damage that the month of March caused" (Rak 908).

8. *scorriato* (Neap.): an instrument for pounding grain similar to a threshing flail, "formed by two bars held together by a leather strap" (Guarini and Burani 535).

tongue, which was the key that had opened the warehouse of this misfortune, since if he had spoken well of that young man he might have had the same good luck as Lise. And, moreover, that speaking well of someone is merchandise that costs nothing but is wont to yield incredible earnings.

"Finally, Lise comforted him by telling him not to look for greater amenities than those given to him by the heavens, because his little chest was enough to fill up thirty misers' houses until they burst; because he would be master of all of Lise's fortune, since a generous man's treasurer is the heavens; and because, even if another brother would have hated him for the cruelty with which he had treated him during his time of misery, he nevertheless believed that Cianne's meanness had been the wind of prosperity that had brought him to this port. And, therefore, he wanted to show him his gratitude and intended to recognize this favor.

"When Cianne had listened to all of this, he asked to be pardoned for the disaffection that he had demonstrated in the past, and after making a shopkeeper's agreement they enjoyed their good fortune together. And from then on Cianne spoke well of everything, no matter how wicked it was, for *the dog burned by hot water will always be afraid of cold*."

3

PRETTY AS A PICTURE

Third Entertainment of the Fifth Day

Betta refuses to get married but finally models a husband with her own hands. He is stolen from her by a queen; after a thousand difficulties she finds him, gets him back by means of her great art, and brings him home.

When Cecca had finished her tale, which everyone liked enormously, Meneca, who was aiming[1] to shoot out her own, saw that everyone was ready to listen with perked-up ears, and she spoke in this manner: "It has always been more difficult for man to keep what he has already acquired than to acquire new things, since in one case Fortune concurs and often gives injustice a hand, whereas in the other it takes brains. That's why you can often see people without any sense rise to prosperity but then for lack of wits roll back down again, just as you'll be able to clearly see from the tale that I'm about to tell you, if you're sharp.

"There once was a merchant who had a single, only daughter, whom he greatly wanted to see married. But however much he played this lute he always found her a hundred miles away from his motifs,[2] since that monkey brain of a women hated all tails. She banned the passage of any man through her territory as if it were a no-trespass zone or a private hunting ground: her tribunal was always closed for the holidays, her schools always on vacation, her banks always shut down for court festivities, so that her father was the most afflicted and desperate man in the world.

"When he had to go to a fair one day he asked his daughter, whose name was Betta, what she wanted him to bring back for her, and she said to him, 'My daddy, if you love me bring me half a quintal of Pal-

---

AT 403: The Black and the White Bride, AT 425: The Search for the Lost Husband, and AT 533: The Speaking Horsehead. This tale shares several motifs with Grimm 88 ("The Singing, Springing Lark"). In the original the title reads "Pinto Smauto"; literally, "Painted Enamel," though "pinto" can also mean "pretty" or "elegant."

1. *che steva a cavalletto* (Neap.): the *cavalletto* was a fork used to support a harquebus or other firearm (Croce 481).

2. *recercate* (Neap.): a type of musical composition (see tale 1.1 n17 and tale 3.10 n3) vs. "searches."

ermo sugar and the same of ambrosian almonds, with four or six
flasks of scented water and a little bit of musk and amber, and also
bring me about forty pearls, two sapphires, a few garnets and rubies
and some spun gold, and, above all, a modeling bowl and a silver
scalpel.'

"Her father marveled over this extravagant request, yet so as not to
contradict his daughter he went to the fair and returned with every
single item she had asked for. Once she had these things she shut herself in a room and set herself to making a large quantity of almond
paste and sugar mixed with rose water and perfume, and then she
began to model a splendid young man, for whom she made hair from
the spun gold, eyes from the sapphires, teeth from the pearls, and lips
from the rubies, and she endowed him with so much grace that the
only thing he was missing was speech. After that was done, since she
had heard that another statue had come alive due to the prayers of a
certain king of Cyprus,[3] she prayed to the goddess of love for so long
that the statue began to open its eyes and, as her prayers became
more insistent, he started to breathe, and after breath came words,
and finally all of his limbs loosened up and he began to walk.

"Happier than if she had acquired a new kingdom, Betta hugged
and kissed him and, taking him by the hand, brought him before her
father and said, 'Daddy, my lord, you have always said that you are
eager to see me married, and so to make you happy I have chosen the
husband of my heart's desire.' Upon seeing this beautiful young man
come out of his daughter's bedroom when he hadn't seen him go in,
her father remained speechless, and when he beheld this beauty so
great that he could have charged a coin a head to come and admire
it,[4] he gave his consent that the marriage take place and prepared
great festivities.

"Among those who showed up was a great and unknown queen,
who, when she saw the beauty of Pretty as a Picture—for Betta had
given him this name—became infatuated with him, and it was no
laughing matter. Pretty as a Picture, who had opened his eyes to the
wickedness of the world only three hours before, wasn't yet capable
of muddying any waters, and he accompanied the female guests who
had come to celebrate the marriage to the stairs, just as his bride had
told him to. As he was doing the same with that lady, the queen, she
grabbed his hand and took him very quietly out to the coach-and-six
that was waiting for her in the courtyard, and then she pulled him in
and gave orders to leave for her own land, where that simpleton

3. I.e., Pygmalion.
4. "Like the 'phenomena' or 'monsters of nature' in booths at a fair" (Croce 483).

Pretty as a Picture, not understanding what had happened to him, became her husband.

"After Betta had been waiting for him a while and didn't see him come back, she sent a man down to the courtyard to see if he was talking with someone; she had another go up to the terrace to see if he had gone to get some air; she peeked into the john to see if he had gone to pay respectful tribute to his vital needs. But then, when she couldn't find him, she immediately imagined that, beautiful as he was, he had been stolen. After she issued the usual proclamations and no one came forth to reveal his whereabouts, she resolved to go search the world for him herself, disguised as a poor woman.

"And thus she set off walking, and after several months she reached the house of a kind old woman, who received her with much affection. When she heard of Betta's misfortune and saw that she was pregnant besides, she felt such pity for her that she taught her three little formulas: the first was 'tricche varlacche, ca la casa chiove'; the second, 'anola tranola, pizze fontanola'; the third, 'tafaro e tammurro, pizze 'ngongole e cemmino.'[5] She told Betta to use them only in times of great need, and she would reap great benefits. Although she was astonished by this trifle of a gift, Betta said to herself, 'Those who spit in your throat[6] do not want to see you dead, and those who take should never cause bother; every little bit helps. Who knows what sort of good luck is hidden in those words?' And with this she thanked the old woman and set out walking again.

"After a long journey she arrived at a lovely city called Round Mountain. She went straight to the royal palace, where she asked, for the love of God, for some lodging in the stable, since she was close to giving birth. When the ladies-in-waiting heard this they gave her a little room off the stairs, and from there the poor thing saw Pretty as a Picture go by, which filled her with so much joy that she nearly slid right off the tree of life. And since she found herself in such a great state of need, she decided to try the first of the old woman's formulas. As she said 'tricche varlacche, ca la casa chiove,' there appeared be-

---

5. For the last two, which are words from children's games, see the introduction to day 2. The first is also probably the name of a game; the *triccaballacco* was a rudimentary wooden instrument of Moorish origin (Croce 484). "Ca la casa chiove" means "for the house is raining"; on the whole the expressions are nonsensical. There is a discrepancy in form between the formulas as they appear here and their appearance later in the tale. Here, in the original, the second and the third read: "ariola tranza, pizza fontanza" and "tafate tammuzzo, pizza 'ngongole, e cemmino."
6. "The common practice of blowing or spitting in the mouth of a person who has fainted, connected with the belief that by doing so the life-spirit would be restored" (Rak 922).

fore her a pretty little golden cart that was encrusted all over with jewels and moved by itself around the room, and it was a wonder to behold. When the ladies-in-waiting saw this they told the queen, who, without wasting any time, raced to Betta's room; at the sight of that beautiful object she asked Betta if she wanted to sell it, for she would give her however much she asked. Betta answered that although she was ragged, her own pleasure was more important to her than all the gold in the world and so, if the queen wanted the little cart, she would have to let her sleep one night with her husband. The queen marveled at the folly of this poor girl, who went around in a pile of rags but wanted to give away such a treasure on a whim, and she decided to snatch up this fine mouthful and, drugging Pretty as a Picture with some opium, to leave the poor little girl happy but badly paid.

"As soon as Night fell—when the stars came out to exhibit themselves in the sky and the fireflies on earth—the queen gave Pretty as a Picture the sleeping draught and had him put to bed next to Betta; he did exactly what he was told to, and no sooner had he thrown himself onto the mattress than he began to sleep like a dormouse. The hapless Betta, who had thought that she would make up for all her past woes that night, saw that she had no audience and started to complain in a loud voice, reproaching him for everything she had been forced to do because of him. And the afflicted girl never closed her mouth, nor did the sleeping boy ever open his eyes, until the Sun came out with its etching acid[7] to separate the shadows from the light, and the queen came down and took Pretty as a Picture by the hand, saying to Betta, 'So, are you happy?' 'May you yourself have this sort of happiness for your whole life,' Betta answered under her breath, 'because I just spent such a dreadful night that I'm going to remember it for a few days.'

"But not being able to resist, the miserable soul wanted to try a second time with the second formula, and when she said 'anola tranola, pizze fontanola,' there appeared before her a golden cage, which held a splendid bird made of gold and precious stones that was singing like a nightingale. When the ladies-in-waiting saw this and informed the queen, she wanted to see for herself. She asked the same question she had asked for the little carriage and Betta answered the same way she had the first time, and the queen, who had already foreseen and figured out what the sneaky girl was up to, promised to let her sleep with her husband. And after she took the cage and the bird, and night arrived, she gave Pretty as a Picture the usual sleeping draught

---

7. *l'acqua de spartire* (Neap.): aquaforte, or nitric acid (lit., "dividing water").

and sent him off to sleep with Betta in the same room, where she had ordered that a lovely bed be prepared. When Betta saw that he was sleeping as soundly as someone whose throat had been cut, she began the same lament again, saying things that would have moved a paving stone to pity; and lamenting and weeping and ripping herself apart, she spent another night filled with torment. As soon as it was day the queen went down to get her husband, leaving the hapless Betta, who was biting her hands over the joke that had been played on her, cold and icy.

"But when Pretty as a Picture went out the next morning to pick a few figs in a garden outside the city walls, he was approached by an old junk seller who lived on the other side of the wall from Betta's room and hadn't missed a word of what she had said, and he related point by point the tribulations, the weeping, and the laments of the miserable beggar woman. Upon hearing this the king, who was already beginning to change his mind about things, imagined what must have happened and decided that if he were sent to sleep with the poor little soul another time, he would not drink what the queen had prepared for him.

"Now since Betta wanted to try a third time, she pronounced the third formula, 'tafaro e tammurro, pizze 'ngongole e cemmino,' and out came an armful of cloth of silk and gold and sashes embroidered with golden seashells, and it was finery more beautiful than even the queen herself would have been able to put together. When the ladies-in-waiting caught a glimpse of those things they informed their mistress, who attempted to negotiate for them as she had for the other things. She received the same answer from Betta—that if she wanted the goods she had to let her husband sleep with her—and the queen said to herself, 'What am I going to lose if I satisfy this vulgar girl in order to steal those beautiful things away from her?' She took all the riches that Betta offered her, and that evening—as soon as Night arrived after liquidating the debts it had contracted with sleep and rest—she gave the sleeping draught to Pretty as a Picture.

"But he kept it in his mouth and then pretended to go and empty his bladder, and spit it out in another room. When he went to lie down next to Betta, she started up with the same tune, explaining how she had molded him out of sugar and almonds with her own hands, how she had made his hair out of gold and his eyes and mouth out of pearls and precious stones, how he was in debt to her for the life given to him by the gods as a result of her prayers, and, finally, how he had been robbed from her and how she, big and pregnant, had gone looking for him and had encountered more hardships than the heavens usually allow baptized flesh to endure. And, moreover, how she had slept for two other nights with him, in exchange for two treasures, without being able to say a single word to him, and how this was the last night for her hopes and the terminus for her life.

"Pretty as a Picture, who was awake, heard these words and started to remember as if in a dream everything that had happened, and he embraced and comforted her as best he could. And—since Night had gone out with its black mask to direct the dance of the stars—he got up very quietly, entered the room where the queen was lost in a deep sleep, and took all the things she had stolen from Betta and all the jewels and golden coins in her strongbox as compensation for the suffering she had caused. Then he returned to his wife, and they left that very moment and walked until they were beyond the borders of the kingdom, where they rested themselves in excellent lodgings until Betta gave birth to a lovely baby boy.

"When she was able to get out of bed, they set off for her father's house, where they found him alive and healthy and as sprightly as a boy of fifteen at the joy of seeing his daughter again. The queen, finding neither her husband nor the beggar girl nor her jewels, tore herself to shreds, and there was no lack of those who said *those who deceive should not complain if they are deceived.*"

4

THE GOLDEN TRUNK

Fourth Entertainment of the Fifth Day

Parmetella, daughter of a poor peasant, encounters good fortune, but due to her excessive curiosity she lets it get away. After a thousand torments she finds her husband at the house of his mother, an ogress, and after undergoing great dangers they live together happily.

There was more than one of them who would have given a finger of their hand to be able to have the power to make a husband or wife just as they desired; the prince in particular would have liked some sugar paste next to him instead of the pile of venom that was sitting there. But since it was Tolla's turn to play the game, she didn't wait for the official summons to pay her debt but began to speak in this manner: "When people are too curious and want to know too much, the fuse that blows up the powder magazine of their fortunes is always lit. Quite often those who mind other people's business fail at their own, and more times than not those who go digging for treasure with excessive curiosity find themselves with their faces pushed into the sewer, like what happened to the daughter of a vegetable farmer, in the manner that follows.

"There once was a vegetable farmer who was so terribly poor that for all he sweat and toiled he was barely able to buy his bread.[1] One day he purchased three little sows for his three daughters, so that they could raise them and have a little something for their dowries. Pascuzza and Cice, the older daughters, took their sows to graze in a lovely pasture, but they didn't want Parmetella, the youngest daughter, to go with them, so they sent her off to graze her animal elsewhere.

"Parmetella took her little animal into a wood—where the shad-

---

AT 425A: The Monster (Animal) as Bridegroom. See Penzer for motifs in common with Grimm 88 ("The Singing, Springing Lark") and other tales (2:128). See also Gonzenbach 15. This is one of several tales of *The Tale of Tales* that bear close resemblance to the story of Cupid and Psyche, as told by Apuleius in *The Golden Ass*.
1. *scire da pane a vennere* (Neap.): a play on words ("to go from Pan to Venus") (Rak 942) vs., perhaps, "to go from [consuming] bread to selling it."

ows heroically resisted the Sun's assault—and upon arriving at some pasture land in the middle of which flowed a little fountain—innkeeper of cool water that with its silvery tongue invited the passersby to drink half a measure—she came across a tree with golden leaves. She took one and brought it back to her father, who with great joy sold it for more than twenty ducats, which allowed him to stop up a few holes. And when he asked her where she had found it, she said, 'Take it, sir, and ask no more, or your fortune will be ruined!' The following day she returned and did the same thing, and she went on stripping the tree of its leaves for so long that at the end it was completely plucked, as if it had been sacked by the winds.

"When autumn had passed and she realized that the tree had a great golden trunk that she wouldn't be able to pull up with her hands, she went home and returned with a hatchet, and set to work baring the roots all around the base of the tree. Then she lifted up the trunk as best she could and found a beautiful porphyry staircase underneath, and since she was immeasurably curious she followed it down to the bottom. After walking through a large, terribly dark cave she came to a lovely plain on which stood a splendid palace, where your feet trod on nothing but gold and silver and you saw nothing before you but pearls and precious stones. Parmetella stared at all of those lavish riches as if she were in a daze, and, not seeing any sign of movement on such beautiful premises, she went into a room hung with a number of pictures in which were painted many beautiful things: in particular, the ignorance of men considered wise, the injustice of those who hold the scales of justice, and the crimes punished by the heavens, all things that seemed so real and alive that it was astonishing. And in that same room she found a lovely table set for a meal.

"Feeling her stomach rumble and not seeing anyone there, Parmetella sat down at the table and began to dig in like a great lord. But just as she was chewing most happily, in came a handsome slave, who said, 'Stop, do not leave; I want you for my wife, and I will make you the happiest woman in the world!' Although Parmetella was spinning the fine thread of fear, she nevertheless took heart when she heard this nice promise, and, agreeing to what the slave had proposed, she was immediately given a diamond carriage pulled by four golden horses with emerald and ruby wings, which took her for a ride in the air to amuse her. And as personal maids she was given a number of monkeys wearing golden robes, who immediately began to dress her from head to toe as elegantly as a spider, so that she looked just like a queen.

"But when night fell—and the Sun, wanting to sleep on the shores of the river of India unbothered by horseflies, put out the light—the slave said to her, 'My darling, if you want to go nightie-night, get into this bed. But after you wrap yourself up in the sheets put out the candle, and be careful to do as I tell you if you don't want to tangle things up.' Parmetella did this and then fell asleep, but no sooner had her eyes been sprinkled with poppy dust than the slave, who had become a beautiful young man, got into bed by her side. Waking up, she felt her wool being carded without a comb and thought she would die of fright, but when she realized that it was merely a civil war, she kept still under the blows. But—before Dawn came out to look for some fresh eggs to appease her little old lover—the slave jumped out of bed and got back his dark veneer, leaving Parmetella quite eager to know what sort of glutton had sucked up the very first egg of such a pretty spring chicken as herself.

"The next night arrived, and she went to bed and put out the candle as she had done the previous night, and, as before, the handsome young man came and lay beside her. After he grew tired of romping around and fell asleep, she took out a flint she had prepared, struck it on some tinder, flared up a match, and lit the candle. Then she lifted up the covers and saw that the ebony had turned to ivory, the caviar to the milkiest milk, and the coal to whitewash. At the sight of such beauty she stood there with her mouth hanging open, considering and contemplating the most beautiful brushstroke that Nature had ever given to its canvas of marvels. But the beautiful young man awoke and began to curse Parmetella, saying, 'Alas, I'll have to perform this accursed penance for another seven years because of you, since you wanted to stick your nose into my secrets with such curiosity! Go away now, beat it, get lost, disappear, and go back to your rags, since you weren't capable of recognizing your own luck!' And as he was saying this he slipped away like quicksilver.

"The poor girl, all cold and icy, lowered her head to the ground and left the house, and outside the grotto she encountered a fairy who said to her, 'Oh, my child, my soul weeps for your misfortune! You're being sent to your slaughter, for you'll be going over the Bridge of Hair,[2] you poor thing! But to keep yourself from danger, take these seven spindles, these seven figs, this jar of honey, and these seven pairs of iron shoes, and walk without ever stopping until they're all worn out. Then you'll see seven women spinning from the balcony of a house down to the ground, with their thread wound on dead peo-

---

2. "This recalls the bridge 'al sirât,' which spanned the middle of hell, and was narrower than a hair and flatter than a sword blade. Every soul had to pass the test of going over it, according to some Islamic belief" (Croce 491). It also appears in the dream of the converted thief in Franciscan legend (see Francesco d'Assisi, *Fioretti* 26; cit. Rak 942).

Stanno a canna aperta a tenere mente e contempranno la chiù bella pennellata c'avesse dato mai la Natura 'ncoppa la tela de la maraveglia. [She stood there with her mouth hanging open, considering and contemplating the most beautiful brushstroke that Nature had ever given to its canvas of marvels.]

ple's bones. And you know what you need to do? Stay crouched down and very quietly, as the thread is lowered, take the bone off and attach the honey-smeared spindle to it with a fig in the place of the spindle holder, so that when they pull it up and taste the sweetness they'll say, "May whoever sweetened my little mouth find their little fortune sweetened, too!" And after these words they'll say, one after the other, "O you who have brought me these sweet things, show yourself!" And you answer, "I don't want to because you'll eat me!" They'll say, "I won't eat you, may God save my serving spoon!" And you dig in your heels and be stubborn, and they'll continue, "I won't eat you, may God save my spit!" And you keep as still as if you were being shaved. They'll go on, "I won't eat you, may God save my broom!" And don't you believe a word of it, and even if they say, "I won't eat you, may the heavens save my chamber pot," you close your mouth and don't say a peep, or else they'll make you shit your life away. Finally they'll say, "May God save Thunder-and-Lightning, I won't eat you!" And then you climb up there, and you can be sure they won't harm you.'

"After listening to this, Parmetella began to walk though valleys and up mountains, so far that after seven years her iron shoes had worn out. She arrived at a large house that had a little loggia hanging off it and saw the seven women spinning, and when she had done everything the fairy had advised her to do, after a thousand peek-a-boos and hide-and-seeks, the oath of Thunder-and-Lightning was finally uttered, and she climbed up and showed herself. At this, all seven of them said, 'Oh, you traitorous bitch, you're the reason our brother has been in the grotto for seven and now seven more years, far from us, with the body of a slave! But don't worry, for even if you have succeeded in confiscating our throats with an oath, at the first chance we get we'll make you pay for the old and the new! You know what you need to do now? Crouch down behind that cupboard, and when our mother, who without a doubt would gobble you right up, comes in, go up behind her and grab her tits, which she carries like saddlebags on her shoulders, and then pull as hard as you can and don't let go until she swears on Thunder-and-Lightning that she won't hurt you.'

"Parmetella did this, and after the mother swore on the fireplace shovel, the foot stool, the clothes rack, the reel, and the dish rack, she swore on Thunder-and-Lightning, and Parmetella let go of her tits and showed herself to the ogress, who said to her, 'I could kick myself! But you better dig a straight row, traitor, because the first time it rains I'll have you thrown in a gutter stream!'[3] And, poking around

---

3. *a la lava* (Neap.): see tale 1.8 n10.

with sticks for an opportunity to wolf her down, one day the ogress took twelve sacks of beans that were all mixed up and jumbled to-gether—there were chickpeas and chicklings and peas and lentils and kidney beans and fava beans and rice and lupins—and said to her, 'Here you go, traitor, take these beans and sort them so that each kind is separate from the others, and if they're not done by this eve-ning I'll eat you up like a three-penny fritter!'

"Poor Parmetella sat at the foot of the sacks and said, weeping, 'Oh, my dear mother, that golden trunk has cost me so much! This time it's really over for me! This blackened heart has become a rag, and all because I saw a black face become white! Alas, I'm ruined, I'm done for, there's no possible remedy; it looks to me like I'm going to be in that stinking ogress's gullet any minute now! And there's no one who can help me, no one who can give me advice, no one who can comfort me!'

"Now as she was tearing her hair out, all of a sudden Thunder-and-Lightning appeared before her like a lightning bolt. He had fin-ished the period of exile imposed on him by the curse, and even though he was angry with Parmetella his blood was not made of water, and when he saw her wailing like that he said, 'Traitor, what have you to cry about?' And she told him how his mother had treated her so badly and of her intentions to rub her out and then eat her up. To which Thunder-and-Lightning answered, 'Arise and take heart, for it will not be so!' And, throwing all the beans on the ground, he caused a river of ants to come forth. They immediately began to pile all the beans into separate groups so that Parmetella was able to gather one kind at a time and fill the sacks.

"When the ogress came back and found the job done, she fell into a state of despair, saying, 'That dog Thunder-and-Lightning did me this nice service, but you'll pay me the difference. Take these ticks, which are for twelve mattresses, and fill them all with feathers by this evening or else I'll chop you to pieces!' The poor soul took the mat-tress covers, sat on the ground, and had begun not only to howl but also to tear at herself and to make two fountains of her eyes when Thunder-and-Lightning appeared and said to her, 'Don't cry, traitor! Leave it to this fellow; I'll guide you to your port. Now mess up your hair, spread the mattress covers on the ground, and start to cry and moan and scream that the King of the Birds[4] is dead, and you'll see what happens.' Parmetella did this, and there suddenly appeared a cloud of birds that darkened the air, and as they beat their wings they

---

4. See introduction to day 1 n21.

sent basket after basket of feathers falling to the ground, so that in less than an hour the mattresses were full.

"When the ogress came and saw what had happened, she blew up so violently that she was about to split her sides, and she said, 'Thunder-and-Lightning is starting to get on my nerves, but I'll be dragged around on a monkey's tail if I don't trap her someplace where she won't be able to get away from me!' With this, she told Parmetella, 'Run, roll on down to my sister's house and tell her to send me the musical instruments, since I've married off Thunder-and-Lightning and we want to have a celebration fit for a king.' And on the other end, she sent word to her sister that when the traitor came to get the instruments she should immediately kill her and cook her, and that she would come so that they could eat her together.

"When she saw herself ordered to do lighter work Parmetella grew quite cheerful, for she believed that the weather was starting to get milder—oh, how wrong human judgment is!—but then on the way she ran into Thunder-and-Lightning, who when he saw her hurrying along said to her, 'Where are you headed, you wretched thing? Don't you see that you're going to slaughter, you're making your own shackles, you're sharpening your own knife, and you're measuring out your own poison, since you're being sent to the ogress so that she can eat you up? Listen, then, and don't doubt what I say: take this loaf of bread, this bundle of hay, and this stone, and when you get to my aunt's house you'll see that there's a Corsican hound that will come at you barking and try to bite you. Give it this loaf of bread, and you'll shut its trap. When you've gotten past the dog you'll find an untied horse that will come at you and try to kick and trample you. Give it this hay, and you'll bind its hooves. Finally, you'll find a door that slams continuously; prop it open with this stone, and you'll take away its strength. Then go upstairs, where you'll find the ogress holding a baby girl in her arms. She'll have lit the oven so that she can roast you, and she'll say to you, "Hold this baby, and wait while I go upstairs to get the instruments," but you should know that she's going to sharpen her fangs so that she can tear you apart piece by piece. Throw her little daughter into the oven without mercy, since she's ogre meat, get the musical instruments from behind the door, and slip out before the ogress comes back, or else you'll be done for. But be warned that the instruments are in a box that you must not open unless you want trouble and then more trouble.'

"Parmetella did everything that her lover had advised her to do, but as she was returning with the instruments she opened the box, and suddenly a flute here, a shawm there, some bagpipes over here, a recorder over there, began to fly through the air making a thousand sounds, and Parmetella ran after them clawing her face to shreds. In the meantime the ogress came down, and when she couldn't find Parmetella she went to a window and cried out to the door, 'Crush that traitor!' And the door answered, 'I don't want to hurt the unfortunate girl, for she propped me open!' Then the ogress yelled at the horse, 'Trample that crook!' And the horse answered, 'I don't want to trample her, for she gave me some hay to chew on!' Finally the ogress called the dog over, saying: 'Sink your teeth into that coward!' And the dog answered, 'Let the poor little thing go, for she gave me a loaf of bread!'

"Now as Parmetella went shouting after the instruments, she ran into Thunder-and-Lightning, who gave her a real dressing-down and said to her, 'O traitor, when are you ever going to learn, at your own expense, that you're in this situation because of your accursed curiosity?' As he was saying this he called the instruments with a whistle and shut them back up in the box, and then told her to bring them to his mother. When the ogress saw Parmetella she screamed, 'O cruel destiny, even my sister is against me, and refused to do me this favor!'

"Meanwhile, the new bride arrived. She was a plague, a cancer, a harpy, and an evil shadow, with a pug nose and buck teeth; she was an owl, a cracked barrel, and stiff as a pole, so that if you put a hundred flowers and garlands on her she would have looked like a tavern that had just opened.[5] Her mother-in-law prepared a great banquet for her, and since her intentions were bad, she had the table set near a well, where she placed her seven daughters, each with a torch in her hand. She gave Parmetella, however, two torches, and had her sit on the edge of the well, with the idea that if she got sleepy she might fall to the bottom.

"Now while the food was coming and going and the blood was beginning to heat up, Thunder-and-Lightning, who was sitting there like an unwilling bride, said to Parmetella, "O traitor, do you love me?' And she answered, 'All the way up to the terrace!' And he replied, 'If you love me, give me a kiss!' And she, 'God help me, may it never be! May the heavens preserve that fine thing sitting next to you for a hundred years, with health and baby boys!' And the bride answered, 'It's quite clear that you'll always be a wretch, even if you live to be a hundred, if you find kissing such a handsome young man disgusting. I myself let a shepherd smooch with me for two chestnuts!'

"When he heard this fine news, the bridegroom flew into a rage and swelled up like a toad, so that the food he was eating got stuck in

---

5. "Branches and wreathes of flowers and leaves identified taverns, and especially recently opened ones" (Rak 942).

his throat. Nevertheless, he pretended the tripe was heart and swallowed the pill, thinking that he would settle his accounts and pay off his debt later on. But when the tables had been cleared he dismissed his mother and sisters, and he, the bride, and Parmetella were left together before going to bed. As he was having Parmetella take off his shoes he said to the bride, 'My wife, did you see how this fussy girl refused to give me a kiss?' 'She was wrong,' answered the bride, 'to back off from kissing you, since you're such a handsome young man. I, on the other hand, let myself be kissed by a boy who looks after sheep, for two chestnuts!'

"Thunder-and-Lightning could contain himself no longer; with lightning flashes of disdain and thunderbolts of actions, when the mustard reached his nostrils he grabbed a knife and slit his wife's throat. Then he dug a grave in the cellar, buried her there, and, hugging Parmetella to him, said, 'You are my joy, you are the flower of all women, the mirror of all honorable ladies! And so turn your eyes to me, give me your hand, offer me your mouth, join your heart to mine, for I want to be yours as long as the world is still the world!'

"As he was saying this they went to bed, and they remained there, taking their pleasure, until the Sun released its horses of fire from the barn of water and sent them to pasture in the fields sown by Dawn. When the ogress came in with some fresh eggs to cheer the newlyweds and to say, 'Blessed are those who marry, and take a mother-in-law!' she found Parmetella in the arms of her son, and after hearing how the business had been conducted she ran straight to her sister's so that they could orchestrate a way to get rid of that speck in their eye without her son being able to help her.

"But when she discovered that out of grief for the daughter who had been baked in the oven her sister had thrown herself in, too, so that the stink of something burning was infecting the whole neighborhood, such was her desperation that she transformed from an ogress into a ram and banged her head against the wall so many times that her brains came splattering out. And when Thunder-and-Lightning had restored peace between Parmetella and her sisters-in-law, they were all happy and content, proving the truth of the saying: *those who resist win.*"

5

SUN, MOON, AND TALIA

Fifth Entertainment of the Fifth Day

Talia dies because of a little piece of flax and is left in a palace, where a king chances to pass by and causes her to have two children. The children fall into the hands of the king's jealous wife, who orders that they be cooked and served to their father and that Talia be burned. The cook saves the children and Talia is freed by the king, who has his wife thrown into the same fire that had been prepared for Talia.

Although the story of the ogresses might have solicited a bit of compassion, instead it was the cause of pleasure, for everyone was happy that Parmetella's affairs had gone far better than expected. After this tale it was Popa's turn for deliberating, and since her feet were already in the stirrups she began to speak in this manner:[1]

"There once was a great lord who at the birth of a daughter named Talia summoned all the wise men and fortune-tellers of his kingdom to predict her future. After conferring a number of times, they concluded that she would find herself in great danger because of a little piece of flax. And so the king issued a prohibition aimed at avoiding that baleful encounter: in his house neither flax nor hemp nor anything of the sort was to enter.

AT 410: Sleeping Beauty. This is an early version of the "Sleeping Beauty" tale, which was followed subsequently by Charles Perrault's "The Sleeping Beauty in the Wood," with which it bears close resemblance, and Grimm 50 ("Brier Rose"), which eliminates the whole second part and ends with the heroine waking up to her prince.
1. This is one of the few tales missing a moralizing introduction, which typically follows the description of the reactions of the listeners to the preceding tale. Although there is not one in the original edition of 1636 and its reprint in 1644, in subsequent editions a new paragraph is added, which Croce includes in his 1925 translation. It reads: "It has been seen again and again that, for the most part, cruelty serves as an executioner to he who exercises it, nor has it ever been seen that he who spits at the heavens does not get it back on his own face. And the other side of this coin, innocence, is a shield made of the wood of the fig tree on which every sword of malice is broken and leaves its tip, so that just when a poor man believes himself to be dead and buried he finds himself being reborn in flesh and bones, as you will hear in the tale that I am about to tap from the barrel of memory with the spigot of this tongue" (cit. Croce 498).

"But when Talia came to be a big girl and was looking out the window one day, she saw an old woman who was spinning pass by. Since she had never seen a distaff or a spindle and was greatly pleased by all that winding, she became so curious that she had the woman come up and, taking the distaff in her hand, she began to draw the thread. But then, by accident, a little piece of flax got under her fingernail and she fell dead to the ground.

"At the sight of this the old woman started running, and she's still jumping down those stairs. And when the hapless father heard of the accident that had occurred, he paid for that pail of bitter wine with a barrel of tears and had her placed inside that same palace, which was in the country, seated on a velvet chair under a brocade canopy. Then he closed the doors and abandoned forever the palace that had been the cause of such great sorrow, so as to thoroughly erase every memory of this misfortune.

"But some time later a king who was out hunting lost his falcon, which after it escaped flew in a window of that house. When it didn't respond to his call the king knocked at the door, since he thought people lived there. After knocking for a long time he had a harvester's ladder brought, intending to scale the house himself to see what was inside. He climbed up and looked all over the place and, not finding a living soul, just stood there awhile like a mummy. Finally he arrived at the room where Talia sat, as if enchanted, and when he saw her he thought she was asleep. He called to her, but no matter what he did and how loud he yelled she did not wake up, and since her beauty had enflamed him, he carried her in his arms to a bed and picked the fruits of love. Then he left her in the bed and returned to his kingdom, where he did not remember what had happened for a long time.

"After nine months Talia unloaded a pair of babies, one a boy and the other a girl, who looked like two bejeweled necklaces. They were cared for by two fairies that had appeared in the palace, who would place them at their mother's teats; one day, when they were trying to suck but couldn't find the nipple, they grabbed her finger and sucked so long that the piece of flax came out. Talia felt like she was awakening from a long sleep, and when she saw those jewels beside her she offered them her tit and held them as dear as her own life.

"And while she did not know what had happened to her and how it was that she was alone in that palace with two children by her side and people who brought her things to eat without her being able to see them, the king, who had remembered her, found an occasion to go hunting and came to see her. Finding her awake and in the company of two painted eggs of beauty, he was stunned with joy and told

Talia who he was and what had happened. They made friends and a strong bond was established, and after staying several days with her he took his leave with the promise that he would return and take her away with him. He then went back to his kingdom, where he mentioned Talia and the children at every chance he got, so that when he was eating he had Talia in his mouth and also Sun and Moon, for those were the names he had given the children, and when he went to bed he called for the one and the other.

"The king's wife had already become a little suspicious after her husband's delay in returning from the hunt, and when she heard all this talk of Talia, Moon, and Sun she felt burned by something other than the sun. And so she called her secretary and said to him, 'Listen here, my boy: you're between Scylla and Charybdis,[2] the jamb and the door, the club and the prison bars. If you tell me who my husband is in love with I'll make you rich, and if you hide it from me I'll make sure you're found neither dead nor alive.' Her crony was on the one hand all shaken up by fear and on the other fleeced by interest, which is a blindfold on honor's eyes, a veil on the face of justice, and a crowbar on words given. He thus gave her bread for bread and wine for wine, at which the queen sent the secretary to visit Talia on the king's behalf and tell her that he wanted to see the children. Talia sent them to him with great joy, and that heart of Medea ordered the cook to slit their throats, make various little dishes and delicacies out of them, and then serve them to her poor husband. The cook, however, was of tender lung, and when he saw those two lovely golden apples he took pity on them and gave them to his wife to hide, instead preparing two goat kids in a hundred different sauces.

"The king came home, and the queen had the food served with great gusto. While the king was eating with great gusto, too, and exclaiming, 'Oh, on the life of Lanfusa,[3] this dish is so good! Oh, on the soul of my grandpa, this other one is so tasty!' she kept on saying, 'Eat up, for you're eating what is yours.' The king paid no attention to this refrain two or three times, but finally, when he heard the music keeping up, he answered, 'I know that what I'm eating is mine, since you didn't bring a thing with you to this house!' and he got up angrily and went out to the nearby countryside to unleash his anger.

---

2. *Sciglia e Scariglia* (Neap.): "Scylla was a maiden transformed into a monster, with the head and body of a woman and the tail of a fish, who devoured six of Ulysses's companions (Homer, *Odyssey* 12). After she was killed by Hercules she was reborn in the sea god Forco, of whom she was daughter, and lay in ambush in the Strait of Messina. Carybdis, which also appears in the myth of the Argonauts, was the whirlpool situated on the other shore of the strait" (Rak 954).

3. See eclogue 1 ("The Crucible") n4.

"In the meantime the queen, not yet satisfied with what she had done, called the secretary back and had him summon Talia with the excuse that the king was waiting to see her. Talia came the instant she heard this, eager to find her light without realizing that only fire awaited her, and she appeared before the queen, who with a face like Nero's, livid with rage, said to her, 'May you be welcome, madam slut!⁴ So you're that fancy piece of trash, that weed with whom my husband takes his pleasure! So you're that bitch who makes my head spin like a top! Go on, you've reached purgatory, and I'm going to make you pay for the pain you've caused me!'

"When Talia heard this she began to apologize, saying that it wasn't her fault and that the king had taken possession of her territory when she was under a sleeping spell. But the queen, who had no intention of listening to excuses, had a huge fire lit right there in the courtyard of the palace and then ordered that Talia be thrown onto it. Seeing that things had taken a bad turn, Talia fell down on her knees before the queen and begged her to at least give her the time to take off the clothes she was wearing. Not so much out of pity for the poor girl as to retrieve those gold-and-pearl-embroidered clothes, the queen said, 'Get undressed; that I will allow you to do.' Talia began to undress, letting out a shriek with every piece of clothing she took off. And when she had taken off her dress, her skirt, and her jacket, and was about to take off her petticoat, she let out the last shriek while they dragged her off to supply the ashes for the laundry tub where Charon⁵ washed his breeches.

"At that very moment the king ran in and, discovering this spectacle, demanded to know the whole story. He then asked about his children and heard his own wife, who reproached him with betraying her, tell him of how she had gotten him to devour them. When the hapless king heard this he fell prey to desperation and began to cry, 'So I was the werewolf that attacked my own little sheep! Alas, why didn't my veins recognize the springs of their own blood? O renegade Turk, what kind of a ferocious thing did you do? Just wait; you're going to end up as compost in a broccoli plot, and I won't be sending this face of a tyrant to the Colosseum⁶ for her penance!' And as he

---

4. *Troccola* (Neap.): from the Neapolitan *trocula,* a rattle or clapper, and so by association a chatterbox, busybody, or woman of little consideration (Penzer 2:131). Also the name of a character in tale 4.7.

5. In Greek and Roman mythology, the ferryman who transported the souls of the dead across the River Styx to Hades.

6. *Culiseo* (Neap.): The Colosseum, Rome's great amphitheater, was begun by Emperor Vespasian and finished by his son Titus in 90; according to Christian legend, it was the site of barbarous cruelty. Basile also puns on *culo* (ass).

was saying this he ordered that she be thrown into the same fire lit for Talia, together with the secretary who had been an instrument in the bitter game and a weaver of the wicked plot. He was intending to do the same with the cook who he thought had chopped up his children, but the cook threw himself at the king's feet and said, 'Actually, my lord, the service I performed for you would deserve a pension[7] other than a furnace full of coals, a subsidy other than a pole in the ass, an entertainment other than to blacken and shrivel in a fire, and a profit other than to mix the ashes of a cook with those of a queen! This is certainly not the great thanks that I expect for having saved your children in spite of that sack of dog bile, who wanted to kill them so that what was part of your body would return to that same body.'

"When he heard those words the king was beside himself and thought he was dreaming, nor could he believe his own ears. He finally turned to the cook and said, 'If it is true that you saved my children, you may rest assured that I will free you from turning the spit and that I will place you in the kitchen of this heart, where you can turn my desires as you please and claim for yourself a prize so great that you will consider yourself happy to be in this world!' While the king was speaking these words the cook's wife, who saw the state of need her husband was in, brought Moon and Sun before their father. And, playing the game of three with his wife and children, he sent out a whirlwind of kisses first to the one and then to the other, and when he had given the cook a large reward and named him his gentleman-in-waiting he took Talia for his wife. She enjoyed a long life with her husband and children, and recognized after all her ordeals that for those who are lucky, *good rains down even when they are sleeping.*"

---

7. *chiazza morta* (Neap.): This, as well as *aiuto de costa* (subsidy) and *trattene-miento* (entertainment), is a term of Spanish origin, relative to military pensions and other forms of assistance. See tale 1.7 n29.

6

SAPIA

Sixth Entertainment of the Fifth Day

Sapia, the daughter of a great baroness, makes a wise man out of the king's son Carluccio, who hadn't even been able to learn the alphabet. When he receives a slap on the cheek from Sapia, Carluccio decides to take revenge by marrying her, and after a thousand torments he has three babies with her and, without realizing it, they are reconciled.

The lord prince and the princess were full of joy when they saw Talia's affairs come to a happy end, for they never would have believed that amid such a tempest she could find a safe port. And after they ordered Antonella[1] to unsheathe her tale, she took hold of it in this manner: "There are three species of idiots in the world, each of which deserves more than the other to be put in the oven: the first is those who do not know, the second those who do not want to know, and the third those who think they know. The idiot about whom I am about to talk to you is of the second species, who does not want knowledge to enter his noggin and thus hates those who teach it to him, trying, like a modern-day Nero,[2] to cut off their bread supply.

"There once was a king, the king of Closed Castle, who had a son so thickheaded that there was no way to get him to learn the ABCs, and whenever anyone talked to him about reading or learning, he would blow up; neither screaming nor beatings nor threats served any purpose. And so his poor father was swollen like a toad with anger, and he didn't know what to do to stimulate the wits of this wretch of a son so as not to have to leave his kingdom in the hands of

---

AT 891: The Man Who Deserts His Wife and Sets Her the Task of Bearing Him a Child. Penzer notes similarities with the frame of the *Panchatantra*, in which there are three ignorant sons, and discusses the "spite marriage" motif in Shakespeare's *All's Well That Ends Well*, *Decameron* 3.9, as well as other lesser-known variants (2:138). See also Straparola 7.1 ("Ortodosio Simeoni") and Gonzenbach 36.
1. In the text, Ciulla.
2. Possibly a reference to Nero's rejection of Seneca.

Mamelukes,[3] for he knew that it was impossible to fuse ignorance and the governance of a kingdom.

"During those same times there lived a daughter of the baroness Cenza, who, due to the great knowledge that she had accumulated in thirteen years, had acquired the name of Sapia. Word of her virtuous qualities got to the king, and he came up with the idea of entrusting his son to the baroness so that she could put him under the tutelage of her daughter, since he thought that the girl's company and competence could have some positive effects.

"And thus, once the prince was installed in the baroness's house Sapia began to teach him the sign of the Holy Cross, but when she saw that he left all those lovely words behind and that all of her fine reasoning went in one ear and out the other, she couldn't help but give him a nice slap on the face. Carluccio, for that was the name of the prince, was so humiliated by this slap that out of disgrace and spite he did what he had refused to do for caresses and kindness, and in a few months he not only knew how to read but had made so much progress in the study of grammar that he had learned all the rules. His father was so delighted that he was walking on air, and he removed Carluccio from that house and sent him off to study other, more important subjects, until he became the wisest man in the whole kingdom. But Sapia's blow had left such an impression on him that when he was awake he saw it before his eyes and when he was asleep he dreamed of it, so that he decided either to die or to avenge himself.

"In the meantime Sapia had reached a marriageable age and the prince, who was waiting with lighted fuse for an opportunity to take revenge, said to his father, 'My lord, I acknowledge that I received my being from you, and for this reason I am obliged to you all the way up to the terrace. But I also recognize that I am just as obliged to Sapia, who gave me the good life, and therefore, since I cannot find a way to pay her adequately for such a large debt, if it pleases you I would like to take her for my wife, and I assure you that by agreeing to this you would secure a mortgage on my person.' When the king heard his son's decision he answered, 'My son, although Sapia does not have all the carats she should have to be your wife, nonetheless, if her virtue is placed on the scales with our blood, they weigh so much in her favor that we can make this deal. And thus you are happy, and I am well paid.'

---

3. Originally slave soldiers, they were an important part of the armies that won control of various Muslim states in the Middle Ages. Famous for the violence they used, in many circumstances, to control court politics, they came to rule Egypt from the thirteenth to the sixteenth centuries and continued to be powerful until the nineteenth century (vs., in common usage, fool).

"As soon as the baroness had been summoned Carluccio had the marriage contract drawn up, and after festivities worthy of a great lord, he asked the king if he would do him the favor of finding him some isolated quarters where he could stay with his wife. Eager to make him happy, the king had a splendid palace, separate from his own, prepared for him. After Carluccio brought Sapia there he locked her in a room and gave her little to eat and even less to drink, and, worst of all, he refused to pay her his debt, so that the miserable thing was the most desperate woman in the world and could not understand the reason for the bad treatment that had started the moment she had entered that house.

"One day the lord felt like seeing Sapia, and he went into her room and asked her how she was. 'Put your hand on my stomach,' answered Sapia, 'and you can see how I am, although I didn't do a thing to deserve being treated in this manner, like a dog. What was the point of asking me to be your wife if you wanted to keep me worse than a slave?' At these words the prince answered, 'Don't you know that those who commit an offense write it in dust, and those that receive one carve it in marble? Remember what you did to me when you were teaching me to read, and know that the only reason I wanted you for a wife was so that I could make a sauce of your life and avenge myself of the insult I received!' 'And so,' replied Sapia, 'after I sowed so well, I'm harvesting so poorly! If I slapped you, I did it because you were an ass and I thought it would wisen you up: you know that those who love you make you cry, and those who do not make you laugh.'

"If the prince had been seething over the slap before, when he saw himself reproached for his own stupidity he now caught on fire, and what made it worse was that while he had thought Sapia would admit her guilt in the matter, what he saw instead was that she answered back blow for blow, as bold as a rooster. And so he turned his back on her and left, in a worse state than before, and when he came back a number of days later and found that she had the same attitude, he went away even more stubbornly than the first time, determined to make her stew in her own broth like octopus and then punish her with a stick of cotton wool.

"In the meantime the king signed a transfer on his life's property atop the column of a bed of torment, and since the prince was now master and arch-master of all of his estates he decided to go and take possession of them in person. He summoned a cavalcade of soldiers and knights worthy of serving him and set off with them on his journey.

"The baroness got wind of her daughter's hard life and decided to find a prudent solution to this dilemma. First, she had a tunnel made under the prince's palace, by means of which she came to poor little Sapia's aid by bringing her some refreshment. When, several days in advance, the baroness learned of the new king's departure, she had lavish carriages and livery prepared, and after dressing her daughter to perfection and putting her in the company of some ladies, she sent them off on a shortcut so that they would end up where Sapia's husband was to stop, but a day before him. Sapia then took a house across from the palace that had been prepared for the king and placed herself, all decked out and elegant, at the window. When the king arrived and saw this flower of the stewpot of the Graces, he immediately became infatuated with her. And he dug and dug until he managed to get his hands on her, and, leaving her pregnant, he gave her a beautiful necklace in memory of his love.

"The king departed to visit the other cities of his kingdom and Sapia slipped back to her house, where nine months later she gave birth to a lovely baby boy. When the king returned to the capital of his kingdom he went back to see Sapia, thinking that she had already passed away. But instead he found her fresher than ever and ever more obstinate in telling him that she had left the prints of her five fingers on his face in order to make a wise man out of an ass.

"The indignant king left, and since he had to go out of the kingdom again on another trip, Sapia, advised by her mother, did the same thing she had done the first time, and after she took her pleasure with her husband she received a precious bejeweled headpiece and became pregnant with another baby boy whom, upon arriving home, she unloaded when the time was ripe. And when this business had repeated itself a third time, she was given a thick chain of gold and precious stones by the king, who left her pregnant with a baby girl that reached port in due course. Upon returning from his travels, the king found that the baroness, who had given her daughter a sleeping draught, had spread the word that she was dead. But after sending her off to be buried, she deftly had her taken from the grave and hidden in the house.

"The king then celebrated with great ceremony another marriage to a lady of noble lineage, and brought her to the royal palace. But while they were celebrating with stupendous festivities, Sapia and her three children, who were three gems, appeared in the main hall, and, throwing herself at the king's feet, Sapia asked him to be just and not deprive these children of the kingdom, since they were of his own blood.

"For a long time the king just stood there like a man who was dreaming. Finally, realizing that Sapia's wisdom reached to the stars and seeing that when he least imagined it he was being presented with three bastions for his old age, his heart grew tender, and, after giving that other lady a great kingdom and a marriage to his brother, he took Sapia for his wife, thus letting everyone in the world know that *the wise man dominates the stars.*"

7

THE FIVE SONS

Seventh Entertainment of the Fifth Day

Pacione sends his five sons out into the world to learn a trade, and when each of them returns with some special skill, they go and free the daughter of a king, who has been kidnaped by an ogre. After various adventures, as they are arguing about who has given the greatest proof of deserving her for his wife, the king gives her to the father, since he was the plant from whence all the branches grew.

When Antonella's tale was over it was Ciulla's[1] turn to speak, and after getting comfortable on her chair she had a look around her and then began to speak graciously: "Those who stay and tend to the hearth have the brains of a cat: if you don't walk you can't see anything; if you don't see anything you can't learn anything; if you get lost you learn to find your way;[2] practice makes the physician and getting out of bed makes one awake, as I'll show you in the royal trial of a tale that follows.

"There once was a respectable man named Pacione, who had five sons who were so inept that they weren't good for anything, such that their poor father, who could no longer provide for them, resolved one day to get them off his back and said to them, 'My sons, God knows I love you, since, after all, you issued from my own loins, but I am an old man who can work but little and you are young fellows who eat too much, and I can no longer support you as I did before. Each man for himself and the heavens for all! So, then, go out and find yourselves a master and learn how to do something, but take care not to agree to serve for more than a year, and when the time is over I will be at home waiting for you to show me your skills.'

"When the sons heard this resolution they took their leave, and,

---

AT 653: The Four Skillful Brothers. See Straparola 7.5. Penzer comments on the "joint efforts" motif seen already, e.g., in tale 1.5, and notes its great popularity in both East and West (2:143). See also Morlini 80 and Grimm 129 ("The Four Skillful Brothers").

1. In the text, Luccia and Iacova, respectively.
2. Wordplay: *chi va spierto deventa aspierto* (Neap.): "he who wanders becomes an expert."

bringing with them a handful of rags for a change of clothes, each of them set off in a different direction in search of his fortune. At the end of the year they all met, as arranged, at their father's house, where they were received with great hugs, and their father immediately set the table and sat them down to eat. Right when they were digging into the best of it they heard a bird singing, and the youngest of the five sons got up from the table and went outside to listen. When he came back the tablecloth had been removed, and Pacione was starting to ask his sons, 'Now then, comfort this heart a bit, and let's hear what fine skills you've learned in all this time!'

"Luccio, who was the first of all thieves, said, 'I learned the art of stealing, and I've become the ringleader of sly dogs, the master laborer of thieves, and a member of the trade council for the roguish arts. You won't find the equal of this fellow; there's no one who has my expertise in smoothing down and folding up cloaks, bundling up and carrying off laundry, sticking my hook in pockets and emptying them, neatening and cleaning out shops, shaking down and hauling off purses, sweeping and vacating chests: wherever I appear I'll show you miracles of light-fingeredness.' 'My word, what a good boy,' answered his father. 'You've learned to play cards like a merchant, to exchange a counterpoint of the fingers for a receipt of the shoulders,[3] a turn of the key for the strokes of an oar,[4] and a climb up a window for a lowering of the rope![5] Woe is me! Better if I had taught you to work a spinning wheel, so that now you wouldn't be making me spin the fine thread of fear in these intestines. For I can imagine that I might see you any minute in the middle of a court wearing a little paper cap;[6] or else, when your gold is found to be copper, with an oar in your hand;[7] or, if you escape that, dangling, at the end, from a rope!'

"That said, he turned to Tittillo, the second son, and said, 'And you, what fine trade have you learned?' 'I've learned how to make boats,' answered his son. 'That's more like it,' replied his father. 'That's an honorable trade by which you can earn a living. And you, Renzone, what do you know how to do after all this time?' 'I know,' said his son, 'how to shoot a crossbow so straight that I can take out a chicken's eye.' 'Well, that's something,' said his father. 'At least you can get by with your hunting and earn your bread that way.' And, turning to the fourth son, he asked him the same thing and Iacuoco

---

3. I.e., to receive strokes of the whip for stealing.
4. I.e., oar strokes in prison galleys for break-ins.
5. I.e., the rope of a noose.
6. I.e., "whipped by his jailers, with a paper mitre on his head" (Croce 510).
7. *scopierto a ramme* (Neap.): *ramme* were false coins of gold-plated copper (Guarini and Burani 570). Basile puns with *rimmo* (oar).

said, 'I know how to recognize an herb that can resuscitate the dead.'
'Good boy, for the life of Lanfusa!'[8] answered Pacione. 'This is our
chance to leave our poverty behind us. We'll be able to make people
live longer than the ruins of Capua!'[9]

"And when he finally asked his last son, whose name was Menecuccio, what he knew how to do, he said, 'I can understand bird language.' 'So it was for a good reason,' replied his father, 'that while we
were eating you got up to listen to that sparrow chirp. But since you
boast that you can understand what they say, tell me what you heard
that bird say up in the tree.' 'It was saying,' answered Menecuccio,
'that an ogre has kidnaped the daughter of the king of High Gulf and
taken her out to a reef, and no one has been able to get any news of
her, and her father has issued a proclamation saying that whoever
finds this daughter and brings her to him will have her for his wife.'
'If that's all there is, we're rich,' said Luccio, raising his voice, 'because I've got the courage to get her out of the ogre's hands!' 'If you
trust you can do it,' his father proceeded to say, 'we'll go to the king
this very instant, and if he gives us his word that he'll keep the promise, we'll offer to find him his daughter.'

"And thus, after they all agreed to this, Tittillo immediately made
a fine boat, and they got aboard and set sail. Upon reaching Sardinia,
they requested an audience with the king and offered to recover his
daughter, at which they received renewed confirmation of the promise. They then set off for the reef, where they had the luck to find the
ogre stretched out in the sun sleeping, with his head on the lap of the
king's daughter, whose name was Cianna.

"At the sight of the boat approaching, Cianna was so happy that
she wanted to jump up, but Pacione signaled to her to keep quiet, and
when they had placed a big stone on the ogre's lap they lifted Cianna
up, put her in the boat, and began to work the water with their oars.
But before they had gotten very far from shore the ogre woke up and,
not finding Cianna by his side, lowered his eyes toward the shore and
saw the boat carrying her off. At this, he immediately transformed
into a black cloud and began racing through the air to catch up with
the boat. Cianna, who was familiar with the ogre's arts, knew that he
was coming hidden in a cloud, and her fear was so great that she
barely had the time to warn Pacione and his sons before she lost her
senses and died.

"Renzone saw the cloud getting closer and took his crossbow in

8. See eclogue 1 ("The Crucible") n4.
9. *lo Verlascio de Capoa* (Neap.): "the amphitheater of Capua; also used as a general
expression for anything ancient, or a ruin" (Croce 589).

hand. He shot an arrow straight into the eye of the ogre, who from the great pain fell out of the cloud like a hailstone and hit the ground with a boom! And when, after standing there with their eyes glued to the cloud in astonishment, they turned to the boat to see what Cianna was doing, they saw that she had stretched out her feet for the last time and withdrawn from the game[10] of life. At the sight of this Pacione began to tear out his beard, saying, 'Now we've lost the oil and our sleep! Now we've thrown our labors to the wind and our hopes out to sea! This one here has gone to pasture, and we're going to die of hunger; she's said good night and we're going to have a bad day; she's broken her life thread and we're going to break the cord of our hopes! It's quite clear that a poor man's plan never succeeds; it's quite easy to prove that he who is born unlucky dies unhappy! There you have it: we free the daughter of the king, we get back to Sardinia, we win her for our wife, we have a royal celebration, we get the scepter, and we're knocked down flat on our asses!'

"Iacuoco listened to this dirge and then listened some more. Finally, when he saw that the song was lasting too long and that his father was going to play counterpoint on the lute of his pain right up to the rosette, he said, 'Just a minute, sir. We intend to go to Sardinia and live with greater happiness and satisfaction than you believe!' 'The Grand Turk may have that satisfaction!' answered Pacione. 'When we bring Cianna's corpse to her father, he'll have something counted out for us, but it won't be money, and whereas others die with a Sardinian smile on their face, we'll die with a sardonic[11] cry!' 'Quiet!' replied Iacuoco. 'Where have you sent your brain to pasture? Don't you remember the trade I learned? First we land; then let me look for the herb I have in mind and you'll see big things happen.'

"His father took heart at these words, hugged his son, and pulled on the oars just as hard as he was pulled by desire, so that in a short time they reached the coast of Sardinia. Iacuoco got out, found the herb, and ran back to the boat. When he had squeezed its juice into Cianna's mouth, she came back to life right away, like a frog that after being in the Grotto of the Dogs is then thrown into Lake Agnano.[12] And so with great joy they went to the king, who couldn't get his fill

---

10. *trucco* (Neap.): see tale 1.10 n20.

11. "Allusion to the various powers (exhilarant, aphrodisiac, toxic) of the 'sardonic herb,' a plant of Sardinia" (Guarini and Burani 573). See also introduction to day 1 n8.

12. "In the famous 'Grotto of the Dogs,' near Naples, experiments were performed in which animals were made to lose their senses by inhaling the carbon dioxide of which the cave is full, and then plunged into the waters of the nearby Lake of Agnano to see if they could be revived" (Croce 513).

of hugging and kissing his daughter and of thanking those good people who had brought her back.

"But when they requested that he keep his promise, the king said,
'To which one of you am I to give Cianna? This is no chestnut cake
that can be portioned out into slices; it is the lot of only one of you to
get the bean in the cake, and the others can take a toothpick.' The
first son, who was a shrewd one, answered, 'The reward, Sire, should
be in proportion to the effort; and so you must see which of us deserves this tasty morsel, and then mete justice as you see fit.' 'You
speak like Roland,'[13] answered the king. 'Tell me, then, what you
have done, so that I might avoid seeing things crookedly and be able
to judge straight.'

"When each had told of his trials, the king turned to Pacione and
said, 'And what part did you have in this matter?' 'It seems to me that
I had a big part,' replied Pacione, 'since I raised these sons of mine
into men and drove them so hard that I made them learn the trades
they now know, and if I hadn't they would be a bunch of empty baskets instead of the beautiful fruits that they are today.'

"After hearing one side and the other and chewing and ruminating
over the reasons of this one and that one and seeing and considering
what seemed right, the king ruled that Cianna should go to Pacione,
since he was the root origin of his daughter's salvation. So he said and
so it was done, and when the sons had each received a handful of
money with which to earn a living, their father became like a fifteen-
year-old boy again out of happiness, and this proverb was a perfect
fit for him: *If two fight, the third one wins.*"

13. See tale 1.1 n7.

8

NENNILLO AND NENNELLA

Eighth Entertainment of the Fifth Day

Iannuccio has two children with his first wife, then marries a second time. His children are hated so much by their stepmother that she takes them to a wood, where after they get separated Nennillo becomes the beloved courtier of a prince and Nennella is shipwrecked and swallowed by an enchanted fish. When she is cast onto a reef, she is recognized by her brother and married off richly by the prince.

When Ciulla had finished her race, Paola[1] prepared to run hers, and after she generously praised the tale of the other woman, who had portrayed Sapia's good judgment so realistically,[2] she said, "Hapless is the man who has children and hopes to take care of them by giving them a stepmother: he brings home the machine of their ruin, since a stepmother who casts a kind eye upon the children of another has never been seen. And even if by some accident one were found, you'd have to put a stick in the hole[3] or say that it was a white crow. But among the many that you may have heard mentioned, I will tell you about one who can be put on the list of unconscionable stepmothers, and I think you will deem her worthy of the punishment she bought for herself with hard cash.

"There once was a father named Iannuccio who had two children, Nennillo and Nennella, whom he loved like the pupils of his eyes. But after death used the silent file of Time[4] to break the bars that kept his wife's soul imprisoned, he took an ugly hag for his wife, an accursed bitch[5] who, as soon as she set foot in her husband's house, began to act like a horse that wants the stable all to itself, saying, 'Why do you

---

AT 327A: Hansel and Gretel, and AT 450: Little Brother and Little Sister. See Perrault, "Little Thumbling," and Grimm 15 ("Hansel and Gretel"); Penzer gives other Italian versions (2:149).

1. In the text, Paola and Carmosina, respectively.
2. The comments on the previous tale refer, in fact, to tale 5.6.
3. As is done to signal a memorable day.
4. Like the one used by the king of Chiunzo (tale 4.7) to file the chain that bound Marziella to the siren.
5. *canesca* (Neap.): Guarini translates as shark (from the Calabrese *caniscu*) (576).

think I came here, to pick lice off someone else's children? That's all
I need now, to take on this bother and have these sniveling brats always around! Oh, if only I had broken my neck before I came to this
inferno, where the food is bad and the lack of sleep even worse because of these troublesome bugs! Who could stand such a life? I came
as a wife, not as a servant girl! We need to hit upon a solution and
find a new address for these pests, or I'm going to find a new address
for myself! It's better to turn red once than to turn white a hundred
times! Let's fix this marriage up once and for all, for I'm firmly resolved either to get something out of it or to break it off once and for
all.' The hapless husband, who had begun to feel a little affection for
this woman, said to her, 'Don't be angry, my dear wife, for sugar is
dear. To make you happy, tomorrow morning before the cock crows
I'll remove the cause of your tribulation.'

"And so the next morning—before Dawn had hung the red Spanish coverlet from the window of the East, to shake out the fleas—he
took the children by the hand, put a nice basket full of things to eat
on his arm, and took them to a wood, where an army of poplars and
beech trees laid siege to the shadows. When they got there Iannuccio
said, 'My little ones, stay right here; eat and drink with cheer and if
you need anything just keep your eyes on this trail of ashes that I'm
sowing, for it will be the thread that will get you out of the labyrinth[6]
and bring you home at a trot.' And after giving each of them a kiss he
returned home, crying.

"But—at the hour when all animals are convened by Night's officers to pay Nature the rent for the rest they need—the little ones, perhaps frightened of staying in that solitary place—where the waters of
a river beating the impertinent stones that presented themselves before its feet would have made Rodomonte tremble with fear—set off
without a sound on that little path of ashes, and it was already midnight when they arrived home walking very, very slowly.

Pasciozza, the stepmother, acted not like a woman but a Fury from
hell, raising her shrieks to the sky, stamping her feet and slapping her
hands, snorting like a skittish horse, and saying, 'What kind of nice
stuff is this? Where did these little snot-nosed brats pop up from? Is it
possible that there exists no quicksilver to remove them from this
house?[7] Is it possible that you want to keep them and make this heart
of mine burst? Go on, get them out of my sight this instant, for I intend to wait for neither the cock's music nor the hen's tears! Otherwise, you can pick your teeth and dream of sleeping with me, and

6. The mythical thread of Ariadne led Theseus out of the Cretan labyrinth.
7. See tale 5.1 n6.

tomorrow morning I'll just slip away to my family's house, since you don't deserve me! And yet I didn't bring such nice furniture to this house so that it could be shat on with the stink of someone else's asshole, nor did I give you such a rich dowry so that I could become the slave of children who aren't mine!'

"The unfortunate Iannuccio, who saw that the boat had been poorly launched and things were heating up dangerously, that very moment took the little ones back to the wood, where he gave them another little basket full of tidbits to eat, and said to them, 'You see, my dears, how much that bitch of my wife, who entered my house to ruin you and to drive a nail into my heart, detests you. And so stay in this wood, where the most merciful trees will be your ceiling against the Sun, the most charitable river will give you drink without poison, and the kindest soil will give you mattresses of grass that pose no danger. And when you do not have anything left to eat, you can come look for help on this straight little path that I'm making for you out of bran.' That said, he turned his face the other way so that the poor little things wouldn't see him crying and lose heart.

"Once they had eaten the things in the basket, they wanted to go back home, but since a donkey, the son of bad fortune, had gobbled up the bran that had been scattered on the ground, they got so far off the path that for several days they wandered astray in the wood, feeding on acorns and chestnuts they found on the ground. But since the heavens always keep a protecting hand on innocents, a prince chanced to go hunting in that wood, and Nennillo, when he heard the barking of the dogs, was so frightened that he hid away inside a hollowed-out tree trunk, whereas Nennella started running so fast that soon after she left the wood she found herself at the seashore, where she was stolen away by some pirates who had left their ship to search for firewood. The head pirate took her home with him, and his wife, who had just lost a baby girl, treated her like a daughter.

"But let us return to Nennillo. After holing himself up behind the bark of that tree, he found himself surrounded by dogs whose howls were so deafening that the prince went to see what was going on. When he found that lovely boy, so little that he couldn't even tell him who his father and mother were, the prince had him loaded onto the packhorse of one of the hunters and took him back to the royal palace, where he ordered that he be brought up with great care and educated in virtue. Among other things he had him learn the trade of meat carving, so that before three or four years had passed he became so accomplished in this art that he could have split a hair in two.

"In the meantime it was discovered that the pirate who held Nennella was thieving the seas, and it was planned to take him prisoner; but since he was friends with the scribes, to whom he had thrown many a sop, he took to his heels beforehand with his entire household.[8] And perhaps it was heavenly justice that deemed that he who had committed crimes at sea, at sea would pay his punishment: he embarked on a light vessel, and as soon as it was in the middle of the sea, such a strong gust of wind and violent outbreak of high waves hit the boat that it overturned and they all kicked the bucket. Only Nennella, who, unlike the wife and children, shared no blame for his thieveries, was able to escape danger, for at that very moment a large enchanted fish found itself in the vicinity of the boat, and it opened its great cave of a gullet and swallowed her right up.

"And just when the girl thought her days had come to an end, she discovered astonishing things in the belly of that fish: splendid countrysides, breathtaking gardens, and a house fit for a lord and endowed with all the comforts, in which she lived like a princess. One day the fish carried her in its mouth to a reef, where, since it was the time of the summer when the humidity is greatest and the burning heat strongest, the prince, too, had gone in search of some cool air.

"While a tremendous banquet was being prepared, Nennillo went out onto one of the balconies of the palace, which was built at the top of this reef, to sharpen some knives, a job he loved to do and which did him honor. When Nennella saw him through the fish's gullet she cried out in a muffled voice, 'O brother, my brother, the knives are sharpened and the tables set, but I don't like living inside of this fish without you!' Nennillo paid no attention to the voice the first time, but the prince, who was on another loggia, turned in the direction of the wailing, saw the fish, heard the same words again, and was beside himself with wonderment. He sent a handful of servants to see if there was some way they could trick the fish and pull it in to shore, and when he heard that same phrase 'my brother, my brother' repeated over and over again, he finally asked each and every one of his people if any of them had lost a sister. Nennillo answered that he was starting to remember, as if in a dream, that when the prince had found him in the wood there had been a sister, but he had received no further news of her. The prince told him to go over to the fish and see what it was; perhaps this good fortune was directed at him.

"When Nennillo went over to the fish it lay its head on one of the rocks and opened its mouth six spans wide, and out came Nennella, so

---

8. The scribes would have written the proclamation announcing that the pirate was wanted.

"Frate mio, frate mio . . ." ["O, brother, my brother . . ."]

beautiful that she looked just like a nymph in an *intermedio*[9] coming out of an animal of that sort after the spell of some wizard. The king asked what this was all about, and she began to tell of their hardships and of their stepmother's hatred for them, although they were able to remember neither their father's name nor where their home was. And so the king had a proclamation issued: whoever had lost two children named Nennillo and Nennella in a wood should come to the royal palace, where they would receive good news of them.

"Iannuccio, whose heart was always heavy and inconsolable since he thought his children had been eaten by a wolf, raced off to the prince with great joy and told him that he was the one who had lost those children. When he told him the story of how he had been forced to take them to the wood, the prince bawled him out and called him a muttonhead and a good-for-nothing who had let a sissy of a woman step all over him until he was reduced to the point of casting out two jewels like those children of his. But after he nearly broke Iannuccio's head with those words, he administered a poultice of consolation by showing him the children, whom the father could not stop hugging and kissing for half an hour. The prince had him take off his modest cape and dressed him like a gentleman, and then he summoned Iannuccio's wife and showed her those two golden spikes of wheat, asking her how she thought someone who harmed them and put them in danger of death would deserve to be treated. She answered, 'If it were for me, I'd put that person in a sealed barrel and roll it down a mountain.' 'There, you've got it!' said the prince. 'The goat has turned its horns against itself! Come on, then; you've pronounced your sentence and now you'll pay for having shown these lovely stepchildren such hatred!'

"He thus ordered that the sentence that she herself had decreed be carried out, and then he found an exceedingly rich nobleman who was a vassal of his, to whom he gave Nennella as wife, and a daughter of another nobleman for Nennillo, and set all of them up with incomes sufficient to support themselves and their father, so that they would never again need the help of anyone. And when she had been planked up in a barrel, the stepmother lost the planks of her life, and for as long as she had breath she shouted from a hole: '*Troubles and woes may come slow to those who await them, but then one good one comes and makes up for them all!*'"

---

9. A short theatrical or musical piece, usually inserted between the acts of a longer play or opera and commonly performed at court festivities.

9

THE THREE CITRONS

Ninth Entertainment of the Fifth Day

Ciommetiello does not want a wife, but when he cuts his finger over some ricotta he gets the desire for one with a white and red complexion, like that of the mixture of ricotta and blood. And thus he wanders through the world, and at the Island of the Three Fairies receives three citrons. When he cuts one of these he obtains a beautiful fairy who conforms to his heart's desire; after she is killed by a slave he takes the black girl in place of the white one. This betrayal is discovered and the slave is made to die, and the fairy, who returns to life, becomes queen.

It is impossible to say how much Paola's tale pleased the company, but it was Ciommetella's[1] turn to speak, and when she had gotten the sign she spoke in this manner: "That sage man truly spoke well when he said, 'Do not say all you know, and do not do all you can,' because the one and the other bring unknown danger and unexpected ruin, as you will hear about in the case of a certain slave girl—with respect for Madam princess—who, because she did a poor girl all the harm possible, defended her case so badly that she ended up being the judge of her own error, sentencing herself to the punishment she deserved.

"The king of High Tower had a son who was like his right eye, on whom he had built the foundation for his every hope, and he could not wait to find a good match for him and to be called grandpa. But this prince was so disaffected and so aloof that whenever anyone talked to him about a wife he would shake his head, and then you'd find him a hundred miles away.

"When his poor father saw his son unwilling and obstinate and his own stock treated like shit, he was more incensed, seething with fury,

---

AT 408: The Three Oranges. This tale reappears in Lorenzo Lippi's *Malmantile racquistato* (1676), as well as in Carlo Gozzi's theatrical fairy tale *L'amore delle tre melarance,* and has numerous variants in the East and West (which Penzer lists in part). The motif of the red and white girl is found in tale 4.9, and that of the supplanted bride in the frame tale and tale 3.10. Penzer notes that "a fruit from which a maiden comes out is an old idea among storytellers," offering examples from the *Ocean of Story* and other Indian collections, among others (2:158).

1. In the text, Carmosina and Iacova, respectively.

spitting mad, and swollen with rage than a whore who has lost her client, a merchant whose partner has gone bankrupt, or a farmer whose jackass has died. For his son was not moved by the tears of his daddy, he was not softened by the prayers of his vassals, nor could he be budged by the advice of respectable men who put before his eyes the happiness of he who had generated him, the needs of his people, his own interest, and the fact that he was going to put an end to the line of royal blood. But with the perfidy of Carella,[2] the stubbornness of an old mule, and a hide that was four fingers thick where it was thinnest he dug in his heels, plugged his ears, and stopped up his heart, so that even a call to arms would not have moved him.

"But since more usually transpires in an hour than in a hundred years, and you can never say, 'I'm not going down that road,' it happened that one day when they were all together at the table the prince was about to cut a ricotta cheese in half, and as he was concentrating on some crows that were flying by he cut one of his fingers by mistake, so that when two drops of his blood fell onto the ricotta they blended together to create a color that was so beautiful and full of grace that—whether it was Love's punishment that had been lying in wait for him or the will of the heavens to comfort that respectable man, his father, who was not as bothered by his domesticated hernia as he was tormented by this wild colt[3]—he got the fancy to find a woman as white and red as that very ricotta stained with his blood. And he said to his father, 'My sir, if I do not have a little something with this sort of complexion, I'm done for! Never has a woman moved my blood, and now I desire a woman like my own blood. Resolve yourself, therefore: if you want me healthy and alive, allow me the comfort of wandering through the world in search of a beauty that may equal that of this ricotta; otherwise I will finish my race and go to ruin.'

"Upon hearing this bestial resolution the king felt the house collapsing on his shoulders, and he went stiff and turned one color after another. When he was himself again and could speak, he said, 'My son, viscera of this soul, pupil of this heart, bastion of my old age, what sort of delirium has seized you? Have you gone out of your mind? Have you lost your brain? It's either an ace or a six! You didn't want a wife so that you could deny me an heir, and now you feel like having one so that you can banish me from this world? Where, just where do you want to wander, like a stray animal, consuming your life and leaving your home behind? Your home, your little hearth,

---

2. "Probably an emblematic character of popular chronicles" (Rak 1014).
3. Wordplay: *polletra* (hernia) vs. *pollitro* (colt).

your little fart? Don't you know how much travail and danger those
who travel encounter? Oh, my son, do away with this whim; listen to
me! Let it not be your desire that this life be beaten to the ground,
this house fall plumb down, this state end up in shambles!' But these
and other words went in one ear and out the other, and it was as if
they were all thrown to sea. When the poor king saw that his son was
a crow in the belfry, he gave him a nice handful of scudos and two or
three servants and told him that he could go, feeling, as he did so, his
soul tear away from his body. And he went out onto a balcony and,
crying like a cut grapevine, followed his son with his eyes until he
lost sight of him.

"After the prince departed and left his father sad and embittered,
he began to trot across fields and woods, mountains and valleys, and
plains and hills, seeing various towns, dealing with diverse peoples,
and always keeping his eyes open in case he should see the target of
his desire. At the end of four months he arrived on a shore in France,
where, after he left his servants in the hospital with migraines of the
feet, he embarked alone aboard a Genoese coaster and set off in the
direction of the Strait of Gibraltar, where he took a larger vessel and
sailed on toward the Indies.[4] And from kingdom to kingdom, province to province, land to land, street to street, house to house, and
hole to hole he continued to seek the exact original of the beautiful
image painted in his heart.

"He shook his legs and rolled his feet until he arrived at the Island
of the Ogresses, where, when he had dropped anchor and set ashore,
he encountered a very old, very thin woman, who had a very ugly
face. He told her what had dragged him out to those parts, and the
old woman was amazed when she heard of the fine whim and the
whimsical chimera of this prince, and the hardships and risks that he
had undergone in order to rid himself of it, and said, 'My son, beat it
out of here, for if my three sons, who are a butcher shop for human
flesh, catch sight of you, I wouldn't value your life at three little coins;
half alive and half roasted, a baking pan will be your coffin and a
belly your grave! So move your feet like a hare, and you will not go
too far before you find your fortune.' When the prince heard this he
was in a fright, frozen with dread, terrified, and stunned, and without even saying good-bye he put the road between his legs and began
to consume the soles of his shoes. He finally arrived in another land
where he encountered another old woman, worse than the first, who,
after being told of his affairs from A to Z, said to him, 'Vanish from

---

4. This is the only transoceanic voyage in *The Tale of Tales;* its end point is the Indies, or the New World.

here immediately unless you want to be served as a snack to my ogrelet sons, but get going, for night is upon you, and if you go a little farther you will find your fortune.'

"Upon hearing this, the poor prince began to kick up his heels as if he had boils on his tail, and he walked so far that he encountered another old woman. She was sitting on top of a wheel with a basket full of little pastries and candies on one arm; she was feeding these to a bunch of donkeys that were jumping around on the bank of a nearby river and doling out kicks to some poor swans.[5] When the prince arrived before this old woman, he salaamed her[6] a hundred times and then told her the story of his wanderings. The old woman, comforting him with kind words, fed him a meal so good that he licked his fingers, and when he had gotten up from the table she presented him with three citrons that looked like they had just come off the tree, together with a nice knife, and told him, 'You can return to Italy, for you've filled your spindle and found what you are looking for. Leave, then, and at a short distance from your kingdom cut open one of the citrons at the first fountain you find. A fairy will come out and say, 'Give me something to drink!' and you be right there with the water or else she'll slip away like quicksilver. And if you're not fast enough with the second fairy open your eyes and be ready with the third; make sure you don't let her get away and give her something to drink immediately, and you'll have a wife that's your heart's desire.'

"The prince was full of joy, and he kissed that hairy hand that looked like the back of a porcupine a hundred times. Then he took his leave of the old woman and departed from that land, and when he got to the coast he sailed off toward the Columns of Hercules,[7] and when he had entered our seas, after a thousand storms and dangers he landed at a port that was a day's journey from his kingdom. Upon arriving in a beautiful little wood—where the shadows served as palace to the meadows so that they would not be seen by the Sun—he got off his horse at a fountain that with its crystal tongue whistled for people to come and refresh their mouths. Here he sat on the Persian carpet of grass and flowers, pulled his knife out of its sheath, and began to cut the first citron. And like a flash of lightning out came a ravishingly beautiful girl, as white as creamy milk and as red as a cluster of strawberries, saying, 'Give me something to drink!' The prince was so flabbergasted, open-mouthed, and amazed at the

---

5. "A metaphor for the man of letters, deriving from several classical sources that had entered into vogue" (Rak 1014).

6. *liccasalemme* (Neap.): the Arabic greeting "peace to you."

7. The Strait of Gibraltar.

beauty of the fairy that he was not quick enough to give her the water, so that she appeared and disappeared in the same instant. That this was like a club falling on the prince's noggin may be understood by anyone who has ever desired something great and, once it was in their grip, lost it.

"When he cut the second citron the same thing happened, and this was the second blow he received on the temple, so that, making two little trickles of his eyes, he poured out tears drop for drop, brow to brow, blow for blow, face to face, and eye to eye with the fountain, not yielding a crumb. And in the midst of all these laments, he said, 'May I be damned; how wretched I am! Twice I let her get away, as if I had arthritis in my hands; may I get the palsy! And whenever I move I'm like a rock, while I should be running like a greyhound! Just look what a fine job I've done! Wake up, poor man, there's one more, and at three the king wins! This knife will either give me the fairy or do something that won't smell very good!' As he was saying this he cut the third citron; the third fairy came out and like the others said, 'Give me something to drink!' The prince immediately held the water out to her, and there in his hands was a girl as tender and white as curds and whey, with a streak of red on her face that made her look like an Abruzzo ham or a Nola salami. Never had such a thing been seen in the world: it was a beauty without measure, a whiteness beyond all imagination, a grace superior to all others. Jove had rained gold onto her hair,[8] and Love had used that gold to make arrows for piercing hearts; Love had stained[9] that face so that some innocent soul might be hanged there on the gallows of desire; the sun had lit two bowls of lights in those eyes so that bangs, rockets, and firecrackers of sighs would be set off in the chests of all who beheld her; Venus and her whole temple[10] had alit on those lips, coloring the rose so that it might prick with its thorns a thousand enamored souls; Juno had squeezed her tits on that breast so that human desires might there be nursed. In short, she was so beautiful from head to toe that it was impossible to find a more splendid creature, and the prince did not know what had happened to him. Beside himself, he gazed at this beautiful fruit of a citron, this beautiful cut of a woman blossomed from the cutting of a fruit, and said, 'Are you asleep or awake, O Ciommetiello? Is your vision enchanted, or did you put your eyes on backward? What a white thing has come out of a yel-

---

8. As he had rained himself, in the form of a shower of gold, into Danae's lap.

9. *fatto na magreiata* (Neap.): see tale 1.2 n17.

10. According to Croce, "the text reads *tempio,* but it should be *tempo,* i.e., with the color of her menstrual blood" (527).

low rind! What a sweet paste from a sour citron! What a robust shoot from a tiny seed!'

"Finally, when he realized that it was not a dream and that he was playing for real, he embraced the fairy and gave her a hundred and then another hundred kisses and hugs, and after they exchanged a thousand amorous words about this and that, words that like plainchant were counterpointed by their sugary little kisses, the prince said, 'I do not want, dear heart, to bring you to my father's land without luxuries worthy of your beautiful person and without a train suitable for a queen. And so climb up this oak tree, where it looks like nature has made a cavity in the form of a little room that suits our very needs, and wait for me until my return, for without delay I'm putting on wings and before this bit of spit dries I'll be back to take you to my kingdom, dressed and accompanied as befits you.' And after performing the necessary ceremonies, he departed.

"In the meantime, a black slave had been sent by her mistress with a jug to get some water at that fountain. When by chance she saw the image of the fairy reflected in the ripples of the water, she thought it was herself and, full of wonder, began to say, 'What you see, unfortunate Lucia, you be so beautiful and mistress send you to get water and me put up with this, O unfortunate Lucia?' As she was saying this she broke the jug and then went back home, and when she was asked by her mistress why she had done her this bad service, she answered, 'Went to little fountain, jug banged against stone.'

"Her mistress swallowed this hogwash, and the next day gave her a nice little barrel and told her to go fill it with water. When the slave returned to the fountain and again saw that beauty shining in the water, she said with a great sigh, 'Me no thick-lipped slave, me no Allah lover,[11] me no wiggle ass;[12] me so beautiful and me bring barrel to fountain?' And saying this, whack! again, and she smashed the barrel into a thousand little pieces. She returned, all grumbly, and said to her mistress, 'Donkey gone by, banged into barrel, fell on ground, broke all to pieces!'

"When the poor mistress heard this she could no longer keep her calm, and she grabbed a broom and bruised the slave up so good that she felt it for quite a few days afterward. And then she took a goatskin and said, 'Run, and hurry up, you ragged slave, cricket leg, bro-

11. *pernaguallà* (Neap.): "A caricatured way of referring to the character of Lucia in the course of the dances of the *moresca, catubba,* Sfessania, and Lucia, . . . probably a deformation of the middle-eastern expression 'witness of Allah' or 'half-moon of God'" (De Simone 933).

12. *culo gnamme gnamme* (Neap.): "Allusion to the stereotype of the shambling Moor" (Guarini and Burani 589).

ken ass; run, and no dawdling, no hide-and-seek with Lucia.[13] Fill this with water and bring it back immediately, or I'll grab you like an octopus and give you such a beating that you'll always remember my name!'

"The slave kicked up her heels and ran off, for she had experienced the lightning and was afraid of the thunder. But as she was filling up the goatskin she again saw the beautiful image, and said, 'Me be stupid to get water: better if Giorgia marry! This no beauty for to die angry and serve cross mistress!' As she said this she took a long pin that she had in her hair and began to pierce the goatskin, so that with its hundred jets of water it looked like a trick fountain in a garden.[14] At the sight of this the fairy began to split her sides laughing, and when the slave heard the laughter she raised her eyes and discovered the ambush, and said to herself, 'You be reason for me beaten, but you not care!' and then said to the fairy, 'What you doing up there, pretty girl?' The fairy, who was the mother of courtesy, poured out everything that she had on her chest, leaving out not an iota of what had happened to her with the prince, who she was expecting to arrive any hour now, any moment now, with clothes and a train to take her to his father's kingdom, where she would take her pleasure with him.

"When the slave heard this she grew cockier and, deciding that she would try to win this hand, replied to the fairy, 'Since you wait for husband, me come up and comb head and make you more beautiful!' And the fairy said, 'May you be as welcome as the first of May!' and as the slave scrambled up she put out her little white hand, which grasped by those black sticks looked like a crystal mirror in an ebony frame. When the slave got up there and began to fix the fairy's hair, she pierced her memory with the pin; feeling herself pricked, the fairy shouted, 'Dove, dove!' and she became a dove, raised herself in flight, and flew away. The slave stripped herself naked, made a bundle of the rags and tatters she had been wearing, and hurled it a mile off. And sitting atop that tree just like her mother had made her, she looked like a statue of jet in a house of emerald.

"In the meantime the prince returned with a great cavalcade, and when he found a barrel of caviar where he had left a vat of milk, for a long while he was out of his senses. He finally said, 'Who put this ink blot on the royal paper where I planned to write my happiest days? Who draped with black mourning the freshly whitewashed

---

13. *nè cierne-Locia* (Neap.): lit., "watching Lucia," but also pun on *geneaolgia*, i.e., "don't make it as long as a genealogical tree" (Guarini and Burani 589).

14. Trick fountains and other water games were popular in seventeenth-century gardens.

house where I thought I would take all my pleasures? Who would
have me find this touchstone where I left a silver mine destined to
make me rich and blissful?' When she saw the prince's marvel, the
cunning slave said, 'Not to marvel, my prince, for presto! Me be enchanted, one year white face, one year black ass!'

"The prince, poor man, saw that there was no remedy for his trouble, made the sign of ox horns, and swallowed the pill, and when he
had gotten coal-face to come down he dressed her from head to toe,
giving her a complete makeover and decking her all out. And with a
lump in his throat and bile in his gorge, swollen with rage and incensed beyond belief, he set off for his land. There they were received
by the king and the queen, who had traveled six miles out of their
kingdom to meet him, with the same pleasure a prisoner feels when
he receives the sentence of *sospendatur*.[15] And although they witnessed the fine demonstration offered by their crazy son, who had
voyaged so far in search of a white dove only to bring home a black
crow, they could not, nevertheless, do without him, and so they gave
up their crown to the newlyweds and put the golden tripod atop that
face of coal.

"Now while fabulous festivities and astounding banquets were
being prepared, and the cooks were plucking ducks, slitting the
throats of suckling pigs, skinning baby goats, larding roasts, skim-
ming soup pots, pounding meatballs, stuffing capons, and making a
thousand other tasty morsels, a pretty dove appeared at a little window of the kitchen and said,

Cook in the kitchen,
What is the king doing with the Saracen?

The cook took little notice of this, but after the dove came back a second and a third time and did the same, he ran to the table to tell of
this marvelous thing; when she heard this music, the lady gave the
order that the dove be seized immediately and without a moment's
delay made into a gratin.

"The cook went off to do this and finally managed to catch the
dove, and when he had done bitchy-dear's[16] command and heated the
dove so that he could pluck it, he then threw the water and the feathers into a flower pot on a balcony, where before three days had passed

---

15. *sospennatur* (Neap.): " 'may he be hanged,' the formula used to condemn someone to execution by hanging" (Croce 530).

16. *Cuccorognamma* (Neap.): "a nickname of uncertain meaning: perhaps from
cucco (darling, but also cuckoo) and *rognamma* (scabies, mange)" (Guarini and Burani 592).

there sprung up a lovely little citron tree, which grew tall in four snaps.

"Now it happened that while the king was looking out a window that faced in that direction he saw the tree, which he had never seen before, and he called the cook to ask him when and by whom it had been planted. When he had heard the whole story from master Ladle, he began to have suspicions about the matter and ordered that under penalty of death no one touch it, and that it be tended to with great care. After a few days three splendid citrons similar to the ones the ogress had given him appeared, and as soon as they were full grown he had them picked. Then he locked himself in a room with a large glass of water and the same knife that he always carried at his side, and he began to cut. The same thing happened with the first and second fairies that had happened the other time, and when he finally cut the third citron and gave the fairy something to drink, as she asked, he found in front of him the same young lady he had left up in the tree, from whom he learned of all the bad things done by the slave.

"Now who can recount even the smallest part of the jubilation that the king felt in the face of this good fortune? Who can recount the delight, the glee, the joy, the pleasure in which he reveled? Let's just say that he was swimming in sweetness, bursting from his skin, heading toward seventh heaven, and floating in ecstasy; and after he pressed her in his arms he had her finely dressed from head to toe, and then took her by the hand and brought her to the middle of the hall where all the courtiers and people of his land were gathered in honor of the festivities. Calling them over one by one he said, 'Tell me, what sort of punishment would someone who harmed this lovely lady deserve?' One responded that that person would be worthy of a necklace of cord, another that it should be a collar of rocks, another a mallet that played counterpoint on the old hide of her stomach, another a little sip of scammony,[17] another a choker of millstones: there were those who said one thing and those who said another.

"He finally called the black queen to him, and when he asked her the same question she answered, 'Deserve to burn, and throw ashes from castle top!' When the king heard this he said, 'You have written your bad fortune with your own pen! You have cut off your foot with your own hatchet! You have forged your own chains, sharpened your own knife, and dissolved your own poison, since no one has caused her more harm than you, you bitch dog, you snout face! Do you know

---

17. *Convolvolus scammonea*, an Asian plant (though a variety is also found on Mediterranean shores) from whose root was extracted a resin used in purgatives (Rak 1015).

"Cuoco de la cocina / che fa lo re co la saraina?"
["Cook in the kitchen / What is the king doing with the Saracen?"]

that this is the lovely young thing you stuck with your pin? Do you know that this is the pretty dove whose throat you slit so that you could cook her in a pan? What do you think, Cecca, of this nag? Give yourself a shake; you're done for now! You sure took a fine shit! Those who do evil should expect evil, and those who cook branches ladle out smoke.' As he was saying this he had her carried off and placed, as alive as could be, onto a large pile of wood, and when she had turned into ashes they scattered her from the top of the castle into the wind, proving the truth of the saying: *Those who sow thorns should not go barefoot.*"

END OF
THE TALE OF TALES

Conclusion of the Introduction to the Entertainments Corresponding to the Tenth Entertainment of the Fifth Day

Zoza tells the story of her misfortunes. The slave, when she feels her keys being played, snips and cuts with her tongue so that the tale will come to an end. But in spite of her the prince wants to hear it, and when his wife's betrayal is discovered he makes her die good and pregnant and then takes Zoza.

Their ears were all hanging as they listened to Ciommetella's tale; part of the group praised the ability with which she told it, while others murmured and accused her of poor judgment, since she shouldn't have broadcast the disgraceful actions of someone so similar to the slave princess, and they said she was running a great risk of ruining the game.

And Lucia truly acted like a Lucia,[1] wiggling all over as the tale was told, and from the agitation of her body could be understood the tempest in her heart, since she had seen in the tale of the other slave the spitting image of her own deceits. But although she immediately made sure all conversation was eliminated and was intending to stage a fine show of resentment at the right time and place, in part because she couldn't free herself of the tales after the doll had put such a fire of desire for them in her body—just like those who are bitten by the tarantula[2] cannot free themselves of the music—and in part so that

---

1. See introduction to day 1 n6.
2. "There exists a vast literature on 'tarantulism,' or the bite of the tarantula and the cure of the bitten through music and dance. See, for example, Francesco Berni, *Orlando innamorato* II, XVII, 6–7: 'As in Puglia they are wont to do against the poison of those animals whose bite drives people to be possessed by madness and are commonly called the "tarantulated"; and you must find someone who will play a while until he finds a note pleasing to the bitten person, who then begins to dance, and dancing, sweats, and thus drives the dreadful plague from himself'" (cit. Croce 590). More recently, see, e.g., the writings of the anthropologist Ernesto de Martino, in particular *Sud e magia* (Milan: Feltrinelli, 1959).

she would not give Tadeo any reason to suspect her, she swallowed the egg yolk.

But Tadeo, whom this pastime had begun to please, indicated to Zoza that she should tell her tale, and she, after paying her compliments, said, "Truth, lord prince, has always been the mother of hatred, and therefore I would not like my obedience to your commands to offend anyone who is here, since, not being accustomed to fabricating inventions and weaving fables, I am constrained by nature and by accident to tell the truth. And although the proverb says, 'Piss clear and make a fig[3] at the doctor,' knowing that truth is not always received in the presence of princes I tremble to say something that might make you fume with anger."

"Say what you will," answered Tadeo, "that lovely mouth can issue nothing that is not sugary and sweet." These words were daggers in the heart of the slave, and she would have shown the sign of it if black faces, as white ones, were the book of the soul, and she would have paid a finger of her hand to have her stomach empty of those tales, for her heart had become blacker than her face, and fearing that the last tale had been an announcement of the bad fortune to come, she presaged the bad day right from the morning.

In the meantime Zoza began to enchant those present with the sweetness of her words, and told from beginning to end of all her woes. She began with her own natural melancholy, which had been the unhappy augury of what later happened to her, since from the cradle she had carried the bitter root of all those terrible calamities that in the key of a forced laugh had forced her to shed so many tears. She then went on to tell of the old woman's curse, of her anguish-filled wanderings, the arrival at the fountain, her crying like a cut vine, and the sleep that had betrayed her and caused her ruin.

When she heard that Zoza was approaching the matter in a round-about way but still moving forward and saw that the boat was taking a dangerous course, the slave shouted, "Quiet mouth, be still, or me punch belly and little Georgie kill!" Tadeo, who had by now discovered land, could no longer keep his calm, and removing his mask and throwing his harness to the ground, he said, "Let her tell it to the end, and that's enough of this cape twirling about little Georgie and big Georgie, because after all, I'm not alone, and if the mustard goes to my head it would be better if you met up with the wheel of a carriage!" And when he ordered Zoza to continue in spite of his wife, she, who wanted nothing other than this signal, went on to tell of the emptied pitcher and of the slave's deceit in taking her good fortune

---

3. See tale 1.10 n25.

out of her hands. As she was speaking she burst into tears, and there was not a person present who was able to remain unmoved when this blow hit.

From Zoza's tears and the silence of the slave, who had become mute, Tadeo understood and fished out the truth about the matter. And after giving Lucia a worse dressing-down than he would have given a donkey and making her confess to the betrayal with her own mouth, he immediately ordered that she be buried alive, with only her head above ground, so that her death would be more tortured. He then embraced Zoza and had her honored as his princess and wife, and notified the king of Hairy Valley so that he could come to the festivities. And with these new nuptials the greatness of the slave and the entertainment of the tales came to an end—much good may it do you, and to your health!—and I left, one foot after the other, with a little spoonful of honey.[4]

The End

---

4. The last line simulates the transition from the fictive universe of the tales to the reality of the oral storyteller, who after finishing his or her tale would offer the audience good wishes and leave, modestly rewarded for the effort.

Selected Bibliography

EDITIONS OF *THE TALE OF TALES*

Neapolitan Editions of *Lo cunto de li cunti:* Princeps (in five volumes)

Lo Cunto de li Cunti overo Lo Trattenemiento de' Peccerille. De Gian Alessio Abbattutis. Naples: Ottavio Beltrano, 1634. [day 1]

Lo Cunto de li Cunti overo Lo Trattenemiento de' Peccerille. De Gian Alessio Abbattutis. Iornata Seconna. Naples: Ottavio Beltrano, 1634. [day 2]

Lo Cunto de li Cunti overo Lo Trattenemiento de' Peccerille. De Gian Alesio Abbattutis. Iornata Terza. Naples: Lazzaro Scoriggio, 1634. [day 3]

Lo Cunto de li Cunti overo Lo Trattenemiento de' Peccerille. De Gian Alesio Abbattutis. Iornata Quarta. Naples: Lazzaro Scoriggio, 1635. [day 4]

Lo Cunto de li Cunti overo Lo Trattenemiento de' Peccerille. De Gian Alesio Abbattutis. Iornata Quinta. Naples: Ottavio Beltrano, 1636. [day 5]

Other Neapolitan Editions

Lo Cunto de li Cunti overo Lo Trattenemiento de' Peccerille. De Gian Alesio Abbattutis. Naples: Ottavio Beltrano, 1637. [reprint of day 1]

Lo Cunto de li Cunti overo Lo Trattenemiento de' Peccerille. De Gian Alesio Abbattutis. Iornata Seconna. Naples: Ottavio Beltrano, 1637. [reprint of day 2]

Lo Cunto de li Cunti overo Lo Trattenemiento de' Peccerille. De Gian Alesio Abbattutis. Iornata Prima [Seconna, Terza, Quarta, Quinta]. Naples: Camillo Cavallo, 1645. [days 1–5, published separately]

Lo Cunto de li Cunti overo Lo Trattenemiento de' Peccerille. De Gian Alesio Abbattutis. Iornata Cinco. Naples: Camillo Cavallo, 1654. [days 1–5]

Il Pentamerone Del cavalier Giovan Battista Basile, overo Lo Cunto de li Cunte: Trattenemiento de li Peccerille. Di Gian Alesio Abbattutis. Naples: Antonio Bulifon, 1674.

Il Pentamerone Del cavalier Giovan Battista Basile, overo Lo Cunto de li Cunte: Trattenemiento de li Peccerille. Di Gian Alesio Abbattutis. Rome: Bartolomeo Lupardi, 1679.

Il Pentamerone Del cavalier Giovan Battista Basile, overo Lo Cunto de li Cunte: Trattenemiento de li Piccerille. Di Gian Alesio Abbattutis. Naples: Mechele Loise Mutio, 1697, 1714, 1717 [?], 1722.

Il Pentamerone Del cavalier Giovan Battista Basile, overo Lo Cunto de li Cunte: Trattenemiento de li Peccerille. Di Gian Alesio Abbattutis. Naples: Jennaro Mutio, 1728.

Il Pentamerone Del cavalier Giovan Battista Basile, overo Lo Cunto de li Cunte: Trattenemiento de li Peccerille. De Gian Alesio Abbattutis. Naples: Stamparia Muzejana, 1749.

Il Pentamerone Del cavalier Giovan Battista Basile, overo Lo Cunto de li Cunte: Trattenemiento de li Peccerille. Di Gian Alesio Abbattutis. Naples: Giuseppe-Maria Porcelli, 1788.

Lo Cunto de li Cunti di Giambattista Basile. Ed. Benedetto Croce. Naples: Biblioteca Napoletana di Storia e Letteratura, 1891. [days 1 and 2 only]

Lo Cunto de li Cunti overo Lo Trattenemiento de peccerille; Le Muse napoletane; e Le lettere. Ed. Mario Petrini. Bari: Laterza, 1976.

Principal Translated Editions of *Lo cunto de li cunti*

Italian

Il Conto de' Conti: Trattenemiento a' Giovani. Naples: Nicolò Migliaccio, 1747. [with woodcuts]

Il Conto de' Conti: Trattenemiento a' Fanciulli. Trasportato dalla Napoletana all'Italiana favella, ed adornato di bellissime Figure. Naples: Cristoforo Migliaccio, 1754, 1769. [with woodcuts]

Il Conto de' Conti: Trattenemiento a' Fanciulli. Trasportato dalla Napoletana all'Italiana favella, ed adornato di bellissime Figure. Naples: Gennaro Migliaccio, 1784, 1792, 1794, 1804. [with woodcuts]

Il Conto de' Conti: Trattenemiento a' Fanciulli. Trasportato dalla Napoletana all'Italiana favella, ed adornato di bellissime Figure. Naples: Michele Migliaccio, 1821. [with woodcuts]

Il Conto de' Conti: Trattenemiento a' Fanciulli. Naples: Gennaro Cimmaruta, 1863.

Lo Cunto de li Cunti (Il Pentamerone) di Giambattista Basile. Intro. and notes Benedetto Croce. Naples: V. Vecchi, 1891.

Il Pentamerone. Ed. and trans. Benedetto Croce. Bari: Laterza, 1982 [1925].

Lo cunto de li cunti. Ed. and trans. Michele Rak. Milan: Garzanti, 1986. [bilingual edition]

Il racconto dei racconti, overo Il Trattenimiento dei piccoli. Ed. Ruggero Guarini and Alessandra Burani. Milan: Adelphi, 1994.

Il cunto de li cunti. Ed. and trans. Roberto De Simone. 2 vols. Turin: Einaudi, 2002.

German

Der Pentamerone oder: Das Märchen aller Märchen. By Giambattista Basile. Trans. Felix Liebrecht. Foreword by Jacob Grimm. Breslau: Josef Max und Komp, 1846.

Der Pentamerone oder: Die Erzählungen der Frauen des Prinzen Thaddäus. By Giambattista Basile. Ed. Paul Heichen. Berlin: Neufeld and

Mehring, 1888. [recasting of Liebrecht's translation; only forty tales included]

Giambattista Basile: Das Märchen aller Märchen oder: Das Pentameron. Trans. Felix Liebrecht. Munich and Leipzig: Georg Müller, 1909.

Das Märchen der Märchen: Das Pentameron. Ed. Rudolf Schenda. Trans. Hanno Helbling, Alfred Messerli, Johann Pögl, Dieter Richter, Luisa Rubini, Rudolf Schenda, and Doris Senn. Munich: Beck, 2000.

French

Le conte des contes. Trans. Myriam Tanant. Paris: L'Alphée, 1986.

Le Conte des contes, ou, Le divertissement des petits enfants. By Giambattista Basile. Trans. Françoise Decroisette. Strasbourg: Circé, 1995.

English

The Pentamerone, or The Story of Stories, Fun for the Little Ones. By Giambattista Basile. Trans. John Edward Taylor. Ill. George Cruikshank. London: David Bogue, 1848. 2nd ed., 1850. Rpt., London: R. A. Everett and Co., 1902.

Il Pentamerone, or The Tale of Tales. Trans. Sir Richard Burton. 2 vols. London: Henry and Co., 1893. Rpt., New York: Boni and Liverwright, 1927.

Stories from The Pentamerone by Giambattista Basile. Ed. E. F. Strange. Ill. Warwick Goble. London: Macmillan, 1911.

The "Pentamerone" of Giambattista Basile. 2 vols. Ed. and trans. Norman Penzer. London: John Lane and the Bodley Head, 1932.

NEAPOLITAN DICTIONARIES

Andreoli, Raffaele. *Vocabolario napoletano-italiano.* Naples: Istituto grafico Editoriale Italiano, 1993.

D'Ambra, Raffale. *Vocabolario napolitano-toscano domestico di arti e mestieri.* Bologna: Forni Editore, 1873.

D'Ascoli, Francesco. *Nuovo vocabolario dialettale napoletano.* Naples: A. Gallina, 1993.

De Ritis, Vincenzo. *Vocabolario napoletano lessicografico e storico.* 2 vols. Naples: Dalla Stamperia Reale, 1845–51.

Galiani, Ferdinando. *Vocabolario delle parole del dialetto napoletano.* Ed. F. Mazzarella Farao. 2 vols. Naples: Porcelli, 1789.

Marulli, G., and V. Livigni. *Guida pratica del dialetto napolitano.* Naples: Stabilimento Tipografico Partenopeo, 1877.

Rocco, E. *Vocabolario del dialetto napoletano.* Naples: Ciao-Chiurazzi, 1882–91.

Rohlfs, Gerhard. *Dizionario dialettale delle Tre Calabrie.* Halle and Milan: Niemeyer and Hoepli, 1933–39.

Salzano, Antonio. *Vocabolario napoletano italiano/italiano napoletano.* Naples: Società Editrice Napoletana, 1989.

Volpe, Pietro. *Vocabolario napoletano-italiano.* Bologna: Forni Editore, 1869.

CRITICAL WORKS AND WORKS CITED

[N.b.: I have included, predominantly, critical works in which Basile and his work figure significantly.]

Aarnes, Antti. *The Types of the Folktale: A Classification and Bibliography*. Trans. and enl. Stith Thompson. Helsinki: Suomalainen Tiedeakatemia, 1961.

Accademia della Crusca. *Vocabolario degli Accademici della Crusca*. Venice: G. Alberti, 1612.

Ademollo, A. *La bell'Adriana*. Città di Castello: S. Lapi, 1888.

———. *I Basile alla corte di Mantova*. Genoa: Tipografia dell'Istituto dei Sordo-Muti, 1885.

Agamben, Giorgio. *Infancy and History: The Destruction of Experience*. Trans. Liz Heron. New York: Verso, 1993.

Ansani, Antonella. "Beauty and the Hag: Appearance and Reality in Basile's *Lo cunto de li cunti*." *Out of the Woods: The Origins of the Literary Fairy Tale in Italy and France*. Ed. Nancy L. Canepa. Intro. Nancy L. and Antonella Ansani. Detroit: Wayne State UP, 1997.

Aprile, Renato. *Indice delle fiabe popolari italiane di magia*. 2 vols. Florence: Olschki, 2000.

Asor Rosa, Alberto. "Giambattista Basile." *Dizionario biografico degli italiani*. Rome: Istituto della Enciclopedia Italiana, 1971.

———. "La narrativa italiana del Seicento." *Le forme del testo: La prosa*. Vol. 3, part 2 of *Letteratura italiana*. Gen. ed. Alberto Asor Rosa. Turin: Einaudi, 1984.

Basile, Giambattista. *Le avventurose disavventure*. Venice: Sebastiano Combi, 1612.

———. *Le Muse napoletane*. Naples: Gio. Domenico Montarano, 1635.

Benson, Stephen. *Cycles of Influence: Fiction, Folklore, Theory*. Detroit: Wayne State UP, 2003.

Bernari, Carlo. "Basile Cortese Sgruttendio: Che passione!" *Belfagor* 40 (1985): 429–47.

Boccaccio, Giovanni. *Decameron*. Ed. Vittore Branca. Turin: Einaudi, 1980.

Boudineau, Marie-Christine. *Animaux et féerie dans "Lo Cunto de li Cunti" de Giambattista Basile*. Villeneuve d'Asq: Press Universitaires du Septentrion, 2000.

Broggini, Barbara. *"Lo cunto de li cunti" von Giambattista Basile: Ein Ständpoet in Streit mit der Plebs, Fortuna under Höfischen Korruption*. Frankfurt: Lang, 1990.

Caccavelli, A. "Fiaba e realtà nel *Pentamerone* di Basile." *Scritti vari pubblicati dagli alumni della R. Scuola Normale Superiore di Pisa per le nozze Arnaldi-Cesaris Demel*. Pisa: Pacini-Marotti, 1928.

Calabrese, Stefano. "L'enigma del racconto: Dallo Straparola al Basile." *Lingua e stile* 18 (1983): 177–98.

———. "La favola del linguaggio: Il 'come se' del Pentamerone." *Lingua e stile* 16 (1981): 13–34.

————. *Gli arabeschi della fiaba: Dal Basile ai romantici.* Pisa: Pacini, 1984.

Calcaterra, Carlo. *Il Parnaso in rivolta: Barocco e Antibarocco nella poesia italiana.* Bologna: Il Mulino, 1961.

Calvino, Italo. *Fiabe italiane.* Turin: Einaudi, 1956.

————. "La mappa delle metafore." *Il Pentamerone* by Giambattista Basile. Ed. and trans. Benedetto Croce. Bari: Laterza, 1982.

————. *Sulla fiaba.* Turin: Einaudi, 1988.

Campagna, Nino. "Die 'Orchi' bei Basile: Menschenfresser oder wilde Männer, die 'hässlich von Ansehen, aber schön von Herzen sind.'" *Zauber Marchen: Forschungsberichte aus der Welt der Märchen.* Ed. Ursula and Heinz-Albert Heindrichs. Munich: E. Diederichs, 1998.

Canepa, Nancy L. "Basile e il carnevalesco." *Giambattista Basile l'invenzione della fiaba.* Ed. Michelangelo Picone and Alfred Messerli. Ravenna: Longo, 2004.

————. "Entertainment for the Little Ones? Basile's *Lo cunto de li cunti* and the Childhood of the Literary Fairy Tale." *Marvels & Tales* 17, 1 (2003): 37–54.

————. *From Court to Forest: Giambattista Basile's Lo cunto de li cunti and the Birth of the Literary Fairy Tale.* Detroit: Wayne State UP, 1999.

————. "From Court to Forest: The Literary Itineraries of Giambattista Basile." *Italica* 71, 3 (1994): 291–310.

————, ed. *Out of the Woods: The Origins of the Literary Fairy Tale in Italy and France.* Intro. Nancy L. Canepa and Antonella Ansani. Detroit: Wayne State UP, 1997.

————. "Ogres and Fools: On the Cultural Margins of the Seicento." *Monsters in the Italian Literary Imagination.* Ed. Keala Jewell. Detroit: Wayne State UP, 2001.

————. "'Quanto 'nc'è da ccà a lo luoco dove aggio da ire?': Giambattista Basile's Quest for the Literary Fairy Tale." *Out of the Woods: The Origins of the Literary Fairy Tale in Italy and France.* Ed. Nancy L. Canepa. Intro. Nancy L. and Antonella Ansani. Detroit: Wayne State UP, 1997.

————. "Translating Basile's *The Tale of Tales:* Notes on Cultural Hybridization from the Baroque to the Postmodern." *Marvels & Tales* 16, 2 (2002): 263–82.

Chlodowski, Ruffo. "Il mondo della fiaba e il *Pentamerone* di Giambattista Basile: Dai sistemi narrativi del Rinascimento al sistema narrativo del barocco nazionale italiano." *Cultura meridionale e letteratura italiana. I modelli narrativi dell'età moderna.* Ed. P. Giannantonio. Naples: Loffredo, 1985.

Clements, Robert J., and Gibaldi, Joseph. *Anatomy of the Novella: The European Tale Collection from Boccaccio and Chaucer to Cervantes.* New York: New York UP, 1977.

Cocchiara, Giuseppe. *Popolo e letteratura in Italia.* Turin: Einaudi, 1959.

Comoth, R. "De *Lo cunto de li cunti* de G. B. Basile aux *Contes* de Perrault." *Rivista di Studi Crociani* 10 (1973): 64–69.

Coppola, Emmanuele. *Giambattista Basile nacque a Giugliano nel 1566.* Giugliano: Quaderni Culturali Centro Studi A. Taglialatela, 1985.

Crane, Thomas. *Italian Popular Tales*. Ed. Jack Zipes. New York: Oxford UP, 2003.

Croce, Benedetto. "Allusioni a usi e costumi nel Pentamerone." *Archivio Storico per la Province Italiane* 17 (1931): 359–69.

———. "Giambattista Basile e il *Cunto de li cunti*." *Lo cunto de li cunti*. By Giambattista Basile. Ed. and intro. Benedetto Croce. Naples: Biblioteca Napoletana di Storia e Letteratura, 1891.

———. "Giambattista Basile e l'elaborazione delle fiabe populari." *Il Pentamerone*. Ed., intro., and trans. Benedetto Croce. Bari: Laterza, 1982 [1925].

———. *I teatri di Napoli dal Rinascimento alla fine del secolo decimottavo*. Ed. Giuseppe Galasso. Milan: Adelphi, 1992.

———. *Saggi sulla letteratura italiana del Seicento*. Bari: Laterza, 1911.

———. *Storia dell'età barocca in Italia*. Bari: Laterza, 1929.

Croce, Giulio Cesare. *Le astuzie di Bertoldo e le semplicità di Bertoldino, seguite dai Dialoghi salomonici*. Ed. Piero Camporesi. Milan: Garzanti, 1993.

Decroisette, Françoise. "Les jeux de l'imagination et du savoir." *Le Conte des contes, ou, Le divertissement des petits enfants*. By Giambattista Basile. Trans. Françoise Decroisette. Strasbourg: Circé, 1995.

De Martino, Ernesto. *Sud e magia*. Milan: Feltrinelli, 1960.

Di Francia, L. *Il Pentamerone di G. B. Basile*. Turin: Migliotti e Besso, 1927.

Doria, Gino. "Croce e Basile." *Il Pentamerone ossia La fiaba delle fiabe*. By Giambattista Basile. Trans., intro., and ed. Benedetto Croce. Bari: Laterza, 1974.

Duval-Wirth, Geneviève. "Fonction de la metaphore et du mythe chez quelques auteurs du XVIIe siècle Italian." *Studi Secenteschi* 18 (1977): 81–104.

Fulco, Giorgio. "La letteratura dialettale napoletana: Giulio Cesare Cortese e Giovan Battista Basile." *Storia della letteratura italiana. Vol. V: La fine del Cinquecento e il Seicento*. Ed. Enrico Malato. Rome: Salerno Editrice, 1997.

———. "Verifiche per Basile: Materiali autobiografici e restauro di una testimonianza autobiografica." *Filologia e critica* 10, 2–3 (1985): 372–406.

Galiani, Ferdinando. *Del dialetto napoletano: In appendice Francesco Oliva, Grammatica della lingua napoletana*. Ed. Enrico Malato. Rome: Bulzoni, 1970.

Getto, Giovanni. *Barocco in prosa e poesia*. Milan: Rizzoli, 1969.

Giambattista Basile: Archivio di letteratura popolare. Ed. Luigi Molinaro del Chiaro. Vols. 1–9. Naples, 1883–93.

(Le) Glorie degli Incogniti overo gli huomini illustri dell'Acedemia de' Signori Incogniti di Venetia. Venice: Francesco Valuasense, 1647.

Gonzenbach, Laura. *Beautiful Angiola: The Great Treasury of Sicilian Folk and Fairy Tales*. Trans. and intro. Jack Zipes. New York: Routledge, 2004.

———. *The Robber with a Witch's Head: More Stories from the Great*

Treasury of Sicilian Folk and Fairy Tales. Trans. and intro. Jack Zipes. New York: Routledge, 2004.

———. *Sicilianische Märchen*. 2 vols. Ed. Otto Hartwig. Leipzig: W. Engelmann, 1870.

Grimm, Jacob and Wilhelm. *The Complete Fairy Tales of the Brothers Grimm*. 2 vols. Trans. and intro. Jack Zipes. Illus. John B. Gruelle. New York: Bantam, 1988.

———. *Kinder- und Haus-Märchen*. 3 vols. Ed. Heinz Rölleke. Stuttgart: Redlam, 1980.

Grizzuti, Umberto. *Le "Pentamerone" de G. B. Basile et "Les contes de ma Mère l'Oye" de Charles Perrault: Considerations*. Naples: Società Editrice Dante Alighieri, 1934.

Guaragnella, Pasquale. *Gli occhi della mente: Stili nel Seicento italiano*. Bari: Palomar, 1997.

———. *Le maschere di Democrito e di Eraclito: Scritture e malinconie tra Cinque e seicento*. Fasano: Schena, 1990.

Harries, Elizabeth Wanning. *Twice Upon a Time: Women Writers and the History of the Fairy Tale*. Princeton: Princeton UP, 2001.

Imbriani, Vittorio. "Il Gran Basile: Studio biografico e bibliografico." *Giornale Napoletano di Filosofia e Lettere, Scienze morali epolitiche* 1 (1875): 23–55; 2 (1875): 194–219, 335–66, 413–59.

———. *La novellaja fiorentina*. Livorno: F. Vigo, 1871.

Leach, Maria, and Jerome Fried, eds. *Standard Dictionary of Folklore, Mythology, and Legend*. New York: Funk and Wagnalls, 1972.

Lippi, Lorenzo. *Il Malmantile racquistato*. Florence: Stamperia di G. T. Rossi, 1676.

Magnanini, Suzanne. "Between Fact and Fiction: The Representation of Monsters and Monstrous Births in the Fairy Tales of Gianfrancesco Straparola and Giambattista Basile." Diss., U of Chicago, 2000.

Malato, Enrico, ed. *La poesia dialettale napoletana: Testi e note*. Preface Gino Doria. 2 vols. Naples: Edizioni Scientifiche Italiane, 1959.

———. *Opere poetiche by Giulio Cesare Cortese*. 2 vols. Rome: Edizioni dell'Ateneo, 1967.

Martorana, Pietro. *Notizie biografiche e bibliografiche degli scrittori del dialetto napoletano*. Naples: Chiurazzi, 1874.

McGlathery, James M. *Fairy-Tale Romance: The Grimms, Basile, and Perrault*. Urbana: U of Illinois P, 1991.

Morlini, Girolamo. *Novelle e favole*. Ed. Giovanni Villani. Rome: Salerno Editrice, 1983.

Moro, Anna. *Aspects of Old Neapolitan: The Language of Basile's "Lo cunto de li cunti."* Munich: Lincom Europa, 2003.

Nigro, Salvatore S. "Lo cunto de li cunti di Giovan Battista Basile." *Dal Cinquecento al Settecento*. Vol. 2 of *Letteratura italiana: Le Opere*. Turin: Einaudi, 1993.

———. "Dalla lingua al dialetto: La letteratura popolaresca." *I poeti giocosi dell'età barocca*. Ed. Salvatore S. Nigro and Alberto Asor Rosa. Bari: Laterza, 1979.

Ong, Walter. *Orality and Literacy: The Technologizing of the Word.* New York: Methuen, 1982.

Ovid. *The Metamorphoses.* Trans. and intro. Horace Gregory. New York: Viking, 1958.

Pedullà, Anna Maria, ed. *Studi su Basile e Perrault.* Naples: Edizioni Scientifiche Italiane, 1999.

Petrarch, Francesco. *Petrarch's Lyric Poems: The* Rime Sparse *and Other Lyrics.* Trans. and ed. Robert M. Durling. Cambridge, Mass.: Harvard UP, 1976.

Petrini, Mario. *La fiaba di magia nella letteratura italiana.* Udine: Del Bianco Editore, 1983.

———. *Il gran Basile.* Rome: Bulzoni, 1989.

———. "Per una traduzione del *Cunto de li cunti.*" *Italianistica* 17 (1988): 527–33.

Picone, Michelangelo, ed. *Passare il tempo: la letteratura del gioco e dell'intrattenimento dal XII al XVI secolo.* Rome: Salerno Editrice, 1993.

Picone, Michelangelo, and Alfred Messerli, eds. *Giovan Battista Basile e l'invenzione della fiaba.* Ravenna: Longo, 2004.

Pitrè, Giuseppe. *Biblioteca delle tradizioni poplari siciliane.* 25 vols. Palermo: L. Pedone-Lauriel, 1871–1913.

———. *Fiabe, novelle, e racconti popolari siciliani.* 4 vols. Palermo: L. Pedone-Lauriel, 1875.

———. *Fiabe e leggende popolari siciliane.* Palermo: L. Pedone-Lauriel, 1888.

———. *Novelle popolari toscane.* 2 vols. Florence: G. Barbera, 1885.

Porcelli, Bruno. "Per un'edizione delle opere di Basile." *Italianistica* 6 (1977): 60–79.

———. "Il senso del molteplice nel *Pentamerone.*" *Novellieri italiani dal Sacchetti al Basile.* Ravenna: Longo, 1969.

Praz, Mario. "Il *Cunto de li cunti* di G. B. Basile." *Il giardino dei sensi.* Milan: Mondadori, 1975.

Rabelais, François. *Gargantua and Pantagruel.* Trans. Burton Raffael. New York: Norton, 1990.

Raimondi, Ezio. *Anatomie secentesche.* Pisa: Nistri-Lischi, 1966.

———. *Trattatisti e narratori del Seicento.* Milan and Naples: Ricciardi, 1960.

Rak, Michele. "Fonti e lettori nel *Cunto de li cunti* di G. B. Basile." *Tutto è fiaba.* Ed. Giorgio Cusatelli. Milan: Emme Edizioni, 1980.

———. *Immagine e scrittura: Sei studi di teoria e storia dell'immagine nella cultura italiana del Seicento.* Naples: Liguori, 2003.

———. *La maschera della fortuna: Letture del Basile toscano.* Naples: Liguori, 1975.

———. *Logica della fiaba: Fate, orchi, gioco, corte, fortuna, viaggio, capriccio, metamorfosi, corpo.* Milan: Mondadori, 2005.

———. *Napoli gentile: La letteratura in "lingua napoletana" nella cultura barocca (1596–1632).* Bologna: Il Mulino, 1994.

———. "Il racconto fiabesco." *Lo Cunto de li Cunti.* By Giambattista Basile. Ed., intro., and trans. Michele Rak. Milan: Garzanti, 1986.

————. "La tradizione letteraria popolare-dialettale napoletana tra la conquista spagnola e le rivoluzioni del 1647–48." In vol. 4.2 of *Storia di Napoli*. Naples: Edizioni Scientifiche Italiane, 1974.

Richter, Dieter. "Geschicten, wie die alten Frauen sie zur Unterhaltung der Kleinen erzählen: Basiles *Pentamerone* und die höfische Inszenierung des Populären im Barock." *Das fremde Kind: Zur Entstehung der Kindheitsbilder des bürgerlichen Zeitalters*. Frankfurt: Fischer, 1987.

————. "Multimedialità e multifunzionalità della fiaba attraverso la tradizione: 'Il corvo' di Giambattista Basile tra Italia e Germania." *La luce azzurra: Saggi sulla fiaba*. Milan: Mondadori, 1995.

Rodax, Yvonne. *The Real and the Ideal in the Novella of Italy, France and England*. Chapel Hill: U of North Carolina P, 1968.

Rotunda, Dominic P. *Motif-Index of the Italian Novella in Prose*. Bloomington: Indiana UP, 1942.

Russo, Ferdinando. *Il Gran Cortese: Note e critiche su la poesia napoletana del Seicento*. Rome: Modernità, 1913.

Sanguineti White, Laura. "Spazio, tempo e personaggi ne *Lo cunto del cunti*." *Forma e parola: Studi in memoria di Fredi Chiappelli*. Ed. Dennis J. Dutschke et al. Rome: Bulzoni, 1992.

Sannazaro, Iacopo. *Arcadia*. Ed. Francesco Erspamer. Milan: Mursia, 1990.

Sarnelli, Pompeo. *Posilicheata*. Ed. Enrico Malato. Firenze: Sansoni, 1962.

Schenda, Rudolf. "Basile, Giambattista." *Enzyklopädie des Märchens* 1 (1977): 1296–1308.

————. "Basiles *Pentamerone*: Mediterrane Lebenswirklichkeit und Europäische Literaturtraditionem—Ein Nachwort." *Das Märchen der Märchen: Das Pentameron*. Ed. Rudolf Schenda. Trans. Hanno Helbling, Alfred Messerli, Johann Pögl, Dieter Richter, Luisa Rubini, Rudolf Schenda, and Doris Senn. Munich: Beck, 2000.

————. "Basiles Pentamerone neu übersetzen?" *Fabula* 39 (1998): 219–42.

————. *Folklore e letteratura popolare: Italia—Francia—Germania*. Rome: Istituto della Enciclopedia Italiana, 1986.

————. "Giambattista Basile, Neapel und die mediterranen Erzähltraditionem: Ein Meer ohne Märchenhaftigkeit." *Fabula* 40 (1999): 33–49.

Speroni, Charles. "Proverbs and Proverbial Phrases in Basile's *Pentameron*." *University of California Publications in Modern Philology* 24, 2 (1944): 181–288.

Straparola, Giovan Francesco. *Le piacevoli notti*. 2 vols. Ed. Donato Pirovano. Rome: Salerno Editrice, 2000.

Tarzia, Fabio. "Il *Cunto* di Giovan Battista Basile e l'ideazione di un nuovo genere letterario." *Letteratura e utopia II*. Annali del Dipartimento di Italianistica Università di Roma "La Sapienza." Rome: Editori Riunti, 1996.

————. "Il cunto di tutti i cunti: Giambattista Basile e la proposta del modello fiabesco." *La novella baroca con un repertorio bibliografico*. Ed. Lucinda Spera. Naples: Liguori, 2001.

Tatar, Maria, ed. *The Classic Fairy Tales*. New York: Norton, 1999.

Testaferri, Ada. "Baroque Women in Medieval Roles: The Narrative Voices in Basile's *Pentamerone*." *Rivista di Studi Italiani* 8 (June–Dec. 1990): 39–45.

Thompson, Stith. *Motif Index of Folk-Literature*. 6 vols. Bloomington: Indiana UP, 1955–58.

Tutto è fiaba. Proceedings of an International Conference on the Fairy Tale. Ed. Giorgio Cusatelli. Milan: Emme Edizioni, 1980.

Valente, Vincenzo. "Per una migliore intelligenza del napoletano di G. Basile." *Lingua nostra* 40 (1979): 43–49.

———. "Note critiche al testo del *Cunto* di G. Basile." *Lingua nostra* 49 (1988): 33–39.

———. "Il *Cunto* di G. Basile: Vicende editoriali e interpretative." *L'Italia dialettale* 52 (1989): 199–205.

Venuti, Lawrence. *The Scandals of Translation: Towards an Ethics of Difference*. New York: Routledge, 1998.

Warner, Marina. *From the Beast to the Blonde: On Fairy Tales and Their Tellers*. New York: Farrar, Straus and Giroux, 1995.

Warnke, Frank. *Versions of Baroque: European Literature in the Seventeenth Century*. New Haven: Yale UP, 1972.

Zago, Ester. "Giambattista Basile: Il suo pubblico e il metodo." *Selecta: Journal of the Pacific Northwest Council on Foreign Languages* 28, 1 (1977): 78–80.

———. "Note alla traduzione di Benedetto Croce del *Pentamerone* di Giambattista Basile." *Merveilles & Contes* 1–2 (1987): 119–25.

Zipes, Jack, trans. and intro. *Beauties, Beasts and Enchantment: Classic French Fairy Tales*. New York: Meridian, 1991.

———. *Breaking the Magic Spell: Radical Theories of Folk and Fairy Tales*. Lexington: U of Kentucky P, 2002.

———. "Of Cats and Men: Framing the Civilizing Discourse of the Fairy Tale." *Out of the Woods: The Origins of the Literary Fairy Tale in Italy and France*. Detroit: Wayne State UP, 1997.

———, ed. *The Oxford Companion to Fairy Tales*. New York: Oxford UP, 2000.

———, ed. *The Great Fairy Tale Tradition: From Straparola and Basile to the Brothers Grimm*. New York: Norton, 2001.

INDEX